Book One Of The Godwars:

Forbidden Magic

Also by Angus Wells in Orbit

THE FIRST BOOK OF THE KINGDOMS:
WRATH OF ASHAR

THE SECOND BOOK OF THE KINGDOMS:
THE USURPER

THE THIRD BOOK OF THE KINGDOMS:
THE WAY BENEATH

Book One Of The Godwars:

Forbidden Magic

ANGUS WELLS

ORBIT

An Orbit Book

First published in Great Britain in 1991 by Orbit Books
A Division of Macdonald & Co (Publishers) Ltd
London & Sydney

All characters in this publication are fictitious
and any resemblance to real persons, living or dead,
is purely coincidental.

Typeset by Leaper & Gard Ltd, Bristol
Printed and bound in Great Britain by
BPCC Hazell Books
Aylesbury, Bucks, England
Member of BPCC Ltd.

ISBN 0 7474 0490 9

Orbit Books
A Division of
Macdonald & Co (Publishers) Ltd
165 Great Dover Street
London SE1 4YA

A member of Maxwell Macmillan Publishing Corporation

For Liz and Laurence, Linda, Sylvia, Nick and Rob,
who joined in battle with the witch...
And, after all, what is a lie? 'Tis but
The truth in masquerade.

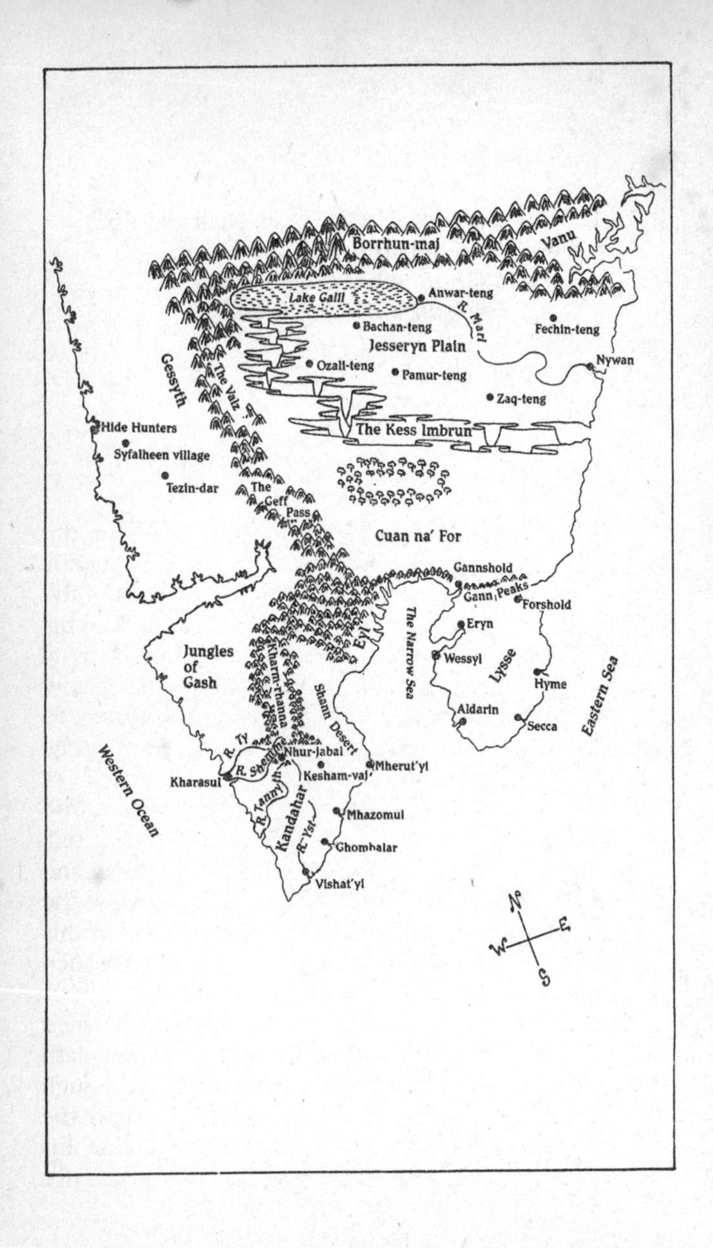
Borrhun-maj
Vanu
Lake Galil
Anwar-teng
R. Marl
Bachan-teng
Fechin-teng
Jesseryn Plain
Gessyth
The Valz
Ozali-teng
Pamur-teng
Nywan
Zaq-teng
The Kess Imbrun
Hide Hunters
Syfalheen village
Tezin-dar
The Geff Pass
Cuan na' For
Gannshold
Gann Peaks
Forshold
The Narrow Sea
Eryn
Wessyl
Lysse
Eyl
Jungles of Gash
Kharm-rhanna
Shann Desert
Hyme
Eastern Sea
Aldarin
Secca
Western Ocean
R. Ty
R. Shemme
Nhur-jabal
Kesham-vaj
Mherut'yl
Kharasul
R. Tannyth
Kandahar
R. Yst
Mhazomul
Ghombalar
Vishat'yl
N
E
W
S

ONE

BYLATH den Karynth, Domm of Secca, Lord of the Eastern Reaches and Chosen of Dera, stared moodily from the embrasure, his expression saturnine, as if the breeze that skirled about the palace walls enhanced his naturally dour temperament. Fingers callused by a sword's hilt tugged at his leonine beard, the yellow streaked with grey now, like his hair, and fell in a fist to the stone of the sill. Below him, on the sanded practice ground, his sons worked under the vigilant eye of Secca's weaponsmaster, Torvah Banul the younger, the object of the Domm's dissatisfaction. He grunted, nodding, as Tobias parried a cut of Torvah's, and riposted to land his blunted blade neatly against the older man's ribs, eliciting a smile of approval from his father. Tobias was cut from the same cloth; the den Karynth blood ran true in his veins.

Of Calandryll, the Domm was less sure. It seemed too often the boy was of stranger stock - though Bylath had no doubt he sprang from the same seed - as though he were a throwback or a changeling. He bore the characteristic yellow hair of the den Karynth line, his body beneath the heavy padding of the protective gambeson was muscular and tall like his father and brother, but it was his attitude rather than any physical differences that set him apart, as was obvious when Torvah turned towards him, gesturing with his sword. Where Tobias sprang eagerly to battle, evincing a ready joy in such manly arts, Calandryll was lackadaisical, negligent; Bylath sighed as the word effete entered his thoughts. He was skilled enough with the blade, but he showed no enjoyment in its use, no will to win. He answered Torvah's probing attack with a halfhearted parry that left his flank open to a thrust, avoiding that only by dint of agile footwork, then awaiting Torvah, rather than taking the fight to the weaponsmaster. It seemed the aggression that was so much a part of Bylath's nature had entered Tobias alone, leaving none to spare for Calandryll. Bylath's hands clenched in angry fists as he watched. If Calandryll only showed the application he devoted to books on the practice ground; if he only spent the time he gave to useless scholarship learning the arts of governance, there might be hope for him. But he showed no interest in the duties of his bloodline: had he not informed Bylath only yesterday that his dearest wish was to be left alone with his books? That he preferred the palace archives to the practice sand? The Domm ground his beard between his teeth, a decision forming. Such bookish ways were suitable to philosophers or pedagogues, not to one of High Blood.

He turned from the window, drawing his robe tighter about him as he stalked the balcony, Torvah's admonitory shout ringing like confirmation in his ears.

'Dera's love, Calandryll! You hold a blade, not a book!'

He strode to where the balcony descended in a winding stairway to the lower levels of the palace, his expression sending servants scurrying from his path, straightening the rigid backs of the guardsmen stationed along the corridors, and came to a door of black wood, inscribed with arcane symbols of scarlet and green. Thrusting it open he paused, eyes narrowing in the dim light cast by nine smoking torches set in sconces of black metal about the walls of the windowless chamber, their effluvium pinching his nostrils, the flickering shadows they cast seeming to hide things better unseen. At the centre of the room a man looked up from behind a dusty table on which rested several skulls, the mummified remains of a blind cat, and a jar containing the tiny corpse of a still-born child. He was small and bald, his eyes bird-like above a wart-infested nose, blinking nervously as he rose to greet the Domm.

'Lord Bylath? You seek an augury?'

Bylath grunted an affirmative, wondering if the paraphernalia displayed was necessary, or merely artifice.

The man came from behind the table, scuttling to close the door, his black robe flapping, prompting Bylath to think of spiders, or carrion birds. For all that he was Domm of Secca, and consequently ruler of the most powerful city in all eastern Lysse, he felt uncomfortable in the presence of the necromancer.

'I have made a decision regarding my sons, Gomus,' he declared. 'I would have it confirmed.'

Gomus nodded, dragging a stool from the darkness; sweeping a sleeve across its surface. Bylath glanced at the proffered seat with a look of distaste and settled himself. Gomus moved to the far side of the table and studied the Domm across the piled skulls.

'And it is?' he asked, his voice papery as his yellowed skin, as though neither had seen day's light in too long a time.

'Tobias must inherit,' Bylath said. 'That's obvious. I would make Calandryll a priest.'

'A priest?' Gomus murmured. 'He will not welcome such office. The priests of Dera have no time for books.'

'What he wants has nothing to do with this,' snapped

the Domm. 'Had he shown more aptitude for the blade I'd have sent him to Forshold; but he's no soldier.'

'No,' agreed the necromancer diplomatically.

'And there's no room in the palace for a scholar-prince,' Bylath continued, seeming unware of the brief interruption, 'his presence would threaten Tobias - there are families enough who would see the den Karynth brought down. I'd not give them a puppet to use against my announced heir.'

'Surely Calandryll would never lend himself to such treachery,' Gomus murmured. 'He's bookish, yes; but never a traitor.'

The Domm made an angry gesture, the movement causing something skulking in the shadows to hiss. 'Not willingly,' he agreed, 'but his head's so firmly in the clouds he'd likely find himself used unwittingly.'

'I think you underestimate him,' Gomus ventured.

Bylath snorted: the necromancer smiled deprecatingly.

'And for all he's a milksop, I'd not see him slain,' the Domm went on. 'There's little love lost between him and his brother, and should Tobias consider him a threat he'd not hesitate to use the Chaipaku.'

'No,' Gomus murmured, nodding vigorously.

'As a priest he'd be no threat,' Bylath said. 'As a priest he must renounce all worldly ties.'

'Including his books,' Gomus said; then frowned: 'What of marriage, Lord Bylath? Does he not entertain hopes in that direction?'

'He makes cow's eyes at Nadama den Ecvin. But that's no more than puppy love, and I've other plans for that maiden - Tobias favours her and she returns his affection. I'd see them wed and bind the den Ecvins to the den Karynth.'

'A wise move,' Gomus complimented; Bylath grunted, fleshy lips twisting in a sour smile.

'Wise moves secure bloodlines, sage. With the den

Ecvins joined by marriage, Tobias will stand inviolate.'

'And you would have me cast an augury on this?' Gomus asked.

'I'd know where the spirits stand,' Bylath nodded.

'Your wish,' Gomus simpered, 'is my command.'

'Yes,' said Bylath, wiping at eyes rendered tearful by the pungent smoke.

He watched as the necromancer busied himself with the tools of his occult trade, rising to bring a stubby candle of nigrescent wax from a shelf, a phial of dull green jade from a locked trunk, a stick of scarlet chalk from a drawer. He cleared a space on the cluttered table and selected a bleached skull, surrounding it with a chalk circle, inscribing symbols in a minute hand around the circumference, another, thicker, circle to contain them. Unstoppering the phial, he took a pinch of yellow powder that he sprinkled between the fleshless jaws, into the sockets of the eyes. He set the candle atop the cranium and lit a taper from a torch, using it to light the candle.

Pale greenish light flickered and Gomus passed his hands through the flame, murmuring softly. The candle began to melt, glistening ebony wax dripping over the bone. As it touched the eye sockets and the jaw, they glowed a dull red, as though fire burned within the empty cranium.

'The Lord Bylath, Domm of Secca, asks for guidance,' the necromancer intoned. 'Do you who are dead hear him?'

'I hear him.'

The answer was the beat of sullen waves on a forsaken shore; a cold wind rustling the leafless branches of a withered tree. Bylath shivered, suddenly cold.

'Ask,' Gomus advised.

Bylath cleared his throat: familiarity with the forms of necromancy did nothing to render the asking easy.

'I would see my elder son, Tobias den Karynth, secure,' he said hoarsely. 'I would marry him to Nadama den Ecvin.'

'He shall wed Nadama den Ecvin; he shall be Domm of Secca after you.'

The voice was everywhere and nowhere. Bylath heard it in the pulsing of his blood, the pounding of his heart, rather than through his ears. It seemed to reverberate in the tissue of his flesh; he shuddered.

'And I would make my younger son, Calandryll, a priest,' he said.

'Calandryll shall serve Dera.'

The timbre of the voice shifted. Bylath wondered if he heard dry laughter.

'He will offer no threat to Tobias?'

'Tobias shall inherit what you leave,' came the whispery answer. 'Calandryll shall not contest him'

Bylath realised that, despite the chill he felt, he was sweating. 'My thanks,' he said.

'I was summoned - I had no choice but to answer. I have no choice save truth - I tell you what you want to hear.'

The stub of candle liquefied, black wax coating the skull. The wick flickered and went out; the red light behind the eye sockets died; the voice tailed into silence. Bylath shook himself.

'That last,' he murmured, 'What did that mean?'

The necromancer shrugged.

'The dead are enigmatic.'

'But it was the truth?'

Gomus nodded.

'As you heard - the dead have no choice save truth.'

'Then I am confirmed.' Bylath rose, anxious to be gone now. 'Tobias shall inherit and Calandryll shall be a priest. My thanks, Gomus,'

'I exist only to serve,' murmured the necromancer, smiling obsequiously as Bylath hurried from his red-lit chamber.

*

Though spring had barely touched the coast of Lysse and waves still winter-strong beat irritably against the harbour walls a warm breeze pervaded the streets of Secca, rendering Calandryll acutely conscious of the disguising cloak he wore. It was the least obtrusive he could find amongst the many displayed in the extensive wardrobes of the Domm's palace, yet still more opulent than those few he had seen as he made his furtive way from his father's halls, and made all the more noticeable by the general absence of such garb in the narrow alleyways of the Seers Gate.

Several times he had become aware of eyes upon him and wondered if he was recognised, or noted for the richness of his dress, hunching in on himself, the deep blue folds of the cloak drawn close across his chest as he hurried past the observers, tempted to cover his thick blonde hair but aware that a raised hood on so warm a morning must only call down additional attention. Bylath or Tobias would have been instantly recognised, though it was unlikely either the Domm or his eldest son would have ventured to this part of the city unless on some official errand, and unthinkable that they would come alone, unaccompanied by armed guard or servants. The younger son, however, was less known and, he felt, considerably less conspicuous. The Domm had told him often enough that save for the yellow hair inherited from his mother, and a general similarity of feature, he lacked those characteristics that set the den Karynth apart from the populace of the city they governed, and certainly he lacked his father's regal air of massive confidence or his brother's stature; so perhaps he might succeed in reaching his objective without word returning to the Domm.

He hoped so, for Bylath would undoubtedly take it amiss that his youngest son should seek out a spaewife amongst the common folk; and take it worse should he learn the reason. Calandryll grinned uneasily at the thought, torn between fear of the Domm's anger and the spice of defiance.

There were seers enough resident within the palace. Diviners of the future in sundry arcane manners: the interpretation of entrails, the casting of rune-writ bones, the reading of cards; an astrologer, a necromancer, a chiromancer; and the Domm consulted them all. Calandryll might have gone to any of them to obtain a prediction of his future, but then, without doubt, word of that small rebellion would have been given to Bylath, and he did not want that. Nor was he by any means sure that such a prediction would be honest: he suspected the palace soothsayers tailored their auguries to the desires of the Domm. He wanted honesty, unbiased, not hindered by fear of his father's displeasure.

So he had awaited an opportune moment, disguised himself as best he was able, and slipped from the palace to make his way through Secca to the Seers Gate.

Now he reached the maze of passages that wound below the city walls, close by the harbour, and paused, studying the buildings confronting him. Like all the structures contained within the ramparts, they stood two storeys high at most, flat-roofed, with winter-stripped vines and budding shrubbery visible above the retaining walls. Window shutters were thrown open to permit entry to the promise of spring carried on the warm breeze. This close to the harbour the promise was accompanied by the smell of fish, and tar, and the odour of garbage was not entirely concealed by the sewers Calandryll's great grandfather had ordered built.

Those smells, however, only added to the excitement he felt, and he savoured them as eagerly as the bouquet of some prized Aldan vintage. The sons of the Domm had little truck with the ordinary life of their city, their own being confined largely to the palace, to the endless preparation for future duties, and the mansions of

Secca's aristocracy. Tobias, Calandryll was sure, would have found such smells offensive and would be horrified that his brother could take such pleasure in them. Calandryll smiled at the thought and strode determinedly beneath the quarter marker hung on slightly-rusted chains across the street.

A few passers-by glanced at him, but he was too eager now to worry about recognition, and most of the folk he saw were sufficiently engrossed in their own business that they paid him scant attention. He moved down the narrow street studying the frontages for the sign of Reba. She, according to those servants he had - discreetly, he hoped! - questioned, was the most reliable spaewife to be found beyond the confines of the palace, and her mark was a crescent moon encircled by stars. He set a hand on the purse at his belt, his fingers brushing the unfamiliar hilt of the shortsword he wore, the touch renewing his nervousness, reminding him that the poorer quarters of Secca were, even under his father's stern rule, not entirely safe. That, he thought, his smile growing rueful, was something Tobias would not have worried about: for all his arrogance and pride, the Domm's elder son was an excellent swordsman, which Calandryll was most definitely not.

He shook the doubt away and continued past the stuccoed fronts. He had come too far to let such weak-spined concerns stay him now, and surely footpads and thieves preferred the darker hours, when they might more easily evade the watchmen. He would find Reba and have her read his future. Then he would have choices to make, based on firmer footing than his own emotions. He pressed on, ignoring the blandishments of those diviners not busy with clients, seeking the star-circled crescent.

He found it where an alley bisected the street, suspended from a pole of dark iron, its wood ancient, the silver of the moon yellowed by age, three stars hidden beneath the white smears of birds' droppings. It was an unimpressive sign, though no less so than the building itself which was narrow, one storey high, with weary vines trailing from the roof and a single blank window beside a closed door of stained wood and hinges pitted with rust. The wall that faced the alley was devoid of openings and inscribed with graffiti of obscene imagination, the frontage pale blue stucco, pocked like a diseased face, revealing patches of bare, sand-coloured stone.

Calandryll swallowed the doubt he felt and tapped on the door.

'Enter.'

The voice was faint, coming from deep inside the house, and somehow younger than he had expected, softer, almost musical. He pushed the door open and went in.

Darkness veiled his eyes and he fumbled warily for his sword, hearing the door thud shut behind him, his nostrils pinching at the cloying scent of incense. He blinked, trying hard to see into the gloom and finding it impossible. He reached out with his left hand, his right still on the sword's hilt, and felt rough plaster beneath his fingers.

'You seek to know your future?'

The voice was louder without the intervention of the door and he moved towards it through the darkness, cautiously, hand still brushing the wall.

'I do,' he said in answer.

'Then come here.'

The house was deeper than he had thought, standing outside; there were interior rooms, passages, that distorted her voice. He asked, 'Where is here? I cannot see you.'

A laugh answered him and she said, 'I am sorry - I forget.'

He frowned, hearing the scrape of flint on metal, seeing a tiny spark of light glitter ahead. Then a glow as a lamp of scented oil was lit, revealing a curve in the passage and dark rooms to his right.

'I am here. Can you see now?'

'Yes.' He moved towards the light, ducking beneath an arched doorway, entering a small room filled with shadows, the single lamp illuminating only the centre, the low table on which it stood, and the face of the woman beyond it.

'Is that sufficient? Would you prefer more light?'

He nodded, and when she offered no response said, 'I would. Unless your art requires darkness.'

'Light or dark, it matters not.'

She rose, lifting the lamp, and he saw that she was not the crone he had anticipated but a woman barely in her middle years, who might have been beautiful were her face not marked by plague scars. Hence the gloom, he thought, spaewives are as prone to vanity as any woman. He bit off the thought as he watched her move to the wall, one hand touching the lamp set there in a gentle caress as she ignited the wick. She moved on slowly, her free hand trailing along the wall just as he had sought that reassurance in the darkness, lighting sufficient lamps that the room grew bright and he could see the blankness of her eyes and that she was blind. The servants had not mentioned that and he felt his cheeks flush, embarrassed.

He smiled apologetically and said, 'Forgive me, I did not know.'

'You are courteous, but why should you? I see in other ways.'

She returned to the table and set the lamp aside, dropping smoothly to the cushions piled there. A motion seated Calandryll opposite her. He found the blind gaze of her eyes disconcerting, more so than the ugly pitting of her skin - plague was not unknown in a city occasionally subjected to siege - and sought to regain his composure by studying the room and her dress. Reba remained silent, as though accustomed to such pauses, and he saw that her hair was long and red, glossy as burnished copper, her gown green, fastened at throat and waist with vermilion cords. The room was empty of those artifacts he associated with divination. There was no crystal ball, nor caged bird or cabbalistic charts, no cards spread before her, no polished skulls. Rather, it was a simple, undecorated chamber, the walls white, the floor plain wood, a reddish hue not unlike her hair, the only furniture the table and the piled cushions, those simple, their colours primary.

'Are you disappointed?' Her tone hinted amusement. 'Am I not grand enough for the son of the Domm?'

'I . . . No.' he shook his head, then gasped: 'How did you know that?'

She laughed aloud and the sound hid her disfigurement.

'I am a spaewife, Calandryll. I saw your coming yesterday.'

'I was not sure yesterday,' he said, slowly.

'But still I saw it. I should be a poor seeress had I not. Would you not agree?'

He nodded and chuckled, her calm and her amusement reassuring. 'I would,' he said, 'do others know?'

Reba shrugged. 'That I cannot tell, though I would doubt it. A seer can usually forecast only specific events - those things of direct import, or those for which prediction is requested. Does it worry you?'

Now he shrugged.

'I should prefer my father did not know.'

'Presumably the reason you come to me, not the palace soothsayers.'

'They would inform my father. And I doubt their predictions.' He paused, not sure what etiquette applied, wondering if she would assume his doubts encompassed her own abilities. 'I mean, they seek to please the Domm and so adjust their divinations. At least, I think so.'

He sounded confused to his own ears, but Reba nodded as though she understood, accepted. She said mildly, 'The Domm is a harsh master, or so I hear - you should not blame them.'

Calandryll nodded his agreement: those who failed to please the Domm found their employment rapidly terminated.

'You will say nothing?' he asked.

Reba shook her head, no longer laughing, solemn now. 'What passes here is no one's business save mine and my client's.'

'Good,' he murmured, 'I would have no word of this go back to the palace.'

'None shall,' she promised, 'not from my lips.'

He realised, not without a shock of surprise, that he trusted her. Exactly why he could not say, but something in her even tone, the calm set of her scarred features, reassured him. He smiled afresh and tapped the purse at his side. He did not know what she charged for her services, nor how he should broach the subject of payment: he was the son of the Domm and had few dealings with such mundane matters.

'The cost is one gold var. Three should the augury prove difficult.'

He stared at her, again surprised, wondering if this was an aspect of her second sight. She laughed as though she saw his expression and said, 'I heard the sound of coins. And it is usually the first question.'

Fresh doubts assailed him, the explanation so simple it prompted him to wonder if his burgeoning confidence in her was misplaced. The servants he had questioned might well have warned her of his interest; and some watcher in the street might have recognised him, brought her swift word of his approach. Nonetheless he drew a var from his purse and placed it in her outstretched palm.

She closed her fist on the coin, holding it a moment before dropping it carelessly on the table. 'Give me your hands,' she said.

He reached out and she took his hands, folding them between her own. Her skin was soft and warm, the touch oddly comforting. He saw her smile again and once more felt embarrassment rise as she said, 'No one told me of your arrival, Calandryll. There is no watcher on the roof, nor in the street; nor did the servants inform me. Listen: I am a spaewife through accident, not choice. My talent was given me, not sought. Perhaps it was in compensation for the loss of my sight, I do not know, but it is a true talent.

'I was wife to Drum, a tavern keeper, until the plague took him. The same plague marked me and took my sight. Keeping a tavern when you cannot see is difficult, and there are few who welcome a woman scarred as I am serving their ale. I sold the tavern, which kept me for a while, then my talent became apparent and I came here. Now I am a spaewife and I can foresee your future, or some part of it. You may not like what I see, but I shall tell you only the truth that is revealed to me.

'Does that resolve your doubt? If not, take back your var and leave.'

She let go his hands and he felt a sudden chill, as if the contact had warmed him; suddenly afraid that she would dismiss him. 'It resolves my doubts,' he said, 'though I have questions I would ask.'

'Ask them.'

'I have heard the arguments of my father's seers, and those of philosophers and scholars, and disagreement exists. Some say the future is pre-ordained and cannot be altered. That a man's path is fixed from the moment of his birth; that a governing pattern controls us all. Others claim there is no pattern and that a man's actions determine his future. Or that the future is a series of alternatives, constantly branching, and that some of those branches may be foreseen, others not. What do you say?'

'That certain immutable truths appertain,' she replied, 'and so a pattern of a kind does exist. That it is often hidden, even from seers. That a diviner can usually see some distance along that pattern, can foresee the branching for some way - that distance depending on his, or her, ability - but that none can foresee it all, simply because it is too large, the branching growing too intricate to comprehend.'

'Then the future is uncertain?'

'To an extent.'

'Then why am I here? Why should I bother consulting you?'

Her laughter was light as a fountain's fall, amused, though empty of any hint of mockery.

'Because you are worried and you seek reassurance. Because you face a decision that is difficult to make and perhaps dangerous. Because you desire guidance you can find nowhere else. Because you are more than a little afraid of your father.'

The words held only truth and Calandryll sighed, admitting it.

'You are the youngest son of the Domm of Secca,' Reba continued. 'Your elder brother, Tobias, has reached his majority and soon will be confirmed as the Domm's succcessor. In two years you attain majority and are expected to follow the traditional path, though your training for the office you are expected to choose must commence with Tobias's confirmation. You do not wish to enter the priesthood, and you are in love.'

Everything she said was true. Calandryll stared at her in silence, awed.

'You would follow a scholarly path, were you able. You prefer books to blades and would be left alone to pursue those interests; but your father would make you a priest to avoid the possibility of your becoming a rival to your brother. The priesthood is sworn to celibacy, but you would marry - if she will have you and if you are allowed. You are not sure of her agreement and you know your father would object.'

'Bylath will not agree to my becoming a scholar,' he blurted, unable to restrain himself, resentment edging his voice. 'And Tobias would wed Nadama himself. The den Ecvin family is powerful - if Nadama took me as her husband they would support me; but then Tobias would see me as a threat. Even though I have no wish to be Domm.'

'You might flee,' she said mildly. 'To Aldarin or Wessyl; Hyme, perhaps. Secca is not the only city in Lysse.'

'But I am, irrevocably, the son of Secca's Domm: a potential threat. Another city would likely see me as a tool to use against my father, or Tobias. In any other city I might be held hostage. Or given back to Secca. And Tobias would surely brand me a rebel.'

'And your father will not allow you to become a scholar.'

He heard the pity in her voice and felt the weight of his youth, anger stirring. 'My father has little use for scholars; less for a son who prefers books to swordwork or, as he puts it, "the furtherance of Secca's interests". He knows I am no soldier and would make me a priest, but - the Goddess knows! - I want only to be left alone. To marry Nadama if she will have me, and study.'

He broke off, aware that his voice rose, part angry, part anguished, afraid that he whined, embarrassed again.

'It is no easy thing to be the Domm's son,' Reba said gently.

'No,' he agreed. 'People think it must be a grand thing - the wealth, the power, the luxury. But I would sooner have freer choice.'

'Yet you come to me, and surely that is a limitation of such free choice.'

Calandryll thought for a moment before shaking his head. 'I do not think so,' he said slowly. 'I do not ask you to *tell* me what to do, but to predict my future so that I may reach those decisions I must make with as much knowledge as I am able to gain.'

'Said like a true scholar,' Reba murmured. 'Give me your hands.'

Once more he extended his arms and she took his hands, this time placing her palms against his, their fingers twining in a curious intimacy. It seemed a tingling pricked against his skin and for an instant his vision blurred, her face became indistinct, the room grew dark. Then he saw her clearly again, the lanterns' light filling her blank eyes with pinpoints of dancing gold as she began to speak.

'I cannot read you so clear as some, but more choices than one lie ahead. There is love, but perhaps not the love you anticipate: love has many forms. I see struggle, disappointment, but happiness, too. You will encounter two who will have great impact on your life. For good or ill, I cannot say. I perceive travel - a quest for which your scholar's mind suits you well.

'You must bear your father's anger, and your brother's; be strong in the face of their wrath and you shall triumph. I ...'

Her voice faltered and she shook her head, untangling her fingers from his.

'I can see no more. Should you wish me to plumb further, it will cost two varre. And I can offer you no promise of greater clarity.'

Without hesitation he set the coins on the table. Reba nodded, then rose, going to an alcove from which she lifted a box of ornate design, dark red lacquer and golden chasings. She set it down and raised the lid, removing a silver censer, a pouch, and a gallipot. Deftly, almost reverently, she set the censer on the table between them and from the pouch took a pinch of powder, sprinkling it over the silver. She opened the gallipot and dug inside with a forefinger.

'Open your mouth.'

Calandryll obeyed and she said, 'Your tongue.'

He extended his tongue and she smeared a daub of ointment there. It tasted bitter. She touched her own and lidded the pot, setting it aside, then brought a taper from the box and lit the powder. Calandryll anticipated some dramatic flash of smoke and flame, but none came, only a thin wisp of white that was disturbed by their breath.

'Breathe deep,' Reba advised.

The smoke was odourless, tasteless, and he felt no effect from its inhalation. Reba, however, commenced to sway gently from side to side, the golden flecks filling her eyes becoming agitated, seeming to swirl and twist of their own accord. Calandryll found them hypnotic, staring fixedly at her face, so that he was startled when she spoke again, the more so for the deepness of her voice, a low baritone that was more masculine than female, as though some unseen entity spoke through her, her lungs and throat and lips merely the vessels of its expression.

'You will seek that which cannot be had and find disappointment. But you will gain much; more than you lose. You will learn by those things you reject and find that friendship is the strongest bond.

'There is water - beware the water, Calandryll! You must cross it to find what you seek, though men say it does not exist. There is danger, but you will be protected, not alone. There is a teacher, though you may not welcome his lessons. Trust him! And one will come after, also to be trusted.

'You will travel far and see things no southern man has seen, perhaps no man at all. There is ... No! I cannot see it ... It hides behind itself. It is forbidden ... I cannot ...'

The voice grew harsh, choking. Reba began to cough, and the strange spell was broken. The smoke wavered and died; Reba's teeth snapped closed with an audible *crack*! and she shook her head, hair swirling wild about her face. Her head hung down, features veiled by the curtain of her long tresses. Her shoulders trembled and she braced herself against the table as though pressed down by the burden of her augury.

'There is wine.' A motion of her lowered head indicated the door. 'Please.'

Alarmed, Calandryll sprang to his feet, a knee banging painfully against the table. He ignored the sudden ache, limping from the chamber into the darkness of the passage. Dim light showed to his left and he stumbled towards it, finding a door, opening that to find himself in a kitchen, an open window revealing a small garden, a well, sunlight and birdsong. A flagon of wine stood on a table, earthenware cups beside. He took the flagon and two cups, carrying them back to Reba's audience chamber.

She had regained her composure, though her face was pale, the pockmarks stark against the pallor. He filled both cups and set her hands about one. She drank the wine in a single swallow and held out the cup that he might pour her more. he drank his own in three drafts, refilled her cup again and waited.

'Perhaps you had best heed your father.' Her voice regained its natural tone as she spoke. 'There is one branch that holds great danger.'

'Tell me,' he urged, as intrigued as he was wary. 'You spoke in riddles before.'

Reba shook her head; smoothed her hair. 'I spoke as clear as I saw. The branchings are complex - and something clouds them. You will meet a man who will become your friend, your ally. You may not see that, at first, but you will learn to trust him. You will journey with him; far.'

'Across water?' he prompted. 'Even though water is dangerous? To Eyl? Or Kandahar?'

'Farther. This journey goes farther than any man has gone.'

'Why is water dangerous?' he asked.

'It is the domain of Burash.'

'The Sea God?' Calandryll gaped. 'What offence have I offered Burash? Why should he harm me?'

'I cannot see that.' Reba shrugged. 'A power clouds my vision. I see only that dangers await you.'

'Eyl I might reach overland,' he murmured. 'Even Kandahar, though the Shann lies in the path.'

Reba nodded. 'Yes, but you will cross water. if you follow this path.'

'I have a choice?' he demanded.

'There is always choice,' she returned. 'Though in your case it is limited by desire.'

'I can obey my father?' he muttered.

'One choice.'

He ducked his head, curtly. 'What is the thing I travel for?'

'I could not see that. It is thought to be lost, though what it is, I cannot tell you. You will be told.'

'By this friend I am to find?'

'Perhaps.' She shook her head helplessly. 'So much is vague; unclear. There is a great destiny ahead, should you choose this path.'

'But not a scholar's life?'

Reba smiled, a wan expression. 'You may learn things unknown. More than Secca's greatest scholars. More than the philosophers of Aldarin.'

That possibility at least appealed and he smiled at the prospect. Had she not spoken of this unknown friend teaching him? 'I can make sacrifice to Burash,' he murmured. 'Propitiate the god.'

Reba nodded slowly. Calandryll frowned as one disturbing doubt intruded. 'What of Nadama?' he asked.

'She may be gained, or lost,' the spaewife said. 'I perceive that you are not sure of her decision. Tobias, too, seeks her hand, and I cannot predict which of you she will choose, not from you alone.'

It was as though she could see the disappointment in his eyes for she added, 'What I see of her future is clouded by your desire for her. Were you to bring her here ...'

'She would not come,' he said quickly.

'Then I cannot say,' Reba murmured.

He accepted that. 'Should I take this path,' he wondered, 'do I take it in duty to my father, as ambassador of the Domm? Or as my own man?'

'As a seeker,' she returned, without hesitation. 'Outlawed from Secca.'

'Banished?'

Such thought had crossed his mind; it was inevitable should he reject his father's wishes. That or a life imprisoned behind the walls of Dera's temple, denied the books he loved, his life given over to religious observance, the rites of worship, a celibate prisoner in a luxurious cage. But to hear it said out loud, so firm, without hint of doubt or hesitation, that made it real. Real and frightening.

'Yes,' Reba said.

'But with true friends.'

'Yes,' she said again. 'Truer friends than any you have known. They will set you on the path, if you choose it.'

'The alternatives remain unpalatable,' he said, endeavouring to affect a nonchalance he did not feel.

'But perhaps more ... comfortable. Certainly less dangerous.'

He snorted his dismissal. 'As a priest? I have considered that and I reject it. Perhaps I should take that path you suggested first, and flee. Even though it makes my life forfeit.'

But that would be without Nadama. She would never leave Secca: he knew he spoke from anger, or resentment; he was not sure which.

'Does it not depend on Nadama?' asked the spaewife.

Calandryll sighed agreement. 'Yes, it does.'

'Should she accept your proposal, her family would protect you. Your father would risk civil war should he seek to annul the marriage.'

'I would not plunge Secca into war,' he said forlornly.

'It seems your choice is narrow,' Reba said, 'If all depends on Nadama.'

'I love her,' he returned, as if that answered the question he heard in her voice. 'And if she'd have me, I'd gladly renounce all family claims. Perhaps my father would accept that.'

'Then approach her,' Reba advised. 'I can do no more than tell you what I see. Should she accept you, then a new path opens.'

Calandryll grunted thoughtful agreement. Now the shock of her prediction had passed he thought more clearly, and that part of him that needed to analyse, to probe and find answers, reasons, prompted him to question her further.

'You spoke of branching paths - and I agree the future must be thus - but it seems you saw only one for me. Does that mean I am pre-destined to take it?'

'No.' Reba shook her head. 'It is only the most probable. What you told me, what I learnt of you, of what you want - all those things combine to illuminate the most likely. The ultimate choice remains yours.'

'This friend who will - *may*,' he corrected himself, 'set me on this path, does he not figure? Will he not influence what I do?'

'He - or she - perhaps,' Reba allowed. 'But you may reject him. Or her.'

'A woman?' Calandryll grew intrigued, almost despite himself. 'Do you say I shall forget Nadama? Meet another woman?'

Now Reba sighed. 'Perhaps. I saw two friends in that future that revealed itself. One was a man; of that there is no doubt. The other was not clear - man or woman, I cannot say.'

'Friends, a dangerous quest for some unknown prize,' he murmured, 'travel to distant lands, banishment. These are romantic notions, but I had hoped for a clearer scrying.'

'Were you a more common man you might have had that,' she replied, 'but you are not. You are the son of the Domm, and that shapes your future. I can offer you no better, Calandryll.'

'Can you offer me no more?' he demanded. 'I have varre enough.'

Reba made a dismissive gesture and his embarrassment returned.

'I am sorry. I intended no offence.'

'It does not matter.' She smiled afresh. 'And your coins would make no difference. I saw what I saw and I cannot see more. The paths branch before you, and which one you take only you can decide. I can offer only that illumination revealed to me.'

'So be it,' he agreed. 'But these friends - how shall I recognise them?'

'You will know them when you meet them,' she said confidently.

'And Burash?' he asked. 'Should I sacrifice to the Sea God?'

'It cannot hurt,' she said. 'Nor prayers to Dera. Now, forgive me, but I am wearied. I can tell you no more, and you had best regain the palace before you are missed.'

'Yes.' he accepted the dismissal. 'Thank you, Reba.'

She nodded in a way that suggested she was not sure

such gratitude was warranted.

'May all the gods favour you,' she called as he left. 'I will pray to Dera that your choice is the right one.'

He moved back along the corridor, eyes narrowing as he stepped into the street and bright sunlight struck him. Glancing up, he saw the sun had advanced across the sky, estimating that he had spent perhaps one hour with the spaewife. That left him time: his father was in conference with the ambassador of Aldarin, concerning the activities of the Kand pirates, which the coastal cities anticipated would increase with the cessation of the winter storms, and those debates would last throughout the day, probably longer. Tobias would be in attendance, and it was unlikely his absence would be noticed by anyone in a position to reprimand him. He had, he knew, a reputation for vagueness - unreliability, according to his father; dreamy as a love-struck girl, according to his brother - and it was not unusual for him to disappear on some erudite mission, forgetful of appointments, ignorant of time's passage until hunger recalled him to the everyday world. He would be expected to attend the banquet that night, but until then he was free to spend the day as he chose.

He chose to think, and for that purpose set out for the city wall, knowing that there he might find solitude.

The alley that flanked Reba's house continued on the opposite side of the street, cutting across the Seers Gate in the direction of the harbour, and he followed it, grinning at the sheer imagination of the graffiti decorating the buildings. He saw few people until the alley emerged into a wider avenue, one of the larger thoroughfares circling the city like the radial strands of a spider's web, linked by the smaller streets, the Domm's palace at the centre. The roadway marked the boundary of the Seers Gate and the commencement of the Merchants Quarter. The buildings were larger here, bright-striped awnings extending over wide pavements busy with pedestrians, the road active with carriages and chariots, the warm air loud, fragrant with the odours of spices, leather, dyes, cloths, metal; the myriad goods offered for sale. Calandryll hurried across the avenue, dodging traffic, and made his way between two emporiums to the broad military road running beneath the wall, designed to allow swift movement of troops to any part of the perimeter in the event of siege.

Civilian vehicles were scarce on the road and he crossed it easily. On the far side the wall bulked towards the sky, barracks and stables and armouries built into the foot, the wall itself wide as a sizeable house to defeat siege engines or sappers. Soldiers lounged in the sun outside the barracks, but none offered Calandryll more than a cursory glance as he crossed the road and commenced the ascent to the ramparts.

The steps at this point were narrow and steep, angling vertiginously between a stable and a storehouse, ending beside one of the small blockhouses that guarded each stairway. Five legionaries looked up from a game of dice as Calandryll came panting onto the wall, grinning as he paused to regain his breath. The officer took in his cloak and clothes and nodded in greeting.

'A fine day for a stroll along the wall.'

He appeared to consider Calandryll some minor aristocrat.

'Yes.' Calandryll nodded, thinking that Tobias would have been instantly recognised. Before the officer had chance to mark any resemblance, he walked on.

The breeze was stronger up here, coming off the sea, tangy with the scent of ozone, and he gathered his cloak about him as he crossed to the farther perimeter and peered down.

The Eastern Sea was a metallic grey, flecked with

white where waves broke, spray bursting across the long mole that protected the harbour. Ships rocked there, mostly caravels that plied the coastal trade northwards to Hyme and Forshold, or south and west to Aldarin, then on to Wessyl and Eryn, but also three-masters awaiting the shifting of the wind that would carry them across the Narrow Sea to Eyl and Kandahar, and fishing boats, dwarfed by their larger companions. Mangonels stood ominous at the farthest extent of the mole and to either side of the harbour itself, and beside the Sailors Gate a sizeable blockhouse warded that entry to the city. There had been no fighting since Calandryll's childhood, the cities of Lysse maintaining a somewhat precarious peace since the last siege when Bylath had resisted Aldarin, and the Kand pirates preferred to attack merchantmen crossing the Narrow Sea to storming a fortified metropolis, but the Domm allowed no relaxation of his defences and so both mangonels and blockhouse were fully manned.

Calandryll's gaze wandered from the activity of the harbour to the more ponderous movement of the sea, its grey surface vaguely menacing in the light of Reba's prediction. There was always some measure of danger where that element was concerned; indeed, although Secca adhered to the worship of Dera, there were temples dedicated to Burash in the Sailors Gate, and few mariners set sail without making some offering to the god of the waters. Burash was an unpredictable god, whimsical in his moods and given to violent rages. If he was to make the journey Reba had forecast, he would sacrifice to Burash.

If . . .

If he chose that path it would be without Nadama. Of that he was certain: the farthest she had ever travelled was to her family's holdings beyond the city wall and she had made it obvious that nothing would persuade her to venture further when he had tentatively raised the topic. If, therefore, she accepted his suit he must remain in Secca, and if he did that it must be at risk of his brother's enmity, his father's wrath. But married to Nadama he would have the support of the powerful den Ecvin family to protect him.

If...

He was no great swordsman, nor did the notion of finding himself an outlaw appeal; less so the idea that he might be hunted by assassins, deemed a threat by his brother.

If his father would only break with precedent and allow him to pursue a scholarly path he might be happy. Even should Nadama refuse him; he loved books as well - *almost* as well - as he loved her, and should he lose her to Tobias he might drown his sorrow in the sea of knowledge. But the Domm would not agree, of that he was certain, and the wheel turned full circle, back to the two choices.

He pushed away from the parapet and began to walk along the wall, unaware of the wind that ruffled his long hair, his head down, deep in thought.

Reba had spoken of a quest, yet told him he could choose to ignore it. Were he to take that path it must, it seemed, mean banishment and the loss of Nadama. Were he to ignore it, it must mean the acceptance of the fate outlined by his father, a life of tedious religious duty. Unless Nadama should accept him.

It seemed that his decision must rest with her. Until he knew for sure whether or not he had her, he could not decide. Yet Reba had said he would encounter a man who would set him on the path of adventure, of learning, and he did not know when that meeting might take place. What if it came now? How could he choose, unsure of Nadama's intentions? What if he should encounter the man now?

He looked up, half expecting to find his mysterious potential comrade, but saw only gulls along the wall, rising in a squall of raucous objection as he approached. He could not wait, he decided; the matter must be settled. He would approach Nadama and demand a decision, and then make his choice. He felt better for that, his stride quickening, cloak billowing behind as he raised his head and smiled. Then he faltered as it occurred to him that he was afraid. That it seemed, whatever answer he received, he must lose something. What was it Reba had said? *You will seek that which cannot be had and find disappointment. But you will gain much; more than you lose.* Did that mean he would lose Nadama? Did soothsayers always speak in riddles?

His smile faded and he looked once more towards the sea. The waves seemed to mock him and he turned from them, looking inwards across the city. The view offered no better answers. He saw the bustle of a prosperous metropolis, the streets angling towards the great white edifice of the Domm's palace, ringed by a sward of green, the inner courts hidden behind high walls. The seat of government, to which all Secca looked for guidance; the seat of power.

He had no wish for power, nor any desire to govern. He was happy to leave all that to Tobias, yet neither his father nor his brother would concede the same freedom to him. He was, he knew, a disappointment to his father; to his brother ... he was not sure what he was. A potential threat, certainly, for Tobias was hungry for the title of Domm, and any sibling could become a rival; it seemed that consideration outweighed what love his brother felt. In the matter of Nadama, too, there was rivalry: both sought her favour, but so far she refused to choose between them.

He mouthed a curse heard in the palace stables, teeth clenching in frustration. Whichever way his mind turned his thoughts came back to Reba's enigmatic prophecy. What did it mean? How did it help him?

He clasped his hands behind his back, shoulders hunching as he forced some measure of scholarly discipline on his troubled mind. He needed logic now: to consider his options and arrive at the most sensible decision, weighing all things as dispassionately as he was able. It appeared that loss of some kind was inevitable, so a choice must exist in the nature of that loss. He might win Nadama and lose his freedom; or lose Nadama but be free. Which did he want?

It was impossible to decide until he knew her mind and he returned to his original thought: before any choice could be made he must have an answer from Nadama. That must be his first point of reference; it was the logical step. She must choose and then he would be free to choose. He nodded, agreeing with himself, and his pace quickened again, moving towards the inevitable watershed. Nadama would attend tonight's banquet: he would ask her then.

He fought the trepidation that mounted with each step, striding grimly along the wall towards the stairs that descended into the Coopers Gate and thence to the palace that was his home. Or his prison: he was no longer sure which.

TWO

CALANDRYLL was too deep in thought to remember to conceal his return to the palace, forgetting that he had left by the ostlers' gate and consequently approaching the great ceremonial arch that granted entry to the main courtyard. It was only the clatter of halberds against shields as the guards stationed there offered him formal salute that reminded him of his mistake, and by then it was too late to rectify the error. Nor was he sure that he wished to, despite the rush of apprehension that filled him as he thought of his father's displeasure should the Domm learn his youngest son had gone wandering the poorer quarters alone. He waved a casual response and continued on across the yard, oblivious of the amused looks the guards exchanged. Like all the palace folk they were accustomed to the vagaries of the younger heir and had long given up any expectations of disciplined or dignified behaviour where he was concerned. Calandryll's a dreamer, they said amongst themselves, not like Tobias. It's lucky he was the second born, for he'd make a poor Domm.

Calandryll himself shared that opinion without

resentment, though now, for all his abstracted air, he felt positive. He had thought the matter through and arrived at what he believed was the only logical conclusion. What worried him was the outcome: it seemed he must lose either way.

He nodded absently as more guards saluted, passing through the wide copper-clad doors into the first of the palace's receiving rooms, crossing that to a corridor busy with servants preparing the halls for the forthcoming banquet. They bowed as he passed, not so deeply as they might for Tobias or his father, but he scarcely noticed that and would not have cared had he been aware of the lack of respect. They liked him well enough and that was sufficient.

He left the bustle behind as he climbed the stairs to his private quarters, pleased to have regained the palace without, so far as he knew, his father learning of his absence.

The door closed behind him, he breathed a sigh of relief and shed his cloak, tossing his swordbelt onto a convenient chair. The familiarity of the room was comforting, reassuring, and the books and scrolls and parchments that covered one wall were like old friends, supportive of his decision. Though that, he thought, was at present only a decision to make a decision and it occurred to him that he should look his best if he was to approach Nadama. He went through the outer chamber to his bedroom. The windows had been opened and his bed made, the books littering the table tidied; the room was pleasantly warm, airy, sunlight tinting the white walls with gold, glinting off the surface of the tall cheval glass standing beside his wardrobes. He placed himself before the mirror and studied his image critically.

A tall youth - no, he decided, a young man - looked back, slim and reasonably muscular. His hair was untidy, shining gold in the sunlight and in need of cutting, framing a long face in which the large brown eyes were the most dominant feature. He was not, he thought, unhandsome. Perhaps not so obviously good-looking as Tobias, and certainly less commanding, but not ugly. His nose might be broader and his jaw perhaps a fraction more square, his ears smaller, but his mouth was wide enough and his teeth even. He grinned at himself, squaring shoulders he knew had a tendency to slump, deciding that he was not, all things considered, unattractive. He would summon a barber and have his hair dressed. Take a bath. And choose clothes for the evening.

Then ... His doubts returned and he saw his grin fade. If he were Nadama, which brother would he choose? He turned from the mirror, going to the wide windows opening onto the balcony. Below was a walled garden, vines climbing the stonework, bushes offering the first green of spring, flowers thrusting tentative stalks up through the dark earth, a small fountain at the centre. That, he remembered, had been a favourite place of his mother's: he could just recall her playing with him there, before she died, a victim of the plague, perhaps the same outbreak that had scarred Reba.

How would she have advised him?

He had not known her long enough to hazard a guess; he had been a child when she died and all he could remember was a feeling of warmth, of protective love, arms to which he ran when Bylath grew angry. There were portraits about the palace, and sculptures, but those were formal representations, depicting a dignified woman, her thick hair encircled by the Domme's coronet. They told him what she had looked like, not how she thought; they were not the mother he dimly remembered.

It seemed that, for all his swift temper, Bylath had been different then; softer, more approachable. Her death had struck him hard and he had withdrawn, become austere, unyielding, as though he feared to commit to fondness again, seeing in his sons the potential for pain that walks hand in hand with love. Had that withdrawal not taken place, Calandryll thought his life, his outlook, might well be different. Tobias, two years older, had accepted it, finding in military training, the anticipation of power, the consolation denied by their father. Calandryll, on the other hand, had been hurt, withdrawing in turn from his father, increasing the emotional distance between them, seeking solace in those things his mother had loved, chief amongst them books, learning, the acquisition of knowledge beyond those matters immediate to the welfare of Secca. That love had increased with the passing years, prompting Bylath to despair of ever making a warrior of his son.

In some ways it worked to Calandryll's benefit. It was not unknown for a Domm to exile younger sons in Gannshold or Forshold, the two great citadels that guarded the landward approaches to Lysse, fearing they might rise against their elder brothers, rivals for the title. Equally, it was not unknown for the elder brother to employ assassins to dispose of the potential contender: Calandryll had heard rumours that the current Domm of Wessyl had used the mysterious Chaipaku to rid him of two siblings, whilst it was common knowledge that the Domm of Hyme had hired the Brotherhood of Assassins to eliminate four members of his family. Such threats did not exist in his case, he thought: Bylath clearly considered him too poor a warrior to send him north and Tobias showed only contempt for his bookish brother.

Were he to remain in Secca it seemed the priesthood must be his destiny, unless he won the support of Nadama's family. He sighed and turned from his contemplation of the garden, going back into his chambers. The sand clock told him he had still some hours before his presence would be required and he determined to spend them making himself as presentable as possible. He tugged on the cord beside his bed, knowing that somewhere in the bowels of the palace a bell would ring, summoning a servant, and settled in a chair with the book he had been studying the previous night.

It was Medith's *History of Lysse and the World*, from which he had sought to glean insights into the thinking of the ambassador he was soon to meet, and while he considered it less erudite than Sarnium's *Chronicles of the Southern Kingdoms*, it was interesting enough that he became engrossed, and was startled by the appearance of the servant.

'My lord?'

The man studied Calandryll with less respect than he would have given Tobias, his manner vaguely suggestive of more pressing urgencies than attendance on the Domm's younger son. Calandryll looked up, marking his place, and set the book down.

'A bath. And a barber. And is there anything to eat?'

'The Domm has taken luncheon, my lord; and the kitchens are preparing tonight's feast. You were not to be found.'

'Did my father ask for me?'

Calandryll reviewed excuses, aware that his cheeks reddened.

The servant paused as if considering the matter, then shook his head. 'No, my lord. He ate with the ambassador and your brother. I might find something.'

'Please,' Calandryll nodded, thinking that if Tobias had voiced the request the man would be gone now.

'In what order, my lord?'

Calandryll bit back a sigh: he must endeavour to be more authoritative. He said, 'Food first, then a bath. Then the barber.'

The man bowed. 'Yes, my lord.'

Calandryll watched him go and returned to the book. One advantage of Medith's work was its more recent maps, his cartography of greater precision than Sarnium's. Secca lay to the east of the Lyssian domains, on a rough line with Aldarin, Wessyl to the north, and higher on the coast the great inlet that protected the shipyards of Eryn. Eyl and Kandahar lay across the Narrow Sea, Aldarin ideally situated to enjoy the benefits of trade with both, whilst Secca's commerce was mostly with the other coastal cities and the distant Jesseryn Plain. Aldarin might, if her Domm so chose, cut the trade routes, so a treaty that would secure Secca's sealanes to Kandahar was a worthwhile prize.

Kandahar occupied the southern tip of the peninsula extending into the Southern Ocean, and whilst nominally at peace with Lysse, still afforded anchorage to the Kand pirates whose annual depredations threatened all Lyssian trade. Thus it was in the interests of both Secca and Aldarin to forge a naval alliance presenting a unified front when the corsairs began their raids.

Satisfied with his summary, he let his eyes wander over the map, thinking of Reba's prophecy of travel to distant lands. Neither Eyl or Kandahar seemed distant enough, but not even Medith showed much more of the world. Beyond the Gann Peaks, which marked Lysse's northern boundary, Kern was depicted as prairie, the grassland surrounding the vast central forest of the Cuan na'Dru, the mountains of the Valt to the west and the Jesseryn Plain to the north across the chasm of the Kess Imbrun. Of that mysterious land nothing was known, those traders venturing so far confined themselves to Nywan, the closed city at the mouth of the Marl. The peninsula containing Eyl and Kandahar, the Shann desert between them, was split by the spine of the Kharm-rhanna, the western coast wholly occupied by the Jungles of Gash. Northwest, from the great barrier of the Valt to the sea, lay Gessyth, of which

Medith said only, 'it is a forbidding land best left be, all reeking swamp where strange creatures dwell, the outcasts of the gods with no love of men. Three of my crew died here, and I fell sick close unto death.'

There was another map, Calandryll remembered, a more detailed work, tucked away in a dusty corner of the palace archives. He had noticed it once before whilst searching for a chart of the Lyssian coastline, but paid it scant attention. At the first opportunity he would seek it out. In case Nadama refused him.

He closed Medith's book as the servant returned, bearing a tray of beaten copper on which a platter of cold meat and some fruit rested.

'Water is now being drawn,' he anno: ıced, and left with a cursory bow. Calandryll realised that he was hungry.

He was biting into an apple when two more servants lugged in a cauldron of steaming water, two women behind with cold. The men deposited the contents of their burden in his tub and the women stood waiting for instructions. He dismissed them. It seemed decadent to allow another to bathe him, and his love for Nadama rendered him oblivious to the other services they offered.

The barber was waiting when he emerged and he sat, watching strands of hair fall about his feet, returning desultory responses to the man's professional chatter. That task completed, the barber applied a razor to Calandryll's cheeks, finally allowing his subject to examine his handiwork.

'Thank you.'

Calandryll waved a hand in dismissal, staring at his image. He looked tidier, but not greatly improved. It would have to suffice; short of divine intervention he could look no better. He glanced at the sand clock, seeing the gains filtered close to the mark of the dining hour, and went to his wardrobes.

Customarily, his dress was careless, but tonight he gave some thought to his apparel, selecting and discarding outfits until he was satisfied with his choice. He drew on a loose shirt of white Seccan silk, and dark blue breeches that he fastened with a maroon belt, its formal sheath decorated with silver threading, the dagger it held hilted with mother of pearl, boots of blue-dyed leather stitched with silver to match the sheath, and finally a tunic lozenged with maroon and blue. He studied himself afresh, self-conscious of his unusual finery, then nodded in satisfaction, and filled a goblet with Aldan wine.

Three glasses bolstered his confidence and when he heard the great gong bell, and gave himself a final examination, he decided he looked handsome enough to sway Nadama. He descended the stairs resolutely, resisting the impulse to hurry.

He reached the ground floor of the palace and strode across the tiles to the smaller banqueting hall. Ambassadors did not merit the grandiose feasting accorded some visiting Domm or ranking monarch, only those nobles directly concerned with the negotiations attending, with their immediate families, though there were enough of them for the hall to seem crowded. Nadama's father, Tyras den Ecvin, would be there, accompanied by his wife and daughter. Calandryll's heart quickened at the thought.

The guards ringing the outer hall saluted him as he passed and he gestured in response, halting beneath the arched entrance. Dusk began to darken the sky and lanterns had been lit along the walls, braziers of sandalwood committing perfumed smoke to the air. Bylath sat at the High Table, raised three steps above the floor on a dais of black marble, facing the arch, the ambassador to his right, Tobias at his left. An empty chair waited beside the ambassador. Calandryll hung back, scanning the hall. The foremost of the Domm's counsellors occupied the tables at the pedestal's foot and he found Nadama there.

She was lovely. The lanterns struck golden highlights from her luxurious auburn hair, piled high to emphasise the slender paleness of her neck. Her eyes sparkled and her lips were spread wide in a smile, and as she turned to speak with her mother Calandryll swallowed at the taut stretch of white silk across her breasts. Taking a deep breath and essaying what he hoped was a dignified expression, he entered the hall.

Bylath glanced up as he approached the High Table, murmuring something to the man on his right. The ambassador was tall, even seated, and slim, his features handsome in a hawkish way, dark eyes bright in a tanned face, his hair cut short, a dramatic contrast to the robe of pale blue and gold he wore. He glanced in Calandryll's direction and nodded. Tobias looked towards his brother and added a word of his own, smiling. Guessing that some comment on his tardiness was made, Calandryll felt his cheeks redden, instinctively quickening his pace. He caught Nadama's eye as he passed her table and smiled, delighted that she returned his unspoken greeting.

'So, you come at last.'

Bylath studied his son with cool grey eyes, a hand toying with the pendant of his office. Calandryll felt his blush deepen, muttering an apology as he reached his place.

'My younger son, Calandryll,' Bylath announced to the ambassador. 'Calandryll, this is Lord Varent den Tarl of Aldarin.'

'My lord.'

Calandryll bowed formally before seating himself; Varent answered with an easy smile.

'Doubtless lost in some book,' Tobias remarked with casual malice.

'Study is no bad thing,' murmured Varent, and

Calandryll flashed the dark-haired man a grateful look.

'But unnecessary to one destined for the priesthood,' Tobias responded.

Varent's shoulders rose a fraction and he brushed his dark beard as if considering the comment. 'Knowledge is power,' he remarked equably. 'Even should the priesthood be his destiny, he loses nothing in study.'

Tobias snorted, and for an instant he appeared a mirror of his father, broad shoulders hunching, his handsome face creased with a dismissive smile. He was tall as Bylath, who yet retained the heavy musculature of his prime, the hand that cupped his goblet large and thick fingered, his yellow-gold hair thick about a face seemingly carved from dark standstone. Calandryll felt himself a wan facsimile of his parent; a poor copy of his brother. He sought to hide his embarrassment behind his wine cup.

'What do you study?' asked Varent amiably.

Calandryll decided he liked the Aldarin ambassador. He said, 'I was reading Medith.'

'The *History of Lysse and The World*?' Varent nodded. 'An excellent work, though I consider Sarnium a more reliable chronicler.'

'Medith offers better maps,' Calandryll returned promptly, his confidence mounting as he felt himself on familiar ground.

'True,' allowed Varent, 'in Aldarin we have his original charts. Should you ever honour our city with a visit, I should be pleased to show them to you.'

Calandryll beamed at the prospect but then felt his smile freeze as his father said, 'The priests of Secca do not leave the city. Calandryll will take up residence in the temple.'

It sounded as though his future had been decided: it firmed his own decision to approach Nadama. He looked to where she sat, barely hearing Tobias say, 'That way I can keep an eye on him,' not needing to turn his head to know that a mocking grin curved his brother's lips.

Nadama smiled at him and he felt his confidence soar, Reba's prophecy momentarily forgotten. If she would have him, the future must hold happiness.

'You appear disturbed,' Varent remarked softly. 'Does the priestly life not appeal?'

Calandryll tore his gaze from Nadama, turning to the ambassador, about to give a negative reply. Beyond Varent he saw his father's eyes upon him and said dutifully, 'As the Domm wills.'

Bylath smiled tightly. Varent nodded, recognising he touched upon an area of argument; diplomat that he was, he changed the subject.

'Do you consider the Kand pirates a threat to Secca?'

'They threaten all our cities,' Calandryll answered, forcing himself to speak calmly. 'Though their depredations are less immediately felt in Secca, we need the iron of Eyl and open trade routes. Should the corsairs succeed in establishing dominance of the Narrow Sea, or threaten the coastline, then we must share the suffering of Aldarin.'

Varent nodded approvingly.

'An allied naval force! Your son speaks sense, my lord Bylath.'

'We are agreed on this,' Bylath said.

'You have decided?' asked Calandryll.

'Today,' said Tobias.

'Aldarin contributes twelve galleys,' Varent offered, 'and we draw up treaties of non-aggression between our cities.'

'Twelve from us,' Tobias expanded as though the credit belonged to him alone, 'and twelve from our ally - surely sufficient to ward our sealanes. Though when I am Domm we shall renegotiate - I favour a more aggressive policy.'

'Your brother would attack the Kands in their

strongholds,' explained Varent.

'Too great a risk of war with Kandahar,' Bylath said. 'Though the notion has its appeal.'

'Strike to the heart!' Tobias declared fiercely. 'Teach the corsairs a lesson and end their threat once and for all.'

Bylath favoured his eldest son with an approving smile, but he said, 'Let us take this thing one step at a time. Alliance first, to secure our trade routes; it would be unwise to overreach ourselves.'

'Of course,' Tobias agreed quickly. 'I speak of the future, when our allied navy will be stronger.'

'What is your opinion?' Varent asked politely.

Calandryll frowned, thinking. It was unusual that his views should be sought on such matters, and he would have preferred to study Nadama, contemplating how he should approach her, but he felt his father's eyes on him, as though the Domm saw his reply as a test of some kind.

'I think,' he said slowly, 'that caution is the wisest policy. Should we go to war with Kandahar we should be the weaker side. The concept of our cities joining in alliance is unusual enough that we should first establish the navy. Let us see how that fares before we attempt so ambitious a venture as direct attack.'

'Cautious as ever,' Tobias grunted.

But Calandryll saw that for once he had his father's approval. Encouraged, he continued, 'There will, inevitably, be problems at first. Who commands? How shall the supportive levies be organised? Shall the ships be built in the yards at Eryn, or in our own cities? Does Eryn join the alliance?'

'Eryn remains neutral,' said Bylath. 'They'll build our galleys, but not man them; nor join us.'

'Eryn sits safe in the north,' grumbled Tobias. 'The corsairs make no sallies so deep into the Narrow Sea and Eryn lacks the spine to fight with us.'

'Why should she?' asked Calandryll. 'The Kand pirates are no threat to Eryn.'

'And this alliance is unprecedented,' agreed Varent. He turned to Bylath: 'Your son has a good head on his shoulders, my lord. He'd make a fine diplomat.'

'He's to be a priest,' said Bylath flatly, bringing Calandryll back to earth. 'Tonight I announce it.'

Calandryll saw the satisfied expression on Tobias's face and felt his spirits sink afresh. Decisions had clearly been made in his absence, and whilst they were hardly unexpected, their immediacy emphasised his dilemma. He sought solace in contemplation of Nadama: if she agreed to marry him, the influence of the den Ecvin family could change his future.

'It cannot be so bad,' Varent murmured, his tone pitched low enough that only Calandryll might hear him. 'Even as a priest you must surely find time to study.'

Calandryll shook his head mournfully.

'In Secca, my lord, the priests are denied such luxuries - their only study is the worship of Dera. And I would marry.'

'That lovely maiden?' asked Varent, following his gaze.

'If she will have me.'

The Aldarin ambassador nodded thoughtfully. 'And does your father know of this desire?'

'No,' Calandryll murmured, turning to face Varent, 'Nor would I have him know until I have her answer. Her family has sufficient influence they might sway my father's decision.'

'So you would kill two birds with the single stone,' the ambassador whispered, smiling. 'Fear not, Calandryll - your secret is safe with me.'

'If she will have me,' he repeated.

'You think she might refuse?' Varent studied him speculatively.

'I have a rival.'

Dark brows rose, framing an unspoken question. Calandryll said, 'My brother.'

Varent's eyes hooded, though the smile remained fixed on his lips. Calandryll paid it scant attention, though it occurred to him that Varent did not particularly like Tobias.

'What will you do should she refuse?'

It was on the tip of his tongue to mention Reba's prophecy to the ambassador. There was something about Varent that elicited trust, and Calandryll thought he might obtain sound guidance from the older man. Was he, perhaps, the friend Reba had forecast? But it was too soon, he was not yet sure enough, he said, 'I do not know, my lord.'

Varent's dark eyes were contemplative as he studied Calandryll's face and it seemed he was about to speak, but Bylath claimed his attention and he turned to answer the Domm. Calandryll applied himself to the food set before him and for a while he was ignored, left to his own thoughts, which turned like a dog chasing its own tail back to Nadama.

He was relieved when the eating was done; then alarmed again when Bylath rose to his feet, compelling the hall to silence. He had no need of a crier to gain attention. His height and natural air of command was impressive enough.

'We have today agreed treaties of great import,' the Domm announced, 'unprecedented in the history of Lysse. Secca joins in alliance with Aldarin that we may defeat the Kand pirates.'

A roar of approval greeted the declaration. Bylath gestured for silence.

'Eryn will build the ships, but they will be manned by the warriors of our two cities. We have yet to decide the levies needed to finance the venture, and so my counsellors shall attend me on the morrow.' His eyes scanned the hall as though warning those nobles likely to object to such taxation, daunting as swords. 'But know now that my son, Tobias, shall command the ships of Secca with the title of admiral.'

There was a rattle of applause. Calandryll glanced at his brother, knowing this was the source of Tobias's self-satisfaction. Learning there was more to come.

'In proof of my faith I name Tobias, formally, my successor. He shall be Domm of Secca after me.' He paused as fresh applause greeted the proclamation, waiting until it died to say, 'At the Feast of Dera he shall be ordained heir.

'Further, my younger son, Calandryll, shall assume the duties of the priesthood. Know that I, Bylath den Karynth, Domm of Secca, declare it so.'

He sat as cheering filled the hall. It dinned against Calandryll's ears, drumming home the stark realisation that his future, so far as his father and brother were concerned, was determined. He had no say in the matter: alliance with Aldarin might be a new thing, but in Secca the world turned as it always had. He thought of the endless round of duties that must inevitably follow, should his father have his way, and the only consolation he could find was in hope of Nadama's acceptance. He could envisage no way in which Reba's prophecy knitted with his father's plans.

'Congratulations.'

Tobias's mocking voice interrupted his self-absorption and he looked up to find his brother at his side, realising that musicians had struck up a tune, bringing folk onto the floor even as servants hurried to shift the tables, making room for the celebrations.

'And to you,' he offered, automatically.

'It was decided today,' Tobias said. 'Had you shown more interest, father might have wished you in attendance. But as you have not ... Well, it is the custom. And you will be where I can watch you. Guide you.'

'Yes,' he muttered, grimly.

'Of course,' Tobias grinned, 'you'll have no time for your bookish nonsense. Save the study of religious observance. I'll see to that.'

He slapped Calandryll's shoulder with amiable menace and flourished a bow in the direction of the Domm and the ambassador.

'My lords, will you excuse me? A lady awaits.'

Grinning hugely he sprang from the platform holding the High Table to Nadama's side. Calandryll's jaw clenched tight as he watched her rise, her smile glorious. For Tobias.

He sat dumbly as they moved to the centre of the floor, Tobias's arm about her waist, hers about his, their feet moving as though guided by a single mind, Nadama's eyes radiant on Tobias's face. Had he been utterly wrong? Had he misinterpreted her affection? That his brother was a rival he had known, but he had not expected to see such adoration in her eyes. Not for Tobias.

'We have a saying in Aldarin,' he heard Varent murmur sympathetically, '"The vine bears many grapes".'

'But not for priests,' he answered dolefully, unable to tear his gaze from the couple.

He did not think to offer excuses as he heard the music end and rose to his feet, ignoring courtesy as he left the table to push through the waiting dancers, confronting the woman he loved.

'You will excuse me?'

He took Nadama's arm without awaiting a response, leaving Tobias standing as the musicians began a second tune. He was, at least, as good a dancer as his brother.

That did not help as he sought the words he was suddenly afraid to utter. Perhaps he had misunderstood her expression. He swallowed, steeling himself.

'Congratulations.' Nadama spoke before he was able to organise his confused thoughts. 'Are you not pleased with your appointment?'

'No,' he answered, apprehension making his voice gruff. 'I have no wish to be a priest.'

Abruptly he was sorry: this was not the way to approach it.

'Forgive me. I had hoped ...' He broke off. 'I don't know what I hoped.'

'It is customary,' she said, smiling in a manner that quickened his heartbeat.

'A priest is celibate,' he muttered, cursing his confusion. 'A priest may not marry. Nor study, save religious tracts.'

Nadama nodded, still smiling, swirling in a flurry of skirts, returning to his arms, her perfume heady as she drew close.

'I admit you are an unlikely priest.'

'I should not be able to marry,' he protested.

'Why should that trouble you?' She was smiling still, though not the way she had smiled at Tobias. 'Are there not ways in which the priests ... satisfy ... those desires?'

He felt a coldness knot tight in his belly. He stared at her, feeling that his heart climbed his ribs to lodge in his mouth.

'I want to marry.'

'You? Whom do you favour? And how shall you refuse the Domm's command?'

Did she pretend confusion? Did she play some game? Did she not understand? The cold spread, presentiment ugly as a tumour. He thought he heard the desperate thudding of his heartbeat; felt she must surely hear it, too; must surely know what it was he asked.

'You,' he said, 'I want to marry you. Did your father speak to mine about this business of the priesthood ...'

'Calandryll ...'

A warning rang in her voice; he ignored it, committed now, speaking before the cold numbed his tongue and he lost the power of speech.

'I love you. I want to marry you. Please?'

'Calandryll!' She moved as far away as his grip on her arms would allow: the distance was a chasm. 'You are fond of me, I know that ... But this is madness. I am promised.'

'I love you. Will you marry me?'

The music stopped. Tobias stood beside them, a hand extended. Nadama took it, granting Calandryll one sorry glance before her smile returned, like the sun rising, bathing Tobias in its radiance.

He watched them walk towards the High Table. Saw Tobias speak with Bylath. The Domm rise.

Silence descended again.

Bylath said, 'It appears there is further good news: tonight my son has chosen a bride. I give my blessing to their union. Nadama, daughter of Tyras and Roshanne den Ecvin, shall wed Tobias.'

Calandryll stared, dumbstruck. It seemed his heart beat a dull threnody against his ribs, threatening to empty his stomach over the floor. Tobias raised Nadama's hand to his lips; Bylath beamed, embracing her. Varent offered his felicitations; Tyras and Roshanne stepped beaming onto the dais. Calandryll felt himself carried towards them as the crowd surged forwards. He stared at them. Heard a voice he barely recognised as his say, 'May Dera bless you.'

It was automatic, a reflex empty of feeling: he felt only pain. He could stand no more. Nadama's smile hurt too much, a knife of happiness that turned in his gut; Tobias, smiling hugely, said something he could not hear through the pounding in his ears. He turned away, ignoring his father's angry cry and the curious glances of the others as he stumbled from the hall with the taste of ashes in his mouth.

*

He had no idea how he came to be at the Seers Gate, no memory of quitting the palace or of the streets he had traversed. The moon hung gibbous above, streamered with rack, the wind that drove the cloud was cold, chilling the sweat that plastered fresh-barbered hair to his forehead, his shirt to his back. The guana-whitened sign creaked on its moorings, the sound like malign laughter, the frontage of Reba's house dark and forbidding. He was aware that he pounded on her door only when the lilting voice bade him stop, and then he stood panting, hands knotted in desolate fists, seeing the door open, the spaewife a dark mass against the lightless shadow of the corridor.

'Who is it? Who calls so angry at this hour?'

In his despair, his anger, he had forgotten she was blind. He said bitterly, 'You do not know?'

'Calandryll?' She stepped a pace towards him, into the moonlight, her eyes twin mirrors of the milky disc. 'Why do you come here so late?'

He closed the distance between them, fists raised as though to strike her, lowering them to thud against his hips. Reba stood her ground, head cocked.

'You call yourself spaewife and you do not know why I come?'

'I am a spaewife; no, I do not.'

Her voice was calm. It seemed her blindness armoured her and that very tranquility leached the anger from him, leaving only despair in its place. He groaned, close to tears that he fought to dam. Reba stood back.

'You had best come in.'

He went past her into the darkness, pausing as she drew the door closed, sliding bolts into place, brushing by him to lead the way to the room where they had sat that morning. She found the tinderbox and struck flame to a lantern, pushing it towards him.

'Light the lamps if you wish.'

He took the bowl and applied its wick to the lanterns set about the chamber. Their light was mellow. revealing the plague-scarred seeress dressed in a sleeping gown, overlaid with a green robe. Her hair was unbound, long and straight, her face calm as her voice.

'There is wine in the kitchen, if wine you need.'

He carried the lamp through; returned with the same flagon and the two cups. This time it was he who drank the faster, aware that much more, after what he had consumed at dinner, would tip him over into drunkeness. It seemed a sound enough idea, but first there were questions.

'She refused me. She is to marry my brother.'

Reba nodded slowly. 'I read loss.'

'You did not tell me I should lose Nadama.'

He choked on her name and wiped a hand across his eyes, filling his cup afresh.

'I told you all I saw,' the spaewife said evenly. 'I told you your future is clouded - that you have choices.'

'They narrow apace,' he retorted, voice hoarse with bitterness. 'Nadama is to marry Tobias and I am ordered to become a priest.'

'Those were options you outlined yourself,' Reba murmured.

'I did not *believe* them!'

Reba sighed. 'Calandryll, you are young and you are a stranger to disappointment. I saw loss - I told you that! - were you not ready?'

'No.' He stared at her, head moving slowly from side to side. 'No, I was not. I thought ...'

He broke off, stifling a sob. Reba said, 'You thought you would have what you most desired and so you saw my prophecy from that viewpoint alone.'

He grunted a reluctant affirmative. 'Now I have nothing.'

'Now you have choices to make.' Her voice was still

musical, but harder now, carrying the ring of battle horns. 'What I read of your future still stands; it is for you to choose whether you take that path or not. Nadama has chosen her own path - does that not free you in a way?'

'I wanted her,' he muttered. 'I *love* her.'

'And you have always had what you wanted.' There was a distinct edge now, a clarion like a challenge. 'You have lived behind the palace walls; with servants, luxury. Whatever you have wanted has been there for the taking. Did you think to have your Nadama so easily?'

Welling tears dried on his cheeks and his mouth hung open: there was truth in what she said.

'I thought ...' He faltered, shaking his head helplessly.

'You thought because you love her, she must return your affection. It is common enough; so is loss. *Nadama has chosen Tobias.* That is a fact you must live with.'

'You did not foresee it,' he said, resentfully.

'I saw both loss and gain. You chose the interpretation.'

'Yes.' Reluctantly. 'Yes, I did.'

'And now it is for you to choose the path your life will take. What I saw suggests you need not accept this duty you find so odious.'

He laughed sadly. 'Your prophecies are vague, Reba.'

'The pattern, as I told you, is complex.'

'It is beyond me.' He sighed, then asked, 'This comrade I shall meet, the one with whom I shall - *might* - travel? Tonight I encountered the ambassador of Aldarin and he spoke of showing me maps - could he be the one?'

'Perhaps.' Reba shrugged. 'Perhaps not. I think that Aldarin is not very far.'

Calandryll drank more wine, though slower now, calming. There was iron in the spaewife's tranquility, an immovable quality that imposed a degree of calm on his disordered thoughts. 'I should have known had he been the one,' he murmured. 'Should I not?'

Again Reba shrugged. 'Perhaps. I think that tonight your judgement has been clouded.'

He remembered Varent's words, 'He said "the vine bears many grapes".'

'And so it does,' she answered, 'and the beach has more than one pebble. I am older than you and I tell you you will get over Nadama. I speak not as a seer, but as a woman. You will find this hard to believe, but it is so.'

She was right: he did not believe it. He said, 'I think I shall not. And if I cannot, then I would go away from her. I cannot bear the thought of seeing her with Tobias.'

Reba smiled and said, 'Perhaps you begin to choose already.'

Calandryll grunted and said, 'This journey you foresaw? This quest to far lands?'

'Perhaps. Perhaps your feet already tread the path. Perhaps you cannot see it yet.'

'Perhaps,' he allowed.

'What will you do now?' she asked.

He thought for a moment before replying, 'I think I shall get drunk.'

'That is no answer. Not to me or yourself.'

'But it is an attractive alternative.'

He was calmer now, but the pain was still there, a knife turning in his heart, hot as a furnace, cold as the grave. Reba sighed. 'For a little while, perhaps; but sooner or later you must sober up.'

'Will you read my future again?'

She shook her head. 'No, Calandryll, I will not. One prophecy in a day is sufficient. There will be nothing new, and you know what you need to make your choice.'

'Then may I drink your wine?'

'Not that, either.' Her voice throbbed, a dull base note. 'I would not have the Domm's son drunk in my house. I cannot afford your father's anger.'

Resentment came back like a fresh-opened wound and he pushed to his feet.

'Then I shall leave you, spaewife, and find a more hospitable place.'

Reba's head lifted as though her sightless eyes followed him. The bass became a clarion again.

'Calandryll! Go back to the palace and get drunk there if you must. The streets of Secca are not safe that you may wander them without danger. Better, find watchmen and have them escort you home.'

'Back to that palace that shelters me from your world?' he demanded. 'From the real world?'

'For now,' she agreed.

'You say I have choices to make. Very well, I shall make this one.'

He turned, ignoring her cry of warning, and stumbled into the corridor. He found the door and fumbled with the bolts, dragging the portal open. Cold air struck his face and he halted, head swimming, the shuttered windows across the narrow street wavering, resolving into distinct outlines only when he concentrated, blinking.

'This is foolishness,' he heard Reba say to his back. He shook his head and walked away.

The odours that had excited him that morning were dulled now by the dampness of the wind, overlaid with the salt tang of the ocean, the street itself changed by night and moonlight. Doorways and signs that had been glamorous in the sun were dimmed, like closed eyes; the mouths of alleyways were maws of darkness, vaguely threatening, oblivious of his heartache. He staggered past them, moving instinctively towards the wider avenue that marked one boundary of the Seers Gate.

Where were the taverns? Where could he find wine to dull the pain? Not in the palace: that was more prison than ever now, and he rejected the possibility. Likely the feasting continued. Nadama would be in Tobias's arms, dancing, that smile he had thought was his directed at his brother. Tyras and his father would be drinking in celebration of the union; and Bylath would be furious with him for leaving as he had. Tobias would crow and he could not bear that. No, he would find some place to drown his sorrow and face the Domm, face the pain, tomorrow. He snorted bitter laughter as inspiration struck. Down from the Seers Gate, beyond the Merchants Quarter, lay the Sailors Gate, and sailors drank. The port garrison lay there, too, and soldiers, off duty, drank. Yes: the harbour was the place to go; there would be taverns aplenty there.

His feet unsteady, he turned back, finding the alley he had traversed earlier, following it through to the Merchants Quarter, taking that broad thoroughfare eastwards.

The wind grew stronger and he shivered, sobering a little in the cold. He did not want to be sober, for then he knew he would think of Nadama and Tobias and the knife would turn afresh in his heart, carving new agonies. He saw a cat studying him warily over the carcass of a rat and halted, returning the animal's hostile stare. The cat's tail furred and it spat a challenge, as though it feared he might contest its prize. Yellow eyes glared, then the feline sank long fangs into the bloodied hide and carried the body swiftly off into the darkness. Calandryll shrugged and continued on past the shuttered warehouses.

It seemed he walked for hours before he saw light ahead and quickened his pace, breaking into a ragged run that brought him unsteadily into a plaza where lanterns defied the night and tavern signs boasted all a thirsty mariner might desire. He turned in a circle, staggering, regaining his balance with flailing arms, as he surveyed the inns. He chose the closest and smoothed his tunic, ran careless hands through his hair, before pushing through the door.

Cold and damp were instantly replaced by heat and the heady reek of liquor. Calandryll blinked, an owl caught in the flare of the hunter's torch, and peered, no less owlishly, about. Rough wooden tables were scattered across a floor spread with sawdust stained with spillage. Men sat there, tankards and cups before them, answering his examination with varying degrees of interest, a few women amongst them, their interest more obvious, more predatory. The ceiling was low, hung with lanterns that he stooped to avoid, their light augmented by the lowering flames of the logs burning in a wide stone hearth. The remnants of a calf roasted on a spit, listlessly turned by a child in threadbare shirt and torn breeks, his feet bare and dirty. To the right was a long table, behind it a fat, bald man in a greasy apron; behind him tapped barrels and shelved flagons, tankards and mugs hung like trophies from wooden pegs.

'Master?' Watery eyes took in Calandryll's finery. 'What's your pleasure?'

'Wine. Strong wine.'

'I have a vintage from the Alda valley that'll please your palate.' The innkeeper produced a dusty bottle, a goblet of cheap glass that he polished briefly on a soiled cloth. 'Try that, young master.'

Calandryll sipped. The wine was, indeed, strong. He emptied the goblet and nodded, taking the bottle. There were tables enough empty that he found a place close to the fire, near a low doorway that led into the bowels of the tavern.

'Would you eat, master?'

He shook his head, waving a dismissal, and the fat man returned to his desultory polishing of the bar. Calandryll filled his goblet and stared around.

The other drinkers were mostly seamen, he thought, from the cut of their clothes and the heavy rings that decorated their ears. Many wore swords, all had daggers; several were clearly drunk. There were a few mercenaries, no doubt in the employ of local merchants, dressed in protective leather, long blades strapped to their sides or hung across their backs. The women had the look of doxies, their gowns cut to reveal breasts bound high, cheap jewellery glittering about their throats and on their fingers. They studied Calandryll with professional eyes. He smiled at nothing and drank, refilled the goblet and drank again. He could not help comparing the women with Nadama, so he drank some more to drive away that hurtful memory.

In a while the flagon was empty and he called for another, slumping in his chair with outflung feet as the fat man brought the bottle.

'It's to your liking, master?'

'It's to my liking. It's a most excellent wine. My compliments on your cellar.'

His voice was thick and he chuckled at the sound, at his joke. The innkeeper beamed obsequiously and left him. Calandryll sank lower in his chair, grinning, oblivious of the wine that stained his shirtfront, grateful for the dulling of the pain.

He emptied half the second flagon and forgot that he was drunk. A torpor that was almost pleasant weighed his limbs, the goblet heavy in his hand as he raised it, the fire warm at his side. He stared around with bleary eyes and a slack-mouthed smile, the other occupants blurred shapes, their conversation a distant groundswell. When he set the goblet down it tilted, falling on its side, spilling wine like bright blood across the cracked surface of the table. He studied it, watching the redness spread and begin to drip to the floor, over his outthrust legs. He chuckled, then sniffed and began to weep, becoming immediately angry with himself so that he lurched straighter in his chair, wiping a careless sleeve over his face.

He set his goblet upright and filled it once more, his movements cautiously exaggerated, pleased at the success of the manouevre. As he raised the smeared glass he saw a shape disengage from a group about a nearby table and move towards him, coalescing as it approached into the form of a woman.

She was more than a few years older than he, with hennaed hair and vermilion lips, eyes accentuated with kohl, the lashes like spikes. Her gown was cut low and waisted high, bright yellow, cinched with a wide corset of black leather. She leaned towards him, affording a clearer view of her breasts, and his nostrils flared at the waft of cheap perfume and sweat that drifted from her. She smiled, exposing stained teeth.

'You drink alone. You're too handsome to drink alone.'

Calandryll blinked, resolving the three images that wavered before him into a single, more comprehensible form, and replied forlornly. 'Nadama doesn't think so.'

The woman took this as an invitation and settled herself in a chair to his left.

'Then Nadama is foolish. My name is Lara.'

He said, 'Lara,' thickly, turning to peer at her through the wine-fog misting his vision.

He saw that she held a glass and filled it. She swallowed and smiled some more.

'Nadama was your sweetheart?'

'I love her,' he answered solemnly, 'but she is to wed my brother.'

'Then you'd best forget her,' Lara advised. 'Shall I help you forget her?'

Calandryll frowned, enunciating his reply with difficulty.

'I don't think I can.'

'Oh, you can,' Lara declared. 'Come with me and you'll forget every woman you've ever had.'

His frown deepened and he said, 'I haven't had any others. I haven't even had Nadama.'

Shrill laughter rang in his ears and she leant closer, a hand on his thigh. 'A virgin? Are you really a virgin?'

He felt his honour was somehow questioned, but he could only answer, 'Yes.'

'Well then,' Lara shifted her chair until her breasts pressed against his arm, her hand stroking his leg, higher, her mouth close to his cheek, 'it's time you became a man. Come with me.'

'Where?' he asked.

Lara tossed her head in the direction of the door. 'There are rooms back there. Old Thorson asks only fifty decima for the night; and I ask but a single var.'

Calandryll turned towards her, then away as breath redolent of stale wine and decay assailed his nostrils. Dimly it occurred to him that he carried no money; slightly less dimly that he felt no wish to bed this blowsy doxy.

'Thank you,' he said primly, 'but no.'

'Don't be shy.' A hand brushed his hair, another his crotch. 'I'll show you what to do.'

'I know what to do,' he said.

'Then come,' urged Lara, taking his free hand. 'We'll bring your bottle with us and I'll give you a night you'll not forget. You'll remember me long after you've forgotten Nadama.'

A rush of panic filled him and he tugged his hand from her grasp, shaking his head: 'No!'

Lara's stroking became more insistent. 'Don't be shy,' she repeated, 'Come with me.'

He swallowed a mouthful of wine, feeling himself

respond to her touch despite the distaste he felt. Lara chuckled and said, 'If it's the money, then I'll bed you for half a var. Because you're a virgin.'

'It's not the money,' he said, regretting it as he saw her smile fade, 'Well, it is.'

'Half a var?' Her tongue licked briefly over her lips. 'A young noble like you surely has half a var.'

'No.' Calandryll smiled apologetically. 'I don't have any money.'

'What?'

Her hand quit its stroking as she sat back, upright, dark-ringed eyes widening in outrage.

'I don't have any money,' he said. 'Not with me.'

'Cheapskate!' Lara's voice was strident, attracting the attention of the other drinkers. 'Who d'you think you are? You come here, drinking, and you've no money? Dera rot your manhood! Do you nobles think you can come down here and lord it over us honest folk?'

The tavern keeper, Thorson, appeared at the table, his moon-face apprehensive.

'What's the trouble? I don't want the watchmen in here - I run an honest tavern.'

'Honest? You talk about honest?' Lara was on her feet now, arms akimbo, face flushed. 'As him about honest! What's he had? Two flagons of that Aldan and no coin to pay with!'

Thorson seemed torn between fear of offending Calandryll and fear of losing his profit. Nervously he asked, 'Is this true, master?'

Calandryll nodded. 'I fear so. But I have this ring.'

He began to fumble with the signet, but Thorson shook his head after glancing at the thing. 'That's no use to me.' The honorific "master" was gone now. 'I take that and the watchmen'll be asking questions. It's strictly coin here.'

'Tomorrow,' Calandryll offered, nervous now, seeing others join the inn keeper, an ominous semi-circle about his table, 'I can bring you coin tomorrow.'

Thorson shook a ponderous head. Lara snorted cynical laughter.

'You believe that, Thorson, and you'll believe anything. This bastard'll cheat you and laugh about it tomorrow.'

'You have no coin at all?' asked Thorson.

'None.' Calandryll heard the onlookers mutter angrily and felt his apprehension grow. His head began to ache. He attempted a placatory, wary, smile and said, 'I can pay you tomorrow. I promise.'

'Nobles' promises are like wind,' sneered Lara. 'They blow away.'

'Yes,' agreed a voice from the crowd, 'It's coin you demand from us, and coin you should demand from him.'

'I am,' snapped Thorson, 'and he hasn't got any.'

'He says,' returned another voice, scornfully 'but I'll wager he's got a purse on him somewhere.'

'Search him,' advised another. 'Strip him down and search him.'

'I don't!' Calandryll shouted, frightened now. 'I swear it. In Dera's name! I'll pay tomorrow.'

'Bugger Dera,' said someone else, 'this bastard comes down here lording it over us in his finery and looks to cheat honest folk. He needs a lesson.'

'I don't want the watchman in here,' Thorson warned.

'Who needs the watchman?' asked a voice. 'We'll teach him a lesson ourselves.'

Calandryll rose, pushing back his chair. It hit the wall and he felt his knees falter. His head pounded. 'Please,' he said, 'I swear I'll pay you tomorrow. I'll bring money from the palace.'

'The palace!' Lara hooted. 'Listen to him - the palace! He'll tell us he's the bloody Domm next.'

'Bloody nobles!' cried an angry voice. 'Get him!'

'No, please!'

Calandryll thrust out defensive hands as the table was dragged away. The flagon, the goblet and Lara's cup tumbled to the floor in a spray of breaking glass. Hands fastened on his tunic. He heard someone shout, 'Watch out! He's got a knife.'

He had forgotten the dagger and would likely not have used it even had it not been snatched from the sheath and tossed aside. Fleetingly he thought that Tobias would have remembered that, and used the weapon, but then a fist hit his cheek and he thought only of the pain.

It got worse as more fists struck him, filling his belly with a surging nausea that doubled him over, barely aware of the blows that crashed against his back. He realised that he was on the floor when sawdust joined the taste of blood in his mouth and a boot thudded hard into his ribs. He struggled to rise, but was knocked down, drawing knees to his chest, arms protective about his head. They began to kick him, warming to their sport, boots landing against his back and thighs and chest.

Then, abruptly, it ended and he heard a harsh voice say, 'That's enough!'

'Who says?' came a snarling answer.

'I do.'

Calandryll lowered his arms, peering from swollen eyes at a pair of well-worn black boots, cracks like friendly wrinkles striating the leather. He looked up, at leathern breeks, a wide swordbelt hung with falchion and long dagger, a shirt of soft leather beneath a tunic of the same material, all black. He could not see the man's face because he turned as he spoke, eyeing the crowd.

'You'll stop us?' There was contempt in the question.

Confidence in the reply: 'If I must. He's had enough. He's learnt his lesson.'

'Give him some more,' Lara urged.

Calandryll saw a tanned hand descend to the hilt of the falchion, then gasped as steel rustled against leather. The falchion slid from its scabbard, smooth as a striking serpent, lamplight glinting briefly on the blade. It flickered out and a man shouted, sword clattering loud in the sudden silence.

'I'd prefer not to kill you.'

The voice was accented, not from any Lyssian, the statement flat, as though no doubt existed that the implicit threat could be made good. Calandryll heard the thud of a sword rammed home into scabbard.

'Stand up.'

He spat blood and got his hands under him, fingers splayed wide on the dirty floor. It hurt, but he got to his feet, swaying, moaning as he straightened his back and a fiery pain shot through his side. One eye was closing, the other blurred as he saw that he was of a height with his saviour, that the man's hair was as long and black as his clothes, drawn into a loose queue like a horse's tail. The eyes that swung momentarily towards him were a startling blue, surrounded by tiny wrinkles as though accustomed to narrowing against the glare of the sun, set deep in a face tanned near as dark as his shirt; the nose flattened where some old blow had broken it; the mouth wide, drawn back from even teeth.

'Can you walk?'

He tried a tentative step and nodded, the motion spilling blood from his nose.

'Then walk to the door. No one will stop you. Eh?'

The grunted question was emphasised by the falchion: Calandryll moved towards the door.

His rescuer paused, studying the crowd, knees slightly bent, his blade extended as he backed away.

Thorson asked, 'What about the wine he drank?'

The man laughed curtly. 'Take his knife in payment, it's a pretty enough blade. Now leave him be, and don't think to follow us.'

He moved swiftly to the door, finding Calandryll still there, shouldering the younger man roughly through.

'Quick!' he urged. 'They'll likely find their nerve in a moment and there's more than even I can handle.'

He locked a hand on Calandryll's arm and hurried his bloodied charge across the plaza to the closest alley. Calandryll had no choice but to match his lengthy stride, despite the agony that lanced his body with each step. The stranger dragged him along the alley as angry shouts echoed behind, ducking into a smaller passageway, then turning again, winding a way deeper into the maze of passages.

At last he halted and Calandryll slumped against a wall, panting, clutching at his aching ribs.

'It's unwise to come coinless into the Sailors Gate,' his companion advised, then chuckled, 'and none too bright for innocents like you to bring coin.'

'I'd have paid tomorrow,' Calandryll grunted, probing teeth with tongue.

'Let Thorson keep your dagger,' said the man. 'And learn to use a blade if you intend to wear one.'

Calandryll nodded, moaned.

'I owe you thanks.'

The man shrugged: 'Accepted. Now - I'd best see you safe home.'

Calandryll groaned at the thought. Suddenly the notion of returning to the palace, bloody and dishevelled, his dagger lost, was more than he could bear.

'No,' he muttered. 'I mean - please? - not like this. Tomorrow. I'll return tomorrow.'

The man studied him critically, then grinned. 'I take it this is no habit of yours?'

'No.' Calandryll shook his head, groaning afresh at the pain that buffeted the interior of his skull. 'I've never done this before.'

'Best not do it again. But you've a point - you look a mess.' He paused, chewing his lower lip, then shrugged again. 'Very well, I've a room with space for another on the floor. Come on.'

He hauled Calandryll from the wall, supporting the young man as he tottered. Calandryll felt mightily grateful for the arm that held him upright: he was not sure he could walk any further unaided.

'My name is Calandryll,' he said. 'How are you called?'

'Bracht,' said the man. 'I am called Bracht.'

THREE

SUNLIGHT shone in a dust-filled band from the window set high in the wall, forcing reluctant consciousness on Calandryll. It illuminated his face, filling his closed eyes with a fierce red that seemed to burn a way into the nethermost regions of his skull. He groaned, reaching for the tasselled cord that would bring a servant, cool water to slake the thirst drying his mouth, some restorative potion for the pounding that assailed his head. His hand struck rough plaster and the shock opened his eyes, wincing as the light struck louder gongs of pain from the templates of his confused mind. Squinting, he saw that there was no bell cord, only a white-washed wall, a plain wooden sill beneath the casement admitting the offensive brilliance. He groaned again, sitting up, instantly regretting the movement, and rubbed at his temples, struggling to pin down memories that danced like fireflies through the tortured convolutions of his whirling head. He had been in a tavern and there had been a woman, a fight. He gasped, turning to examine the room. He was not in the palace; someone had rescued him from a beating. Bracht - yes, that had been his name. A dark man, dressed all in black; a mercenary. And Bracht had agreed to let him sleep here because he had been afraid - or ashamed - to return to the palace.

Where *here* was, he had no idea. It looked to be a room in some cheap inn or lodging house. There was a bed, neatly made, a single chair, a wash-stand, a small cupboard; the floor was uncarpeted, plain boards, scarred and dusty; the ceiling low, the angles of the obtruding beams suggesting the room was located high, beneath the roof. He lay on a blanket, another covering him; of Bracht there was no sign.

He shuddered, regretting the excesses of the night before; regretting more the confrontation that must be inevitable on his return, and pushed the blanket away. He was naked beneath its dun coloured wool and ugly bruises discoloured his ribs and thighs. He looked at the wash-stand, praying that the ewer held clean, cool water, and began to rise. It seemed then that daggers drove between his ribs and the muscles of his legs screamed in agony: he fell back, panting, twisting awkwardly to avoid the light burning his eys. Closing them seemed the wisest course, so he did that, and fell asleep again.

When next he woke, the sun had shifted across the sky and the window no longer cast its radiance on his face, though his head still throbbed and it seemed his body was wrapped in heated bands that creaked a painful protest at every moment. His thirst was worse, his tongue furred and swollen in a mouth seemingly filled with sand. He gritted his teeth, feeling at least one loosened, and rolled onto his belly. Rising on hands and knees was an effort that brought sweat to his brow, standing an exercise he doubted he could complete. The muscles of his belly protested, and when he straightened his back he thought his spine must break. Bent over, shuffling like an old man, he crabbed a way to the wash-stand and grasped the ewer in shaking hands. The water that spilled into the bowl was tepid, stale, but he drank it as though his life depended on it, then filled the bowl again and dunked his face.

Such rudimentary ablutions went a little way towards clearing his head and he examined the room again, wondering where his clothes might be. He found them in a cupboard, folded neatly, though stained with wine and blood. His fingers told him the gore had likely come from his nose and lips, which felt swollen, horribly tender, and he shuddered afresh at the notion of presenting himself to his father in such condition. Sighing, unsure which part of his body felt worse, he tugged on his soiled clothing and stumbled to the door.

It opened on a low-roofed corridor that appeared to circuit three sides of the building, a narrow staircase offering a way to the levels below. He descended with both hands on the banister, each step jarring shafts of agony through body and mind, arriving finally at a hall running the length of the building. The sound of voices came from behind a door and he went through into a kitchen, where the smell of food managed to inform him that he was hungry and to nauseate him simultaneously. He hung on the door, blinking, and a large woman, her hair bound up in a turban of dirty white pointed an accusatory ladle in his direction.

'Food's not ready yet.'

'Bracht?' he succeeded in mumbling.

'The swordsman? In the yard, playing with his toys.'

The ladle swung to indicate the farther end of the hall and Calandryll grunted thanks and began to shuffle awkwardly towards the open door there.

Outside the sun was bright, a fresh onslaught against his aching head, the air sweet with the promise of spring and stables. He halted, noticing that the hand he raised to shade his eyes trembled. He leant wearily against the door frame, peering across a cobbled yard, horses staring incuriously back at him from the stalls on the far side, racked barrels standing against one of the high surrounding walls.

Bracht stood alone at the centre, the falchion extended, the curved blade glittering. He was stripped to the waist, sweat lending a sheen to his dark skin. Muscles rippled on his shoulders and back as he executed a series of delicate, almost terpsichorean steps, the sword feinting, thrusting, riposting against some invisible opponent. He spun, sweeping a sideways cut, and saw that he was observed.

'Calandryll!' He seemed unaware that the falchion shifted to a defensive position even as he called the greeting. 'You wake at last.'

Calandryll nodded and the blade lowered, Bracht grinning as he slid the steel into its sheeth.

'How do you feel?'

'Awful.' He grinned weakly as the man came towards him, seeing as he approached that pale scars streaked his ribs and chest. 'My head pounds and my body's in torment.'

'You were beaten hard, and I suspect you've little head for liquor.' Bracht smiled as he spoke, crossing to a water butt, splashing his face and torso. 'You've nothing broken, though - you'll mend.'

He fetched a strip of cloth from beside the butt and towelled himself dry; pulled on his shirt. Calandryll waited, vaguely resenting the absence of any hint of sympathy. Bracht laced his shirt and came to face the younger man. studying him critically.

'A healer can supply ointment for the bruises and in a week or so you'll look yourself again.'

Calandryll felt a rush of alarm. 'A week? How do I look now?'

'As if some drunken sailors used you for a kickball. You'll not be kissing any maidens until your mouth heals, though I doubt they'd want you to with a face like that.'

'Dera help me!' Calandryll moaned.

'It's not permanent,' Bracht chuckled.

'My father will flay me,' muttered Calandryll. 'He'll have me watched! I'll never be able to leave the palace!'

'The palace?' Curiosity flickered in the blue eyes. 'You spoke of the palace last night. Who are you?'

'Calandryll den Karynth, son of Bylath,' he answered.

'The Domm?' Bracht whistled. 'That was no boast, then?'

Calandryll shook his head; and groaned anew as the movement reminded him that it hurt. 'No,' he said, 'my father is a Domm of Secca, and I am in grave trouble.'

'I sense a story.' Bracht jabbed a finger in the direction of the hall. 'And stories are best told on a full stomach and a mug of ale.'

'I cannot eat,' Calandryll complained, 'and ale ... ugh.'

Bracht ignored him, turning him with a hand upon his shoulder to steer him back into the inn, along the hall to the spacious dining room. 'Trust me,' he advised, 'I suspect I have more experience of these things than you.'

Calandryll allowed the man to settle him in a comfortable chair and watched as he crossed to the serving hatch. This place was more salubrious than the tavern of last night, the air redolent of pine from the fresh sawdust sprinkled on the floor, the windows open to admit the faint scent of early honeysuckle from the vines covering the outer facade, and the scattering of men and women already seated at the wooden tables ignored him after their initial examination.

Bracht returned with two mugs, one surmounted with ale froth, the other containing a dark liquid.

'Drink.' He indicated the second mug. 'It'll clear your head.'

Calandryll doubted that, but when he sipped the bitter liquid he was surprised to find it palatable, the drumming inside his skull abating, the nausea that roiled his stomach easing. Bracht downed a healthy measure of ale and wiped the white moustache from his upper lip, lounging back in his chair.

'So, tell me.'

It seemed to Calandryll that he owed the swordsman at least that much, and there was something about the man that prompted confidence: he began to speak, sipping the restorative, explaining the events that had brought him to the Sailors Gate.

Bracht rose when he was done and fetched two more mugs over, soon followed by bowls of stew. Calandryll found that appetite overcame revulsion, and that the stew was good, further settling his stomach.

'You've a problem,' Bracht remarked equably. 'What do you propose to do about it?'

'I don't know.' Calandryll's reply was mournful.

'Best think of something. If Nadama's lost to you and you've no desire to become a priest, you'd best find some other course.'

'If I flee Secca - even if I was able to get away Tobias would likely employ Chaipaku to hunt me down.'

Bracht's response lacked sympathy, as if the notion of such danger was something he took for granted: 'Life is complicated in Lysse, my friend. In Cuan na'For things are simpler.'

'Cuan na'For?' Calandryll stared at the man, his own curiosity aroused now, overwhelming his self-pity. 'We name your homeland Kern. You belong to the horse-clans?'

'I did. I was born Asyth. I left my clan because ...' Bracht's blue eyes clouded for a moment, a shadow passing over his features. 'I had reasons.'

He fell silent and Calandryll saw that he did not wish to discuss those reasons. No matter: it was exciting enough to encounter a Kern; the land to the north was largely a mystery, the horseclans' contacts with Lysse confined to the trading of the animals they herded to market at Gannshold or Forshold. 'How came you here?' he asked.

Bracht shrugged. 'I had a fancy to see the world, so I stole some horses and brought them to sale in Forshold. Unfortunately the owners followed me - I had a choice between continuing on my way or facing thirty angry warriors, so it seemed the wiser course to take my money and wander Lysse. Money doesn't last long here and I took employment with a merchant, which is how I come to be in Secca.'

'You're a mercenary,' Calandryll murmured, intrigued.

Bracht nodded: 'My sword is for hire. Though at the moment there are no takers.'

'Perhaps ...' A thought crossed Calandryll's mind. 'Perhaps my father might find a place for you.'

'In the Palace Guard?' Bracht grinned, shaking his head. 'My thanks, but no - I've no taste for ceremony and less for taking orders.'

'What will you do then?' Calandryll asked.

'Something will turn up.' Bracht wiped the last of his stew with a hunk of bread. 'If not here, then in Aldarin, perhaps; or Wessyl. Perhaps I shall go to Eyl.'

'Varent spoke of my visiting the library in Aldarin.' Calandryll glanced up as a woman set fruit before them, removing their emptied plates, memories of Reba's prophecy stirring. 'Perhaps we might journey there together.'

'Would your father allow that?'

The blunt reminder dampened Calandryll's risen spirits and he experienced a sudden return of depression: Aldarin was far from Nadama. But she, he told himself resolvedly, was lost to him, there was nothing to keep him in Secca save the odious future mapped out by his father. If Bracht could wander freely, why not him?

'I could run away,' he said defiantly.

'Could you?'

The Kern's tone suggested he doubted it and Calandryll stared at his newfound friend: 'Why not?'

'You seem,' Bracht said bluntly, 'ill-equipped for adventuring.'

'I'm healthy. Likely I could find employment.'

'As what?'

'As ...' Calandryll paused, frowning, '... as a tutor, perhaps. Or an archivist.'

'I know nothing of such things.' Bracht shrugged carelessly. 'I can neither read or write, but it seems to me that a swordsman has a better chance in the marketplace.'

'You're unemployed,' Calandryll retorted, irked by the Kern's dismissal of his skills.

Bracht took no offence. Instead he shrugged and said, 'At the moment. That will change.'

'I could do something.'

'No doubt. But even the roads of Lysse are dangerous, and you are no warrior.'

The response sounded patronising to Calandryll and he bristled, youthful pride offended. Did no one take him seriously? 'Varent would help me, I think,' he said.

'Is Varent not your father's guest? Assuming he would be prepared to chance offending the Domm, how can you approach him without first returning to the palace? And if you do that, did you not say your father will confine you there?'

These words were pragmatic enough that Calandryll was brought forcibly back to earth. For a few moments he had seen a possible answer to his unhappiness, but now Bracht's casually spoken words dismissed that solution. He experienced a flash of irritation.

'There is Reba's prophecy. She spoke of travel - a quest.'

'Ah, yes,' said Bracht, 'the spaewife.'

'You doubt her?'

'I prefer to put my trust in my blade,' the Kern returned. 'It has been my experience that soothsayers unfold paths too complex for my liking.'

'Perhaps,' said Calandryll, studying Bracht with renewed interest, 'you are the one she spoke of.'

'No!' Bracht raised defensive hands. 'I'm a freesword, no tutor of innocents. I seek honest employment, not some vague quest. I'll see you safely returned to the palace, but there our ways separate.'

'As you wish,' Calandryll said stiffly, thinking that perhaps the Kern laughed at him; resenting it. 'Escort me to the gates and I'll see you rewarded. Will ten varre suffice?'

'Amply.'

It seemed Bracht took no offense. Why should he? Calandryll thought. He was, after all, a mercenary. Doubtless he had acted on a whim when he came to the rescue, or perhaps he had foreseen the opportunity of reward. Most likely that and nothing more; no fated meeting, but the natural opportunism of a hired sword. 'Then perhaps we should leave,' he said, disappointed.

Bracht nodded and they rose, Calandryll gloomy again. If the Kern was not the one foretold by Reba, then perhaps it *was* Varent the spaewife had meant. He would, he decided, return to the palace and face Bylath's wrath, but after that he would approach the ambassador. The sole certainty he felt was the antipathy that filled him at the idea of entering the priesthood. Limping, he followed Bracht out into the street.

It was a quarter with which he was unfamiliar and he trailed the Kern in sullen silence as the man strode purposefully - likely thinking of his reward, Calandryll decided - through a labyrinth of sidestreets and alleys.

They crossed a corner of the Merchants Quarter and entered an avenue devoted to pleasure houses, the lewd promises of the signs hung above the doorways reminding Calandryll of the doxy in the tavern. He grimaced at the memory, battered mouth pursing in distaste. If Bracht frequented such low establishments, he doubtless considered Calandryll no more than a pampered boy, the Domm's spoilt son. It was foolish to have thought he might be the comrade foreseen by Reba.

Then his dark musings were interrupted by a shout and he looked up to see a squad of watchmen approaching. There were five of them, surcoats emblazoned with the emblem of Secca over mail shirts, swords at their sides and curve-billed halberds on their shoulders. The officer shouted again and Calandryll realised the cry was directed at Bracht.

The mercenary halted. Calandyll stopped alongside. On both sides of the avenue passersby paused to watch and women hung from balconies, idly studying the entertainment.

The watchmen drew up facing the pair, halberds at the ready now. Their captain stepped forwards, his features stern.

'Lord Calandryll? Praise Dera we've found you. There are search parties all over the city.'

Calandryll felt embarrassed by the attention. He saw folk pointing at him; heard a woman call, 'Shall I tend those bruises, sweet?' He felt his cheeks flush.

'What happened to you?' asked the watchcaptain. 'This bravo put those marks on you?'

He was about to say, 'No,' but Bracht spoke first, clearly angered by the groundless accusation.

'You've a quick tongue.'

'Hold yours,' returned the officer curtly, 'I'm talking to Lord Calandryll.'

'He saved me,' Calandryll interposed, seeing that the Kern's hand dropped to his swordhilt. 'He rescued me from a beating.'

The watchcaptain studied Bracht insolently. 'A

mercenary, eh? What are you, a horseherder?'

'A Kern,' Bracht responded tightly, 'Yes.'

The officer grunted. 'Well, the young lord's safe now. You can leave him with us.'

'There's a matter of ten varre,' Bracht said.

'A mercenary,' the captain repeated, this time lading the word with contempt. 'And you want your money, eh?'

'Yes,' Bracht said.

'Not enough you get the honour of saving the Domm's son?' the watchman demanded.

Bracht's answer was a shrug.

'I promised him,' Calandryll said. 'He saved my life.'

'I've orders to bring you to the palace,' said the watchman. 'Nothing about paying some Kern mercenary.'

'He can come with us,' Calandryll decided. Then, turning to Bracht, 'Come to the palace and I'll see you paid.'

Very well,' the Kern agreed.

Calandryll had hoped that he might slip unobserved into the palace, at least change his bloodied, wine-stained clothing and bathe before confronting his father, but it was not to be. The watchcaptain marched his squad resolutely up to the gates and loudly presented his charge to the officer of the Palace Guard waiting there. Calandryll found himself the object of the guards' attention, discipline holding their faces straight but amusement clear in their eyes. The officer in charge looked him up and down, then stared at Bracht, raised brows framing a question.

'I owe him money,' Calandryll muttered. 'He saved my life.'

Bracht grinned at the officer, who nodded and said, 'If you will follow me, Lord Calandryll?'

'I need fresh clothes,' Calandryll declared.

'I have orders to bring you directly to your father,'

the officer returned, and spun about, barking orders that brought a squad of five soldiers to attention, an unwelcome guard of honour that gave Calandryll no choice save to be herded into the palace buildings.

He was brought to a chamber and left to await the Domm, Bracht inspecting the room with casual interest, as though the palaces of Lysse were as familiar as her taverns. He turned, offering no obeisance, when Bylath entered, Tobias at his side. The Domm's face was flushed with anger, growing a deeper red as he studied his younger son and his unexpected companion. Tobias seemed amused.

Bylath waved a hand, dismissing the guardsmen, and stared at Bracht.

'Who in Dera's name is this?'

His voice was tight with barely-suppressed rage. Calandryll felt his head begin to ache again and licked his lips, but before he could speak, the mercenary said, 'I am called Bracht. A warrior of the clan Asyth, of Cuan na'For. Your son owes me ten varre.'

'A Kern mercenary?' Tobias spoke, contemptuous laughter in his voice. 'Do you consort with barbarian freeswords now, Calandryll?'.

Bracht stiffened, blue eyes fixed hard on Tobias's face. Calandryll thought he might return some insult in reply and began to gabble, 'He saved my life! They were beating me and he stopped them. He gave me shelter and I promised him ten varre.'

'You place small value on your life,' Tobias said.

He was about to add more, but Bylath raised a hand to silence him, glowering at the Kern.

'This is true?'

Bracht nodded. Bylath clapped his hands and a door opened to admit a blank-faced servant.

'Ten varre,' snapped the Domm. 'Quickly!'

The servant departed and the quartet stood in silence, only Bracht seeming at ease, as if undaunted by the prestigious company. Calandryll shifted from foot to foot, nervously probing his loosened tooth. The servant returned with a small pouch; Bylath gestured in Bracht's direction and the coins changed hands.

'My thanks,' the Kern said, ducking his head in vague approximation of a bow.

'Thank you for your service,' Bylath grunted. 'You may go.'

Bracht glanced at Calandryll, smiling. 'Farewell, Calandryll.'

'Farewell,' he replied. 'And thank you.'

The Kern nodded and followed the waiting servant to the door. Calandryll squared his shoulders, awaiting the onslaught of his father's wrath.

It was a short wait.

'You,' Bylath said, spitting the words, each one a whiplash, 'are the son of the Domm of Secca. You have a position; you are expected to set an example. You have duties. Chief amongst those duties is obedience. Without obedience there is nothing, only chaos. The observance of protocol is a part of that obedience. But a part, it seems, that you choose to ignore. You were summoned to attend a banquet of double importance. It was to celebrate our agreements with Aldarin, and to honour your brother's betrothal. You chose to insult both our guests and your own family!'

He broke off, snorting as though outrage stilled his tongue. Beside him, Tobias stood smugly, enjoying his brother's discomfort. Calandryll stood in silence, trepidation and resentment mingled.

'You insulted Nadama, who shall one day be Domme,' Bylath continued. 'You insulted her family. Are you without any loyalty? Do you have no respect?'

He paused, but when Calandryll offered no reply he went on, 'You disappoint me, boy. I've long given up any great expectations of you; Dera knows, you're useless enough. You're no warrior and you show no interest in the affairs of state, but - thank the goddess! - I can rely on your brother in those matters. But I do not expect insults from you! When you're ordered to attend a banquet I expect you to remain. I do not expect you to disappear. Nor to return looking like ... like ...'

'Some common brawler?' Tobias suggested, then sniggered as he added, 'Though Calandryll is hardly the type to seek a fight.'

'What happened. Where were you?' Bylath roared. 'Who was that mercenary? Do you prefer the company of freeswords?'

Calandryll saw that an answer was expected. He licked his lips.

'I went to the Sailors Gate,' he said. 'I went to a tavern, and when they found out I had no money they set upon me. Bracht stopped them. He ...'

'What in Dera's name were you thinking, going to the Sailors Gate?' Bylath interrupted, the notion of his son mingling with commoners fuelling his rage.

'I was ...' Calandryll faltered, reluctant to admit his reasons, reluctant to give Tobias that further satisfaction, unwilling to admit his visit to Reba, 'I was ... upset.'

'By all the gods!' fumed Bylath. 'You were *upset*? My son insulted me bcause he was *upset*?' He stepped a pace closer and for a moment Calandryll thought he would lash out. Instead, his voice dropped ominously. 'What *upset* you, boy?'

The diminutive was offensive. Tobias's smile was offensive. Calandryll shrugged. Bylath raised a hand. Dropped it as Calandryll took an instinctive step backwards.

'What upset you, boy?'

'I love Nadama,' he blurted.

His father stared at him, dumbstruck, face purpling. Tobias laughed out loud.

'What?' asked Bylath, as though the idea was ungraspable.

'I love Nadama. I thought ...'

'She's to marry your brother.' Bylath shook his head.

'Still, I love her.'

'What have your feelings to do with this?' Bylath asked, and somehow that unfeeling question cut deeper than his anger: Calandryll stared at him in silence.

'You're to enter the priesthood.'

'No.'

He was surprised to hear himself say it; almost as surprised as his father.

'No? What do you say, *no*?'

'I do not wish to become a priest.' Now the words came in a flood, fear banished by resentment, by the unfairness of it all, by his father's lack of feeling, by Tobias's mocking grin. 'I feel no calling. Why must I be a priest? I want to study. Why can't I study? Why should I be celibate? I want ...'

Bylath's hand punctuated the sentence, cutting it short, sending Calandryll staggering sideways, crying out as the force of it drove his damaged lips hard against his teeth. Something broke then, not physical, and at first he did not realise what the blow had shattered or what it strengthened by its breaking. He felt involuntary tears moisten his eyes, heard, dimly through the ringing in his ears, Tobias say casually, 'He weeps. Poor little brother.'

Bylath said, 'What you want has nothing to do with this. You will obey me. Do you understand that, boy? *You will obey me!*'

He shook his head, less in negation of his father's demand than in dismissal of his tears, in chagrin. Then he gasped as Bylath clutched his dirtied shirt, snatching him upright, drawing him close enough that spittle landed on his face.

'You will obey me,' the Domm repeated. 'And I say you shall be a priest.'

He released his hold and Calandryll tottered back.

'There will be no more discussion. No more argument. You will obey. Now go to your quarters and remain there until I send for you.'

Calandryll stared at him for a moment, then turned and stumbled to the door, shoulders slumping, tasting blood salty on his tongue. As he left he heard Bylath say, 'Thank Dera you were the firstborn,' and Tobias's answering chuckle.

He found his way to his chambers with downcast eyes, ignoring the curious stares of servants and soldiers, wanting then only solitude. Inside, he tugged the bell cord and collapsed onto his bed. When a servant appeared he asked that a bath be drawn and a healer attend him, and began to pull off his soiled clothing. Outside, the day waned towards evening, cloud blowing up from the Eastern Sea, grey as his mood.

He was in the tub when the healer came, rising stiffly to present himself to the woman's ministrations, wincing as she probed his ribs and examined his damaged mouth, her expression carefully indifferent. It occurred to him that all the palace must know by now of his humiliation. She layed her hands on the bruises, her brown eyes assuming the blank stare of total concentration, becoming unfocussed as she murmured softly, drawing out the pain until all he felt was a dull aching, forgettable. She applied unguents and wound a bandage soaked in some aromatic preparation about his torso, advising him to avoid rigorous exercise for the next few days. When she was gone he dressed in shirt and breeks and lowered himself into a chair with Medith's *History of Lysse and the World* open on his knees.

He turned the pages idly, his interest dimmed by the confusion of his thoughts. If he obeyed his father, then he was condemned to the cloistered life of the priesthood, his studies limited to the religious texts permitted the order, to a life of celibacy and ritual. Should he disobey, what would happen? If Reba had spoken true then a quest lay before him. But a quest to where? With whom? The spaewife had spoken of comrades and for a little while he had thought Bracht was the one foretold, but the Kern had shown no interest, save in the promised reward. Varent, then? Was the ambassador of Aldarin the one? He might - perhaps - be safe there, but as Reba herself had said, Aldarin was not far distant; and would Varent risk jeopardising the alliance, chance Bylath's wrath, by helping him? It seemed unlikely. Perhaps Bracht's scepticism had been well-founded.

No! He would not accept that: he had a choice between acquiescence and freedom. The problem was to find the path the spaewife had foretold; take the first steps along that road.

But how?

That he could not say, and he closed the book, setting it aside as he rose and limped to the window.

Dusk was falling and bats darted about the palace walls, flittering shapes in the growing darkness. The cloud had increased, the undersides silvered by the waxing moon, blown up in great billows by the wind that rustled the foliage below. He shivered, thinking that if he was to find the path he must openly disobey his father, that such disobedience must outlaw him from Secca, from everything he knew, all that was familiar and safe. It was a great step to take and it frightened him. He moved back from the window as a knocking announced the servant come to light the lamps in his chambers, and called for the man to enter. Another, he felt certain, who knew of Bylath's wrath and all that had transpired that day. He watched the man as the lamps were lit, wondering if he laughed, or if his bland expression hid sympathy. The servant offered no comment and Calandryll watched him depart, wondering now if his father intended the further humiliation of denying him food. Like a wilful child, the thought fuelled his resentment. He would not accept the role forced on him! He *would* take the path Reba had offered.

He filled a cup with water, sipping slowly as he paced the confines of his chambers, determined now, but no wiser as to how to go about his rebellion.

He was still pacing when servants arrived with food and wine, their eyes failing to meet his as they set out the repast, filing out with no word spoken. As they went through the door, he saw that two guardsmen stood in the corridor outside: he moved towards the portal.

The guardsmen shifted, blocking his exit. They were burly men, shoulders wide beneath their breastplates, and they filled the doorway. Calandryll halted, staring at them.

'I would leave.'

'Forgive me, Lord Calandryll, but you are to remain here. The Domm has ordered it.'

The larger of the two spoke, his voice carefully neutral. Calandryll's hands bunched into frustrated fists.

'What?'

'The Domm has ordered that you remain in your chambers. We are instructed to guard your door.'

Humiliation blanched his cheeks and he ground his teeth, wincing as pain lanced his jaw. 'I am not allowed to leave?' he demanded, his voice husky.

'The Domm has ordered that you remain in your chambers,' the guard repeated doggedly; at least he had the grace to look shamefaced as he said it. 'We are ordered to see that you do.'

Calandryll slammed the door: it was all that he could think of doing.

Like a child, he thought. My father confines me to

my quarters like a child. He was close to tears and might well have cried had anger not proven the stronger emotion, strengthening his determination to rebel. He crossed to the windows and threw them open, going out onto the balcony. It was a short enough drop to the garden, and from there he could find a way out of the palace. Where he would go, he had no idea: he was too angry, too humiliated, to think beyond that single act of rebellion. He set his hands on the cool stone of the balustrade, preparing to straddle the low wall, then halted as low-voiced conversation drifted up on the night air and moonlight glinted on metal, seeing two more guards lounging in the shadows. He peered at them, scarcely able to believe that he was imprisoned, though that was what it amounted to, the realisation bringing a curse to his lips, the expletive attracting the attention of the men below. They looked up, faces pale beneath the shadowing beaks of their helms. Did one smile? Calandryll could not tell: he spun round, going back into his chamber, the window crashing shut behind him with sufficient force the thick glass rattled in its frame.

Helplessly, he slumped in a chair, picking at the food. He must be the laughing stock of the palace. Of all Secca when servants and guardsmen spread the word of his confinement. He pushed the plates away, the wine ignored, and sought solace in his books. There he might find some information that would help him in his plight.

He was determined, more than ever now, to evade the destiny his father set for him, but if he fled Secca he would likely, as he had told Bracht, find himself hunted by the Chaipaku: he turned to Medith's dissertation on the brotherhood.

'Of the Chaipaku, or the Brotherhood of Assassins, the historian had written, 'few facts are surely known, the sect guarding jealously its rituals and privacy, whilst about its activities there grows a plethora of legend. That they are assassins of awful repute is common knowledge, though their crimes are seldom prosecuted and their ways mysterious.

'The sect originates in Kandahar, that land itself a haunt of corsairs and brigands with little in common with the civilized domain of Lysse, though even the folk of Kandahar go in fear of the order. They were initially priests dedicated to the worship of the Ocean God, Burash, whose bloody rituals earned the displeasure of their fellow Kands, persuading the Tyrant Desmus to proclaim such practices beyond the pale of law. In consequence the sect, or brotherhood (no female may become Chaipaku), became outlaw, continuing its practices in secret.

'Numerous members deserted the sect at this juncture, whilst many more were slain on the Tyrant's orders, those most devout in their abnormal beliefs concealing themselves amongst the ordinary folk of Kandahar. The Tyrant Manorius (seventh of that title) sought to destroy the sect forever, appointing his brother, Taroman, to that duty, but sadly Taroman met with little success, himself dying of a fever commonly ascribed to Chaipaku poisons. Some measure of order was established under the eighth Tyrant, Geromius, to the extent, at least, that the sect was no longer able to openly flaunt the Tyrant's law. It did, however, spread secretly throughout Kandahar, establishing cells in all the major cities, and, so some claim, within the boundaries of Eyl and Lysse, though this I doubt.

'What, however, is certain is that the Chaipaku, no longer devoting themselves exclusively to worship of Burash, but seeking victims where they might, became assassins of dreadful repute. Their services are available to any able to meet their price and able to gain audience with one of the sect. This, so some claim, may be accomplished through the offices of the priests of

Burash, though such relationship is denied. That they may be contacted by those unscrupulous enough to employ such means appears proven by the murders of such as Krim, Domm of Hyme, Gareth of Wessyl, the heirs of Balthan, and Roldan of Eryn, whose deaths are described elsewhere in this work. The mysterious demise of Telek, the ninth Tyrant of Kandahar, is also attributed to the Chaipaku (see Tyrants of Kandahar).

'Rumour has it that in modern times the Chaipaku are dedicated from birth, parents relinquishing all natural rights that their children may be raised unaware of their origins, believing Burash to be their progenitor. They are versed in all known forms of combat and the poisoner's art, and believed equipped of superhuman abilities. Certainly, it seems that they are able to conceal themselves with remarkable talent, to come and go undetected, and largely able to escape the consequences of their abominable deeds. Their awesome reputation rests to large extent on the grim fact that not one has ever been taken alive, death being the preferred option to capture.'

Calandryll paused, wondering if Tobias knew how to contact the Brotherhood. Then started as fingers scraped against the glass at his back.

He dropped the book, its antique pages crumpling as he rose from the chair with hair prickling on his neck, turning with widened eyes to the window. A man stood there, dressed in black, a shadow against the darkness of the sky. Thoughts of the Chaipaku dried Calandryll's throat as he opened his mouth to shout for the guards, and the figure raised both hands, palms towards its face. Light glowed briefly, emanating, it seemed, from the flesh itself, and the gaping youth saw Varent den Tarl's features illuminated.

His shout died stillborn as he recognized the ambassador of Aldarin and Varent smiled, gesturing for him to open the tall window. For long moments he stood in shocked silence, unable to do more than stare. Varent gestured again and the light died; Calandryll moved, almost unwilling, to the window, his hand rising seemingly of its own accord to the latch. The smell of almonds hung briefly on the night air as he swung the frame open.

'Thank you.' Varent stepped into the room, affable as though he paid no more than a courteous visit to an acquaintance, as though his appearance, impossible as it was, was perfectly normal. 'I do not think it a good idea to attract the attention of your ... guardians.'

He beamed, going to the table, where he lifted the decanter and savoured the bouquet.

'Excellent,' he murmured, filling a goblet, 'your father at least maintains a fine cellar.'

Calandryll gaped, struggling to speak. Varent sipped wine, nodding appreciatively, his handsome features radiating amusement.

'Are you,' Calandryll swallowed hard, 'Chaipaku? Have you come to kill me?'

Varent laughed softly and shook his head. 'Chaipaku? No, my friend, rest easy on that score. And as for killing you - quite the opposite: I come to aid you.'

'Aid me?' Calandryll took a step backwards, glancing nervously at the door.

'There's no need to summon the guardsmen,' Varent said amiably. 'I intend you no harm.'

'How ...' Calandryll shook his head in amazement, '... how did you reach the balcony unseen?'

Varent shrugged, dropping the black cloak he wore to a chair. Beneath, his clothes, too, were black, a dull shade that blended well with the night.

'Magic,' he said negligently. 'Simple magic.'

'Magic?' Calandryll felt foolish: he could do no more than echo the ambassador's words. 'Simple magic?'

'Insofar as any magic is simple,' Varent nodded. 'My powers are no great thing.'

'But,' Calandryll gasped, '... the guards ... the balcony.'

'I would have come directly into your chambers, but I really need to see a place before I can materialise there,' Varent returned. 'Luckily, I was able to catch sight of your balcony from my own chambers. So there I came, and here I am. The guards heard nothing, and these clothes ... well.' He indicated his subfusc garments with a careless hand. 'Hardly fashionable, but most effective when concealment is required. Why don't you sit down? You look as though you might faint.'

Calandryll sat, more a collapse than a deliberate movement, and Varent drew a chair up, facing him.

'Some wine? It really is a delicious vintage.'

Calandryll shook his head helplessly and the ambassador smiled, helping himself to a second glass.

'I imagine you have little taste after last night, eh? Your father waxed most wrathful on the subject, and your face tells me you suffered for your escapade.'

'Escapade,' echoed Calandryll.

'I gathered from your father's ... forgive me, but *ranting* seems the only appropriate word ... that the announcement of your brother's betrothal to the lovely Nadama prompted you to seek solace in the poorer quarters of Secca.' Varent sipped more wine; smacked his lips. 'I understand you were set upon by some band of irate tavern hounds and rescued by a mercenary. Really, Calandryll, you should choose your company more carefully. Though you certainly enliven an otherwise dull visit.'

'Dull visit,' he heard himself say.

'Oh, I have made the necessary treaties, and that was one reason for my presence. I really am Aldarin's ambassador, by the way. In case you doubt my credentials.' Varent waved a dismissive hand, chuckling. 'But there was another reason, and in that you may help me. In return I think I can help you.'

'Help me?' Calandryll mumbled.

'Indeed.' Varent reached out to pat his knee. 'Are you sure you will not venture a glass? You appear most disconcerted.'

'Magic,' he mouthed.

'Ah!' Varent tapped his aquiline nose. 'Am I to understand you are not particularly familiar with the wizardly arts?'

Calandryll shook his head.

'I am hardly a wizard,' murmured Varent modestly, 'what small talent I have was largely learnt from another but, though I say it myself, I do have a certain skill.'

Calandryll nodded mute agreement.

'It serves a purpose,' Varent beamed. 'This clandestine visit, for example. No doubt you already know your father confines you to your chambers. Did you know you are forbidden visitors? Or that the servants are forbidden to speak to you? Bylath really is a somewhat disagreeable man. Forgive such criticism, but I feel his reaction overstated, and I really did want to speak with you.'

'Why?' Calandryll managed to ask.

Varent reached for the decanter before responding, his dark eyes twinkling as he returned his gaze to Calandryll's gaping face.

'Because you appear to be the only scholar of any character here. Oh, there are your tutors, I know, but they are terrified of the Domm and had I enquired of them, word would doubtless have got back to your father. No, I need your help - you are positively the only one.'

He lounged back in his chair, black-clad legs extended, ankles crossed. Calandryll continued to stare at him, intrigued and still more than a little frightened.

'I formed that opinion last night,' Varent went on. 'You struck me as a young man of considerable learning, and your comments on Medith and Sarnum impressed me. More - you are familiar with the palace archives.'

'The archives?'

'Indeed. The archives. They contain a map I should dearly like to study.'

'A map?' said Calandryll.

'A map,' nodded Varent. 'No doubt ignored in some dusty corner that perhaps only you have explored.'

'Would my father not show it you?' Varent's attitude was so casual Calandryll found his confidence returning, the shock of the man's abrupt appearance abating; a degree of suspicion rising.

'I doubt he knows its whereabouts,' came the answer. 'And the ambassador of another city - even one now allied with Secca - is unlikely to obtain permission to roam at will through her archives. Who knows what secrets he might find?'

'What map?' Calandryll demanded.

'It is an ancient chart,' smiled Varent. 'A thing of no consequence to anyone save historians. Or wizards.'

Calandryll's suspicion must have showed on his face, because the man chuckled again and said, 'I do not ask you to betray your home city, my friend. The map is of no value to Secca, save as an antiquity. And I think neither your father nor your brother place much importance on such matters. No, this chart will not be missed, nor damage Secca with its removal. Quite the opposite, in fact.' He raised a hand as Calandryll opened his mouth to speak. 'Hear me out and then decide whether or not you wish to aid me. If not - well, I shall have to ask the Domm if I may inspect the archives, and when he refuses, I shall depart empty-handed. And you will remain here, to become a priest.'

It was sufficient bait that Calandryll was instantly alert. Varent smiled, nodding.

'Yes, I know what fate awaits you and I offer to help

you escape it. Further, I can offer you the protection of Aldarin should you choose to aid me.' He glanced at the discarded book. 'I see that you were reading of the Chaipaku. You fear Tobias might employ the Brotherhood against you? I can offer a measure of protection from them, too. Aid me and you'll be far from their clutches. Now, will you hear me out?'

Calandryll nodded, eager now: surely Varent must be the one Reba had foretold.

'Good.' The ambassador nodded, leaning forwards with elbows on knees, the goblet cupped between his hands. The bantering tone left his voice and his eyes fixed with a hypnotic intensity on Calandryll's face. 'As a scholar you are doubtless familiar with the gospels. Have you read Rassen? Excellent - you will understand all the better. As that somewhat dull scribe puts it, the gods of our world - Dera, Burash, Brann and the rest - are relative newcomers. Before them were the brother gods, Tharn and Balatur; and before them, the first of all the gods - Yl and Kyta.

'As Rassen has it, Tharn and Balatur were the children of Kyta and Yl - if gods have children, which I rather doubt - and were worshipped when the world was young. As seems to be the way with both gods and men, they grew vain in their supremacy, and rivalry mounted between them.' He shrugged, smiling, as if these notions amused him. 'But you know all this; you know that Tharn envied his brother god and fell upon him, that warring bringing chaos to all creation, leading the First Gods to intervene when Tharn proved victorious, condemning both victor and vanquished to oblivion.'

He paused, studying Calandryll as if expecting an answer of some kind. Calandryll nodded: all this was common knowledge to any scholar or historian.

'Well,' said Varent, serious again, 'there is a warlock - his name is Azumandias - who seeks to raise the Mad God Tharn.'

He paused, as if the very thought was terrifying, his eyes burning darkly as he stared at the dumbstruck youth, the enormity of the idea harshening his aquiline features. When he spoke again his voice was ominously low.

'Think on it, Calandryll - the Mad God raised! We speak of the world's ending - insanity combined with godly power! Even insane, Tharn is mightier than any of the younger gods, though I doubt his successors would accept their inevitable relegation. More likely, they would oppose Tharn. And such a conflict would undoubtedly destroy the world.

'Azumandias himself is mad, of course - he thinks to control the god with his grammaryes, but he will succeed only in unleashing cataclysm. Unless he is stopped.'

He broke off, shaking his head. Calandryll sat bemused, the concept so vast, so awesome he was robbed of speech. He waited for Varent to continue, wondering what part he had to play.

'There is, however, hope,' the ambassador continued. 'Azumandias has secured those spells necessary to raise the Mad God, but not the means of locating his resting place.

'I, though, know how they may be found.

'It was Azumandias taught me the magical art: I was a willing pupil until he sought to suborn me to his purpose, but when I discovered the full extent of his ambition I knew that I must oppose him. I had learnt sufficient of his design that I was able to commence my own researches, and thus I discovered the means by which he may be thwarted.'

'The chart?' whispered Calandryll.

'No, although it is vital to our purpose,' Varent said; Calandryll noticed the plural. 'It is not so easy - the chart, studied in conjunction with my own documents, reveals the key to Azumandias's defeat. When Yl and

Kyta banished their children, they hid them well, binding them with spells. Azumandias has discovered the spells, but not the tombs. There is a book - the Arcanum - that reveals the locations. It is hidden in Tezin-dar.'

'Tezin-dar?' Calandryll could only gape.

'Indeed; in Tezin-dar,' said Varent.

'But Tezin-dar is a fable,' Calandryll objected. 'The Arcanum is a fable. They are no more than legends. Medith denies their existence; even Rassen doubts their reality.'

'It is real,' Varent said firmly. 'Tezin-dar lies somewhere in Gessyth, deep in the swamplands. Perhaps the least accessible place in the world, but it does exist.'

'And the chart shows where,' Calandryll said.

Varent nodded solemnly and raised his goblet in a toast. 'You are quick: I like that. That is one reason I approached you - you have the wit to comprehend.'

'But surely, if all this is true, you need only inform my father,' Callandryll suggested. 'He could not deny you access, knowing this.'

'Your father is a man of this world,' Varent returned. 'Do you think he would believe me? Or would he suspect some deep plot on the part of Aldarin? Some manouevre to advantage my city at cost to Secca?'

It was true: Calandryll nodded.

'Besides,' Varent added, 'even if the Domm did believe me - granted me access to the archives - he would hardly leave the rest to me. He is a warrior, a man of action. His response would be to send an expeditionary force to Gessyth, probably led by your brother. And that would alert Azumandias, whose own response would certainly be to employ magic against us. For the same reason, I dare not reveal what I have learnt to any in Aldarin. Azumandias has occult spies abroad, and should he suspect I know so much, I should be dead within the hour. No, my friend, force of arms is not the answer here.'

'What then?' asked Calandryll, his voice hushed.

'The Arcanum must be destroyed,' said Varent. 'Before Azumandias gains its knowledge, it must be destroyed. But cunning is required. Quick minds and scholarly knowledge will prevail where armies may not. This is a task for one or two, no more. The book must be found and destroyed before Azumandias learns of it.

'Now - do you aid me? Or leave the field to Azumandias?'

FOUR

CALANDRYLL stared at Varent, his thoughts in turmoil. He did not doubt that the ambassador spoke the truth, but that truth was of such terrifying magnitude. A crazed magician bent on raising the Mad God? Surely that must mean cataclysm, the destruction of the world. And Varent sought his help. His alone …

You must cross the water to find what you seek, though men say it does not exist … There is a teacher … You will travel far and see things no southern man has seen … Reba's words came back to him … *You will seek that which cannot be had and find disappointment …*

That much was already true: Nadama was lost to him, and only disappointment lay ahead in Secca. Surely Varent was the teacher. Surely this was the quest the spaewife had described. He nodded solemnly.

'What would you have me do?'

'I knew you were the man!' Varent beamed. 'I want you to find me the chart.'

Disappointment: was that all?

'I am confined to my chambers,' he replied, that knowledge dampening his enthusiasm.

'I'll speak on your behalf - seek to mollify your father. After all, I *am* an honoured guest. Then, when you're released, find the map and bring it to me.'

'How shall I recognise it?' Calandryll asked.

'It was drawn in the time of Thomus, by Orwen; it is marked with both the seal of the Domm and the sign of the mapmaker. The Domm's seal you surely know. Orwen's sign looks thus ...'

Varent raised a hand, forefinger extended, and traced a shape in the air between them. Silvery brilliance, like moonlight spun in a web, sparked from his fingertip, inscribing a design that hung, glowing, before Calandryll's face.

'You will remember it?' asked Varent, and when Calandryll nodded, closed his fist, the glittering tracery extinguishing.

'Then what?' asked Calandryll.

Surely he had a larger part to play?

'Then,' said Varent, rekindling his optimism, 'I'll return favour for favour, as I promised. Come to my chambers the day I leave and I'll take you with me.'

'To Aldarin?'

Only that far?

'I'd ask more of you.' Varent's eyes twinkled as he spoke, full of promises. 'I cannot depart Aldarin, for fear Azumandias would discover my absence and set magical hounds on my trail. That would be disastrous. No, my friend, what I ask of you is a great thing, an awesome duty. You are familiar with the Old Tongue - you are one of the few men able to recognise the Arcanum. I want you to go to Tezin-dar.'

You will travel far ... see things no southern man has seen.

It was the prophecy! It had to be!

'Yes!' he said eagerly.

'There will be danger,' Varent warned.

Calandryll shrugged, dismissing such concern. Then

thought of the spaewife's words again ... *One will come after, also to be trusted ...*

'Might I not hire a bodyguard?' he wondered.

'An excellent idea,' agreed Varent. 'You know of one? A trustworthy man?'

Bracht had saved him, and the Kern was unemployed.

'There is a man called Bracht,' he said, 'a Kern free-sword.'

'Your rescuer?' Varent's lips pursed in thought; he nodded. 'Kerns are dependable. Where is he to be found?'

Calandryll frowned. What was the inn called? 'He had a room in a house on the edge of the Merchants Quarter. At the sign of the Wayfarer, I think.'

'I shall make enquiries,' promised Varent, and eyed Calandryll warningly: 'But he can know nothing of our true purpose, lest he alert Azumandias. Let him think you flee Secca on some erudite mission. He will accept that?'

'I think so,' said Calandryll.

'Good, I shall seek him out,' Varent murmured. 'And now, perhaps I should leave you, lest someone discover us together. Remember: secrecy is our best defence against Azumandias's glamours.'

He rose, draping his dark cloak about his shoulders, then extended his hand, taking Calandryll's.

'Praise Dera I met you, Calandryll. Together we'll defeat Azumandias.'

Calandryll returned his grip, smiling. It was gratifying to be treated as a man. 'Yes,' he said firmly.

Varent nodded and turned to the window. Calandryll stepped close as he went onto the balcony. The wind rustled the night-black folds of the cape and the man shimmered, and was gone, leaving behind that faint odour of almonds.

Calandryll stood for long moments staring at the

empty balcony, then closed the window, smiling. The first step was taken, the quest begun. He would escape the priesthood. He would show his father, show Tobias, that he was no boy, but a man now, with his own destiny to follow. He would return a hero. And what would Nadama think of him then? He was too excited to contemplate sleep and flung himself into a chair, reaching for the fallen book, turning urgently to those pages in which Medith discussed the gods.

'In the beginning, before this world was formed,' he read, 'there were the First Gods, and they were Yl and Kyta, the All-Powerful. They dwelt within the Void, formless until it pleased them to assume shape and substance, becoming male and female. It also pleased them to shape this world, and the sun and the moon, the stars and all things that lie in the heavens and the waters and on the earth. Thus was the Void filled and no longer an empty place.

'Because they had taken male and female form Yl and Kyta joined, and from their union came children, lesser than their parents, yet themselves gods, and they walked upon the world.

'These children of the First Gods were the brothers, Tharn and Balatur, and their form was perfect.

'The Children of the First Gods grew and felt the power they possessed, asking of their progenitors that they be given worshippers, that their power and their godhood be known. So it was that Yl and Kyta took earth and water and from that stuff shaped humankind to please their children, as fond parents seek to grant their offspring playthings, for such are men to the gods. And in this way were men created and set within the world, which was a fecund place where none wanted for food or drink or shelter, knowing only the ways of paradise, and they worshipped the brother gods in the ways demanded by Tharn and Balatur.

'But in time the Children of the First Gods grew

wearied of this perfection and asked of their parents that they create like beings, that they might walk amongst equals. But Yl and Kyta refused, saying, "No, for we have made you and you are sufficient." And their children waxed wrathful, for there were none other like them in all the places of the firmament and they felt alone. In their pride they sought to create beings of their own making, but that was a power possessed of Yl and Kyta jealously and none others, and the creatures thus shaped were strange and malformed, and hideous to the eyes of men.

'Now the First Gods saw that the beings of their childrens' shaping could not live with men and banished them to the lonely places of the world that they might offer no harm to men, nor offend with their ugliness and their unhuman ways. So it is said did those things which inhabit the jungles of Gash and the swamps of Gessyth and the forest Cuan na'Dru in Kern, and all the lonely places of the world, come to be where they are, that they might follow their own strange ways and offer no harm to men, save those men that venture where they dwell.

'This Balatur accepted, seeing that his parents were wise, but Tharn was angered and cried out saying, "Why do you deny us?" and "Why do you hold this power to yourselves?" and "Why should we not be as you?" And he determined that he would do as he wished, turning his face from the guidance of his parents and seeking to create as had the First Gods, which is their right alone.

'But Yl and Kyta took such power from him and from Balatur that they could no longer fashion the changeling things and Tharn's anger waxed until it became a madness and he sought to persuade his brother to his cause, but Balatur spoke out, saying, "No, for our parents are wiser than we and I shall obey them," and then did Tharn become lost in his madness, waxing wrathful, and fell upon his brother in terrible fury. And Balatur must then defend himself, or fall before his brother and see all the folk of the world ground down beneath the heel of Tharn. In that time were mountains destroyed and chasms cleft where none had been before, and seas boiled dry, whilst others filled the land. And the time of paradise ended, men huddling in fear of the godly strife, fearing that they must die beneath the feet of their gods, who fought in ways beyond the comprehension of men that were terrible to behold.

'Then did Yl and Kyta once more intervene, coming between their children that they should not utterly destroy the world and all the creatures therein, seeking to pledge peace between them. But Tharn was gone into madness and would not listen to the words of the First Gods, and a great sadness fell upon Yl and Kyta for they perceived that their children were lost to them and bent solely upon destruction. Then did they seek in their hearts for an answer, and it grieved them, for it was a hard thing to see the creation of their loins bereft and mad. But also did they see that should they leave Tharn and Balatur to their ways, the world must go down into ruin, and yet they could not find it in their hearts to slay their child, yet were he left to pursue his course he must destroy all, Balatur and the world, both. And they feared that did they bind the one brother, then might the other take his place, for they saw that their children held overmuch power, and that is a thing that corrupts when one alone holds all.

'They debated long, and with much pain agreed a course whereby they set upon the brother gods a mighty glamour that sent them down into sleep, and they were entombed in hidden places and their resting places set about with spells that they should not wake again but languish in the oblivion of limbo, their names forgotten by men, which is a very great punishment for a god.

'And then the world knew peace again, and men multiplied and wandered the ways of the world, but godless.

'Then did Yl and Kyta see that men need gods, and from their dreaming shaped those newcome deities who are the Younger Gods, limiting their powers that they might not visit upon men and strife done by Tharn and Balatur. And those gods are Dera, whose fruitful bounty blesses Lysse; and Horul, who is both horse and man and revered by the folk of the Jesseryn Plain; and Burash, the Lord of the Waters, who is worshipped in Kandahar; Ahrd, the Holy Tree, which the people of Kern hold in awe; and the Iron God, Brann, whose blood is said to fill the mountains of Eyl with precious iron. But in Gash and Gessyth there were no gods, nor are there now, for the creatures of those lands are strange.

'Then did Yl and Kyta perceive that they had visited grief upon the world when they created their children, and mourning went into the Forbidden Lands, where only gods may dwell, leaving men to worship as they would. But ere they left for that place they caused to be written down a memorial to their lost children, recording those hidden places where they lay, and that tome they set in a secret place, guarded, and it is the book named The Arcanum.

'So stand the gods now.'

Calandryll yawned, the close-scribed words blurring, and set the book aside. Medith offered no great insights, his interest being more with the physical than the theological, and his dissertation did little more than echo the religious tracts promulgated by the Derans. He had never thought much on such matters, and deemed the Arcanum a legend, like the lost city of Tezin-dar: but now Varent's words lent fresh light to the ancient scriptures and he shuddered at the thought that Azumandias might find the book and raise the Mad

God. It was a terrifying notion.

A second yawn stretched his jaws wide and he rose, stretching, feeling the dull ache of his healing ribs, and glanced at the window. Outside, the night was black, the moon no longer visible. He yawned again, exhaustion overcoming excitement, and tugged off his clothes, clambering gratefully beneath the sheets, where, within moments, he was sleeping soundly.

He dreamed, though of what, he could not remember when sunlight woke him, save that he had been on board a ship and frightened. He rubbed his eyes, grunting as a fist pounded on his door and servants - still silent - entered with his breakfast and kettles of hot water. He bathed, careful not to wet his bandages, and dressed, wondering if he should set clothes aside against his departure; deciding against such preparation for fear it might alert his father to his intentions.

In the spring-warm light of the new day Varent's words felt no less alarming, nor any less appealing, and he ate his breakfast deep in thought, wondering when he might get the chance to explore the palace archives.

Two guards still stood patiently beyond his door, and two others in the garden below. He had no visitors, save the healer, who pronounced herself satisfied with his recuperation, and the servants who brought him food. That night he slept frustrated, his enforced isolation strengthening his determination to aid Varent, as much for the sake of rebellion as to thwart Azumandias's monstrous plan.

For three more days he remained confined to his chambers, then was summond to appear before his father. His bruises were healed by now, paling memories of the beating, and the bandages removed. He dressed carefully, hoping to impress with a sober demeanour, and went, excited and more than a little nervous, to the interview.

Bylath waited alone in his own quarters and Calandryll was grateful that Tobias was not present: facing the Domm was difficult enough without his brother's mocking grin to spite him.

He stood in silence as his father sprinkled sand over the ink of a document and pressed his seal to the wax. Bylath was dressed for the hunt, his manner impatient as he shoved the scroll aside and turned cold eyes to his younger son.

'I trust you've learnt your lesson. Or must I set a watchdog on you?'

Calandryll examined the floor beneath his feet, suppressing a grin of excitement.

'Well?' Bylath demanded.

'I've learnt my lesson.'

He composed his features in an expression of subservience, meeting his father's eyes.

'I hope so.' Bylath rose, leathers creaking, and walked to the window. 'There will be no more of these escapades.'

'No,' agreed Calandryll.

Bylath nodded; grunted. 'Very well - you're free within the palace. But you will not leave here, do you understand?'

'I understand,' he said dutifully.

'The gatemen have orders to turn you back, should you attempt to leave. And if you do ...'

The Domm's features hardened, the threat of severe punishment implicit in his eyes: Calandryll shook his head.

'I'll not attempt to leave.'

'Good. Perhaps I may enjoy a day's hunting without wondering what fresh disgrace you'll inflict on our name.'

'None,' he promised; sincerely.

Bylath nodded again.

'So be it. You may leave me. But tonight I expect you

to attend the dining hall - without dramatics!'

'No, I promise,' Calandryll said. 'Thank you.'

His father waved a hand, dismissing him, and he turned, marching across the tiles to the door, struggling against the shout of triumph that threatened to burst out.

He resisted the impulse to hurry directly to the archives and went instead to the balcony overlooking the palace's great entry hall. Tobias was there, dressed in brown hunting tunic, a dirk on his waist and Nadama on his arm. She was lovely, the moss green of her tunic and loose pantaloons complementing the rich auburn of her hair, her eyes sparkling as she answered some jest of his brother's. Tobias threw his head back, laughing, and saw Calandryll, murmuring something to Nadama. She, in turn, looked up, her smile knifing his heart so that his hands tightened on the balustrade, the knuckles blanching. What will she think when I return? he wondered. She'll not laugh at me then. He forced himself to smile, and saw Tobias bow mockingly. Then Varent appeared, dressed in motley, a cap rakish on his black hair. He saw Tobias laughing and looked to where Calandryll stood, raising a hand in greeting, dark eyes alive with their shared secret. Calandryll answered his wave and nodded, and the ambassador ducked his head, engaging Nadama in conversation.

Bylath came striding along the balcony then, favouring Calandryll with an admonitory glance.

'Remember what I told you.'

'Yes, father,' he returned, and watched the Domm go down the wide stairway, gathering the hunting party about him as he went out to where the horses stood in readiness. Calandryll waited until the clatter of hoof-beats had receded, then hurried to the archives.

There were two repositories within the palace, one a spacious chamber lined with shelves on which rested those documents, parchments, scrolls and books used with some regularity, either for the purposes of governance or for pedagogic reasons, and consequently frequented by the palace librarians, scribes and scholars, its contents indexed and ordered. The other was located in the cellars, near Gomus's gloomy chamber, and seldom used. Here were placed the antique documents, deemed useless by the pragmatic Bylath, the old maps and mouldering books accumulated over the years by successive Domms, the material of no immediate importance, stored randomly. To Calandryll it was a treasure house filled with wonders and he had passed many happy hours delving amongst the alcoves and cobwebbed shelves.

A low-roofed doorway granted ingress to this elder reliquary, hinges creaking a protest as he swung the door open, pausing to fetch a lantern from the adjacent corridor before descending the steep stone stairs that went down into the shadowed bowels of the palace. He heard things chitter a protest as he lit the ancient lanterns set in rusted sconces along the walls, their radiance exposing a cavernous vault, buttressed with low arches festooned with spiders' webs, the niches piled high with the forgotten memorabilia of Secca's past.

Calandryll moved down the vault, careless of the dust that settled on his face and clothes, the design Varent had shown him bright in his mind's eye. There was no particular organisation down here, save that imposed by time itself, no index to guide him, no catalogue to which he might refer, but still he thought he could without much difficulty locate that area in which the documents collected by Thomus would be found. That Domm, he remembered, was the fourth to hold power in Secca: he walked purposefully towards the farther reaches of the vault.

Yes - he was right: when he checked the ancient

scrolls in one grimy alcove they bore the seal of Thomus. So, where might the chart be found? He began to rummage amongst the relics.

It was hard to resist the impulse to examine each aged document, but he was anxious to complete his search before his father returned. He might not get another chance before Varent must depart for Aldarin, and if he was to accompany the ambassador, he must find the map. He ignored the books, forcing himself to think sensibly despite his excitement. A map would most likely be rolled, perhaps contained within a protective cylinder, and so he turned to an alcove where tubes of cracked and ageing leather were stacked one upon another in a great careless mass.

He started at the top of the pile, lifting the first cylinder down and extracting its contents. Dust tickled his nose and he sneezed noisily, the exhalation arousing more clouds so that his eyes watered and he rubbed grimy hands over his face. Gently, careful of the parchment's age, he unrolled a blueprint of the city's sewage system: he replaced it in its tube and set the cylinder on the floor. The next contained a street plan; after that an architect's drawing of the palace's west wing; then a chart of the farmlands abutting the city walls; a map of the harbour; a design for a temple never built; a fanciful structure of incomprehensible purpose. The pile at his feet grew. His hair was thick with dust, his shirt streaked with grime. Some tubes emitted only blackened flakes that fell like ashes to the floor, others spilled the long-dried husks of dead insects. Calandryll began to wonder if he would ever find the chart Orwen had drawn.

He cleared the alcove and hurriedly replaced the cylinders, fearing that someone might discover his search. A second proved equally disappointing, but halfway down the third pile he found a map marked with the chartmaker's seal.

He stared at it, comparing the design with his memory of that drawn on thin air by Varent. As best he could tell, this was the one, though how it helped their purpose he could not discern. He wiped his hands on dirtied breeks and carried the chart closer to a lantern, smoothing it with infinite care against his thigh. The paper was very old, oiled but still dangerously brittle, the ink dulled, and he feared that it might dissolve at his touch. It was, so far as he could tell, a map of the world as it had stood at the time of Thomus. Neither Kern or the Jesseryn Plain were shown, and Lysse was depicted in exaggerated size, the great jut of land containing Eyl and Kandahar and the Jungles of Gash a diminutive nub; of Gessyth there was no sign. Confused, he rolled the map again and prepared to return it to its cylinder.

As he did so, he noticed a second scroll inside the tube, like a lining against the leather interior. He set the first map down and began to work the other loose. It was not drawn on paper, but on some finer material, thinner and more supple, that lacked the coarse, brittle quality of the other parchment. It was a hide of some kind he realised as it slid from the cylinder, a creamy yellow inscribed with fine lines and the ornate script of the Old Tongue. Orwen's seal was drawn in still-bright scarlet at the righthand bottom corner. The scale of the domains was still disproportionate, but now Gessyth occupied as much space as Lysse. At the head of the skin the chartographer had written, A mappe of the Worlde drawne by Orwen for the Domm Thomus, favorred of Dera.

Calandryll licked his lips, and spat as his tongue encountered a heavy furring of dust. His inclination was to examine the chart in detail, but he resisted the temptation, fearing to linger overlong and risk discovery: there would be time to study the thing later. Careful of the brittle parchment, he rolled the one map and set it back inside the protective tube. The other he slipped beneath his shirt, against his skin, then set about returning the littered cylinders to the alcove.

When that task was completed and he was satisfied that even if his exploration should be discovered no one could tell what, if anything, he had taken, he walked back down the vault, extinguishing the lanterns as he went.

He emerged filthy, thankful that the passage leading to the depository was empty, and hurried to his chambers. Inside, he set the map almost reverentially on a table and looked at himself in the mirror. Excited brown eyes stared back from a mask of grime surmounted by a lank mop of near-black hair. His shirt and breeks completed the picture, and the brown leather of his boots was hidden beneath a mantle of sediment.

A glance at the window showed a sky darkening towards evening, threatening the return of the hunting party: he disrobed, piling his soiled clothes in a cupboard before tugging the bell cord to summon a servant.

A man came, eyeing Calandryll with open curiosity.

He said, 'Hot water. And quickly,' surprised at his own authority, though no less so than the servant, who nodded and hurried away, clearly taken aback by his new sense of command.

The water came and Calandryll dismissed the servants, immersing himself in the tub and scrubbing furiously at his hair and skin. He would have liked to study the chart, but soon, he knew, his father would be back and he wanted to take no risk of giving further offence.

Considerably cleaner, he dried himself and selected fresh clothes. Bylath had not indicated whether or not a formal occasion was planned, so he compromised, selecting a shirt of dark blue cotton and matching breeks, short boots of black leather, and a loose tunic of green. He combed his hair, smiling, albeit ruefully as he thought that the last time he had taken such care with his appearance he had sought to impress Nadama.

Well, now she would wonder where he had gone; perhaps even fret over his disappearance. And when he returned - a hero! - she would likely regard him in a new light. The thought pleased him and his smile grew broader. It was still there when he was summoned to dine.

It was not a formal occasion. The servant sent to fetch him informed him that Bylath awaited his presence in one of the smaller halls, and when he entered he saw that the Domm sat with Varent and Tobias at a round table, the others occupied by only the closest of his father's advisers. Nadama was not present and he was uncertain whether that was a relief or a disappointment as he bowed courteously.

He was placed between Varent and Tobias, the ambassador beaming a greeting, his brother regarding him with disinterest. Bylath eyed him for a moment, as though deciding between reprimand and admonishment, and said, 'You owe thanks to the ambassador.'

Calandryll frowned his incomprehension, turning to Varent, who shrugged and smiled effacingly.

'I saw no great reason to have you present,' the Domm announced, 'but Lord Varent pleaded your cause.'

'Thank you,' Calandryll murmured, politely.

'Young men are apt to act without forethought,' said Varent smoothly. 'I am sure Calandryll intended no offence.'

'But nonetheless gave it,' Bylath grunted.

'Aldarin forgives any slight,' Varent returned, smiling, 'and I should prefer to depart Secca knowing that peace reigns in your household.'

Bylath snorted; Tobias grinned and murmured, 'I

believe any insult he may have intended was directed at me. And Nadama.'

The remark was designed to hurt, but Calandryll ignored it, his attention caught by the ambassador's announcement.

'You are leaving?' he asked, hoping desperately that his tone did not reflect the anxiety he felt.

Varent nodded and said, 'Indeed. Gracious though your father's hospitality has been, I must return to Aldarin on the morrow.'

'Your business is concluded, then?' asked Calandryll.

'It is,' said Varent. 'The treaty is signed and I must carry that welcome news back to my own city without delay.'

'You have achieved all you hoped for?'

It was difficult, this double talk: he would have preferred to blurt out his news and ask the diplomat outright how he was to leave Secca undetected. But Varent would inform him; of that he was sure, he told himself. After all, the man could come and go like a shadow in the night, and it was hardly likely he would leave without the chart. And without Calandryll, he would have no chart.

'I believe so,' he heard Varent say, trying to read the man's face, seeking an answer there.

'We have,' said Bylath, bluntly, 'the final details have been ironed out.'

'Perhaps one or two may require amendment,' smiled Varent, 'but I am confident we all have what we want.'

The words were directed at the Domm, but Varent's easy smile encompassed Calandryll like a question. He nodded slightly and saw the ambassador's lids close briefly, as if in confirmation that he understood.

Servants brought food then, and for a little while the table was silent. Varent spooned soup, murmuring some bland comment on its taste. Tobias said, 'We eat fresh venison tonight, little brother. A buck I killed myself.'

'It was an excellent kill,' Varent complimented, 'and a truly enjoyable hunt.'

'Secca has good hunting,' nodded Bylath, beaming as he turned towards Tobias. 'And that second kill! You surpassed yourself; the horn spread on that buck was magnificent.'

Tobias basked in the praise. 'A pity Calandryll did not accompany us,' he remarked. 'He'll have little enough time for such pleasures after he assumes his priestly duties.'

Bylath chuckled sourly. 'Calandryll? He's no huntsman.'

'How did you pass your day?' asked Varent, as if making polite conversation. 'What did you do whilst we rode to the hounds?'

Calandryll shrugged. 'I studied. I examined some old maps.'

'Studied,' Bylath snorted. 'All you need study, boy, is the Deran gospels.'

He did not notice Varent's smile, or the satisfied look the ambassador gave Calandryll.

'You found them interesting?'

'I did,' Calandryll nodded. 'Most interesting.'

'My offer stands,' Varent said. 'Should your father permit it, you are most welcome to examine my own small scholarly collection.'

Calandryll grinned his answer, undaunted by his father's scornful grunt.

'You have my thanks, Lord Varent, but Calandryll is to enter the priesthood - he'll not be free to visit Aldarin.'

'As you wish,' Varent murmured equably.

'We must all accept our duties,' Tobias intoned portentously. 'Must we not, Calandryll?'

'Yes,' he answered evenly, 'we must. Whatever they may be.'

Both Tobias and Bylath glanced at him then, surprised by his apparent acceptance. The Domm frowned, but Calandryll was saved from interrogation by the arrival of the venison, thick slabs of aromatic meat accompanied by great platters of steaming vegetables and salvers of blood-thickened gravy.

'This really is superb,' Varent applauded, skillfully deflecting attention from Calandryll. 'Your kitchens complement your son's skill as a huntsman, Lord Bylath.'

The Domm beamed; Tobias simpered, and the conversation, steered by Varant, returned to the day's sport. Calandryll ate in silence, satisfied that the ambassador had understood his oblique references; satisfied that he had received the answer he wanted.

In his chambers after the dinner had ended and the palace slept, he awaited Varent's arrival in a fury of impatience. The night was clear and the moon full now, lining his balcony with cold silver light. Bats fluttered on silent wings, and in the garden below nightbirds chorused, their song loud through the opened window. The air was warm, the early promise of spring fulfilled. Calandryll paced, pausing only to peer at the map spread on a table. For all the value Varent placed on it, it seemed to show no more than a possibly disputable outline of Gessyth's geography, a seemingly random tracery of lines devoid of annotation: he could not see how it might define the location of fabled Tezin-dar.

'Is that it?'

He gasped as Varent entered the chamber, the warm air momentarily filled with the odour of almonds. The ambassador shed his obfuscating cloak and stepped up to the table.

'Excellent! You have done well, my friend. Now, would you do even better and offer me a cup of wine?

Calandryll gaped, nodding, and filled a goblet. Varent smiled his thanks, sipped, sighed, and said, 'Delicious. Dinner was so tedious! Your brother shares the bovine attributes of the creatures he takes such pleasure in slaughtering. And your father - I can see why you want to leave Secca.'

He emptied his glass and set it aside, resting a companionable hand on Calandryll's shoulder.

'But I digress - the curse of the diplomat! - and you have triumphed.'

'It *is* the map?' Calandryll asked. 'The one you - *we* - need?'

Varent bent over the table, studying the chart.

'It carries Orwen's seal; it shows Gessyth. Yes, my friend, it is the one.'

'But it shows so little,' said Calandryll. 'Where is Tezin-dar? It shows no cities at all, only lines that might mean anything.'

'Ah, but it will.' Varent tapped the yellow skin confidently. 'It will lead us - you! - to the Arcanum. My word on it.'

'But there are no cities marked,' he protested again. 'It appears utterly random.'

Varent tapped his nose. 'Thomus had foresight,' he murmured. 'Alone of all the Domms Lysse has known, he saw that this might be needed. But he was careful! He knew that such a chart fallen into the wrong hands might well prove the undoing of the world, so he took precautions. Do you know how this was drawn?'

Calandryll shook his head.

'Thomus sent Orwen to Gessyth,' the ambassador explained. 'Orwen and a band of his most trusted men. For years they remained in that godforsaken place, and more than half died there. Still more of fevers when they returned. All were sworn to secrecy, and Thomus employed sorcerers to set glamours upon them, that they could not speak of what they saw. He was a wise man, Thomus.'

'But how does it help us?' Calandryll demanded.

Varent chuckled. 'Thomus was a very wise man, my friend. He had Orwen draw two maps.'

Enlightenment dawned: Calandryll chuckled in turn. 'And you have the second!'

'Yes,' said Varent. 'To the unknowing eye, it is no more than some arcane antique - a seemingly random collection of notes jotted on a skin like this. But finer, thinner - transparent, in fact. Of itself, useless, just as this is useless. But place the one upon the other ...'

'And you have a true map of Gessyth,' Calandryll finished.

Varent nodded, beaming.

'The only true map in existence, Calandryll. A map that shows exactly where Tezin-dar is to be found. More, it shows the dangers that lie in wait. Without both, Tezin-dar remains hidden in the swamplands; a legend. The two combined, however, enable staunch-hearted explorers to locate the fabled city; warns them of the perils they must face.'

He paused, his aquiline features growing solemn.

'You have done much already. Are you sure you would do more? Safer to remain in Secca, let there be no doubt of that.'

'And risk Azumandias's success? Risk his raising the Mad God?' Calandryll shook his head. 'No, Lord Varent - I am with you.'

Varent grasped his hands. 'Dera guided me to you, Calandryll, and I thank her that she gave me so stout a comrade.'

Calandryll smiled. Varent gestured at the map.

'Best keep that with you. I do not entirely trust your father to leave my baggage unexamined. Now, as to your ... is escape the right word? I found your mercenary and he will be waiting for us beyond the walls. I have paid him one hundred varre, and promised four hundred more on arrival in Aldarin; another five hundred on your return from Gessyth - his loyalty is secured.

'As for you, my promise stands. Can you gain my quarters unseen?'

Calandryll nodded.

'Good,' said Varent. 'I depart after the morning meal - come to me then.'

'There will be ceremony; my father will escort you to the walls,' Calandryll said nervously. 'How shall I go unseen? I am forbidden to venture beyond the confines of the palace, even. The guards have orders ...'

Varent waved a casually dismissive hand, stilling his protests.

'Trust me. Come to my quarters and I assure you, you shall depart Secca with me.' His dark eyes twinkled with amusement, conspiratorial. 'We play a magical game, Calandryll, and magic shall win you freedom.'

Calandryll would have plied him with further questions, but Varent smiled and retrieved his cloak, draping the sable cloth about his shoulders as he crossed to the window. Once again Calandryll gazed in wonderment as he stepped onto the balcony and murmured a few words in a voice too low to decipher, the moonlit air shimmered, like water disturbed by the submarine passage of a fish, rippling silvery where Varent stood and then was gone, the scent of almonds fading behind him.

He closed the window, bemused by the ambassador's occult talents. Magic was not unknown in Lysse, but by no means common, and those glamours he had experienced were of more mundane variety. He had seen magicians perform for the amusement of the court, producing live animals from thin air, causing borrowed objects to disappear; and the Domm's necromancer had several times raised ghosts on Bylath's command, but he had never witnessed a man transport himself as Varent did. Perhaps that was how the ambassador intended to bring him out of Secca. With that thought in mind, he hid the chart amongst his clothing and prepared to sleep.

He dreamed again, but this time there was no fear,

no apprehension of danger. Instead, he flew above the city, looking down on the close-packed, crowded streets, where his father and brother scurried hither and thither, seeking him but never thinking to look to the sky, where he soared. Excitement filled him as he drifted towards the walls, passing over the ramparts to sail above the fields beyond, and then laughter as Secca dwindled behind him and he tasted the heady wine of freedom.

He woke with the dream fresh in his mind and early sunlight on his face, leaping instantly from his bed so that he was waiting when servants brought hot water and food.

He bathed swiftly and gobbled his breakfast as he dressed. Breeks of supple brown leather and high boots, a loose white shirt, a jerkin of sturdy leather: clothes suitable for travel, but not so obvious that alert eyes might discern his intent. He thought to buckle on a sword, but forewent that protection, deeming it too manifest an announcement of his hopes. He tucked the map beneath his jerkin and, assuming a casual air, left his chambers.

Servants worked in the corridors of the palace, but they paid him little enough attention as he strolled towards Varent's quarters, accustomed to his random wanderings, so that he reached the ambassador's door without attracting undue notice.

Outside, he glanced around. Three women scrubbed the tiled floor, their faces turned from him: he tapped on the door and slipped inside.

Varent awaited him behind the remains of a hearty breakfast. He was already dressed, splendid in blue and gold, the insignia of Aldarin emblazoned on his chest, his dark hair oiled, held back from his handsome face with a fillet of silver. He rose, beaming, as Calandryll entered.

'You were not seen?'

'No.' Calandryll shook his head. 'Only some servants, and they did not see me come in.'

'You have the map?'

Calandryll nodded, patting his jerkin.

'Good.' Varent beckoned. 'Now come here - it is time to effect your disguise.'

He moved close to Calandryll, his hands raised, palms outwards, and began to murmur softly. The smell of almonds wafted on the air. Varent extended his hands, cupping Calandryll's cheeks, the touch intimate and oddly embarrassing. Calandryll felt his skin tingle, his hair prickle; Varent placed both hands on his head, still murmuring: a droning undertone. The odour of almonds grew stronger, then dissipated. Varent stepped back.

'It is done: you will not be recognised. Stay close to me and any who see you will assume you one of my retinue.'

Calandryll looked down: his clothes remained unchanged. He turned to a mirror: saw himself. He frowned.

'Trust me,' urged Varent. 'You see yourself as you are because you know yourself. To anyone else you now appear a somewhat homely fellow, with brown hair and a sizeable wart on your chin. I rather like that touch.'

'Shall I remain so?' Calandryll asked warily.

'No!' Varent laughed, shaking his head. 'Once we are beyond your father's boundaries I shall change you back. I promise!'

Calandryll nodded, nervous now despite his excitement.

'We need only await your father's summons,' Varent said, confidently, 'and then we shall be gone. There's no need to look so wary - my word on it.'

Calandryll nodded again: he was anxious to go, to end this waiting. His mouth was dry now and his heart beat alarmingly against his ribs. For all Varent's casual confidence, he was still not entirely sure of success, and the servant who brought the announcement that the Domm awaited the ambassador seemed both the harbinger of good tidings and the bringer of alarming news; he was not certain which.

'So, let us go.'

Varent clapped him on the shoulder and strode confidently from the chamber, leaving Calandryll no choice but to follow in his wake.

In the corridor outside, the ambassador's small retinue waited, accompanied by an honour guard of palace soldiers. Varent beamed at them, offering cheerful greetings, and walked leisurely to the wide staircase that descended to the main entry hall. Calandryll stayed close behind the tall man, his heart pounding loud enough, he thought, it must sound an alarum of his escape.

Bylath waited for them near the doors, dressed formally in a robe of green, a heavy ceremonial chain about his neck. Tobias stood beside him, wearing light armour, a sword on his belt, a silver helm in the crook of his arm. Behind, a squadron of twenty lancers stood at attention, silent and stern as the Domm bade his guest farewell.

Calandryll stood listening to the formal exchanges, his eyes downcast. He felt sweat bead his brow; swallowed hard as his father's eyes strayed in his direction, and gaped as they passed over him without the slightest hint of recognition. He raised his head then and stared at Tobias. His brother glanced at him incuriously, a cursory look devoid of comprehension: no more than the casual inspection of a faceless servitor. He heard his father offer apologies for his absence, and Varent dismiss it, then they were moving out through the doors into the courtyard beyond.

A small, gaily decorated wagon stood there: Varent's

servants loaded the baggage on board and the ambassador nudged Calandryll.

'Take the wagon.'

He climbed onto the seat beside a solemn-faced driver wearing the livery of Aldarin and clearly too conscious of the occasion to engage in casual conversation. His taciturnity suited Calandryll, who settled himself comfortably, beginning to enjoy the benefits of his disguise.

Varent mounted a tall chestnut horse, caparisoned in blue and gold to match his clothes, flanked by Bylath and Tobias, and the ambassador's retinue took up position behind. The lancers mounted, forming into two squads at the head and rear of the party, and Bylath nodded to Tobias, who raised a hand and bellowed the order to proceed.

The wagon's driver shook his reins, calling to the four matched white horses, and the beasts lunged against the traces, the metal-shod wheels rumbling over the flagstones of the courtyard, accompanied by the clatter of hooves. Ahead, the palace gates stood open, guardsmen lined in ceremonial columns with upraised halberds, saluting as the riders went past.

Calandryll began to smile as the shadow of the arch crossed his face and he saw the broad avenue leading through Secca stretch out before him. Townsfolk stood there, waving and cheering as the party moved at a walk into the town: obviously Varent's magic was as strong as promised.

They paraded the avenue and passed into the Lords Gate, where nobles stood on their balconies to see them go by. Calandryll saw Nadama there, lovely in a white gown, her hair caught up in a net of gold filigree, and his smile waned as Tobias bowed in his saddle, the greeting answered enthusiastically. She did not see Calandryll, her gaze rapturous on his brother, and he slumped, his excitement dulled by the knowledge that he would not see her until he returned; that she could not know of his great quest until it was done.

But then ... What would she think then? Might her smile not be for him?

He consoled himself with the thought as the wagon rumbled on through the quarter into the Fletchers Gate, then through the Bridlesmith Gate into the Brewers Quarter and the city walls loomed ahead.

The sun was shining out of a clear blue sky, painting the white stone of the walls with an overlay of golden light, glinting on the armour of the legionaries paraded along the ramparts. The massive bulk of the west gate swung open and the column halted as Tobias raised his hand. Calandryll sat, forgetting Nadama as his excitement rose afresh, watching Bylath lean across in his saddle to embrace Varent; Tobias take the ambassador's hand. Then they were moving again, the lancers parting to either side, Varent lifting his chestnut to a brisk trot, his own escort matching pace. Calandryll passed his father, passed Tobias, looking at them both, their own eyes focused on the figure of the ambassador.

Then they were behind him, lost as the wagon passed beneath the walls, shadowed, then rolling into sunlight again. The gate swung shut and the driver spoke for the first time.

'Be good to get home, eh? Secca's not a bad place, but you can't beat Aldarin.'

'No.' Calandryll smiled vaguely, turning on the seat to look back.

The walls of his home city stretched wide across the plain, high and white as the hopes of his boyhood: he was leaving, he felt, more than a place behind him and for a moment he experienced a pang of regret. Then his smile broadened as he thought of the consternation that must arise when Bylath discovered him gone. What would the Domm assume? That he had somehow managed to slip past the palace guards to lose himself in the city? Would there be a hue and cry? Would the watchmen scour Secca for him again? Surely no one would believe he had ridden out under their very noses with Varent: he began to chuckle.

'You're pleased about it,' said the driver, assuming his laughter was at the thought of returning to Aldarin.

'Aye,' he answered, 'I am. Very pleased.'

The driver grinned at him. 'I don't remember your face. You been with Lord Varent long?'

'No, not long,' Calandryll said.

'Thought you must be new. What's your name? I'm Shadim.'

'Calandryll,' he replied.

'Calandryll.' Shadim savoured the name. 'Doesn't Domm Bylath have a son of that name?'

'Yes,' Calandryll said.

'You related?' Shadim chuckled, enjoying the notion. 'Bylath sow some wild oats for your mother to reap?'

'No,' Calandryll said quickly.

'No offence meant,' Shadim offered mistaking Calandryll's tone.

Calandryll smiled, shaking his head.

'I take none.'

'Good. Be a miserable journey if you had.'

Calandryll nodded, his attention caught by the figure of Varent. The ambassador had reined in and now stood watching the column go by. As the wagon drew level, he turned his horse close and waved to Calandryll.

'Come down: we've business to attend to.'

Calandryll nodded, ignoring Shadim's curious glance as he rose from the seat, springing eagerly to the ground as the driver hauled on the reins to slow the team. Varent waved the wagon on and called to one of the rearward horsemen.

'Darth, ride the cart a while.'

The man nodded obediently and halted, dismounting. He walked his animal to where Calandryll waited and passed the reins over, running to catch up with the wagon. Calandryll climbed astride the borrowed horse, curious.

'We go to meet your mercenary friend,' Varent announced. 'And return you to your own form.'

'Your men ...' Calandryll began, silenced by Varent's hand.

'Will assume my warty retainer has been sent on ahead,' the ambassador explained, 'whilst two hired men have joined us. They're accustomed to my little intrigues.'

Without further ado he heeled his horse to a canter; Calandryll followed. They had soon left the slow-moving column behind, riding at a swift pace along the well-tended road that arrowed through the farmlands surrounding Secca. By late afternoon they came in sight of a caravanserai set in a sheltered hollow and Varent reined in.

'I suggest,' he said, smiling, 'that I restore your own face. As you know the Kern, he might be confused by the disguise.'

Calandryll ducked his head in agreement and swung to the ground. Varent climbed down and raised his hands. He began to murmur and Calandryll smelled almonds on the warm air. Then Varent touched him again and he felt his skin tingle, his hair seeming momentarily to stand on end.

'A distinct improvement,' smiled the ambassador. 'The wart was a nice touch, but most unsightly. An effective disguise, though; do you not agree?'

'My father saw me,' Calandryll said, shaking his head, 'and ... and yet did not.'

'He saw what we wanted him to see,' Varent remarked casually. 'Magic is a useful art, Calandryll.'

'Yes,' he agreed, chuckling at the deception.

'Now,' Varent set a foot in the stirrup, 'let us find out if the Kern is to be trusted. Or if he has taken my hundred varre and run away.'

Calandryll swung into the saddle and cantered after the ambassador.

The caravanserai was built around a well, three of its defensive walls given over to stables and storehouses, the third containing living quarters. A groom took their animals and Calandryll followed Varent into the cool, airy interior of the common room. A handful of travellers looked up as they entered and the landlord eyed Varent's somewhat opulent clothes speculatively.

'There's a party of twelve will be here later,' the ambassador called. 'We'll require stabling and beds.'

'I'll see to it, my lord,' the man promised.

'Now,' Varent looked around, 'is the Kern here?'

'There.'

Calandryll pointed to the farther wall, where a black-clad figure lounged, boots resting on a stool. The Kern had a pot of ale before him and his falchion at his side and he was studying them with a mixture of surprise and irritation.

'You did as I asked.' beamed Varent.

'You paid me,' said Bracht.

'A man of honour.' Varent drew up a chair.

'You expected less?'

'No!' Varent shook his head. 'A Kern's word is his bond, don't you say?'

Bracht studied the ambassador with cold blue eyes. Calandryll sat, sensing anger in the freesword. Unbidden, the landlord brought two pots of ale.

Varent raised his to his lips and drank. Calandryll said, 'Greetings, Bracht.'

The Kern ignored him. Varent murmured, 'Excellent. A fine ale.'

'You said nothing of him.' Bracht indicated Calandryll with a jut of his chin.

'I told you you were hired to guard a traveller,' Varent said. 'Calandryll is the one.'

'The son of the Domm of Secca?' Bracht shook his head. 'How long before his father comes looking? And if he finds me with Calandryll I'm gallows meat.'

'The Domm has no idea where he is,' said Varent placidly. 'Nor any reason to suspect that I secreted him from the city.'

'Even so,' said Bracht.

'Even so, you have taken my money,' said Varent. 'And can earn a great deal more.'

'There is that,' Bracht allowed.

'A thousand varre,' said Varent. 'A great deal of coin.'

Bracht stared at his mug as though weighing choices, then shrugged.

'So be it.'

'Good,' Varent smiled. 'Now, shall we eat?'

FIVE

'WHY do you object to me?' Calandryll demanded.

He had seized the chance to speak to Bracht alone when the Kern went to the stables to check his horse. Throughout the wait for Varent's men, and the subsequent meal, the mercenary had exhibited a cool antipathy towards him, despite agreeing to Varent's terms, and Bracht's hostility disturbed him: he had anticipated a warmer welcome.

Bracht shrugged without speaking, sweeping a curry-comb over the glossy back hide of his stallion; Calandryll refused to go unanswered.

'We'll be spending enough time together - if you're unwilling, perhaps you should speak up.'

Bracht swept the comb over the horse's croup and surveyed his handiwork.

'I took Varent's money; I agreed to accept the commission. Is that not enough?'

'No!' Calandryll was vaguely surprised by his own self-assurance: it seemed to grow momentarily. 'It is not enough. I'd not have ill-feeling between us.'

Bracht smoothed the mane and shouldered the stallion aside, doling oats into the manger. He dropped the currycomb into a pouch and tossed that to the straw outside the stall, then, leaning against the rails, he studied Calandryll critically.

'I have no ill-feeling towards you, Calandryll; not in the way you think.'

'Then in what way?'

Bracht grinned tightly. 'Varent came to me with an offer,' he said. 'He offered me one thousand varre to act as bodyguard to a traveller bound for Gessyth. That's more than I could hope to make in three, four years as a freesword. I accepted, and so I am bound - as Varent said - by my word. I know little of Gessyth, but what little I do know suggests it is a dangerous land - I assumed I was to guard some merchant enterprise, but I find I am to escort you.'

'And you would sooner hire out to some fat-bellied trader?'

Bracht shook his head, chuckling softly. 'A trader bound for Gessyth is unlikely to be fat-bellied; more likely a merchant-adventurer. A man who knows how to use a blade. I find my charge is the son of Secca's Domm - who will likely be sought by his father, but more important, a ...' He caught himself, looking directly into Calandryll's angry eyes, '... a young man who knows little of swordwork; by preference a scholar.'

'That's why Varent needs me,' Calandryll snapped. 'Because I *am* a scholar. Because I can read the Old Tongue, I can recognise the ...'

He broke off, aware that he gave away perhaps more than Varent wanted the mercenary to know.

'Recognise what?' asked Bracht, and he realised he had gone too far: the Kern's blue stare demanded explanation.

'A book,' he muttered, as angry with himself now as with the Kern. 'A rare, antique document that Lord Varent would acquire for his collection. And I *can* use a sword.'

Bracht ignored that, his eyes narrowing.

'Varent pays me one thousand varre to acquire a *book*?'

Calandryll nodded: 'A very rare book. A unique book. Lord Varent is,' he extemporized, 'a collector.'

'How much does he pay you?' Bracht asked.

Calandryll shook his head. 'Nothing. I undertake the mission because I am a scholar. And he helped me escape Secca. Dera, Bracht! My father would make me a priest.'

'I can understand your reluctance to accept that office,' the Kern allowed, 'But to venture to Gessyth without pay?'

He shook his head, grinning in disbelief. It seemed he considered Calandryll a fool to undertake such a mission without reward and the younger man felt his cheeks grow warm, embarrassment and anger mingling. 'There are more important things than money,' he said irritably.

'Of course,' Bracht agreed. 'But not many.'

'I am not a mercenary!'

'No.' The Kern went on grinning. 'That's for sure.'

'What do you imply?' Calandryll demanded.

'I watched you beaten in the tavern,' came the answer, 'and saw that you cannot defend yourself. From what I hear, Gessyth is a land of monsters, fraught with danger - I'd prefer my charge was able to use a sword at least a little.'

'I can use a sword,' Calandryll repeated.

Bracht's thick eyebrows rose in unspoken doubt.

'I *can*!' said Calandryll, red-faced with anger now: the Kern's calm stare was as infuriating as Tobias's mockery. 'I'll show you! Wait here.'

He spun round, intent on borrowing a blade; Bracht's even voice halted him at the stable door.

'This is no place to demonstrate your swordsmanship: I'll wait for you in the barn.'

He jutted a thumb in the direction of the adjacent building: Calandryll nodded curtly and stalked across the moonlit courtyard toward the common room. Varent and his men sat drinking there, the ambassador's dark eyes curious as Calandryll approached.

'I need a sword,' he said.

'Why?' Varent asked, curious.

'Bracht doubts my ability to survive our journey - I'd show him I can protect myself.'

'He's a freesword,' Varent murmured, 'You've no hope of defeating him.'

'I'd convince him,' Calandryll snapped, impatient in his anger. 'He awaits me in the barn. Will someone lend me their blade?'

The ambassador's men looked to their master for instruction; Varent pursed his lips in thought, dark eyes enigmatic, then slowly nodded.

'Very well - take mine.'

He slid a sabre from a sheath inlaid with silver chasing, the slanted quillons carved with ornate scroll-work, the pommel a globe of gold. Calandryll nodded his thanks, hefting the weapon; it sat easily in his hand. Varent's men moved to follow him as he turned for the door, but Varent waved them back. 'This needs no audience,' he murmured, too soft for Calandryll to hear, 'leave them be.'

'The Kern'll cut him to pieces,' the man called Darth protested.

'No,' Varent shook his head. 'The Kern may teach him a lesson, but he'll not harm the boy. Leave them to it, and let us find our beds - the hour grows late and I'd leave this place early.'

Calandryll breathed deep as he re-crossed the courtyard, seeking a measure of calm. Realistically, he knew that he was no match for Bracht: he was no soldier, let alone a swordsman of the mercenary's standard, but he had been required to practice often enough on his father's orders, and he hoped at the least to show the Kern he was not entirely helpless.

He entered the barn. Bracht had lit several lanterns and moonlight penetrated through the high windows at front and rear, providing sufficient illumination that they might fight without excessive difficulty. Heavy pillars supported a hay-filled loft, the aisle between them wide, stretching unhindered down the length of the building. The Kern waited by the door, kicking it shut behind Calandryll. He held his falchion loosely in his right hand.

'Put this on.' He tossed a heavy gambeson of the kind worn in practice to Calandryll.

The younger man caught the jacket, scowling, setting Varent's sabre aside as he slid his arms into the padded sleeves, lacing the cheststrings tight. Bracht wore a similar garment over his black leather shirt, and an infuriating smile.

'Remember, we do not fight for blood,' he warned, 'Let there be no cuts to the head.'

'I have fought in practice before.' Calandryll assumed the stance of a duellist. 'On guard!'

Bracht shook his head, though his eyes did not leave Calandryll's face.

'Your first lesson - if you intend to kill a man, don't warn him.'

'I do not intend to kill you.'

'No.' Bracht smiled. 'But still.'

'It seems hardly honourable to attack without warning,' Calandryll said.

'Sometimes honour takes second place to staying alive,' murmured Bracht; and sent the falchion darting at Calandryll's chest.

He jumped back, bringing the sabre across in a defensive sweep. Bracht's blade floated over the sword, forcing it to the side, exposing Calandryll's ribs. The falchion landed flat: the blow stung and Calandryll grunted. He sidestepped, anticipating a second blow, and feinted an attack. Bracht riposted, this time lifting Calandryll's weapon high, the falchion slapping across his belly.

'I think,' the Kern said mildly, 'that you'd be tripping on your entrails now.'

Calandryll forgot his discipline as he saw the free-sword's smile. Teeth clenched, he brought Varent's sabre down, turning the cut as Bracht's sword moved to block it, seeking to drive in over the mercenary's guard. Bracht was too fast: his blade shone in the lamplight, twisting, rolling over Calandryll's to touch the younger man's chest.

'Another lesson - control your anger. Anger makes a swordsman reckless.'

He backed away, letting Calandryll come to him, thwarting each attack with an effortlessness that infuriated Calandryll. It seemed there was no way past his defence, each attack met with a counter, parry and riposte, the falchion a living thing in his hand, darting with a serpentine ease that left Calandryll panting.

'Also,' he declared amiably, 'you should seek to learn your opponent's limits. Not simply charge him.'

Calandryll dragged a hand across his sweating brow and raised the sabre in a defensive stance. Bracht advanced and the blades met again. Calandryll was unsure this time how the falchion found his ribs.

They fought on, Calandryll's breath becoming ragged, perspiration shining on his face, the sabre growing heavier in his hand. He would have given up, conceded victory, had pride not fuelled his anger. Several times he thought he must win through to score a hit, but somehow his blade was always turned, his attack ending with the mercenary's blade slapping anew against side or chest or belly.

'I think,' Bracht said after a while, still smiling, his breathing even, 'that by now you'd be dead.'

Calandryll nodded despite himself and extended his sword. Bracht raised his left hand.

'Enough, my friend. I'll concede that you're not without some talent.'

'What?'

Calandryll lowered the sabre, gaping: it seemed Bracht had taught him how little he knew. The Kern chuckled and said, 'You've much to learn, but the makings are there. Perhaps I can make a freesword of you before we reach Gessyth.'

'You withdraw your objections?'

Bracht bowed and for a moment Calandryll thought he was mocked by the courtesy, but then the Kern said, 'You're not the milksop I thought - yes, I withdraw my objections.'

'And you'll teach me bladework?'

'I'll do my best,' the Kern promised. 'Now, let's drink some ale together to seal that bargain.'

Calandryll nodded: he had, he felt, passed a test and now the freesword offered a measure of friendship. He sought to accept the offer.

'I've a thirst,' he admitted.

'Then let's slake it,' Bracht said, sheathing his blade.

They began to douse the lanterns, working their way from the rear of the barn towards the door. They were halfway along the wide aisle, the rearward portion shadowed, when Calandryll caught the waft of almonds on the dusty air. He turned, staring about, anticipating the appearance of Varent, but the ambassador was nowhere in sight. The odour grew stronger and he saw the air between his position and the door shimmer, the silvery moonlight rippling with a mercurial insubstantiality.

'What is it?'

Bracht appeared to sense his apprehension, swinging to face him with a hand on the falchion's hilt, his swarthy features alert.

'I am not sure.' Calandryll pointed to where the shimmering air began to coalesce. 'Magic, I think.'

Bracht followed his gesture and mouthed a low-voiced curse as his sword slid free; Calandryll gasped, raising Varent's sabre.

The air no longer shimmered, but grew solid, figures fashioned from the depths of darkest nightmare taking form. There were four of them, shaped in obscene semblance of men, but lacking any element of humanity. Wolfish heads sat on bullish necks, those columns descending into massive shoulders, like the arms, corded with muscle that bulged the grey, reptilian skin. From the hips extended long legs, feathered and bird-like, ending in scaled yellow feet from which jutted curved talons. The creatures' eyes were red, and their jaws were lined with fangs, parting to emit slimy streamers of luteous drool. Each one held a long, black-bladed sword. The smell of almonds gave way to a midden stink as the hideous quartet advanced.

Calandryll stared, horrified. Bracht snatched the lantern he had been on the point of dousing and hurled it at the centremost abomination. The fragile glass shattered, bathing the monster with oil that ignited, flame washing over the grey torso, wreathing the furred skull in a corona of fire. The thing flung back its head and roared an ear-splitting bellow of pain and fury, its midnight blade scything wildly as it stumbled against its companions, interrupting their advance. Bracht shouted a challenge and sprang to the attack, his falchion slicing deep across the chest of the closest monstrosity, the cut sending a spray of black blood high into the air. The beast ignored the wound, bringing its sword round in a sweeping arc that would likely have severed the Kern's neck had he not ducked beneath the swing to drive his own blade into the feathered abdomen. His wrist twisted as he withdrew the falchion, opening a gaping wound in the apparition's belly, the black blood pulsing in thick gouts that seethed where they splashed over the floor.

The burning horror still staggered, still roared, as its skin crisped, peeling from the bones, and for long moments Calandryll could only stare, frozen in disgust. Then a black sword swung towards his face and he reacted without thought: the sabre rose, deflecting the blow, though the force of it jarred his arm. He cut again as the sword was swept to the side, gagging on the stench of the awful thing as he stepped close, slashing across the ribs. Saliva splattered his cheek, burning, and he ducked, dancing clear of the blow that shivered great splinters from one of the barn's uprights. Red eyes empty of any emotion save hate stared at him as a third cut arched at his chest. He parried, feeling his blade knocked away, and the creature snarled in triumph as it drew back its massive arm, preparatory to splitting him. He flung himself to the side, barely evading the thrust, and the ebon sword imbedded deep in the splintered pillar. Faster than he had believed he could react, he brought the sabre up in a two-handed grip; and down as if the sword were an axe.

The thick wrist was severed, the hairy grey hand still clutching the hilt as it was parted from the arm. A thick jet of the black blood spurted from the stump and the monster, propelled by its own inertia, staggered forwards. Calandryll reversed his stroke, the sabre rising to intersect the ribcage. A shriek of outrage dinned against his ears as the beast toppled; then became a grunt as he drove the sabre into the exposed back, twisting savagely, experiencing a fierce, bloody pleasure as he felt the blade grate on bone.

He spun, seeing Bracht carve a gory wound across the chest of the fourth monstrosity, dancing back as the gutted beast attacked from the side. The thing should have been dead: entrails hung stinking from the raw-lipped opening in its belly and its leathery torso was curtained with the outpouring from Bracht's first stroke. It still moved, however, joining its companion to press the Kern hard, back along the barn. The burning creature stood in flames, howling, its sword dropped as it clawed at its chest and face, blunt nails tearing loose long strips of hide, its blood sizzling noisome. Calandryll ignored it, darting to Bracht's aid.

He saw the mercenary parry an attack and hack his falchion viciously across a reptilian belly, spinning as the second blade angled at his skull, turning that blow to step inside the monster's reach and ram his sword between the ribs. He pivoted, dragging the abomination with him as he yanked his weapon clear, point darting between open jaws to plunge deep into the throat. Calandryll attacked from behind: a double-handed blow that clove down into the shoulder. His victim snarled and spun to face him: the sabre was torn from his grasp, point jutting from the thing's chest. He leapt back. Bracht, still engaged with the hideously wounded brute, shouted, 'Behind you!' and he turned again to find the aberration he had thought he had slain advancing.

Black blood welled from the sundered ribs and the feathered legs were slimed with the stuff, the taloned feet leaving seething imprints on the floor as it came forwards. Both arms were outthrust, the stump of the wrist sending thin spurts of blood at his face, the remaining hand clawed, ready to seize him and drag him in range of the champing jaws. Charnel breath assaulted his nostrils and he sensed more than he heard the whistle of the sword that descended at his back and flung himself sideways.

He landed heavily against a stall as the sword struck the stone floor of the barn, sparks showering in pyrotechnic display, and for an instant the two awful creatures faced one another. Then both turned towards Calandryll.

He pushed away from the stall, running back along the aisle. It seemed the perverted beasts were impervious to wounds: Bracht still fought with a creature that bled from its ravaged throat, bone showing where the falchion had opened its ribs, great gashes across its belly; the two that lumbered after him should be dead: one was split from abdomen to sternum, the other wore Varent's sabre in its back. But all lived. The only one that took no part in the battle was the creature Bracht had set aflame: that had ceased its howling and now lay in a crumpled, charred mass at the centre of the barn. Calandryll snatched a lantern from its peg and flung it at the armed monstrosity.

Savage delight filled him as burning oil bathed the aberration in long tongues of flame. He saw its advance falter, the lupine jaws part in a roar of agony: he took a second lantern and hurled it at the handless beast. That, in turn, yowled and began to beat at the fire that wreathed its grey torso. Swiftly, he darted across the aisle, grabbing a third lantern, a fourth, sending them both in whirling arcs at the flaming horrors.

The barn was abruptly lit with hellish effulgence. Pale moonlight was lost in the glow of the ghastly living torches that roared and staggered in an agonised dance that filled the place with flickering red light, shadows capering wildly as the jet sword flailed, striking the unarmed monstrosity.

He looked for Bracht. The mercenary was agile as a cat, and his proficiency with a blade was indisputable, but the ghastly thing that pressed him was supernaturally strong, and undaunted by its wounds. Pure swordskill kept the Kern alive, but in time even he must tire, and then fall victim to the sweeping blows of the black sword. Calandryll glanced round: there were no more lanterns. He could think of nothing save to shout, 'Fire slays them!'

Bracht answered with a tight grin, sidestepping a

blow that would have gutted a slower man, and danced backwards. The abomination came after him: he parried a cut and retreated down the barn. The monster followed: Bracht paused, luring it on. He parried a vicious attack, riposted a cut to the belly, and continued his retreat. Each dancing, backwards step brought him closer to the flaming creatures. Calandryll shouted, 'Ware the flames!' and he risked a glance at the burning monsters.

The survivor scuttled forwards, jet blade raised high. Calandryll screamed, 'No!' as Bracht seemed to slip on the seething floor, lurching a step back, then falling to his knees as the dark sword descended. The Kern rolled, falchion ramming upwards into the monster's feathery groin, the force of the thrust combining with the momentum of the beast's own attack to lift it off its feet, tumbling it over the mercenary into its burning companions. It toppled against the closest creature, embracing the thing as it fought to regain its balance, howling as it felt the fire touch its hide. Its howling grew fiercer as the flames took hold and it spun in a wild circle, black sword striking the other, that in turn flailing mindlessly so that for a moment the two things fought one another.

Bracht rose smoothly to his feet, poised to counter an attack that failed to materialise. Instead, all three creatures staggered in helpless circles, rippling at their own skin, dark blood spitting and sizzling, the wounds they opened in themselves seeming to fuel the flames until they fell down, wailing now, and crumpled to ash.

Through the stink of their spilled blood Calandryll caught the waft of almonds and saw the fiery air shimmer. Then, suddenly as they had come, they were gone. The scent of almonds faded; the stench of burning blood dissipated. Clean moonlight lit the barn and the air once more smelled of hay and leather. It was as if no battle had been fought.

'Ahrd!' Bracht sighed, shaking his head. 'What were those things?'

Calandryll shrugged. Varent's sabre lay unsullied on the floor and he stooped to retrieve the blade. It should have been nicked, should have been stained, but it was pristine. He looked to where the dark sword had imbedded in the pillar, but that, too, was gone, the wood unmarked where it had struck. He shook his head, staring at Bracht. Then felt his belly roil and doubled over, emptying his dinner onto the stone. Shuddering heaves racked him and he felt Bracht grasp his shoulders as tears filled his eyes and he spat sour bile between his feet.

'You fought well,' he heard the mercenary say, 'and thought fast.'

He nodded wordlessly, wiping at his eyes as cold terror chilled him. He had not thought - had not had time - to be afraid until now, but now the hideous enormity of the sorcerous attack struck home. The beasts had materialised as readily as Varent had appeared on his balcony, and they had clearly intended to kill him - would have succeeded had Bracht not reacted so swiftly, or he not thought to use fire against them. Where had they come from? Were they Azumandias's creatures? If they were, then Varent's enemy must already suspect his part in the quest; must - the thought induced another wave of nausea - know where he was, be able, perhaps, to see him.

Could that be possible? He spat and swallowed, gagging at the bitter taste, and stared wildly around.

'They're gone,' Bracht said, mistaking his purpose. 'We defeated them.'

'Dera!' he gasped. 'Can he find us? I must speak with Varent.'

'Can who find us?' Suspicion rang in the Kern's voice. 'What have you withheld?'

Now guilt joined Calandryll's fear: surely Bracht had

a right to know what they faced. But Varent had urged secrecy upon him, and if Bracht suspected the true nature of their quest, then he might rescind his promise. Calandryll shook his head.

'No one,' he mumbled. 'I hope Lord Varent may offer some explanation; no more than that.'

What friendship he had seen in the mercenary's eyes departed; they grew cold as a winter sky. He fastened a hand in the lacings of Calandryll's gambeson and hauled the younger man upright, his face set in angry lines.

'I have agreed to escort you to Gessyth in search of this ... *book*. No sooner do I learn my charge is a runaway from Secca than I'm attacked by demons. They howl and burn, but none hear them, none come to aid us, and you speak of someone finding us. There's more here than I've been told - and I'd know what.'

Calandryll nodded helplessly, frightened by the Kern's cold anger. It seemed his wits deserted him in the aftermath of the sorcerous onslaught: he could think of no ready explanation.

'Please,' he muttered. 'Please, Bracht, we'll go to Lord Varent.'

The Kern held him at armslength, his eyes still wintry. Then he grunted, releasing his grip.

'Now.'

Calandryll tottered on weakened knees, unable to do more than mumble his acceptance.

'Come.'

Bracht's tone was cold, brooking no disobedience as he strode towards the door, and Calandryll went after him, feeling sweat cool on his face as they stepped into the moonlit courtyard. 'Wait,' he asked as he saw the well, drawing up a bucket of fresh water that he used to rinse his mouth and bathe his face.

He felt a little better composed after that and followed the grim-façed Kern into the caravanserai.

The common room was deserted save for two

drudges curled by the banked fire. Bracht ignored them, leading the way to the stairs that climbed to the sleeping quarters. He found Varent's room and hammered on the door. It opened to reveal the ambassador wearing a robe of saxe blue silk and a curious expression. 'You need not have returned my sword until morning,' he murmured, 'but come in. You'll take a glass?'

Without awaiting a reply he filled three cups. Calandryll accepted gratefully, drinking deep, then spluttering as fire burned in his throat.

'Distilled wine,' said Varent sympathetically. 'A powerful brew and best sipped; but a most excellent nightcap.'

Calandryll fought his coughing to silence and took a second cautious mouthful. Bracht tossed his down in a single swallow and faced Varent. His eyes were cold and hard, his tone, when he spoke, no less so.

'We were attacked,' he announced. 'By demons.'

'Demons?' Varent's eyebrows formed twin arches over his dark eyes. 'I heard nothing.'

'There were four of them,' said Calandryll, 'but we despatched them.'

'Thank Dera,' Varent declared earnestly. 'Do you sit down and tell me exactly what happened.'

Succinctly, Bracht outlined the attack. Varent listened in silence, then nodded thoughtfully, turning to Calandryll.

'Might your father, or your brother, have done this?'

It did not occur to him that so ready an explanation would provide ample reason for the appearance of the creatures and without thinking he shook his head.

'How could they know where I am? Even if they did, they would not send demons against me. There are no wizards of such ability in Secca.'

'Are you sure?'

He failed to recognise the undertone of irritation in

Varent's question and nodded.

'Absolutely.'

The ambassador's dark eyes clouded for a moment and he reached for the decanter, topping their glasses. His gaze met Calandryll's, angry, and the younger man saw that he had made a mistake: to claim Bylath or Tobias as the originators of the creatures would have explained his admission to Bracht, avoided further amplification. He shrugged, sighing: the alcohol calmed his fluttering stomach, but in place of terror came a great weariness; he found he longed to sleep.

'At least you survived,' Varent murmured.

'But were still attacked,' said Bracht, his voice cold, 'which prompts me to wonder why.'

'Why?' Varent said.

'Yes,' insisted the Kern. 'Whoever sent those creatures must wish us dead - why?'

Varent raised a hand to indicate the mercenary should elaborate. He appeared at ease, his features composed in lines of concern and relief, though in his dark eyes there remained the glitter of suppressed irritation.

'You came to me with the offer of a small fortune,' Bracht went on, 'and then I never thought to wonder why you sought me out. It did not occur to me that the young man I'd saved suggested it, but now I learn that my charge is the son of Secca's Domm and you want him to obtain some antique document from Gessyth. No sooner do we meet than creatures from the pit attack us, and when they are defeated Calandryll wonders if some mysterious *he* can find us - presumably to send the beasts against us. There's more to this quest than you've revealed and I'd know what we face. Or part company now.'

'Despite your given word?' asked Varent.

'I gave my word thinking to face mortal dangers, not the creations of sorcery.'

Bracht's voice was cold, his expression unyielding. For long moments he and Varent locked eyes, then the ambassador sighed. 'You've proved yourself a doughty swordsman,' he admitted. 'Very well - Calandryll is a scholar and can read the Old Tongue. Few can boast that accomplishment and he is one of the few capable of recognising what I want. Your task, as ever, is to guard him.'

'He mentioned this mysterious book,' Bracht nodded. 'A valuable document, I believe?'

'To a collector,' agreed Varent smoothly.

'Valuable enough that someone sends demons to thwart us?'

Varent shrugged. 'It would seem so,' he conceded.

Bracht shook his head, steel in his eyes as he studied the ambassador.

'I have taken your coin and given you my word, but,' he paused ominously, '*I will not swallow lies*! Now, do you tell me the truth, or do we part company here and now?'

Calandryll saw Varent's handsome features stiffen; his hand tightened on the cup he held, and when he spoke his tone matched Bracht's, ice for ice.

'I am the Lord Varent den Tarl of Aldarin and no man calls me liar.'

'Should you choose to challenge me, I'll meet you gladly,' Bracht returned, his gaze unwavering.

They stared at one another, engaged in a silent battle of wills. Calandryll realised he held his breath; then Varent smiled.

'You've a prickly sense of honour for a freesword, Bracht.'

The Kern did not answer the smile: his face remained cold as he said, 'I've a keen sense of survival, Varent. And when demons attack me, I want to know why.'

'Perhaps they sought Calandryll.'

'Perhaps, but as you point out - I am hired to guard him.'

'Indeed.' Varent ducked his head; sighed. 'So be it - I had thought to keep this secret, but I perceive I deal with a man a cut above the usual mercenary.'

'I'd know my enemies,' said Bracht, the compliment ignored.

'Then know that your enemy is a mage called Azumandias,' Varent said, undeterred by the freesword's hostility. 'A wizard of some power, who lusts for the same thing I seek. It is called the Arcanum and it is rumoured to lie in the city of Tezin-dar, which - as you perhaps know - is supposedly a fable.'

He paused, sipping the distilled wine; Bracht waited, not yet mollified.

'Azumandias is a fanatic,' Varent continued in a solemn tone, fixing the Kern with his eyes. 'A madman, who seeks the book that he might use it to raise the Mad God, Tharn. Should he succeed in that, the world is ended. I seek to prevent his insanity.'

'A book can do this?' Bracht demanded; he seemed unimpressed.

'The Arcanum makes it possible,' said Varent, 'It is the key to the resting places of Tharn and Balatur. Azumandias already has the spells that will rouse the Mad God - he cannot be allowed to obtain the Arcanum!'

'The Mad God is a thing of the past, banished to oblivion by the First Gods.'

Disbelief rang in the Kern's voice: Varent shrugged, spreading his hands.

'So the world believes. But Azumandias - and I - know better. If he should succeed in locating the book, he will uncover Tharn's resting place and use his magic to wake the god.'

Bracht stared at the ambassador; reached for the decanter, helping himself.

'And this book, this Arcanum, lies in Tezin-dar? A legendary place? It seems to me we hunt the wind.'

'It is no fable,' Varent said earnestly. 'Tezin-dar exists and the Arcanum is there; of that I am certain. Calandryll secured me a map that - with one I already hold - will show the location of Tezin-dar. Go there with Calandryll and bring me the Arcanum - or see the world destroyed.'

Bracht sipped the distilled wine. Calandryll studied his face, willing him to agree. He asked, 'Why do you not go there yourself? Why does Aldarin not raise an army to secure the book?'

Varent smiled briefly.

'Your wits are as quick as your sword, my friend, but that I cannot do. Like you, Aldarin's Domm is by no means sure the Arcanum exists, and should I endeavour to persuade him to such a venture word would undoubtedly reach Azumandias. An army is a clumsy thing: its raising would give my enemy time to use his magicks against me; perhaps enable him to secure the charts. No, I cannot risk that. Secrecy is my greatest weapon - the Arcanum must be destroyed and with your aid Calandryll may find Tezin-dar and bring out the book before Azumandias has chance to thwart us.'

'Why?' Bracht demanded, suspicion in his voice.

'Why? I do not understand,' said Varent.

'Why bring out the book?' the Kern amplified. 'Why not destroy it there?'

'If it were only that easy,' Varent murmured regretfully, 'but the Arcanum is a magical thing itself. Spells render it indestructible by normal means. Only magic may destroy it.'

'And you have such magic?'

Varent nodded, 'I do.'

Bracht lounged in his chair, feet thrust out, his expression speculative. 'You ask much,' he said. 'You ask that I escort the errant son of Secca's Domm to Gessyth

- itself a place of unknown dangers - to find a city men call legend and secure a book you say may raise the Mad God. Already demons have opposed us, sent - you say - by a crazed warlock who seeks the book himself. What other dangers might we face along the way?'

'I cannot tell you.' Varent fixed the mercenary with a dark stare, his handsome face grave. 'I can only ask that you agree to do this. In return I offer my undying gratitude. And five thousand varre.'

Calandryll was unable to stifle a gasp of surprise: it was a fortune. Bracht's face remained calm, revealing nothing. He said, 'That is a very high price.'

Varent nodded. 'Enough to compensate you for the additional dangers?'

Bracht smiled then, a tight grin empty of humour. 'You offer much, Varent.'

'The fate of the world lies in the balance,' answered the ambassador. 'Do you accept?'

Bracht ducked his head.

'Half when we reach Aldarin; the rest on my return. Whether we secure the book, or not.'

Varent's lips pursed and for a moment Calandryll thought he would argue, but then he shrugged and smiled and said, 'Done. Your word on it?'

'You have it.'

'Excellent!' Varent was once more affable. 'I am delighted we are able to settle this ... misunderstanding.'

'Yes.' Bracht rose. 'And now I would sleep. Hopefully undisturbed.'

'I doubt Azumandias will attack again,' Varent said. 'Not for some days - the raising of such creatures as you described requires effort, and likely his strength is depleted. Besides, I'll change our route so he'll not be able to guess our whereabouts. And once in Aldarin, you'll be protected.'

'Good.'

Bracht moved to the door. Calandryll rose to follow him, glancing at Varent. The ambassador waved a hand, dismissing him, and he went with the Kern into the darkened corridor.

Their rooms were adjacent and as they reached them Calandryll frowned, turning to Bracht.

'Would you have reneged?' he asked.

Bracht's face was shadowed, rendering his expression unreadable. 'I'd not anticipated demons,' he murmured, 'but nor had I expected to find the son of Secca's Domm placed in my charge.'

'What difference does that make?' wondered Calandryll.

'You don't see?' He thought Bracht grinned then. 'Had I refused, what do you think Varent would do? He need only send word to your father that I aided your escape and I'm outlawed in Secca. He's the ambassador of Aldarin, so I'd likely find myself outlawed there, too. Two cities placing a price on my head? Those are heavy odds; powerful enemies. This way at least I have an ally in Aldarin.' Now Calandryll was sure he grinned. 'And five thousand varre, besides.'

'Is the money so important?' Calandryll sought to probe the darkness that hid the Kern's face. 'Does the quest not excite you?'

'The money sweetens it,' Bracht said. Then added as if in explanation, 'I've no great liking for Varent.'

Calandryll sighed: it had not occurred to him that the two comrades of Reba's prophecy would be other than friends, but he heard in the Kern's tone an implacable coldness. It appeared that Bracht had weighed Varent and found him wanting. At least, he thought, the freesword accepted him, and he was surprised to find himself thankful for that: they had little enough in common, but he realised that he wanted the Kern's friendship. He yawned, unable to conceal his weariness.

'Sleep,' Bracht advised, amiably enough.

Calandryll nodded drowsily and opened his door, half expecting to discover something monstrous inside the chamber. He saw only a plain room, moonlight falling across a mightily tempting bed. He stepped inside, aware that Bracht waited at the door, hand on the falchion's hilt: he smiled his thanks.

Bracht nodded and said, 'We'd best find you a blade tomorrow.'

'Yes.' He watched as the mercenary turned to his own chamber, and closed the door.

The very simplicity of the room helped dispel his apprehension. It was a place to rest, not a venue for magic, and Varent had said Azumandias was likely weakened by the conjuration. He trusted Varent: there would be no further assault. He crossed the slightly-creaking boards and dropped wearily to the bed, bending to unlace his boots and tug them off. A small wardrobe provided space for his clothes and a cache for the map, and he climbed beneath cool sheets, seeing the full moon beaming enigmatically from a sky of darkest blue velvet pocked with stars. That same moon had lit the barn when Azumandias's demons attacked ...

A sudden thought widened his sleep-heavy eyes: when Varent had materialised on his balcony the ambassador had explained that such magic enabled him to transport himself only to a known location. Therefore Azumandias must be familiar with the caravanserai.

He frowned, the thought denying him the sleep his body craved. To do that, Azumandias must have visited the place ... might therefore have visited every potential stop along the way ... might be able to produce demons anywhere. For a moment he felt the chilly grip of dread. Then he smiled, remembering that Varent had foreseen that possibility and announced his intention of altering their route. He turned his face from the moonlight, drawing the comforting sheet up to his chin, alarm fading as welcome sleep crept over him. Until a further doubt crept in: how could Azumandias have known he would be in the barn?

And why send demons against him?

Why not attack Varent?

Without the ambassador, the whole quest must surely falter. He and Bracht were merely agents, Varent the mastermind, so why direct the attack against the lesser players?

The thoughts disturbed him, rendering sleep, for all he craved its peace, elusive, the lack of answers setting him to turning restlessly, his mind refusing to let go the problem. Varent's magic protected him, he decided at last: that must explain it. Or part of it: he was still wondering how the wizard could have known where he would be as exhaustion overcame him and at last he drifted into welcome slumber.

Sunlight had replaced the moonglow when he woke, a little after dawn to judge by the noise that rose from the courtyard and the height of the sun in the cloud-flecked blue sky. He thrust back the sheets and climbed from the bed, washing and dressing swiftly. The map lay where he had left it in the wardrobe. He stared at it for a moment, then settled it against his skin, beneath his shirt: it seemed the safest hiding place for now. Satisfied, he hurried to the common room with the questions that had plagued him rising afresh in his mind.

The spacious room was mostly empty, Varent beaming a welcome from a table set against one wall where he sat alone, beckoning. Calandryll was pleased Bracht was not there, or any of the ambassador's men: he felt a need to discuss his doubts in some measure of privacy.

'Your ordeal seems to have left no lasting marks,' Varent greeted him. 'Break your fast with me - this fruit is truly delicious.'

He pushed a bowl of apples across the table and

called for the landlord to bring another mug. Calandryll helped himself to the fruit, and the fresh-baked bread, as Varent filled the mug with steaming tea.

'Where's Bracht?' he asked.

'Tending his horse,' said Varent cheerily, 'what they say about Kerns is true, you know - they place the comfort of their animals above their own.'

He sliced an apple with a slender dagger; added a sliver of yellow cheese. he appeared completely at ease, as if he had forgotten the events of the previous night. Calandryll said, 'I was thinking about the demons.'

'I'm not surprised,' Varent murmured smoothly, 'but as I told you, I believe we may safely dismiss such threat for a while.'

'No.' Calandryll shook his head. 'I was thinking about *how* they came to be there.'

'Indeed?' Varent raised a napkin to his lips. 'By courtesy of Azumandias, I assume.'

Calandryll frowned. Varent was the picture of relaxed urbanity, his manner suggesting that he found the subject more than a little tedious.

'How could he know where I was?' he insisted.

'He is a powerful wizard,' Varent said, helping himself to bread.

Calandryll refused to let it go: 'You suggested he had guessed our whereabouts.'

'You've an enquiring mind, Calandryll; I like that!' Varent nodded, smiling. 'You are wondering how he could have known we should halt here? Apply that scholarly logic - this is the first waystation on the route from Secca to Aldarin; Azumandias has travelled extensively in his search for Orwen's charts and no doubt he anticipated I should make this my first halt.'

'How could he know when you would arrive?' Calandryll demanded.

'A spy.' Varent shrugged casually. 'He might well employ some human agent in Secca who released a pigeon to alert him; or, perhaps, an occult agent. Either way, he needed only use logic to deduce that my party would halt here.'

Calandryll's frown deepened; Varent's smile grew broader.

'You wonder why he did not attack me? How he knew of your presence? Again, the answers lie within the realm of logic - the creatures you described are unpredictable and might have destroyed the chart and me together. Azumandias would assume I hold it, which is why it is best you keep it; also, he cannot be certain how strong my own powers have become. As for your presence, he would have learnt of that from his spy.'

'Then he might alert my father to your part in my escape.'

Calandryll paled at the notion of Bylath sending a squadron of legion cavalry to bring him back: the prospect was somehow worse than the thought of facing monsters. Varent's laughter reassured him.

'No,' said the ambassador, 'had he chosen that ploy, we should have been halted before leaving Secca. I'd wager that Azumandias suspects I have the chart and wanted me to bring it out of Secca. But he acted hastily! He's shown his hand now and I can guard against further assaults.'

Calandryll nodded: the explanation seemed rational enough; he wanted to believe Varent, but one doubt lingered still.

'When you came to me in my chambers,' he said carefully, 'you told me it was necessary to know the place.'

'Indeed,' Varent responded equably. 'Blind transportation is horribly dangerous. One might materialise immured in a wall; or fused with a chair, say. Even magic is governed by certain physical laws, one of which is that two objects may not occupy the same space without disastrous results.'

'Then Azumandias must have familiarised himself with the barn.'

Varent nodded.

'How could he know I would be there?'

For an instant the dark man's equanimity faltered. His eyes hooded and he raised his napkin again, hiding his mouth.

'You *do* have an enquiring mind,' he said at last. 'How did Azumandias know you would be in the barn? Well, perhaps it was a lucky guess; or perhaps he left some occult spy here. Dera, Calandryll! Your logic outpaces me! I had not thought of that! Thank the goddess that you did.'

Abruptly he was on his feet, his handsome features troubled. Calandryll pushed his unfinished breakfast away, following him as he strode towards the door. Coins were flung carelessly to the landlord, his thanks dismissed with a hurried wave as Varent surged into the courtyard.

The wagon was already loaded, the ambassador's men saddling their mounts. Bracht stood by his stallion, his blue eyes curious as Varent, with Calandryll close on his heels, hurried to the cart and clambered beneath the gaudy canopy. Calandryll took the opportunity to toss the practice jerkin on board as Varent opened a small, ornately carved box and rummaged amongst the contents.

'What's amiss?'

Calandryll turned as Bracht led the black horse over.

'Lord Varent believes Azumandias may have some magical spy watching us.'

The Kern glanced round, hand dropping to the falchion. Varent emerged from the wagon and brought his left hand to his mouth, murmuring softly. He blew and a cloud of pinkish dust rose from his spread palm, surrounding him in a roseate aura. He lifted his right hand, setting a disc of thick glass held in a silver frame to his eye. Slowly, still murmuring, he turned in a circle, surveying the courtyard.

'He's a mage?' Bracht demanded.

Calandryll nodded. 'He has magical powers.'

The Kern grunted sourly: it appeared such talent reduced Varent further in his estimation.

'There was something,' Varent declared, 'but it has gone. Dera! I should have thought of this last night.'

'It would,' said Bracht quietly, 'have saved us some trouble.'

Varent seemed not to hear him; he returned the glass to the wagon and beamed at Calandryll.

'All is well, thank the goddess. No doubt Azumandias placed a spy here, but your defeat of his emissaries banished it.' His smile shifted to encompass Bracht. 'You both served me well - my thanks.'

Calandryll returned his smile, grateful for the praise, his doubts resolved. Bracht merely nodded, his face expressionless.

'So, let us leave,' Varent suggested. 'Calandryll, take Darth's horse again. Bracht - you'll stay close?'

'I'm paid to stay close,' said the mercenary, reaching to his saddle. 'Here, Calandryll, take this.'

He tossed a sheathed sword to the younger man. Calandryll caught it and fixed the belt about his waist. He drew the sword, hefting the weight. It was a lesser weapon than either Bracht's falchion or Varent's sabre, but it sat comfortably enough in his hand. The blade was straight, the steel gleaming dully with the milky look of good Eylian craftsmanship, the quillons slightly curved and rounded at the ends, the hilt wrapped in worn leather, the pommel a small globe of dull steel. He swung it a time or two, experimentally, then sheathed it.

'You owe me five varre,' Bracht said.

'Dera, man!' Varent looked down from his horse. 'Do you think of nothing but money?'

'I'm a freesword,' the Kern answered coolly.

'I've no coin,' Calandryll apologised.

Varent snorted, fumbling in his sabretache. Irritably, he flung coins in Bracht's direction. The mercenary caught them deftly, grinning as he slipped them into a pocket. 'My thanks,' he murmured, and swung astride his stallion.

Calandryll mounted, thinking with regret that Reba's prophecy had said nothing about the comrades he would find being friends, and heeled Darth's horse into line as the cavalcade trotted out through the gates.

Varent headed the column, leading them out onto the broad highway linking Secca and Aldarin. The farms that fed the city lay behind them now, the land ahead open territory, and soon they passed the great stone piles marking the boundary of Secca's influence. Despite Varent's assurances, Calandryll breathed a sigh of relief as he saw the indicators of his father's domain go by. He felt safer now: past those markers Bylath's legionaries had no power; they could not demand his return. He began to grin, his mood lifting. The sky above was blue, streamered with high cirrus, wheeling birds black specks against the azure, their song a chorus of liberation. Before him spread a vista of undulating grassland, sprinkled with woods, a broad river winding, no less blue than the sky, in leisurely curves, the paved road ending on its bank, becoming a wagon trail of hard-packed black earth on the farther side.

They forded the waterway and Varent indicated that they should swing south, across open meadowland.

'If Azumandias has planned any further surprises,' he explained, 'they'll be on the road. We'll take the lesser trails and be in Aldarin before he knows it.'

'What of his mystic spies?' asked Bracht.

'What of them?' returned Varent cheerfully. 'Not even Azumandias can guess our path. We're safe for the moment: trust me.'

Bracht grunted what might have been an affirmative and allowed his horse to fall back, putting a little distance between them. He seemed dissatisfied and Calandryll eased his own mount alongside.

'Why do you dislike him so?' he queried.

The Kern shrugged and shook his head, not speaking.

'I trust him,' Calandryll insisted, 'and he's offered only friendship.'

'That serves his own purpose,' Bracht murmured. 'He needs you because you speak the Old Tongue and now, it seems to me, you're in his power.'

'How so?' Calandryll stared at the mercenary. 'He brought me out of Secca - saved me from the priesthood; risked my father's anger. Was that not the act of a friend?'

'And should you refuse his quest? What then?'

'The spaewife foretold the quest,' Calandryll argued. 'Varent must be one of the comrades she said I should meet; you must be the other.'

'Perhaps, but that does not answer me,' Bracht insisted, 'You're in his power.'

Calandryll frowned his incomprehension.

'You've fled from your father,' Bracht explained, 'and cannot return to Secca. You're without money - by Ahrd! Varent had to buy that sword for you! The horse you ride, he provided; the food you eat, he buys. Did you not agree to Varent's quest, you'd be a wanderer, a footloose vagabond. You've nowhere to go but Aldarin; and only Varent to rely on when you arrive. Without him, you'd likely starve. Do you say you're not in his power?'

'What if I am?' Calandryll grew defensive. 'Aren't you?'

'He pays me,' Bracht said bluntly.

Did the quest mean no more to him than that?

'I trust him. I have faith in him.' Calandryll's voice was cold.

Bracht shrugged again, doubt written clear on his swarthy features.

'It is said in Cuan na'For,' he remarked, 'that a wizard has many faces, and keeps his true face hidden.'

Calandryll found his scepticism irritaing. Curtly he demanded, 'And what does that mean?'

'That I do not trust him,' Bracht answered evenly.

'Then why do you agree to accompany me?'

Bracht smiled, ignoring the vexed tone.

'Because he pays me,' he repeated.

SIX

AT first the journey, for all its promise of adventure, was a nightmare that not even its high purpose could assuage. Calandryll had seldom spent more than a few hours on horseback, riding to the hunt or in ceremonial parades, and now found himself rising beneath a sky still grey to saddle his borrowed mount and ride out at dawn, halting briefly at noon to eat and rest before pressing on until dusk. It seemed that every muscle in his body protested the hardship, and this was compounded by the nights spent in the open, a blanket his only covering, the ground his bed. He had never passed a night in the open before; indeed, had never spent a night outside the city, and the discomfort weighed heavy, rendered the worse for Bracht's silently critical appraisal of his awkwardness. Pride forbade that he complain, however, and so he suffered in miserable silence.

The circuitous route Varent chose meant that the waystations of the marked road were denied them, and the wagon, barely large enough to accommodate one person, was reserved for Varent's use. Calandryll, like the rest of the party, slept rough on a saddle blanket.

The nights were not unduly chill for the early promise of the spring had fulfilled itself, and the woodlands they traversed provided ample timber for fires, but still the hard ground was a far cry from the comfort of his bed and before long he found the excitement of such an adventure outweighed by the sundry lumps that dug into his ribs and the dew that each morning soaked his hair and face, and sometimes, when he had kicked off his blanket, his clothes. He wished that he could settle with Bracht's stoic indifference: the Kern simply rolled his blanket around himself each night and, his sword cradled like a lover in his arms, went soundly to sleep. So far as Calandryll could tell, he was not troubled by disturbing dreams.

His own lingered as he rose, rubbing moisture from his face, groaning as his muscles protested, his back aching as he straightened, the thought of another day in the saddle looming like the threat of punishment. Some were vague, so nebulous that they left behind only a feeling of apprehension, an inarticulate wariness, but others remained vivid.

Initially they were of the wolf-headed monstrosities, nightmare images of fanged mouths and hate-filled red eyes, of fire and battle, but these he could understand, and after the first shock of waking he was able to dismiss them. Others troubled him far more.

Chief amongst them was the image of Varent's handsome face smiling as he described the quest, then turning as the man prepared to leave, revealing a hidden face that snarled, laughing, becoming the visage of the lupine demons, his black cloak swirling, becoming a pair of vast, nigrescent wings that raised a great wind as the figure flew upwards, a bat with a wolf's head, spiralling into the sky, its mocking laughter echoing behind it. Sometimes he would hear Bracht's voice then, saying, 'A wizard has many faces'; and sometimes he would dream of the freesword, falchion in hand, the other scooping coins, his blue eyes filled with contempt and accusation. Sometimes he dreamed of Reba, the spaewife's musical voice repeating the words of the augury, and then he would see both Varent and Bracht emerge from the shadows behind the blind seeress, both beckoning him, requiring him to choose between them. He would turn to Reba then, seeking her guidance, and she would shake her head, dissolving into the candle's flame, leaving him, alone, to choose between the waiting figures.

Less often, the infrequency surprising him, he dreamed of Nadama. He would see her somewhere in the palace, in a garden or an empty hall, and she would raise her arms, smiling, and he would move towards her only to find his limbs leaden, dragging slowly as he sought to run, Tobias striding past him to sweep the girl up in his embrace, their kiss a lingering insult, their close-pressed bodies abruptly hidden behind the bulk of his father, Bylath lifting a condemning hand to point at him, his leonine features set in lines of outrage.

On all of these occasions Calandryll would wake sweating, the blanket crumpled about his feet or tossed aside, and lie staring at the night sky, listening to the snoring of Varent's men and the soft shuffling of the tethered horses, simultaneously longing for the sleep his body craved and dreading that descent into confusion. He wished that he might consult a dream-speaker, but knew that such interpretation would not be available until he arrived in Aldarin, composing himself once more to sleep only to find the camp waking when it seemed he had just shut his eyes.

He would rise then, reluctant to discuss the troublesome nocturnal visions, and dully eat his breakfast as he struggled to respond in kind to Varent's diplomatic apologies that no greater comfort was available, aware of Bracht's critical gaze as he wearily readied his borrowed horse and climbed without enthusiasm into the saddle. The two men had little to say to one another, Varent mostly remaining with the column whilst Bracht was constantly at Calandryll's side. The mercenary was polite enough, and Varent appeared satisfied with him, but when they halted the Kern's silence, for all that the ambassador ignored it, seemed pointed. Calandryll felt that he studied Varent, awaiting some justification of his distrust.

He was pleasantly surprised, after some seven days of journeying, to find that his aches began to decrease, that his limbs began to respond more readily as he saddled his borrowed horse and climbed astride; no less that the riding itself grew increasingly enjoyable. His humour improved then, and as it did, the dreams became less frequent, his sleep deeper, so that he once more began to assume his natural cheerfulness.

'You toughen,' Bracht remarked one day when he urged his horse to a canter, riding out ahead of the cavalcade, the mercenary dutifully accompanying him.

'Yes,' he agreed, unwilling to admit how uncomfortable he had been.

Bracht put it bluntly into words: 'You were soft.'

'I am not accustomed to sleeping rough,' he allowed.

'You're more used to beds than the ground,' the Kern responded. 'To cities and servants; to luxury.'

It was indisputably true, but Callandryll refused to acknowledge that veracity. His feelings towards the Kern were ambiguous: he felt a need to prove himself to Bracht, to augment the acceptance he had felt after the battle with the demons, but at the same time could not forget that the freesword rode with him for pay, no other reason. Bracht's mistrust of Varent rankled, for Calandryll had faith in the ambassador and the coolness that stood between them irked him, stemming, he felt, from Bracht's unreasonable dislike of Varent. He drove his heels hard against the gelding's flanks, lifting the animal to a gallop. The horse was willing enough, but no match for the Kern's big stallion: Bracht matched him easily, riding as if melded with the beast.

'But now you harden,' the Kern shouted over the windrush.

It sounded almost like a compliment and Calandryll turned his face, grinning. Bracht smiled back and Calandryll felt a flush of pleasure, the more determined to win the freesword's respect.

They thundered across the broad meadow ringed round with stands of slender birch, the trees silvery in the morning light, the sun shining warm out of a bright blue sky, white cumulus bulking across the western horizon, where land and sea met. Birds sang amongst the timber, more scattering from their path, and Calandryll gave himself over to the sheer pleasure of motion. It was as though the troublesome dreams were left with the column that receded behind them, the purity of the carefree gallop washing away all doubt, leaving only the quest ahead, Bracht's welcome comment reassuring him, firming him in his resolve. He stretched low over the gelding's outthrust neck, willing the animal to greater speed.

Ahead, the flanking woodland closed in the meadow, the grass becoming an avenue of sun-dappled green, down which they raced neck-and-neck. Calandryll glanced at Bracht, seeing the Kern sitting upright in the saddle, the reins held almost casually in his left hand, the thick tail of his glossy black hair streamered out behind him. He was smiling still, his stern features relaxed, his own pleasure writ clear.

Then sunlight gave way to shadow as the ground dipped and the wide-spaced birches were replaced with denser, older trees. Ash and beech and oak filled a broad bowl, the timber spreading up the ridge-sides, heavy boughs thrusting out to hide the sky. Bracht reined the stallion down to a walk, gesturing for Calandryll to follow suit as the trail became a winding path overhung with gnarled limbs that might easily sweep an incautious rider from his saddle. Beneath the horses' hooves the ground was rich with humus, black and muffling so that the sound of their passage became an aural match to the obfuscation of the light. There was a solemnity to the forest, the air still, cut through with occasional shafts of brightness, prompting Calandryll to think uncomfortably of a temple, its dark interior lit only by the high, narrow windows. Birdsong was a distant chorus, muted, it seemed, by the bulk of the great trees. Calandryll realised that he held his breath, as though the weight of timber imposed a sense of reverence, and when he next glanced at Bracht, he saw that the Kern was no less impressed.

They rode slowly through a vault of beeches and found themselves in a clearing as abruptly sunlit as the entrance to the forest had been shaded. Bracht halted, Calandryll at his side, staring at the enormous tree that dominated the glade. It was an oak of proportions to suggest tremendous venerability, boughs spreading in a mighty corona from a trunk so wide rooms might have been cut into its interior. Beneath the span of its limbs the ground was thick with winter-fallen leaves, a carpet of dry yellow that contrasted with the fresh green of the springtime shoots rising to meet the sun. Bracht dismounted and Calandryll followed suit, aping the mercenary as he tethered his stallion and moved on foot towards the tree.

Dead leaves crackled beneath their boots but there was no other sound. No birdsong or hum of insects, no rustle of breeze, disturbed the silence, as though the sheer solidity of the tree absorbed everything about it. There was an expression on the Kern's face Calandryll had not seen before, a look of awe; of reverence. He watched as Bracht approached the massive oak, arms raised as if in homage, setting his palms against the furrowed trunk, murmuring in a language he recognised as the tongue of Kern, in which he caught only the one word: 'Ahrd.'

For long moments Bracht stood, resting his weight against the tree, as Calandryll waited, then he straightened, turning a solemn face to his companion.

'I have never entered the Cuan na'Dru, never seen the Holy Tree, but I think this must be kin to Ahrd. I think this must be a sign, though of what I do not know.'

Calandryll frowned: he knew the folk of Kern hailed the tree, Ahrd, as their god, but he had not thought of Bracht as at all religious; and it seemed strange to worship a thing inanimate. Nonetheless, he could not deny the power that emanated from the vast growth. In that sunlit glade it was a tangible thing; it seemed he inhaled it with the rich, loamy air, felt it in the green-tinted light that bathed his face: he nodded.

Then gasped, clutching at his sword, as a voice said, 'Bracht understands.'

It was as if the tree itself spoke, or the woodland, for the words were soft as the rustle of wind through leaves, the faint rattle of stirred branches. He felt his skin prickle and saw the Kern draw his falchion, light glinting on the polished blade as he spun, ready to meet an attack, and realised that his own blade was out, raised in defence.

Gentle laughter whispered across the clearing and the same voice said, 'I offer you no harm. Rather, I would protect you.'

They both turned, eyeing the surrounding ring of beeches, seeing no one. Calandryll looked to the oak, anticipating some hidden archer; a volley of shafts. The voice said, 'Put up your swords; you are safe here,' and Bracht lowered his blade, studying the tree.

'Ahrd?'

His voice was hushed. Calandryll, raised in worship

of Dera, was less ready to accept such an explanation.

The voice came again, out of nowhere, out of everything around them. It seemed to emanate from the air itself, from the oak, from the sunlight.

'Put up your swords. There is no danger here, not for you.'

Bracht sheathed the falchion; less readily, Calandryll returned his straightsword to the scabbard. The sun seemed to shine brighter then, filtering through the wide-spread boughs to fill the glade with a gentle, green-hued radiance. Calandryll sniffed, anticipating the scent of almonds, that olfactory warning of sorcerous materialisation: he smelled only the rich, woodland odours. They grew stronger as the light increased, momentarily dazzling him so that he was not sure of what he saw, could only guess, still suspecting trickery. It seemed the great bole of the oak shifted as though filled with some inner, mobile life, the wrinkled wood bulging, roots wavering from the soil, a shape forming that came out of the tree itself, stepping confidently towards them. He set a hand to the hilt of his sword; felt Bracht's grip on his wrist, stilling him. The figure came closer, growing clearer with each step, and he gaped, staring at it.

It was formed in roughly human guise, but clearly no fleshly being, as though crude-carved from the oak, a dendriform thing. Its skin was the seamed grey of ancient wood, green-leaved twiglets sprouting from the gnarled round of its head, cracks for eyes and mouth, the torso a wooden trunk extending narrow arms that ended in thin twigs, the legs like roots, their bases thick with earth and dead leaves.

'You came to me in peace and I would send you away in like manner,' it said.

'Ahrd?' Bracht repeated softly.

'Not Ahrd,' said the creature, 'but Ahrd's kin, as you thought.'

Bracht raised a hand, the fingers spread wide in a gesture Calandryll recognised as obeisance. The gentle laughter sounded again, serene as the oak itself; strong, too, as that massive growth. It washed over them, warm as sunlight, reassuring: he felt his doubts dissolve.

The being halted, facing them, and he saw that the twin columns of its legs did, indeed, penetrate the soil, driving down roots as if seeking the sustenance of the earth. He stared at that part of it he thought of as a face and it seemed to smile, though that might have been no more than the play of sunlight on the gnarled surface.

'Listen,' it advised, 'and be warned. Deception cloaks your path and you must choose your friends with care. Beware the face of lies and hold no secrets one from the other, for you are bound as root to branch and the one may not survive what you face without the other. Remember that when the deceiver spins his web: trust is your ally and your strength.'

'You speak of Varent?' asked Bracht.

'I speak of wizards and of gods,' the creature answered.

'You speak in riddles,' Calandryll said. 'Can you not speak clearer?'

The twigs atop the thing rustled as though in negation. 'I cannot,' it declared. 'There are ... limitations. Were Bracht not born of Cuan na'For, I could not speak at all. Now go - I can tell you no more.'

The voice faded, soft as a dying breeze. The tree-being turned, roots tearing from the soil, and walked away. Calandryll stared, watching as it trod ponderously to the oak, seeing it embrace the great trunk, the light shimmer again as it merged, becoming one with the tree as if it had never been. He looked at Bracht, who raised his hand again, towards the tree, spreading his fingers, then bowed and walked towards the horses.

'This is a holy place,' the Kern murmured.

'It is a strange place,' Calandryll allowed.

'You saw the soul of the tree,' said Bracht. 'You heard Ahrd's kin speak.'

'I saw a creature formed of magic.' Calandryll looked back: the oak stood noble in the clearing, but now it seemed no more than a very ancient tree and his doubts returned. 'But I have seen much magic lately.'

'You doubt its warning?' Bracht demanded.

'I heard riddles,' he returned.

'It spoke of Varent.'

Bracht's voice was firm. Calandryll studied his face and shrugged.

'Or of Azumandias.'

'You are of Lysse,' said Bracht. 'What do you know of Ahrd?'

'I know the tribes of Kern worship it - him? - though few have seen the tree,' Calandryll answered. 'Do you not call it the Holy Tree? It is supposed to lie within the Cuan na'Dru, is it not? And none dare enter there.'

'You worship Dera - have you ever seen her?' Bracht countered.

Calandryll shook his head. 'No, but Dera was born of the First Gods - who can doubt her?'

'She is a goddess of Lysse,' Bracht said. 'Ahrd is the god of Cuan na'For.'

'We are in Lysse,' Calandryll responded.

'You say that was not a warning sent by Ahrd?'

Calandryll heard the conviction in the Kern's voice; read it in his eyes. He shook his head helplessly.

'I am not sure what it was. Perhaps Azumandias sent the thing to confuse us.'

'Varent said Azumandias could not find us. How could he know we should come to this place?'

'I know not.' Calandryll felt confused. 'You say it warned us against Varent?'

'Aye, I do.'

Bracht nodded. Calandryll stared at him, confusion mounting. 'Why do you mistrust him?' he asked.

Now Bracht shrugged.

'He has an air - something about him.'

'That you dislike. Is that reason enough for your suspicion?'

'Suspicion has often kept me alive,' Bracht said.

'But still you accept his coin.'

Accusation crept into his voice; Bracht ignored it.

'Why not? He pays me well.'

Calandryll snorted, growing angry.

'And so you accept his commission. Even though you distrust him.'

'I may be wrong,' Bracht admitted. 'But now ... I heard the *byah* speak.'

'*Byah*?' Calandryll frowned.

'The spirit of the tree. Ahrd's manifestation.'

'Ahrd is a god of Kern,' said Calandryll, 'and we are in Lysse. You cannot be sure Azumandias did not send the thing.'

'I *know*,' Bracht said, simply.

'Dera!' Calandryll raised his arms in frustration. 'Whoever sent it - Ahrd, Azumandias; Dera herself for all I know! - it spoke in riddles that you choose to hold against Varent. How can you say for sure it did not warn against Azumandias?'

Bracht shrugged; Calandryll sighed.

'If you believe that, why don't you leave his service?'

'I gave my word,' Bracht said, frowning as if he considered the question unnecessary.

'To a man you don't trust?'

'Until he proves me right,' Bracht nodded.

'I don't understand you.'

The Kern grinned tightly. 'Is there no honour in Lysse?'

'Of course,' Calandryll answered stiffly, sensing insult.

'I took his coin and gave my word in return,' Bracht explained. 'Until he shows himself treacherous I'm bound by that.'

'It might be too late then,' Calandryll said.

'Perhaps,' Bracht nodded, 'but still - I gave my word.'

'And that binds you.'

'Yes,' Bracht said, 'it binds me. What am I without it?'

Calandryll studied his face. The Kern's answering stare was guileless and after a few moments the younger man shook his head, seeing that Bracht would not be shaken from his conviction: his honour was a binding thing and he would serve Varent until such time as the ambassador showed himself false. But that time would not come; of that, Calandryll was certain. Varent's purpose was honorable and sooner or later Bracht must accept that. Of the *byah's* purpose he felt less certain. He had felt no doubts when the tree creature spoke, but now that it was gone he was less confident. Its warning had been ambiguous: it had offered no direct hint that it spoke of Varent, so why should it not have referred to Azumandias? That seemed, to him, the logical conclusion if it was, as Bracht believed, a manifestation of Ahrd. But how could the Holy Tree hold power in Lysse? Might it not, as he had suggested, be some further trick of Azumandias's? He determined to discuss the apparition with Varent as soon as he was able.

'Come.'

Bracht's voice roused him from his musings and he mounted the gelding, following the Kern back through the forest to the ridge where they had first descended into the dense timber.

The column was close, winding through the birch-lined avenue, Varent riding alongside the wagon in conversation with Darth. 'I think,' Bracht murmured as the cart approached, 'that my suspicions are better kept to ourselves.'

Calandryll ducked his head in agreement: if Varent knew of the Kern's mistrust he might well dispense with him, and Calandryll was loath to forfeit the free-sword's company.

'But I would discuss the *byah* with him,' he said.

'As you wish,' Bracht agreed. 'Though not my interpretation of its warning.'

Calandryll nodded and they waited for the column to reach their position, then Bracht gestured towards the timber.

'The trees grow thick down there. It will be hard going for the wagon.'

'I know a path,' smiled Varent. 'You enjoyed your gallop?'

'Yes,' Calandryll answered, 'it was ... enjoyable.'

'But?'

Varent's dark eyes studied his face and he frowned, glancing at Bracht. The Kern offered no response so he said, 'We encountered magic.'

Varent's brows rose enquiringly, inviting explanation. Calandryll brought his mount alongside, flanked by Bracht. 'There was a glade,' he offered, 'with a great oak at its centre. A being - Bracht named it a *byath* - came from the tree and spoke to us.'

'I have heard of the *byah*.' Varent leant forwards in his saddle, looking past Calandryll to the silent Kern. 'Are they not manifestations of Ahrd?'

'Yes,' said Bracht.

Varent beamed as though delighted with this confirmation.

'A *byah*! Would that I had been with you,' he declared wistfully. 'They appear only to worshippers of the Oak, I understand. If I remember correctly they are benign creatures, likely to offer sound advice. Did you receive such?'

'It told us to beware of lies,' Calandryll nodded. 'It said that deception cloaks our path, and that we should trust one another.'

'Sound advice, indeed,' smiled Varent, 'when you face the mendacity of such as Azumandias. The *byah* appear only rarely, I believe, and I doubt it would show itself again. What do you think, Bracht?'

'I think it accomplished its purpose,' the Kern answered. 'It will not appear again.'

'A pity.' Varent sighed. 'I'd dearly love to see such a being. But the tree remains - will you guide me to it?'

'You seem unsurprised,' Calandryll said, himself somewhat taken aback by the ambassador's cheerful acceptance of the creature.

'No,' Varent said, 'Why should I be? from what I have read, Ahrd is the father of forests and his presence may be found everywhere the great oaks grow. Just as Burash holds sway over all the oceans, so is Ahrd present in the forests.'

'But surely Lysse is Dera's domain,' Calandryll said.

'Indeed,' Varent agreed, 'but still there is room for other gods. I have a most interesting work on the subject of theogony in my library. By Marsius- do you know it?'

Calandryll shook his head.

'I shall find it for you when we reach Aldarin,' Varent promised.

'Might Azumandias not have conjured the *byah*?' Calandryll wondered.

'Not here.' Varent waved a hand, indicating the trees that now surrounded their path. 'How could he know our whereabouts? No, my friends, we are safe from his glamours for the moment.'

Calandryll glanced sidelong at Bracht, hoping the freesword was satisfied with this response. Varent accepted the manifestation too readily to fear it: his interest was that of the scholar. Had he thought the creature warned against him, surely he would have shown some sign of alarm, would not wish to visit the site of its appearance. And he appeared supremely confident that it was not some conjuration of his rival. If anything, his words agreed with Bracht's own beliefs, save in their diverse interpretations of the warning.

Bracht was wrong, he decided: as he suspected, the Kern's dislike clouded his judgement. Reassured, he nodded, smiling; he was fortunate to have encountered Varent.

'Well,' the ambassador asked, 'will you show me this wondrous oak?'

Calandryll looked again at Bracht, not quite ready to agree without the Kern's approval, and saw him duck his head, turning his stallion from the line of march. Varent called to his men to proceed, following the mercenary into the depths of the forest.

They reached the glade and dismounted. The oak stood majestic at the centre, but now it seemed only a tree, huge, impressive in its age and vast size, but otherwise mundane. The sunlight seemed brighter here only because of the space around the tree, and the earlier stillness, the solemn silence, was replaced with birdsong and the gentle rustling of a breeze. Varent walked towards the oak, staring up at the spreading branches. Calandryll saw Bracht watching the man, as though anticipating some revelation of falsity, some confirmation of his suspicions, but Varent appeared merely a scholar, fascinated by the vast growth. He drew close, touching the bole, smiling as a squirrel chattered from a branch, and paced slowly around the trunk.

'Do you still believe the *byah* warned of him?' Calandryll whispered.

Bracht nodded without speaking; Calandryll grunted, frustrated by the Kern's irrational obstinacy.

'Magnificent!' Varent came towards them, beaming delightedly. 'If a *byah* was to appear anywhere, it must surely be from such a splendid tree.'

He halted, turning to study the oak afresh. Bracht said, 'You seem familiar with the ways of Cuan na'For.'

Varent ducked his head absently, absorbed in his observation.

'I have made a study of most religions. As I

mentioned to Calandryll, Marsius is quite fascinating - you should read him.' He laughed briefly, waving an apologetic hand. 'Forgive me, I forget you cannot read.'

Bracht said nothing and Varent went to his horse.

'Fascinating. I am pleased to have seen it, but now we should rejoin the others.'

He mounted the chestnut, favouring the glade with a final glance as if hoping something might yet appear, then urged his mount back through the beeches. Calandryll followed, Bracht at the rear, his swarthy face impassive, and they trotted after the column.

For two days and a half they traversed the forest, emerging on the scarp of a ridge that descended through thinning stands of birch to a grassy plain. Feral cattle grazed there, and horses, scattering from their approach with tossing horns and wild-waving manes. They forded three shallow streams and floated the wagon across a river, spending the remainder of that day on the far bank, drying clothes and gear, their horses content to crop on the lush grass, Varent's men welcoming the leisure. Calandryll enjoyed no such respite, for Bracht declared that it was time he improved his swordskills and as he no longer suffered from the aching muscles and stiffness that had at first plagued him, he had no reason to argue. They were, after all, drawing steadily closer to Aldarin and the real start of the quest, when swordwork might well be needed.

From noon to dusk, and then each evening when they halted, the Kern drilled him in the finer points of swordplay as Varent and his men looked on, calling advice and shouting encouragement. Calandryll was pleased to find that he grew more limber with each passing day: he had, as Bracht had remarked, hardened, and he did his best to give a good account of himself as he faced the mercenary.

Bracht's praise as he improved delighted him and he was surprised to find that he took a pleasure in their duels that he had never known under the instruction of Torvah Banul on the practice grounds of his father's palace. Sleep, too, was a newfound boon, for when they cleared the forest his dreams ceased altogether.

He had thought them gone, but after the visitation of the *byah* they returned, as though the trees themselves sent visions, though of what he was uncertain. He would drift comfortably into sleep only to find himself standing once more in the clearing, moonlit in his dreaming, silvery light filtering through the branches of the great oak, the night silent and still all around. The *byah* would emerge from the substance of the tree and walk towards him with upraised arms, the twigs of its fingers spread wide so that he was unsure whether it raised its limbs in warning or threat. It would speak, but the words always got lost in the wind that blew then, cold and fierce so that the dendriform creature stood shaken by the gust, returning slowly, as if defeated, to blend again with the oak. As it merged, Bracht and Varent would come from the shadows at the oak's base, each man beckoning him, calling him to join them, to left or right of the tree, and he would stand undecided, knowing he must choose between them, but not knowing to which one he should go.

This dream stayed with him until they reached the grasslands, as though the power of the tree ended there, and once the forest lay behind them he slept untroubled.

He decided, finally, that the dream was not a sending of the *byah* but a product of his own making, the result of his increasingly divided loyalties. He remained confident that Varent's purpose was unimpeachable, but Bracht's mistrust was implacable, and that still disturbed him. A bond grew with the Kern, begun when they fought the demons together, cemented by his own guarding of the freesword's doubts, strengthened by the hours spent together. He no longer saw the mercenary as merely a hired man, motivated by desire for Varent's coin, but as a friend; and Bracht no longer evinced that vague contempt for his softness, his inexperience, seeming to regard him increasingly as an equal, a comrade. It was as though, with their sharing of the *byah's* warning, he had passed a further unspoken test, earning himself a higher place in Bracht's estimation, and he valued that.

On the other hand, he trusted Varent, enjoying the ambassador's urbane company no less than the Kern's. At night, after sword practice was ended, and often as they rode, Varent would discourse on the history of Lysse, the religions of their world, a myriad topics in which the ambassador was well-versed as any pedagogue, and Calandryll delighted in his erudition as keenly as he found himself enjoying Bracht's more physical tutoring.

It was a time he thought of later with some nostalgia: a time of innocence, almost idyllic.

They crossed the plain and saw low hills rising before them, the grass ending, giving way to more arid terrain: hard, reddish brown earth scattered with thrustings of grey and black stone, as if the land was pared to the bone. Still there was no sign of human habitation, nor any magical visitations as they wound a devious route amongst the knolls, climbing steadily to emerge after three days on a windswept plateau. Varent called a halt there, pointing ahead.

'Aldarin lies beyond this grass,' he announced. 'On the Alda.'

Calandryll squinted into the heat-hazed distance. The wind was strong, rustling his lengthening hair, whipping his horse's mane and tail, and on its gusting he could smell the ocean. Far off to the west the land fell down to meet the Narrow Sea, verdant green merging with the blue, and ahead the plateau stretched lush with spring grass. He saw buildings, painted blue, a shade akin to Varent's tunic, squat and walled, like tiny fortresses, flat roofs bright beneath the cloud-flecked sky.

'Ranches,' Varent explained, 'that provide the city's meat.'

He seemed enthusiastic, eager to reach his home city, his men no less so, and they commenced the crossing of the plateau at a brisk pace.

They encountered drovers, dark-tanned men in tunics and breeks of weather-beaten leather bearing long lances and riding sturdy ponies, who called greetings as they recognised the emblems decorating the wagon, but Varent steered them past the ranches and they camped in the open still, for the two days it took to cross the high grazing land.

Around mid-morning on the third day the plateau fell away in a sweeping slope that ran down to a broad valley, farms and vineyards spread along both sides, the ribbon of the Alda glittering silver blue all down its length. At the foot, where the river met the sea, stood Aldarin.

Like Secca - like all the cities of Lysse - the place was walled, its buildings contained within the circle of the ramparts. Calandryll saw the paved road running alongside the river, disappearing into great gates of metal-barred timber, mangonels threatening the approach. On the farther side, visible from the vantage point of the slope, was the harbour, spreading to either side of the walls within the bay formed by the valley. Ships lay at anchor there, toy-like in the distance, the ramparts of the city extending in two sweeping horns to encompass the bay, blockhouses at their extremities. It was a well-defended place, clearly able to withstand siege, yet festive, the houses colourful, the streets bright and busy.

The air was fresh, sweetened by the perfumes of the vines and tangy with the salt-smell of the blue-grey sea as they followed a drovers' road that wound down the slope to join the highway. By noon they were at the city gate, halting as a squad of mail-clad soldiers under the command of a captain raised pikes in salute to Varent.

'Welcome, Lord Varent,' the officer declared, bowing. 'Your journey was successful?'

'Most successful,' Varent replied, 'The Domm will be pleased with the outcome.'

The officer nodded. 'You require an escort, my lord?'

'I think not,' Varent said, smiling. 'My own retinue is sufficient, and I'd visit my palace before attending the Domm.'

'As you wish, my lord.'

The captain barked an order and the soldiers formed into ranks, clearing a way into the city. Varent headed the column, Calandryll and Bracht behind as they passed beneath the arch of the walls into a broad market square, gay with stalls and crowded, the folk there parting to let them through. An avenue paved in blue stone led out of the plaza, running between warehouses, straight as the roads bisecting Secca, opening onto more squares bright under the noonday sun, then on through quarters that reminded Calandryll of his home, all bustling, alive with activity.

Varent turned onto a narrower highway as they approached the centre and soon they rode through gardens and past houses attesting to the elevated status of their owners, set back behind protective walls, cool and spacious after the busy streets. Varent halted before a magnificent edifice, its roof and upper storey visible beyond a wall of white-washed bricks, its gates painted a vivid azure. He shouted and men in tunics of blue and gold swung the gates open.

They bowed, murmuring deferential greetings, and Varent rode between the gates into the courtyard.

'Welcome to my home,' he said, dismounting.

Calandryll and Bracht climbed down as servants came running to attend their master. Varent turned to the Kern.

'No doubt you'll wish to inspect the stables, though I assure you your horse will be well tended.'

He tossed his own reins to a servant. Calandryll found another waiting to take his, but after a moment's hesitation he shook his head, eliciting a chuckle from the ambassador, an approving nod from Bracht.

'I'll await you inside.'

Varent seemed to find his refusal amusing and he experienced a flush of embarrassment, as though he had chosen sides. The animal was not, after all, his, though he had groomed it and tended it - another of Bracht's lessons - since that first day in the caravanserai. He smiled apologetically and followed the Kern across the yard.

The stables were set to the rear of the house, a long row of spacious stalls shaded by a tiled portico, redolent of sweet-smelling hay and horseflesh. Varent's men left the wagon there for the house servants to unload, leaving their animals to the grooms and disappearing into the building. Calandryll unsaddled the gelding and rubbed it down, checking that the manger was filled and the trough supplied with sufficient water, grinning as it occurred to him that he had never devoted so much time to a horse: it seemed Bracht's influence was rubbing off. Then, satisfied, he joined the Kern and together they followed a patiently-waiting servant into the house.

The building was smaller than the Domm's palace in Secca, but, if anything, more luxurious. High windows admitted the sea-fresh air and the hall in which they found themselves was scented with the plants that grew in great urns of jade and malachite, standing on a floor patterned with blue and gold mosaics, the walls a soft blue that merged with the cerulean of the ceiling to produce the impression that they walked through a submarine garden. Beyond was a corridor where marble busts stood in niches, each one lit by the sun that entered from an artfully-cut embrasure on the opposite wall, ending at a door faced with beaten copper. The servant opened the door and ushered them through, into a cool, airy room where Varent waited.

Here, the walls were white, the floor polished wood layed in chevron patterns, a hearth set with unlit logs to one side, windows to the other. Varent lounged in a high-backed chair, the light accentuating the fine-drawn planes of his aquiline features, his feet thrust out, dusty boots resting on a lacquered stool. He smiled as they entered, rising to fill three silver goblets with rich, red wine, gesturing at the seats arranged in a semi-circle about the hearth.

'A toast,' he declared, 'to our safe arrival. Azumandias cannot touch you here.'

Calandryll accepted the goblet he offered, Bracht the other.

'I suggest we eat,' Varent said. 'Or would you prefer to bathe?'

Bracht said, 'Eat,' Calandryll nodded his agreement.

'So be it.' Varent settled himself comfortably and sipped his wine. 'The servants will show you to your rooms and provide anything you wish. I must leave you for a while - the Domm will require news of my dealings with Secca, and I shall likely return late, if not tomorrow. One thing I would impress on you, however - so long as you remain within these walls Azumandias cannot harm you.' He glanced at Bracht, an expression part warning, part apology, as though he understood the Kern's dislike of sorcery. 'I have set spells to ward this place, but outside you are in danger. Azumandias must surely learn of my arrival and will watch this house. Do not leave here, on peril of your lives!'

'Azumandias is in Aldarin?' Bracht asked.

'Perhaps.' Varent shrugged. 'Certainly his agents are – and his power is considerable, as you know.'

'Why not kill him?' the freesword demanded bluntly. 'Put a blade between his ribs and have done with it.'

Varent laughed.

'Would that it were so simple, my friend. But it is not! Azumandias is a mightier wizard than I can hope to be and he guards himself with magic. And there are laws in Aldarin - the punishment for murder is the gallows.'

'The man who sent those demons against us respected no laws,' Bracht retorted.

'No,' agreed Varent, patiently, 'but what proof is there Azumandias sent them? Save for you and Calandryll, they came and went unseen. And should I produce you as witnesses, Azumandias must know for sure you are here. At present he must wonder; at the least, be unsure where you are.'

'It takes no wizard to guess we'll be here,' Bracht argued.

'Probably,' Varent nodded, 'but he cannot be certain. I have estates beyond the city and I might have secreted you there. Whilst you remain behind my walls he cannot know for sure.'

'Your servants?' the mercenary demanded. 'The men who rode with us? They might talk.'

Varent beamed approvingly. 'Your caution is admirable,' he applauded, 'but you need not fear on that score - my people are trustworthy. They will give nothing away.'

'And when we leave?'

Varent raised a conspiratorial finger. 'When you leave,' he said, 'you will go swiftly to the harbour. A ship will be waiting and with luck you'll be gone before he knows it.'

'When will that be?' Bracht asked.

'Soon,' promised Varent. 'I must locate a suitable vessel - a trustworthy captain - before you may safely depart.'

'So until then,' Bracht said slowly, 'we are prisoners.'

'Hardly prisoners,' Varent chuckled. 'Honoured guests. I think you will find your sojourn comfortable enough.'

Bracht grunted and drained his goblet. Calandryll asked, 'What of the charts?'

'The charts,' smiled Varent, 'Yes, the charts. Immediately my business with the Domm is concluded we must study them. Then I must find a ship. Likely, I shall be required at the palace most of tonight. In the morning, then?'

Calandryll nodded, satisfied. Varent said, 'Now, shall we eat?' and rose, ushering them from the room.

He was an agreeable host, maintaining a flow of casual conversation throughout the meal that precluded any further discussion of their plans, and Calandryll found himself relaxing, enjoying his sophistication and ready wit. Bracht remained taciturn, but that was not unusual, and he offered no objection when Varent declared that he must attend the Domm and left them in the care of his servants.

They were shown to adjoining rooms, where baths were drawn and women in fine silk robes waited to assist them. They were attractive, but Calandryll dismissed the pair intent on bathing him and climbed alone into the tub, disturbed by their presence: their fair faces and luscious bodies reminded him of Nadama. It was strange, he mused as the hot water lapped about him, that he had not thought of her in days, yet it was her rejection that had set him on this path. Had she preferred him, would he still be in Secca? Certainly, he would not have run from the palace to get drunk in the Sailors Gate; and if he had not done that he would never have met Bracht; perhaps Varent might not have offered him the means to escape the destiny decreed by his father. Reba had outlined the path he might take, but that was not predetermined, and if Nadama had accepted his suit he might never have taken those first steps along the path that brought him here.

He wondered what his father did now. Did watchmen scour the city? Did patrols search the countryside? Perhaps Bylath had news from the caravanserai; but what if he did? Would he send a mission to Aldarin, demanding the return of his errant son? Would even Bylath dare accuse Varent of aiding his escape? It seemed unlikely: political expediency would surely override the risk of such insult. And Varent need only deny it: the Domm of Aldarin was hardly likely to suspect his own ambassador. So he was safe under Varent's protection.

He grinned at the thought of his father's rage; then felt the smile dull: he was safe only so long as he *was* under Varent's protection, just as Bracht had said. Without Varent he was lost, no better than a refugee, outlawed from his home city and perhaps hunted by the Chaipaku.

That new thought chilled him and he rose, water splashing from the tub. Then shook his head, fighting a surge of panic.

There is a teacher ... Trust him ... And one will come after ...

He tracked wet footprints across the tiled floor as he concentrated on the words of Reba's prophecy. They had to refer to Varent and Bracht. The one had come offering him escape, refuge, offering fulfilment of the spaewife's vision; the other was a comrade, a sword to guard his back. Bracht's dour warnings stemmed from his dislike of Varent, nothing more. He was safe whilst Varent protected him: he grunted, irritated with himself; irritated that Bracht should place such doubts in his mind.

What was it the *byah* had said?

Trust is your ally and your strength.

Well, he trusted Varent. If Bracht chose not to, that was the Kern's affair.

You must choose your friends with care.

The tree creature had said that, too, and he had chosen Varent. For every pessimistic argument of Bracht's there was a positive view: it depended on the observer. His logic pleased him and he walked from the bathroom into the chamber, seeking fresh clothes.

Varent's servants had taken his own travel-stained garments for cleaning, but there was a well-stocked wardrobe from which he selected a shirt of fine white cotton and breeks of dark blue, a pair of boots, and a loose tunic of grey silk. He decided the chart would be safe enough here, leaving it in the wardrobe, and went in search of Bracht.

His knock was answered by a muffled voice that he took as an invitation to enter and he pushed the door open, stepping into the room. Bracht and a yellow-haired girl looked up from a confusion of sheets and he felt his cheeks grow hot, mumbling an apology. The mercenary grinned.

'Varent's hospitality is everything he promised.'

Blushing, Calandryll sprang back, closing the door, feeling the warmth that pervaded his face grow deeper as the girl's shrill laughter rang in his ears, echoed by the Kern's deeper chuckling. He cursed, angry with himself, uncertain whether he was angry once more with Bracht or merely envious, and decided to find the library Varent had described.

A servant showed him to a chamber filled with books, shelves rising from a floor of polished pine to the white-plastered ceiling, a single window spreading light over a desk of mahogany, a padded leather chair drawn up before the bureau, two others set either side of a cold hearth.

The books were catalogued and he had no difficulty

in finding the tome Varent had mentioned, Marsius's *Comparison of Religions*, and settled at the desk, rapidly immersed. Bracht found him there as dusk fell, engrossed in his studies. The Kern was smiling cheerfully; Calandryll closed the book.

'Our host's servants are most enthusiastic,' Bracht grinned, leaning against the desk. 'Rytha offers some small compensation for this confinement.'

'I'm pleased you're ...' Calandryll sought the right word, '... satisfied.'

'With her, yes,' Bracht nodded, rising to peer from a window. 'With other things, no.'

'What troubles you now?' Calandryll demanded.

Bracht turned to study his face, frowning curiously.

'The girl offends you?'

'No!' he said, a little too quickly. 'Why should you not avail yourself of the ... amenities?'

Bracht shook his head, a quizzical grin exposing white teeth. 'Did you not?' he asked.

'No. I ... No, I didn't.'

The Kern seemed about to say something, but thought better of it and shrugged instead; Calandryll sought to change the subject, embarrassed by his inexperience.

'What troubles you?' he repeated.

'Confinement.'

Bracht went to a chair; dropped into it. Calandryll said, 'Varent explained why we must remain here.'

'Indeed,' Bracht nodded. 'And most convincingly.'

'Then why do you protest?'

Bracht shrugged again. 'We come to Aldarin by secret ways; in the city we must remain behind his walls. It smells too much of prison.'

'Hardly a prison,' Calandryll argued, 'and Lord Varent explained the reasons.'

'Do you notice that when you take his side you honour him with a title?'

The question was mildly put, but still Calandryll felt himself blush, irritation stirring afresh. He shook his head dismissing it.

'He seeks only to protect us from Azumandias. Dera, Bracht! You've seen what he can send against us!'

'"Deception cloaks your path and you must choose your friends with care"' Bracht quoted. 'You heard the *byah*, Calandryll.'

'Yes!' he snapped, 'and I believe it spoke of Azumandias.'

'I believe it spoke of Varent,' Bracht returned, his voice still mild.

Calandryll shook his head, sighing. 'We come full circle again. Have you witnessed evidence of treachery? What has Lord Varent done to earn this mistrust?'

'Perhaps nothing,' Bracht murmured. 'Perhaps I am wrong, but it seems to me that a man who sends demons to do his work takes a straightforward path. Deception is less obvious.'

'That's sophistry,' Calandryll declared.

Bracht frowned, uncomprehending.

'Your argument trips on its own subtlety,' Calandryll explained. 'Who else sent the demons but Azumandias? Their very appearance confirms Lord Varent's integrity.'

'I am certain of only one thing: Varent wants the Arcanum,' said Bracht, 'Of that I'm certain, if of little else. He plays some game of his own with us as pawns.'

Calandryll shook his head wearily, tiring of the Kern's unrelenting suspicion. 'I play the part willingly,' he said.

'As do I, for now,' Bracht returned, grinning as he added, 'Five thousand varre buys my trust. Until I know more.'

'And should you learn more?' Calandryll wondered. 'Should you be right?'

Bracht's smile grew wolfish.

'Then we'll hold the book, and that must be the key

to this riddle. When that's in our hands, we'll see where Varent stands.'

Calandryll sighed, not knowing what he could say to convince the freesword of Varent's honesty.

SEVEN

VARENT did not return that night, so Calandryll and Bracht ate in lonely splendour, attended by servants who were politely deferential and tactfully vague when the Kern attempted to question them about their master. All he was able to extract from them was that Lord Varent den Tarl was the scion of one of Aldarin's oldest families, unwed, and a trusted adviser to the Domm, Rebus. Of Azumandias they professed ignorance, and when questioned on the subject of Varent's own occult talents murmured smooth replies that left the freesword little the wiser. Eventually, to Calandryll's relief, Bracht gave up and concentrated on the excellent meal; at least until they had finished eating and the servants had left them alone with a decanter of the distilled wine, in a comfortable withdrawing room off the dining hall.

'They protect him,' Bracht declared obstinately.

Calandryll shook his head in resignation. He was enjoying the luxury of Varent's mansion, knowing that soon they must embark for Gessyth and such comforts would lie behind them: he would have preferred to savour the liquor in peace.

'They have nothing to tell you,' he said.

Bracht fixed him with a blue stare and said, 'You trust too easily.'

'And you suspect too readily,' he countered.

The Kern shrugged and rose to his feet, crossing to a window. Outside, the night was dark, moonless behind rolling banks of cumulus blown in from the sea, the sounds of the city muffled by the protective walls. Lanterns lit the room with a mellow glow, striking highlights from the richly polished furniture, a fire burning in the hearth, reminding Calandryll of the comforts of his home. He thought of fetching a book from Varent's well-stocked library, contemplating an hour or two of literary indulgence before finding his bed, but Bracht gave him no chance.

The freesword turned from the window and moved towards the door, pausing as Calandryll asked, 'Do you retire?' Thinking that he likely sought the girl, Rytha, or some other compliant wench. But Bracht shook his head and said, 'No. I'd take a stroll.'

'Where?' Calandryll enquired; a turn about Varent's gardens might be pleasant.

'Into the city,' Bracht said.

'You heard Lord Varent,' Calandryll protested. 'He warned us that Azumandias likely watches this house.'

'And may send more demons against us?' Bracht suggested. 'I've thought on that sending, and it occurs to me that Azumandias's demons are somewhat clumsy - four could not defeat us, and they were slow-moving creatures. Should I encounter any, I'll turn tail.'

'Dera!' Calandryll came to his feet. 'Can you not wait a little while?'

'No,' said Bracht, and quit the room.

Calandryll hurried after him, his protests falling on deaf ears as the Kern strode to his chamber and secured the falchion about his waist. Calandryll snatched up his own blade, not sure whether he acted from loyalty to

Bracht or to Varent, but determined that the Kern should not go unaccompanied.

'Perhaps you should remain here,' Bracht suggested.

'No.' Calandryll grew obstinate now. 'If you're determined to ignore Lord Varent's wishes, I'll go with you.'

Bracht nodded and returned down the corridor, Calandryll close on his heels. They found the entrance hall and went out into the courtyard. The air was chilly, salt-scented and promising rain before dawn, a solitary nightbird serenaded the starless sky. As they reached the gates two men stepped from the shadows beneath the arch, positioning themselves before the portal. The lights shining from the mansion glinted on mail shirts and half helms.

'I'd go into the city,' Bracht said.

'Forgive me, but Lord Varent left orders that no one is to leave.'

The man spoke politely enough, but an obdurate note underlined his statement.

Bracht said, 'Stand aside.'

'Lord Varent left orders,' the guard repeated. 'I believe they are for your safety.'

Calandryll heard the angry intake of the Kern's breath and feared he would attack. Instead he asked, 'Are we prisoners, then?'

'I obey Lord Varent's orders,' the guard intoned doggedly. 'I understand the city is dangerous for you.'

'I believe I can take care of myself,' Bracht snapped.

'No doubt.' The guard remained unmoved, unmoving. 'But my orders are clear.'

The Kern studied the two armoured men as though weighing his chances of felling them. They, in turn, set themselves shoulder to shoulder, hands on sword hilts.

'Bracht,' said Calandryll, warningly.

'What's amiss?'

Calandryll turned to see Darth approaching, three others of Varent's retinue with him.

'We are denied the freedom of the city,' Bracht responded.

Darth chuckled, shrugged, and said, 'Lord Varent protects you, man.'

'I can protect myself,' grunted the freesword.

'Against blades, no doubt. But against magic?' Darth lowered his voice, glancing at the gates. 'Lord Varent has enemies who'd see you slain, I think. Come back to the house and drink with us, if you've a mind. And I believe Rytha anticipates warming your bed.'

He winked as he said it, grinning. His companions smiled, but Calandryll saw that they ranged themselves, albeit casually, between Bracht and the gates.

'Come on,' Darth urged, indicating the two guards with a thrust of his chin. 'These fellows only do their duty.'

'And you?' Bracht demanded.

'I serve Lord Varent,' Darth said. 'And he's left orders ...'

Bracht fingered his sword, then shrugged: 'So be it.'

Calandryll breathed a relieved sigh as the mercenary allowed Darth to lead him back across the courtyard into the house. He followed, but when Darth suggested he join them, he shook his head, declaring his intention of retiring with a book, and went to the library.

He fetched the copy of Marsius from the shelf and carried it to his chamber. He hoped to find some reference to the Arcanum in the weighty tome that would furnish more information, but it told him nothing he did not already know and after a while he set the book aside, yawning, promptly falling into a sound and dreamless sleep.

Sunlight woke him and he rose, wondering if Varent had returned from the palace. When servants brought hot water and the announcement that his host awaited him, he bathed and dressed quickly, eager to hear what news Varent brought.

The ambassador was settled comfortably in the dining hall, breaking his fast with fresh-baked bread and fruit. He smiled as Calandryll entered, motioning the younger man to a chair. Calandryll sat, helping himself to food.

'I understand there was some small misunderstanding last night,' Varent murmured.

'Bracht had a yen to explore the city.' Briefly Calandryll wondered if he should advise Varent of the Kern's misgivings; but then dismissed the thought: it would be a betrayal of Bracht's confidence.

Varent sighed as if he considered Bracht a necessary but troublesome adjunct to their purpose. 'Our Kern friend has an independent nature,' he murmured. 'Surely I explained why that is not possible?'

He studied Calandryll's face speculatively, his own radiating a mixture of resignation and mild irritation.

'Yes,' Calandryll agreed, 'but Bracht has little fondness of confinement.'

'Sadly needed,' Varent said, 'At least until I've arranged your passage. The sooner the better, I think.'

Bracht came into the room then. Calandryll saw that his eyes were somewhat bloodshot, purple crescents darkening the tan beneath. Varent offered a greeting that was answered with a grunt as the freesword slumped into a chair.

'I understand you've found favour with Rytha.' Varent smiled.

It seemed to Calandryll he sought to bridge the gap between them, showing the mercenary a greater courtesy than their respective positions warranted. If so, Bracht appeared unaware of the gesture, or chose to ignore it: he nodded and said, 'Your guards refused to let us out.'

'I thought we had agreed you'd not leave,' Varent said, unruffled.

'I'd not thought to find myself a prisoner.'

'A guest,' said Varent smoothly. 'Whose welfare I'd protect.'

Bracht glanced at him and filled a mug with aromatic tea.

'I was saying to Calandryll, I'll find a ship as soon as possible.' Varent raised a napkin to his lips. 'And once you've finished eating we'll examine the maps.'

'There's my money, too,' said Bracht.

'Indeed. Half on arrival in Aldarin, as we agreed.'

Bracht nodded.

'Less the one hundred already paid.'

'A trifle,' said Varent.

'Less that,' Bracht insisted.

'You're scrupulous,' smiled Varent. 'A matter of honour?'

'Aye.' Bracht nodded again, staring at the ambassador. 'Honour is important, do you not agree?'

There was a hint of challenge in his voice and Varent met it with a frozen smile, then ducked his head: 'Aye, it is.'

'Shall we sail direct to Gessyth?' asked Calandryll, seeking to deflect the confrontation he feared might explode.

'I think not.' Varent shook his head. 'At this time of year there are few captains who will risk Cape Vishat'yi, so I'll book you passage to Mherut'yi. From there you'll travel overland to Nhur-jabal, and on to Kharasul. The Kands maintain a trade route between Kharasul and Gessyth - there's a settlement built on a headland from which you can strike into the swamps.'

He paused to peel an orange, fastidious; then glanced at Bracht with the corners of his wide mouth rising a little.

'I'll provide you with coin to buy your way. And when you reach the outpost you can likely hire men to ferry you inland.'

'Who lives there?' the Kern asked.

'Hide hunters,' Varent returned. 'They trap the swamp dragons and sell the hides to the Kand traders. The skins make excellent armour.'

Bracht frowned and asked, 'Are they men?'

'Some,' Varent informed him. 'Outcast Kands, mostly.'

'And the rest?'

'Halflings.'

Calandryll had never seen a halfling. 'What are they like?' he wondered.

'Strange, I believe,' said Varent. 'Some are quite human in appearance, but others ...'

He shrugged.

'The makings of the younger gods,' grunted Bracht.

'Exactly.' Varent nodded. 'But doubtless you can deal with them.'

'Doubtless,' Bracht said, as if there were no doubt. He pushed his plate away. 'Now shall we examine these maps?'

Varent smiled his agreement. 'But first your payment - I'd see you satisfied on that score.'

'Good,' Bracht said, grinning for the first time.

Varent led them from the dining hall to a wood-panelled chamber with a single window set high in the wall shedding light on a cluttered desk at which sat a bald man in the blue and gold tunic of a household servant. He looked up as they entered, blinking short-sightedly over the rims of large spectacles.

'Two thousand, four hundred varre, Symeon,' Varent said.

The bald man's nose twitched. Calandryll saw that the quill he held had splattered ink over the tip.

'In single coins, or decuris?'

Varent glanced at Bracht, who said, 'Decuris.'

Symeon studied the mercenary for a moment, as if debating whether or not to obey the order, then wiped an ink-stained hand on his tunic and rose slowly from his chair to kneel before a metal door set into the wall.

He brought a key from his breeches and swung the door open, dragging out a chest that he deposited on the floor. Hiding it with his body, he began to count the heavy gold coins into a leather sack.

Ponderously, he relocked the chest and returned it to the recess, locked that door, and then straightened, wheezing slightly, the sack in his hands.

'Twenty-four decuris. Count them if you like.'

He passed the sack to Bracht, who shook his head.

'I have no reason to mistrust you.'

Calandryll felt the comment was addressed to Varent. And that it lacked one word: *yet.*

If Varent sensed it he gave no sign. 'Now,' he said, 'let us examine the maps.'

They left Symeon with his accounts and went to the library. There, Varent latched the door and took several books from the shelf. It seemed that he exposed only a section of the wall, but when he turned a knob carved on the facing of the shelves, a panel sprang open and he brought out a packet of waxed paper bound with scarlet ribbon.

He brought the packet to the table and tugged the ribbon loose. Inside was a sheet akin to the chart Calandryll had taken from the archives in Secca, but finer, virtually transparent, marked with a delicate, spidery script, Orwen's seal bright scarlet at the foot. Varent pushed the protective wrapping aside and smoothed the map, his touch reverential, looking to Calandryll with brows raised in silent question.

Calandryll unlaced his shirt and withdrew the matching chart, handing it to Varent. The ambassador set one over the other, weighting the corners, and smiled triumphantly.

'Dera's blood, my friends, we have it!'

Calandryll and Bracht drew close, studying the map. One overlaying the other, the combined charts showed Gessyth in greater detail than anything in Medeth or

Sarnium, in greater detail than any map Calandryll had ever seen. Orwen had been painstaking in his depiction of the coastline of the Western Ocean and the interior of Gessyth, marking those places along the coast of Gash where a boat might find anchorage and fresh water, the sweeping bays that scalloped the perimeter of the swamplands; the promontory containing the hide hunters' settlement was marked. It was a chart of minute detail, scribed with annotations in the antique language of the Old Tongue: Calandryll studied it in awe.

'It *is* there,' he murmured, touching the scarlet blemish marked, *Tezin-dar.*

'Did you doubt it?' Varent tapped the charts. 'See? As I promised, he shows the route to take. And warns of the dangers.'

Calandryll stared, struck as much by the maps' antiquity as the details the long-dead cartographer had included. It was a thing of wonder a priceless treasure in its own right. And it showed the way to legendary Tezin-dar.

'Dera,' he whispered, touching a nervous fingertip to a line of script, 'He warns of dangers enough.'

'Do you translate them?'

Bracht's question interrupted his amazement and he said, 'Flesh-eating trees,' absently, ignoring the Kern's snort as he continued, rapt, to study the wondrous document, 'Swamp dragons; insects of some kind; poisonous flowers; flesh-eating fish.'

The Kern grunted, less impressed with the age of the charts than the information they imparted. 'Useful,' he agreed. 'Do we take these with us?'

'Best transcribe them onto a single sheet,' said Varent. 'Calandryll, do you undertake that task? While I find you a ship?'

Calandryll nodded without speaking, still caught in the mysteries of the fabulous map.

'I'll find you paper and pens,' Varent promised.

For the next three days Calandryll was engrossed in his task. Varent provided him with materials and ensured that he was left alone in the library, whilst Bracht wandered fretfully about the mansion or amused himself with the compliant Rytha. Calandryll devoted himself wholeheartedly to the copying of the charts. It was far more complex than he had anticipated, and several times he destroyed his efforts, deeming his transcription insufficiently accurate. His life and Bracht's might well depend on the precision of his work and he was determined to recreate Orwen's fabulous maps in the minutest detail. His hand and eye, however, lacked the ancient cartographer's skill and just as he thought he had succeeded, he would notice some line drawn slightly out of true and, with a groan of frustration, consign his efforts to the hearth and start over again. Finally he hit on the notion of obtaining paper so fine he was able to read the charts through it, tracing their details to his satisfaction. Then he used a blunted quill to inscribe the minutiae on a thicker sheet, inking in the faint impressions and adding Orwen's notes after.

At last he was satisfied with the accuracy of his copy, and though his head throbbed and his eyes ached with the effort of poring over the map, he felt triumphant. That evening he showed his work to Varent.

The ambassador sat staring at the original charts and the copy, eyes flicking from one to the other before he nodded, smiling.

'Superb! You've captured it all.'

Calandryll sighed with relief. Bracht, ever pragmatic, asked, 'Is there news of a ship?'

'A Kand merchantman docked yesterday,' Varent nodded. 'I've spoken with her captain and tonight we meet again. If he's willing, you'll sail when he leaves.'

'How long?' The Kern demanded, anxious to be gone.

'Three days, perhaps.' Varent shrugged. 'He's a cargo to sell and goods to buy. Can you curb your impatience until then?'

Bracht grunted an affirmative, staring at the ambassador with a quizzical expression on his swarthy features.

'So,' he said thoughtfully, 'we likely have a ship. We have the map, and you'll provide us with the means to purchase our passage across Kandahar and on to Gessyth. If the halflings or the swamp dragons or those sundry other perils the map mentions don't kill us, we'll likely find Tezin-dar. What then?'

'Then you locate the Arcanum,' Varent said, 'And bring it out.'

Bracht snorted cynical laughter. 'And shall such a thing lie unguarded?' he asked. 'Simply for us to take?'

Varent's face grew serious. He leant forwards in his chair, dark eyes solemn as they met the Kern's.

'I do not know,' he said. 'I know nothing of Tezin-dar beyond that knowledge already given you. I cannot say what awaits you there, or how difficult it may be to take the book. I only know that if you fail, Azumandias will eventually locate it and seize it. And if he does ...'

He broke off, shaking his head as though the very thought appalled him.

'You must use your wits,' he continued at last. 'I can offer you no more advice than that.'

'Should we be opposed,' Bracht said, 'our situation will likely be parlous.'

'Dera knows, you speak true,' Varent said softly, seriously. 'But I see no alternative. Should Azumandias lay hands on the Arcanum he'll raise the Mad God and bring the world down in ruin.'

'We must attempt it,' Calandryll urged. 'Can you stand by and watch the world destroyed?'

Bracht glanced at him, a tight smile curving his mouth. He shook his head: 'I do not say we give up. I say only that we may not succeed.'

'We must do our best,' Calandryll said. 'Let us face the problems when they arise.'

'Do you recall that first bout we fought?' Bracht asked mildly. 'I told you then that a good fighter seeks to learn his opponent's limitations, not simply charge him.'

'There's little alternative here,' Calandryll protested. 'We know nothing of Tezin-dar, so how can we study our opponents?'

'Unfortunately, Calandryll is correct,' interposed Varent. 'Until you reach Gessyth there is no way of telling what opposition you may encounter.'

Bracht grunted, nodding.

'I don't like it,' he murmured.

'You've come too far to renege now,' Calandryll said.

Blue eyes fixed him with a cold stare and Bracht said, 'I do not speak of reneging. I've agreed to accompany you and that I'll do. But it seems we walk blind into Tezin-dar.'

'You're my only hope,' Varent said, his voice earnest as the look he cast Bracht's way. 'The Arcanum *must* be destroyed.'

The Kern nodded, turning to the map. 'Assuming we succeed in taking the book, it's a long way from Tezin-dar to the coast if we're pursued.'

'Must we return to the coast?' Calandryll indicated Tezin-dar with a fingertip; moved it to the Valt mountains. 'Might we not flee to the Geff Pass and cross into Kern? Follow the mountains to the Gannshold crossing and come south through Lysse?'

'The Geff?' Bracht shrugged. 'In Cuan na'For that place is called Hell Mouth. It's the domain of creatures to chill the blood. And beyond lies the territory of the Lykard.' He laughed, once; a cold bark. 'I am not very ... popular ... with the Lykard.'

Calandryll stared at him, inviting amplification, but Bracht shook his head. 'Best return the way we know - we'll travel faster.'

'You'll do it, then?' Varent asked.

'I gave my word,' said Bracht, bluntly.

Varent relaxed visibly, his smile returning. 'There's some small measure of protection I can offer,' he said. 'If you'll accept magic as an aid.'

Bracht eyed him for a moment, then nodded.

'I think we'll need whatever aid you have.'

'Wait here.'

Varent rose, hurrying from the room. Silence fell with his departure, Bracht sitting with dour mien, Calandryll lost in his own thoughts. He had been carried, he realised, on a wave of excitement that had left him little time to contemplate what he faced. The purpose was noble - of that he had no doubt - and Varent had offered an escape from the odious fate planned by his father. With Bracht at his side, and his own burgeoning swordsmanship, he had assumed they would simply enter Tezin-dar and carry off the Arcanum, to return in triumph to Lysse. That was the stuff of legend, the material of the balladeers, but now, looking at Bracht's sober face, he forgot that romantic optimism.

'You believe we may die,' he said softly.

'Yes,' Bracht answered. Then grinned: 'But all men must die. It's no reason to give up.'

Calandryll nodded, presentiment twisting a cold, hard knot deep in his belly.

'Are you afraid?' Bracht asked, still grinning.

He thought for a moment, then nodded: 'Yes.'

'Good,' said the mercenary, 'a little fear will make you careful.'

'And a lot?' he wondered.

'Will likely kill you,' Bracht informed him cheerfully. 'Control your fear and it becomes an ally. Let it overwhelm you and you're dead.'

Calandryll was no longer sure whether the chill he suddenly felt represented a greater or lesser weight. The hazards in their way seemed real now, rendered so by the freesword's blunt practicality, by the realisation that, in the final analysis, they did not know what they faced. But he was committed: he could not turn back; not now. The fate of the world rested with them: if they failed, Azumandias would secure the Arcanum and raise the Mad God. That must not be! He squared his shoulders, forcing a smile to his lips.

'I'll play my part,' he declared.

'No doubt,' said Bracht, to Calandryll's disappointment, unimpressed.

The door opened then and Varent entered, a small box of dark wood inlaid with silver in his hand. He set it down and sprung the clasp, revealing an interior lined with purple velvet on which rested an innocent-looking stone, drilled through to allow its attachment to a simple leather thong. Varent removed it, holding the thong, the stone revolving slowly, a dull carnelian, save for a hint of fire that seemed to flicker tentatively within its heart.

'This serves a double purpose,' he advised them. 'The talent required for the practice of magic is a rare commodity, and even those gifted with the power may not employ it without arduous training. This stone, however, serves to channel latent ability, enabling the wearer to utilise the simpler spells - with it, you will be able to render yourself invisible. In addition, should you encounter some glamour, the flame within will burn bright and the stone grow hot. Should that happen, you will know that wizardry is close. I would urge you to wear the stone at all times.'

Calandryll nodded; Bracht frowned his incomprehension. Varent smiled and hung the red stone about his neck, murmuring soft, guttural words.

Where he stood the light shimmered, momentarily iridescent, and he was gone, the scent of almonds drifting on the still air. Calandryll stared, concentrating on the spot. He could see the walls of the ambassador's library, see the window, but between there was a faint area of disruption, as if the light itself stirred, as if the very stuff of the air was somehow agitated. Had he not known that Varent stood there he would likely not have noticed, but by squinting, by forcing his tired eyes to focus on the spot, he could just perceive the shape of a man. Varent spoke again, and once more the room was perfumed with almonds as he reappeared.

'Perhaps this is the way to the Arcanum,' he suggested.

'Useful,' Bracht allowed warily.

'Perfect!' Calandryll declared enthusiastically.

'You must know the words,' said Varent, removing the stone. 'You must fix them in your minds and your pronunciation must be exact. Of course, should you shed the talisman, the spell is broken.'

He repeated both incantations, slowly, emphasising the strange, tongue-twisting syllables. Calandryll attempted to reproduce them, succeeding in a vague approximation.

'Lower,' Varent advised, 'and the words must roll together, the emphasis always on the second syllable.'

Calandryll tried again, eager to master the spell. Bracht was less enthusiastic, his innate dislike of magic making him an unwilling pupil, though on the urging of Calandryll and Varent he did his best to pronounce the arcane words.

It was not easy, the consonants fricative, the vowels drawn out, the language seemingly designed for throats other than human. They practised until Varent was satisfied, then Calandryll was allowed to attempt the magic. He felt excited as he hung the stone from his neck and murmured the words. And felt his skin tingle, his nostrils filled with the scent of almonds.

'Excellent,' Varent applauded.

Calandryll grinned delightedly and began to move about the room. He felt no different, nor were any of his senses dulled by the magic, but he could see from the way Bracht's eyes darted, trying to locate him, that the Kern was unsure of his whereabouts. Grinning, he positioned himself close to the man and mouthed the releasing spell. He felt the strange prickling again, smelled almonds as he materialised at Bracht's shoulder, the freesword starting back in alarm. Chuckling, Calandryll removed the stone and passed it to Bracht.

The Kern took the talisman gingerly, clearly reluctant to attempt the glamour. 'It may save your life,' Varent said, and Bracht nodded, passing the thong over his head.

He mouthed the spell: nothing happened. He repeated the strange words, and still remained visible. A third attempt met with no better success and he shrugged, an expression close to relief on his tanned face. Caladryll said, 'Try again,' but Varent shook his head.

'I fear your comrade lacks the basic talent essential to the spell. No matter - you are the one who speaks the Old Tongue, and when you reach Tezin-dar it will be you who recognises the Arcanum; and I have but the single stone.'

'Take it.' Bracht loosed the stone from his neck and handed it to Calandryll. 'I'd sooner trust in my blade.'

He eyed the magical artifact dubiously, obviously pleased to be rid of it. It was, Calandryll thought, the first time he had seen Bracht disconcerted.

His own enthusiasm had replaced all doubts and he turned to Varent, beaming. 'With this we'll succeed,' he declared fiercely. 'We'll bring the Arcanum out of

Tezin-dar and thwart Azumandias.'

'Let us hope so,' said Varent, returning his smile. 'Remember those words, my friend. Practice them, for the success of your quest may rest on them.'

'I shall,' Calandryll promised.

'How shall he recognise the book?' Bracht asked.

'The stone will tell you. The same magic that protects it will reveal the Arcanum. When the book is close the stone will burn. Now,' Varent glanced at the darkening sky, 'I had best leave you - the Kand awaits me, and I'd arrange your passage before he's too drunk to remember our agreement.'

He bowed formally, answered in kind by Calandryll, with a curt nod from Bracht, and was gone again.

Calandryll hung the stone about his neck once more, gleefully delighted with his newfound magical talents. Then halted in midspell as he saw Bracht's sour expression, his enthusiasm dampened.

'What troubles you?' he asked. 'Dera! Lord Varent's given us the answer to your doubts, a way into Tezin-dar, yet you wear a face to curdle milk.'

'I've no love of magic,' Bracht responded gloomily. 'Even though it aids us, I don't like it.'

'As Lord Varent said, I'll be the one to use the stone.'

Calandryll repeated the spell, and began to stride about the room, chuckling.

'No good comes of magic,' Bracht grumbled at the empty air.

Calandryll reappeared. 'Then let's eat,' he suggested. 'Perhaps food will put you in a better mood.'

Bracht nodded and they made their way to the dining hall.

Two days later they prepared to leave. The sun had not yet risen and mist hung thick in the courtyard of Varent's mansion, lending their departure a spectral, clandestine air that Calandryll felt was entirely suitable to their purpose. Aldarin still slumbered as they stowed what little baggage they brought with them in the carriage Varent provided and waited on the ambassador. Calandryll wore the red stone at his throat and the map folded into a satchel he slung across his back. The money Varent had given them - ample for their needs - was divided between them, and Bracht's pay was secured in a pouched belt beneath his jerkin. They watched as the ambassador prepared a spell he promised would confuse Azumandias's spies, drawing faint symbols in blue chalk on both sides of the carriage and the hooves of the horses, then sprinkling some colourless liquid over animals and vehicle alike. Satisfied, he turned to face them.

'The Kand captain's name is Rahamman ek'Jemm and his ship is the *Sea Dancer.* He sails on the dawn tide. Darth knows the mooring.' He nodded in the direction of the driver. 'I have paid ek'Jemm fifty varre and you will give him the same amount when you land at Mherut'yi.'

He took Calandryll's hand in both of his, his aquiline features solemn as he added, 'You embark on a heroic quest. Find Tezin-dar and bring me the Arcanum, and we'll end this threat forever. The fate of the world lies in your hands! May Dera ward you both.'

He encompassed Bracht in his look; the freesword answered with an impassive stare. Calandryll said, 'Trust in us, Lord Varent.'

'I do,' came the answer. "Now go, lest you miss the tide. I remain here to decoy any spies of our enemy.'

He released his grip and Calandryll clambered into the carriage, Bracht close behind. Varent raised a hand in farewell and Darth flicked the reins, easing the team towards the opening gates.

They turned onto the street, mist or magic - Calandryll was not sure which - muffling the hoofbeats, the avenue shrouded, the mansion soon lost in the swirling brume. Neither spoke as they traversed the city, as if the weight of their mission stilled their tongues, the enormity of what they attempted become more real now the journey was begun. Calandryll thought of Reba's prophecy, so far come true: he had lost Nadama but gained two comrades, and he would, soon, travel far.

Over water.

Beware the water.

'Dera!' he groaned. 'I'd forgotten that.'

'What?' Bracht looked up from his own musing.

'The spaewife warned of water - I'd planned to sacrifice to Burash.'

Bracht shrugged. 'Perhaps the Kand boat carries an altar.'

'Perhaps.' Calandryll fingered the red stone nervously. 'I hope so.'

He looked to the carriage windows, seeing only the mist, cut here and there with the faint glow of lanterns as folk rose, hearing a dog bark, smelling the moist, salt-tainted air.

'There'll be temples enough in Kandahar,' Bracht said.

'Still, I wish I'd remembered.'

He turned to watch the shapes of buildings drift by, obscured by the fog, mysterious, the roadway empty, the sun not yet even a promise. Droplets hung like jewels on the budding leaves of trees, and when they crossed a park the greensward shone a ghostly silver, phosphorescent in the eerie light. He realised they had reached the city wall when the carriage halted and soldiers came like wraiths out of the obscurity. Darth exchanged a few words; a document was examined. Calandryll heard Varent's name mentioned, then a postern was opened and the carriage trundled through a tunnel lit red by torches.

The familiar sound of surf breaking against stone told him they moved along the mole. A breeze stirred off the sea, the smell of salt stronger, mingled with the harbour odours of tar and wet rope and fish. The mist began to break, masts visible, bobbing on the tide, and the bulwarks of ships, creaking at their moorings as though waking and anxious to sail. The carriage halted again and Darth sprang down.

'The *Sea Dancer* lies there.'

He pointed to a dark bulk that seemed to hang suspended in the swirling grey, three masts standing tall, sails slapping fitfully in the rising breeze.

Calandryll and Bracht descended to the slippery cobbles, their baggage on their shoulders.

'My horse,' the Kern turned to Darth, 'Should I not return, he's yours.'

'My thanks.' The man nodded. 'Dera guide you.'

'Ahrd is my god,' the Kern said.

Darth shrugged.

Calandryll said, 'A favour?' and Darth ducked his head.

He brought a varre from his satchel; passed the coin to the man. 'Make sacrifice to Burash. Ask that he look with favour on our journey.' He would have preferred to attend the matter himself, but this might do.

'As you wish,' Darth said, then turned as a bulky figure came towards them.

'Are you my passengers?'

His voice was harsh, the Lyssian he spoke shaped by the tongue of Kandahar. He was short and fat, his girth accentuated by the heavy green cape he clutched about him, black-bearded, a golden hoop hung from either ear, a white cloth wound about his head.

'You are Rahamman ek'Jemm?' Calandryll asked.

'Ship's master Rahamman ek'Jemm,' the Kand corrected. 'You'll address me as captain whilst aboard my vessel.'

'We're your passengers,' Bracht said. 'Captain.'

Ek'Jemm grunted, studying them as though calculating their weight, then nodded.

'Come on board. The tide's on the turn and I'd be gone.'

Without further ado he spun about and strode away. Calandryll saw that he walked with a rolling gait. He moved to follow; realised that Bracht hesitated and glanced at the mercenary. The freesword appeared nervous, reluctant to climb the gang-plank revealed by the clearing mist.

'I've never been on a ship,' he muttered.

Calandryll suppressed a laugh: in this at least he had an advantage.

'You'll grow used to it soon enough,' he promised.

'Burash rot you! Do you come on board or do I sail without you?'

The captain's voice boomed from above and Calandryll beckoned his companion. Bracht sighed noisily and began to climb the gangplank.

Rahamman ek'Jemm met them at the head, gesturing sternwards. 'Wait there. I've a tide to catch, so you stay out of the way.' It seemed an afterthought to add, 'You share a cabin, but that I'll show you later.'

He bustled off, his gait no longer odd, better suited to the swaying deck than their own landlubbers' walk, bellowing orders as he went. Calandryll led the way aft, past busy sailors galvanised to action by their captain's roaring, and found a place beneath the high poop. He dropped his baggage and settled himself against the planking, Bracht at his side.

The *Sea Dancer* was a sizeable craft of typical Kand design, wide-bellied, with poop and forecastle overlooking the main deck, arbalests mounted on both. Her three masts carried square sails that rose now to the accompaniment of ek'Jemm's shouting, filling as they caught the wind and the vessel turned ponderously from the harbour. Instantly her swaying was more pronounced and Calandryll heard Bracht groan, turning to see the Kern pale beneath his tan.

'Sea sickness passes,' he advised cheerfully, refusing to allow the mercenary's discomfort to dampen his own growing enthusiasm.

Bracht's only response was a heartfelt sigh and Calandryll climbed to his feet to watch Aldarin disappear behind them.

The city was still hung with tatters of mist, but now the walls were visible, rising out of the grey, the sky beyond brightening as the sun approached the horizon. At the farther end of the river valley a band of reddish gold stretched from hillside to hillside, surmounted by a growing swathe of blue that extended itself as he watched, spreading out to swallow the grey. Then pure brilliance shone down the length of the Alda as the sun came up, driving off the last vestiges of fog to bathe the city in golden light. He turned, looking ahead, and saw the moon low on the western horizon, the sky there still dark, but brightening as day overtook the world. Soon the sky was blue, long ribbons of pristine white cloud strung out high overhead by the same wind that carried them towards Kandahar, and he felt excitement grip him: now the quest was truly begun.

A moan from Bracht tore him from his observation and he saw the Kern rise awkwardly, stumbling to the bulwarks to hang over the surging ocean, shoulders heaving as he emptied his breakfast into the waves.

'Landlubber.' Rahamman ek'Jemm's harsh voice rang contemptuous in his ear. 'What is he, a Kern?'

Calandryll nodded.

'You're not afflicted?' the captain demanded.

'No.' he shook his head. 'I've sailed before, though not on so grand a vessel.'

That seemed to please the Kand, for his plump face creased in a brief smile and he nodded approvingly.

'The old *Sea Dancer*'s a stout craft, sure enough. What've you used? Those little toys you Lyssians call boats?'

He thought of the small craft he had sailed in Secca's harbour and said, 'Dinghies. A caravel, once.'

Ek'Jemm snorted. 'Coastal craft. You need a ship with heart to cross the Narrow Sea.' He stabbed a finger in Bracht's direction. 'When he's empty I'll have a man show you your cabins.'

'Thank you,' Calandryll said. 'Do you carry an altar to Burash, captain?'

The Kand showed surprise, green eyes narrowing until they were almost hidden in the fleshy folds of his face.

'You're a Dera-lover if you're from Lysse. And you're no seaman, why d'you want to sacrifice to Burash?'

'I travel over water, and the sea's his domain.'

The explanation was sound enough: the Kand nodded, gesturing at the ocean. 'We need no altars when he's all around us. The ocean's his temple.'

Calandryll nodded. 'Are there forms I need observe? What might he accept?'

'The priests have rituals,' ek'Jemm rumbled, 'but Burash'll hear you if he's in the mood to listen, and there's no priest on board. The sacrifice? What's precious to you? Give him something precious.'

Calandryll thought for a moment. A book would be precious to him, but he had none with him; the map, the red stone, they were too precious to give up. He might need his sword. 'Might this be accepted?' he asked, drawing the signet from his ring finger.

Ek'Jemm shrugged: Calandryll decided the ring must do. He walked to the rail, standing upwind from the heaving Bracht, hand extended over the waves.

'Hear me, Burash,' he murmured. 'I ask that you favour this journey. We travel your domain and I ask that you grant us safe passage over all your waters.'

He opened his hand, the ring glittering as it fell to the waves. He hoped it was enough: it was all he could do.

He turned away, finding Bracht's eyes on him. The Kern's face was tinted with a greenish hue and he sucked air as though he thought each breath might be his last. Calandryll anticipated criticism, but all Bracht said was, 'Does that buy me respite from this malaise? Ahrd, but I'd not thought sea travel could be so foul.'

Calandryll was about to reply, but the mercenary turned away, hanging over the rail again, racked.

'I've a nostrum might help,' ek'Jemm announced, calmly studying the Kern, 'and I'll have a bucket placed in your cabin.'

'Thank you,' Calandryll answered on behalf of his comrade: Bracht was in no condition to speak.

The captain grunted a reply and left them, climbing the companionway to the poop deck. The *Sea Dancer* gathered speed, the deck pitching and rolling as she gained the open sea, her sails bellying, the masthead pennants snapping briskly. Seagulls wheeled overhead, an aerial escort, their shrill cries cutting through the steady slap of water against her prow and the steady rumble of the wind-filled canvas. Calandryll clutched a stay, bracing against the roll, hair streaming in the breeze. He was exhilarated: there was a pure excitement to sea travel that stretched his mouth in an eager smile as he felt salt spray dash his face and filled his lungs with air tangy with ozone.

He looked to where Bracht hung miserable over the rail and saw that the Kern's stomach was empty, his retching dry now. Too much of that could damage his insides, and ek'Jemm had made no mention of carrying a ship's healer: he set a hand to Bracht's shoulder.

'We'd best go below. You'll feel better in your bunk.' Bracht nodded dumbly and Calandryll said, 'Wait here,' leaving him to climb the companionway.

Rahamman ek'Jemm stood spraddle-legged behind the wheel, a seaman at his side ready to take the helm. The captain had shed his cape and stood in portly splendour of yellow and black, the tails of his headdress fluttering. He glanced at Calandryll with vague irritation, as though passengers were not welcome in this lofty place.

'I'd see my comrade to his bunk,' Calandryll said.

Ek'Jemm nodded and bellowed. 'Mehemmed!'

Calandryll felt his sleeve tugged and turned on the ladder to find a shirtless youth of about his own age clambering unceremoniously past him. A dark brown face glanced curiously his way, flashing a toothy grin, and the Kand sprang onto the poop.

'Captain?'

'Show this one and his puking friend to their cabin. And make sure they've got a bucket.'

Mehemmed ducked his head and turned towards Calandryll, who said, 'You promised a nostrum, too, captain.'

Rahamman ek'Jemm frowned, taken aback.

'You understand the tongue of Kandahar?'

'And speak it,' Calandryll replied in the same language.

Ek'Jemm snorted and said, 'When you've shown our passengers to their cabin, go to mine and bring them the blue bottle from my medicine chest. Three drops in a little water, morning, noon and night.'

This latter was directed at Calandryll, who smiled his thanks and descended to the deck, Mehemmed close behind.

They fetched Bracht from the rail and helped him across to the hatchway. Calandryll stooped to collect their gear and Mehemmed eased the pale-faced Kern down into the bowels of the ship. The air was musty and Calandryll was pleased to find their cabin had a port: he opened it as Mehemmed settled Bracht on the bunk below.

'I'll bring the nostrum and the bucket,' Mehemmed promised.

'Oh, Ahrd preserve me,' Bracht moaned. 'Had I known it would be like this ...'

'Best hope the sea stays this calm,' Mehemmed grinned, and ducked through the low hatchway.

Calandryll tossed their gear onto the second bunk and looked around. The cabin was small, the two bunks occupying most of its space, storage lockers beneath them and a narrow aisle between. The ceiling was low enough he had to stoop, so he sat down, torn between amusement and sympathy for Bracht's condition.

Mehemmed returned with a bucket and a small flask of blue glass, a carafe and a beaker. He filled the beaker and carefully measured three drops from the flask into the water, handing the remedy to Bracht. The Kern drank it and grimaced.

'It tastes foul,' Mehemmed chuckled. 'But it'll cure you.'

'Unless I die first,' Bracht moaned, and fell back.

'He'd best eat,' the Kand youth advised, 'I'll fetch you something.'

He brought a plate of bread and cold pork: Bracht glanced at it once, shook his head, and turned away.

'He needs something in his stomach.' Mehemmed looked to Calandryll for support. 'Shall you feed him?'

Calandryll nodded and took the plate. The Kand seemed reluctant to leave, lingering by the door with a curious expression on his narrow face.

'He's your bodyguard?' he asked.

It was the simplest explanation: Calandryll nodded.

'And who are you?'

'My name is Calandryll.'

He thought it best not to give his family name, for fear his father had sent word of some kind to Aldarin: there might be a reward for his return.

'You're a merchant?'

They had discussed this with Varent, deciding that their journey should be explained away as a trade mission, he an emissary sent to establish business links with the merchants of Kandahar, Bracht his bodyguard: he said as much.

Mehemmed grinned: 'He's a poor bodyguard if you're to travel by sea. You'd have done better to hire a Kand. Burash put salt in our blood.'

'He's capable enough,' Calandryll replied defensively. 'At least on land.'

'Then best hope no corsairs cross our path,' the youth declared cheerfully, and left them.

Calandryll stowed their gear and settled to persuading Bracht to eat. The Kern succeeded in swallowing a few mouthfuls before he pushed the plate away and bent over the bucket.

'We should've ridden overland,' he groaned when he was done.

'That would take months,' Calandryll protested. 'We'd need to cross half Lysse, then swing south through Eyl. And then the Shann desert would lie before us. This way, we'll tread dry land in Mherut'yi in little more than a week.'

'A week!' Bracht mumbled. 'Shall I live so long?'

'You'll survive,' Calandryll promised.

Bracht moaned again and turned his face to the wall.

In a while he slept and Calandryll left him to go back on deck. The *Sea Dancer* moved at a brisk pace, the coastline of Lysse fading to stern, lost in the fusion of sea and sky. The wind blew steady from the northeast and ek'Jemm had set all his canvas to take full advantage of the blow. Whatever cargo he carried back to Kandahar provided solid ballast, for the ship sat low in the water, that thought provoking a grin as Calandryll wondered how Bracht might have fared had the vessel sailed with empty holds, riding high and rolling like a wave-tossed cork. He did his best to stay out of the sailor's way, although his natural curiosity prompted him to inspect the craft as much as possible and he roamed the deck and lower levels until a gong informed him that food was served.

He ate on deck with the crew, Rahamman ek'Jemm dining alone on the poop, and found himself the object of curious glances, though only Mehemmed made any attempt at conversation, that mostly a string of questions about the cities of Lysse. He realised that these men spent the larger part of their lives on the water, plying the trade routes between Kandahar and his homeland or the coast of the great peninsula. The food was simple after the luxurious fare of Varent's mansion, but he enjoyed it, his appetite sharp, and when he was done carried a platter below to Bracht. The freesword was awake again, accepting a further dose of the nostrum and even holding down a few mouthfuls of beef, though his humour was not improved and when he declared himself unable to eat more Calandryll left him to sleep.

He went back on deck, wishing he had been able to bring at least one book with him, for boredom threatened as the crew went about their duties, too busy to spare time for a passenger, and he realised that the crossing likely meant days of enforced idleness. He fetched his sword from the cabin and engaged in the exercises Bracht had taught him, ignoring the embarrassment induced by the crew's obvious amusement as he slashed and cut the empty air.

Then his practice was interrupted by Mehemmed.

'The captain wants you,' the youth announced. 'Quick.'

Curious, Calandryll sheathed his blade and climbed to the poop. Ek'Jemm had given the wheel to his helmsman and stood beside the stern arbalest, a spyglass raised.

'Lord Varent said you act as his emissary,' he

declared. 'That you travel to Mherut'yi on merchant's business.'

'Yes,' Calandryll agreed.

'To negotiate contracts,' the captain said.

'Yes.'

Calandryll wondered what disturbed the Kand seaman.

'Secret business?'

'Yes.'

'Might you have rivals in this venture? Might they know of your departure?'

Calandryll stared at the man's plump face, an ugly suspicion dawning. He shrugged: 'Perhaps. Why?'

Ek'Jemm handed him the spyglass and pointed astern.

'You see it?'

He peered down the leather-bound tube, the lenses producing a blurred magnification that at first defeated his inexperienced eye. Then he focused on a dark shape resting low in the water, the image growing clearer as he concentrated. A single mast supported a square sail, the prow curving high, carved in semblance of some ocean creature, the body of the craft low and lean. It had a rakish look, as if designed for speed.

'That craft has the lines of a warboat,' ek'Jemm announced. 'It seems corsairs follow us.'

Calandryll lowered the glass and faced the captain, his heart beating dully. 'Do the corsairs sail so early?' he asked.

'No.' The Kand shook his head. 'Mine is the first craft to make the spring crossing. And no pirate vessel came after. That warboat set sail from Lysse.'

'Perhaps it lay in wait.'

Calandryll hoped the captain would agree: if not, the vessel was likely sent by Azumandias. It might carry the warlock on board. But Rahamman ek'Jemm disappoined him. He shook his head again and said, 'No. It sailed from Lysse. I think it chases you.'

Calandryll passed the spyglass back.

'What will you do?'

'Pray to Burash we can outrun her. If not, fight. Or …'

He paused, studying Calandryll speculatively.

'Or?'

'Give them what they want,' ek'Jemm said calmly. 'I'll not lose my ship for one hundred varre.'

EIGHT

'YOU made a bargain!' Calandryll stared at the man, aware that outrage - or trepidation, he was not sure which - lent his protest a shrill edge. He cleared his throat, self-consciously deepening his voice. 'You undertook to bring us safe to Kandahar.'

Ek'Jemm ducked his head in the direction of the warboat, without the spyglass no more than a speck on the blue horizon.

'I undertook to carry two passengers to Mherut'yi. There was no mention of pursuit.'

Calandryll clutched the hilt of his sword, wondering if he should draw the weapon: set the point to the Kand's throat and insist he fight if necessary. He dismissed the impulse as senseless: were Bracht with him they might bring it off, but even were the mercenary fit enough to back him they would still face all of ek'Jemm's crew; and their pursuers. He thought of offering a bonus, but dismissed that, too. The funds Varent had provided were needed to get them to Gessyth: without them, they would be stranded in a foreign land. And what coin he did carry was scarcely sufficient to compensate ek'Jemm for the risking of his vessel. If the captain knew how much they carried, he might take it for himself. It seemed diplomacy was his only resort.

'Lord Varent would take it ill should you deliver us into the hands of his enemies,' he said, doing his best to make his voice coolly threatening, 'You'd likely find yourself banned from Aldarin harbour.'

The Kand studied him for a moment, lips pursed, then said, 'How should Lord Varent find out?'

'He'd know,' said Calandryll. 'My word on it.'

Ek'Jemm chuckled, glancing astern.

'You've nerve enough, I'll grant you that. And there's time in hand to make such decisions - that sea wolf's fast, but she'll not catch us for a day or two if this wind holds. Perhaps we can outdistance her. If not, well ... I'll decide then.'

'It would be worth your while to fight,' Calandryll promised rashly, 'Lord Varent would reward you well.'

Ek'Jemm nodded. 'Perhaps. But what good is a reward if I lie with Burash?'

Calandryll could think of no appropriate answer and the Kand chuckled again, humourlessly. 'You see my dilemma? I've a boat and crew to think of. Best pray we can outrun her.'

Calandryll grimaced, turning to stare aft. The sky was darkening, the sun already touching the western horizon, and the warboat was lost in the obfuscation.

'The *Sea Dancer*'s fleet enough,' ek'Jemm said, a trifle more kindly, 'perhaps we can lose her in the night. Perhaps our arbalests will put her off.'

He patted the great crossbow affectionately, then turned back to the wheel.

'Now clear my deck. Keep out of my crew's way - we've some sailing to do; and light no lanterns.'

Dismissed, Calandryll climbed from the poop, returning to the cabin, where Bracht lay sleeping.

The confined space stank, and before waking the

freesword Calandryll carried the bucket topside, emptying its contents over the rail. It seemed a sense of tension already gripped the crew, several turning accusing faces in his direction as he made his way back to the hatch, though none spoke. The burgeoning twilight that obscured the pursuing warboat was fading rapidly into night, the sun no longer visible and the west painted orange along the line of the horizon. To the east, darkness reigned, the moon risen and stars spread like bright-glittering jewels across the heavens. No running lights were lit on the *Sea Dancer*, but between the phosphorescence of the ocean and the starshine he saw that men moved about the forwards arbalest, readying the weapon. He ducked through the hatch and clambered down to the cabin.

Bracht stirred as he entered; a dark shape in the shadowy interior. Calandryll set the bucket down, cursing as he rose to bump his head against the low ceiling.

'Is there no lantern?' asked the Kern.

'We run without lights,' Calandryll said, and explained the situation.

'Azumandias?' Bracht grunted. 'Did Varent's magic not conceal our tracks, then?'

He seemed almost pleased at the prospect of such failure, as if it justified his distrust of magic. Calandryll shrugged, the gesture unseen in the darkness, and found the nostrum, administering a further dose. Bracht drank the potion and swung his feet to the floor, groaning. He was clearly too weak to fight and Calandryll pushed him back.

'There's nothing you can do,' he advised. 'Ek'Jemm says it will take the warboat a day or two to catch us if the wind holds, and we might lose her in the night. Better that you rest.'

The Kern sighed and fell back across the bunk. 'If we'd gone on horseback, like civilized folk ...'

'The same would likely have happened,' Calandryll interrupted. 'If it *is* Azumandias sent that boat, then he should surely have pursued us overland.'

'Where I could fight,' Bracht grunted obstinately. 'Not lie here with this cursed sea sickness.'

'Perhaps ek'Jemm's nostrum will cure you before the warboat catches us,' Calandryll offered, hoping to console him. 'Perhaps it's not Azumandias's craft. If not, then it's after the *Sea Dancer* and ek'Jemm will have to fight.'

Bracht refused to be consoled. 'So I've a choice between that fat Kand handing me to Azumandias and going to a watery grave fighting corsairs,' he muttered. 'Neither option appeals.'

His tone was mournful: sunk in misery, he seemed such a far cry from the proud horseman Calandryll had come to know it was difficult not to laugh despite their predicament. Calandryll resisted the temptation, however. He said, 'We might win a fight. The ship carries arbalests at prow and stern.'

'If Azumandias is on the warboat, he'll use magic,' Bracht argued. '*If* ek'Jemm chooses to fight.'

'Together, we could make him,' Calandryll suggested. 'If we held him at swordpoint we could force him.'

'To what end?' Bracht grunted despondently. 'I suppose Azumandias could use magic to sink this tub.'

'Then he'd lose the map.' Calandryll patted his satchel. 'And that must be what he wants. If the warboat *does* seek us, Azumandias must take us alive to obtain the map.'

Bracht nodded, a wan smile curving his mouth.

'You think ahead of me. If that's the case, perhaps we stand a chance.'

'Yes,' Calandryll declared, with more enthusiasm than he felt: as he had thought earlier, to hold Rahamman ek'Jemm at swordpoint would mean holding off the entire crew, presumably in the midst of a sea battle. It seemed, on consideration, a forlorn hope, but at least it cheered the Kern. He settled himself more comfortably on the bunk, clutching his sheathed sword as though the falchion lent him strength, nodding to himself.

'Yes, that's it - we must gain that ... what's it called?'

'The poopdeck,' Calandryll supplied.

'The poopdeck and inform ek'Jemm that we'll slit his throat if he attempts to hand us over. That's your part; I'll watch the crew. If you're right, Azumandias won't dare sink us, knowing the map goes to the bottom with us. That way, we might reach Mherut'yi alive.'

'With Azumandias still on our heels,' Calandryll said practically.

'Yes,' Bracht allowed, 'but once on land we stand a better chance. And what other do we have?'

'None,' Calandryll agreed.

Mehemmed's face appeared in the hatchway then, nostrils wrinkling as he smelled the cabin. 'I've brought you food,' he said in thickly-accented Lyssian. 'And I'll fetch something to clear the stink.'

He set two platters down and disappeared, returning moments later with several tapers. He thrust a couple into chinks in the planking and struck a spark from a tinderbox, lighting them. Sweet-scented smoke drifted from the glowing tips, rapidly overwhelming the sour odour of Bracht's vomit.

'That's better,' the Kand youth declared, grinning. 'How d'you feel?'

'Nervous,' Bracht grunted.

Mehemmed chuckled. 'It's exciting isn't it? I've sailed with the captain five voyages now and we've never been chased.'

Calandryll stared at him, noticing that he wore a long dagger sheathed in his sash, surprised by his enthusiasm.

'Aren't you afraid?' he asked.

'I suppose so.' Mehemmed shrugged. 'But it's still exciting. I doubt the warboat can catch us, anyway - we're running under full sail and the captain thinks the wind will hold for a while. Likely we'll lose the warboat tonight.'

He nodded in confirmation of his own optimism and left them alone. Calandryll found he was in good appetite and was pleased to see Bracht consume a modest portion of the stew without losing it afterwards. When they were done, he carried the plates to the galley, handing them to a sour-faced Kand who took them with a grunt, refusing to meet his eyes. It seemed that Mehemmed was their only friend amongst the crew, for when he went on deck the sailors kept studiously out of his way, as if they feared he might deliver them to misfortune, and he heard several low-voiced conversations on the subject of ill-starred passengers. He was glad he wore his sword; and surprised at the comfort he took from the weapon. Not very long ago he had considered the blade a miserable nuisance, the practice sessions with Torvah Banul a tiresome interruption of his studies, but now he took comfort from the tough leather-bound hilt, the weight of the steel on his belt. Ideally, he hoped the *Sea Dancer* would leave the warboat behind in the night, but if not ... as he had agreed with Bracht, they would force Rahamman ek'Jemm to fight.

He looked to the poop, but the Kand captain was hidden behind the angle of the high deck and all he saw was the star-pocked sky and the swelling crescent of the moon. He turned, staring at the sails, seeing them filled, the masthead pennants driven out straight by the northeasterly wind, the stays cracking like whips through the steady surging of sea against the prow. There, outlined against the starry sky, he saw two men leaning against the arbalest, and wondered if ek'Jemm planned to use them, or if their presence was merely bluff.

There was nothing he could do and he returned to the cabin, throwing himself on the bunk, where he fell rapidly asleep.

He dreamed for the first time in weeks, of a low, lean vessel with a square sail of midnight black that followed him remorselessly, turning when he turned, drawing ever closer no matter how hard he sought to escape it, a man in a billowing black cloak standing behind an arbalest at the prow, aiming the crossbow towards him. He seemed not to be on board a ship, but swimming, or somehow himself a craft, perhaps a dinghy or a caravel, something that lacked the turn of speed necessary to evade the bolt that shot from the great bow, hurtling over the water in a shimmer of light ...

That woke him, piercing his closed lids so that he cried out, sitting up, at first not knowing where he was, then shaking his head as he blinked and saw the cabin, sunlight reflecting off the sea, bright as the bolt's sharp point.

Bracht still slept and he rose quietly, finding his way to the deck, where sailors drew buckets of sea water for their morning ablutions. The day was clear, the sky blue and brilliant, unsullied by cloud, the sun a handspan above the eastern horizon, already hot. He washed and felt the wind that still filled the sails cool on his skin. He drew on his shirt and made for the companionway.

Rahamman ek'Jemm stood by the wheel as though he had stood there all night, and would stand there throughout the whole voyage, though now a wide-bladed sword was belted on his sizeable waist. His green eyes narrowed as Calandryll's head appeared.

'With your permission, captain.'

Calandryll climbed onto the poopdeck as he spoke, giving the Kand no chance to refuse him. Ek'Jemm shrugged and beckoned him forwards.

'It's still there.'

He stabbed a thumb to the northeast. Calandryll

squinted into the glare and saw nothing.

'Here.' Ek'Jemm thrust the spyglass towards him. 'She's hull down on the skyline. We've kept distance, no more.'

Calandryll took the glass and raised it to his eye, wincing as the new-risen sun was magnified, traversing the horizon until he located the dark square of sail. It seemed to him the Kand was pessimistic: surely the warboat had fallen back a little?'

'If we can only hold distance we must reach Mherut'yi before she closes,' he said.

'If this wind holds,' ek'Jemm nodded, 'but only if it holds.'

'Do you think it will?'

The blow seemed strong enough to him; the sails still strained, full-bellied, and the pennants stood out straight from the mastheads.

'Perhaps.' The Kand was less sanguine. 'I smell a change coming.'

'If we lose way, surely the warboat must.'

Ek'Jemm favoured him with a patronising glance.

'If the wind shifts, or drops, we must tack to maintain headway. That sea wolf carries oars - she'll come straight on.'

'Can rowers catch us?' he asked incredulously.

'Ycs,' said ck'Jemm, bluntly. 'If they get close enough, they'll overhaul us.'

Calandryll gestured at the arbalest. 'If they must use oars, can you not cripple them?'

The Kand shrugged.

'If we're lucky, but a warboat's hard to stop. You'd best hope Burash accepted that offering you made.'

'Yes,' he agreed, and went in search of breakfast.

He carried two plates to the cabin, finding Bracht awake, measuring the nostrum into a beaker of stale water.

'I feel recovered,' the freesword declared. 'We must

obtain more of this when we sail for Gessyth.'

He seemed closer to his old self. The greenish pallor that had coloured his face was faded and his eyes were brighter. Calandryll saw that the bucket stood empty, and when he set the plates down, Bracht took one without demur. He tossed the slab of salted pork out through the window, but ate the bread and cheese. Better still, he kept it down, and when he was finished, declared his intention of going on deck. Calandryll lit another taper as he buckled on the falchion, then led the way up into the sunlight. Bracht paused at the outer hatchway, then took a deep breath and stepped onto the deck.

Almost immediately he faltered, looking wildly round for something to clutch as the *Sea Dancer* rolled beneath his feet. Calandryll took his arm and helped him to the rail, which he held firmly, bracing himself against the swaying planks.

'Ahrd knows,' he muttered grimly, 'this is no way for a man to travel.'

Calandryll grinned, delighted that his comrade regained his composure.

'Now,' said Bracht, 'I'd see this boat that chases us.'

Ek'Jemm was irritated by their presence, but passed the Kern his spyglass, smiling maliciously as Bracht tottered uncomfortably to the arbalest, steadying himself against the crossbow as he peered through the glass.

'So that's a warboat,' he murmured. 'What's that carved on the bow?'

'The bow?' Calandryll snatched the glass from his hands. 'You can see the bow?'

He adjusted his weight, compensating for the pitch of the deck, and saw the slender craft had gained on them. It no longer lay hull down below the horizon, but was closer, the dragon's head prow clearly visible.

'Give me the glass.'

Ek'Jemm's harsh voice rang in his ear and he passed the telescope to the Kand.

The man stood for long moments with the leather tube pressed to his eye, then grunted, turning to peer up at his sails.

'Burash rot them,' he muttered. 'It's as I feared.'

'The wind drops,' Calandryll told Bracht. 'And the warboat carries oars.'

Bracht followed the captain's gaze and nodded, glancing at Calandryll, who in turn stared at the sails. It seemed that in the time they had emerged from their cabin and climbed to the poop the wind had lessened. It still blew, but the *Sea Dancer* lost headway. Ek'Jemm bellowed orders and seamen clambered aloft, adjusting the canvas. The captain mouthed a curse and ordered his helm brought over. The vessel swung slightly to starboard, the sails filling again. Ek'Jemm said, 'Go below.'

'We'd sooner remain here,' Bracht answered.

The Kand fixed them with an angry glare. Bracht smiled tightly, left hand loose on the falchion's hilt, right clutching the arbalest for support. Ek'Jemm snorted laughter. Calandryll moved to the side, not sure what might come next; not sure that Bracht was yet ready to fight over the swaying deck.

'You'd threaten me?'

Ek'Jemm appeared torn between disbelief and anger.

'We'd not be handed over like cattle for the slaughtering,' said Bracht.

'I think,' said the captain, 'that if you draw that sword you'll fall down.'

As if to emphasise his point, he barked a further command in his own language and the *Sea Dancer* swung to port, her deck canting. Calandryll braced against the roll and kept his footing. Bracht shouted and lost his hold on the arbalest, falling to the deck and sliding across the planks to fetch up against the taffrail.

Ek'Jemm chuckled; Bracht hauled himself upright. His pallor had returned and Calandryll realised that he was less recovered from the malaise than his actions suggested. Will power had brought him to the poop and it was determination that now locked his left hand to the rail, his right to the falchion's hilt. His piercing blue eyes blazed furiously from the dulled tan of his face as he drew the sword.

It seemed to amuse ek'Jemm: a thick-lipped smile creased his plump cheeks and he nodded as if in appreciation of the Kern's courage. Then Calandryll saw him gesture with his left hand and the helmsman turned the wheel a trifle more. It was only a small adjustment in the great hoop's revolution, but it tilted the deck at an even steeper angle. Calandryll himself staggered, arms flailing as he struggled to retain his balance; Bracht was flung hard against the rail, almost losing his blade as he teetered, close to toppling over into the waves. Calandryll slithered across the deck to snatch a handful of his leather shirt and drag the freesword back to safety. Close up, the Kern's tan was once again tinted with green, his forehead and upper lip glistening with a fine sheen of feverish sweat.

'I think,' ek'Jemm said in a curiously mild voice, 'that you had best sheath that sword before you go overboard.'

Bracht mouthed a curse and attempted to fight his way up the slope of the deck to the Kand. Ek'Jemm shook his head, as if admonishing a wilful child, and barked an order. The two sailors manning the arbalest came nimbly across the planks, wide, curve-bladed swords in their hands.

Bracht turned to face them, tearing loose of Calandryll's grip, and found himself sliding backwards again.

'No doubt a freesword like you could carve both my fellows on land,' ek'Jemm said, his voice no longer mild, 'but you stand on the deck of my craft and here you don't stand a chance. Now sheath that Burash-damned blade!'

Calandryll saw that it was useless to protest or fight: he nodded to Bracht, reaching out to steady the Kern.

Reluctantly - and not without difficulty - Bracht slid the falchion into its scabbard. Ek'Jemm spoke to the helmsman and the *Sea Dancer* righted, the deck flattening again. Calandryll and Bracht stood shoulder to shoulder against the taffrail, facing the two armed sailors. Ek'Jemm shouted and two more swordsman came scurrying up the companionway.

'Under the sea laws of Kandahar I could hang you for that,' said the captain, 'but I won't. I admire your courage, if not your stupidity. Now take off those swords.'

Four weapons gave threatening weight to his command: Calandryll and Bracht unbuckled their swordbelts and tossed them to the deck.

'These remain here,' said ek'Jemm, and switched to Kandaharian again. 'You men take them below. Lock them in their cabin.'

Calandryll translated, and the four sailors prodded them down the ladder and back into the bowels of the ship. The cabin door banged shut and they heard a bolt slide home. Bracht flung himself furiously onto his bunk, his pallor hidden beneath a dark flush of anger. Calandryll bent across him to peer from the window. The angle of the *Sea Dancer*'s course afforded him sight of the pursuing warboat. It was closer now, no longer a speck but a distinct shape, visible to the naked eye: he wondered how long it would take to catch them. He fell onto his own bunk, staring at Bracht.

The Kern lay with his hands folded across his stomach, eyes fixed on the boards above, his hawkish features set in harsh lines. Calandryll said, 'There was nothing else we could do.'

'He took my sword.'

Bracht's voice was flat, unyielding. Calandryll shrugged.

'We had no other choice. He'd have ordered us killed had we refused.'

'No one takes my sword,' Bracht snarled, 'No one!'

At least, Calandryll thought, the freesword's rage supplanted his malaise. 'He'll likely return it,' he said. 'If we evade the warboat.'

'With the wind dropping?'

Bracht snorted and rolled on his side, presenting his back to Calandryll. The younger man opened his mouth to speak again, but then thought better of it, holding silent as he stretched out, staring helplessly at the planks above him: there seemed nothing they could do save wait: that, and hope.

The day passed slowly. The *Sea Dancer* altered course from time to time, swinging to starboard, then back to a port tack, the warboat intermittently visible, still some distance off, but clearly narrowing the gap between the vessels. Around noon a silent Mehemmed brought them food and fresh water, and Bracht took more of the nostrum. Calandryll wished he had a book, but contented himself with a careful study of the map.

'You waste your time,' Bracht said, irritable.

'Perhaps,' Calandryll returned, himself irked by his comrade's sullen attitude, 'Perhaps not.'

Bracht rose on one elbow to peer from the window. 'It's closer,' he said. 'Before long it'll overhaul us and that fat coward will hand us over.'

Calandryll set the map aside, kneeling on Bracht's bunk to study the warboat. It was, indeed, closer: he could see the black rectangle of the sail, like the vessel of his dream, clear against the blue of the afternoon sky, the sleek hull below, curving up to the figurehead.

'It's a sea dragon,' he murmured.

'What?' Bracht frowned.

'The prow - it's carved in the shape of a sea dragon.'

Bracht grunted.

'If he does,' Calandryll said softly, 'I'll toss the satchel overboard. The coin it holds is weighty enough to sink it - at least Azumandias won't get the map.'

'He'll have us instead,' Bracht said.

'So?'

Calandryll regained his bunk as the *Sea Dancer* turned, fighting the fear the Kern's flat statement roused; affecting calm.

'So you've studied the chart,' Bracht said, 'and doubtless it's fixed in that scholar's mind of yours. And Azumandias is a warlock - of great power, Varent said. Do you not think he'll use magic to leach the knowledge from you?'

Calandryll swallowed hard: that possibility had not occurred to him. He licked his lips nervously. There were sages who claimed that a man's mind retained all he saw, all he read; that every experience of his life was kept within some indefinable mental receptacle. And he had done his best to memorize the chart. If the sages - if Bracht - were right, then Azumandias *would* draw out that knowledge: he could not resist magic.

He nodded, steeling himself, and said, 'Then I must go down with it.'

Bracht stared at him.

'That's a thing said easier than it's done.'

'Azumandias must not gain the chart,' he said fiercely. 'He must not find the way to the Arcanum. He'll likely kill us, anyway. That, or something worse. I'd sooner drown than let him raise the Mad God.'

'Noble sentiments,' Bracht murmured, and for a moment Calandryll wondered if he mocked, 'but perhaps there's another way.'

'What? We're prisoners here, unarmed. What other way is there?'

'The stone,' Bracht said, 'and Varent's spell.'

Calandryll frowned, shaking his head.

'What good invisibility?'

'If ek'Jemm proposes to hand us over, he'll likely have us brought on deck. The ... poop's? ... the most likely place - from there we'll be in clear sight. Use the stone and disappear! Hide. This tub's large enough a man who can't be seen should be able to hide.'

'And you?'

Bracht shrugged, white teeth exposed in a cold grin.

'I'm a Kern freesword hired to escort you. I can't read; I've not studied the map. what can I tell Azumandias, save what he already knows?'

'He'll kill you,' Calandryll said.

'Probably, but it appears I face death whichever way I turn.'

'He'll know,' Calandryll protested. 'He'll know there's magic afoot.'

Again Bracht shrugged.

'But perhaps he'll not be able to find you. Who knows? Perhaps he'll send ek'Jemm to the bottom and you'll drown anyway. Perhaps he'll choose to let the ship go - hope to hunt you down in Kandahar. It seems the only chance we have.'

'*I* have,' Calandryll corrected.

'The only chance to prevent Azumandias laying hands on the chart, then. It's worth taking.'

Calandryll nodded; reluctantly.

'Yes.'

'Be ready,' said the Kern, and stretched back on the bunk, closing his eyes.

Calandryll fingered the red stone at his throat. It was cold to the touch and when he raised it he saw only a glassy ovoid like an overlarge, crimson teardrop, a hint of flame faint within its depths. He tucked it back beneath his shirt and folded the map back inside the satchel as he pondered Bracht's suggestion. It was a desperate plan - and one, it seemed to him, that had little chance of success - but it was, as the Kern had pointed out, the only one they had alternative to his suicide. Perhaps he *would* be able to hide on the *Sea Dancer*, and if Azumandias wanted the map, the warlock was unlikely to risk sending it down with a sinking ship. But could he evade the wizard's magic? Would the spell Varent had taught him conceal him from occult investigation? That he could not know until the time came.

He studied Bracht, abruptly melancholy. It seemed the mercenary was prepared to die, leaving him a chance to live, to continue their mission, and the thought of going on without the blunt-spoken free-sword depressed him. For all Bracht's doubts, for all his mistrust of Varent, he had come to like the Kern. He truly believed the man was one of the comrades fore-told by Reba. He sighed, remembering the spaewife's warning that water offered danger: had he sacrificed properly to Burash, might they have avoided this impasse? Was it his omission that had brought them to this point? He sighed again and stretched out on the bunk, the satchel for a pillow.

He realised that he had drowsed when the door opened to admit Mehemmed with the evening meal. The cabin was dark, and when he looked to the window, the warboat was lost in the night.

'It's still there,' said the young sailor. 'Closer now. I think that by dawn they'll be within hailing distance.'

His voice was carefully neutral, as though he feared to show any hint of weakness to the seaman Calandryll saw stood just beyond the hatch, but there was a flicker of sympathy in his eyes and he smiled as he set the tray down.

'Will your captain use his arbalests?' Bracht asked.

Mehemmed shrugged, the movement conveying all such responsibilities to his captain, and ducked out of the cabin. The door closed and the bolt thudded home.

Calandryll saw that a flask of wine was included amongst the items on the tray: he filled the two mugs, passing one to Bracht.

The Kern grunted his thanks, dosing himself with the nostrum before downing the alcohol.

'At least he feeds us,' Calandryll said. Bracht nodded and began to eat.

After, there was little to do save rest on the bunks and talk until sleep took them.

'Tell me about Kern,' Calandryll asked.

Bracht sniffed and said, 'Kern is your word for it, a southern word. We call it Cuan na'For, which means the Land of Horses.'

'The forest is the Cuan na'Dru, is it not?' Calandryll prompted when his companion fell silent. 'What does that mean?'

'The Heartland,' came the answer. 'The Cuan na'Dru is the great forest that surrounds Ahrd. That's a sacred place, tended by the Gruagach, who were created when the world was young. The folk of Cuan na'For seldom venture there, for the Gruagach are jealous guardians and apt to treat intruders unkindly.'

He laughed curtly and emptied the last of the flagon into his mug.

'They tend to kill people. They are strange creatures - devoted to their wardship of the Holy Tree - but they care for Ahrd. The rest?' He sighed fondly. "Oh, it's a fine, free place, unlike your home. We have no cities, but live in tents and follow our herds over the grass. It's foaling time now, and the grass will be lush. The sun will shine and the wind will blow; the rivers will run blue, and my clan will follow the horses north.'

'You said you were Asyth,' Calandryll murmured into the darkness. 'There are five tribes, I believe.'

'The Asyth, the Lykard, the Valan, the Helim and the Yelle,' said Bracht. 'The Asyth raise the finest horses and the stoutest warriors.'

'Are you at war with the Lykard?' asked Calandryll

'Not when I left,' said Bracht. 'Why?'

'When I spoke of leaving Gessyth by the Geff Pass you said the Lykard were enemies.'

Bracht chuckled.

'Mine; I am not much loved by the Asyth, either.'

'Why not?'

There was a long silence, then the Kern said, 'It is a personal thing.'

Calandryll frowned but made no attempt to press the matter: it was obvious that Bracht had no wish to discuss it. Instead, he asked, 'Were you a warrior?'

'We are all warriors,' Bracht said. 'Sometimes the clans fight one another, and we steal horses - that's the way of Cuan na'For - and sometimes the Jesserytes cross the Kess Imbrun to make war.'

'It's strange that the folk of Kern - Cuan na'For,' Calandryll amended, 'worship a tree when you raise the finest horses, whilst the Jesserytes worship Horul.'

'The Horse God?' Bracht sniffed again, dismissively. 'The Jesserytes are a strange folk. It's said they worship a horse because they couple with them, but I think that may not be true. We worship Ahrd because we have always worshipped Ahrd.'

He yawned sleepily. Calandryll asked, 'Have you fought them?'

'Aye, at times,' Bracht answered. 'When the mood comes on them they seek to cross the Kess Imbrun after our horses and our women, and we join to send them back. Or give them to the crows. But those are little more than skirmishes - we've fought no great war since the High Khan Tejoval sought to invade us, in my grandfather's time. He brought an army over the rift, vowing that he would burn the Cuan na'Dru and Ahrd with it. All the clans sent warriors then, and we destroyed the Jesseryte army. The old men say it was a mighty battle and the rift river was red with Jesseryte blood. They say the crows got too bloated to fly then.'

The bunk creaked as he shifted, yawning again. Calandryll wondered how he could be sleepy: he felt too nervous to contemplate slumber. He asked, 'Have you ever been in love?'

Bracht sighed and said, 'Do you think of your Nadama?'

Now Calandryll paused, taken aback. The question had sprung unbidden to his lips, and he was not sure why he had asked it. He realised that he had not thought of Nadama since ... When was the last time? Since their encounter with the *byah*? Since the dreams along the trail to Aldarin? He said, 'No.'

'I thought I was,' Bracht said, 'Once. But ... something happened.'

His voice grew flat and Calandryll sensed that he touched on another forbidden subject. 'I think,' he said slowly, 'that I have accepted she's lost to me. She might be wed to Tobias by now; certainly by the time I return.'

If I return.

He was surprised by his own acceptance, by the absence of that knife that had turned each time he thought of her. It was gone now: it seemed that imminent danger, the possibility of death, cauterized the wound. He conjured an image of her face and found it blurred, as though time and distance eroded the edges of his memory. He felt a weight was lifted, something in his soul freed: he chuckled.

'Good,' said Bracht.

'Aye,' he agreed, 'it is.'

'And so is sleep,' said the Kern.

Calandryll nodded in the darkness, hearing Bracht change position, the bunk creaking. Through the port he heard the steady, soothing slap of waves against the hull, the low, slow groaning of timbers. He closed his eyes.

Dreaming, he found himself standing on the deck of

the *Sea Dancer*, the sun bright on his face, the wind died away to a listless murmur that draped the sails like wet sheets hung from the spars. All around, the Narrow Sea glistened, smooth as a millpond, and the crew moved past him, unseeing. Rahamman ek'Jemm stood behind the wheel with Bracht at his side. The mercenary's hands were bound and when Calandryll called his name he gave no sign that he had heard, staring at the black boat that drew steadily closer, driven by great black oars that swept the waves in silence, a figure in a black cloak standing at the prow, one hand caressing the dragon's head. The boat came alongside and the figure sprang on to the *Sea Dancer*'s deck. Calandryll could not see its face. A hand beckoned and ek'Jemm bowed, pushing Bracht to the companionway. The black-cloaked figure towered over the Kern as he was shoved rudely forwards, then reached out, grasping him by the waist, lifting him. Calandryll began to run as the monstrous figure held Bracht high, turning to the rail, but his legs were jelly and the planking of the deck seemed to buckle and give way under his feet. He shouted, but no one heard and all he could do was watch as Bracht was tossed over the side, to the warboat that was no longer a vessel, but a huge, black dragon that raised a gaping, many-toothed maw to accept the body. Calandryll shouted again and this time the black figure turned towards him and he saw red eyes burning within the smoky shadows of the face. He struggled to draw his sword, but the blade was mired in the scabbard as firmly as he was mired to the deck, and all he could do as the relentless figure strode towards him was raise his hands in protest, feeling fingers like steel claws lock about his wrists, lifting him as they had lifted Bracht ... Who said, 'You dream! Calandryll, you dream!' pinning his flailing arms down on the bunk.

He opened his eyes and saw the Kern's face close, his

breath redolent of ek'Jemm's nostrum.

'Dera!' he mumbled, wiping sweat from his brow. 'I thought ...'

He shook his head, the dream already fading, the images breaking as the mist had broken in Aldarin harbour, swirling and dissipating, lost even as he tried to hold them.

Bracht let loose his arms and pointed to the window. 'I think you had best ready yourself.'

He crossed to the port, squinting into the brightness of a new day, and groaned. The warboat stood off the starboard quarter, its sail furled, the sweeps that drove it like giant drumsticks beating a relentless rhythm on the skin of the sea. He could see the figurehead. See the bulging red eyes and the flared nostrils, the carved fangs, painted white, a curling scarlet tongue between the black lips. Circular shields decorated with a variety of fanciful designs hung along the bulwarks and behind the prow and amongst the oarsmen stood archers, shafts notched ready. He felt a vibration from above, heard a dull *twanging* sound, and saw a bolt whistle through the morning air. It raised a splash to port of the warboat.

'Ek'Jemm uses the arbalest,' he cried. 'Perhaps he means to fight.'

'Perhaps I misjudged him,' Bracht said, 'Perhaps his bolts will frighten them off - if they be no more than ordinary corsairs.'

A second bolt fountained a glittering column no closer than the first and the warboat veered rapidly to starboard, cutting around the *Sea Dancer*'s stern with an agility the larger vessel had no hope of matching. Calandryll saw the archers raise their bows. The arrows were brief, dark flashes against the blue sky. He heard a man scream, the sound shrill as a seagull's cry, and the dark boat was gone from sight.

He turned as the hatch opened and a hulking seaman

armed with a cutlass filled the doorway. Behind him stood three more: hope faded.

'You're to come topside.'

The man stood back, cutlass poised. His order required no translation: Bracht glanced at Calandryll and smiled.

'Ahrd be with you, and your own goddess.'

'And with you.'

Calandryll wanted to say something more in reply but could not find the words. He slung the satchel from his shoulder, briefly touched the talisman concealed beneath his shirt, and stepped into the narrow corridor. Bracht followed him, menaced by the sailors' heavy blades, and they clambered out onto the deck, to the companionway, and up to the poop.

Rahamman ek'Jemm stood with folded arms and dour face beside the helmsman. A bare-chested Kand stood miserably by the arbalest; another lay moaning on the deck, two arrows protruding from his right leg. The warboat was already past the merchantman, swinging wide around her bow, gone past before the arbalest mounted there had time to sight and fire.

'I tried,' ek'Jemm said, 'and that's the result.'

He pointed to the wounded seaman, the shafts bristling from deck and mast and sails.

Bracht grunted and said, 'You give up easily, captain.'

The Kand turned cold green eyes on the freesword. 'As I told your comrade, I'll not forfeit my ship for a miserable one hundred varre. If it's you they want, they'll see you now and I'll give you to them. If not,' he shrugged, 'then we'll fight.'

As if to emphasise his point a second volley of arrows arched into the azure. They seemed to hang for a moment, suspended at the apex of their flight, before rattling onto the *Sea Dancer*'s deck.

'A warning,' ek'Jemm murmured, studying the dark shafts that thrust from the planking.

The warboat came back along their port flank, dancing over the waves, driven by the steady sweeping of the oars. Calandryll saw that the stern rose up, fashioned in the shape of a dragon's tail, a massive, paddle-like rudder at its base. Two men held shields raised to protect the helmsman. The archers stood on a small deck behind the prow and on a raised aisle that ran like a spine down the length of the warboat, the oarsmen sat on recessed benches to either side. They appeared to follow the orders of a slim figure wearing fine silver mail that glittered proudly in the sun, the face hidden beneath the shadow of a beaked helmet.

'That's their captain?' Bracht asked. And when ek'Jemm grunted an affirmative: 'Give me a bow and I'll kill him.'

The Kand studied him speculativly, as if considering the possibility, then shook his head.

'A wounded animal's worse than a healthy beast.'

'Two shafts at most,' Bracht said confidently, 'and he's dead.'

'The deck of a ship's no steady platform,' ek'Jemm returned.

'Nor's the back of a running horse,' said Bracht. 'I can do it.'

Ek'Jemm smiled briefly and shook his head again. 'No,' he said firmly, 'I'd not anger them. If you're all they want, I escape easy.'

Bracht's eyes blazed contempt; the Kand ignored him, turning to stare at the warboat.

The dark craft swung dramatically to port, cutting close under the merchantman's stern. Calandryll stared at the armoured figure commanding the archers, wonder if he looked on Azumandias; wondering then why a mage should employ so physical a means of attack when surely magic must serve him better than arrows. Something about the stance, the drape of the hauberk, was wrong and he gasped as realisation dawned.

'That's a woman!' he cried. 'The captain's a woman!'

'No woman commands a Kand warboat,' ek'Jemm grunted.

'No corsair vessel sails out of Lysse,' Calandryll snapped. 'But this one did, and that's a woman.'

The figure raised gloved hands then, removing the helmet, and his point was proven: a thick spill of flaxen hair tumbled loose, framing a strong face from which eyes grey as storm-tossed waves studied the *Sea Dancer*, a wide, full-lipped mouth issuing a command that slowed the warboat.

'Burash take me!' ek'Jemm muttered. 'You're right.'

'And she's lovely,' Bracht said softly. 'Ahrd, but she's a beauty!'

The woman seemed oblivious of their stares and the arbalest alike, contemptuous of the danger, although ek'Jemm might then have hit her square, or bowmen picked her off. Her order brought her craft almost to a stop, drifting close under the merchantman's stern, protected there from the great crossbow. She tossed her helm to the deck and cupped her hands about her mouth.

'You carry two passengers, captain - I'd have them.'

Her voice was melodious, carrying clear across the gap between the vessels.

'You'll leave my ship be?' ek'Jemm shouted.

'I have no quarrel with you,' the woman called. 'It's your passengers I want. Hand them over and you're free to go your way.'

'I've a man wounded,' the Kand returned.

The woman's face clouded for an instant, then she cried, 'I regret that, but you fired on us.'

Calandryll could not help staring at her and would

likely have done so even had she not represented such a threat: her beauty compelled attention. He started when he felt Bracht's hand grip his arm.

'Be ready,' warned the Kern.

He nodded, instinctively reaching for the stone at his throat, mouth opening to utter the spell. Then gaping as he felt the smooth surface burn his fingers, looking down to see the dull red transformed to flame, as if he clutched fire.

Abruptly, the air about him shimmered, filled with the heady scent of almonds, stronger than he had ever smelled it, cloying in his nostrils. The air seemed brilliant, as though the risen sun fell from the sky to hang between the two vessels. He heard Bracht shout; ek'Jemm cry out. Then he, too, shouted as he saw the sea boil, a great surge of turbulent water rising from the gap between warboat and merchantman, as if some vast, unseen beast rose from the depths, angry. Water seethed, rising to hang in a swirling, glittering pillar that joined sea and sky. A sheet of liquid drenched the poop, draping a rainbow across the *Sea Dancer*'s stern, and he felt his hair torn back by a wind that sprang from nowhere. Dimly through the spray he saw the warboat engulfed by the spout, tossed like a cork, spun round and round, the archers tumbling like stricken pins to the deck, falling into the scuppers. He saw the woman thrown against the prow, embracing the dragon's neck, pressing herself hard against the wooden effigy as her long legs flung over the side. For an instant he thought she must lose her grip and topple into the maelstrom, but then the very spinning of her craft hurled her back onto the deck and she rolled inelegantly across the planking to crash down amongst the terrified oarsmen.

The warboat was lifted by the wave, the sweeps in disarray, the furled sail ripped loose to flap uselessly, a torn rag in the grip of elemental fury. Then the air reverberated with an ear-splitting blast and the spout was gone. The warboat fell seawards, taking on water as it crashed against the waves. The wind grew stronger and he saw the impossible happen: saw nature divided against itself. The *Sea Dancer*'s sails filled, drumming with the rhythm of the wind, the merchantman gaining headway, surging away from the warboat which was driven in the opposite direction by a gusting no less fierce than the gale that propelled the cargo vessel. Waves crashed over the ducking prow, the black sail, tattered now, driven out straight, the oars helpless. He heard ek'Jemm shout again, and saw the portly Kand stagger to the wheel, lending his bulk to aid the helmsman, holding the *Sea Dancer* stern-on to the ferocious wind.

Within moments the warboat was a dwindling speck, then it was a blur on the skyline, then gone. Calandryll realised that he still clutched the red stone. He released his grip and the wind dropped. He looked about. Bracht clung soaked to the arbalest, a wide-eyed seaman on the weapon's other side. The four armed sailors sprawled gaping against the taffrail. Ek'Jemm and the helmsman clutched the wheel as if fearing they might be torn loose and swept overboard. The wounded sailor lay at their feet mumbling a prayer to Burash, and all along the deck men hung from sheets, or held the rails, not quite believing in the calm that fell. Calandryll alone had sought no support: he stood brace-legged on the poop, dazed by the magic that had saved them.

'Burash protect us,' ek'Jemm said slowly, his voice hushed as he stared at Calandryll. 'What are you?'

Calandryll shook his head. The wave, the wind - neither had been things of his conscious making: he had no better idea than the captain what had happened. He opened his mouth to speak, but Bracht intervened.

'You'd have done better to have listened to him, captain.' The freesword said quickly, casting a warning glance in Calandryll's direction. 'But now that you've seen what he can do, perhaps we may have our weapons back?'

Ek'Jemm nodded dumbly, motioning in the direction of the gape-mouthed sailors.

'Their swords. And quick!'

The weapons were brought and they buckled them on, the sailors eyeing them with a newfound respect that bordered on open fear. Calandryll looked at Bracht with eyes widened by amazement; the Kern winked. The wind still blew, no longer a gale, but strong enough. Ek'Jemm asked wonderingly, 'Are you a mage?'

Calandryll caught Bracht's eye and shrugged.

'Would you have him demonstrate again?' asked the mercenary.

The Kand swallowed and shook his head.

'That was sufficient. Why did you not tell me?'

'I prefer to travel incognito,' Calandryll extemporized: it was not, entirely, a lie.

'Had I known, I would not have ... Forgive me ... Lord Varent made no mention of it ... I could not know.'

Calandryll found that he enjoyed the man's discomfort: it was some small recompense for his imprisonment. 'I would not have it published abroad,' he said. 'And I trust you will hold your tongue - see that your men keep it to themselves, too.'

It was a slender hope: to ask a crew that had just witnessed so miraculous an event to remain silent was ... as unlikely as the maelstrom or the gale, he decided. Nonetheless, ek'Jemm nodded enthusiastically.

'As you command.'

'We are merely two passengers travelling to Kandahar on private business,' Calandryll said. 'No more than that - you understand?'

'Aye. Indeed, aye!' Ek'Jemm's head bobbed vigorously,

threatening to dislodge his headdress. 'Two passengers. Quite.'

'Good. And now we shall leave you.'

He grinned at Bracht and led the way down to the deck. The sailors still avoided them, but now it was out of respect, as if they feared the unleashing of further magicks, and they found a place amidships where they might speak privately. Calandryll was surprised to see anger and suspicion in the Kern's eyes. His amusement at ek'Jemm's newfound humility evaporated, replaced by confusion.

'How did you do that?' Bracht demanded harshly. 'Are you a mage? Have you hidden that talent from me?'

'Dera, no!' he answered. 'I have no more idea than you how it happened. I touched the stone and the sea boiled - I know no more than that.'

Bracht stared at him for a while. 'Your word on it?' he asked at last.

'My word,' Calandryll promised. 'I am no wizard, if that's what you fear.'

'Then how?' Bracht frowned, his innate distrust of sorcery writ clear.

Calandryll shrugged helplessly.

'I was about to speak the incantation - as you suggested! - and I saw the sea boil. I know no more than that. Dera, Bracht! If I was a wizard I'd have used magic to persuade ek'Jemm against handing us over. Or sunk that warboat before it reached us. I'd have used my own magic to flee Secca! I understand this no better than you.'

'But you touched the stone,' the Kern persisted.

'To hide,' Calandryll answered, 'only that.'

'Then how was the magic worked?' The freesword's anger was diminished somewhat, but suspicion still grated in his voice. He fixed Calandryll with a hard blue stare.

Calandryll thought for a moment, then said,

tentatively, 'Lord Varent spoke of my possessing the ability to work magic - do you not remember when he first gave me the stone? - so perhaps, in moments of danger, some power is released. But how, I cannot say. I sought only to become invisible as we agreed.'

'Varent taught you how to become invisible,' Bracht said, 'Nothing more?'

'And the only spell I know is the one he taught us,' Calandryll said earnestly, 'I swear it. Perhaps the magic of the stone reacted with Azumandias's magic. I swear I know not how it happened.'

'Was Azumandias on that warboat?' Bracht's eyes narrowed. 'Who was that woman?'

'Lord Varent said Azumandias is a man. Who the woman might be, I have no idea.'

Calandryll spread his hands, indicating incomprehension. Bracht stared at him thoughtfully.

'If Varent uses us, perhaps Azumandias uses the woman.'

'Perhaps,' Calandryll agreed, 'and if so, she's far behind us now. Or sunk.'

Bracht nodded. Then: 'But why use the woman? Varent's excuse for our employment was the fear of discovery, that Azumandias might uncover his plan. Azumandias needs no such delicacy.'

'Dera!' Calandryll shook his head. 'I've no better notion than you why he should. But surely he must - she was no ordinary corsair: she knew we were on board; asked ek'Jemm to hand us over. Who else would send her? She must be the agent of Azumandias.'

'Likely she is,' Bracht agreed, 'and followed us out of Aldarin. But still I do not understand why Azumandias himself does not pursue us.'

'Nor I,' said Calandryll. 'Save that Lord Varent holds him in Lysse by some means.'

Bracht's fingers drummed briefly on the falchion's hilt as he ducked his head. 'Perhaps,' he allowed.

'At least we escaped her,' said Calandryll.

'Through use of sorcery.' The Kern's face grew dark again. 'I've no love of magic.'

'You were the one suggested I employ such means!' Calandryll protested.

Bracht shrugged, and grinned as he recognised his own inconsistency. 'As a last resort,' he said. 'To save you from a watery death.'

'Whatever the reason, it saved us all.'

'Aye, there's that,' the Kern admitted, his grin becoming a full-fledged smile. 'And ek'Jemm accords us more respect now. But still I wonder who the woman was.'

'Likely we'll never know,' Calandryll said.

He was wrong, but then, basking in the relief of their escape, he could not know that both their destinies were inextricably linked with the mysterious woman.

NINE

TWILIGHT hung a curtain of soft, velvet blue over the coastline of Kandahar as the *Sea Dancer* entered the harbour at Mherut'yi. The sun was dropped behind the barrier of the central mountains, the rimrock marked by a swathe of fiery orange, and the sky to the east darkened with the advancement of night. The town huddled low along the flat shore, obscure save for random pinpricks of brilliance that cut through the drapery of the dusk where lanterns burned in scattered windows. Calandryll, accustomed to the walled cities of Lysse, was surprised to see no fortifications other than a fortalice illuminated by the beacons that flared along the mole protecting the anchorage, no ramparts or watchtowers, or any other sign of defensive construction. He had know that Mherut'yi was no metropolis, but the settlement he saw as they drifted past the mole was tiny by the standards of Secca or Aldarin, little more than an outpost on the edge of the Shann desert. He heard Rahamman ek'Jemm shout orders and anchors splashed at bow and stern, the merchantman easing leisurely to a halt and swaying gently at her moorings. The favourable wind that had carried them steadily

across the Narrow Sea since the encounter with the warboat struggled briefly with the breeze off the desert and gave up, the masthead pennants hanging listless, the ship creaking softly. With that cessation of movement the air grew hot and dry, redolent of the sand that spread wide to the north. Calandryll paid the captain and, Bracht close behind, followed him down a ladder to the boat that came out to meet them.

'You have lodgings?' the Kand enquired as they were rowed to the dock. 'I can recomment a decent inn - the Sailor's Rest has clean beds and sets a fair table.'

'Thank you.'

Calandryll glanced at Bracht, who frowned a silent negative and stared ashore as if entranced with the prospect of once again finding himself on dry land.

'I stay there myself when I'm in Mherut'yi,' said ek'Jemm, affable to the point of deference since witnessing Calandryll's apparent display of magical talent. 'I can promise you the finest quarters available.'

Calandryll nodded absently. He had no intention of using the inn: better, he and Bracht had decided, to conceal their tracks from the start. Ek'Jemm went ashore alone only to clear his vessel with the harbour authorities; once that formality was dispensed, his crew would come off, and within the hour they would be talking about their adventures. Before long word of the two mysterious travellers would be out on the waterfront, and soon spread through the town. He would find some discreet hostelry to spend the night and in the morning purchase horses and take the Tyrant's road inland to Nhur-jabal.

'Thank you,' he repeated, 'but we have . . . plans.'

Ek'Jemm shrugged, plump features torn between the desire to please and curiosity.

'As you wish. Your business is in Mherut'yi? Or elsewhere? I sail for Ghombalar with the morning tide should that be convenient.'

Bracht spoke from the bow without turning his head. 'Our business is private, captain. And we'd have it remain so.'

The Kand's face stiffened at the rebuke, then reformed an obsequious smile.

'Of course. You can rely on me.'

Bracht grunted. Calandryll said, 'The contracts we negotiate on Lord Varent's behalf are delicate, captain. The fewer who know of our arrival, the better.'

'Yes, of course.' Ek'Jemm nodded eagerly. 'I understand.'

Calandryll suppressed a smile and watched the dockside loom from the shadows.

The boatman sprang to the wharf, mooring the dinghy, and they climbed stone steps to the quayside. Bracht sighed as he trod solid ground again, turning as a squad of soldiers in leathery armour marched from the nearby fortalice.

'Allow me,' murmured ek'Jemm, pushing past to present himself to the officer in command. 'They know me here.'

'I am Rahamman ek'Jemm, master of the merchant ship, *Sea Dancer*,' he declared formally, 'en route to Ghombalar with a cargo of Aldan wine. These gentlemen took passage with me. They come to negotiate trade agreements on behalf of the Lord Varent den Tarl of Aldarin.'

The officer took the papers ek'Jemm offered and gave them a cursory glance before turning his gaze on Calandryll and Bracht. He was tall and thin, his face dark beneath a scarlet puggree wound about a conical helm. He wore a breastplate and greaves of hard red leather, and a curved sword was sheathed at his side. His men carried hooked pikes.

'You are?'

Calandryll recalled the protocol demanded when greeting a minor functionary: he ducked his head briefly, hands spread, assuming a business-like manner.

'I am Calandryll, factor to Lord Varent. This is my bodyguard.'

The officer glanced at Bracht, then returned his attention to ek'Jemm.

'You vouch for them?'

'Most certainly,' said the captain.

The officer eyed them, with bored disinterest and nodded: 'Very well, you may go.'

'Thank you.' Calandryll bowed again, and smiled in ek'Jemm's direction. 'Our thanks, captain. Should our negotiations succeed, I'll recommend you to Lord Varent.'

'Thank you,' beamed the Kand, bowing deeply. 'And remember - should you decide to favour the Sailor's Rest you need only mention my name.'

Calandryll nodded and led the way past the soldiers, mildly confused by a footing that no longer rolled and shifted beneath him. Ahead lay a barrier of pale stone warehouses. Indeed, it seemed that Mherut'yi was built exclusively of the same yellowish stone, save for the docks and the mole and the fortalice, which were of harder-looking, grey stone. The buildings were low, with shallow, shingled roofs, their windows shuttered against the oppressive wind, set square on to a geometric pattern of right angled dirt streets. The lights they had seen as they approached were hidden now and they wandered for a little while amongst the warehouses before emerging on a plaza where stunted trees stood dusty at the centre, their arrival greeted by a desultory yapping from five lean-flanked dogs stretched beneath the trees. The lanterns and the sounds of music coming from the surrounding buildings suggested they had found Mherut'yi's taverns, and the few folk they saw were mostly sailors or fishermen from their dress, studying the travellers incuriously, as though foreigners were no strangers here. There was no sign that the town mounted any watch patrols and the streets were lampless: they decided to enquire in a tavern about hostelries.

The place they chose was called The Mermaid and had sawdust on the floor and sweet-smelling smoke hanging thick in the air, drifting from numerous pipes to hang beneath the low ceiling in a haze of swirling blue, the smokers smiling indolently as the narcotic took effect. Several gaudily-dressed women, their hair and necks and wrists heavy with beaten gold jewelery, eyed them speculatively as they approached the plank counter, reminding Calandryll of the doxy whose irritation had first brought him to Bracht's attention.

The Kern, too, was reminded, because he grinned and murmured, 'This time pick your company more carefully.'

Calandryll's only answer was a shame-faced smile.

'Friends, what's your pleasure?'

The innkeeper was stouter than ek'Jemm, but taller, his scalp glistening sweat through a thin layer of oiled black hair. He wiped thick-fingered hands on a bright yellow shirt, displaying stained teeth as he beamed, using the pidgin tongue called the Envah that was the lingua franca of the Narrow Sea.

'Ale,' said Bracht in the same dialect. 'And information.'

The man nodded and drew two pots of dark beer. Calandryll noticed that the pots were fashioned of the same leathery material as the soldiers' armour. He guessed it was swamp dragon hide.

'This'll cut the dust.' The innkeeper slapped foam from the pots. 'The gaheen's started blowing and that makes a man thirsty.'

Calandryll realised he spoke of the hot, dry wind coming off the Shann. Both Medith and Sarnium mentioned that in spring northern Kandahar was plagued with the gaheen. He sipped the ale: it was warm.

'You're not Kands,' the man declared amiably. 'what are you? From Lysse?'
Calandryll nodded. Bracht said, 'Cuan na'For.'
'Kern?' the innkeeper's smile grew wider. 'We don't see many Kerns here. You merchants?'
Bracht grunted an affirmative and asked, 'Where's a good place to stay?'
'Depends what you want,' the man shrugged.
'Clean sheets. No bugs.'
'One thing about the gaheen, it kills the bugs,' the innkeeper chuckled. 'Gives us other problems, but it does kill the bugs. Now - someplace to sleep. You have money?'
Bracht nodded. The man pursed his lips and said, 'Mother Raimi's got soft beds, and she's a devil for washing. Good cook, too. Tell her Hammadrar sent you. You'll find her place three streets across and one left. The Sign of the Peacock. You want another pot?'
Bracht shook his head and Calandryll saw that he had emptied his mug: he swallowed his own ale and set the pot down.
'Remember - tell her Hammadrar sent you,' the innkeeper called as they walked out.
The wind was stronger as they recrossed the plaza, and very dry, tingling on their skin, skirling dust along the narrow streets in miniature whirlwinds. Calandryll spat grit, a passage from Medith springing to mind: 'The gaheen (the devil wind) is said to drive men mad, and certainly it is a most irritating breeze, bringing as it does, a material taste of the Shann desert. Fortunately, it afflicts only the northern parts of Kandahar.'
Well, before long they would be riding inland, hopefully away from the gaheen, and so far they had encountered no madmen. Nonetheless, he was grateful when the bulk of buildings checked the prickly gusting.
They left the taverns behind and passed a series of shuttered emporiums, the streets empty, ghostlike as

full dark fell. Then lights showed ahead, brighter as they turned into the street described by Hammadrar. Here, signs clattered listlessly, advertising beds and food and baths. They saw one bearing an ornate depiction of a peacock, the paint dulled beneath a layering of dust, and went inside.

The windows were shuttered and glass-encased lamps burned on the walls of a sizeable room, its floor spread with gaily-patterned carpets, empty chairs and tables along the walls, a small counter to one side. As the door swung shut behind them a bell tinkled and a bead curtain hung across an entrance behind the counter was thrust aside to reveal a small, very dark woman dressed in a robe of startling vermilion and cyan. In contrast to her tanned skin, her hair was silver, held in a net of fine gold mesh.

'Welcome to the Sign of the Peacock,' she said. Her voice was thin and high, birdlike. 'I'm Mother Raimi.'

Calandryll bowed politely and said, 'Hammadrar recommended you to us.'

Mother Raimi nodded and asked, 'You want rooms?'

'If you have them.'

Trilling laughter answered him. 'All you want,' she chortled. 'With the gaheen blowing, Mherut'yi's empty. You can take your pick.'

He translated for Bracht and the woman switched to the coastal argot.

'A room apiece and dinner will cost you one var each. A bath, fifty decimi.'

'We'll take it,' he said.

'Good. Follow me.'

She disappeared through the curtain, re-emerging from a side door to beckon them into a long corridor running the length of the building.

'Dining room. Baths.' She swung her head to indicate the facilities, each movement jangling the necklace she wore. 'I'll give you rooms at the back - they're the quietest rooms.'

Such consideration seemed unnecessary, given the sleepy atmosphere of the town, but she showed them to chambers facing one another across the corridor, announcing that baths would be drawn and dinner served when they were ready. Unlike Hammadrar she showed no interest in their origins or their purpose in Mherut'yi, merely opening each door and fetching a lantern from the hall to ignite those inside. Calandryll smiled his thanks and examined his quarters.

After the cramped cabin on the *Sea Dancer*, the room seemed spacious. A carpet that was only slightly worn covered most of the floor, the windows were shuttered and the lantern cast long shadows over the wide bed. Beside it stood a small table with a ewer, a chest of drawers on the other side, a wardrobe against one wall. The air smelled vaguely musty. 'Not been used in a while,' Mother Raimi explained, 'and with the gaheen blowing it's best to keep the shutters closed.' She bustled off. He tossed his baggage on the bed and sat down, wondering if all the towns of Kandahar were as dry and dusty and dull as Mherut'yi.

A knock and Mother Raimi's shrill voice announced that their baths were ready and he joined Bracht in the corridor, his sword and the satchel in his arms. He was pleased to see that the Kern took the same precautions, his falchion on his waist. They followed the woman to the bathroom, where a single vast tub filled the air with steam.

After the cold salt water on the *Sea Dancer* it was sheer luxury to bathe in the hot tub and the mild embarrassment he felt at sharing his ablutions with the freesword was rapidly forgotten as he sank into the steaming liquid.

'Tomorrow we find a stable,' Bracht said through the steam. 'How far to Nhur-jabal?'

Calandryll pushed wet hair from his eyes and

shrugged. 'Some weeks. Less to Kharasul.'

Bracht nodded, grinning. 'At least we travel in a civilized manner. It'll feel good to get back on a horse.'

'A boat could reach Kharasul faster,' Calandryll murmured.

'You think of that warboat?'

He nodded and Bracht said, 'That wind blew it away. Even if it rode that storm, how could she know we travel to Kharasul?'

The Kern's spirits were raised now that he was on land again and Calandryll felt somewhat guilty for his own vague apprehension. 'How did she know we were on the *Sea Dancer*?' he asked.

'Azumandias's spies,' said Bracht, refusing to allow his good humour dampened. 'The warboat hid along the Lyssian coast and set out after us when she got word. And now she's likely been blown back to Lysse.'

'You're probably right,' Calandryll allowed.

'If not,' said Bracht, 'we'll face her when the time comes. But until then, let's make the best of things. I'm hungry for decent food after ek'Jemm's slop.'

He climbed from the tub, towelling himself cheerfully, and Calandryll followed suit. Then, dressed in clean shirts, they found the dining hall, where the innkeeper's promise concerning the standard of Mother Raimi's cuisine was fulfilled. She served them a rich fish soup, and then thick slabs of a gamey pie accompanied by cold vegetables. Cheese and fruit followed, and they drank three bottles of some tangy Kandaharian wine, after which they both felt pleasantly replete and more than a little drowsy. The prospect of exploring Mherut'yi held little interest, and as they preferred to remain anonymous they decided to find their chambers and make an early start come morning.

Calandryll undressed and propped his sword beside the bed, tucking the satchel beneath the pillows. He snuffed the lanterns and climbed gratefully beneath the sheets, delighted to find them clean and free of dust. He grew daily less concerned with such comforts, the luxury he had known in his father's palace dimming in his memory - and given what lay ahead, that was to his advantage - but it was still pleasant to once again sleep in a bed wider than the *Sea Dancer*'s bunks, with crisp linen and soft pillows. He yawned, listening to the faint droning of the gaheen outside the shutters, and drifted readily into sleep.

He was not sure what woke him, thinking at first that he roused from some dream and rolled over with a sigh, slitted eyes ascertaining that no light showed at the window to herald dawn, grunting comfortably as he composed himself to return into slumber. Then faint sound drew him back from that tempting threshold. He grunted again, less comfortably, and forced his sleep-blurred eyes to open. The room was dark, his adjusting vision slowly picking out the dim outlines of the window, the ewer on the table, the wardrobe, the chest of drawers. The gaheen murmured through the sleeping street and he decided it was that he heard: he burrowed his head deeper into the pillow, hand reaching to touch the satchel beneath. And heard a board creak. Sharp, cold fingers of apprehension danced the length of his spine. The hair on his neck prickled as realisation forced him to acknowledge that someone - or something - was in the room. He shivered as he thought of the wolf-headed creatures Azumandias had sent to the caravanserai, suddenly - incongruously - aware that he was naked. He forced himself to lie still, resisting the impulse to snatch at his blade, savouring the air. It smelled hot, but there was no scent of almonds. Would there be, had the conjuration already manifested? He clenched his teeth, feigning sleep as he opened his eyes a fraction, peering from under hooded lids into the gloom. The room was still. There was nothing there that should not be: perhaps he had dreamt it all.

Then a shadow moved between the wardrobe and the door, detaching itself from the angle of the cupboard and the wall. It was a man-shaped shadow, a more solid black than its surroundings, and it moved towards him.

He could contain himself no longer: with a shout that was part outrage and more fear, he lurched from the bed, snatching at his sword. His fingers locked about the hilt and he swung the weapon up, sending the scabbard flying across the room. It clattered against the door and dropped to the floor. The shadow was on the far side of the bed and he saw steel glint briefly as it propelled itself across towards him, agile as some hunting cat. It rolled over the crumpled sheets, landing on its feet before him, a long, narrow-bladed dagger darting at his ribs. He swung the sword again, hearing steel ring on steel, and jumped back as the shorter blade thrust for his belly. He sucked his stomach in, bending and turning, and felt a brief stab of pain that was instantly forgotten as the blade drove at his throat. He danced away, terror lending him strength as he countered the blow, cannoning against the shutters, the latch stabbing viciously beneath his shoulder.

The shutter banged open a fraction, permitting pale silver moonlight to enter the room. In its band he saw a lean figure dressed in shirt and loose pantaloons of midnight hue, the head wrapped round with a bandage-like hood in which only the eyes were visible. They were cold and dark; implacable. He backed away and his attacker dropped to a crouch, advancing with a silent, scuttling motion, the dagger weaving a hypnotic pattern before his face. He raised his sword defensively and felt it swept aside by the dagger, twisting his head barely in time to avoid the blade that stabbed at his eyes.

Turned, he had no chance to avoid or deflect the foot that lashed at his knee. He shouted as he felt the kick slam hard against the bone, pain erupting in a fiery explosion, paralysing his leg so that it gave way under him and he fell heavily to one side. He struck the wardrobe and thudded to the floor, struggling to raise his sword as he saw the dagger flash towards him, then halt in midstroke as the door burst open and Bracht charged into the room.

The Kern was naked, his long hair wild about his face, the falchion outthrust. His blue eyes took in Calandryll, helpless on the floor, and the black-clad figure poised above him, and he roared a battle-cry, turning the direction of his charge towards the assassin. The dagger rose to parry his attack, but the momentum of his charge drove the figure back, clear of the fallen Calandryll. Sparks glittered as falchion and dagger met. The assassin backed, seeking room to manoeuvre; Bracht followed him - or her, Calandryll was not sure - across the chamber. A second time, a third and then a fourth, the dagger turned the freesword's blows. Calandryll pushed awkwardly to his feet. Fire burned in his knee and he could feel warm liquid oozing down his belly. He ignored it as he leant against the door, the straightsword held before him. He saw Bracht cut at the assassin's head and the figure duck, slashing at the Kern's abdomen. Bracht danced clear and cut again, his stroke again deflected. The shadowy shape rolled back across the bed, darting towards Calandryll even as the falchion slashed the sheets. *Chaipaku* burned in his mind. He raised his sword, knowing he had no chance against one of the Brotherhood and yelped as fire blazed in his damaged knee and he felt his leg give way.

Time seemed to slow then and he saw the deadly game played out as if he were a spectator, indifferent to his own fate, protected by the very knowledge that he was about to die. He fell below the assassin's thrust and saw the force of the blow lodge the dagger deep in the panelling of the door. Saw Bracht roll, no less nimble than the Chaipaku, over the bed to land on his feet behind the assassin. Saw the falchion driven forwards by all the strength of the freesword's powerful shoulder, all his weight behind the blow. He saw the killer turn, spinning with inhuman speed, left hand dropping to sweep the blade aside, right thrusting stiffened fingers at Bracht's face. And saw that not even the Chaipaku was fast enough to beat the Kern.

Bracht swung his head clear of the murderous blow, stabbing his sword at the killer's midriff. The falchion pierced the ribcage. Calandryll saw the tip emerge from the assassin's back. Then the door shuddered in its frame as the body was slammed against the wood. He saw Bracht snarl with animal ferocity as he twisted the blade loose, and winced as hot blood splattered his naked chest. A strangled moan erupted from beneath the hood and the figure took a single step forwards. Bracht swung the falchion in a savage cut and more blood sprayed from the belly. The assassin tottered. The Kern cut back and the figure grunted, abruptly limp, the knees folding, clawed hands dropping. It fell heavily to the floor. Bracht drove the falchion into its back and it jerked, bare feet drumming briefly on the blood-stained carpet. Then it was still. Bracht tugged his sword loose and turned to Calandryll.

'You're wounded?'

'I ... Yes ... I don't know ...'

He shook his head as time resumed its normal passage and he realised that he heard a fist pounding on the door, Mother Raimi's fluting voice demanding entry.

Bracht tossed the falchion aside and hauled him to his feet. He groaned as he put weight on his knee. The Kern lowered him to the bed. He was dimly aware that he still clutched his own sword. The door opened to reveal Mother Raimi, dressed in a loose gown of irridescent green that shimmered in the light of the lantern she held. Its glow showed her the body and the two naked men, the blood that oozed darkly over her carpet. She screamed, and two more faces, one male, the other a woman's, appeared behind her. The woman echoed Mother Raimi's scream; the man mouthed an oath.

Bracht said, 'He was attacked,' indicating Calandryll.

Mother Raimi said, 'Surinim, fetch the lictor. Quick!'

Bracht took the lantern from her and brought it close to Calandryll, studying his blood-spattered torso.

'A scratch. No more.' The Kern touched his knee. 'A kick?'

He nodded. Bracht glanced over his shoulder and said, 'Bring cloths and cold water. There's a healer in this godforsaken town?'

Mother Raimi nodded dumbly.

'Then send for him.'

'Her,' the silver-haired woman corrected automatically, staring. Calandryll was suddenly aware that she was brought from her sleep to a room where a corpse lay on the floor and two naked men, one smeared with blood, sat upon the bed: he began to laugh.

Bracht slapped his face and said, 'Now! Cloths, cold water, and then the healer. Do it!'

The old woman started as though his hand had landed on her cheek. She nodded to the gaping woman at her back and said, 'Go, Lyhanna,' in a muted voice.

Calandryll stopped laughing and began to shiver. Bracht tugged the sheet across his midriff and he stared as the white linen grew slowly dark. The Kern rose, ignoring his own nudity, and retrieved his blade. 'I'll dress,' he said, and left the room. Mother Raimi stared at Calandryll, her eyes huge, her mouth moving silently.

'I was attacked,' he said, aware that his teeth chattered. 'I was asleep and I woke to find him here.' He gestured at the corpse. 'He tried to kill me.'

Lyhanna came back then and set wadded cloth and a pitcher of water on the floor by the door. She appeared unwilling to enter the room.

'He tried to kill me,' Calandryll repeated. 'He would have killed me had Bracht not stopped him.'

Mother Raimi nodded, her eyes not leaving his face. She seemed afraid to move or speak, as if he might spring from the bed and attack her. Bracht pushed her gently aside. He was dressed in his black leathers, the falchion sheathed on his waist, his dark hair bound in its customary ponytail. He crossed to the bed and soaked a cloth in water, wadding it about Calandryll's knee.

'Hold it there,' he ordered.

He lit the room's lanterns and knelt beside the corpse. Calandryll watched as he turned the body over. Mother Raimi gasped as the ravaged belly was exposed.

Bracht said mildly, 'He was hard to kill. I wonder who he was.'

He drew the hood clear of the face and Calandryll gasped as he saw Mehemmed's features exposed.

'He's just a boy,' Mother Raimi said softly.

Bracht said, 'He's a dead assassin.'

Calandryll said, 'Why? Was he Chaipaku?'

Bracht shrugged.

Mother Raimi said, 'I want no trouble here. Not with the Chaipaku. You'd best leave at dawn.'

Bracht glanced at Calandryll and said, 'If he can walk.'

Calandryll said nothing: he was staring at Mehemmed with his thoughts in turmoil.

'Why did he wait 'til now?' Bracht murmured. 'Why not while we were at sea? And the woman on the warboat - did she know him?'

Calandryll licked his lips: an ugly suspicion began to dawn.

'At sea, he might have been found out,' he suggested. 'Perhaps he waited until now so that he could flee when ek'Jemm sets sail. Perhaps he had nothing to do with the woman. Perhaps he was sent after me, not ...' He slid a hand beneath his pillows, touching the satchel.

Bracht frowned and said, 'Your brother? Your father?'

'Perhaps,' Calandryll nodded.

'And the woman serves Azumandias. So perhaps we are hunted by wizard and Chaipaku, both.' Bracht grinned humourlessly. 'It seems I shall earn my pay.'

Calandryll looked at the corpse again. Mehemmed was about his own age, likely younger. Had Tobias sent him? He was about to speak when boots thudded in the corridor outside and the officer they had seen on the quay entered, flanked by six soldiers, Surinim peering curiously over their shoulders. Mother Raimi favoured him with a grateful look, as if she at last felt safe.

'Who killed him?' the lictor demanded curtly.

'I did,' said Bracht.

'He tried to kill me,' said Calandryll.

The officer studied them both, his dark face expressionless, then he nudged Mehemmed's body.

'Chaipaku,' he said thoughtfully. 'Why should the Brotherhood hunt you?'

Calandryll shrugged helplessly. Bracht said, 'Our rivals - Lord Varent's rivals. Likely they hired him.'

The lictor nodded. 'Rahamman ek'Jemm said you were on some secret mission for this lord of Aldarin. Do you bring your trade wars to Kandahar?'

'We sought no trouble,' Bracht said. 'Calandryll was attacked while he slept.'

'But still I have a corpse,' the lictor said. 'And albeit it's a Chaipaku, there are still questions that require answers. You'd best come with me.'

'He's hurt.' Bracht spoke quickly, glancing at Calandryll. 'He can't walk.'

Calandryll groaned in confirmation. The lictor glanced at Mother Raimi, who said, 'I've sent Lyhanna for the healer.'

'We'll wait,' the lictor decided. 'If Suleimana declares him unfit to walk, then he can stay here.'

'And Bracht?' Calandryll asked.

'Finds lodging in my cells,' said the lictor. 'Until the district podesta tries his case.'

'What case?' Bracht demanded angrily. 'A Chaipaku assassin attempted to kill the man I'm hired to guard - I did my duty, no more.'

The lictor shrugged, turning to draw the dagger from the woodwork.

'Likely that's true, but I've a duty, too. And that requires me to hold you until the podesta can investigate. Until then, you're my guest.' He smiled briefly. 'You'll save a var or two on your bed and board.'

'We have business to attend,' Calandryll protested.

'If you can't walk, you can't travel,' came the unyielding answer. 'The podesta should arrive within three weeks and you'll likely be free to go then. But until then ...'

He shrugged expressively. Calandryll and Bracht exchanged glances. The Kern smiled coldly. "It seems we must wait,' he said, nodding in the direction of the watchful soldiers.

Calandryll ducked his head, silently cursing Tobias, or Azumandias, or whoever had employed the Chaipaku to hunt him. He had not anticipated their whereabouts would be so quickly discovered, and the thought of kicking his heels in Mherut'yi until the podesta arrived chilled him afresh: if Mehemmed had been able to find him, despite all Varent's precautions, then so might another of the brotherhood. Or the mysterious woman.

The soldiers parted then, admitting a stern-featured woman wearing a light cape and carrying a large leather bag. She pushed the hood back to reveal a head of thick auburn hair, glancing at the lictor.

'Well, Philomen, I can see one's beyond repair, so who is it I attend at this ungodly hour?'

The lictor bowed, pointing at Calandryll.

'That one, Suleimana. They say his knee's damaged.'

The woman nodded and shed her cape. She wore a plain brown robe beneath, smoothing its folds as she settled herself on the bed beside Calandryll. She glanced briefly at his leg and said, 'This may hurt.'

He winced his agreement as she probed his knee, then moaned as she took his ankle in both hands and turned his leg back and forth.

'It's not broken,' she declared. Then smiled fleetingly as she added, 'You'd have screamed if it were - the knee's a delicate thing.'

'Can he walk?' the lictor asked.

'Burash, no!' the woman shook her head. 'Not for a day or two, and then he'll be limping for a while. I'll set a compress on it, but he'd best stay here in bed for the next two days. After that, I'll see.'

She pushed her sleeves back and set the palm of her right hand flat against the cut on his belly, her eyes closing as she murmured softly. Calandryll experienced a faint stinging, then the woman removed her hand and he felt nothing.

'There's no poison,' she remarked casually, and set both hands about his knee.

Her eyes closed again and a look of intense concentration gripped her face. He grunted as her hold tightened, then sighed as the pain abated. She loosed her grip and opened her bag and began to rummage through the contents. Calandryll watched as she produced a pot from which she smeared some pungent ointment over his bruised flesh. It burned a little, then dulled to a pleasant warmth as she wound a bandage about the joint.

'Drink this.' She passed him a phial of colourless liquid. 'You have money?'

He nodded and drank. The potion tasted bitter. Suleimana said, 'Good, you owe me two varre. One more for each visit. Now, let me dress that cut.'

She daubed some other unguent over the wound and wrapped a bandage about his waist.

'Clean that blood,' she advised, 'then sleep. Stay here until I say you can walk. Raimi will bring you your meals.'

Mother Raimi nodded as though accepting an order. Calandryll said, 'Thank you.'

The healer smiled again and shook her head.

'Your money's all the thanks I need.' She closed her bag and stood up. 'Now - unless there's another needs me - I'll return to my bed.'

'No,' the lictor said, standing aside as she strode regally past him. He fixed a stern eye on Calandryll. 'You'll remain here. Your companion comes with me.'

His men moved closer to emphasise the order. Mother Raimi asked, 'What about ... that?' pointing nervously at the body.

'Two of you haul it out,' commanded the lictor.

Calandryll watched the body dragged unceremoniously from the room. Mother Raimi stared aghast at her ruined carpet. 'You,' the lictor said to Bracht, 'come with me. And leave your sword here.'

The Kern glowered, and for a moment Calandryll feared he would refuse. He sighed his relief as Bracht unlatched his swordbelt and flung it irritably to the floor. The lictor beckoned him. His men angled their pikes menacingly. Bracht nodded, offering no further protest. Instead, he looked to Calandryll.

'Visit me when you can walk.'

Calandryll ducked his head, understanding the message.

The next two days passed slowly. When he tried to stand, pain lanced his damaged knee and he was forced to acknowledge Suleimana's diagnosis, reluctantly accepting her advice and remaining supine on the bed. A nervous Lyhanna came in the morning to scrub the soiled carpet, avoiding his eyes and answering his questions with grunted monosyllables until he gave up the attempt to engage her in conversation. Mother Raimi brought him food, Surinim at her back with a stout cudgel, and they were no more forthcoming than Lyhanna. It seemed he was allowed to remain only because the healer had spoken against moving him, and he spent the day alternately cursing his immobility and worrying about the attack. He had too much time to think, and his thoughts spun circles about themselves, like mad dogs snapping at their own tails.

Was the Chaipaku sent by Tobias?

Or by Azumandias?

If the latter, then why send the warboat after the *Sea Dancer*? Had Azumandias sought to further his chances of success by employing both the woman and the Chaipaku?

Or was it Tobias who sent the assassin?

Would his father use such methods?

He was not sure Bylath would stoop so low, but Tobias ... Yes, his brother would not hesitate to eliminate a threat to his accession. But that had to mean Tobias had known he was in Aldarin - could he have found out so fast? Or did the Chaipaku themselves have some means of passing information that swiftly? Carrier pigeons, or perhaps magic. He ransacked his memory for information, but could not recall any mention of the Brotherhood using magic.

He lay on the bed, staring through the opened window at the small yard behind the hostelry, feeling the dry heat of the gaheen, lost in the maze of his troubled thoughts. Had Mehemmed simply recognised him as one sought by the assassins and seized the opportunity to strike? That likely meant his face was known to all the Chaipaku: that particular thought chilled him, for it magnified the dangers of his journey to a horrible extent. Magic and Bracht had saved him this time: the next the Kern might not be so quick. Certainly not whilst he was incarcerated in the lictor's jail. Calandryll clasped the sword rested across his hips and cursed his injury. Fit, he had been no match for the killer. Unable to walk he had no chance at all should a second appear.

That night he slept fitfully with the sword cradled in his arms and his hand was on the hilt when Suleimana came back.

'I am no Chaipaku,' the healer declared. 'Had I wished to kill you, the draft I gave you would have been poison. Philomen is not very bright and I could have told him the blade that cut you was envenomed.'

He nodded, relinquishing the sword as she settled herself on the bed and opened her bag.

'Why do they seek you?'

She unwrapped the bandage as she spoke, her eyes critical of his knee. He saw that her rich auburn hair was streaked with strands of grey.

'I travel on secret business,' he replied vaguely. 'There are trade contracts to be negotiated.'

The woman snorted, turning sceptical eyes towards him.

'Ghombalar or Vhisat'yi are Kandahar's trade centres, and the *Sea Dancer* sailed for Ghombalar yesterday.'

He shrugged, watching as she prodded his kneecap. It felt only slightly sore now.

'We travel inland.'

Suleimana applied fresh ointment.

'There's nothing inland save farms. Unless you travel to Nhur-jabal.'

'We do.'

He was reluctant to reveal even that much, but it seemed that further prevarication would merely heighten her obvious suspicion. She nodded and wound a clean bandage about his leg.

'Now let me see your belly.'

He leant forwards so that she could unwind the cloth. The wound was already healing, the skin puckered and pink.

'A fraction lower ...' She chuckled; Calandryll blushed. 'But you were lucky. It's little more than a scratch - in a day or two it'll be no more than a story to tell your children.'

She smeared a salve over the cut and circled him with a fresh swathe of linen.

'And my knee?'

'More serious,' she said briskly. 'I'll have Surinim cut you a staff and you can walk a little tomorrow. But not for long! When it begins to ache, you must rest. Strain it and you'll limp all your life. You were lucky it didn't break.'

'How long before I can travel?' he asked.

'You Lyssians.' She shook her head. 'Do you think of nothing but business?"

'How long?' he insisted.

'At least a week before you can walk unaided. Probably three before it's full-healed.'

His face registered his alarm. Suleimana shrugged, returning her unguents to the bag.

'Your comrade remains in Philomen's care until then at least. The podesta makes his circuit and he's not known to hurry. And he'll want to interview you.'

'Three weeks,' he muttered.

Suleimana nodded.

'There are stables in Mherut'yi?' he asked. 'I can buy horses?'

'Old Dahammen has horses for sale,' she said, 'but riding will do that knee no good. And Philomen will not permit you to leave.'

'He's the only authority in Mherut'yi? Is there none higher?'

The healer chuckled.

'No. Philomen is our lictor and a lictor's the highest official we merit here. You should have stayed aboard the *Sea Dancer* and travelled on to Ghombalar if you're in such a hurry.'

'But I didn't.'

'No; and now you must remain here until the podesta declares you free to go.'

'You think he will?'

She pursed her lips, then ducked her head.

'The one your fellow killed was Chaipaku, and killing them's no crime. Aye, the podesta will release you once the formalities are done. But Philomen will hold you until then - he likes to demonstrate his authority from time to time.'

'Might he change his mind?' he paused, not sure how she would take it, or if she would report back to the lictor. 'Might money change it for him?'

'No. Philomen's none too bright, but he's honest. Don't try to bribe him.'

He nodded. Suleimana smiled again, rising.

'Curb your impatience. Three weeks is not so long.'

A lifetime, he thought. Long enough for the Chaipaku to find me; or the warboat to reach Mherut'yi. He said, 'I suppose I must.'

'Yes,' she said, businesslike again. 'And now - you owe me three varre.'

He handed her the coins.

'Thank you, I suggest you visit me in two days time. And be careful not to exert yourself.'

He nodded again and she quit the room, leaving him alone.

Three weeks! It was too long to wait: an impossible time. He must test his knee and when he could walk, purchase horses; free Bracht. He lay back, wondering how he would do it. Presumably the Kern was held in that stronghold on the mole. With Varent's magic to aid him he should be able to gain entry … find Bracht … the key … Was the freesword held in a cell? How to bring him out? The talisman would render only one of them invisible. He shook his head, refusing to be daunted. He would succeed! He had to, because the fate of the world depended on it. As soon as he could hobble he would penetrate the fortalice and decide a stratagem.

A little happier, he waited for his evening meal.

The next morning Surinim appeared with a staff. It seemed that Suleimana must have reassured the man, for he carried no cudgel today and he smiled shyly as he set the stave beside Calandryll's bed. Calandryll thanked him and, as soon as he was gone, dressed and clambered awkwardly to his feet. A dull throbbing drummed in his knee when he stood, but he was able to limp, resting his weight mostly on the wooden pole, along the corridor to the entrance of the hostlery. Mother Raimi watched him as he fumbled with the door and he smiled at her, the greeting sending her scurrying back behind the protection of the bead curtain as he hobbled into the street.

The sun shone bright out of a sky that seemed scoured to a steely blue-silver by the relentless gaheen. Within his room he had not realised how fierce the wind was, but now he felt its hot, heavy strength and understood why it was called the devil wind. It burned in his mouth as he breathed, bombarding his face with grit so that he blinked and spat, turning his head to avoid its onslaught. He began to sweat, feeling his lengthening hair slap damp against his neck, the strap of the satchel an irritation across his chest. The street was empty; indeed, Mherut'yi seemed empty, a somnolent place where dust skirled along the narrow thoroughfares and people hid from the oppressive gusting. He wiped his mouth and set out to explore the town.

The investigation did not take long. Even slowed by the frequent need to halt and rest when his knee threatened to fold under him, he succeeded in patrolling the environs by nightfall. He found the stable Suleimana had described and negotiated the purchase of two horses and tack with Dahamman, explaining to the old man that he would collect them when the podesta freed Bracht. He ate in a dusty inn and afterwards limped to the waterfront, disappointed to find that the proximity of the sea offered no respite from the gaheen. The harbour was empty save for a few fishing boats and he leant against the wall of a warehouse as he studied the grey bulk of the fortalice. It was the tallest structure in Mherut'yi, two stone storeys rising above the harbour, the lowest level cut with narrow embrasures and the upper with wider, barred openings. The roof was flat and there was a single door granting entry on the landward face. Soldiers lounged about the door, but paid him no more attention than a glance. He wondered where Bracht was held, but decided against attempting entry until later, hobbling back to the hostelry in time for dinner.

The following morning he rose early and wandered the town again, familiarising himself with its pattern until he was confident he knew the fastest route out. The townsfolk had the habit of sleeping through the worst of the heat, leaving the place largely deserted for hours after the noonday meal. Despite Suleimana's advice he decided that he would not delay: there was no time to waste, lest Azumandias or the Chaipaku find him. If he could only effect Bracht's escape they should be able to ride clear before Philomen even knew they were gone. The Kern's gear was already transferred to his room: it remained only to free his comrade.

On the appointed day he sought Suleimana again.

The healer examined his knee and pronounced it on the way to mending. The cut on his stomach was almost gone, only a narrow red line attesting to the wound.

'Exercise the knee,' she advised, 'but not too much. There's no need to return here - you can apply the unguent yourself. Smear it on the bruise every two days, and change the bandage, and you'll be fit enough by the time the podesta releases you.'

He smiled his thanks, thinking that he would not wait so long, and paid her. Then, barely able to suppress his mounting excitement, he returned to the hostelry. It was the hottest time of the day and the folk of Mherut'yi kept themselves behind closed shutters until the worst of the heat had abated, the streets deserted until the ferocity of the gaheen eased a little. He ate and announced his intention of following the local custom by sleeping the afternoon away, asking that he not be disturbed. Behind his closed door he gathered their gear in a single bundle and counted out what he owed Mother Raimi. His sword was belted on his waist and he slung Bracht's falchion over his shoulder. Then he mouthed the spell Varent had taught him and felt his skin tingle, the scent of almonds powerful in his nostrils. Still unaccustomed to the use of magic, he found it hard to believe that he was truly invisible as he started towards the door, and paused as it dawned on him that he no longer limped. His knee no longer ached. In fact, it felt sound as ever and he grinned as he threw the staff to the bed: it seemed the faint fire of the red stone flowed through the damaged tissue, healing and strengthening. Still smiling, he traversed the corridor, slipping silently out into the empty street.

Mherut'yi slumbered in the noonday sun, even the dogs seeking respite from the savage heat, and he was thankful for the solitude as he made his way briskly to the stable. There was no sign of Hadamman as he entered, nor as he saddled both horses and led them out, breathing prayers to Dera and Burash both as he took the reins and headed for the harbour. The narrow alley between two warehouses provided a hiding place for the animals, its mouth shaded as he studied the fortalice. A solitary guard stood by the open door, leaning on his pike, the tails of his scarlet pugree drawn across his nose and mouth. Calandryll took a deep breath and set out across the cobbles.

The guard rested in the scanty shade of the blockhouse wall. Calandryll drew steadily closer, afraid the pounding of his heart beat loud enough to alert the soldier. He halted close enough to touch the man, staring at him. The Kand stared idly back, seeing nothing. The grin returned to Calandryll's lips as he tiptoed past into a spacious, shadowy chamber that occupied most of the stronghold's lower level. It was some kind of guard room, to judge by the tables, still littered with food, at the centre, and the bunks, each one holding a sleeping soldier, set along the walls. A narrow flight of stone steps led up to the second level and he guessed that Bracht was held there: he began to climb.

He paused again at the head, studying this second storey. Grey stone surrounded a bare central area, a further flight of steps leading to the roof, heavy doors set deep in the walls. One, across the hall, was cut with a small grille and he guessed that was the cell holding Bracht. He started towards it, then stopped as a door to one side opened and Philomen emerged.

The lictor wore a flowing robe of a scarlet to match his puggree, but his head was bare now, oiled black hair loose to his shoulders, his feet bare. He paused at the door, turning to speak, and Calandryll heard a feminine voice answer, the indistinct words eliciting a smile from Philomen. He crossed the open space, still smiling, and Calandryll flattened against the wall, holding his breath, as the lictor passed directly before him. The man's eyes looked straight at him - through him - and Calandryll voiced silent thanks to Varent for the spell. He watched as Philomen entered a room across the hall, reappearing moments later with a flagon of wine that he carried into the chamber. The woman laughed as the door closed, and Calandryll let out his breath in a long, slow sigh.

He crossed to the grille and peered in. Sunlight shone bright through the bars covering the outer window, illuminating a spartan chamber containing tiered bunks. Bracht lay on a bunk to one side of the window, asleep. Calandryll examined the door. It was held by a sturdy lock: there was no sign of the key. He called Bracht's name softly, praying no other would hear. Bracht sat up and said, 'Calandryll?'

He nodded, raising a finger to his lips before he remembered the Kern could not see him.

'Aye,' he whispered. 'Here.'

Bracht climbed from the bunk, approaching the door. He seemed no worse for his incarceration, only irritated.

'You use Varent's spell?'

'Aye,' he repeated.

Bracht grunted and said, 'Then get me out of here.'

'I need the key.'

'The lictor has it. He keeps it on his belt.'

'Dera!' he muttered.

'You're invisible,' Bracht said.

'But Philomen's behind a closed door. With a woman.'

The Kern glowered at the empty air beyond the grille, his blue eyes angry.

'Then he's other things on his mind. And I'd not stay here any longer. Get me out!'

Calandryll nodded, sighing.

'Wait here.'

'I can do little else.' said Bracht.

'I'll try,' Calandryll promised, and crossed to the door he had seen the lictor use.

He pressed his ear to the wood, but could hear nothing through its bulk. He saw a ring set above a lock like that on Bracht's cell and hoped no key was turned on the inside. He took the ring in his hand, took a deep breath, and eased the ring a half circle round. The soft *click!* of falling tumblers seemed to echo off the stone walls. He held his breath, ready to spring back should the lictor appear. Then, heart pounding, he gently thrust the door inwards. Bars of light striated a darkened room. He saw the corner of a bed. Two pairs of bare feet, entwined. Heard the panting of the woman and Philomen's heavier breathing. He eased the door a fraction wider and slipped inside.

Instantly, he was overcome with acute embarrassment. He felt an insane desire to giggle as he saw hirsute buttocks moving rhythmically above the paler hue of the woman's thighs. Her arms clutched the lictor to her and her face showed over his shoulder. Calandryll saw that she was pretty in a nondescript way, her eyes wide, unfocussed in pleasure.

Philomen's scarlet robe lay crumpled on the floor, beside it a gown of purple and white. The lictor's armour hung from a stand by the shuttered window, his swordbelt on a peg. On the belt was a bunch of keys. Calandryll swallowed and trod carefully towards them.

He heard Philomen's breathing quicken and the woman moan, 'Oh, Philomen! Philomen!'

He glanced over his shoulder, cheeks warm, and snatched the keys from the belt. He froze as they jangled, but the pair on the bed were too entranced to allow extraneous sound to intrude on their preoccupation and he jammed his prize beneath his own belt.

'Philomen!'

The woman's voice was louder as he returned to the door.

'*Philomen!*'

He slipped through as the lictor groaned, his last sight of the Kand his hairy buttocks.

Philomen's heavy breathing became a gasp of pleasure that drowned the sound of the closing door and Calandryll hurried to Bracht's cell. He tried three keys before he found the one he needed and sprung the door open. Bracht jumped back as the wood threatened to smash against his face, eyes narrowing as he tried to define Calandryll's outline.

Calandryll dropped Bracht's sword on the bunk. As he released the falchion it became visible. The Kern, grinned, buckling it on his waist.

'Ahrd,' he murmured, 'I'd not thought to be so grateful for Varent's magic.'

'We still have to get out,' Calandryll said. 'And the lower hall's full of soldiers.'

'Awake?' Bracht crossed to the door.

Calandryll said, 'The lictor is across the hall,' and grinned despite the tension, 'but occupied. The guards sleep below. One mans the door.'

Bracht nodded, smiling grimly.

'One I can deal with easily.'

'I'd not see him killed,' Calandryll said.

'If I can silence him ...' The Kern shrugged.

'He's not our enemy.' The thought of seeing an innocent man die sat ill with Calandryll. Bracht said, 'Would you see our quest ended here? Do you think you can cross Kandahar alone? With the Chaipaku hunting you?'

'Even so,' Calandryll protested.

'You've a delicate conscience,' murmured the freesword, 'but this is not the time to debate it. You've bought horses?'

He nodded again, unthinking, and said, 'Yes. Across the square.'

'Good,' Bracht murmured, 'Come.'

He drew his sword and stepped out of the cell. Calandryll eased the door shut, locked it, then quietly secured the lictor's door before dropping the keys inside the cell. At the head of the stairs Bracht halted, beckoning. Calandryll drew close.

'Invisibility has its advantages,' the Kern whispered, 'but I can't see where you are. Stay close.'

Calandryll said, 'I'm at your back.'

Slowly, step by step, they descended to the guard room. Calandryll felt his heart thud against his ribs, his eyes darting over the supine soldiers, willing them to remain asleep.

They reached the stairway's foot, sunlight a bright promise outlining the rectangle of the exit. Then, from above, a furious shout rang through the fortalice and a locked door was rattled in its frame. The sleeping guards stirred. Bracht snapped, 'Philomen wakes!'

The soldiers, too, rising groggily from their bunks as the lictor's angry bellowing grew louder, their eyes widening as they saw the prisoner with sword in hand, impossibly freed from his cell.

Calandryll shouted, 'Take the man on the door. I'll hold them.'

Bracht paused an instant and he shoved the Kern forwards. 'They cannot see me,' he gasped. 'Go!'

Bracht grunted and sprang to meet the startled watchman, ducking under a clumsy pikeswing to drive the hilt of his falchion against the Kand's jaw. Calandryll was grateful the freesword heeded his wish and left the man alive even as he snatched a halberd from its rack against the wall and flailed the haft in a sweeping arc across the ankles of three charging soldiers. They went down in a sprawling mass, their shouts echoed by their slower companions, who saw impossibility piled on impossibility, a halberd swinging of its own accord. One cried, 'Sorcery!' and several halted their pursuit, faces wary, hands shaping protective signs. Calandryll flung the halberd at them and darted to a table, upending it to send plates and food and wine flagons tumbling over the floor. The panic he read in the Kands' eyes encouraged him, and he darted about the room, hurling missiles at random. It must seem, he thought, that some occult force came to Bracht's aid, and he sought to enhance that impression with a strident howling. Several of the guardsmen cowered in unfeigned terror; a braver few moved after Bracht.

Calandryll saw that the Kern had overpowered the man at the door and was now running for the warehouses. He seized another pike and flung it underhand at the pursuing soldiers. Two tripped and more fell over them, piling in the doorway. Calandryll turned a second table and sprang across the fallen guards. One began to rise and he kicked the man, unthinking, in the chest, then raced after Bracht.

The freesword was astride one horse, the reins of the other in his hand, his eyes intent on the confusion in the fortalice. Calandryll halted, mouthing the releasing spell. The air shimmered, once more redolent of almonds, and he became visible again. Bracht passed him the reins and he swung into the saddle.

'Can you ride?' the Kern demanded urgently. 'Is your knee healed?'

Calandryll said, 'It seems the stone heals me.'

'So be it,' Bracht nodded, still suspicious for all that magic had freed him. 'Now let's ride - fast and far.'

Calandryll needed no further bidding. The soldiers' fear of magic, and the confusion he had wrought, was soon overcome by the more immediate fear of their lictor's wrath: they were flooding in an angry tide from the fortalice.

'Follow me,' he shouted, heeling his mount to a gallop.

They charged through the quiet streets, the habit of siesta masking their escape as they traversed Mherut'yi and reached the outskirts.

'We ride for Nhur-jabal?' Bracht asked. 'Which way?'

Calandryll pointed to where the highway led out of the little town, a ribbon of packed dirt winding into the heart of Kandahar. Bracht nodded.

'You did well,' he called over the pounding of the hooves. 'I owe you thanks.'

Calandryll beamed, flattered by the freesword's praise: proud of himself.

TEN

THEY rode as hard as they dared in the oppressive heat, a dust cloud marking their flight, Bracht setting the pace, sweat shining on the horses' hides as they thundered away from Mherut'yi. When the town was lost in the haze behind them the Kern slowed, but he did not permit a halt until the rim of the sun touched the distant buttresses of the Kharm-rhanna range and twilight's blue shadows crept across the land. He turned off the dirt highway then, finding a hollow in the desolate terrain that afforded partial shelter from the gaheen. The wind still assaulted them, beading their faces with sweat, plastering shirts to prickling backs and dusting them with its burden of grit. It clung to their damp skin, lodging in eyebrows, finding its way into their mouths and under their clothes, reminding them of the luxury of water and soap as they huddled hungry, watching the horses crop on the sparse grass that filled the hollow. Calandryll had filled two canteens, but packed no food, deeming that too obvious an announcement of his intentions, and his stomach grumbled a protest as he crouched under the lee of the slope.

'We'll ride through the night,' Bracht decided, apparently unaffected by the discomfort. 'Perhaps tomorrow we can buy food; or hunt something.'

'Can we risk buying it?' Calandryll wondered. 'What of Philomen?'

'The lictor?' Bracht chuckled. 'Unless some other key can be found, he'll be with his woman a while longer than he anticipated. Then he must organise his men, and I doubt he'll stray far from Mherut'yi. He'll make some token pursuit then turn back. If we put sufficient distance between us tonight, we should be safe.'

'From him, at least,' Calandryll nodded. 'But what of the Chaipaku?'

The Kern shrugged. 'Against them, we must be on our guard,' he said, his smile fading. 'I'd not anticipated the Brotherhood's intervention.'

'Tobias must have employed them,' Calandryll shuddered. 'But how could they know so fast?'

The elation he had felt at their escape waned as he thought of Mehemmed: the prospect of crossing Kandahar with the Chaipaku hunting him was daunting. Bracht glanced at him and shook his head. 'The ways of the Brotherhood are mysterious. Who knows how they communicate? But there's little point in brooding on it.'

Calandryll tore moodily at the stubbly grass, his expression troubled now.

'But if we must pass through Nhur-jabal ... the other towns along the way to Kharasul ... how can we avoid them?'

'Perhaps we can't,' Bracht offered, 'but we need not concede them the victory. We've defeated one - we can do it again.'

'*You* can,' Calandryll said morosely. 'Had you not heard me, I'd be dead.'

'But you're not,' said Bracht. 'You survived his attack.'

'Barely.' He touched his throat, where the red stone hung beneath his shirt. 'And were it not for Lord

Varent's magic, I'd be scarce fit enough to ride.'

'And were it not for you, I'd still languish in Philomen's keep,' the freesword returned. 'Ahrd, man! We've escaped capture by that warboat and a Chaipaku attack. We've left Mherut'yi behind us. We can cross Kandahar if we're careful.'

'And Kharasul?' Calandryll demanded. 'What then?'

'Then we find a ship to take us north,' said Bracht, 'just as we planned. We sail for Gessyth and find Tezindar. We take the Arcanum and ...'

He fell silent. Calandryll frowned as he gestured at the red stone. 'And?' he prompted, vexed by the Kern's suspicions.

'I've yet to be convinced of Varent's honesty,' Bracht continued. 'I still believe the *byah* spoke of him. I say we take the Arcanum and hold it safe until we can be certain he intends to destroy it as he says.'

Calandryll sighed his frustration: he had thought Bracht's doubts forgotten. 'Were it not for Lord Varent I'd still languish in my father's keep,' he said. 'Were it not for Lord Varent, we'd be prisoners on that warboat - or dead. Were it not for Lord Varent, you'd still be in Mherut'yi.'

'He needs us,' said Bracht flatly. 'He needs you to find the Arcanum and me to guard you. We're useful to him.'

'Dera!' snapped Calandryll. 'Your suspicions are groundless.'

'I heard the *byah*,' Bracht said doggedly.

'Which warned of Azumandias. Or Tobias, for all I know.'

Bracht shrugged, his eyes unrelenting.

'You think he'd use the book to raise the Mad God?' Calandryll shook his head helplessly. 'Only a crazy man would attempt so lunatic a thing - and Lord Varent is obviously sane.'

Bracht shrugged again, not speaking, stretching on his back to stare at the darkening sky. Calandryll sighed.

'What do you propose then? After we've secured the book?'

'I don't know,' Bracht admitted. 'But until Varent convinces me of his honesty, I'd not hand him so powerful a thing as the Arcanum.'

Calandryll plucked a second handful of grass; flung it from him, watching the yellowed blades flutter on the breeze.

'Perhaps you believe he spies on us through the talisman?'

Bracht shook his head, ignoring the sarcastic tone.

'No,' he said evenly, 'I think the stone gains power from the wearer. I think it uses your eyes, your ears.'

'And what,' Calandryll asked wearily, 'brings you to that conclusion?'

'You have the talent,' Bracht said, his voice calm. 'I could not use it, remember? Varent said then I lack the aptitude. But you are able to disappear; you wore it when that storm arose; it mends your knee. I believe you channel its magic.'

Calandryll gaped, dumbstruck.

'Do you say I am a magician?'

'I believe you have occult power. That ability Varent spoke of.'

'Then do you mistrust me as you mistrust all magicians?'

Bracht chuckled then, shaking his head. 'I trust you, Calandryll, and I believe you honest.'

Something hung on the tail of his words: Calandryll frowned, staring at him.

'But?'

'Power corrupts.'

'You think me corrupted?'

'No.' Bracht rose on one elbow to smile at his companion. 'But I think you may be seduced by Varent's promises.'

For a moment Calandryll felt resentment return. It

seemed the Kern judged him, the blunt statement suggesting Bracht weighed him and found something wanting. Then he dismissed the thought, refusing it a hold: his background set him closer to Varent, to the man's way of life, than Bracht could understand. The Kern's doubts were no more than that. He was, after all, a wandering mercenary, outcast from his own land, almost a barbarian. Likely he viewed all Lysse with suspicion. He was a friend though, of that Calandryll had no doubt - Reba's prophecy had foretold his coming, as it had foretold Varent's - but still there were differences between them, and likely would always be. He touched the stone, grateful for the relief it gave his damaged knee, and thought to take the additional precaution of applying the healing ointment too: he rubbed the stuff in, rewinding the bandage as Bracht checked the animals. Dusk was falling rapidly into night now and the gaheen eased, the air losing that furnace intensity imparted by the wind. A near-full moon hung above the eastern horizon and stars began to appear in the great sweep of dark blue above them, the land assuming a spectral quality, the road a band of blackness flanked by silvered grass. They mounted and continued in the direction of Nhur-jabal.

Bracht held them to a steady canter as the moon rose higher, the shod hooves drumming on the packed dirt. Distances that had seemed of little account on the maps Calandryll had studied assumed a physical reality as they progressed through the night. From Mherut'yi to Nhur-jabal, assuming they stuck to the road, was roughly the same distance as from Secca to Aldarin, the journey to Kharasul as much again. From the west coast of Kandahar to the swamps of Gessyth was a journey he preferred not to contemplate: few Seccans travelled much beyond the city walls and he began to feel very lonely as he followed the silent Kern through the night. The terrain was flat and empty of features, the sweep of the plain rendered the more immense by darkness. To Calandryll, it felt as though they traversed a limbo, the only living creatures in that great spread of land, or ghosts, doomed to ride forever, their destination always unattainably ahead.

After a while Bracht slowed to a walk, resting the animals, then picking up the pace again, alternating until the moon was lost in the grey opalescence of approaching dawn. He called a halt then, riding a little way off the road to a stand of gnarled and windswept trees where they dismounted and hobbled the horses. It seemed they had left the gaheen behind, for the air was still, the grey mist undisturbed by any breeze. Calandryll rubbed his mount down and left it to crop as he wrapped himself in the saddle blanket and stretched on the hard ground.

He woke to find the sun on his face, still low in the sky, but warm, five curious birds studying him from the branches of the stunted trees, taking flight as he pushed to his feet and groaned at the protest of saddle-stiffened muscles. Bracht was already awake, combing his long hair. Calandryll wondered how the freesword could so easily ignore the pangs of hunger as he thought longingly of Mother Raimi's breakfasts. He stretched, kneading limbs deadened by the long hours in the saddle. Looking around, he saw that they camped on the great plain still, the land bleak, arid, as if kin to the desert wastes to the north. There was no sign of habitation, the occasional clumps of trees the only disruption of the terrain, and those sad echoes of the luxuriant timber of Lysse. He drank a little water and rubbed a moistened hand over his face, telling himself that at least the gaheen no longer blew. Nor was there any sign of pursuit, and Brach set an easier pace as they continued along the road.

Around midmorning they forded a small stream, where they watered the horses and filled their canteens, taking time to strip and wash the dust away before continuing westwards.

The character of their surroundings began to change after a while, imperceptibly at first, no more than a thickening of the grass, its colour changing subtly to a healthier green. The road began to climb at a gradual angle and then to dip, and the flat plain gave way to an undulating landscape mounded with small hillocks. The stands of timber grew more numerous, the trees less stunted by arid soil and wind, and wild flowers appeared in bright clusters. In the afternoon they saw cattle browsing in the distance, great heavy-muscled beasts with wide-spread horns and dark hides. A bull watched from a hummock, raising his head to bellow a challenge and they quickened their pace. As the sun neared its setting they saw a solitary building, its white walls painted rose by the waning light. It had the look of farm and fortress both: a low, square structure, surrounded by a chest-high fence of sturdy palings, the windows cut deep, with heavy shutters.

'We'll ask their hospitality,' Bracht decided.

Calandryll, thinking of cool water and hot food, nodded enthusiastic agreement.

They rode towards the building, slowly for fear of alarming the occupants, halting at the gate. Through its arch they could see a well and a stone-built barn beyond the house. Pigs and chickens rooted in the yard and a huge red dog barked furiously from the porch. A man appeared, murmuring something that silenced the hound, and two youths, so similar in looks they could only be his sons stepped out to flank him. They both held short, deeply curved bows, red-fletched arrows nocked to the strings. The man studied the newcomers for a moment, then beckoned them on, coming to meet them by the well, the dog at his heels. The archers remained on the porch.

The man was tall and thin, his face weatherbeaten to

the colour and texture of ancient leather, his eyes set deep and dark beneath craggy brows, eyeing them with a mixture of curiosity and suspicion. A broad-bladed knife was sheathed on his waist, the belt cinching a robe of faded green, his left hand resting idly on the hilt.

'Greetings, strangers.'

His voice sounded like his face looked: harsh and hard.

'Greetings,' Calandryll returned in the language of Kandahar, 'We've ridden far and should welcome a decent meal and a bed. We can pay.'

'From Mherut'yi?'

The farmer's face remained expressionless. Calandryll nodded.

'Not many travel overland from Mherut'yi.'

Calandryll shrugged.

'We have business inland.'

'Better to take ship to Mhazomul or Ghombalar, and a riverboat inland.'

'Our business is … delicate. We prefer to avoid the obvious trade routes.'

The man's eyes narrowed.

'You don't look like merchants.'

'We come to negotiate trade contracts. I am called Calandryll. This,' he indicated his companion with a wave, 'is Bracht.'

'You're Lyssian?'

'I am. My comrade is from Cuan na'For.'

'He speaks our language?'

'No.' Calandryll shook his head, 'but he understands the Envah.'

The man nodded and turned his head slightly.

'Denphat, check the roof.'

The younger bowman grunted an affirmative and disappeared back inside the house. Moments later he appeared on the roof, moving slowly along its perimeter with his eyes fixed on the surrounding terrain.

'Nothing I can see,' he called.

'Then come down.' The man gestured at the well. 'Those horses need watering - help yourselves. I am called Octofan.'

'Our thanks, Octofan,' smiled Calandryll, dismounting.

The farmer nodded and walked around them to the gate. He swung it shut and dropped a bar in place, sealing the opening. Denphat and the other youth continued to study them in silence down the length of their shafts. The red dog watched them with parted lips, as if ready to attack on a word or any sudden movement.

'You're cautious,' Bracht said, emptying a bucket into the trough beside the well.

Octofan shrugged without speaking, waiting until the horses had drunk their fill, then leading them to the long, low structure of the barn. The red dog followed at his heels. His two sons came after, standing in the doorway as their father indicated stalls.

'Put them up here. Help yourself to hay.'

He stood back as they stripped off the saddles and led the horses into the pens, patient as they rubbed the animals down and forked hay into the mangers. When they were done he said, 'There's a wash-house at the back. Food'll be ready soon.'

They washed under the wary eyes of his sons, then Octofan beckoned them onto the porch and escorted them into the building. It was cool and airy inside, the floor the same thick stone as the walls, the odours of meat and vegetables rising from pots on a cooking range tended by a grey-haired woman in a worn blue gown. She turned to examine them, her face expressionless as Octofan's. Calandryll bowed; Bracht ducked his head.

'I'll not have swords at my table,' she said.

'My wife, Pilar.' Octofan indicated a row of hooks by the door. 'Hang them there. These are my sons, Denphat and Jedomus.'

The youths had lowered their bows on entering the house and now they loosened the strings, setting the bows down on a table by the wall, nodding silently to the unexpected guests. Bracht and Calandryll unbuckled their swordbelts and hung them on the pegs.

'Sit down. Jedomus, bring that pot of ale.'

They settled at the long table that occupied the centre of the room. Octofan took the head, his sons to either side, and filled clay pots with dark beer. Calandryll and Bracht drank gratefully.

'They've come from Mherut'yi,' Octofan informed his wife as she set a loaf of steaming bread before him. 'On some Lyssian business.'

'They're not ...?' Pilar's raised brows framed a question.

'They offered to pay.'

The woman nodded as though this confirmed something. Calandryll fetched a coin from his satchel.

'Is one var sufficient? We'd purchase provisions for the journey, too?'

Octofan began to slice the bread, using the knife he wore. He said, 'Three varre is ample.'

Calandryll pushed the coins across the table. Octfan picked them up, examined them, and dropped them into a pocket of his robe. Pilar brought a pot of stew from the range and began to dole it into bowls. Calandryll felt his mouth water as the rich odour struck his nostrils. His stomach rumbled and he smiled apologetically.

'You came without provisions?'

Octofan spooned stew as he spoke. Calandryll followed suit, too hungry to concern himself with good manners and not sure how to explain their lack of supplies. Bracht saved him.

'We were attacked,' he said, adjusting the truth, 'and lost our supplies.'

The farmer and his wife exchanged glances. Octofan said, 'The road from Mherut'yi to Kesham-vaj is plagued by brigands.'

Bracht nodded. Pilar said, 'Sathoman,' in a low, angry voice.

'Sathoman is their leader?' asked Bracht.

'Aye,' Octofan grunted. 'Sathoman ek'Hennem, may Burash rot his soul.'

'He's the reason for your caution?'

Bracht indicated the bows Denphat and Jedomus had discarded: Octofan nodded.

'Sathoman ek'Hennem is a noble gone bad. The lictor of Mherut'yi didn't warn you?'

Bracht shook his head. 'We found the lictor ... unfriendly.'

'Philomen,' said Pilar, her tone dismissive. 'He's no better than Cenophus. They're supposed to patrol the roads - protect folk like us - but what do they do? They sit safe in their keeps and barely venture out save to gather the Tyrant's taxes. And when they do that, they eat us out of house and home. Nor ever pay for what they take.'

She smiled briefly at Calandryll.

'Cenophus is a lictor?' Bracht asked casually.

'Lictor of Kesham-vaj,' said Octofan. 'He claims our land falls under Philomen's jurisdiction. Save when it's time for tax-gathering.'

'And this Sathoman is a local brigand?' murmured the Kern.

'The son of Mandradus ek'Hennem,' said Octofan. 'Mandradus was Lord of the Fayne until he took the wrong side in the Sorcerer's War. He fell at the battle of the Stone Field and the Tyrant declared his lands and all possessions forfeit. Sathoman swore he'd revenge his father's death and declared himself rightful master of the Fayne. He claims it's his right to extract a toll from travellers. And herdsfolk, too, Burash damn him!'

'Lictor and Sathoman both claim their tax,' Pilar added bitterly.

'Does the Tyrant not act against outlaws?' Calandryll asked.

Octofan glanced at his wife and laughed sourly.

'The Tyrant sits safe in his palace, and Nhur-jabal is a long way from the Fayne. So long as his taxes come, he's content to leave such matters to his lictors.'

'And neither Cenophus or Philomen have the taste for battle?' Bracht said softly.

Octofan fixed suddenly suspicious eyes on the Kern. 'You've not heard of the Sorcerer's War?'

'I come from Cuan na'For,' Bracht returned, 'and I've travelled in Lysse. I know little of Kandahar.'

'The Tyrant Iodrydus declared sorcery outlawed,' Calandryll supplied. 'Save for those wizards licensed by himself, he placed severe limitations on their employment - the lords of Kandahar were required to give up their court magicians, and they rebelled. It was called the Sorcerer's War.'

Bracht nodded thoughtfully. 'Does this Sathoman still employ a wizard?' he asked.

'A mage called Anomius,' said Octofan. 'Neither Cenophus or Philomen will risk his magic. You were lucky you didn't face him when Sathoman's cutthroats attacked you.'

'Indeed,' the Kern murmured.

'And Sathoman's stronghold is nearby?' enquired Calandryll.

'To the north,' Octofan said, 'Though he spreads his net wide, across all the Fayne.'

'Hopefully we'll not encounter him,' said Calandryll, remembering to add, 'again.'

'Few survive an encounter with Sathoman, with or

without Anomius,' Octofan offered dourly. 'You'll not likely escape a second time.'

'Is he likely to be on the road?' Bracht asked.

Octofan shrugged, pushing his emptied plate away. Pilar rose and began to collect the dishes.

'Who knows where Sathoman will be? Perhaps you'll meet him, perhaps not. Best pray to Burash you don't.

He rose to fetch a pipe and a pouch of the narcotic tobacco to the table. Denphat and Jedomus pushed their chairs back and left the room. Calandryll saw that both took a bow. He shook his head as Octofan offered a pipe; Bracht did the same.

'Why does the Tyrant not send his own wizards to aid the lictors?' asked the Kern.

Octofan sucked smoke, holding his breath a moment before releasing it in a sweet, blue cloud and saying, 'Most fled Iodrydus's edicts, and those who remain the Tyrant prefers to keep close. Some few ward the larger towns, but he'd need an army of sorcerers to dig Sathoman out of Fayne Keep - I suppose that as long as the lictors collect his taxes he sees no advantage in it.'

'And so folk like us suffer,' Pilar said from where she scrubbed dishes. 'Cenophus collects taxes; Sathoman collects what he wants. At least he leaves us enough to live on. Just.'

'Is it not the way?' asked Octofan, his voice slightly slurred. 'The farmers always suffer.'

'It's different in Lysse,' Calandryll offered.

'You live in walled cities.'

It sounded like an accusation and Calandryll could think of no suitable response: he shrugged. Octofan slumped in his chair, drawing deep on the pipe, filling the room with its smoke. Pilar finished her cleaning and took a chair at his side, filling a pipe of her own. Bracht helped himself to more ale. Calandryll yawned, pleasantly full and growing drowsy. In a while the door opened and Denphat and Jedomus came in. They set their bows down and helped themselves to their father's tobacco. Outside the moon painted the yard with silver light. The red dog scratched on the porch and the pigs grunted. Somewhere a cow lowed; a bull snorted. Finally Octofan set his pipe aside and rose loose-limbed to his feet.

'You can sleep in the barn. I'll see you provisioned in the morning.'

'Thank you.' Calandryll was grateful for the dismissal: he wanted nothing more than to sleep now. He bowed in the direction of the table: 'My thanks for a fine meal, Goodwife.'

Pilar nodded, smiling languidly, saying nothing. Bracht handed him his swordbelt and Octofan took a lantern, opening the door. The red dog stirred, growling, and the farmer gestured it to silence, leading the way across the yard to the barn. He let them inside and left them there amongst the sweet scents of hay and horseflesh. Moonlight entered from narrow windows cut high in the front wall, revealing the straw mounded at the far end. They spread their blankets and stretched on the makeshift bed: it was mightily comfortable after the hard ground of the Fayne. He closed his eyes, but Bracht's soft voice denied him instantaneous sleep.

'So, to the dangers of the Chaipaku and Azumandias we can add a brigand and a renegade wizard.'

'At least,' he replied, 'sorcery's outlawed in Kandahar. That should please you.'

'Then you'd best keep that red stone well-hid,' Bracht chuckled. 'Lest we add the Tyrant to our list.'

'Aye,' he mumbled, burrowing deeper into the straw.

He was not sure at first what woke him, thinking that the sun rose and shone into his eyes, then that someone held a lantern close to his face. Close enough he could see the red glow of its flame through his shuttered lids and feel its heat against his chest. He stirred, throwing a protesting arm across his face. Surely it was not yet dawn - did Octofan come to wake him? He grunted and opened his eyes to darkness, the blue-velvet stillness of the earliest hours, yet lit by a faint red glow. Not before his eyes, but below them. From his throat! Where the red stone hung. He gasped, right hand scrabbling for his sword's hilt even as he rolled from his blanket, his mind screaming *Chaipaku!*

He was on his feet, unsteady in the shifting straw, sword drawn, knees bent in the fighter's crouch Bracht had taught him before he was fully awake. He saw the aisle of the barn, the sleeping horses in their pens, the yard beyond the door lit by a moon preparing to vacate the sky. He spun, stumbling in the straw, and saw the Kern's dark form, filled for an instant with the awful dread that his comrade was slain in his sleep, almost laughing with the relief Bracht's soft snore brought. He turned full circle, his wary eyes finding nothing amiss, no sign of imminent danger. No black-robed figure prepared to attack, nor lictor's soldiers. A horse broke wind; out in the night an owl hooted.

He blinked, racing mind calming, and touched left hand to the stone. It was warm to the touch, and when he drew it from beneath his shirt its glow was fiery. He let it drop. Varent's words loud in the ears of his mind: *Should you encounter some glamour, the flame within will burn bright and the stone grow hot. Should that happen, you will know that wizardry is close.*

He sniffed, but smelled only horses and hay: no scent of almonds. He took a step to the side, a step closer to Bracht, and kicked the sleeping Kern ungently. Bracht's steady breathing faltered, then quickened. He moved suddenly off the blanket, the falchion glittering in the waning moonlight as it slid from the sheath, rising defensively as the freesword came to his feet. He stared about, caught Calandryll's wide-eyed gaze, and frowned a question.

'Magic,' Calandryll said, slow and soft, 'There's magic abroad.'

He touched the stone again and Bracht nodded as he saw its glow.

'Where? I see nothing.'

Calandryll shook his head.

'I don't know. But the stone ...'

'Aye.'

Bracht moved off the piled straw onto the firmer ground between the pens. His blue eyes darted over the horses; returned to Calandryll, then up to where the loft hung heavy with baled hay.

'There. By Ahrd, what is it?'

His voice was hushed. Calandryll looked to where the falchion's tip pointed, and gasped.

In the darkest corner of the barn, farthest from the door, where the moonlight that filtered through the openings in the wall could not reach, something hung glowing. It was like the witchfire he had seen dancing on the masts of ships before a storm, silver as a polished blade, but not flickering: solid; unmoving. It was shaped like man and bird conjoined, its form growing clearer as his eyes adjusted to the gloom. It sat - or perched, he was not sure which - on the edge of the loft. Prehensile toes gripped the edge of the platform, bent knees concealing the body, which hunched forwards as though strained by the bulbous head. Ethereal wings were folded behind, framing that strange skull - if the thing had such corporeal substance as bone beneath its shimmering hide - which seemed all eyes, huge and round and impenetrably black. There was no indication of a nose, but below the dominant orbs he saw a slitted mouth, and on either side of the head, great fan-shaped ears.

He gaped. The thing stared back. Then, sudden and silent, it rose, launching itself from the loft.

The wings spread like silver sails, curved and angled,

more bat's than bird's; the legs stretched behind in facsimile of a tail and he saw vestigial arms folded across the narrow chest. It swooped towards him and he ducked, raising the straightsword as does a man swatting at a fly. The creature darted effortlessly clear, its blank eyes never leaving his face, rising to swoop again, this time over Bracht's head.

The Kern swung the falchion viciously and again the weird creature avoided the blow. Calandryll thought he heard a whistle, almost beyond the range of human hearing, trill from the lipless mouth. Then the wings beat and it sped for the door, through into the night beyond. He saw Bracht spin round, running after, and followed, in time to see the thing climbing into the sky above the sleeping farmhouse, lost against the panoply of stars.

He looked at the talisman: it glowed no longer.

'It's gone,' he said, hearing his voice shake.

'What was it?' Bracht lowered the falchion. 'Have you seen its like?'

Calandryll shook his head. 'Not seen, but I've read of such beings. They are called *quyvbal* - sorcerous creatures used as spies by wizards.'

From the porch the red dog growled a warning. Bracht stared at the sky, then turned back into the barn. 'I think,' he said, 'that perhaps Azumandias has found us. Or the one called Anomius.'

'Sathoman's wizard?' Calandryll frowned. 'Why should he seek us? How could he know we are here?'

'This journey of ours raises more questions than I can answer,' Bracht shrugged. 'Perhaps the mage sensed our presence. Or perhaps he look for us for reasons of his own. Perhaps he allies himself with Azumandias. Or Varent, for all I know.'

'Should we flee?'

'I think not.' Bracht shook his head. 'If whoever sent that thing could find us here, he - or she, perhaps? -

can find us again. We need those provisions Octofan promised, so we'd do as well to wait for the dawn.'

Calandryll glanced at the sky. After the appearance of that strange creature dawn felt a long way off. 'At least it didn't attack us,' he said.

'No,' Bracht agreed, 'but why did it spy on us? We ride watchful from now on.'

'Perhaps Octofan can shed some light on it,' Calandryll suggested.

'Perhaps Octofan told it of us,' said Bracht. 'And if he knew of the sender he may be an enemy. I think we'd best keep silent.'

Calandryll nodded and stretched on the straw, all thought of sleep forgotten. It seemed they must regard all they encountered with suspicion, every Kand a potential enemy: it was an oppressive thought. He was glad when the velvety darkness opalesced into the misty grey of dawn, and gladder still when the sun broke through and he heard the strident crowing of a cock announce the commencement of the day.

Pilar appeared, nodding a brief greeting as she began to collect eggs, and then Octofan, stretching and yawning, Denphat and Jedomus at his back. They, in turn, greeted the two wayfarers before going about their farmyard tasks, none seeming suspicious as Bracht and Calandryll availed themselves of the wash-house and prepared their horses for departure, seeing the two sons ride out to tend the cattle as Pilar called them to a substantial breakfast and her husband presented them with provisions sufficient to carry them through to Kesham-vaj: dried meat and a sack of vegetables, flour and salt, a little sugar.

'You can buy more there,' he said, 'if Sathoman doesn't stop you along the way. The town's some three or four days' ride from here if you make a good pace.'

'Are there other holdings?' Bracht asked.

Octofan shook his head.

'Not close to the road. There was a caravanserai, but Sathoman burnt it down and Anomius cursed it and it was never built again. Folk avoid it.'

Calandryll nodded, studying his face, but saw no hint of treachery in the deep-set eyes. He thanked the farmer and they carried the sacks out to the waiting animals. Octofan lifted the bar and swung the gate open. 'Burash ward you,' were his parting words as they quit his yard, following the track down to the road.

The sky was a soft blue, empty of cloud save to the northwest, where piling billows marked the line of the mountains, the sun a golden coin still low to the east. The irritation of the gaheen was replaced with a gentle breeze, pleasantly cooling, that rustled the grass verging the road, and magic seemed a thing of the night, driven off by the dawning of a bright new day. Birds sang from the trees dotting the rolling landscape, and high above them more flew, spiralling and swooping against the blue. There seemed no danger in that gentle countryside, though the land rolled and ridged in a manner that could hide riders between the folds, their presence unmarked until they chose to appear. Calandryll saw that Bracht rode with a hand close to the falchion's hilt, his eyes scanning the way ahead, turning in his saddle from time to time to study the road behind.

They saw only Denphat and Jedomus, who waved from a low hillside where they herded cattle back towards the farm, soon lost amongst the ridging. All morning, until they halted to rest the horses and eat, they saw no other sign of human life, only the scattered cattle and watchful hares, the birds above. Nor any other until late in the afternoon.

The sun westered towards its setting, shadows long across the land and the air still, silent but for the buzz of insects. Birds still hung above them and ahead they saw a descending spiral, falling from the azure to a place hidden behind a ridge. The road ran up the eastern face, through a small stand of timber where black birds perched, lost to view after that: Bracht reined in.

'Carrion eaters.' He pointed towards the black column, eyes narrowed in suspicion and distaste. 'We'd best ride cautious. And not straight on.'

He turned his mount off the road, cutting through the high grass parallel to the ridge. Calandryll followed, glancing warily at his chest, where the red stone hung. It remained dull: no hint of fire warned of wizardry, and he decided that if peril lay ahead it was danger of man's making, not occult origin. He set a hand to his sword's hilt, easing the blade in the scabbard, ready to draw. He saw Bracht halt and brought his own mount alongside. The Kern gestured him down, passing him the reins of both animals.

'Wait here,' Bracht's voice was low, a murmur lost in the rustling of the breeze, 'whilst I climb the ridge.'

He frowned a protest, but the freesword's hand gestured him to silence.

'I am paid to guard you. Perhaps Sathoman waits on the other side; perhaps there is nothing more than a dead cow - but those birds come down to feed on something, and I'll take a look. Wait for my signal. And if it's to run, get on that horse and ride back to Octofan's holding! Do you understand?'

Calandryll nodded and watched as the Kern began to climb the gentle slope. He dropped on his belly as he approached the crest, worming his way upwards until he was able to peer over, to see whatever lay beyond. After a while he rose, beckoning Calandryll forwards. Calandryll mounted and urged his horse up the slope, leading Bracht's. The Kern walked down to meet him, taking the reins. Both animals began to fret, sawing at their bridles with flattened ears and rolling eyes, snorting nervously.

'Dismount,' Bracht ordered curtly.

Calandryll obeyed.

'What is it?'

Bracht simply led the way to the crest and inclined his head to the hollow beyond.

'The blood's fresh enough they can smell it. Hold firm lest the beast run.'

Calandryll felt his horse begin to plunge as the Kern spoke, fighting it to a standstill even as he stared, not sure the trembling he felt came from the animal or himself.

Ravens and crows came down out of the sky to strut the trampled grass about the road where it dipped between the ridges. The air was loud with their croaking, the grass shadowed by their wings. They moved amongst the corpses of some twenty men and as many horses, perching on arrow-feathered chests, bloodied armour, tearing and tugging, too intent on their feasting to attend to the watchers on the ridge. Swords jutted like grave markers from the ground, as did lances with scarlet pennants a brighter red than the gore that decorated the animals and the dead soldiers. Calandryll saw that they wore the scarlet pugrees of lictor's men, the same conical helms and leathery breastplates as Phillomen's guards.

'What happened here?' he asked softly, grimacing as the breeze shifted a fraction, carrying the charnel reek to his nostrils.

'I think perhaps Cenophus came looking for taxes; or Sathoman,' Bracht answered. 'I think he found Sathoman.'

He walked a little way along the ridgetop, towards the trees, pointing.

'See? There, where those two lie?' He indicated two soldiers fallen close to the road, close to arrow-studded horses. 'They were the scouts. Ambushed from the cover of the trees. Thirty, forty men hid to either side of the road. As the soldiers approached the hollow, they attacked.'

Calandryll followed his pointing hand, seeing trampled grass, dung busy with flies beyond the bodies. Bracht brought his hands together.

'They struck from both sides at once. With archers in the timber. Those,' he indicated three men fallen halfway up the slope, five others some distance off along the hollow to the north, 'tried to escape. The rest had no chance.'

'They were slaughtered,' whispered Calandryll.

'Their officer was careless,' said Bracht. 'He led them into ambush.'

Calandryll tore his gaze from the carnage to the Kern's face. It was cold, unmoved by the massacre. He shuddered: Bracht had likely seen such sights before; he had not and he was abruptly aware of the sickly-sweet odour of recent death, the sound the beaks made as they ripped at flesh. He spat and swallowed, fighting the bile that rose in his throat.

'This happened no more than yesterday,' Bracht said.

'How can you know?'

He hoped his voice came out steadier than it sounded, willing himself to look, not to turn and vomit.

'They're still fresh. There's meat still on them.'

Calandryll groaned.

'What do we do?'

'Likely it was Sathoman attacked them. We've not met him on the road, so he's either between us and Kesham-vaj or out there.' Bracht indicated the rolling landscape, the hollows shadowed now as the sun fell lower in the sky. 'We seek to avoid him. Wait here.'

Before Calandryll had opportunity to protest the Kern was in the saddle, moving at a trot along the ridge. He paused amongst the trees, his presence bringing a chorus of alarm from the bloated crows, walking slow across the dirt of the road, then on. Calandryll clutched his nervous mount, nervous himself now, anticipating a return of the ambushers, wishing Bracht would return. He watched as the black-clad man went down the ridge and up the farther side, his worry growing as Bracht disappeared from sight, his relief expressing itself in a long sigh as the Kern showed again, on the road, where it topped the ridge.

He halted on the crest and waved Calandryll over.

Calandryll mounted and brought his animal at an angle down the slope, unwilling to ride in amongst the bodies. Crows and ravens screamed protest as he passed by them, some taking flight, most too bloated to fly. He reached the road and joined Bracht on the crest.

'They're ahead of us.' The Kern pointed to the south-west. 'They grouped along the hollow and took the road towards Kesham-vaj.'

'Dera!' Calandryll gasped. 'They lie between us and the town?'

'Perhaps,' Bracht shrugged. 'Perhaps they turned off. Octofan said Fayne Keep lies to the north.'

'Please Dera - please Burash! - they've done that,' Calandryll hoped.

'I'll know if they have,' Bracht said. 'Or if they haven't. Meanwhile, we'd best move on.'

Calandryll was more than happy to accept the suggestion: he wanted to be a long way from the bloody hollow when they made camp.

The horses seemed of like mind, for they rose eagerly to a canter, calming only when the scene of slaughter was well to the rear. By then the sun was close to its setting, the sky darkening in the east, lit by the globe of a full moon. The dark spiral that marked the hollow was lost against the encroaching night and Calandryll felt a little easier until Bracht slowed his mount to a walk, staring up.

'I think,' he said slowly, 'that we are observed.'

Calandryll craned his head back, seeing only the open sky and the solitary shape of a bird hanging there: he shook his head, frowning.

'Since we left the holding we've seen birds overhead,' Bracht said. 'All day. Now all are gone save that one.'

'So?' asked Calandryll.

'So night approaches and birds roost,' Bracht replied. 'But not that one.'

Calandryll looked up. The bird still hung there, wings spread to catch the updraft. He brought the red stone from under his shirt and said, 'It does not glow. It shows no sign of magic.'

'Even so,' Bracht looked around, 'tonight we keep a watch.'

They found a place where a timbered ridge curved sharply, the angled flanks providing cover on two sides, hiding them from the road. Bracht set Calandryll to gathering wood while he scouted the environs, returning to announce the absence of obvious danger, crouching to shape a small fire, not large enough that its glow might be seen above the banks. Shadow filled the declivity and above, the sky grew dark. Calandryll peered upwards, but if the bird Bracht had seen was there, it was lost against the burgeoning night.

'They're still ahead of us,' Bracht said, 'around forty men, holding to the road as if Kesham-vaj's their destination.'

'How far ahead?' Calandryll asked as the Kern struck tinder to the twigs, coaxing a little flame into life.

'A day.' Bracht shrugged, 'Perhaps two - they set an easy pace.'

Calandryll watched as he spilled water into a pot, added vegetables. Soon a simple stew bubbled, and cakes of journey bread baked over the fire.

'Why do they ride for Kesham-vaj?' he wondered. 'Surely brigands would not dare attack a town.'

Bracht stirred the pot, his face underlit by the flames, hard-planed, his blue eyes thoughtful.

'If that was Cenophus back there, perhaps Kesham-vaj stands undefended. In Mherut'yi, Philomen commanded no more than twenty men - perhaps all Kesham-vaj's soldiery died there on the road and Sathoman looks to invest the town.'

'Then Kesham-vaj is an obstacle,' Calandryll murmured. 'If Sathoman lays siege - or holds the town - he's not likely to grant us passage through.'

'No,' Bracht agreed, 'but the road's our swiftest way to Nhur-jabal and a detour will cost us time. You have that map Varent provided?'

Calandryll nodded and brought the chart from his satchel, spreading it close to the flames.

'The caravanserai is here.' He tapped the mark, tracing the dark line of the Tyrant's road, 'And the highway here. Kesham-vaj, here, then the road runs on to Nhur-jabal.'

'And these?' Bracht asked, indicating the thinner inscriptions that ringed the area. 'What do they tell you?'

Calandryll studied the markings. 'The land rises steadily,' he said. 'The caravanserai lies at the foot of a plateau. Kesham-vaj a little distance from the rim. The plateau spreads to here,' he traced a line, 'and then descends into hilly country before rising again to Nhur-jabal.'

'This is the road?' Bracht drew a finger along the darker line; Calandryll murmured an affirmative. 'Then if Sathoman posts men on the crest, they'll see us coming. Horsemen must be in clear sight; in arrow range. What's this?'

He tapped a shaded section that circled half the plateau's south-western perimeter.

'Woodland,' Calandryll said. 'With no trails marked.'

'And time needed to cross it,' grunted Bracht. 'Nhur-jabal is here?'

He set a fingertip on the point where the Kharmrhanna

thrust a spur into the heart of Kandahar.

'Yes,' Calandryll confirmed. 'See here? The road from Kesham-vaj runs arrow-straight to Nhur-jabal. The country between is broken - hills and woodland. There might well be trails, but they're not shown.'

Bracht grunted again, resting back on his heels, staring into the fire.

'We'll chance the road,' he decided after a while, 'but by night. With any luck, Sathoman will be occupied with the town and we'll gain the highland unnoticed. Then ride around.'

'And if they sight us?' Calandryll wondered.

Bracht grinned.

'Then we turn tail and run. Back down the slope and then south to circle through the woods. With a town to take, they'll likely not bother chasing two men.'

He seemed satisfied with his plan, and with no better strategy to offer, Calandryll nodded agreement. The Kern tasted his stew and pronounced it ready: they ate and Bracht suggested Calandryll take the first watch.

The night was warm enough, and the fire, small though it was, cheerful. Calandryll settled with his sword across his knees, watching the stars spread out above. From time to time he glanced at the red stone, but it gave no sign of nearby magic and he decided that the bird Bracht had seen was only that: a bird. The revulsion he had felt at sight of the massacre faded, and in time he grew bored, rising to climb the ridge and study the night-black land spread before him. There was no sign of life, no fires burning to mark the men ahead, nor sounds to warn of danger, and he returned to the fire and his vigil, waking Bracht at the agreed hour.

The Kern roused him while grey dawn still filled the declivity, passing him a mug of tea and a bowl of warmed-over stew. They ate and saddled their animals, returning to the road as the sun eased its way above the horizon.

'It's still there.'

Bracht pointed upwards, to where the solitary speck hung, seemingly motionless, against the brightening sky. Calandryll narrowed his eyes, seeking to define the shape, but it was too high, no more than a hint of wings, a fan-shaped tail. He checked the talisman, but still it gave no indication of sorcery, and he could only shrug, wondering if his companion was overly cautious.

By noon he began to share Bracht's doubts, for the bird still paced them and it seemed that any normal avian must surely have lost interest by now.

That night they camped by a stream, sheltered by willows, again taking turns on watch, and as dawn broke the bird was there again, an irritation now, setting the hairs on Calandryll's neck to prickling with the feeling of eyes upon him.

It remained as they sighted the ruins of the caravanserai, fire-blackened by the roadside. The white stone of the walls was scorched where flame had scoured the interior, the roof fallen in, the windows dark pits, their sills smeared with melted glass like frozen tears. Weeds overtook the yard, and grass, trod down by horses, their dung not yet so old the flies failed to gather, the well poisoned by a long-rotted carcass. Bracht entered the desolate place on foot, emerging to announce that Sathoman's men - if it was them they followed - had camped within the tumbled stones a night past. Calandryll studied the wreckage, wondering what manner of man this rebel lord was, that he would destroy a travellers' resting place, even to the extent of fouling the well. It was a mournful relic in a lonely land, and he was glad when they had left it behind.

By late afternoon they saw the plateau bulking ahead. The road approached the foot and then turned, winding in a zig-zag up the scarp, wide enough to permit wagons to pass, paved for most of its way, and all of it under easy bowshot from any archers posted at the summit. The cloud they had seen billowing over the Kharm-rhanna had drawn closer, offering some chance of obfuscation of the waning moon. Bracht reined in amongst a stand of slender birches, their pale leaves rustled by the wind that drove the cloud, studying the road.

'I'd sooner the moon was gone,' he remarked, 'but if all goes well, that cloud should aid us. We'll wait here 'til full dark and then go on. Best get what sleep you can.'

Calandryll unsaddled his horse and tethered it, stretching on the grass, listening to the buzz of insects, staring up through the trees. The bird was still there, a silent, omnipresent observer, but when he turned to inform Bracht, the Kern was asleep. He shrugged and sighed, too nervous himself to find such easy respite.

As dusk fell they ate cold meat and journey bread, secured their packs, and sacrificed a blanket to the wrapping of bits and buckles, the muffling of the hooves. The promised cloud drifted across the rim of the plateau, silvered by the moon, but laying a filigree pattern of shadows and shifting light over the way ahead.

'Slow and quiet,' Bracht warned as they mounted, 'and when we close on the crest, we go on foot. Be ready to silence your horse.'

Calandryll nodded, dry-mouthed, and followed the freesword out from the trees, towards the ascent ahead. By night it looked far longer, a killing ground for bowmen, and he wondered hopelessly if they had not done better - wiser, at least - to chance the delays of a detour. No, he told himself, pushing pessimism and fear aside, they must reach Kharasul and take ship for Gessyth as swift as they might. If Azumandias had sent the mysterious woman to take them - and she had survived the magical storm - her warboat was likely already closing on Cape Vishat'yi, and if she should reach Kharasul before them ... He pushed that fear aside, too: danger lay ahead, likely waiting for them, and he must concentrate on the task in hand, without digression.

He rode after Bracht, matching the Kern's easy pace. The road angled upwards, winding to left and right, the stones of its paving grooved where wagon wheels had cut the blocks, the blanket-swathed hooves thudding dully. Small trees and bushes thrust out from the scarp, affording some small measure of cover, the wind stronger, scudding cloud in welcome streamers across the moon so that they moved spectral, lit and then shadowed, like phantom riders toiling towards some waiting destiny. It seemed a breath-held eternity, each moment lived in anticipation of a warning shout, a bowstring's twang, the whistle of an arrow, the flash of pain that would tell of shaft finding target. And yet, in a way he did not properly understand, it was easier than facing magic. Sorcery, for all he used Lord Varent's stone, remained a mystery, a dark, unknown thing. He had faced the demons, back in Lysse, a lifetime ago it seemed, and his stomach had emptied after; and that thing in Octofan's barn, though it had offered no harm, had left him unnerved. There was that element of the unknowable in sorcery, the notion that dark powers might rise to do far worse than harm his flesh. Now, as he climbed behind Bracht, he though only of physical hurt, of attack against which he might, no matter in how small a way, take some measure of defence. He rode on, halting when the Kern halted, dismounting to take the reins of both horses as Bracht continued on foot.

Time passed, the wind chill at this elevation, and Bracht returned, a solidity emerging from the darkness, hair and face and clothes all better suited to such work than Calandryll's, his boots silent as he came up, setting his mouth close to Calandryll's ear.

'There were two guards.' *Were* two? 'The rest are camped beyond, outside the town. We crest the rim and ride south, around.'

He passed the Kern the reins and they led the horses up the final slope, the road angling at the last past a great stone pillar to devolve upon the flatland of the plateau. Beside the pillar, resting against the stone as if at ease, sat a man, a bow across his outthrust legs, his chin on his chest. Moonlight lit him briefly and Calandryll saw the dark stain that covered his chest. Across the way, between a clump of bushes and a windblown tree was another, lounging, it seemed, with his back against the tree, an arm flung careless over a bough. A closer inspection revealed loose, lifeless legs, the string of his bow wound supportive about the trunk, the same dark stain beneath the dropped chin.

'You killed them both,' he whispered.

'Yes. Otherwise they'd have seen us.' Bracht favoured him with a curious stare, as though he had stated the obvious. 'Now come; this way.'

He turned from the two dead brigands as the Kern moved along the rim of the plateau, not yet daring to mount, Sathoman's men too close to risk a gallop. Kesham-vaj stood some little distance off, a huddle of low, stone houses, similar to Mherut'yi, but larger, and lit far more brightly by the fires that burned inside and those beyond the buildings. In a ring around the town the brigands had erected tents, and bonfires, invisible from below, but atop the plateau providing sufficient light he could see the horses tethered on picket lines and the groups of men who watched, waiting like hungry wolves for their prey to weaken. Sparks cascaded upwards, incongruously cheerful, and he heard voices raised, shouting across the distance between the fires and the town.

'We must walk around,' Bracht's whisper tore him from his study. 'Likely most of the night. But by dawn we should be clear. If they see us, mount and run westwards.'

He nodded and trailed after the Kern, through the scrub that decorated the rim, glancing constantly at the fires. He was unaware of the red stone at his throat, too intent on moving in silence, too aware of the brigands' proximity, to notice when the stone began to glow.

He felt its heat in the instant that light burst before them, as though some separate bonfire was lit directly in their path, smelling almonds then and cursing as his horse shied, rearing and screaming, seeing Bracht's animal do the same, the freesword clinging grimly to the reins, falchion in hand even as he swung into the saddle. He felt a hot wind gust, hurling him to the ground, hooves flailing above him as the horse fought free of his grip and charged madly into the night. He saw Bracht turn, fighting his panicked animal, and lift from the saddle as if plucked by some giant, unseen hand.

The Kern thudded to the ground and the same wind sent him rolling, over and over until he struck Calandryll, then the gusting shifted, blowing from above, downwards, pressing them flat, helpless against its force. The timbre of the shouting about the bonfires altered as men came running, and the light faded, the wind dying as threatening swords ringed them and a mild voice announced in faultless Lyssian, 'I have been waiting for you. I am called Anomius.'

ELEVEN

'INTRIGUING,' Anomius continued, as if no time had passed, no cords been bound about their wrists or angry hands dragged them to the ruins of a building, once a cowshed by its smell, lit by the glow of the fires outside, all shifting shadow within, 'a warrior of Cuan na'For and a young noble, unless I miss my guess, of Lysse travelling together. With a magic stone, a small fortune in gold coin, and a map of Gessyth that purports to show the location of fabled Tezin-dar. Intriguing. Absolutely intriguing.'

He paused, studying them speculatively, a small man, unimpressive in his soiled black robe, strands of age-yellowed hair escaping from beneath his headdress to coil about a sallow face in which watery eyes sat too close to a bulbous nose. They stared back, not speaking, resting against the wall.

'Adventurers? Seekers after the lost city's gold? Or something else? Rumour has it that Tezin-dar holds secrets forgotten since the gods fought. Power then? Do you seek the grammaryes of the Old Ones?' He smiled, pale lips exposing stained teeth, eyes twinkling with something that might have been amusement - or madness - speaking again without awaiting reply, more interested, it seemed, in h own musings than in any response. 'And yet not versed in the occult arts - no warlocks, for sure. Are stone and map stolen, then? Trophies? Happenstance thefts from some Lyssian mage, taken up in hopes of fortune? And the coin - from the same source?' He chuckled softly, a twittering, avian sound, and shook his head. 'That stone might have saved you, boy, had you known better how to use it. It warned you of my little watcher, did it not? Back there in the cowherd's barn? You frightened him, you know, for he's a timid creature. But my bird you could not frighten. Did you see him, watching you, his eyes mine? No matter: you are come here and now I shall have answers of you.'

'Arrhiman and Laphyl are dead.'

A figure blocked the doorway, hiding the light, the voice angry. Anomius shrugged carelessly and stepped aside.

'My lord Sathoman ek'Hennem, Lord of the Fayne.'

'Burash!' Sathoman grunted, 'Give me light. Am I a bat that I can see in the dark?'

'I forget, my lord, that you lack my ability.'

Anomius raised a hand and brilliance sparkled in his palm, spreading to illuminate the shed. Calandryll stared at the renegade lord. Sathoman was huge, perhaps the largest man he had ever seen, his head close to what remained of the roof. He stood bareheaded, a mane of reddish hair falling about a dark and furious face, mingling with beard and thick moustaches so that he appeared wild, like some beast, or changeling. Heavy brows overhung deep-set eyes, the black glinting in the light of the wizard's magical torch. He wore a cuirasse of dragon's hide, red as his hair, and vambraces of the same hue on muscle-corded arms, greaves on columnar legs. A longsword was sheathed on his waist, and a hand axe. He eyed the prisoners:

Calandryll felt as must a sheep, inspected by a butcher.

'Kill them.'

Sathoman turned away, halted by the wizard's soft voice.

'Unwise, my lord; yet.'

'What?'

The great head swung to face Anomius, hairy lips parted in a snarl of animal ferocity. The wizard smiled, untroubled.

'My lord, I warned you of their coming. Arrhiman and Laphyl were careless - they should not have let the Kern get close.'

'The Kern slew them? Then kill him. Have your way with the other.'

'I think not,' Anomius said. 'I sense a joining here - a shared purpose - and something else. I think the one useless without the other.'

'Riddles,' Sathoman barked. 'Burash's eyes, mage, why must you always talk in riddles?'

'It is my way,' Anomius replied, unabashed.

'And it is my way to execute those who slay my people,' roared the giant. 'Arrhiman and Laphyl lie with slit throats and I've a town to take. Burash, man, we've planned this long enough! It was your magic brought that cursed lictor out where we could kill him and now I need you to pave a way into Kesham-vaj. Kill them - or watch as I do it.'

He drew his sword. The blade glittered in the unnatural light: Calandryll felt his stomach clench, his mouth dry. From the corner of his eye he saw Bracht tense and knew that even bound, the Kern would not go easily.

'My lord - wait!' Anomius needed to crane back his head to meet the giant's eyes, but in his manner there was nothing of subservience; rather, Calandryll sensed, he focussed his will on Sathoman. 'Now or tomorrow, what does it matter when they die? We have them and they shall not escape. You've my word on that – and you know my word is good.'

Beneath the mild tone there was a hint of steel: Sathoman faltered, chewing at his moustaches. Calandryll licked his lips.

'They offer no threat, not now,' the wizard said. 'Kesham-vaj shall be yours, and from Kesham-vaj you'll hold the road. Command the way into the Fayne. You'll hold the Tyrant at bay - Kesham-vaj's the gate to the eastern Reaches, just as I told you. I'll give you Kesham-vaj; and Mherut'yi, after. You'll rule the Fayne undisputed, and all the eastern coast from the Shann desert to Mhazomul. These two are no threat to that.'

The sword lowered. Sathoman glowered at the diminutive mage; then sheathed the blade.

'Why plead for them?'

'Not for their lives, my lord. I plead for a little time, no more. I'd know why a Lyssian and a Kern travel Kandahar. Indulge my curiosity - it shall cost you nothing, and perhaps gain you some advantage.'

'You'll give me Kesham-vaj?'

'Within days, my lord. My word on it.'

The giant grunted; shrugged.

'After ...' Anomius smiled, 'Kill them at your will.'

Sathoman nodded slowly, shaggy head turning to settle angry eyes on the prisoners. 'So be it, mage. They're yours for the moment. But I'd make an example of them.'

'Of them and Kesham-vaj, both, my lord.' Anomius inclined his head slightly. Sathoman favoured him with a brief, feral smile and spun on his heel, striding into the night. The wizard returned his attention to Calandryll and Bracht.

'So impatient - all blood and fire, like his father before him. Burash knows, it took me long enough to persuade him to this plan and with success in sight he wants it now. Always now! He'd slay you and regret the loss later - if regret were in his nature.'

He sighed sadly, shaking his head as if discussing the behaviour of a wilful child, folding his hands inside the voluminous sleeves of his robe, for all the world like a pedagogue.

'But we have a little time and much to learn. Shall we commence with names? Who are you?'

Calandryll stared at him, confused by his manner. Anomius clicked tongue against teeth. Bracht said, 'Do you not know, wizard? Does your power not extend to so simple a thing?'

Anomius sighed again, his parchment features mournful.

'The folk of Cuan na'For were ever obstinate. You've witnessed what I can do - would you have me draw out your names with magic? You might not enjoy the experience.'

'I take no joy of bonds or threats of death,' Bracht snarled defiantly.

'So be it.'

Anomius withdrew a hand from his sleeve. Levelled a finger tipped with a blunt, chipped nail at the Kern, and murmured soft words. Bracht gasped, mouth opening. Calandryll felt the red stone pulse heat against his chest, aware of its glow even as he stared, aghast, at his comrade. Bracht struggled against the sorceror's will: his lips drew back from gritted teeth, tendons standing out along his neck, sweat on cheeks and brow, a strangled growling that gradually shaped words bursting unwillingly from his straining throat.

'I am ... Bracht ... ni Errhyn ... of ... the clan ... Asyth ... of ... Cuan na'For.'

'Excellent,' murmured Anomius, lowering his hand.

Bracht coughed, spat, his chest heaving.

'And you?'

The warlock turned to Calandryll.

'I am Calandryll,' he said quickly, seeing no point in

struggle against that power, 'late of Secca.'

Anomius frowned.

'Your family?'

'I am outcast,' he said. 'I have no family.'

'Come,' said Anomius gently, 'we all have family. To whom were you born?'

'Deny him!' Bracht rasped. 'Fight him! We're dead once he's done.'

The wizard swung a negligent hand in the Kern's direction and Bracht shouted, head slamming back against the rough stone of the wall. He began to tremble, palsied, spine arching, his legs thrusting straight, heels drumming furiously against the dirty floor. Spittle flecked his lips and the whites of his eyes showed bright, surrounding the blue. Anomius closed his hand in a fist and Bracht screamed, back bending until he was supported on heels and head alone. It seemed his spine must snap, or his heart burst.

'No!' Calandryll yelled. 'I'll tell you!'

Anomius nodded and gestured, and Bracht slumped, panting, stretched on the floor.

'Calandryll den Karynth. My father is Bylath, Domm of Secca.'

Interest sparked in the wizard's small eyes. His head cocked, bird-like, to one side, a finger stroking his turgescent nose.

'So, the son of Secca's Domm. But outcast, you say?'

'Yes,' Calandryll nodded, eyes flicking from the gasping Bracht to the wizard, 'My father would make me a priest - I fled that fate with my comrade. We took ship to Kandahar to escape. The money, the stone - I stole them.'

Watery eyes came closer, suspicious, the warlock's finger raised in mute threat.

'And the map? How came you by a map men say does not exist?'

'I stole that, too,' he extemporized. 'I was ... am ... a

scholar. I'd read of Tezin-dar and thought to seek the lost city. To win fame.'

Anomius sniffed noisily, finger extending to touch Calandryll's chin, tilt back the head. Then the mage winced, snatching back his hand as though from unseen flame, eyes hooding as they studied the young man.

'I am not sure I believe you. I sense occult power in you, but no matching knowledge.'

'I am no sorcerer,' he said quickly.

'No,' Anomius agreed, 'were you magician, you'd not have fallen so easily to my snare. But still ... you hold things back. Tell me about this stone.'

'I stole it,' he repeated. 'From a palace magician.'

Again the warlock's tongue clicked against his teeth. He shook his head, levelling his finger.

'Tell me the truth.'

Calandryll felt a shock akin to buffetting wind. It seemed that probing fingers explored the contours of his brain, the touch urging truth, softly, but threat behind the caress. He felt his mouth open unbidden, his tongue move to shape the words. Then he felt the stone grow warm against his chest, red glow spreading about his face. The pressure inside his skull eased and was gone. Anomius frowned.

'So.' His voice was thoughtful; soft, like a serpent's hiss. 'So, the stone protects you. And well - I cannot touch it, nor you. Yet, at least. In time, who knows? Meanwhile, your comrade enjoys no such protection - shall you witness his suffering in silence? Shall you watch him die? I sense a bond between you - linked destinies. Shall he be the key that loosens your tongue?'

He pointed at Bracht. Calandryll said, 'Slay him and I've no reason to speak.'

The wizard chuckled, the sound obscene.

'I need not slay him, Calandryll den Karynth. Only turn him a little on the spit of agony. I think his screams might well unlock you.'

'A hired man?' Calandryll struggled to make his tone scornful. 'A Kern freesword? He's a mercenary; a mere bodyguard. And one who led me into your trap. Why should I care for his suffering?'

'But you do,' said Anomius. 'I sense that - and no denial of yours persuades me otherwise. I think I'll put fire in his lungs and listen to his screaming a while. Or shall I melt his eyes? Which do you prefer to witness, Calandryll den Karynth?'

Desperately Calandryll sought some answer, some delaying tactic with which to forestall the warlock. He doubted neither Anomius's ability or intent: did he not speak, he would see Bracht writhe in agony, or die; yet to reveal their purpose in Kandahar seemed likely to end their quest here, in a dung-reeking cowshed. Did Anomius but grasp that what they sought was the Arcanum, surely he would seek the book for himself, or ally with Azumandias: it seemed already clear that he had scant concern for human suffering. He needed time; his mind raced, close to panic, but time was not a commodity the warlock offered.

Until a brigand appeared in the doorway, glancing warily at the prisoners, eyeing the wizard nervously.

'Lord Sathoman asks that you attend him, mage.'

'Why?'

Anomius turned to face the man, his question mildly put, but still prompting the brigand to step back a pace.

'The defenders make a sally - Lord Sathoman would have you deal with them. An example, he said.'

Anomius sighed, head swinging to face Calandryll again.

'It would appear our ... conversation ... must wait. While I am gone, think on what you've seen; and what I can do.' He waved the messenger back, pausing in the doorway to mutter a spell. Calandryll felt the stone warm briefly; smelled almonds. 'This place is bound by magic. Do not attempt to leave it, on peril of your lives.

Remember that Sathoman will treat you unkinder than I.'

He walked away, leaving them in the shadows. Calandryll sighed his relief and looked to where Bracht lay.

'Are you hurt?'

It seemed inadequate; Bracht grunted, forced a grin.

'No. Though I'd not suffer that again. You?'

Calandryll shook his head.

'It seems the stone protects me.' He studied the Kern's face. 'But if he makes good his threat ...'

'A hired man?' Bracht got his legs under him, wriggling up the wall to a sitting position. 'A mere bodyguard?'

'I could think of nothing else. I thought he might leave you be.'

Bracht snorted grim laughter.

'Sadly, not. The cursed wizard saw through that. I think in time he'll have his answers, by one means or another.'

'Should I tell him,' Calandryll mused, 'what then? What might he do?'

'Slay us both, I think,' Bracht said. 'The man's mad. Likely he'd take the map and seek the Arcanum for himself.'

'Would Sathoman let him go? It seems this would-be lord needs his magic.'

Bracht shook his head: 'You heard Anomius - Sathoman seeks to establish himself as Lord of the Fayne. It seems Kesham-vaj's the gateway to the east. Sathoman takes the town to command the road, and once established here it's likely more dissidents will flock to his cause. He takes Mherut'yi and commands the coast - it's civil war we see fomenting and the next step must be to seize the Tyrant's crown. Sathoman will not release the mage.'

'Then if we told Sathoman,' Calandryll suggested.

'He'd have no reason to hold us. We'd die.'

'And if I refuse to tell him, you die.'

'We face a quandary.'

Bracht pushed awkwardly to his feet, crossing to the doorway. Calandryll joined him, warning 'Remember his magic.'

The Kern nodded grimly. 'I've reason enough. But I'd see what goes on.'

Together they peered into a night that aged towards dawn. Beyond the encircling tents the light of the besiegers' fires revealed a town unwalled, but barricaded, carts and wagons, furniture, barrels, anything portable, piled in jumbled heaps between the houses, blocking the entry points. The party they had followed down the Tyrant's road had been no more than a skirmishing band, for Kesham-vaj was ringed with a horde of armed and armoured men. They were spread all round, but where the road entered the town they clustered thickest and it was at that point Anomius went to work.

A group bearing shields moved forwards, the sorcerer at the centre, marching slowly towards a knot of defenders come out from behind their blockade.

'They sought to stampede the horses.' Bracht ducked his head to where the animals fretted on the picket lines, snorting and stamping, made nervous by the fires and the sounds of battle. 'They failed.'

Calandryll saw that the defenders retreated under a hail of arrows that ceased on a word from Anomius. The wizard raised both hands and the shield wall parted, the little black-robed figure stepping out, careless of the danger; or supremely confident of his own invulnerability. He stood for a moment with hands held high and then fire blossomed in the air above him. It drifted slowly forwards, growing. The defenders turned and began to run. The fire, still growing, swept quicker after them, catching them. Men screamed and fell. The fire reached the barricade and faltered, as though held back, then died. On the road charred shapes smouldered.

'Why not burn the barricade?' Calandryll wondered.

Bracht shrugged. 'Perhaps Sathoman wants the town intact. A burned ruin's little good for a stronghold,' he suggested.

'But Anomius could surely use other spells.' Calandryll stared at the sorcerer, speaking now with the giant rebel. 'I think perhaps Kesham-vaj is protected by magic.'

'Octofan said wizardry was outlawed by the Tyrant.'

Bracht hobbled to the rear of the shed, easing down the wall. Calandryll settled beside him, his expression thoughtful.

'Save for those sorcerers employed by the Tyrant himself. What if one were in Kesham-vaj? If it's so important a town - and the Tyrant knew, as he must, that Sathoman uses Anomius - perhaps he set a wizard to guard the place.'

'Perhaps,' Bracht allowed, 'but what good to us?'

'I don't know,' Calandryll admitted. 'Unless it means Sathoman's defeat.'

'Which will likely mean our deaths,' Bracht said. 'If Sathoman withdraws, I doubt he'll carry prisoners with him.'

Calandryll nodded, fighting to banish fear, panic, the depression that threatened to overwhelm him. He sought calm, to still his mind and *think*, to impose scholarly logic on his racing thoughts. Swords would not see them clear of this impasse, so reason was all he had left: he must use it to find a way out.

'Anomius knows I lie,' he said slowly, seeking to use the words themselves to unravel his half-formed thoughts, 'and if I continue to lie, he'll torture you.'

Bracht began to protest, but Calandryll shook his head for silence.

'Listen - we've no means of escaping save that the warlock or Sathoman release us, and they're not likely to grant that boon. But Anomius is interested in the map. Perhaps that's the key to unlock this trap.'

'How so?' Bracht asked. 'Tell him of our quest and he'll either take the map for himself - and kill us - or laugh at our foolishness - and kill us.'

'Perhaps; perhaps not.' Calandryll frowned, concentrating. 'He spoke of forgotten grammaryes, and why should he aid Sathoman save in lust for power? He's cast his lot with a rebel lord who seeks to rule the Fayne and likely - as you said! - all Kandahar. Why do that unless he, too, seeks power? And if he does, then surely the secrets of Tezin-dar must offer him powers undreamt of.'

'You'd give him the means to raise the Mad God? I'd as soon hand the book to Varent.'

Bracht stared at Calandryll, eyes narrowed. Calandryll shook his head.

'Not that, but perhaps the promise of unimagined power.'

'And warrant of our deaths with it.'

'Not if he believes he needs us. He cannot touch the stone, remember. And the stone wards me from his magic. Perhaps it shields me enough that I may ensnare him - promise him the grammaryes of Tezin-dar in return for our freedom. Persuade him that he needs us; that he's better served joining us than aiding Sathoman.'

'That's a desperate plan,' Bracht said softly.

'I can think of no other,' Calandryll returned.

'Nor I,' the Kern admitted, 'but it's a snare that must surely leave us in his power - if he takes the bait.'

'It might at least see us clear of Sathoman,' Calandryll said. 'And whilst we remain here time passes - perhaps Azumandias finds a way to Tezin-dar.'

Bracht nodded, then hissed a warning. Calandryll turned to see Anomius approaching.

The wizard gestured at the doorway and stepped through, spilling light into the shed once more. Calandryll thought that perhaps his shoulders slumped a fraction; that perhaps the practice of magic tired him: certainly, he appeared less vital, and a petulant expression showed on the parchment features.

'So impatient,' he murmured, 'Now, now, now; always *now*. He will not wait and I must use magic where arrows would serve as well. I've promised him Kesham-vaj - you heard me promise that, did you not? but he'd have it now. Not tomorrow, not in time, but *now*!'

'The virtue of patience is a rare commodity,' Calandryll said.

'A philosopher?' Anomius cocked an inquisitive eyebrow. 'No doubt the benefit of your father's palace. You've an education, eh? These men of the ek'Hennem have so little. No more than bandits, were the truth told.'

'Why do you serve a hedge-lord?' Calandryll ventured. 'Surely the Tyrant himself would prize your allegiance?'

'A hedge-lord?' Anomius chuckled softly. 'Best not let him hear that, lad. But yes - of now he is little more than that. But after he's taken Kesham-vaj - ah, then he'll be more. Much more!'

'Tyrant, perhaps?' Calandryll asked.

Anomius stared at him, lips pursed, then smiled, nodding to himself, his mood brightening. He turned, calling for a stool to be brought, and settled himself before them, fussily arranging the folds of his grubby robe.

'My lord Sathoman ek'Hennem is a mighty warrior,' he declared when he was comfortable, his manner pedagogic again, 'men rally to him for what he is, not just the title. When his father died on the Stone Field it was young Sathoman - a youth no older than you at the time - who gathered the ek'Hennem army and swore to deny Iodrydus tenure of Fayne Keep. And he succeeded. Three times he withstood siege - aided, of course, by me! - and after that the Tyrant left him be. Now he rules the Fayne. Almost, at least: the Tyrant's lictors still lay claim to the towns, but that shall soon end. Once Kesham-vaj's fallen we'll hold the road. Take Mherut'yi and our back's protected - all the Fayne will acknowledge Sathoman. Mhazomul, Ghombalar, Vishat'yi we can take at leisure - isolate Nhur-jabal! Yes, I'll make Sathoman Tyrant of Kandahar before I'm done.'

He paused, scratching vigorously beneath his robe, his smile dreamy; demented.

'And that should answer your other question. Of course the Tyrant would prize my services - did he not put me to death for aiding the ek'Hennem cause - but then I should be merely one more sorcerer at court. When I install Sathoman as lord of all Kandahar I shall be paramount sorcerer. All Kandahar shall hail me and the Tyrant's puppet mages shall bow before me!'

'Why did you halt your fire at the barricade?' Calandryll wondered. 'Surely you could have razed the town?'

The warlock's expression darkened a fraction. He sniffed; rubbed at his bulbous nose.

'You saw that, eh? Why do you think?'

'Bracht said you'd have no use for a ruin.' Calandryll smiled apologetically, 'I wondered if perhaps there's magic in the town's defences.'

'Bracht is no fool.' Anomius glanced, nodding, in the Kern's direction. Kesham-vaj commands this highland and Sathoman has the bulk of his army here. Such a force needs a secure base - we need Kesham-vaj intact. As for magic - Yes, there's a wizard of some small ability in the town. It seems dead Cenophus learnt something of our plans and sent word to the Tyrant, who answered his lictor's request with a mage. I could, of course, overcome him, but likely our warring powers would destroy all Kesham-vaj. I prefer to whittle him down and present Sathoman with a town entire. It's a matter of time; no more than a few days.'

'But Sathoman grows impatient,' said Calandryll, encouraged by the wizard's loquacity.

'Always impatient,' Anomius nodded. 'Had I not counselled the division of his forces, he'd have all his army here. But - fortunately for him - he bows to my better judgement: by now Mherut'yi, too, is under siege.'

'Wise counsel,' Calandryll applauded.

'Yes,' Anomius agreed.

'You'll be the greatest sorcerer in Kandahar,' Calandryll said. 'Perhaps in all the world.'

'Undoubtedly.' The wizard beamed; then frowned: 'Perhaps? How do you mean - perhaps?'

Calandryll paused, gathering his thoughts. He felt the bait taken, but the reeling in demanded great care. For all Anomius's pride, his overweening ambition, he was no fool to step careless into so flimsy a snare.

'I've thought on what you said, and I'd not see Bracht suffer,' he declared. 'I doubt that even protected by the stone I could deny you.'

'Wise,' Anomius murmured approvingly, 'that stone's a minor obstacle to one of my ability.'

'Indeed,' Calandryll nodded, 'Nor a thing to be damaged, for it's a key to power and set with protective magicks.'

The wizard's small eyes grew smaller still.

'Explain yourself, Calandryll den Karynth - I find you interest me.'

'I lied earlier, just as you surmised. I thought to deceive you, but clearly that's impossible.'

'Quite,' said Anomius.

'I did not steal the stone - it was given me by a sorcerer of Lysse. Lord Varent den Tarl. He helped me escape Secca and in return I, and Bracht, undertook a quest on his behalf. You've seen the map - would you study it again?'

Anomius's sallow features glowed with fascination. He gestured at where their gear was tossed and the satchel rose in the air, floating to his hands. He drew out the chart, smoothing it over his knees.

'You know, of course, of the cartographer Orwen,' Calandryll said.

'Of course,' Anomius agreed. A fraction too readily, Calandryll thought, as if the ugly little man sought to conceal ignorance.

'Who was commissioned by the Domm, Thomus, to make a map of Gessyth. A map showing the location of Tezin-dar.'

'You say this is it?' Anomius tapped the sheet. 'This is no ancient map, but something new.'

'A copy,' Calandryll said quickly. 'A copy of the chart I took from Secca's archives, and another. The two combined show the way to Tezin-dar. I drew it myself.'

'And this Varent den Tarl employed you and the Kern to go there? To what purpose? Why not journey there himself?'

'Not all magicians have your courage,' Calandryll said. 'Lord Varent prefers to remain safe in Lysse whilst we undertake his mission.'

Anomius snorted contempt.

'And should you succeed, what are you to fetch him?'

Now was the moment; Calandryll heard it in the warlock's voice, saw it in his eyes. He licked his lips, knowing that his life and Bracht's hung on the precarious thread of his words: knew that death was the price of failure. The balance was delicate: to speak of the Arcanum was to give the mage too much, to risk the entry of another player in the world-shattering game - and one who, at the moment, held the upper hand - but he must offer Anomius something, some prize of sufficient worth he might be tempted from Sathoman's service, tempted to free them. He was unaccustomed to such manoeuvreing, to this juggling of truth and half-truth and deceits, but he must find the bait with which to hook the wizard's interest. And swiftly, for their lives depended on it.

'There is a grimoire,' he said carefully, feigning reluctance, 'that Lord Varent claims is as old as time. A book of grammaryes written when the world was young and the Elder Gods ruled. He believes it lies in Tezin-dar; he believes it contains forgotten spells. He said that the wizard who owns it must wield power unimaginable.'

'Ah!' Anomius raised a hand, halting him. 'I repeat - why should he entrust you two with such a mission?'

'I speak and read the Old Tongue,' Calandryll said; quickly, 'And so am able to read the map.'

'The Old Tongue?' Anomius leant forwards, elbow on knee, chin on hand. 'That's a long-forgotten art.'

'And yet I can,' Calandryll returned, 'Do you?'

Anomius shook his head, irritation sparking in his eyes. Calandryll shrugged as best he could with hands bound at his back.

'Because I speak it, and because Lord Varent lacks your daring, he preferred that I should make the journey on his behalf. Bracht accompanies me as body-guard.' He saw irritation replaced with interest again and continued swiftly, 'The one half of the map I *did* steal - from the archives of my father's palace - my father would have me be a priest and Lord Varent offered the better bargain: to bring him that half of the map that he might match it to the half he owned, and he would bring me safe out of Secca. Yet with the way to Tezin-dar shown, he was reluctant to venture on the journey himself. He urged me to undertake it - with Bracht - and bring him the book.'

'He would trust you to fetch it?' Anomius's yellow brow wrinkled, a finger rubbing at his swollen nose. 'Would he not fear you'd keep it to yourself?'

'To what end? I have no knowledge of magic - as you

discerned yourself,' Calandryll said. 'If I possess any occult talent, it is unknown to me.'

'And yet you wear a sorcerer's stone,' said Anomius.

'Given me by Lord Varent. I have no skill with magic.'

Anomius smiled as if pleased to have scored that minor victory. 'This Varent would seem a coward,' he murmured, 'to send others out to seek what he desires. But no matter - tell me of the stone.'

'Protection, so he told me.' Calandryll said, forcing doubt, confusion, aside to concentrate on his deception, 'as you saw. Save by the application of great magic, it may not be removed from me.'

'That much I recognise,' Anomius agreed. 'Though I could do it, the magicks required would render the stone useless. And it has another purpose, no?'

'I think you must be a greater mage than Lord Varent,' Calandryll flattered. 'Aye - the stone will lead me to the grimoire. And when it has, Lord Varent said the book is guarded by magic, against which the stone shall furnish protection.'

'So,' Anomius said gently, his voice soft, 'if what you say is true, you are the lodestone that points to the book.'

'Aye,' Calandryll said eagerly.

'And the book offers the mage who owns it power unlimited.'

'So Lord Varent said.'

'Yet to obtain the book, you are needed.'

'Aye.'

'But not the Kern.'

Calandryll's answer froze on his readied tongue. Like a fish taken by the hook, Anomius was caught, but still he fought, still he was cunning: still the fisherman must use all his wiles to reel him in.

'He is.'

Think! Buy time, but *think*! Give this dangerous little man no reason to slay Bracht - *think*!

'We are bonded,' he said; slowly, then faster as logic came to his aid. Logic and an extension of the tenuous web of half-truths he wove: the whole truth now. 'You saw that yourself - our destinies are linked. In Secca I consulted a spaewife - Reba was her name; she was blind - and she foretold that I should encounter a true companion: Bracht. She scried an augury, that we should travel together. I think that to separate us must be to break that web she discerned and halt the journey. Without Bracht, I shall not find the grimoire.'

'I sensed a joining,' Anomius admitted, 'and honest auguries are not to be trifled with.'

'And,' Calandryll added quickly, 'she said I should meet another. Might that be you?'

The watery eyes fastened on his face. Like leeches, he thought. Anomius said, 'Perhaps,' and he felt the line reel in a little further.

'I never trusted Varent.' That Bracht should speak surprised him: he turned towards the Kern. 'A man - wizard, or no - should take his own chances. Not skulk safe behind city walls whilst others risk their lives for his advantage. I've more respect for a man who faces his foes.'

Like you, hung on the tail of the sentence. Anomius nodded. Calandryll licked dry lips. The shed filled up with silence as the wizard turned his colourless gaze from one to the other.

'What do you say?' he asked at last. 'Do you offer me this grimoire?'

The fish broke water, the line taut: heart pounding, Calandryll extended the net.

'I tell you only the truth - obviously, there is no hiding it from you. I say that we go to seek the grimoire in Tezin-dar. That it offers powers beyond a sorcerer's dreams - but that only we may find it.'

'Your loyalty to this Varent is somewhat ...' Anomius shrugged, '... tenuous.'

'Lord Varent sleeps safe in Aldarin whilst we sit, bound, in a cowshed in Kandahar facing death. What would you do?'

'I'd not have entrusted a beardless youth and a Kern freesword in the first place,' Anomius said, 'But no matter. You say you speak and read the Old Tongue ... and you've that stone - You give me cause to ponder. A man faced with death is likely to make wild promises, but there's such in what you say that you shall live a little longer while I think on your future.'

He rose, black robe rustling, pausing at the shed's door.

'Best that you say nothing of this matter to any other.'

The watery eyes held a threat: Calandryll nodded, Bracht grunting agreement. Anomius quit the shed and the light died with his departure, revealing a sky no longer star-pocked, darkening into the ultimate nigrescence that prefaces dawn. Calandryll looked down at the red stone, wondering if some invisible eavesdropper was left behind, but the stone merely pulsed faintly, indicating the magic that barred the door, and he turned to Bracht, his breath a long, slow sigh of released tension.

'Is he hooked, do you think?'

The fires outside bathed the Kern's stern features in shifting light, his smile a flash of teeth, white against the reddened tan.

'I think you gave him reason to keep us alive a while. I think you a more accomplished liar than I had suspected.'

'Dera!' Calandryll returned the smile. 'I thought each moment he'd slay us. Or dismiss the bait - give us to Sathoman.'

'There's that to consider still,' Bracht murmured, his smile fading. 'Sathoman's bent on conquering the Fayne, and becoming Tyrant.'

'A wizard with a grimoire of ... what did I say?

Unimaginable power ... would make a useful ally.' Calandryll rested his head wearily against the rough stone, staring at the doorway. 'Perhaps Sathoman will consider that. Or Anomius choose to betray him.'

'Both choices leave us in jeopardy still,' Bracht said. 'Think on it - should Sathoman agree to send his wizard after this imagined grimoire it's not likely he'll do it until he holds Kesham-vaj and Mherut'yi, both. And then he'd likely send men in escort. We should travel under guard while perhaps Azumandias comes closer to the Arcanum. If Anomius decides to leave his master, he'll need to get us out by some clandestine means. And then we shall travel with a crazed wizard; who's likely, at the end, to seize the Arcanum for himself.'

'I'd thought no farther than escape from this place,' Calandryll admitted, 'and I could see no other way.'

'Nor I,' Bracht allowed. 'Save that the stone work some magic to whisk us free.'

'It would seem not,' Calandryll murmured. 'Save that it prevents Anomius from extorting the truth.'

'At least we're not given to Sathoman,' Bracht said. 'At least we live another day. And while we live, we can hope.'

He yawned, working himself to a more comfortable position against the wall, and closed his eyes. Calandryll, too, sought sleep, but found such respite elusive. The cords were tight about his wrists and with nothing else to occupy his mind he realised that numbness was replaced with a painful tingling. His hands were swollen and his arms ached; the wall was hard against his back, rough stone probing tensed muscles, nubs forming small focusses of discomfort. No matter how he shifted he could not find ease, and after a while he gave up, staring dully at the doorway.

In time the darkness became grey, then brighter. A few birds began to sing. The wind shifted around and he coughed as smoke from the bonfires wafted into the shed. The brightness grew, dissolving slowly to reveal a blue sky marked along its edges with heavy swells of cloud, the threat of rain. He saw the ek'Hennem soldiery stir, those who had maintained the night-long vigil seeking tents, or simply throwing themselves to the ground, others taking their places about Kesham-vaj. Sathoman emerged from a splendid pavilion, all green and gold and white, still armoured, his hair and beard wild, and stretched hugely, turning to bellow orders. Anomius, who looked to have had no more sleep than the prisoners, came to his side; words were exchanged and the would-be Lord of the Fayne glanced once, blackly, in the direction of the cowshed. Then shouting caught his attention and he set off at a run towards the town, Anomius trotting behind, his robe gathered up to expose pale, spindly legs.

A small black cloud hung low over Kesham-vaj, and it seemed to Calandryll that lightning played within it. It drifted across the town towards the closest fires, slowing and halting, then disgorging such a weight of rain the fires were instantly doused. Men stared up, then screamed as the lightning flashed, descending in vicious tendrils to strike them down. A peel of thunder dinned over the besiegers' camp and the cloud drifted on, sweeping over fire after fire, spilling fresh floods over each, the white-silver bolts blasting more men, the morning filled with the deafening blast of its thunder. Sathoman paused, waiting for Anomius, their conversation clearly angry, the giant gesturing furiously at the cloud, the mage answering with placatory gestures. Calandryll watched as he raised his hands, pale white arms revealed now, and the air about him shimmered. It seemed then that a wind tore at the cloud, like wolves on a sheep, black streamers tearing loose, the lightning dying, until it was no more than a ragged collection of dark streaks, tatters that broke and faded against the blue sky.

'Perhaps the Tyrant's mage is stronger than Anomius suggested,' Bracht said. 'Perhaps our captors face defeat.'

'Shall that be to our advantage?' Calandryll wondered. 'Or not?'

'Who can say?' The Kern flexed cramped shoulders, grunting. 'I think our wisest course is to suborn Anomius.'

'Azumandias may help us there,' Calandryll murmured.

'How so?'

'If Anomius decides he wants the grimoire, he'll not welcome rivals, I think. When next we speak I'll tell him of Azumandias - warn him that another seeks the book.'

'It might well spur him into action,' Bracht agreed, grinning. 'You've a head for intrigue, my friend.'

Calandryll returned his comrade's smile, though his eyes remained troubled. It was a slender hope at best, that Sathoman's wizard should choose to quit his master to risk the journey to Tezin-dar in search of a fictitious grimoire, its existence based on a fragile platform of lies and half-truths. But it was their only hope.

'Look,' Bracht said, catching his attention, 'What does he do now?'

They clambered to their feet and went to the door to gain a better view. Anomius stood with Sathoman beside a smouldering fire. The black cloud had drenched the timber and now dark smoke oozed fitfully from the wet wood. The wizard moved his hands and the smoke thickened, dark tendrils creeping like draggled serpents over the ground, twisting and joining to become a solid column that slithered menacingly towards the town. He went to a second doused pyre and performed the same ritual, producing more oily tentacles, those mingling with the first, the column growing denser, moving implacably towards Kesham-vaj. A third and then a fourth bonfire were treated in the same way, until two snakes of smoke converged on the barricades. Soon the defences were hidden beneath the oily pall, the smoke like flowing water, filtering through gaps, rising to surge over the piled obstacles and fill the streets beyond with reeking darkness. Torches showed dimly in that obscuration, and frightened cries rang out. Sathoman laughed and clapped Anomius on the back, his enthusiasm sending the diminutive sorceror staggering forwards. Then both men turned to the giant's pavilion and disappeared inside.

Calandryll and Bracht settled against the wall again. The morning dragged slowly on, their stomachs reminding them they had not eaten in some time, nor been offered water, the constant pain of bound hands and cramped shoulders going almost unnoticed now.

Towards noon the smoke-serpents began to roil and dissipate, breaking up like the cloud, and Anomius visited them again.

'You saw my little trick?' he asked proudly. 'I find it especially satisfying to turn an opponent's magic against him. There'll be red eyes and roughened throats in Kesham-vaj now. Could your Varent den Tarl do that?'

'I think not,' Calandryll said. 'I think Lord Varent a lesser mage.'

'And your father,' Anomius beamed, flattered, 'does the Domm of Secca employ sorcerers of like power?'

'None to match you.'

Anomius nodded, still smiling, hugely pleased with himself. 'I've his measure now,' he declared. 'I think tonight I'll test him further. Perhaps tomorrow Sathoman's impatience shall be ended.'

'You'll take the town?'

The wizard beamed and tapped his bulbous nose.

'I think it's time. I think we've lingered long enough,

and likely word of these events finds its way to Nhurjabal ere long - perhaps the Tyrant will send an army. I'd see Kesham-vaj secured against that.'

'And then,' Calandryll asked, 'what becomes of us?'

Anomius's smile dissolved into a thoughtful frown, parchment features creasing into a myriad wrinkles, the watery eyes hooding.

'I've thought on your story,' he said softly, 'but I've yet to decide your fate. Sathoman would execute you now, did I not persuade him to delay a while.'

'There's a thing I did not tell you.' Calandryll paused, thirst-furred tongue licking over dry lips, heart beating furiously. 'Lord Varent is not the only one to seek the grimoire.'

'What?' Anger flashed in the warlock's eyes. 'You hold things back? Best tell me all, Calandryll den Karynth, lest I test your faulty memory on your comrade's body.'

'There's a mage - Azumandias, he's called - who knows of the book. And of the map.' Calandryll swallowed, his throat ashy, his mind working furiously. 'He has some inkling of Tezin-dar's location, but needs the stone - needs me! - to reach the grimoire.'

'A race? You say there's a race for this fabulous book?'

'Yes.' Calandryll fought the discomfort of his bound wrists, the hunger that threatened to confuse his thoughts when he most needed cunning, deciding that again truth - or a basis of truth, at least - offered him the most effective ploy in this deadly game. 'On the road to Aldarin he sent demons against us. And when we sailed from Secca we were pursued by his agent. In Mherut'yi, I was attacked by one of the Brotherhood.'

'The Chaipaku take a hand in this?' Anomius demanded.

'It seems so,' Calandryll nodded, regretting the movement when his head spun and began to ache. 'At least, I woke to find one in my room.'

'And lived?'

Anomius was doubtful. Calandryll began to nod again; thought better of it and said, 'As you see - yes. Bracht intervened.'

'You defeated a Chaipaku?'

The wizard transferred his attention to the Kern, his gaze met with a cold, blue stare.

'Yes,' Bracht said, 'I slew him. But he was only a boy.'

'Nonetheless impressive,' Anomius said, 'The Chaipaku are not easy to defeat.'

'At least we are safe here,' said Calandryll. 'Though Azumandias may find some other way to locate the grimoire.'

'With neither map nor stone to aid him?'

Suspicion danced in the small eyes: Calandryll cursed his slip; struggled to find a convincing answer.

'Perhaps not,' he said. 'I know only what Lord Varent told me - that the map shows the way to Tezin-dar, and the stone the way to the book. I am no sorcerer - I know not what powers Azumandias wields.'

'But, like Varent, he seeks the grimoire?' Anomius demanded.

'Aye. And Lord Varent feared him. Feared he might succeed. Perhaps there are other ways; perhaps the stone simply offers the swiftest.'

'More food to nourish thought,' Anomius murmured. 'I'll ponder what you say.'

Without further prevarication he rose and left them alone.

'Does he take the bait?' Calandryll asked.

Bracht frowned. 'He nibbles, I think. I cannot say; but you can do no more.'

The day grew older. The cloud that had edged the horizon swept closer, white hammerheads lofting from the billows. A wind got up, bringing the smells of cookfires to worsen their hunger. Sathoman's men busied themselves about the town, and late in the afternoon Anomius returned, a soldier with him. It seemed a favourable omen that the man brought food: cold meat and bread, a little cheese, a flask of water. He set his burdens down and stood back, hand on sword hilt as the wizard faced them.

'I'll loose your bonds,' Anomius said, 'so that you may eat. The door-spell remains - make no attempt to cross the threshold.'

He pointed at them, each in turn, and muttered something that loosed the cords from their wrists. Calandryll groaned as the freed blood flowed like fire through his fingers. Beside him Bracht flexed his hands, and worked at shoulders cramped by long confinement. Neither touched the food or water until some measure of mobility had returned, but then they drank long and deep, and consumed the food with a voracity that left no room for conversation until the last morsels were gone.

'I doubt,' Bracht said carefully, 'that he would bother feeding men about to die.'

'And our gear remains.'

Calandryll gestured at the satchel, the swords, left carelessly in an angle of the shed's broken wall.

'For what good it does us.' Bracht buckled on his falchion. 'Though perhaps it means something.'

'We can only wait,' Calandryll said, taking his own blade. 'Wait and hope.'

They waited through a night filled with the alarums of battle, both usual and magical. They heard arrows sigh through the darkness, and the shouts of men, attacking and ambushed, the clash of steel on steel. Twice it seemed the sky over Kesham-vaj took fire, and twice a wind not of natural making roared, gusting against the flame. Three times great thunderclaps dinned across the plateau, and once they watched as spectral beasts fought in the sky, things composed of many parts joined in abnormal union, ripping at one another until only shimmering tatters remained, fading back into a night sweet with the scent of almonds, the talisman at Calandryll's throat pulsing fiery. Red-eyed, they saw dawn overtake the darkness, and that misty pearl give way to sunshine that lanced through heavy banks of cloud.

Then Anomius came to them again. Dark shadows ringed his eyes and his sallow skin was blanched with an unhealthy pallor, but he appeared mightily pleased with himself.

'An impressive display, do you not agree?' he asked amiably, settling himself on a stool, uncaring of the blades they wore. 'The Tyrant's mage is close to exhaustion, and he's reached the limits of his ability. I shall have a victory today and Sathoman ek'Hennem shall enter Kesham-vaj as conqueror. My little spy tells me that Mherut'yi has fallen, so once we've taken this place my lord will truly rule the Fayne. Whatever force the Tyrant may send against him, his position is strong. By Burash, am I not a giant amongst sorcerers?'

'Indeed, you are,' Calandryll agreed.

'And you wear your swords as if ready to depart,' Anomius chuckled. 'Or to sell yourselves as dear you may.'

'Which is it to be?' Bracht demanded.

'Blunt,' said the wizard, 'so blunt. The warriors of Cuan na'For have near as little patience as Sathoman.'

'If I face death,' Bracht said evenly, 'I'd know it.'

Anomius chuckled again, a whispering sound, its humour coldly threatening. He scratched an armpit, staring at them.

'With Kesham-vaj taken,' he murmured, 'Sathoman can hold the Fayne without my help. For a while, at least. And did I hold this fabulous grimoire, I'd wield such power as must cause the Tyrant's puppets to bow before me. Yes! And the Tyrant, too.'

He paused, studying them each in turn. Beyond him Sathoman's men readied for an assault, checking armour, whetting blades. Calandryll returned his stare, aware that his heart beat nervously against his ribs, aware that his life - likely even the world's survival - hung on the decision of this little man.

'I think,' Anomius said at last, 'that perhaps I shall leave Sathoman to fend for himself for a while. I think that perhaps I shall journey with you to Tezin-dar.'

Calandryll heard his breath come out in a long sigh and realised for the first time that he had held it.

'Yes,' Anomius continued, 'I do not think your Varent den Tarl worthy of this book. Nor this Azumandias. I shall have it! And you shall bring me to it. Do you make that bargain with me? In return, I offer you your lives.'

'We take it,' Calandryll said.

Anomius smiled and turned to Bracht.

'The men of Cuan na'For hold their word sacred - do you give yours? That you will do all you can to bring me safe to this grimoire?'

Bracht stared at the warlock, and for a long, breath-held moment Calandryll thought he would refuse: that honour would deny him the chance to survive. But then he ducked his head.

'I shall do all I can to bring you to the grimoire.'

'Good,' smiled Anomius, 'I scarce need add that any treachery must unleash my anger. Or that my anger is a terrible thing.'

'We have seen what you can do,' Calandryll said.

'Then you know what I can do to you,' beamed the wizard. 'Now I must leave you - there's a town to be taken. You remain here for a while, but stand ready to flee on my word.'

They nodded and watched him go, making for Sathoman's pavilion. Calandryll turned to Bracht, his gaze worried.

'You gave him your word, and as he said - you hold that high. You took Lord Varent's commission on that, despite your doubts.'

Bracht nodded, smiling. 'I promised to bring him to the grimoire,' he said. 'Only that.'

'So?' Calandryll was confused. 'Does that not bind you to his service?'

'The grimoire is a fiction,' Bracht answered. 'In his arrogance he failed to question you on that - how can I bring him to a thing that does not exist? Besides, he offered no payment for my services.'

Calandryll stared at the Kern, who faced him with solemn mien. Then they both began to laugh.

Chapter TWELVE

THROUGHOUT the morning they watched as Satho-man's men commenced the construction of several massive bonfires. Toiling squads hauled fresh-cut timber in carts and on make-shift sleds from all over the plateau, building the huge pyres facing the barricades, just beyond arrow range. The defenders, apparently sensing some pending occult attack, made one sally but that was driven back by the archers still posted about Kesham-vaj, whilst the remainder of the brigand army concentrated on fetching wood and stacking it in accordance with the warlock's instructions. By early afternoon, when it seemed there could not be a tree left on the highland, Anomius called a halt and the rebels stood down. Food and water were brought to the prisoners, but although Anomius came to release the door-spell, he said nothing, merely smiling and tapping his excessive nose in a conspiratorial manner. They ate by the door, fascinated by the preparations for the assault.

It began in late afternoon.

Anomius, protected by a squad of shield-bearing warriors and bowmen, went to each bonfire in turn, mouthing unheard words and moving his hands in complex gestures that set the air about him to shimmering. Calandryll saw that the red stone glowed fiercer as the wizard performed his rituals. Sathoman stood beneath the shadowing canopy of his pavilion, his huge hand clenching and unclenching on his sword's hilt, his eyes fixed on the tiny sorcerer, a look of savage anticipation on his bearded face. Anomius completed his rites and nodded to a soldier, who bellowed orders that sent a man running to each pyre, torch in hand. The stacked timber ignited, flame climbing hungrily over the wood, the air shining and shimmering as the heat grew, blue smoke climbing wind-tossed towards the cloudy sky. Anomius walked to where Sathoman stood and they spoke a moment, then the giant nodded and settled a dragon-crested morion on his head, beckoning his lieutenants to follow as he strode to where the main body of his force stood ready. Anomius waited until he had taken his place at the head of the phalanx, then raised his arms, wide spread, palms outwards. The stone pulsed stronger: Calandryll tugged it from his shirt as it burned against his chest. The scent of almonds hung cloying in his nostrils. Then flame burst from Anomius's palms, twin balls of fire hanging in the air, his hands transformed to living torches. He brought his arms down, shouting a single word, and incandescent tongues licked out, streaking towards the bonfires, whose roaring changed in timbre, becoming less the crackling and booming of flame-consumed wood than the throaty growling of some living creatures. Each one burned higher, burned fiercer, great sheets of fire lofting, writhing as if possesssed of some sensate energy. And from those conflagrations stepped beings of pure flame, man-like and beast-shaped simultaneously, malformed, malign things that emanated rage and evil as they stood, towering, burning heads turning on columnar necks as if seeking victims to satisfy their dreadful appetites.

Anomius spoke again, and though his words were lost beneath the booming of the fires it seemed the flame-beasts heard him, for each one turned in the direction of Kesham-vaj and began to move ponderously towards the town. Where they trod the ground burned, the trampled grass scorching, the earth itself left black and smoking in their wake. The scent of almonds grew sickeningly sweet; the stone blazed, itself like fire now. Calandryll watched dumb-struck as arrows rained from the defences, useless, burning even before they touched the fiery apparitions. For each entry into Kesham-vaj there was one flame-beast, and they marched implacably towards the barricades, high as houses, looming above those few defenders brave - or desperate - enough to remain.

Those who did perished as the occult creatures reached down, fiery paws indiscriminate as they tore at the barriers, wood and flesh alike burning on their touch. Between the houses the barricades were demolished in a moment, timber blackening and collapsing into ash that swirled within the flaming forms of the creatures, striping them with black and streaks of grey. Metal melted where they were, spears and sword blades running like ice in flame, sizzling in molten droplets to the charred ground, the wielders - those not themselves consumed - running in terror.

A clarion rang and Calandryll saw Sathoman raise his great sword aloft, bellowing a war-cry as he began to run straight for the closest fire-beast.

For one wild instant Calandryll thought the brigand-lord would himself charge to his death, but as he approached the creature it turned and stalked ahead, driving the defenders before it, and, still screaming his war-shout, Sathoman led his men into Kesham-vaj.

Then the afternoon was loud with the clamour of battle, the ek'Hennem forces converging on the town in a savage human wave on the heels of the fire-beasts. Calandryll saw Anomius raise his hands again and the flickering shapes of the monsters he had created flashed and were gone, leaving the field to mortal combat, the heady almond scent clearing, leaving only the wood-smoke smell of the fires. The wizard sagged, shoulders slumping beneath his shabby robe, his chest heaving. A man brought him a stool and he collapsed onto it, head hanging, threatening to dislodge his headdress. He remained thus, seemingly exhausted by his conjurations, until a squad of Sathoman's men herded a robed figure from the town. Then he straightened, sitting upright on the stool as the man was brought before him.

This, Calandryll guessed, was the sorcerer sent by the Tyrant to defend Kesham-vaj. He was a more impressive sight than Anomius, taller and narrow-featured, standing defiantly straight although obviously no less fatigued by his work than the smaller man. His hands were bound and a knotted leather thong gagged his tongue. Unbound grey hair hung about his face, falling to the shoulders of a silvery robe streaked with soot and charred about the hem. As if conscious of the difference in their heights, Anomius remained seated, studying the enemy wizard with head cocked to one side. Then he gestured, murmuring something to the soldiers, and they stood back, forming a loose half circle about the bound man. Anomius gestured again and the wizard was abruptly wreathed in flame, a single choking cry erupting from his lips. In no more time than it had taken Anomius to mouth the spell, the flame was gone, the rival sorcerer with it. A handful of ashes fluttered in the air, caught by the wind and blown away. Anomius spoke again and the soldiers spun as if pleased to quit the wizard's presence, trotting back to the fight.

It went on until dusk, the clash of steel on steel gradually dimming, the shouting fading until silence hung over the plateau. Then the clarion sounded again and a great shout went up.

'I think,' Bracht said, 'that Sathoman is now Lord of the Fayne in more than name.'

'And has the time to think of us,' Calandryll returned. 'Anomius had best act swiftly, unless he's changed his mind.'

Bracht ducked his head in silent agreement, his hawkish features thoughtful. 'If he's not,' he said, 'tonight would be the time to go, while Sathoman basks in his triumph. And if we do, we'd best lay some plan for the future.'

Calandryll's eyes framed a question.

'Anomius is our only hope of escaping this,' Bracht's gesture encompassed the shed and the town together, 'and likely a wizard can ease our passage through Kandahar. But when we reach Kharasul? Are we to take ship with him? Do we take him as companion to Tezindar?'

'Dera, no!' Calandryll shook his head vigorously. 'Should Anomius learn of the Arcanum he'll seize it for himself - and that, I think must be akin to handing the book to Azumandias.'

'Then we must escape him,' Bracht said.

'If we can,' Calandryll agreed.

'Even sorcerers must sleep.' Bracht tapped his sword hilt, a cold smile on his lips. 'And surely even sorcerers can be slain.'

Calandryll stared at the Kern, aware that they discussed what seemed no better than cold-blooded murder. It seemed a long road from Secca to this, the changes in his life perhaps more costly than he wished to pay. But the Arcanum was the prize - the salvation of the world itself the stake in this game - and he nodded reluctant agreement.

'If we must.'

The sounds of revelry came from Kesham-vaj as the

ek'Hennem army celebrated its victory, and for the moment at least it seemed the prisoners were forgotten. The moon, full now, rose to shine fitfully through the gathered cloud and a light rain fell, damping the dying fires. Whatever spell Anomius had cast on the cowshed did nothing to hold out the drizzle and Calandryll and Bracht crouched, miserable and wary, beneath the scant shelter of the broken roof. Food was brought them by a dirty, grinning soldier, Anomius lifting his spell just long enough for the man to thrust the meal inside. Calandryll thought the wizard would speak with them, but he merely glanced at them as before and turned away. In the moonlight, his face was drawn, his eyes like reddened ditch water ringed with purple shadow, giving no sign of his intentions. They ate listening to the drunken shouting of the victors, wondering if the wizard intended to renege on his promise. Of Sathoman ek'Hennem there was no sign, and that at least was favourable: they composed themselves to sleep with blades at their sides, their gear set close by in optimistic readiness.

Bracht was the first to wake when Anomius came again, nudging Calandryll until he stirred from a fitful dream of fiery monsters and trees that spoke, to open bleary eyes on the small figure of the warlock standing in the doorway. Instinctively, he glanced at the red stone, and saw that it held no glow to reveal magic, guessing from that the door-spell was removed.

Anomius tapped a warning finger to his fleshy lips and beckoned them to their feet.

'Sathoman celebrates his victory still,' the warlock murmured, 'and most of his men are drunk. This is, I think, a most propitious time to leave. But first ...'

He moved his hands, muttering, a finger extending towards Bracht. The Kern sprang back, mouthing a curse, then shook his head, eyes glazing momentarily. Anomius smiled amiably. Calandryll saw the stone flicker.

'A simple spell, my friend. We have a journey to go, we three, and I'd not chance your forgetting your vow.'

'Curse you!' Bracht snarled. 'What have you done to me?'

'A geas, no more,' Anomius said. 'I'd place the same upon Calandryll, save that the stone prevents me.'

'What have you done to me?' Bracht repeated furiously, hand fastening on the falchion's hilt.

'Draw that - or any other weapon - against me,' the wizard beamed, 'and you must turn the blade on Calandryll. Attempt to slay me, and your comrade dies.'

The Kern stared at him, rage etched on his face. Calandryll said, 'And I? Should I come against you?'

Anomius studied him, still smiling, and shook his head.

'Your ethics are ... less pragmatic ... than those of Cuan na'For, Calandryll den Karynth. I doubt you're the man to slit my throat whilst I sleep, or slide a blade between my ribs as my back turns.'

'You insult me,' Bracht rasped.

'I take no more than understandable precautions,' Anomius replied evenly. 'After all, do you not betray Varent den Tarl? You need me to escape Sathoman's vengeance; but after? What guarantee - other than your word, which you no doubt gave to your former employer, too - do I have that you'll not betray me likewise?'

His argument - given that they had, not long ago, discussed his murder - was irrefutable: Calandryll could think of no counter. Bracht's lips clamped tight, his eyes blazing dangerously.

'This is no time to debate the matter,' Anomius declared. 'We ride together and I'll protect myself - accept it, or remain here. Likely Sathoman will remember you when he sobers; if you prefer to await his justice ...' He shrugged. 'If not, then let's be gone. I've horses waiting and I'd distance myself from

Kesham-vaj before my lord learns of my departure. Which is it to be?'

Calandryll glanced at Bracht: the Kern shrugged.

'We ride.'

'Then come,' said Anomius, beckoning: they followed the sorcerer from the shed.

The fires, no longer fuelled by Anomius's magic and damped by the steady rain, smouldered fitfully now. Thick banks of cloud masked the sky above the plateau, the moon losing its struggle to pierce the canopy, the ground before Kesham-vaj dark. Those few of ek'Hennem's men not carousing within the town sheltered in their tents, and the three fugitives reached the horses unnoticed. Bracht's chestnut and Calandryll's roan snickered greetings as they stowed their gear behind the saddles, the Kern taking time to check each animal before they mounted. Anomius hauled himself laboriously astride a dark grey gelding and led the way out of the encampment.

They moved at a walk for fear of calling attention down on their escape, past empty tents, the spitting remnants of a bonfire, a line of picketed animals stamping fretful in the rain. Drizzle and darkness were their allies, those and the victory that relaxed the brigands' vigilance, the slow clopping of the hooves muffled by wet ground and the susurration of the rain, the handful of sentries still posted along the perimeter huddling under cover, consoling themselves with ale and wine brought them by sympathetic comrades. They circled the tents to put Kasham-vaj at their backs, crossing fields deserted with the coming of the rebel army, farmhouses standing dark and empty, the animals eaten by ek'Hennem's army. When the town was no more than a blur of light behind, they angled towards the road, quickening their pace.

'How long before we're missed?' Bracht shouted through the rainhiss and hoofbeats.

Anomius, none too happy with their speed, wiped a hand over his face and answered, 'Morning, perhaps. If we're lucky, noon or later.'

'Shall we be off this highland by then?' asked the Kern.

The wizard nodded. 'If we ride all night. And if we can pass the sentinels.'

'Sentinels?' Bracht swung his chestnut closer to the grey. 'What sentinels?'

'Sathoman has twenty men posted at the western edge,' the wizard said. 'To watch and warn against attack.'

'Ahrd damn you!' Bracht cursed. 'You said nothing of watchers there.'

'Can you not use magic against them?' asked Calandryll.

'No major conjuration,' Anomius shook his head. 'I raised fire demons today, and that takes a toll. That and quelling my opponent's counter-spells. I can work no major sorceries until my strength is recovered.'

'You set a spell on me,' Bracht said. 'Or was that a lie?'

'No lie,' Anomius returned, 'but a small spell. To overcome a score of men - or bring us past them unseen - is more than I can do now.'

'Is there another way down?'

Calandryll saw their escape ending soon after it had begun as the wizard shook his head again and said, 'Not off this highland. Only the Tyrant's road. But another way ... perhaps.'

He loosed his left hand from its nervous grip on the saddlehorn just long enough to gesture at his pack.

'I have a bow. By night ... they'll not expect attack from this quarter.'

'You'd see your comrades slain?'

Calandryll stared at the sorcerer's face, glistening in the rain, feeling a loathing for this unwelcome ally.

'I'd have the grimoire,' Anomius replied, unmoved. 'If

a handful of outlaws must die for that, so be it.'

'And when Sathoman learns of it?'

Bracht felt no compunction: Calandryll realised that Anomius had been correct in his assessment of their ethical differences.

'He'll not for a day, at least,' said the wizard; then grinned maliciously, 'And when he does - and finds us gone - he'll likely assume you succeeded in forcing me to free you.'

'And send men after us,' snapped the Kern. 'If we're alive to chase.'

'Of course,' Anomius agreed, 'but by then we'll be off this highland and there are places to hide below. And my strength will be restored - you need only concern yourselves with the men ahead.'

'You've much faith in my swordskill,' Bracht grunted.

'We'll find a way,' Anomius replied evenly. 'Between us, we'll find a way.'

Bracht mouthed a curse that went unheard in the night. Calandryll, riding on Anomius's left, looked across the sorcerer at the Kern. Bracht's face was cold and hard, resolved, as if the attacking of twenty men was already accepted and he thought only of the doing of it, that and the need to get down off this open plateau to the hiding places of the land below.

They rode on, Bracht setting the pace, Anomius bouncing uncomfortably in the grey's saddle, a miserable bundle of dark, rain-sodden clothes, silent now that the decision was made. Calandryll thought of his words: 'I can work no major sorceries until my strength is recovered'. Perhaps that offered some hope of escaping his clutches - if the working of conjurations exhausted him to the point at which he could fashion only simple spells, then perhaps they might flee him at some time when his occult powers ebbed low. Perhaps: for now, there was the problem of passing the sentinels to consider. Twenty, Anomius had said. Bracht could hardly take twenty men with the bow: likely it would come to swordwork. It came to him that he had never killed a man. He began to wonder if he could.

As the night gave way to dawn he found out.

Kesham-vaj lay lost in the darkness behind them, the land around stretching flat, broken only by the half-seen shapes of windblown trees, the plateau's rim hidden in the softening grey that marked the transition between night and day. The rain had ceased, the air cool, fresh with the pleasant scent of wet grass. Anomius slowed his mount, raising a cautious hand.

'We approach the descent. Sathoman's men may hear the horses.'

Bracht reined in, Calandryll following suit as the Kern swung to the ground.

'Give me the bow.'

Anomius groaned as he hiked an awkward leg over his saddle and slid down, reaching up to slide the bow from its wrappings on his saddle. It was heavy-curved, like those Denphat and Jedomus had carried, short enough to be used effectively from horseback. Bracht took it and bent it against his knee, setting the loose string in place. Anomius passed him a quiver of twelve arrows and the Kern examined each one, sighting down the shafts and checking the fletching. He pronounced himself satisfied and turned to the wizard.

'Where will they be?'

'The road's edge is marked by a pillar,' Anomius said, 'Like that where you found Arrhiman and Laphyl. Beyond the pillar the road descends steeply, through a cut. Before the rim, the ground is open for half a bowshot. They'll be there.'

'Armoured?'

'Yes,' Anomius nodded, 'but that bow can pierce armour.'

'Not fast enough,' Bracht grunted, 'but perhaps

enough to divert them. Is there any magic you can use against them?'

'Some,' the wizard admitted. 'But minor spells that I can work only at close range against single men.'

'Then we must ride through them.' Bracht's face was grim in the pale grey light. 'Calandryll, your task is to scatter their horses. Likely they'll be on a picket line - get close and send them running. Then return here. Sorcerer, you'll wait with our mounts ready. When Calandryll returns, you both come fast.'

'And you?' Calandryll asked.

'I'll do what I can to confuse them and meet you on the rim. Come forwards at full gallop. Anomius - you'll use what magic you can then.'

The wizard nodded. Calandryll said, 'What if you're ... delayed?'

Bracht grinned, shrugging. 'Leave that worry to me, my friend,' he advised. 'Once the horses are scattered you need only make the road. If worst comes to worst, I'll meet you lower down. If not ... go on.' He cut short Calandryll's protest with a curt gesture, turning to Anomius. 'Wait here, sorcerer. Keep the horses quiet if you can.'

He beckoned to Calandryll, nocking a shaft. Calandryll drew his sword. His mouth was dry and in his stomach something rebelled, fluttering nervously. Bracht smiled, tightly, and began to move down the road.

A little way along they heard the muted sounds of a waking camp; the snorting of tethered horses and the low-voiced conversation of the guards; saw the dull glimmer of a fire; the dark bulk of a stone column thrusting against the brightening sky. Bracht raised a hand, pointing to the road's edge.

'The horses are there. Use Varent's spell if you must, but turn them loose and set them running. I'll come at them from the farther side.'

Calandryll nodded silently. Bracht placed a hand on his right shoulder, staring at his face.

'They'll not let us past, do you understand?' His voice was soft, but urgent. 'Likely they'll be grouped tight - when I fire, they'll scatter, and some may come after the animals. Kill them. Those left will be on our heels - or carry word to Sathoman.'

Calandryll ducked his head once, not trusting himself to speak.

'Leave me time to get close,' Bracht said, 'and loose the horses when the first man falls.'

He moved swiftly across the road, disappearing into the undergrowth. Calandryll mouthed the words Varent had taught him and felt his skin tingle briefly, the scent of almonds mingling with the freshness of the morning. He began to pace through bushes glistening silvery with raindrops, crouching sword in hand, eyes and ears straining. Birds began to sing, welcoming the dawn, and the rising sun limned the eastern sky with red and gold, its light driving off the insubstantial grey. That cleared to reveal a column of dark stone set beside the road where it fell away from the plateau, hidden by the rim. At the foot of the column the fire flared as branches were added, the sleeping watchers rising, shaking water from their bedding. One walked around the column to fumble with his breeks. Calandryll heard him sigh as he began to relieve himself. Two others busied themselves about the fire and those who had taken the last watch flung themselves down close to the warmth. He saw the horses pegged some little distance off, snickering a greeting to the light, and crept towards them.

There was no warning of Bracht's attack, only the dull thudding sound of an arrow striking home, the exhalation of the man standing by the column as he pitched forwards, a shaft protruding between his shoulders. He struck the stone and fell sideways into a bush, the shrubbery supporting him so that he hung with one arm outflung as if in supplication; or accusation. A man by the fire glanced up, his view obscured by the pillar. Calandryll saw him clearly, a short, plump-featured man, streaks of grey in his black beard, his breast plate decorated with a blue seahorse. He frowned, rising, and stepped a few paces out, peering towards his fallen comrade. Calandryll saw his eyes widen in alarm and his mouth open to shout a warning cut short by the shaft that suddenly jutted from his chest. He toppled backwards, across the fire, sparks scattering as his companions yelled and drew their swords. He broke clear of the bushes and ran for the horses.

They sensed his presence and set to stamping, tugging on the picket line. He slashed it through, hacking to right and left, severing the individual ropes, careless of the plunging hooves, the screaming of the panicking animals. He waved his arms, forgetting they could not see him, and used the flat of his blade to send them charging clear.

A Kand screamed shrilly as an arrow pierced his throat; another fell with a shaft buried deep in his ribs. Three ran towards the scattering horses, one succeeding in snatching up the trailing line. Calandryll charged him, sword raised, slashing the hand that held the horse, reversing the cut to send the man down with bloodied face, spinning to attack the others, who gaped and flailed their blades wildly at their invisible opponent.

He slew them both, mercilessly, all notions of honour forgotten in the urgency of the moment, remembering he was unseen only when they lay dead at his feet. Then disgust gripped him and he voiced the counter-spell, becoming visible again. He began to run back down the road, to where Anomius waited, his black-swathed shape clear now in the burgeoning light.

Suddenly he was confronted by a burly Kand wielding a sabre, a buckler of dragon hide thrust before his torso. He snarled, eyes furious beneath the green headdress he wore, and swung the sabre in a vicious arc at Calandryll's head. Calandryll parried the blow and riposted, his sword turned by the shield. He deflected a second cut, sliding his blade in over the Kand's swordarm to prick the unarmoured shoulder. The brigand fell back behind his shield: Calandryll pressed the attack.

He felt no compunction now, no hesitation: this was honest combat, man to man, both visible, and a fury gripped him as he moved forwards, intent only on removing this obstacle to his freedom. He cut at the brigand's head and ducked the counterstroke, driving the straightsword in at the belly, below the cuirasse. The Kand danced back, and Calandryll feinted an attack to bring the shield out, using that opening to hack at the exposed chest. His blade scored the leathery armour and he darted clear as the sabre threatened his side, turning, spinning, to slash the man's swordarm. It dropped and he drove his blade in hard, into the Kand's side. The brigand yelped as the steel bit home; Calandryll twisted the blade free and cut deep into the man's neck, stepping back as he fell, the morning abruptly bright with the blood that jetted from the wound. He watched as the brigand went down on hands and knees, shaking his head as though realisation of his dying came slowly, perhaps not before he slumped face down, still.

Calandryll left him where he lay, running to the wizard, already in the saddle, springing astride the roan and seizing the reins of Bracht's horse. His heels rammed against the roan's flanks and the gelding sprang forwards, the chestnut snorting a protest as the reins snapped tight. He was dimly aware of Anomius beside him as he sent his mount headlong for the pillar, seeing Bracht come running from the bushes, the falchion a glittering thing that sent two brigands down as the Kern reached the road. He slowed enough that Bracht could mount on the run and they galloped towards the rim, where the road fell out of sight.

More brigands blocked their way and for long moments all was confusion, shouting men struck down by charging horses, swords, and the fire that sparkled from Anomius's outflung hand. Then they were past the pillar and thundering down a road that dropped away from the rim of the plateau in a steep descent that called for concentration as the horses squealed and fought against the reins, dangerously close to tumbling on the gradient. Arrows whistled past them, rattling off the sheer faces to either side, and they crouched low until they rounded a slight curve and found the protection of the scarp.

The sun had topped the eastern edge of the highland now and they could see they went down a cut, the road masoned from naked stone, high walls rising to either side, ending on a sweeping shelf where the slope grew gentler, the road winding down to a broad river at the plateau's foot.

They took it at a run, slowing only when trees set a barrier at their backs, halting the near-winded horses when Bracht declared them out of arrow's range.

Timber grew thicker here than on the eastern ascent, trees encircling high meadows lush with grass and blue streams tumbling down to join with the wider channel below. Spread out below them they saw the heartland of Kandahar, dense forest presenting a patchwork of myriad greens, sewn with the silver-blue threads of rivers, savannah misty in the distance, the line of the Kharm-rhanna a ribbon of blackness between land and sky. It was a beautiful vista: it filled Calandryll with sudden remorse.

He turned in his saddle, eyes swivelling inexorably to the scene of carnage hidden above them.

'I've never ...' he paused, swallowing the bile that rose in his throat, '... never killed a man.'

Bracht nodded.

'The next will be easier.'

Calandryll was not sure he wanted the next to be easier; not sure he wanted a next to come. He spat, shaking his head as if that physical movement might dislodge the memories of steel biting flesh, of blood, and the screams of dying men, telling himself it was foolish to think he might secure the Arcanum without bloodshed; hypocritical to think that only Bracht's hands would be stained. It made no difference, and his stomach churned with the knowledge that men had fallen to his blade.

'Forget them,' Bracht advised. 'Do you think they'd spare a thought for you?'

'I am not them,' he returned.

'No; for sure you are not.' Bracht smiled, echoing his own thoughts, 'But did you believe we'd reach Tezin-dar with blades unblooded? Why did you practise your swordwork, save to use it?'

'I did not think to ...'

He shook his head. Bracht nodded and said, 'Use it on men? Sathoman would have killed us; they'd have killed us. And none spared a second thought for the doing of it. This world of ours is a bloody place, and a man does what he must to survive in it.'

The Kern's voice was gently earnest: Calandryll showed him a brief smile of gratitude, knowing that he sought only to reassure, to assuage a troubled conscience. He murmured, 'But they were not our enemies. They were simply men who happened to be in the wrong place.'

'Yes,' Bracht said, 'in out path. They would not have let us past. They would have killed us, or sent us back to be killed by Sathoman. And then Azumandias would reach Tezin-dar and bring out the book. Would you rather that?'

'No.' Reluctantly, he shook his head. 'Not that.'

'Then we had no other course. Did we?'

'No' he said again. 'But still - men died at our hands.'

'And likely not the last,' Bracht answered, 'It's a thing we had to do. I think your goddess will forgive you.'

But can I forgive myself?

He stilled the thought, staring at his comrade.

'Does it not trouble you?'

'No,' Bracht said.

'Do you wait here, engaged in philosophical debate, until they catch their mounts and come after us?'

Anomius's question brought his attention back to their immediate plight. He looked to Bracht for advice, and the Kern nodded.

'Will they pursue us, or wait on Sathoman's orders?'

'How many were left?' asked the wizard.

'I slew five, I think,' Bracht replied. 'And wounded more.'

Calandryll said, 'Four.'

'Then likely they'll wait on Sathoman.' Anomius beamed, using the tails of his headdress to wipe sweat from his yellow skin. 'You did well, my friends - but still I suggest we continue at our best pace.'

'A day to get down this,' Bracht walked his horse to the road's edge, studying the way ahead. 'And by then Sathoman will know we've escaped.'

'He'll likely search Kesham-vaj first,' Anomius said, 'but when word comes from above he'll know the road we've taken. He'll not risk pursuing us far into the heartland, but I'll feel safer once we're into the woods.'

'We've a day's advantage, then,' nodded the Kern, 'more if he's unwilling to take the road by night. How many might he send after us?'

Anomius shrugged. 'He's the Fayne to hold - perhaps the Tyrant's army marching against him - He'll not send too many.'

Bracht expressed his impatience with an irritable gesture.

'How many is "not too many"? Curse you, wizard, I'd know the odds!'

'A score he could spare,' Anomius replied, equably. 'Perhaps thirty.'

'Thirty on our heels!'

Bracht's voice was flat with anger. The sorcerer smiled, showing stained teeth. 'You forget you have an ally now,' he said. 'One who can deal easily with thirty men.'

'As you dealt with the twenty up there?' Bracht stabbed a thumb back at the plateau. 'I do not remember your helping much there.'

'As I told you - the raising of fire demons is taxing.' Anomius refused to allow the Kern's anger to disturb his complacency. 'But by dawn my full strength will be returned - I can leave ... guardians ... behind us.'

He smiled as he said it, the expression horribly threatening in its confidence; Calandryll wondered what form the wizard's guardians might take, preferring not to ask.

'So, shall we descend?' Anomius enquired, as mildly as if he suggested a pleasurable day's riding. 'There are places aplenty to hide below.'

Without waiting for a reply he heeled his horse, bouncing in the saddle as he commenced the descent, like a bundle of black rags set insecurely on the grey's back.

'Sorcerer he may be,' Bracht grunted, 'but never a horseman.'

It took most of that day to reach the river they had seen, its waters darkening as twilight gathered, night creeping stealthily over the bottomlands, transforming the forest ahead to a looming, shadowy mass, lightless and forbidding. The road ran alongside the river, halting abruptly at a cluster of buildings where lights showed in windows and dogs barked warning of their approach. They reined in, surveying the settlement.

'There's a ferry,' Anomius told them, 'and a tavern. We've the advantage of Sathoman for now, and I'd rest overnight - by dawn my strength will be replenished.'

'By dawn Sathoman could be riding down that hill,' Bracht objected, 'and I'd not lose our advantage.'

The diminutive sorcerer raised a hand, his voice petulant as he said, 'I am not accustomed to riding and I'd take my leisure here.'

'And I'd cross,' said the Kern.

'Tomorrow,' said Anomius, hand moving to point at Bracht, 'and I'd not argue with you.'

Calandryll heard the threat in his voice and thought of the men who had gone down to the strange fire that burst from the warlock's fingers. He edged his horse between them, sending Bracht a warning glance. 'A night's comfort is tempting,' he said, 'and surely Sathoman cannot catch up so fast.'

'A diplomat,' Anomius complimented, and turned an oily smile on Bracht. 'Come, my friend, what's one night? We'll sleep here and cross at dawn. And I'll ensure Sathoman cannot cross after us.'

Bracht glanced at Calandryll, then shrugged. 'So be it; but we leave at first light.'

'Good,' Anomius murmured, favouring the Kern with a watery look as he lowered his hand, 'such questors as we should not argue. I'll arrange our quarters and leave the horses to you - you've more experience of such matters.'

He rode imperiously into the courtyard of the inn, where the dogs set up a racket at his arrival. He looked at them as he had looked at Bracht and pointed a finger: yelping, the dogs turned tail and ran.

'He'd likely have done worse to you,' Calandryll remarked as they watched the little man drop from his horse. 'We'd best remember that.'

'Or leave him behind,' the Kern grunted.

'How?' Calandryll gestured at the ferry lying idle on

the riverbank. 'He'll know if we attempt to cross and use his magic against us.'

'Then when we can,' Bracht said.

'Yes, when we can,' Calandryll agreed, 'but let him use his powers to aid us first. Let him set this spell to ward our trail and then we'll flee his company at the first opportunity.'

Bracht grunted reluctant assent and they led the horses to the stable. A youthful ostler appeared, eyeing them with open curiosity.

'Are you ek'Hennem men?' he asked nervously. 'Word's out the rebel lord's abroad up there.'

His eyes rose to the rim of the plateau, tinged red with the rays of the setting sun. Tinged red, Calandryll thought, with blood. He said, 'No. We're honest travellers in search of beds; no more.'

'I thought ...' the youth grinned apologetically. 'You've the look of warriors, the both of you.'

Bracht chuckled and tossed him a coin. 'Rub them down,' he ordered as they pulled their gear from the saddles. 'Carefully. And feed them oats.'

The boy nodded, gathering the reins as they crossed the yard, watched by the dogs lurking warily by the verandah.

Inside, the tavern was pleasantly cool, unlit logs piled in the hearth, empty save for Anomius and the owner, a fat man, the purple veins on nose and cheeks attesting to his fondness for his own wares. He brought them tankards of dark ale, lingering by their table, curious as the stable-boy, but less easily satisfied.

'You've come from Kesham-vaj?' he asked.

'Indeed we have.'

Anomius's response was swift and amiable, accompanied by a hooding of his pale eyes that clearly warned his companions against speaking up.

'Heard there's trouble up there. Heard Sathoman ek'Hennem's gone to war.'

'From whom?'

The landlord assumed a vague expression, hands wiping absently on his stained apron. 'Folks,' he shrugged. 'Folks say he's raised an army and plans to take the Fayne. Not that he doesn't own it already. More or less.'

'And how do you feel about such a claim?'

'He's welcome to it.' The landlord studied them as if weighing where their sympathies lay. 'His father was Lord of the Fayne and he's that right by blood. Battle of the Stone Field, or no.'

Anomius smiled pleasantly.

'Of course, the Tyrant feels different,' the man continued, encouraged by the wizard's smile, 'and I've heard he's got an army marching against Sathoman. The lictor was out of Bhalusteen this week past, talking about raising levies.'

'Successfully?'

The landlord answered the question with a wink, a finger to veined nose.

'Down here we mind our own business. The Tyrant wants to go to war with Sathoman, let them fight it out themselves, we say. The Tyrants' got his warlocks to call on - why'd he need ordinary folk?'

'Does Sathoman not employ a wizard?' Anomius asked, his parchment features radiating innocent curiosity.

'That he does, and a mighty powerful one, I've heard.' The answer spread Anomius's smile wider across his face. 'They say he's a giant. He breathes flame and fights with a huge axe and magic, both. If you came by way of Kesham-vaj you're lucky you didn't cross his path. You did say you came that way?'

'We did. But there was no sign of fighting - the town was quiet.'

'Just shows, doesn't it?' the landlord remarked, shaking his head. 'Rumours get started and folk start worrying about nothing. I saw you three come in and I began to wonder if you weren't ek'Hennem men, looking the way you do. No offence, friends.'

'Nor any taken,' the wizard smiled. 'We're merely travellers. I hope to conduct business in Nhur-jabal and these are my bodyguards.'

The landlord nodded, eyeing Bracht and Calandryll.

'Well, they look tough enough - and if they brought you safe across the Fayne, they must be good at their work. You saw no sign of Sathoman?'

'None. Perhaps he lurks in Fayne Keep, awaiting the Tyrant's army.'

'Be hard to winkle him out from that fortress. Still, if there is an army on its way I should turn a coin or two.'

'Indeed,' Anomius murmured, 'and more from us if you've baths to offer. We'd wash the trail away and spend the night. In the morning we'll need the ferry.'

'I've rooms and baths, and the ferry crosses at dawn.' The fat man's chins wobbled as he nodded, enquiries diverted by the prospect of profit. 'And I can offer you a better meal than anything in Kesham-vaj. With a fine selection of wines, too.'

'I knew,' Anomius said, beaming at Calandryll and Bracht, 'that this would be the place pass the night.'

'Only place between Kesham-vaj and Bhalusteen,' the landlord chuckled, 'unless you want a bed in some forester's cottage.'

He removed himself then, bustling off to arrange their baths and the meal. Anomius's smile faded as he left, a frown creasing his sallow brow.

'If there's truth in his story,' he murmured, 'we must avoid this army. The Tyrant will send sorcerers, and sorcerers will recognise me for one of their own.'

'A fire-breathing giant?' Bracht asked, his voice bland. 'An axe-wielder?'

'Rumours have their uses,' the wizard responded, ignoring the freesword's mocking tone. 'But another mage will know me on the instant; and ranked against several, even I might lose the battle. We must avoid this army - if it does exist.'

'It must surely march from Nhur-jabal,' Calandryll suggested, 'and there's but the one road suitable to so large a force. How can we avoid it when we must pass through Nhur-jabal to reach Kharasul? Unless you use magic.'

'How so?' asked Anomius. 'The very use must reveal me.'

'Lord Varent used a spell by which he travelled on the instant,' Calandryll said, 'Unseen from one place to another.'

Anomius sniffed noisily, lips down-turned.

'The occult talent manifests in many guises,' he returned, 'and no mage possesses exactly the same powers as another. My own skill - as you've seen - is for aggressive magic. From what you've said of this Varent, I'd hazard a guess his talent is defensive - likely the reason he hesitated to pursue the grimoire himself. No, I cannot transport us to Kharasul by occult means.'

'Then we must ride careful,' Bracht offered.

'And beware the Tyrant's puppets,' Anomius nodded, turning to smile at Calandryll, 'for they'll sense the power in that stone our young friend wears as readily as they sense mine. And he'll suffer the same fate.'

'But I'm no mage,' Calandryll protested.

'But you have a latent talent,' insisted the wizard, 'and they'll see it in you and offer you the choice I rejected: life-long service to the Tyrant or immediate execution.'

Calandryll frowned, both alarmed and intrigued by the wizard's statement. Bracht had made the same suggestion, back on the *Sea Dancer* after the waterspout had taken the warboat, and he had rejected it. Now, for the second time, Anomius had told him he possessed occult talent; and now, even though he was unsure he agreed, and had not an inkling of how to employ such talent if it did exist, it seemed the very suspicion must put him at risk. He turned to the wizard, about to question him, but the landlord appeared again, forestalling such potentially dangerous conversation.

The bowls of soup set before them served as well as his presence to curtail any discussion, the rich, gamey odour reminding them all of hunger so that they ate in silence, concentrating on the food. Trout fresh from the river followed, and then thick steaks of venison, finally wild strawberries, all washed down with wine that was, as the fat man had promised, of excellent vintage. Folk from the little settlement came in as they ate, respecting their privacy until they had finished, but then plying them with questions as to the affairs of the Fayne. Calandryll and Bracht were content to play the parts assigned them by Anomius, leaving the mage to answer, learning more of the affairs of Kandahar as they sipped wine, listening.

The domain claimed by Sathoman ended on the plateau and they were now in the province called the Ryde, its capital, Bhalusteen; beyond that the Kyre, ruled by the Tyrant's city, Nhur-jabal. The Ryde was mostly woodland, peopled by hunters and foresters, whose regard for Tyrant and Sathoman alike was, it seemed, warily contemptuous. The lictor's attempts at raising levies were laughed at, though the notion of an army marching through the woods seemed to irritate them. That Anomius and his 'bodyguards' had crossed the Fayne without difficulty surprised them, but they took it to mean the rumours of war were unfounded, turning to grumble amongst themselves at the intrusion of the Tyrant's army. That, it appeared, was no rumour. Finally they exhausted their enquiries and the travellers were left in peace to take their baths and find their beds.

Calandryll had hoped for an opportunity to speak alone with Bracht, to formulate some plan to rid them of Anomius, but the landlord escorted them all to a single room, where three beds were made ready, and the wizard declared himself satisfied with that arrangement.

He smiled as the door closed, wandering, murmuring, from portal to window, hands tracing elaborate patterns that set the red stone to flickering and filled the chamber with the smell of almonds.

'So,' he beamed when he was done, 'we are secure. I trust you'll not argue my precautions, but I'd not have you flee in the night.'

'What have you done?' demanded Bracht, his dislike of magic showing on his face.

'A few simple spells, my friend,' Anomius informed him, loosing his grubby robe to reveal a no less grubby shirt beneath. 'No one may enter; or leave. And one other - having observed our young companion in battle, I find myself less confident of the delicacy of his ethics, so in the event that he overcome his natural scruples and seek to slay me whilst I sleep I've augmented the spell already set on you, required you to protect me.'

'Against Calandryll?' Bracht shook his head. 'I'd not turn my blade against Calandryll.'

Anomius tugged off his boots. His legs were paler than his face, like old parchment left too long in lightless rooms. Beneath his shirt a paunch swelled, prompting Calandryll to think of a small, ugly toad.

'But you will,' he declared confidently, 'for you'll have no choice. Should Calandryll attack me, you'll slay him.'

Bracht stared at the wizard, his tanned face a mask of rage; Calandryll saw a hand drop to the falchion and said, 'I'll not attack you, Anomius. Do we not need one another?'

'I need you to lead me to the grimoire,' the wizard nodded, unwinding his headdress, 'and without me, you've little chance of crossing Kandahar safely. But still ...'

'I've no great love for magic,' Bracht said angrily, 'and less for spells set on me.'

'Perhaps when I trust you,' Anomius replied, 'I shall remove it. But until such time, I fear you must suffer the ensorcelment. Now I bid you goodnight.'

He climbed beneath the sheets and in moments the room grew loud with his snoring. Calandryll looked at Bracht, shrugging helplessly; the Kern mouthed a curse and flung himself down. Weary, too weary to argue or discuss their situation, Calandryll shucked off his clothes and clambered gratefully into his own bed.

After uncomfortable nights in capitivity and the hard ride down from the plateau, sleep came quickly, bringing, for Calandryll at least, a confusion of dreams. He found himself reliving the skirmish on the plateau, seeing the frightened faces of the brigands as they died, not knowing who slew them, only that they fell to an invisible sword, becoming, in the instant of their dying, Sathoman, who raised his massive blade and roared a battle-shout, that sound transforming him into the flaxen-haired woman, who levelled a blade from the deck of the warboat and called out, her words lost in the rush of swirling water that carried her up and up until she was no more than a dot against a sky filled with the flames of a burning town through which monstrous creatures strode, reaching down to pluck him from the smoke-filled streets even as he mouthed Varent's spell and ran, invisible, from their grasping talons into the arms of Anomius, who laughed and said, 'I am your true companion - the one Reba spoke of.' He tore free and plunged through roiling smoke, pursued now by black-clad men, masked so that only cold eyes filled with implacable hate were visible, his lungs burning, his legs weakening and slowing until he knew that he ran without moving and his pursuers must catch him unless he could somehow reach the great oak that rose before him, its branches stirred by a howling wind, their rustling a message he could not decipher. He strained towards it, knowing that it offered the safety of truth, but the ground before him sloped abruptly and he felt himself falling, down and down, tumbling into a pit towards a pinpoint of light, bright as the sun ...

... Or the faint presentiment of dawn that filtered through the shutters, welcome herald of the new day. He lay, breathing fast, the knowledge that he was awake, in a room in a tavern in Kandahar, Bracht stirring in the bed beside his, Anomius still snoring, though softer now, coming slowly as he opened his eyes and pushed tangled sheets from his legs. He rubbed his face and rose, crossing to the window, reaching for the shutter.

His cry brought Bracht fast from the bed, falchion raised, poised to attack or defend. He shook his head, rubbing at a hand still burning from Anomius's spell.

'I forgot,' he grinned; ruefully.

Bracht grunted, sheathing his blade, and spilled water into a jug, splashing his face.

'You touched the window?'

Anomius peered bleary-eyed from his pillows, yawning noisily; Calandryll nodded. The mage raised a hand and once more the almond scent wafted on the cool air.

'Now that spell is lifted.' Anomius sat up, turning his watery gaze on the Kern. 'But not the other - best remember that.'

Bracht ignored him. Calandryll threw the shutters open, seeing mist hung low along the riverbank, the young ostler scratching his head as he plodded sleepily towards the stables, the tree-thick slope rising above, its upper edge lost in grey. He turned away, using the bowl, and ran fingers through his hair, thinking that soon he must tie it back, like Bracht's. He dressed, and with his comrade waited for Anomius to swathe himself in his grubby robe.

The wizard's toilet was brief and soon they were seated in the common room, breaking their fast with hot bread and steaming tea. The landlord presented them with his reckoning and they went out to the stable, saddling their rested animals and leading them down to the ferry through mist that swirled and began to break as the sun rose and a breeze got up.

The raft stirred in the current as they walked the horses on board, the ferryman a wiry Kand, bare-chested despite the early morning chill. He took their coin and suggested they speed their passage by helping him with the ropes: Anomius held the horses while Bracht and Calandryll each seized a line and began to haul the flat-bottomed vessel across.

The mist was blown away and the sky become blue as they grounded on the farther bank, watching as the ferryman commenced his return journey. He was in mid-stream when Bracht pointed to the road descending from the plateau.

'Riders!' The freesword's voice was urgent. 'Twenty or thirty.'

'Sathoman must have discovered our absence sooner than I'd anticipated,' Anomius said.

'And those men must have ridden through the night. Curse you, wizard! I told you it was foolishness to delay.' Bracht's tone was angry. Anomius merely smiled, rubbing at his bulbous nose. 'We're safe from them here - did I not promise you a night's rest would restore my powers?'

'They've but to reach the ferry and cross,' Brecht said. 'Our lead is cut and if we run, we'll likely charge headlong into the Tyrant's advance guard.'

'They'll get no farther than this spot,' the wizard

replied. 'Do you not trust me?'

The Kern's face was answer enough: Anomius shrugged, shaking his head as if disappointed by such lack of faith.

'Watch,' he said calmly. 'Watch, and learn what I can do.'

THIRTEEN

THE wizard handed Bracht his reins and walked to the water's edge, stooping there, his hands delving into the rich mud. He scooped up a ball of the sludge, kneading it as he ambled casually back to where they waited. Calandryll saw that he worked the stuff into crude semblance of human shape, setting the mannikin down where the ground was dry to complete his rough sculpture. The approaching riders were hidden in the timber and the mage worked without hurry. Squatting over the tiny figure, he spat, working the saliva into the blank face, then drew a small dagger from the folds of his robe and pricked his thumb, squeezing a droplet of blood onto the mud doll. His ragged nails etched an approximation of eyes, a mouth, and then he took a twig, setting that in the shapeless right hand. He began to murmur a spell: Calandryll saw the red stone at his throat pulse fiery, smelled the now-familiar scent of almonds. Anomius straightened, wiping his hands on his robe, smiling as he turned to glance at his unwilling companions.

'Watch,' he commanded, and pointed at the figurine.

It seemed then that fire sprang from his fingers,

washing over the mannekin, the wet mud drying on the instant, baked hard in the supernatural flame. The horses shied, plunging, ears flattened back and eyes rolling, and for an instant Calandryll's attention was diverted. He calmed the roan as best he could, clinging tight to its bridle, and returned his gaze to the little mud figure. It was no longer little: it grew even as he watched, elongating, thickening, the twig it held enlarging in proportion. It was the size of a child, then large as a youth; man-sized, and still growing. It sat up, flakes of dried mud falling from its back, the indentations that were its eyes deep pits now, that glowed with an unholy fire, the twig a cudgel. Anomius spoke again and the thing rose to its feet, clumsy at first, swaying, arms waving, flailing the branch, still growing. It peered around, a massive, red-eyed golem, taller now than Sathoman, towering over the frightened horses, the twig become a staff, thicker around than a normal man might hold. It took a step, a second, as if testing its ability to move, and raised the great club it held, scything the air. Across the river, the ferryman stared in awe, then shouted something and took to his heels, running for the inn. The golem heard him, the globular head swinging ponderously to stare over the sunlit water, an inarticulate cry, neither animal or human. bursting from the ragged gash of its mouth as the club rose, crashing down into the river in a great silver burst of spray.

Anomius spoke again, in a language hard for human tongue to shape, and the creature ceased its roaring, turning to face him. The horses screamed in protest and the wizard motioned them away, beckoning the golem. Calandryll and Bracht, their eyes wary on the monster, lead the horses back into the shade of the timber. On the slope across the river Sathomen's men came into view again, riding hard. Anomius brought the monster clear of the bank, under the shade of a massive cypress, the grey head touching the lower branches. It had stopped growing now and the wizard craned back his head, peering up at the burning eyes, speaking softly. The golem made a grunting sound and turned to face across the river, standing with the club upraised, a misshapen colossus.

'We need dally no longer.' The wizard favoured his creation with a last admiring glance and walked to where Bracht and Calandryll waited. 'They'll not get past him.'

He took his reins from the nervous Kern and clambered astride the grey horse. Calandryll and Bracht mounted, letting Anomius take the lead as they followed the road into the forest.

'There are twenty, perhaps thirty, of them,' Bracht called. 'How can you be sure none will get by ... that?'

Anomius chuckled gaily.

'The ferry will take no more than what? Six riders at a time? My little pet will slay them all - I doubt they'll make more than one attempt. But if they do ...' He laughed again, 'Well, he'll slay them six by six. Have faith, my friends - you ride with the greatest sorcerer in all Kandahar. I'm only sorry we lack the time to wait and watch him at work. He was a splendid creation, do you not agree?'

Neither offered answer and the wizard chuckled to himself, urging the grey horse to a faster pace along the wide roadway cut through the forest. Trees stood tall to either side, oaks and beech and ash spreading limbs across the trail so that they rode through dappled light, occasional shafts of brilliance lancing from a sky mostly hidden behind the foliage, the shadows painted with the woodland's green. Ferns grew luxuriant along the verges, and grass, lush and thick, the air sweet-scented and loud with birdsong, game trails evidence of deer and hares, and the hunting creatures that preyed on them. They held a steady pace, not speaking, until the morning was well advanced and then halted where a stream bisected the road, spanned by an ancient stone bridge, its masonry green with moss. Frogs splashed from the bank as they took the horses down to drink, and a wide-winged heron croaked a protest at their intrusion, flapping heavily away downstream to some more private hunting ground.

They rested there, eating fruit and cheese purchased at the inn and filling their canteens while the horses cropped the grass along the waterside, then started off once more, the sun overhead now, warm, summer approaching fast in this more southerly latitude.

The going was easier than the crossing of the Fayne. There was no gaheen to dry the air and fray tempers, none of the scorching heat that had marked the journey from Mherut'yi to Kesham-vaj, and a plentitude of streams and grazing for the animals. Several times they saw deer start from the road ahead, darting into the cover of the timber, and Bracht promised to bring them fresh venison should Anomius allow him time to hunt.

Calandryll rode mostly lost in thought, trusting to Bracht's keen eye to warn of danger as he pondered the problem set by the wizard. The creation of the golem assured him that Anomius's powers were fully restored and he had little doubt that when they camped the sorcerer would set spells to bind them, to protect himself. Flight seemed impossible - and there were obvious advantages to be gained from Anomius's presence - but somehow, he knew, they must rid themselves of the mage before reaching Tezin-dar. To bring him to the lost city must surely result in his seizing the Arcanum for himself - the fiction of the fabulous grimoire would collapse under closer examination - and that thought was no less horrifying than the likelihood of Azumandias obtaining the book. Azumandias and Anomius must be, he felt, of like temperament: the one remained a mystery, but the other had demonstrated his ruthlessness to undeniable extent. Beneath his false jollity, beneath his unassuming appearance, there was a steely core of utter selfishness, an iron-willed desire to establish himself as effective master of Kandahar. He had betrayed Sathoman ek'Hennem - had mercilessly slain men he likely knew by name - because he believed the lie of the grimoire, believed that possession of that imaginary book would endow him with powers insuperable. Should he come into possession of the Arcanum he would likely, Calandryll felt certain, take Azumandias's path: would seek to raise the Mad God. And in the doing destroy the world. He was not, Calandryll thought, sane, and by some means he must be left behind. Or destroyed.

That thought rang bell-like in his mind: *Anomius must be destroyed.*

Its cold clarity chilled him, for he recognised that its very formulation, his instinctive acceptance of its logical outcome, meant that he had changed. Anomius had sensed it - had said that Calandryll would now kill him without compunction - but he had not accepted that the wizard was correct. Now he knew Anomius was right: had he the chance he would slay the warlock with a clear conscience. He was no longer the mild scholar mocked by Tobias, despaired of by his father. This quest had changed him; beyond the inevitable hardening of rough living, beyond the slaying of men in battle, it had changed his basic ethics. The young man who had mooned over Nadama - it came to him that he could no longer clearly recall her face, that realisation in itself shocking - existed no more. The boy who had suffered Tobias's jibes was gone. He had hardened in ways more than physical: he snorted cynical laughter to think how that would please Bylath; how it would confirm to his brother that he was, indeed, a man to fear. Secca seemed now a distant memory, a life left behind, shed as a serpent sheds its skin. He was by no means sure that ends justified means, but he was certain that he must prevent Anomius from finding the Arcanum. And if the only way to ensure that was by slaying the wizard he would, as the man had sensed, cut his throat while he slept; and deal with any qualms of conscience after the deed.

But how? Anomius protected himself well, and it was unlikely he would allow his guard to slip. Should Calandryll slay him, then the glamour placed on Bracht must set comrade against comrade - and of that struggle there could be only one outcome: Bracht would win. And - if he were prepared to sacrifice himself - Bracht alone could not locate the Arcanum, it would lie waiting for Azumandias. It seemed an impasse, a deadlock born of the wizard's cunning, and he ground his teeth in frustrated anger as he grappled with the problem, for there seemed no solution.

Bracht's voice snapped him from his contemplation and he saw that they rode across a tree-encircled meadow, oaks spreading gnarled branches like suppliant hands all around.

'I said,' the Kern repeated, 'That if the Tyrant's army advances on the Fayne we'd best ride careful. With open eyes.'

Calandryll grinned an apology, reining his horse a little so that Anomius gained distance. Lowering his voice, he said, 'I was thinking of the warlock. Of how we might rid ourselves of his company.'

'I, too,' Bracht returned, studying the black-shrouded figure bobbing on the grey's saddle, 'but with little success. You?'

Calandryll shook his head.

'I'd slay him if I could, but ...'

Bracht nodded, understanding.

'And I cannot. Somehow, then, we must escape him.'

'In such manner that he's not able to follow us.'

'I think,' Bracht said, 'that we can only wait for now,

and watch. If opportunity arises ...'

'Aye,' Calandryll agreed, thinking that it was a forlorn hope.

At least he aids our passage across Kandahar. Perhaps in Kharasul, or on the sea, we might lose him.'

'Unless his presence attracts the attention of the Tyrant's sorcerers and we find ourselves prisoners again.'

'There's that,' Bracht murmured, then smiled, 'But we had little hope of unhindered passage when we began this journey.'

'I'd not,' Calandryll returned, 'anticipated civil war. Nor the Tyrant's wizards ranged against us.'

Such thoughts had occurred to Anomius, too, it seemed, for when they halted that night, in a clearing ringed by great, straight-trunked beeches, he prepared once more to work his magic.

Dusk wove shadows amongst the timber, the aerial denizens of the forest winging to their roosts, wary rabbits watching from the edges of the glade, squirrels furtive in the branches as the sorcerer stood with arms outthrust, his voice raised in a singsong chant. Calandryll and Bracht turned from their tending of the horses to watch, seeing Anomius delve inside his robe to produce a small pouch of leather. Still chanting, he loosed the drawstrings and upended the sack over one palm. Something pale, like the shimmer of frost in early morning light, fell onto his hand and he blew gently on the glowing object, then set it carefully down. Like the golem back on the riverbank, it grew until they saw once again the creature that had watched them in Octofan's barn. It crouched on stubby legs, arms thin as a malnourished child's wrapped about its knees, the misshapen head cocked first to one side and then the other as it fastened huge black eyes on Anomius. He gestured at the sky and they saw the silvery wings spread wide, the creature rise, running awkwardly to gain the speed necessary for flight, the wings beating, bearing it aloft, no longer ungainly, but a graceful, swooping creature of the air. It circled the wizard twice, then rose into the rapidly darkening sky, climbing swiftly above the treetops, a receding glow that soon disappeared beyond the beeches.

'He'll tell us where the army lies,' Anomius promised, settling himself comfortably on the grass.

'And warn the Tyrant's wizards that magic's abroad?' Calandryll asked.

Anomius shrugged negligently. 'Likely they'll assume him a spy of Sathoman's - they know I'm lieged to the Fayne lord, so they'll think him sent from the highlands.'

'And if they send out their own *quyvhals*?'

'Aha!' Anomius clapped his hands delightedly. 'You are familiar with the *quyvhal*?'

Calandryll dropped his saddle; spread his blanket.

'I have read of them. Both Sarnium and Medith mention them; Corrhum, too.'

Anomius nodded, smiling. 'I knew you were a remarkable young man,' he complimented. 'We must talk of this - Sathoman and his followers are more interested in conquest than erudition and I long for civilized discourse.'

Once - in a life left behind - such a compliment might have flattered Calandryll. *Had* flattered him, when Varent paid it, but now he said only. 'We must get a fire going.'

'By all means,' the wizard agreed, 'but after, let us talk. Perhaps over roast venison?'

This latter was directed at Bracht, who met the tacit suggestion with a look of surprise.

'You're not afraid I'll flee?'

Anomius shook his head.

'You gave your word as a warrior of Cuan na'For -

nor do I believe you'd quit your comrade.' He chuckled, his smile a challenge. 'And the spell I set upon you would bring you back. Stray too far and you'll know pain beyond your imagining.'

'The deer may not know my limitations.'

Calandryll saw fury spark in the Kern's blue eyes, Anomius shrugged again and said, 'Find one within the aegis of my spell, then.'

Bracht stared at him a moment longer, then nodded, stringing the bow. Calandryll moved to join him, but the wizard waved him back. 'We need but one deer and you've no bow.' He accepted, mind returning to the thoughts of that afternoon as Bracht faded into the undergrowth. Was the sorcerer's desire to keep him there based on need, rather than the wish for conversation? They could neither of them attack him, save that they fight together, but were they able to escape the wizard's observation ... might his spells be useless then? He said, 'I'll gather wood,' and when Anomius nodded, set to scouring the edges of the clearing for the makings of a fire.

A cheerful blaze begun. Anomius motioned him to the blanket and he squatted, setting a kettle to heat water for tea.

'So,' the wizard declared, his tone conversational, amiable, as though they were two friends idling away the hours before sleep, 'you have read the classics.'

'The library in Secca is extensive,' he murmured, 'and I've a love for books.'

'Mandradus built a sizeable library.' Anomius's voice was nostalgic. 'But Sathoman has little concern for books. You've read Dashirrhan?'

'No.' Calandryll shook his head, busying himself with the kettle. 'Though I've heard of him. Wasn't he a mage?'

'One of the greatest,' Anomius nodded, 'and a historian, to boot. His *Treatise on Magick and Grammaryes* is a marvellous work. It mentions Tezin-dar, of course. But oddly says nothing of the grimoire we seek.'

His voice was mild, but behind his seeming affability Calandryll heard the scrape of steel: he shrugged, adding herbs to the infusion.

'Yet your Lord Varent den Tarl sent you seeking the book. Even though it is not mentioned by Dashirrhan. Or Sarnium. Or Medith.'

Calandryll assumed an expression he hoped was guileless. 'I know only what I've told you,' he said.

Anomius scratched thoughtfully at his grandiose nose. The eyes he turned on Calandryll reflecting the fire's light, suddenly akin to the glowing orbs of the golem.

'Perhaps Varent lied to you. Or you to me.'

'Would you not know, had I lied?'

He forced himself to return the wizard's stare, eyes locking for long moments. Then Anomius smiled, chuckling.

'The stone protects you, boy - I cannot see past it. Were you to remove it, however ...'

'I cannot!' Quickly, Calandryll shook his head, desperately extemporizing. 'Lord Varent made that clear to me, in Secca, when he explained what we must do. The stone itself is magical, and Lord Varent set further spells on it - he impressed upon me that should I remove it, or it be removed, I can no longer locate the grimoire. To remove the stone is to lose the book.'

Anomius was silent for a while. Calandryll stirred the kettle, hoping the lie was convincing. Then the wizard sniffed. 'So be it - I shall not attempt to coerce knowledge.' He chuckled again, his casual tone returning. 'But tell me more of this mysterious grimoire.'

'I have only Lord Varent's word,' Calandryll said, resisting the impulse to express his relief with a sigh, 'He said that the grimoire is one of the forgotten books - that it contains grammaryes used by the gods themselves, and must invest its owner with power unimaginable. He risked my father's wrath, perhaps even war between our cities, to bring me out of Secca, and - as you've seen - he furnished the coin to finance our travels. I took him on his word.'

Anomius's eyes flickered, hooding: Calandryll hoped he saw greed rekindled.

'And so you set out for Gessyth. You and the Kern, alone.'

'Lord Varent feared a larger party must alert Azumandias. That he would endeavour to seize the map.'

'You forget the stone. You say the map is useless without the stone.'

'Azumandias has no need of it. Lord Varent said his powers are such that he could locate the grimoire without its aid.'

'Then so might I.'

Despite the fire's warmth a chill raised hairs on Calandryll's neck: he shrugged, fighting alarm to answer the wizard with some kind of logic, some reasoning that would persuade him.

'Perhaps. But if not . . .'

Bird-like laughter twittered, then Anomius's voice grew cold with threat. 'If this Azumandias has no need of the stone, then likely nor do I,' he said. 'And if I have no need of the stone, I have no need of you or the Kern.'

'No,' Calandryll agreed, the chill joined by sweat now, 'but I think that without the stone it must be harder to find the grimoire. And surely Tezin-dar is guarded - Medith speaks of sentinels; Sarnium of demons at the portals.'

'Aye,' Anomius nodded, 'there is that.'

'So likely the finding must be rendered easier by the stone.'

Again the wizard nodded.

'You argue well, Calandryll den Karynth. Stop trembling now, for I'll keep you with me. Unless I find you've lied.'

He ducked his head, licking lips gone suddenly dry.

'And when you've the book?'

'If what you say is true I'll be the mightiest sorcerer in all the world.'

'And us?'

Anomius shook his head; effected a casual wave.

'You'll find me generous. Why should I harm the two who bring me to such power? You'll be under my protection.'

'In Kandahar?' he asked. 'What of Sathoman? What of the Chaipaku?'

'With such power at my command you'll be safe from both,' Anomius promised. 'I'll make Sathoman Tyrant and buy off the Brotherhood. Perhaps I'll make you Domm of Secca; Bracht overlord of Cuan na'For. You see? You've as much to gain from this as I. We're allies, we three.'

It seemed the moment of danger passed: lust for power seduced the wizard. Calandryll smiled and said, 'And yet you don't trust us.'

The bird-like laughter trilled again. 'Our alliance is born of necessity, rather than choice,' the wizard tittered. 'Neither you or the Kern seem overfond of my company - would you not, in my place, tread cautiously?'

'I would,' Calandryll agreed; honestly.

'Nonetheless we remain allies, so we'd as well make the best of it.'

'Aye,' he said.

'So we travel together and there's an end to it. Serve me well and you'll be well-rewarded. Seek to betray me and . . .'

The wizard's right hand moved and flame gouted high, the kettle seething. It was demonstration enough:

Calandryll sprang back, measuring his length on the grass as Anomius laughed.

'Now let's forget such depressing matters and speak of books, of learning,' he said cheerfully. 'We'll while away the time until Bracht returns with scholarly talk. What do you say to Sarnium's proposition that life began north of the Borrhun-maj?'

Relieved, Calandryll bent his mind to these easier matters and they talked until Bracht appeared, a bloody haunch of venison slung on his shoulder.

'Well done,' Anomius applauded, 'this talking's given me a rare appetite.'

The Kern drew his knife and began to carve the meat, spitting strips over the fire.

'Your creature's not returned?' he demanded.

'Unless he finds urgent need he'll not be back until dawn,' Anomius replied, 'the *quyvhal* range far, and they love the night.'

'And if he sights the Tyrant's army?'

'He'll tell me where it stands and we'll avoid it.'

'And was Calandryll's question answered?'

'Which one?' Anomius asked.

'What if the Tyrant's warlocks send their own *quyvhal*?'

'The creatures have no magical apptitude of their own,' the wizard beamed. 'They are eyes in the night, no more - should one sight us it will see three travellers feasting on roast venison, not magic.'

'You knew of Calandryll's stone through the creature,' argued Bracht. 'When it found us in Octofan's barn.'

'Calandryll made reference to the stone then and the *quyvhal* reported that to me,' Anomius responded, 'That was how I knew.'

Bracht grunted, satisfied, accepting the tea Calandryll offered. He sipped and glanced at the wizard again.

'The army likely lies between us and Nhur-jabal,' he said after a while, 'so to avoid it we must take the forest trails. Do you know them?'

'I have ways to know them,' Anomius answered easily, more intent on the sizzling venison than the freesword's question.

'And the Tyrant's road is the swiftest path to the coast, but passes through Nhur-jabal.'

'Yes.' Anomius nodded absently. 'What of it?'

'Do all the Tyrant's sorcerers ride with the army?'

'I doubt it,' the wizard murmured, and snorted scornfully. 'The Tyrant is a cautious man and he'll remain safe in his palace with sufficient of his pets to ease his mind.'

'Then how do we get by them?' Bracht demanded. 'They'll know you for a sorcerer, will they not?'

'Cautious as ever,' chuckled Anomius. 'And correct - yes, if I go to Nhur-jabal they'll sense my presence.'

'Then how do we reach Kharasul?'

'The road's but one way.' Anomius tapped his nose, smiling. 'Nhur-jabal lies in the foothills of the Kharm-rhanna, where the Tannyth river comes down from the mountains. Above and below the city the river divides - the Yst flows down to Cape Vishat'yi and the Shemme runs west to Kharasul. We must cross south of Nhur-jabal and take passage down the Shemme.'

Bracht frowned, turning the meat. 'A boat?' he demanded. 'There's nowhere to run on a boat.'

'If we avoid Nhur-jabal we'll not need to run,' said Anomius. 'The Shemme's fast-flowing and we'll be past before they know it. Trust me, my friend. And if that venison's cooked, pass me some - I grow faint from hunger.'

As if to emphasise his request his belly rumbled sonorously: Bracht plucked a strip of meat from the flames and passed it across the fire. Anomius took it and began to chew noisily, oblivious of the juices that dribbled down his shallow chin and dripped onto his robe. More fastidious, Calandryll and Bracht used their daggers to carve the meat, using slabs of journeybread for platters.

The night grew older and the moon showed above the glade, a waned yellow-white disc against the star-spread blue-black of the sky. There was no sign of the *quyvhal* and, with hunger satisfied, they rolled themselves in their blankets and slept.

It seemed that Calandryll had come to terms with the bloody necessities of the journey, for his slumber was dreamless, untroubled until the red glow of the stone penetrated his closed lids and he woke, eyes opening to find Anomius squatted before the silvery shape of his magical observer.

Dawn was close, the moon gone and the stars lost in the nebulous grey that replaced the blue velvet of night. Dew glistened on the grass and he heard a horse snort, stamping once. The *quyvhal* was settled on its haunches, the huge black eyes intent on the wizard's face, the slitted mouth open, emitting a high-pitched whistling sound in which Calandryll could discern no words. He saw Bracht awake, like him watching the strange conversation. The fluting ended and Anomius reached out, patting the over-sized head, the *quyvhal* arching its back as might a cat caressed by its owner. Then the wizard opened the leather sack and murmured softly, and the *quyvhal* shrank, dwindling to a glimmer of pale light that hopped into the bag, Anomius tightening the drawstrings and tucking the pouch beneath his robe. He moved closer to the fire, adding timber, and saw that he was observed.

'The army lies between us and Nhur-jabal,' he declared as the fire sprang to fresh life, 'perhaps three days off, by my pet's reckoning. A squadron of cavalry guided by foresters forms the advance guard - half a day ahead of the main body.'

Calandryll yawned, stretching; Bracht moved to the fire, setting water to heat.

'Back at the inn the landlord spoke of a town - Bhalusteen - within a few days ride,' the Kern murmured. 'Must we avoid it?'

'The army will reach Bhalusteen today,' Anomius nodded, hands scratching vigorously beneath his robe, 'so, yes - we'd best take the forest trails.'

'We need supplies,' said Bracht.

'There will be hamlets.'

Anomius appeared unconcerned; Bracht turned to Calandryll.

'You have the map?'

Calandryll fetched the chart of Kandahar from his pack, spreading it on his knees. Bracht and Anomius moved closer, peering over his shoulders.

'We are here.' The wizard set a ragged nail to a spot a little way past the course of the Narn, below the contour lines indicating the plateau. 'Bhalusteen is here; Nhur-jabal, here. We must travel southwards, then swing west again when the army's behind us.'

He described a course that swung in a wide curve through the great central forest, avoiding settlements and marked trails, running well wide of the road. Calandryll saw that it brought them out in the foothills of the Kharm-rhanna, south of Nhur-jabal, where the Shemme separated from the Tannyth.

'We'll lose time,' Bracht said. 'Why not return to the road beyond Bhalusteen?'

'Because there'll likely be a mage left in every town of any size along the way,' Anomius replied, 'and while I could undoubtedly overcome them, such conflict will delay us longer than a detour.'

And leach your powers, Calandryll thought. Aloud he said, 'There are no trails marked where you propose we go.'

The wizard's answering smile was smug. Leaning

closer to the fire he said, 'I told you - I have ways to know them.'

Those ways he demonstrated after they had eaten.

The horses were saddled and the fire stamped to a charred memory, their gear stowed ready for departure. The daylight inhabitants of the forest began to stir as the sun broke through the overcast, blue replacing the grey, banks of white cloud riding a warm south wind high above. Anomius delved in his saddlebags, producing a phial from which he sprinkled a pinch of brownish powder that he clutched in his left hand. His right he raised before him, chanting. For an instant, the birdsong risen in greeting of the new day faltered, then redoubled as feathered forms descended from the trees to flutter about the sorcerer. In moments he was surrounded by a storm of multi-coloured shapes, finches and thrushes, dunnocks, cuckoos, pipits and pigeons, warblers, nuthatches, woodpeckers and tree-creepers all flocking to his call. They scattered on a word as a wide-winged goshawk swooped towards the black-robed figure, settling like a well-trained falcon on his outthrust arm. He cooed softly, opening his left hand, bringing it close to the bird's bright eyes, then blowing, the brown powder swirling about the proud head. The goshawk emitted a single harsh cry and shifted on the wizard's arm, rocking gently to and fro as though momentarily stunned. Anomius murmured softly and flung his arm up, like a falconer setting his bird to course. The hawk spread its blue-grey wings and soared aloft, circling the clearing once, then winging above the trees to disappear westwards. The mage smiled, staring after the bird, and walked to where Bracht held his horse.

Calandryll saw that his watery eyes seemed brighter, but curiously unfocussed, as though he looked beyond his immediate surroundings to sights invisible to mortal eye. He mounted with even less grace than usual and smiled down.

'Now we can find the trails; and know where the Tyrant's army stands. Follow me.'

He shook the reins, urging the grey horse across the glade, away from the road. Bracht and Calandryll moved after him, intrigued.

It seemed the goshawk was their guide, for several times that day they saw the bird ahead, swooping amongst the dense timber, and the wizard led them unerringly to forest paths they might have missed, taking them down game trails and streambeds hidden beneath overhanging foliage, riding without hesitation at thickets that appeared impenetrable until branches were swept aside to reveal the narrow and secret ways of the woodlands. He saw, Calandryll realised, through the hawk's eyes, for when they halted at noon, by a spring that fed a little rivulet trickling amongst leafy oaks, he informed them that the army had reached Bhalusteen and made camp there, and that at least six sorcerers accompanied the force.

'The Tyrant flatters me,' he declared proudly. 'Six warlocks sent against one - my fame grows, I think.'

'And when they reach the highland?' Calandryll asked, curious that the little man could so easily forget his loyalties. 'What of Sathoman then?'

Anomius shrugged, a negligent gesture of dismissal. 'Even with six warlocks, the gaining of those heights will be hard,' he said. 'A handful of men can hold the rim, and then - if need be - fall back on Kesham-vaj. Sathoman will have Mherut'yi by now, and he's still Fayne Keep as his last retreat. And that fortress is warded by spells the six will find mightily difficult to overcome. Sathoman must manage without me for a while.'

'He'll not thank you, though,' Calandryll said.

'Should he be defeated he'll find it a temporary

reverse,' the wizard answered. 'Once I've secured the grimoire I shall return and fulfil my promise - he'll be lord of all Kandahar before I'm done, and he'll thank me well enough for that.'

He spoke no more until nightfall, his attention focussed on the strange communion with the vigilant goshawk, leaving them the chance to talk, low-voiced, of escape.

'He promised reward,' Calandryll informed Bracht, 'In return for our aid.'

'And should he discover the grimoire exists only in your imagination?' the Kern returned. 'What then? His anger? Or worse - his taking of the Arcanum?'

'That must not happen,' Calandryll said firmly.

'If he accompanies us to Tezin-dar, how can it not?' asked Bracht. 'If we bring him to the city, then he must surely realise that there's no grimoire to be had, but a larger prize. And I trust him no more than Varent.'

Calandryll shook his head helplessly. 'How can we escape him?' he wondered. 'He binds us with his magic. You cannot flee him or slay him; and if I attempt his murder, you're bound to kill me.'

Bracht nodded grimly. 'The Tyrant's sorcerers might defeat him, were we able to bring him close.'

'And - if Anomius spoke the truth - recognise whatever power I have,' Calandryll said, 'and thus bind me to the Tyrant's service. Or execute me.'

'There must be something we can do.' Bracht's tone suggested that he did not see what. 'Some way to escape him.'

'I cannot see it.' Calandryll looked to where the wizard jounced awkwardly on the grey horse. 'He has us caught.'

'The warboat had us caught,' Bracht said, 'but we escaped that.'

He glanced at Calandryll as he spoke, his eyes expressing hope and something close to apprehension.

Calandryll said, 'This occult talent he says I have? I told you then I had no knowledge of it, and nor do I now. What happened then I cannot comprehend - if you ask me to use magic against him, I know not how.'

'It would seem our only hope,' Bracht said. 'Save that some other agency intervene.'

Calandryll laughed briefly, cynically.

'Such as Azumandias? Or the Tyrant's sorcerers? It seems that all this journey brings us from pan to fire.'

'And yet we move towards our goal,' Bracht said. 'Were it not for Anomius we'd hang now on Sathoman's gallows. Did he not guide us through these woods we'd ride head-on into Tyrant's army. There's that, at least.'

'You think there's some design in this?'

Calandryll grinned, the angling of his lips expressing disbelief rather than humour. Bracht shrugged and said, 'Perhaps not, but we do cross Kandahar fast.'

That much, at least, was true, for they travelled as swiftly as they might along the road. Swifter, given that the road must bring them to the army and that meeting, certainly, delay them if not halt them altogether. Anomius, thanks to his magic, was a successful guide, bringing them in the days that followed around the Tyrant's squadrons, avoiding the scouts who flanked the army and the wizards left behind in the settlements along the way. Twice they hid from outriders, and three times swung wide of their elected path to avoid outlaw bands, but always they progressed steadily south and then west, drawing ever closer to their destination. By day the wizard rode ahead, seeing through avian eyes, and by night he sent out his *quyvhal*, the spectral creature returning each dawn to report in its strange, fluting voice. What supplies they needed, they obtained from the hamlets they found deep in the forest, small clusters of wooden houses occupied by hunters and charcoal burners, each with a few pigs, or some sheep grazing land cleared for that purpose, a milch cow or two, and little plots were vegetables grew. The folk they met were incurious, content to accept that they were travellers bound for Nhur-jabal with no wish to meet the Tyrant's army on the road. Indeed, it seemed that gave them a kind of bond, for the forest dwellers were private folk with little interest in the doings of such lords as the Tyrant or Sathoman ek'Hennem, preferring to live their lonely lives apart from the ways of Nhur-jabal and the rivalries of the nobility. Their hospitality was plain, but freely given, and the travellers made good speed. As the spring became summer they came in sight of Nhur-jabal.

The terrain grew irregular, the Kharm-rhanna like a great rocky wave, sending ripples into the heart of Kandahar, the woodland climbing and falling into dells until they stood upon the rim of a great river valley. Across the sweep of lowland the forest thinned, breaking like a green dendroid sea on the rocks of the Kharm-rhanna, green giving way to blue-black granite. The great mountain range that divided Kandahar from the jungles of Gash bulked dark across the western sky, the upper peaks lit by the setting sun, burning defiantly fiery as night advanced from the east, the land below already overtaken, shadowed save for the distant sparkling lights of the villages and towns along the banks of the Tannyth river. The land fell away before them to the wide ribbon of the southwards-flowing Yst, foothills dim beyond to west and north. Across the river, as though suspended in the night, they saw the lights of Nhur-jabal, standing on the farther scarp of the valley. They made camp there, where the timber still afforded plentiful cover, and in the morning studied the city revealed by the new day's light.

The goshawk was released from Anomius's enchantment, their path clear enough no winged fore-runner was needed, only cunning and a fair helping of luck. To the north lay the Tyrant's road, emerging from the forest to cross the Tannyth on a massive stone bridge, running on into the foothills to meet Nhur-jabal, where the city stood on a bluff dominating the valley below, protected at its rear by the crags of the Kharm-rhanna, the Tyrant's citadel a guardian over all. Stone-built houses spread across the bluff, tumbling down the sides like some frozen, rocky waterfall, fortress-like in its lofty isolation, its keep the palace that towered above the city, elevated on a shelf that thrust from the mountains, walled and towered, drawbridges granting access to the inner courts. The Tannyth ran eastwards past the foot of the bluff, and across the valley they saw the gap that marked the exit of the Shemme, that river sparkling faintly in the morning sun.

'There's a town beyond the pass.'

Calandryll offered the map to Bracht, who nodded, studying the terrain ahead.

'We'll find a boat there,' Anomius said, 'and ride the river to Kharasul. Thence to Gessyth and Tezin-dar.'

Anticipation leant his voice an unusual stridency and when Calandryll looked at his sallow face he saw the watery eyes burned greedily. 'Can the Tyrant's sorcerers not sense you so close to Nhur-jabal?' he asked, studying the valley warily.

Anomius shrugged, fidgetting as though he wished only to be gone, to cross careless of the danger. He seemed oblivious of the great city sprawling so close.

'We must take a ferry across the river,' Bracht said, pointing, 'and there are settlements on both banks. Horsemen from Nhur-jabal could intercept us at the pass.'

Anomius chopped the air impatiently, parchment features creased in vexation. 'Do you dawdle now, all is lost,' he complained irritably. 'We have no choice save to take the ferry and find the pass. Come - we ride.'

'Wait!' Bracht raised a calming hand. 'If the Tyrant's

as cautious as you say, he's likely got soldiery down there. And if his warlocks learn of your presence ...'

'A risk we must take,' Anomius snapped, interrupting, 'Come!'

'Better to attempt it by night,' the Kern said.

'The ferry stands moored by night,' returned the wizard. 'And we'll attract more attention if we seek to cross then.'

Bracht studied the valley with a practiced eye. 'A day's ride across,' he murmured, ignoring Anomius's angry glare. 'The morning, at least, to reach the ferry; the afternoon to gain the pass. The horses could use rest. The final stretch is uphill, and if we must run they might well falter.'

'We take the chance,' the wizard barked. 'I've too much to gain to dally now.'

'Still I say that darkness is our friend,' Bracht declared, making no move to mount.

Calandryll stared at him, seeing the tanned feautures set in obstinate lines. He glanced at Anomius and saw anger writ clear on the wizard's face. It occurred to him that the Kern provoked the sorcerer with deliberate intent, and wondered why.

Anomius raised a hand, extending a threatening finger at Bracht.

'Do you mount and ride, or suffer my anger?'

'The horses are wearied,' Bracht said. 'We ran them hard through the forest, and if we must flee fresh-mounted men they need a day to rest.'

'Curse you, freesword!' Anomius snarled, and Bracht was thrown back, staggering against the chestnut horse, which shied, snickering in alarm. Calandryll saw the red stone flicker, caught almonds on the moist morning air. He moved to Bracht's side as the Kern gasped, clutching at his chest.

'Shall I slay you?' Anomius demanded. 'Shall I leave you dead here, for the crows to pick your bones?'

Bracht rose on hands and knees, teeth gritted, his voice coming harsh through the clenching.

'The ... horses ... need ... rest.'

He screamed as the wizard worked his violent magic again, falling on his face with hands pressed hard to his breast, knees drawing up to his belly, trembling as pain racked him. Calandryll shouted, 'No! Remember the augury! The spaewife said we are bonded, Bracht and I - without him I'll not reach Tezin-dar!'

'There's that,' Anomius admitted, his voice less strident now. 'So - put him on his horse. But remember, freesword, that if you argue with me you'll know more pain. Worse pain!'

Bracht grunted, slowly straightening as the wizard lowered his hand. Sweat beaded his forehead as Calandryll helped him rise, steadied him as he shuddered, reaching painfully for the chestnut's saddle. He set a foot in the stirrup and hauled himself astride, clumsy as Anomius for the moment. Calandryll passed him the reins and saw that he smiled; grimly. He opened his mouth to ask why, but Bracht shook his head, silencing him, pointing to the roan in tacit indication that he mount without questions.

Calandryll left him as he wished, thinking that Bracht's provocation of the sorcerer had, indeed, been deliberate: he wondered what the Kern thought to gain from such a testing of the wizard's patience.

'Come,' Anomius called, cheerful again now, 'to the ferry.'

A loggers' trail descended through the timber to the Yst river, wide and muddy, marked with the stumps of felled trees, great lengths piled to await collection. Lower down they passed a felling party, waving in answer to the cheerful greetings offered, continuing through the dwindling forest until they emerged on meadowland, where sheep grazed and shepherds' huts stood lonely beside rough pens. By noon they approached the spread of buildings along the riverside, timber structures, with smoke rising lazy into the warm air. The Yst lay ahead, far broader than any river they had so far crossed, with barges moored along the bank, heavy with dressed wood. The ferry lay on the north side and they rode directly to the raft, ignoring the inns and eating houses to which, it seemed, most of the population had repaired.

A bearded Kand lounged on the jetty, munching bread and cold meat, answering their request for passage with the news that two men were needed to man the winches and his fellow was sampling ale. Anomius looked to Calandryll, motioning for him to show coin, and he drew a var from his satchel, tossing it to the man.

'Fetch your partner,' he ordered, surprised at his imperious tone, 'He can drink later - and better for such payment.'

The Kand bit the coin, eyeing them curiously, then shrugged and set down his meal, ambling towards the nearest tavern.

They dismounted, leading the horses onto the raft, and waited for the ferryman. Bracht appeared recovered from the magical attack, his face impassive as he stared north, to where Nhur-jabal stood menacing on the bluff. Calandryll watched him in silence, sensing that some design was afoot, curious as to what the Kern planned. Anomius fidgetted irritably, though whether from impatience or apprehension Calandryll could not tell.

Then the Kand appeared with another and the two men sprang on board and, without further word, set to turning the winches, drawing the heavy cables slowly straight as the ferry eased from the dock into the stream. Now Calandryll turned to watch the city, alarmed as much by the prospect of cavalry galloping to meet them as the fear of magic. The raft swayed, tugged by the current, its progress slow, the slap of water and the creaking of the winches metronomic, ticking off the long minutes of the crossing. The farther bank seemed no closer, the buildings there no larger, as if they hung suspended in midstream, caught in time until the Tyrant's sorcerers should become aware of their presence and magic or soldiery be sent against them. Then, gradually, riverbank and buildings came closer, the ferry drawing inexorably towards the dock. It grounded and they walked the horses up the landing ramp, boots lapped by wavelets as the silent Kands watched them go.

The spur of the Kharm-rhanna holding the pass was clearer now, wooded slopes dark green in the afternoon sun, the gash cut by the Shemme standing bright: a gateway out of Kandahar. Anomius prepared to mount.

Bracht said, 'Can we not eat?'

The wizard turned an angry face on the Kern.

'Would you taste my power again?'

'I'd eat,' Bracht answered. 'We've a long ride ahead and hunger sits ill on my belly.'

Anomius raised a threatening hand, then thought better of it and smiled.

'Later - perhaps when we reach the pass.'

Bracht looked up to where the foothills hung against the sky and shrugged, making no move to mount.

'Remember,' Anomius murmured, his voice falsely affable, 'that distance from me means agony.'

He dragged himself astride the grey and heeled the horse to a trot through the sleepy village. Calandryll turned to Bracht.

'Dera, would you have him work his magic on you again? Do you seek deliberately to anger him?'

'I tire of his commands.'

Bracht grinned and swung astride the chestnut without further explanation. Calandryll mounted and followed him, alarmed now: fearing that perhaps

Anomius's magicks had addled the Kern's mind.

They passed through the village into farmland, increasing their pace as the trail wound amongst fenced fields, the land climbing steadily towards the hills. Anomius kicked the grey to a swift canter and Bracht speeded to come alongside the black-robed man.

'Slower,' he urged, 'you'll wind your mount.'

As if to emphasise his point he reined the chestnut back, prompting an angry grunt from the sorcerer. 'An exhausted horse is useless,' he called. 'Slow down.'

In answer, Anomius turned in his saddle extending his hand again. Calandryll shouted a warning, but even as it passed his lips Bracht jerked upright, holding his seat with difficulty. His lips stretched back from chattering teeth and his suddenly shaking arms sent his horse dancing, circling its own tail. Bracht slumped in the saddle as Anomius lowered his hand, the chestnut shaking its head, snorting nervously.

'Enough!' the wizard yelled, his voice shrill. 'Do you seek to delay me? Do you wish me to bind you with more spells?'

Bracht shook his head; Calandryll saw that he smiled. Or that pain stretched his lips in parody. They rode on, the trail steeper now, climbing up past hill meadows to meet the timberline, the afternoon growing older, their way soon shadowed by tall trees, the sun fleeting through the branches.

'Must we ride hungry?' Bracht demanded. 'You allowed we'd halt to eat.'

And once again Anomius hurled magic at him, rocking him in the saddle until he moaned his acceptance that they should continue. Calandryll feared more seriously that his comrade was addled by the sorcerer's attacks, for he saw that as the pain faded Bracht still grinned, the expression wolfish, as if he found some secret satisfaction in the suffering.

Then they rounded a curve in the trail and saw they

stood upon a shelf thrusting out from the foothills above the Shemme. The river shone silver in the sun, flanked on both sides by high walls of black rock, the spur they crossed angling away northeast to meet the Kharm-rhanna where Nhur-jabal stood upon its bluff, as much guardian of this valley as of that behind them. The trail wound down, serpentine in its descent, the north-facing slopes devoid of timber, to a cluster of buildings.

Anomius chuckled and heeled his horse onwards. Bracht reined back, holding his position, and shouted, 'Best approach with caution, mage.'

Again the wizard flung magic at him: again the Kern smiled his awful grin.

They reached the riverside as the sun drew close to the mountain peaks, the valley shadowed, but not yet full dark, boats visible at the waterside. Anomius made directly for the anchorage, his horse's hooves loud on the cobbles that streeted the little settlement.

Then he reined hard in, mouthing a curse as three men appeared before him. The grey horse reared and the wizard struggled to retain his seat, fighting the animal to a standstill and launching himself with unusual agility from the saddle.

Calandryll stared, hearing Bracht laugh, casting one swift glance at the Kern: seeing his face alight with anticipation, lips curved in a wolfish smile. Then all his attention was focussed on the three men facing Anomius. Two were tall, the third short. All wore long robes of black and silver, marked with cabbalistic designs, their headdresses black, each pinned with a silver star. They bore no weapons; nor needed any he saw as they raised their hands, light sparkling there, the stone at his throat pulsing fiery, the air thick with the scent of almonds.

'Do you think to defy the Tyrant?'

He could not tell which spoke, for their lips moved in

unison, the question rumbling thunder.

'Do you think to escape his justice?'

'Do you think to pass us?'

His horse began to prance and he felt Bracht's hands on him, dragging him unceremoniously from the saddle as Anomius shrieked in fury and met the light that burst from the six outthrust hands with his own fell fire. He stumbled after the freesword as the horses screamed in panic no less than his own and fled the explosion that burst where pale light met red. The smell of burning hung on the air as Bracht thrust him down behind stacked bales, close to the water, and it seemed the heat of it must sear his lungs, the air reeking, the stone he wore fierce against his skin.

Then suddenly unnatural night descended, a foul darkness, stinking of decay, and in it shapes moved, malign things that shuffled and snorted, clacking dagger fangs, eyes glowing redly. The sun was hidden in the occult clouding, the only illumination the bright white light that burned about the three men - sorcerers, he knew; the Tyrant's men, sent from Nhur-jabal - and that growing, taking forms that moved to meet the shadow-beasts of Anomius's conjuring, clashing with them, the air loud with their unnatural shrieking. Darkness and light met in awful battle, rending, tearing. He felt Bracht's hand on his shoulder, urging him on, away from the cover of the bales towards the water. He heard Anomius scream: he could not tell whether in pain or outrage. Then it seemed that tatters of black fell, seething, to the cobbles and the light grew brighter until the sun shone again, orange now, and closer to its setting. He saw the Tyrant's sorcerers standing before Anomius. One, the tallest, clutched his side as though wounded. Anomius snarled, parchment face contorted, feral, and raised both hands.

Fire burned from his fingertips and the hurt man screamed, wreathed in flame, consumed so that only dark ashes drifted to the cobbles. The others answered with blinding light that drove the bulbous-nosed little man back across the harbour, defensive now, fire a wall before him, holding off the light. It seemed he grew within that fire, becoming tall as the golem he had created, and massy as the creature, a hulking man-beast with flaming hair and hands that spat incandescence, his strength increasing, for now the two warlocks staggered back, weaving spells to fend off his magic as he advanced, roaring, towards them.

Light and flame met once more. Calandryll saw the bales behind which he had sheltered take fire, sparks dancing high, thatch igniting on the nearby buildings. He felt Bracht yank him back, closer still to the water. He saw Anomius's face turn towards him, furious, a hand extended. Fire burst from the fingers and he raised his own hands, unaware that he clutched the red stone: a defensive talisman, but surely useless against the wizard's awesome power.

He screamed as the flames washed over him, hearing Anomius's shout through the dinning.

'You'll not escape me! The book is mine and I shall have it!'

His lungs were filled with fire, his ears with the roaring of the flames, his nostrils with the stench of scorching flesh that he knew for his own. The red stone was a coal in his hand.

He knew that he died, and was grateful for the darkness that took him: it was blessed relief from the agony.

FOURTEEN

SO this was death, this gentle ending of pain. It surprised him, even though he had not thought overmuch of what followed after life. To dwell in peace with Dera, the priests of Lysse said, and mostly left it at that, though if pressed they would elaborate a little: to be at one with the goddess; to serve her and bask in her love down all the ages of eternity; to know no suffering, no want; to be without need, content. Vague, and now it seemed the afterlife was not so different from the preceding existence: a blue sky spread above him, streaked with high cloud, long mare's tails blown out by a wind that he felt warm on his face, a sensation of drifting, as if borne on some ethereal vessel, a distant sound, as of water running to some unseen destination. Perhaps, he thought, this was transition; a passage necessary between the world of flesh and that of the spirit, Dera awaiting him at the journey's end. He breathed in air that tasted no different to that left behind, save that it lacked the stink of burning, and sighed, content for the moment to ride between the worlds, grateful that the agony of Anomius's awful fire was gone. He raised a hand and saw it whole, uncharred where he had thought to find roasted flesh, bones blackened by magic, and realised that he lay supine. He sat up.

And cried out as Bracht's voice said, 'So you wake at last. I thought perhaps you'd sleep until we reach the sea.'

He turned to find his comrade smiling at him, seated a little above him, and gaped, saying, 'He slew you, too? We are both dead then.'

Bracht's laughter surprised him no less than the similarity of world and afterlife, and he frowned his incomprehension.

'We are not dead,' the Kern said. 'Look about you.'

Slowly, he craned his head round. Steep walls of rugged granite rose on both sides, tall pines thrusting from declivities where sufficient soil had gathered to support such dendrous life, and between those walls ran a river, not so wide as the Yst but broad enough. They floated down it, he saw now, in a small boat, Bracht at the tiller, he in the bilge. He eased himself up, onto the midships thwart, the movement rocking the craft.

'Careful!' Bracht warned. 'I've little enough skill for this and Ahrd knows, I'd not drown now.'

He stared at the freesword, blinking, thinking to find himself in some trap set by Anomius, or the Tyrant's wizards, and dabbled a cautious hand in the stream. The water was cold and wet: true water as best he could tell; he brought his hand to his lips and tasted it, splashed his face and shook his head.

'We are not slain?'

'We live,' Bracht said firmly, smiling still. 'We go down the Shemme - to Kharasul, if all goes well.'

'Anomius?' he gasped. 'The Tyrant's sorcerers?'

'Two nights and a day behind us,' Bracht said. 'If they live, though all may be dead for what I know. You've slept that time through, like a babe - save that you breathed I thought my plan had failed.'

'Plan?' he mumbled, confused. 'You had a plan?'

Bracht nodded, grinning. 'And one that worked, it seems, for there's been no sign of pursuit.'

The stony walls, the river, the sky, all took on a new reality as he studied them with eyes he now accepted were alive. 'Tell me,' he asked. Bracht chuckled, shrugging, his expression both pleased and a little embarrassed. 'I'd have told you sooner,' he declared, 'save that I suspected your knowing might have thwarted it.'

Calandryll's eyes narrowed. 'You brought his anger down deliberately,' he said, aware that his voice held accusation.

'I did,' Bracht nodded, 'I thought long on it and it seemed the only way to rid us of the cursed wizard. There was risk, I knew, but I saw no other way.'

'Tell me,' he repeated.

'On the *Sea Dancer*, when the warboat came, you denied all knowledge of what happened, but we both saw the woman and her boat swept away - as if some power rose up to protect us. Or you. In Mherut'yi, after the Chaipaku attacked, your injury was healed when you wore the stone. When Sathoman took us, Anomius said he could not touch you with his glamours - that you were protected by the stone.'

'He might have removed it,' Calandryll said, and fell silent as Bracht raised a hand, continuing.

'But he did not. He left you with it and believed your story of the grimoire, even though he had never heard of such a book; even though he seems as widely read as you.'

'How do you know that?' Calandryll wondered.

'In the forest, when I hunted down that first deer,' Bracht grinned, 'I made my kill early. I'd have returned with the meat but that I heard you talking and thought to listen - it's the habit of Cuan na'For to walk wary.

Anomius spoke of books and libraries and denied all mention of the grimoire - yet still he believed in its existence and never thought to question further. That seemed odd to me. At first I thought it merely greed that drove him - his lust for ultimate power - but then I began to wonder if that stone you wear worked on him. You remember that I spoke of a design? That by travelling with the wizard we crossed Kandahar faster than we might alone? I was not sure, save that the stone imbues you with some power you - nor I! - understand.

'A more cautious man - a man in less haste - would not have ventured so close to Nhur-jabal, knowing that sorcerers of equal strength resided there and might - as Anomius himself warned - sense the presence of magic. We might have crossed the river farther down and come to the Shemme by a more circuitous route, but it seemed that greed consumed the wizard the closer we came and he forewent caution in his haste. I decided then to attempt it - by bringing his anger on me I prompted him to work magic that was sensed in Nhur-jabal. I saw that valley and guessed the Tyrant's sorcerers would meet us at the pass, or at the river, brought down by Anomius himself.'

He paused, his grin fading for a moment, replaced with a look close to embarrassment as he studied Calandryll's face.

'The rest was a chance I felt we must take. The warboat, the Chaipaku, Anomius's failure to touch you - all convinced me that the stone unleashes power in you when danger threatens. I trusted in it to protect you then. It did.'

Calandryll gaped, not sure whether he wished to laugh or rail against the Kern for flirting with such danger. It came to him that Bracht had never spoken for so long; that the tanned features were grave, as if seeking his forgiveness; and that Bracht had pondered lengthily on the matter and taken the only course he saw to escape Anomius. He said, 'What happened then?'

'You saw them join in magical battle?' Bracht asked, and when he nodded, 'Anomius became as one with the demons he raised against Kesham-vaj. He said then that such occult workings leached his strength; the Tyrant's wizards, too, I thought, must feel that weakening. I counted on that to see us clear - that and the stone.

'Anomius turned his hand against you and you were lashed with fire. I saw the stone burn, like a shell about you. For a moment I thought us both slain, but then I knew we lived and I was protected, too. Because I held you, I suppose. I threw you into the nearest boat and cut the lines. We drifted clear as the wizards fought, and the last I saw of them was fire in the sky. The town burned, I think.'

Calandryll stared at his reckless comrade - *it's the habit of Cuan na'For to walk wary?* - He smiled, seeing scorched hair, leather shirt cracked as if brought too close to flame.

'You risked much,' he said. 'I thought I died.'

'I feared you had,' Bracht returned solemnly, then grinned again. 'But then you breathed and I saw no sign of burning on you and knew you *were* protected.'

'So now you think me mage?'

'No.' Bracht shook his head. 'I think you have some power beyond your understanding; certainly beyond mine. The stone would appear to release it, and it saved us both so I'll revise my opinion of magic where you're concerned.'

'My thanks,' Calandryll said dryly.

Bracht grinned and said, 'It served us well and if magic dogs us, we're better warned - Gessyth's likely a place even less hospitable than Kandahar, so it may well aid us again.'

Calandryll nodded, then asked, 'A day and two nights you say we've been on the river?'

'Aye,' Bracht replied, 'and without food. What little

we had left went with the horses. Our gear, too.'

'The map?' Calandryll felt alarm renewed. 'The money?'

'The satchel is there.' Bracht pointed to where the sack had pillowed Calandryll's head; patted his waist. 'And what Varent paid me I still carry. We have our clothes and our blades, but all else is lost.'

It seemed a small price to pay to be rid of Anomius: Calandryll shrugged it off.

'We can buy what we need in Kharasul. With map and coin - and the stone - we've enough.'

'Save food,' Bracht said. 'That was no lie when I told the wizard I was hungry.'

'Surely there must be villages along the Shemme?'

'We passed one yesterday,' Bracht agreed, 'but I've no knowledge of boats or rivercraft - I cannot stop this thing.'

Calandryll began to laugh then, his mirth rocking the dinghy: he lived and Anomius was left behind; the notion of Bracht manning the tiller for a day and two nights as the little vessel floated, unstoppable, down the Shemme struck him as hugely amusing.

'I'll take the helm,' he said, 'I have some knowledge of boats.'

Cautiously, Bracht passed the rudder to Calandryll, announcing his intention of sleeping as he stretched along the bilge. Calandryll settled on the stern thwart and guided the craft westwards.

Glancing at the sun he saw that noon approached, and a little while after the disc had passed its zenith he saw a settlement on the bank ahead. He steered the dinghy to a mooring on a stone quay and woke Bracht. Together they found a tavern, where they ate a meal of fish taken from the river, and then obtained sufficient provisions to see them through to Kharasul. No mention was made in tavern or township of occult sightings, nor of Tyrant's craft come seeking fugitives, and they decided they had made good their escape. Anomius was either slain by the Tyrant's sorcerers or taken prisoner - in which event it seemed most probable he would face execution: a fate they could not regret - and no mages in black and silver appeared to bar their going as they set course again. Perhaps they were assumed dead, slain in the glamorous battle: that suited their purpose well enough and, with bellies filled, they felt cheerful as they continued down the river.

Within a week they came to Kharasul and the next stage of the perilous journey.

The city lay on a headland, banded to north and south by the inlets of the Ty and the Shemme. The final thrustings of the Kharm-rhanna ended a half day east of the settlement, the land between the hills and the ocean flat, the river that had carried them there broadening to an estuary in which floated a variety of craft. Merchantmen, the kin of Rahamman ek'Jemm's *Sea Dancer*, lay at anchor alongside caravels out of Lysse and the sleek warboats favoured by the Kand pirates. Fishing boats were drawn up along the shoreline, and small craft made the anchorage busy, cutting close to the dinghy as Calandryll used the last of the Shemme's current to bring them in to the wide stone wharf. The air was sultry, redolent of the jungles that lay across the Ty, in Gash; the sun, close now to its setting, burnished the ocean, painting Kharasul with hues of gold and orange, and seagulls wheeled screaming about the boat as they moored. They climbed steps slippery with tide-tossed seaweed to the wharf and passed between warehouses into the centre of the city.

Kharasul was not unlike Secca, being walled in defence against the strange inhabitants of the jungles who from time to time attempted raids, but rowdier, and seemingly without a city watch; its buildings, crammed together on the headland, stood taller, and the soldiers they saw offered no hindrance to their passing. It was smaller, but no less bustling, and it was soon clear that its districts echoed those of Calandryll's home. To the east lay the mansions of whatever nobility Kharasul boasted, whilst the emporiums of the merchants were located close to the estuary, behind them the taverns and inns; the poorer quarters huddled closest to the Ty, as did the city garrison, and between, at the centre, were the bazaars. It lacked the organisation of the cities of Lysse, its streets random in their direction, running hither and thither so that the newcomers soon found themselves wandering a narrow way overhung by tall, shuttered buildings that by day's light were likely trading houses, but that seemed, as the shadows lengthened, menacing, reminding them that they walked the streets of an unknown city. Calandryll thought of the warboats lying at anchor, and of the Chaipaku, and set a hand to his sword's hilt as they paced the cobbled alley, nostrils pinching, after the clean river air, at the thick, sweet odours that came from gutters and the jungles.

This far to the south the sun set fast and it was suddenly full dark as they emerged onto a square where palm trees grew and a low building surmounted by a slender tower threw light from windows of multi-coloured glass. Calandryll recognised the edifice as a temple to Burash and called Bracht away, urging a change in direction.

'I thought you wished to propitiate the god,' the Kern said, and Calandryll shook his head vigorously, thinking of what Medith said: that some believed the priests of Burash agents of the Chaipaku.

'I gave offering on the *Sea Dancer*,' he replied. 'Let that be sufficient. I've no wish to call attention to our presence.'

Bracht shrugged his acceptance and they turned

from the square, finding their way between more overhanging buildings to where hospitality was offered in the tavern quarter.

They found an inn called The Waterboy, tall and narrow as all the buildings of Kharasul, the common room and kitchen filled all the lowest floor, the remaining rooms piled one upon other, tower-like, with creaking stairways and small balconies linking the chambers. Their room was on the third floor, not spacious, but comfortable enough, with two beds and a little space between, a window there, and a single cupboard. They bathed, the water transported by panting servants to the bath-house on the first floor, and then decended to the common room to eat.

Other Lyssians took their dinner there, but none gave sign of recognising Calandryll, keeping largely to themselves amongst the swarthy Kands and a sprinkling of near-black folk, with huge, yellowish eyes and wide noses that he took to be out of Gash, or halfbreeds. All, he saw, went well-armed, which might be expected of the sailors and mercenaries, but even the merchants who dined there wore swords, and several times he caught the glint of mail beneath parted robes. He and Bracht found a place where a pillar warded their flank, aside from the main part of the room, and as they ate they listened to the babble of conversation, seeking news of events beyond their ken.

Sathoman ek'Hannem, they heard, had taken Mherut'yi, just as Anomius had said, and swore to seize all the eastern coast. The lictor of Kharasul had commandeered merchant vessels to the Tyrant's service and an army marched on the Fayne, but as yet no word had come of its success or failure. Secca and Aldarin founded a war fleet in the shipyards of Eryn and vowed to render the sealanes safe from corsairs, to which purpose the Tyrant gave his blessing - this met with much laughter from the Kands, the general opinion being that the Tyrant bestowed equal blessing on the pirates, whose gold was spent in Kandahar and thus found its way, eventually, into his coffers. A Lyssian seaman objected to this, expressing his displeasure in a loud condemnation of double-dealing rulers and Kands at large. He was carried from the room with a broken nose and an ugly knife wound in his side, that seemed not to merit more than casual interest once the fight was done. Of Gessyth there was little said, except that it was early in the year to venture in that direction and, for all the danger of seeing their craft seized by the lictor, the merchants would wait until the summer was more advanced and the winds consequently more favourable.

This last boded ill for their quest: a speedy departure seemed advisable were they to beat Azumandias to Tezin-dar, and if Anomius had somehow survived he would doubtless come fast on their heels, him or the Tyrant's warlocks. Calandryll was also unpleasantly aware that Chaipaku likely inhabited Kharasul, desirous of his death - and Bracht's, too, for the slaying of Mehemmed. They cleared their plates, emptying a flagon of wine, and retired to discuss the future where prying ears might go frustrated.

The room was warm; not like the skin-prickling heat brought by the galleen in the north, but thick, vapid with the rank odours of jungle vegetation. What breeze there was, stirring from the sea, did little to clear the heavy air and they discarded their leathers, wiping sweat from chests and brows. Outside, the city showed no sign of sleeping, noise rising from the streets below, the inns ablaze with light. Calandryll stared from the window, seeing the jungles across the Ty river gleam with a strange phosphorescence, the sea sparkling beneath a gibbous moon.

'Come morning we'd best seek a boat,' he murmured.

'If such can be found.' Bracht stretched on the bed.

'From what we heard, I doubt there's a merchantman going north.'

'The warboats need not wait on the winds,' Calandryll replied. 'They've oarsmen.'

'And are likely pirates,' said the Kern, 'willing to cut our throats for the coin we carry.'

'We'd need go wary.' Calandryll agreed. 'But we've blades to defend ourselves.'

Bracht chuckled morosely: 'I'd best secure more of ek'Jemm's nostrum, then - should that sickness afflict me again I'll be of little use.'

Calandryll nodded, turning from the window.

'What other choice is there?' He answered his own question as Bracht shrugged. 'Do we wait for the winds to shift, one mage or the other may overtake us. And if we linger here, we may face the Chaipaku again.'

'There's that,' Bracht agreed. 'A warboat, then; if we've no other choice.'

They slept then, as best they could on beds rapidly damp with sweat, the night alive with the sounds of revelry and the stranger cries that drifted from the jungles, finding little respite with the sun's rising, for that brought only a brief freshening of the breeze before the cloying heat descended again. They repaired to the common room where they broke their fast with bread and fruit and cheese, then found their way to the harbour.

Two merchantmen departed as they watched, sails bellying to carry the vessels clear of the estuary, their course southeastwards, three warboats, each flying the Tyrant's flag, moving in escort.

'Conscripted to the Tyrant's cause. Folk say that civil war stirs in the north.'

They turned to find a grizzled man, a carved wooden stump where his left leg had been, grinning at them from a bollard. A pipe jutted from his bearded lips, emitting a faint aroma of the narcotic tobacco favoured by the Kands. He nodded pleasantly, removing the pipe to knock the dottle loose.

'Sathoman ek'Hennem moves on Mhazomul, it seems, and the Tyrant looks to reinforce the garrison there. Poor news for traders, that - they'll find their craft taken for supply ships and transport, and little enough reward for their loss.'

'What do they lose?' Calandryll asked. 'Surely their cargoes are discharged?'

'Surely,' the old man agreed, 'but it's the habit of the captains who venture the early passage round Cape Vishat'yi to lie up here until the winds shift and return with dragon hides. Those sail empty - to Ghombalar, at least; and what they'll get from the Tyrant for that service is poor recompense for an empty hold.'

'And when,' Calandryll enquired casually, 'will the winds shift?'

The old man sniffed, as if tasting the breeze. 'A month at least. Perhaps longer.'

'And no vessel sails north before?'

'Not into the swamp winds,' declared the ancient, tamping fresh tobacco into his pipe.

Calandryll surveyed the sleek hulls of the warboats rocking on the changing tide. 'Those can surely brave the winds?' he asked.

The old man struck a flint, lighting the pipe, puffing vigorously before he replied.

'You're from Lysse?' And when Calandryll nodded, 'Most of those sea-wolves fly the Tyrant's standard - they're come to bring the merchants safely up the coast. And persuade the more reluctant captains of their duty. The rest are corsairs, looking to pick off likely craft. There's no profit for them in Gessyth. Nor would any sane man venture to that god-forsaken place. See this?' He slapped his wooden leg. 'Was a dragon did this to me. I sailed with Johannen ek'Leman on the *Wind's Pride*. A hold full of hides, he promised, and a share for every man of the crew - I paid for my share with my leg! A Burash-damned dragon came after our longboat and put seven of us in the water. Four died and the cursed beast took my leg before Johannen drove it off.' He shook his head, sucking deep on his pipe, calming as the narcotic took effect. 'No, no man in possession of his wits would sail for Gessyth unless there's guaranteed profit.'

'Suppose,' Calandryll said, 'that reward was offered?'

'You'd hire a boat to reach that hell? Why?'

Calandryll smiled, shrugging; offering no explanation. The old man spat, staring at him as if judging his sanity and finding it wanting. 'You'll find none to take you,' he said, weatherbeaten face solemn, 'and if you flaunt such a purse as a sea-rover would demand, you'll find a knife between your shoulders and your coin taken. You want to sail to Gessyth? Wait for the wind to shift and travel with a merchant - if any are left.'

'It would seem none will be,' Calandryll said.

'Likely not,' nodded the old man amiably, 'and likely you'll live longer for it.'

Calandryll smiled grimly: the one-legged man confirmed Bracht's doubts, but still Gesyth was their destination and passage must be found somehow, regardless of the dangers. He ducked his head in farewell, turning along the wharf, the ancient's parting words ringing in his ears.

'You'll find nothing in Gessyth, and death in the going.'

'An unfavourable prophecy,' Bracht remarked.

'We have no choice,' he said.

'No,' the Kern agreed, and they walked in silence along the cobbles, eyes on the vessels moored in the estuary.

The presence of the Tyrant's soldiers was more obvious now, knots of armoured men with the scarlet puggrees wound about their helms standing about the waterfront, their officers in conversation, often heated, with sea captains who protested the seizure of their ships, or accepted the claiming with resignation. A squad of archers was despatched to each vessel and as the morning grew older it became increasingly obvious that passage must be hard to find. At noon they found a tavern and reviewed their situation, deciding that the remainder of the day was best spent in search of some corsair willing to undertake the journey.

It was a decision easier made than implemented, for the warboats not marked with the Tyrant's flag were unmanned and their enquiries as to the whereabouts of the masters were met with evasions, or blank refusals. As dusk approached they had made little headway, beyond learning that they might - perhaps - find some captain willing to lend an ear in the taverns of the Beggars Gate.

They ate dinner in The Waterboy and replaced their sweat-soaked shirts before pursuing their elusive quarry.

The quarter to which they were directed was hard against Kharasul's western edge, as if ostracized, a maze of narrow alleys and small squares, noisome with the reek of liquor and overrun gutters, rats busy amongst the spillage despite the crowds thronging the street. The taverns were no more fragrant, their common rooms smoky, the floors puddled with spilled drink, the men settled at the tables hard-eyed, the women with them no softer. Calandryll realised that he went with left hand about his scabbard, ready to draw the straightsword; and saw that Bracht did the same, his eyes flicking constantly about.

In three taverns the very mention of passage to Gessyth elicited roars of laughter and the suggestion that they find some captain with mind sufficiently addled to undertake the journey, but not to bother sane men; and in others they received the warily sympathetic looks that spoke of doubt as to their sanity. In one a man promised to take them there if they would only purchase him a boat; and in another the landlord warned them away, for fear their throats would be cut. Towards midnight they found themselves in a square a little quieter than the rest, the city wall rising above the plaza, buildings on three sides, painted pale by the gibbous moon. They entered the closest tavern and called for ale, experience by now prompting them to remain silent until they saw some likely prospect.

The drinkers seemed no different to all those elsewhere: swords at their sides and the look of men ready to use the blades on a moment's provocation. Dark-tanned faces eyed them with idle curiosity or open hostility, as if the very presence of two men markedly not of their fraternity was occasion to seek a quarrel. Calandryll thought that had Bracht not stood beside him, he must already fight for his life, for there were no other Lyssians in this quarter and his looks set him clearly apart from the swarthy denizens of the Beggars Gate. He sipped dark ale, his belly already filled, and peered into the smoke-haze, head threatening to swim under the influence of the narcotic fumes drifting on the malodorous air. Then straightened from his stance at the counter as a man sidled close, aware that Bracht, too, set down his mug and let hand fall, casually, to the falchion's hilt.

The man was short and thin, a coil of dark green silk wound about his head, a loose tunic of the same colour belted tight, the belt holding a curved dagger and a shortsword. A livid scar ran down one cheek, from temple to beard, the dead tissue dragging the eye askew. He smiled, showing teeth stained brown, and nodded a greeting.

Calandryll anticipated some invitation to entertainments more exotic than those offered by the tavern, such as they had received several times that night, but instead the Kand said, 'You seek passage to Gessyth,' in a husky tone, more statement than question. He sought to pitch his response at casual level.

'Do you offer such?'

The man beckoned him closer; when he bent his head he caught the waft of stale wine.

'It can be arranged.' Disorganised eyes swept over the room. 'For a price best discussed elsewhere.'

Bracht moved to place himself on the man's farther side. 'Why not here?' he asked.

The distorted eye closed in a grotesque wink and the smile grew broader.

'Too many ears - too many *greedy* ears. The price will be high and should these,' a waved hand encompassed the crowded room, 'learn that you carry gold ...'

He shrugged expressively. Bracht glanced at Calandryll, eyebrows raised: Calandryll nodded slightly. Bracht said, 'They might attempt to take it,' and as the man nodded, 'as might you, did we follow you into some alley where thieves wait.'

'Sirs!' An expression of hurt dignity overtook the scarred features. 'I am an honest man. I followed you here to offer what you seek, having heard you asking elsewhere. Do you choose to believe me a common thief I'll leave you.'

He moved from between them, halted by Bracht's hand on his shoulder. 'Where would you talk?' the freesword asked.

The Kand looked up at the taller Kern, at Calandryll, and smiled again. 'There is a tavern named The Peacock,' he murmured, 'close by the harbour. Do you truly seek a vessel to bring you to Gessyth, I'll meet you there at noon tomorrow.'

'Honest business is best done by day's light,' Bracht said. 'And by men who call one another by their names.'

'Mine is Xanthese,' the man said. 'Ask for me in The

Peacock at noon and a ship shall be yours.'

'At noon,' Bracht agreed.

'And sirs,' Xanthese murmured, 'I'd advise you be gone from here. Your enquiries have raised some ... interest ... and it may be that folk less honest than I might seek to part you from your coin. Walk wary, sirs!'

He touched a hand to his forehead and disappeared into the crowd, swift as a scuttling rat, gone out the door before either moved to halt him. Calandryll looked to his comrade.

'Do we trust him?'

'I think it wisest to trust no one,' Bracht said, 'though he gave sound enough advice - let's quit this place, and keep our eyes open in the streets.'

'But meet him tomorrow?' Calandryll asked. 'At least he offers the chance of a boat, nor sought to lure us into some alley.'

'The only chance, it seems,' Bracht nodded. 'We'll attend this tavern at noon and hear him out.'

He drained his mug; Calandryll followed suit, and together they pushed to the door. None moved to follow them as they crossed the square and entered an alleyway so narrow, the buildings to either side crowding so close, only a thin ribbon of sky was visible above, the way below shadowy. Their shoulders touched as they paced the street, hands on swords' hilts, ears cocked for pursuing footsteps. The alley disgorged into a wider street, where blowsy women called to them from little balconies and drinkers spilled out from the taverns, but no one sought to halt them and, as best Calandryll could tell, there was no one behind.

They reached The Waterboy to find the landlord waiting with a message of sorts: that a woman had come asking after them, seeking a fair-haired young man from Lysse and a dark-haired Kern freesword.

'A blonde woman?' Bracht demanded sharply. 'With hair like melted gold and eyes grey as a storm?'

That he remembered the woman on the warboat so accurately surprised Calandryll as much as the lyrical description; the landlord nodded enthusiastically.

'A real beauty. But with a temper to match a fishwife. I told her The Waterboy's guests value their privacy and she cursed me roundly - I thought she'd draw her blade.' He grinned, scratching his chins. 'I've not seen her like - some warrior woman from Lysse or Kern, I thought. I told her nothing.'

'Good,' Bracht said. Then, 'Was she alone, or in company?'

'Alone,' the landlord said, and chuckled. 'She needed no company, not her. Zarian - he's a fisherman - was in his cups and invited her to join him. When she refused, he insisted - he fancies himself with the ladies - and she left him unmanned.'

Calandryll gasped and the landlord chuckled some more, shaking his head. 'Oh, she didn't cut him - just,' he raised a knee expressively, 'robbed him of such ambitions for a while. Though from the look of her I've little doubt she can use that blade she carries.'

'Did she say anything more?' Bracht asked.

The landlord shook his head: 'No. Just wanted to know if I'd seen you.'

'And you told her no,' Bracht said.

'I did,' the landlord nodded. 'We mind to our business here in Kharasul. Should I have done otherwise?'

'No.' Bracht said. 'And should she come again, let your answer remain no.'

'My word on it,' the landlord promised.

'Our thanks,' Bracht smiled, and beckoned Calandryll to the stairs.

They found their room and latched the door. Calandryll peered from the window, but if the inn was watched he could see no sign of the observers and turned to face Bracht. The Kern's face was thoughtful as he tugged off his boots.

'So, the woman snaps closest on our heels. Best we find this boat Xanthese offers and quit Kharasul as swift we may.'

'I thought her lost when the magic took her,' Calandryll murmured. 'Who is she? Does she act for Azumandias?'

Bracht shrugged.

'For Azumandias or herself, what matter? She's another hound baying on our heels.'

'A hound with a warboat at her command,' Calandryll said glumly.

'Hope then that Xanthese's boat runs swift,' Bracht said, stretching on the bed with head in cupped hands and a contemplative smile on his face. 'But she was lovely, was she not?'

Calandryll stared at him, frowning, hearing frank admiration in his voice. 'You sound moonstruck,' he said; accusingly.

'I was ... impressed,' Bracht admitted, unabashed. 'Cuan na'For has its share of warrior women, but I've not seen her like. Nor is she of the clans.'

'Neither from Lysse,' said Calandryll, 'and certainly not a Kand. Might she be Jesseryte?'

'Those folk are small and dark and ugly,' Bracht informed him. 'I know not from where she comes.'

'Perhaps from beyond the Borrhun-maj,' Calandryll said, vaguely irritated by the Kern's tone. It seemed to him that Bracht hankered almost to encounter the woman, 'Perhaps from Vanu.'

'Then she would be a goddess.' Bracht laughed. 'Certainly she's the look of a goddess.'

'A moment since she was a hound; you elevate her fast.'

Peevishly, he tossed his boots aside, set his sheathed sword beside the bed. Bracht chuckled, smiling at him.

'I give her just due, no more. Should she seek to thwart us I'll fight her as I would any man. But I admit she intrigues me. And you must admit that she is somewhat fairer than most who've sought to halt us.'

That was indisputable: Calandryll thought of Anomius's homely features and nodded, a smile stealing across his lips.

'That I must admit.'

'Then we're agreed,' Bracht said. 'And come noon we'll seek this boat Xanthese offers and - our gods willing - leave her behind.'

They composed themselves for sleep then, lightly, with blades at their sides, aware that the game's pace quickened and departure from Kharasul grew momentarily more vital. The room was no less stifling, the air dense with the jungle odours and those of the streets, the shutters not holding out all the insects that swarmed the night, sufficient entering that Calandryll found slumber hard as they buzzed about his head. He drifted, thinking himself back on the dinghy, floating down the Shemme, then once again on the *Sea Dancer*, that recollection bringing the woman's face before the eyes of his drowsing mind. She was lovely; but she was also an obstacle, another player in their world-shattering game. In sleep he found himself torn between admiration for her beauty and regret that she had not drowned when the maelstrom took her boat.

He woke thick-headed from the ale he had drunk and the narcotic fumes inhaled, eyes heavy from poor sleep. Bracht, more accustomed to taverns and shallow slumber, was in both better condition and mood when they rose, suggesting that they avail themselves of the bath before taking food. Water and a tisane recommended by the landlord restored him somewhat and after eating they lounged about the inn awaiting the approach of noon and their meeting with the mysterious Xanthese.

'Surely,' Calandryll suggested, 'did he intend

treachery he would not arrange to meet us in the day.'

'Perhaps.' Bracht toyed with a mug of wine. 'It would seem so, but then perhaps he seeks to allay our suspicions.'

'Do you trust no one?' asked Calandryll, eliciting a cheerful smile from the Kern, who shook his head and said, 'Few. Very few.'

Calandryll thought to speak of Varent then, and touched the red stone at his throat, its cold surface reminding him of their agreement so that he held silence, letting his thoughts wander as they idled the morning away. Whether Varent played some devious game, as Bracht believed, or was true, as remained his opinion, he set aside in the face of more immediate concerns. If Xanthese's offer was sound and not some trap, then likely they had the means to reach Gessyth soon within their grasp. That was the paramount thing: to quit Kharasul, leaving Anomius - if he lived - and any other hunters behind. Wizards and woman, both. To gain the coast of Gessyth and strike inland for Tezin-dar. Without, he reminded himself, falling victim to cut-throat pirates. That would be difficult: likely they would need to sleep turn and turn about, one always on watch; but he could see no other way with honest sailors taken by the Tyrant or awaiting the shifting of the winds. They had come this far, he told himself, against odds he would have thought a while ago insurmountable. They had eluded the woman once and he had survived attack by a Chaipaku; he had rescued Bracht from Philomen's gaol and they had survived capture by Sathoman ek'Hennem; they had escaped the clutches of Anomius and evaded seizure by the Tyrant's sorcerers: surely they must now succeed in departing this city. And if the woman sought to take them, let her beware. Let treacherous corsairs beware! They dealt not with some soft Lyssian prince warded by a hired man, but with two hardened swordsmen - he would find Tezin-dar and broach the defences of the city; bring out the Arcanum and return to Lysse in triumph.

Perhaps then, he thought, he would compose a volume describing his travels. A work to rival Medith and Sarnium, bound in the finest hide, with a transcription of Orwen's map, and others. That would be a fine ending to this adventure. It did not occur to him that Nadama featured not at all in these contemplations.

'You seem pleased.'

Bracht's voice woke him from the reverie and he blushed, grinning his embarrassment.

'I thought that we near the ending of this quest,' he said.

'The ending?' Bracht shook his head. 'We've a way yet to go before we speak of endings, and I suspect the hardest part lies ahead.'

The flight of fancy fell soundly to earth and Calandryll nodded solemnly, embarrassed afresh by the reminder that some part of him remained, as his brother had so contemptuously declared, a dreamer. Then, briefly, he was reminded of Secca, of Tobias wed to Nadama, she now, perhaps, bearing an heir, and he frowned; then smiled as he realised the memory brought no pain. Indeed, it lifted a weight, for if Nadama should carry Tobias's child, then Secca had an heir and his brother no further cause to send the Chaipaku against him. He turned to his comrade and asked, 'Do we find Xanthese soon?'

Bracht looked to the window, assessing the position of the sun and nodded.

'Noon's an hour off, but aye - let's find this tavern and see how the land lies.'

The Peacock was situated only a few streets away, in an alley linking the tavern quarter with the harbour. It seemed salubrious enough, fresh sawdust on the floor and clean mugs behind the serving counter. Its clientele was a mixture of sailors, merchants and soldiers, those latter reassuring Bracht and Calandryll, their presence rendering treachery, at this juncture at least, unlikely. They called for wine and found a table by the inner wall from which they could watch the door. As the harbour bell tolled noon Xanthese entered.

He paused, squinting, and saw them across the common room, nodding a greeting as he approached.

'Good day, sirs.' He settled himself on a chair facing them, smiling as a third glass was brought and Calandryll poured him wine. 'Your health - and success to your venture. Whatever it may be.'

'You have news for us?' Bracht asked.

The scarred man winked, downing a generous measure of the wine and smacking his lips appreciatively before replying.

'I do, sirs; and good news. A captain of my acquaintance - a reliable man - is willing to take you north. For a suitable reward.'

'How much?' asked Bracht.

'Ah, sirs, there remains the small matter of my own fee.' Xanthese's smile became apologetic. 'It is customary in these affairs.'

'How much?' Bracht repeated.

'Ten varre.'

Bracht glanced at Calandryll and ducked his head: Calandryll brought coins from his satchel, pushing them across the table.

'My thanks, good sirs,' Xanthese said, the coins disappearing beneath his tunic. 'As for the captain, he asks five hundred. For that he guarantees you passage to Gessyth, and your return.'

'He'll wait for us?' Bracht was suspicious.

Xanthese nodded enthusiastically. 'Should he remain here ...' he lowered his voice, glancing towards the soldiers in their scarlet puggrees, 'Well, he'll find his craft taken for less and him no say in it. And every chance of disaster should the Fayne lord raise a navy.

He'd sooner stand off Gessyth's coast than that.'

Bracht nodded. Calandryll asked, 'What guarantee do we have of his honesty? How shall we know he'll not rob us once at sea?'

'Sirs!' the little man declared, his disfigured face assuming an expression of hurt. 'I give you my word he's an honest sailor, with no thought of such treachery.

'Even so,' Bracht said.

'I see that you are cautious men,' Xanthese murmured, 'and I cannot blame you for that. May I suggest a solution to this doubt? There are traders in this city of Kharasul renowned for their honesty - I believe I can persuade my captain to accept a token payment whilst you leave the remainder with a merchant, the balance to be paid on your safe return. Would such resolve your misgivings?'

He studied them as they exchanged glances. Calandryll said, 'It seems a reasonable answer.' Bracht ducked his head in agreement and Xanthese beamed afresh.

'Sirs, to further prove the honesty of our arrangement I shall leave you to find a merchant with whom to deposit your coin.' He raised his hands as if they protested, shaking his head vigorously. 'I'll not give you a name. No - ask of some other and know that Xanthese does not lie.'

'So we shall,' Bracht said. 'Now, how is this captain called and where do we find him?'

The scar-faced man leant closer across the table, lowering his voice again as though afraid the soldiery might learn of their transaction.

'He is called Menophus ek'Lannharan and his boat the *Sea Queen.* He awaits you even now, at the harbour.'

'When can he sail?' Calandryll asked.

'On the tide, do you wish it,' replied Xanthese. 'He'd as soon be gone as wait anchored for the lictor to claim his service.'

'And what boat does he command?'

'A warboat,' Xanthese said, 'a swift warboat. With sturdy oarsmen to fight the wind and sail aplenty to ride her back.'

'And the lictor will allow him to sail?'

Xanthese grinned, conspiratorial now. 'Need the lictor know? Come with me and I'll affect an introduction. Then, doubtless, you'll wish to settle matters with a trader. That done, Menophus stands at your command and you can be out of Kharasul harbour before the sun sets.'

Calandryll looked to Bracht for confirmation: the freesword smiled briefly. Calandryll said, 'So be it. Let's meet this captain.'

'As you bid, good sirs.'

Xanthese rose, draining his cup, and led the way out the door. He brought them down the alley, turning where it crossed another, going deeper into the jumbled ways behind the harbour. Calandryll shifted the satchel to his back, hand on scabbard, aware of the buildings looming overhead, quiet, shuttered against the noonday heat, the sky a thin strip of hazy blue high above. Seagulls screamed from the waterfront but in that narrow road the only sounds were the drumming of their boots and the drone of insects. Xanthese hurried before him, Bracht at his back, their route running parallel to the water, the alleys tortuous as the warren of the Beggars Gate, but, at this hour, unpopulated.

'Best we avoid the lictor's men,' Xanthese called over his shoulder. 'Menophus would as soon no questions be asked. Nor you, either, lest I miss my guess.'

Neither Calandryll or Bracht offered answer and the scarred man took them deeper into the maze until they came to an open place, where the blank walls of storehouses formed a little square with no other exit than the alley down which they had come. Shuttered windows like eyes closed against sight of treachery stood high on the walls and cobblestones glistened in the hot sun. Xanthese scurried to the far side of the square, his shortsword suddenly in his hand, his face no longer obsequious, but harsh, set in lines of undisguised hatred.

Calandryll heard the slide of steel on leather as Bracht drew the falchion, his own blade loosed but an eye's blink later.

'To the side! Put a wall at your back!'

Bracht's voice brooked no debate, no hesitation, and he sprang to obey, suddenly aware of the soft footsteps that padded in the alley behind.

Five men appeared at the mouth, dressed as was Xanthese in loose tunics and breeks, for all the world like sailors or wharf rats, each bearing a shortsword. They spread across the exit and Xanthese moved to join them.

'You die for this!'

Bracht addressed himself to their betrayer, his threat met with a contemptuous smile.

'You think so?' Xanthese was changed. The fawning manner was gone and he seemed taller, even commanding, as if before he had played a part and now revealed himself. 'It shall be you who dies, Kern. You and the Seccan puppy.'

'At the hand of a cringing wharf rat?' Bracht laughed. 'I think not.'

'A cringing wharf rat?' Xanthese chuckled, and for an instant he assumed his earlier demeanour, mocking the freesword. Then, subtly, features and stance shifted again and he was menacing. 'You face Chaipaku now, Kern!'

Calandryll gasped, unable to stem the wash of naked terror that flooded him. He could see it now, in the cold eyes and the professional way they held their swords. This was no ambush organised by some opportunistic thief: these men were of the Brotherhood. He felt sweat slicken his palms even as an awful chill slid unpleasantly down his spine.

'Aye, that frightens you.' Xanthese looked to him now. 'And so it should.'

He heard himself ask, his voice husky, 'Why?'

'Your brother sought our service.' A dagger not much shorter than the sword appeared in Xanthese's left hand. 'It seems he considers you a threat. But then you killed one of us - Mehemmed? He was young - he was told to watch you, to discover where you went - but you slew him and now you pay the price.'

'I slew him,' Bracht said. 'He was careless and I gutted him like a pig. As he deserved.'

Xanthese laughed again, the sound echoing off the high walls.

'Do you seek to anger me, Kern? Do you seek to make *me* careless? You cannot. I am older than Mehemmed and I shall lay your entrails at your feet and watch you die. I shall enjoy that.'

From the corner of his eye Calandryll saw Bracht's lips draw back from his teeth, the expression as much snarl as smile.

'I've not had much practice of late,' he said. And sprang forwards.

He was fast - his move took Calandryll by surprise - but the Chaipaku were equally swift. Shortswords and daggers rose to meet the assault, steel clashing loud on steel, and Bracht sprang back to the protection of the wall, shirt cut, the falchion defensive before him. Xanthese wiped a thread of blood from his scarred cheek and nodded, his own smile feral now.

'Good. But not good enough. And I doubt the puppy's so skilled.'

The raw contempt in his voice grated against Calandryll's terror, stirring anger. The words were true - he knew he stood no chance against these assassins, even with Bracht at his side - and he must die here, but rising like the sun to dispel his fear he felt the heat of rage. He was no threat to Tobias, had no desire to usurp his brother, and yet that false assumption must now leave him dead in this lonely square, the way to the Arcanum left open for Azumandias to take. He cursed his brother and the Chaipaku with heartfelt rage, determining to sell his life as dear he could.

The six Chaipaku advanced.

Bracht said softly, 'Use your magic now. Destroy them with a storm, or fire - but destroy them.'

He shook his head helplessly, gaze darting from the assassins to the Kern, and said, 'I know not how to summon it!'

'Even I cannot defeat six of the Brotherhood.' The falchion shifted like a living thing in the freesword's hand. 'Magic must aid us, or we die here. If you must, render yourself unseen.'

Calandryll hesitated, unwilling to leave his comrade. Even aided by the spell Varent had taught him it seemed unlikely he could slay so many Brothers: the spell offered escape only for him.

'Use it!' Bracht urged. 'One of us at least may survive.'

He waited still, loath to take that path, and said, 'I'd not desert you.'

'Better that than die,' Bracht snapped. 'Use it!'

He opened his mouth to utter the spell, but even as he voiced the first strange syllables the assassins closed, their advance so swift the words died still-born on lips that faltered, gasping as blades flashed in the noonday sun and death sprang ferocious towards him. He forgot the spell as he instinctively raised his own sword, thinking only of defence.

Steel clashed on steel, sparks shining bright, and he danced back, aware of fleeting pain against his ribs, of a warmth and wetness he knew was blood even as he parried. Fear grew, and anger with it, a mounting rage that his brother's groundless jealousy should threaten his quest, should intervene now, to leave him dead in Kharasul after so perilous a journey, after surviving so many dangers. It grew, becoming a consuming thing, as great as the fear provoked by the grinning faces of the Chaipaku as they advanced, confident of slaying him.

Calandryll roared and hurled himself against them, careless of their blades, his own a whirling, thrusting thing propelled by a force he did not understand. It seemed then that he was possessed, for he did not know what he did, only that they fell back before him as if driven by a silent wind so strong it sent them stumbling across the square, their quarry become their attacker. He went after them, riding the magical wind, offensive now, their swords desperate in defence.

'Berserker!' Xanthese barked. 'Dylus - ward the alley! You others take him. Leave the Kern to me.'

He sprang at Bracht as the others moved swiftly to obey. The falchion turned his cut; was itself deflected by a flanking blade. Bracht danced sideways along the wall. Calandryll darted to his left, advancing on the Chaipaku, separating them from Bracht and Xanthese. A Chaipaku grunted as the straightsword drove against his ribs, more surprise than pain in the sound. He spun, blade flailing before him, and Calandryll cut low, seeing the tunic severed, the dull red hue of dragon's hide armour beneath brightened by flowing crimson. The blood seemed to fuel whatever magic aided him and he launched himself at the assassin, sword raised high.

A helm lay hidden by the headdress: Calandryll felt his blade turned, heard the clash. He swung the sword at the unprotected neck, the Chaipaku stunned long enough he made no move to duck. Steel met flesh and crimson blossomed over the assassin's shoulder. Calandryll hacked again, all his strength in the blow, and saw the head roll free, bouncing between the shifting feet of the others, who gaped and struggled to press forward against the force that opposed them. Calandryll saw the body stagger, swordarm working a moment longer before it fell, its blood spraying its companions. He sprang once more to the attack, raining ferocious blows at head and shoulders, held back a while by sheer swordskill: even faced with magic, the Chaipaku were fierce opponents.

Two faced him, moving to either side, the third scuttling to take him from behind, and he saw the two sent staggering, human leaves blown on a glamorous wind. He spun to deal with the other, not knowing whether it was fear or rage or magic that worked his arm. He turned the man's sword and drove his own in a savage slash against the ribs, the power that gripped him lending him such strength that again he saw dragon hide armour sundered, the Chaipaku screaming as ribs broke and steel hacked flesh. He cut again, where armour ended and the neck began. The Chaipaku jerked, his shortsword dropping as his dark eyes dulled. Blood jetted and he fell to his knees, then onto his face. Calandryll turned to meet the survivors, and saw the man, Dylus, who had remained to ward the exit, stiffen, sword and dagger dropping from hands that rose to clutch at the red wound across his throat. He was thrust aside, falling limp as his life drained out. In his place stood the warrior woman, capless, her golden hair drawn back like Bracht's in a loose tail. She wore, as best he could tell, no armour beneath her tunic of white silk, nor any on her long legs, but in her hands was a bloodied sabre, and in her eyes - storm-grey, just as Bracht had said - he saw fierce satisfaction as she charged across the square, the sabre swift as Bracht's falchion, and equally deadly.

One of the Chaipaku sprang to block her; the other faced Calandryll, no longer confident, but fighting with a desperation born of terror, of the knowledge that he encountered a power beyond his understanding. Calandryll was no wiser, aware only that in some manner he did not comprehend, magic again stood between him and defeat. He ducked under a scything blow and countered with a cut that sent the assassin staggering back, not sure whether the mysterious force or his own resolve hurled the man against a wall smeared now with blood.

The woman's eyes flickered in his direction, and a blade cut dangerously close to her side. She turned it with almost casual grace, spinning clear of the attack, parrying the thrust as her foot rose to land between the Chaipaku's legs. He wore no armour there, for he yelped, bending, and the sabre hacked across his exposed neck. He grunted and collapsed onto the cobbles.

Smiling grimly, the woman raised her sabre in salute as Calandryll deflected a blow and sent his straightsword darting over the wielder's arm, hard into the soft belly below the hide armour. He twisted the steel and stepped back as the assassin shrieked, face paling as agony gripped him, then cut, almost casually, to the side of the neck. The Chaipaku's shriek ended abruptly as his head lolled to the side and he fell against the wall, adding his own marks to the stains already left there.

Across the square he saw Bracht turn Xanthese's sword; dance clear of the dagger in the Chaipaku's left hand and riposte a stroke that drove the falchion deep into the assassin's windpipe. Xanthese grunted, an awful choking sound, and spat blood. He made no attempt to retreat; seemed even to reject the knowledge of his death as he attacked again. Bracht parried the blow and backed away, luring the Chaipaku onwards, the red hole in his throat spilling gore over chest and breeks. Hatred drove him, it seemed. Calandryll saw it burning in his eyes; heard it in the ghastly wheezing that came from gaping lips and opened neck.

Bracht took him farther across the square, each step leaching out more of his life. Then the Kern halted and feinted a cut, parried the counterstroke, and thrust forwards, the falchion driving into the lower belly. Xanthese screamed then, as best he could, and fell down on his knees. Bracht kicked his sword aside and swept the falchion hard across the neck: the Chaipaku toppled forwards into the pooling of his own blood.

At the centre of the little square, the woman saluted the Kern's victory.

'You fight well.'

Bracht faced her, sword still in hand, his eyes both suspicious and admiring.

'As do you.'

Calandryll saw that she stood between them and the alley: he hoped, not knowing why, that she would make no attempt to halt them. Her sabre remained on guard, the grey eyes intent on the Kern's face. Like two wary animals, he thought, assessing one another. Dimly he became aware of an absence, of a weariness close to nausea, and knew that whatever unknown power had aided him, it was gone now. He smelled blood, heated by the sun, and spat, eyes straying to the corpses; back to the woman.

'I have sought you,' she said calmly. 'It was fortunate I found you when I did.'

'Perhaps,' Bracht acknowledged.

'The Chaipaku would have killed you,' the woman said. 'In time.'

The Kern shrugged.

'Even with your friend's magic to aid you. Chaipaku are very hard to kill.'

'Aye,' Bracht said, 'but I think we should have slain them, even without your aid.'

'Now they'll claim blood debt.' She smiled briefly. 'Remain in Kharasul and your lives will likely be short.'

'We do not intend to remain in Kharasul.'

'No. You seek passage to Gessyth. To Tezin-dar. You go in search of the Arcanum.'

She smiled as the falchion shifted a fraction, Bracht tensing, the slight stiffening of his features masking surprise. Dera, Calandryll prayed, must we now slay one who came to our aid?

'We need not fight,' she said.

'You seek to stop us,' Bracht returned, his voice wary.

'No - I seek the Arcanum.' Grey eyes fixed solemnly on the freesword's face; shifted just far enough to encompass Calandryll in their gaze. 'I propose an alliance. I have a warboat at my disposal.'

'Why should we trust you?' Bracht asked.

'I aided you.' The sabre swung, indicating the bodies that littered the square. 'And in Kharasul - anywhere in Kandahar - the Chaipaku will hunt you down. Our forces joined, we stand better chance of gaining what we seek.'

'Or we of dying,' Bracht said. 'On your warboat.'

The woman sheathed her blade and said, 'Save that you have my word.'

Bracht ducked his head briefly, his eyes not leaving her face, and surprised Calandryll by sliding the falchion into its scabbard.

'I am Bracht ni Errhyn of the clan Asyth,' he said. 'Of Cuan na'For.'

'And I am Katya.'

Bracht glanced sidelong at Calandryll: shrugged, and said, 'Let us talk of this then, Katya.'

FIFTEEN

THEY followed Katya to the harbour, hurrying to put the square behind them before Chaipaku or Tyrant's soldiers came to question or to kill, not speaking until they reached the safety of the open wharf, where the armoured men in their scarlet puggrees seemed guarantee against further attack. What remorse stirred in Calandryll's conscience at the slaughter they left behind was drowned beneath the questions that seethed in his mind, the doubts he felt concerning the mysterious woman, and when he glanced at Bracht he saw the Kern's face set in contemplative lines, the blue eyes fixed on the woman's slim figure, as if he, too, pondered the reasons for her intervention and found answers elusive. They both kept silent, however, until she halted on the water's edge, beyond earshot of the soldiery, pointing to a sleek black boat, its dragon's head prow familiar.

'I can bring you to Gessyth on that,' she declared, settling easily on a bollard, sheathed sabre across her knees.

Calandryll studied the vessel, seeing it different now to the Kand warboats; subtly, but to an eye with some experience of sailcraft out of no shipyard he could name. He returned his gaze to the woman, curious and more than a little wary.

'My question remains,' Bracht said, 'Why?'

Katya smiled, shoulders rising in negligent shrug.

'I do not think you will find another to take you.'

Her gaze shifted to encompass the harbour. There were noticeably fewer vessels anchored in the estuary now, and even as they watched two merchant men set sail, escorted by four warboats flying the Tyrant's pennant. A squad of armoured men marched by, flanking a ship's crew, towards the longboats that would carry them out to yet another impressed merchantman. And of the warboats that remained, Calandryll wondered, how many can we trust?

'You evade answers,' Bracht said.

'Ask me questions then,' Katya offered, 'and judge my honesty. But I tell you this - you will not find a trustworthy captain to bring you north, and to remain in Kharasul must surely mean your deaths. I do not think you have another choice.'

Bracht nodded, lips hinting at a smile, and settled on a crate, facing her, studying her face.

'Who are you?' Calandryll asked.

'As I told you - Katya.' She smiled then, chuckling softly as she shook her head. 'Forgive me - Bracht is right: I *am* evasive. It has become a habit.'

'A habit that does little to promote faith,' Bracht said.

Katya nodded. 'Aye; but have you been always open?' Her face assumed a gravity then and she said, 'I am of Vanu, beyond the Borrhun-maj.'

'Vanu?' Incredulity echoed loud in Calandryll's voice. 'Surely Vanu is the domain of the old gods. Do you name yourself goddess?'

'No,' she returned evenly, meeting his eyes with a calm grey stare. 'I am flesh and blood, like you; whose name I do not know.'

'Calandryll,' he said automatically.

Katya nodded. 'And why do the Chaipaku seek to slay you?'

'My brother sent them.' Briefly, he explained the Brotherhood's hiring by Tobias, halting at Bracht's frown.

'This does little to allay doubt,' the Kern said. 'You promised answers, then answer this - why do you seek the Arcanum?'

'Our purpose is the same, I think,' she replied. 'The Arcanum leads to the Mad God - whoever owns the book, if they have the knowledge to read it and the spells necessary for the doing of it, owns the means to raise him. And that no sane man would see.' A frown creased her brow and she sighed. 'He stirs yet, I think, sensing in his limbo what transpires here. You've heard the talk of Lysse's war fleet? And the civil war that threatens Kandahar? Is that not chaos stirring?'

'The Lyssian fleet is to defend against Kand pirates,' Calandryll said. 'That, surely, is order, not chaos.'

Katya smiled bitterly and shook her head again.

'A war fleet is a war fleet, and surely the means to ending Kand attacks is to deal with the Tyrant. Who first suggested its founding?'

'Aldarin,' he returned promptly, 'Lord Varent den Tarl came as ambassador to Secca. Tobias is to command.'

'Whilst Kandahar's Tyrant engages in war with the Fayne lord.' Katya ducked her head as if his words confirmed hers. 'And your brother seems, from what you say, no reasonable man.'

Calandryll was reminded of Tobias's bellicose attitude, of his suggestion that the fleet sail on Kandahar itself. He frowned, confused. 'You say that Lord Varent plans war?' he asked.

'I say there would be no better time to attack Kandahar.' Katya shrugged. 'And there are men easier prey to the temptations of chaos than others. Who sent you on this quest?'

Bracht raised a hand then, silencing his answer. 'Questions and more questions, but still few answers. Who sent *you*?'

Katya ducked her head in acceptance, grey eyes clouding. For several moments she stared out across the harbour, then smiled again.

'I haste,' she murmured. 'I feel the chaos winds gather and I'd come to Tezin-dar swift as I may: fear renders me impatient. So - listen, and I shall tell you all I know.'

Tanned hands braced firm on her scabbard and she met their doubtful eyes with even gaze.

'The holy men of Vanu scried an augury that spoke of the Mad God's raising and sent me forth to prevent this. Their scrying foretold a sorcerer of Lysse with means to return Tharn to life, though to accomplish this he had need of the Arcanum. They foresaw two I should encounter, our purpose joined. They sent me to find the book and bring it back to Vanu, that they might destroy it and leave the Mad God forever in limbo. We of Vanu have little to do with your southern kingdoms, but that boat was built and I travelled to Lysse, where I learnt of a fair-haired young man and a warrior of Cuan na'For gone questing for the book ...'

'How?' Bracht interrupted bluntly.

'These same holy men gave me a talisman.' She reached inside her shirt, bringing out a silver chain from which hung a red stone akin to that worn by Calandryll. 'It is a thing of power; it points like a compass to magic. It brought me to Aldarin, and there I learnt of a mage whose ambition waxed large.'

'Azumandias!' Now it was Calandryll who interrupted her, gaping when she shook her head; gasping when she spoke again.

'Azumandias is dead. Long dead. Oh, he sought to secure Orwen's map whilst the ink was still fresh on the parchment, but he was slain by one he trusted - his own son, who lusted for that power himself.'

He could not contain himself. Unthinking, he blurted, 'But Lord Varent learnt his skill from Azumandias! This cannot be!'

The grey eyes found his and in them he saw only sincerity.

'If this Lord Varent studied with Azumandias, then he lives far beyond the years of mortal men and is a sorcerer of very great power. Was he the one sent you?'

Calandryll ignored her question. 'Azumandias sent demons against us,' he said, accusation in his voice. 'If he is dead, how could that be?'

'Do you know it was Azumandias?' she asked.

'Who else?' he snapped.

'Varent,' said Bracht, the flat statement snatching Calandryll's head round to stare in frank disbelief at the Kern.

'Lord Varent? Do you lose your wits? Why should he?'

'We argued then,' Bracht said. 'Do you remember? I found myself hired to guard the runaway son of Secca's Domm and had little liking for that task. I doubted your ability and you borrowed Varent's sword to prove me wrong. He knew what we did and the demons came then - and were easily defeated. Too easily, it seemed.'

'So?' Calandryll frowned. 'That proves nothing.'

'Unless Varent conjured them to persuade me of your worth,' Bracht said. 'My opinion of you was higher after that. Nor should you forget the *byah*'s warning.'

Calandryll shook his head: the suggestion was preposterous. No doubt the *byah* had warned them of Katya.

'This Varent, then, is the one who sent you,' she said, 'And he told you he learnt his skills from Azumandias?'

Calandryll nodded, confusion for the moment rendering him speechless.

'Then perhaps Varent is Azumandias's son. Though he called himself Rhythamun then.'

'This is insanity!' His hand chopped air, dismissing her. 'Lord Varent is ambassador of Aldarin. A noble. Trusted adviser to the Domm. You say he is a patricide? And lived in the time of Orwen? How many hundreds of years have passed since then? Lord Varent sent us seeking the Arcanum that he might destroy it. It is Azumandias who seeks to raise the Mad God.'

'Azumandias is long dust,' she replied, undeterred by his rank disbelief. 'And there are ways a man - a wizard - may live beyond his natural span.'

'Lord Varent shows no sign of age,' he retorted, angry. 'And how should he come full-grown to such prominence in Aldarin?'

'He changed your shape,' Bracht said, voice soft, his eyes moving from one to the other, 'And I never trusted Varent.'

'You sought to slay us.' Calandryll ignored the Kern, glaring at the woman. 'You came against the *Sea Dancer* and sought to end us there.'

'I sought the chart you carry,' she replied, 'or whatever guide you have to Tezin-dar. I did not seek to slay you. Had I sought that I should have sunk your vessel.'

'A man was wounded and more might have died,' he barked, 'when your archers fired upon us.'

'The Kands employed their arbalest,' she returned, 'and my bowmen answered. I had sooner none were harmed - I had no quarrel with the Kands. Nor you, did you but give me what I asked.'

Calandryll snorted disbelieving laughter. Katya said, 'Did I wish your deaths, would I have aided you against the Chaipaku? I could have let them slay you and bargained, after, for what you carry. Their only interest is to see you dead.'

'There's truth in that,' Bracht murmured.

'There's deceit in it!' Calandryll snapped. 'Dera, Bracht! You speak of the *byah*'s warning and choose to name Lord Varent the deceitful one. I say it is she -

she weaves words in a spider's web, to ensnare us. She feared the Chaipaku would take the map, no more. She seeks the Arcanum for her own ends.'

'To destroy it,' Katya said.

'Lord Varent has the same desire,' he retorted. 'Why should we trust you, not him?'

'Wait.' Brach raised a placatory hand. 'Think on this, Calandryll. That I distrust Varent you know; that matter of the demons - did I not say they seemed very easy to overcome? And she might have sunk the *Sea Dancer* - fetched us half-drowned from the waves and taken what she wanted then. And the Chaipaku - aye, why should they not sell her the map? Xanthese himself said they sought only to slay us.'

'You trust her?' He shook his head helplessly.

'I say we hear her out,' Bracht said.

'I can tell you little else,' Katya admitted. 'I have travelled from Vanu in search of the Arcanum, that it be destroyed and its threat forever ended. I do not know what else I can say to convince you.'

'Leave us to find it,' Calandryll muttered. 'Let us return it to Lord Varent, that *he* may destroy it.'

'Your comrade doubts him.' She looked to Bracht, who shrugged, expressionless. 'And if he *is* Rhythamun, then he intends not to destroy it, but to use it. To raise the Mad God himself.'

'We had agreed on this,' Bracht said softly. 'To hold the book against Varent's proving.'

'And now you say we should hand it to her?' Calandryll stepped to the wharf's edge, hands raised in frustration, letting them fall to his sides.

'I say there is sufficient in what she tells us to suggest truth.' Bracht moved to join Calandryll, staring at him, his voice low; earnest. 'And Kharasul has become doubly dangerous now. She, at least, offers us passage to Gessyth.'

'And slit throats,' he returned.

'Perhaps,' the Kern allowed.

Calandryll swung from his observation of the harbour to stare at Bracht, eyes narrowing as he examined his comrade's face. 'You trust her,' he gasped.

Bracht met his gaze and shrugged. 'She's shed blood in our aid - by the ways of Cuan na'For that earns her at least a measure.'

'Your wits are addled! You see a pretty face and throw away your caution. Does lust blind you?'

'No,' Bracht said, calmly, 'though her face is undoubtedly lovely, I see the means to reach Gessyth.'

'Or die,' said Calandryll. 'Or hand the Arcanum to Azumandias.'

'If she speaks the truth, Azumandias is dead,' Bracht said. 'And that must make Varent the liar.'

Calandryll's hands clenched into fists, raised helplessly against such convoluted logic. All hinged on Katya's word, on trust in a woman who had once already sought to halt them, and now - for all he knew - sought only to gain the chart by more subtle means. 'I cannot trust her,' he muttered. 'She weaves words - as we seduced Anomius, so she seduces us ... you.'

'I incline to trust,' Bracht nodded, accepting the accusation. Then frowned: 'And perhaps there is a way to prove her; or reveal her.'

'How?' asked Calandryll.

'In Secca you consulted a spaewife,' Bracht said, slowly, choosing his words carefully, 'and she told you of this quest, did she not? She told you of two comrades, no?'

He nodded. 'You and Lord Varent.'

'Perhaps,' Bracht said. 'Or - perhaps - Katya.'

'Insanity.' He shook his head, rejecting the notion.

'Surely there are spaewives in Kharasul,' Bracht said. 'Let us find one and seek guidance there.'

He faced the Kern, doubt creasing his brow.

'We face the finding of another boat, else,' Bracht urged. 'With the Brotherhood seeking payment of blood debt, and few boats to be found, I think. Is it not the answer? If a spaewife denies the woman, we avoid her and make our way to Gessyth as best we can.'

'Do we secure another boat she'll likely follow us,' he said.

'Likely,' Bracht agreed, 'but with the spaewife's aid we shall know her for friend or enemy.'

It made sense: and surely now expediency must govern their actions. He looked at the estuary, seeing another merchantman haul anchor and turn for the north, warboats riding low to either side. Six dead Chaipaku lay in the square and soon must be discovered: to remain in Kharasul was to die. A scrying would, at least, reveal Katya for Azumandias's agent and end Bracht's insane trust: he nodded acceptance.

'And if she,' he could not help a covert glance towards the waiting woman, 'is proven enemy?'

Bracht's face was solemn as he touched the falchion's hilt. 'In Aldarin I asked Varent why he did not cut his enemy's throat - should she be proven of Azumandias's following, then she answers to me.'

'Your word on it?'

Now Bracht nodded: 'My word on it.'

'Let us find a spaewife,' he said.

The Kern grinned, tightly, and walked to where Katya sat with patient, solemn mien.

'We would seek proof you cannot give,' he said. 'Will you agree to a scrying?'

The flaxen head tilted back, grey eyes on his face, moving to Calandryll's, where he stood at Bracht's side. 'And if she scries me true?'

'We sail for Gessyth,' Bracht said, 'to seek the Arcanum together.'

'And if not?'

Calandryll could not tell whether Bracht's grin was

ironic or regretful, but he saw the freesword's hand touch the falchion's hilt again in unspoken answer. Katya nodded once and rose to her feet.

'So be it. Put me to your test - the sooner we're gone from this place the better.'

They went in silence to The Waterboy, each wrapped in their own thoughts, Calandryll's of what must follow when the spaewife proved him right, revealing Katya for a liar, agent of Azumandias. Lord Varent a patricide, centuries old? It was a monstrous deceit, a lie of dazzling proportion, plausible in its very enormity, an accusation so incredible it begged belief for want of reasonable explanation. And yet it seemed Bracht chose to trust her, though he had dislike of Lord Varent for cause; that and his unhidden admiration of the woman. Calandryll's face set in a scowl as he pondered all she had said, finding for each argument of hers a counter, each firming his conviction that she lied.

The Chaipaku - she could not know for sure that the Brotherhood would sell her Orwen's chart; that she had not sunk the *Sea Dancer* - perhaps she might had magic not saved them; the *byah*'s words - spoken of her, not Lord Varent; holy men of Vanu, their augury - he knew nothing of Vanu, it was a land lost behind the Borrhun-maj, and that she came from there rested solely on her word. His scowl darkened; soon enough she would stand revealed and then Bracht must regain his senses and ... slay her? He was not sure he wanted that: there was blood enough already pooling in their footsteps across Kandahar and she *had* come to their aid, albeit for her own reasons. He thought then of the dead Chaipaku, and for all they were assassins, and would have slain him without mercy, he shuddered as he remembered the savage satisfaction of his steel slicing flesh. 'The next will be easier,' Bracht had said, and the freesword had been right. He had changed -

was changing - and he was not certain he enjoyed what he became.

Such grim contemplation he thrust from his mind as they entered the inn and sought advice of the landlord as to the location of Kharasul's diviners, and one they might trust, eliciting directions and a name that brought them, in the early part of the afternoon, to an inner quarter of the city.

The streets here were a little less noisome than those others they had walked, as if a greater respectability attached to this Seers Gate; and quieter, those folk they passed sober, their faces solemn. The landlord had directed them to a spaewife he named as Ellhyn, whose sign was the moon and sun conjoined. They found it suspended from a blue-painted pole that jutted from the upper storey of a tall building, its stone clean and pale, day-star and lunar disc melded on a background of azure. Two children, brother and sister by their looks, sat casting knucklebones on the step before the open door, staring up as the trio approached. Calandryll moved to pass them and the boy rose, a diminutive guardian.

'What would you here?' he asked, holding station in the doorway.

'We seek the spaewife, Ellhyn,' Calandryll replied. 'This is her sign?'

The boy nodded and motioned his sister inwards, bidding them wait. Within moments she reappeared, whispering to her brother, who beckoned them into the house.

'Mother will see you in a while. Wait here.' He brought them to a simply furnished chamber, a single window looking onto the street, plain chairs of carved wood set along the blue-washed walls.

'Our thanks.' Calandryll bowed, the courtly gesture answered with a grin from the boy, who returned to his sister and their game. In a little while footsteps sounded and they saw a man walk past, leaving. The boy returned and led the way into a corridor cool and shadowy, perfumed with some indefinable herbal scent. At the farther end a door stood open on a chamber tiled in blue and gold and silver echo of the sign outside. Cushions were scattered across the mosaic and a low table of dark blue wood stood at the centre, behind it a woman who smiled and waved them in. She wore a robe patterned with suns and moons, small metal discs in the same design wound through her greying hair, catching light from the single window. Her face was homely, Kand-dark, and cheerful until they entered.

Then it clouded and she said, 'I cannot scry past the magic you wear. Do you seek an honest telling, you must remove it.'

Calandryll nodded and took the red stone from his neck, looking to Katya. She did the same and the spaewife clapped her hands, bringing her attendant son.

'The stones will be safe with Jirrhun,' she said, and both were handed to the boy, who held them, smiling, for a moment, then scurried out.

'Sorcerers' stones,' Ellhyn murmured, 'and power in both. The one to seek, the other to release. Sit down.'

They sat and she studied them each in turn, her eyes calm and black as midnight, settling on Calandryll at the last.

'There is power in you,' she said, 'that you could use without the stone, did you know the way of it. But now you need the stone. And doubt - much doubt, I feel. Fear of betrayal.'

To Katya she said, 'You travel far for what you seek, and fear who else may find it,' and to Bracht, 'Your only magic is your honesty. Your trust is precious.' She paused then, silent for a while, her eyes far away, then smiled again and said, 'My service costs ten of the golden varre you carry.'

Calandryll fetched coins from the satchel and set them on the table. Ellhyn opened a lacquered box that stood there and dropped the coins inside, taking from the box a tasselled cord of woven silk that she spread ceremoniously across the table. She took a knotted end in either hand and bade them each set hand in place about the rope.

'Now ask me what you will,' she said, closing her eyes.

Katya glanced at Calandryll, her eyes challenging. He looked to Bracht, who shrugged, indicating that he should speak.

'I would know,' he said slowly, choosing his words with care, 'if this woman speaks the truth. She says she comes from Vanu and means us no harm.'

Sunlight bathed the spaewife's face in golden light, deepening the creases on brows and cheeks. She nodded once, the trinkets in her hair jangling softly.

'Her name is Katya and she has come from beyond the Borrhun-maj. From Vanu, on a quest after that which you seek, which is ...' Abruptly, sweat glistened on her brow and she shuddered, lips tight against clenched teeth. 'Burash, but there is fell power here! What you seek is better left unfound, lest it bring down all the world. There are others seek that thing, and should they find it ...'

Her voice trembled into silence. Calandryll said, 'Does she mean us harm?'

'No!' Ellhyn's voice came harsh from straining throat. 'No harm from her - aid, rather. Has one of my calling not already told you that two comrades walk your path?'

'Their names?' he asked, in a manner fearing the answer.

'The warrior at your side, Bracht,' the spaewife groaned, 'and the woman you doubt. Katya. Such doubt is madness! She is true, and your ways are one. Trust her!'

A vein throbbed at her temple, starting a tic that trembled one closed eye. Calandryll stared at her, his thoughts in turmoil. *Trust her?* To trust Katya was to believe all she had said; and that was to disbelieve another.

'Lord Varent den Tarl,' he demanded urgently, 'Is there truth in him?'

'The name is unknown.' It seemed the words clogged Ellhyn's throat, each one spat out, laboriously, like bitter seeds. 'But there is a shadow at your back that binds you with deceit ... Lies have been told you by that one ... Not her ... A prince of lies, who would ... No! I cannot!'

The last word was a shriek. Her head flung back, hands snatching from the cord to clasp at her neck, as if the words of the scrying burned, she rocking backwards and forwards as though nursing moral hurt. Jirrhun and the girl appeared in the doorway, the boy darting past them to throw protective arms about his mother, anger on his young face, the girl standing wide-eyed, her gaze accusing.

'Wine, and quickly!' Katya turned, gesturing at the girl.

The child looked at her brother, who nodded, sending her running, returning with a brimming cup that she set upon the table. Jirrhun raised it to his mother's lips and said coldly, 'Leave now.'

Ellhyn shook her head, spilling purple droplets over her robe. 'No, wait.' She sipped a little more and the trembling that shook her abated. She took the cup from Jirrhun's hands and drank deeper, then smiled wanly at her son. 'Thank you, you did well. Both of you. But now, please leave us.'

Jirrhun paused a moment, doubt writ clear on his youthful face, then walked slowly from the chamber, taking his sister's hand. Ellhyn drained the cup and set it down, sighing.

'Burash, but there's a darkness waiting.' The spaewife shook her head again, slowly, as though to clear it. 'A darkness such as can swallow all the world.'

'Of whose making?' Calandryll asked, the question met with a weary sigh.

'Of those long dead.' Ellhyn's hand, shaking, found the lacquered box unbidden, her eyes intent on his face. 'And better left dead.'

He watched as she removed a silver pipe; filled the bowl and struck a spark. The sweet fumes of narcotic tobacco wafted on the hot air: the spaewife's shuddering ceased as she breathed the drug.

'These are riddles,' he said, aware that he had said the same words in another place, far away; longer, it seemed, ago.

'I can offer you no more.' Ellhyn inhaled deeply, grunting her satisfaction. 'I can scry you only what is revealed to me.'

'Do you name Lord Varent betrayer?' he demanded.

'I know not that name,' Ellhyn gestured with the pipe, stem indicating Katya. 'But I tell you this one is true - the second companion foretold.'

This one is true.

Logic collapsed. All his careful arguments shattered against the rock of the spaewife's words. An awful cold settled over him and he clutched his arms across his chest, rocking forwards as does a man deep-chilled and seeking warmth, seeking to reject the cold that was acceptance of her scrying. Dimly he heard Bracht say, 'In Lysse a *byah* spoke of treachery. Was that warning of Varent?'

Ellhyn shook her head once more, in negation now. 'I do not know that name,' she repeated. 'Katya, Bracht, Calandryll den Karynth - these came to me, but not that one. The tree spirits utter only truth, this much I know - did this *byah* say the name?'

'No,' Bracht said, 'only warned against treachery.'

Ellhyn shrugged, sucking deep on the pipe.

'And you perceived no treachery in Katya?'

'Only truth. You three are bound in a design beyond my ability to comprehend.'

This one is true.

And therefore another is not. Another lies: the cold bit deeper and he began to shiver, unaware of the hand Bracht set upon his shoulder. Men lay dead by his hand because he had believed the lie; his own life was forfeit because he had believed the lie. The shivering became a bitter chuckle. How he had prided himself on the deception of Anomius - the cunning web of duplicity he had spun, tangling the sorcerer, a greedy fly ensnared in the spider's mesh of words, of promises, of ambitions. And all the time he was the fly in Varent's web. Saviour of the world? A messenger boy, no more. He groaned, reft by the pain of betrayal, the foundations of his belief, his confidence, shaken.

This one is true.

Katya true; Varent not.

Deception cloaks your path and you must choose your friends with care. Beware the face of lies ... Remember that when the deceiver spins his web ...

The *byah* had spoken, just as Bracht believed, of Varent.

This one is true.

Then likely all she said was true: Varent was no aristocrat of Aldarin, but what Katya told them - a warlock untold ages old and steeped in evil, the ambitions ascribed to Azumandias his. He sought the Arcanum not to destroy it, but to raise the Mad God himself. He would visit chaos on the world; and close - how close! - he came to succeeding, thanks to his unwitting, witless, dupe.

Katya true; Varent not.

The awful knowledge dinned against the walls of his mind. The cold bit harder, fierce as a knife. Insane he had called Bracht for the Kern's faith in the woman: a bitter irony, for Bracht had seen what he could not, seduced by Varent's - Rhythamun's! - soft words, his lying promises. He would have seen Katya slain; would have delivered the Arcanum into Varent's hands. No, not Varent's - Varent den Tarl was not his name and likely not his face, but Rhythamun; and what face owned that name he could not say. He grew aware of a pressure against his lips and opened his mouth, feeling liquid enter, wine that he swallowed unthinking and began to choke. A hand pounded at his back, another wiped his mouth. The cup came again and he drank. A third time. His vision cleared and he saw Ellhyn studying him across the table, her homely face troubled. Bracht knelt beside him, his arm as much comfort as support. He turned to Katya, apology in his eyes and she met him with a smile, her grey gaze clear, no triumph in it, but concern.

'Forgive me,' he mumbled, 'Forgive my doubts.'

The flaxen head ducked in acceptance: she set a hand upon his arm, the pressure of her fingers her answer. He essayed a smile that seemed to stretch his cheeks in rictus grin, a deathshead grimace, lorn of all the confidence he had known, that lost on the spaewife's scrying. He wiped a hand over his face, feeling it wet, and rubbed, embarrassed, at his eyes, forcing his back straight as he faced Ellhyn.

'The stone,' he said, voice hoarse, 'that Varent gave me. Does that grant him power over me? Might he control me through the talisman?'

'The stone is a tool,' she answered, her own voice husky now from the narcotic tobacco, gesturing at the tasselled cord, 'as that is. It unleashes power already yours.'

'Power?' he asked numbly, not wanting such power; wanting nothing of magic and magicians. 'Do you name me sorcerer?'

'No.' The spaewife laughed, briefly. 'It is not so simple, magic. It is a talent - an ability - that some have and others not. To use it requires study, knowledge. Long years of tutelage. There is ability in you, and the stone may sometimes focus that ability, but I do not think you can control it.'

He nodded, thinking that he had believed himself wise, educated, yet Bracht had seen what he had not. Had seen the truth from the start.

'Azumandias,' he rasped, 'do you know that name?'

The spaewife shook her head.

'Rhythamun, then?'

Again, the negative.

'There was much hidden,' she said, the words slurring somewhat, 'and I would not probe that darkness again. It hides things too terrible. Perhaps these names are hidden there - I do not know. I tell you, though, that what you seek is better left lost.'

'For others to find?' Now he shook his head, warmed by the wine, the cold giving way to heat, to anger. 'For the liars and the deceivers to find and use? No. Not that.'

'Then destroy it if you can,' the spaewife told him; told them all. 'That thing opens gateways to abomination.'

'That is our quest,' he heard Katya say. 'To find it that it may be destroyed.'

'Then I wish you well,' Ellhyn said. 'I will offer to Burash, that he aid you. I think you will need such aid, for you are not the only ones who seek this thing.'

'Who else?' asked Katya.

'I cannot tell you,' the spaewife answered. 'The darkness hid them.'

Varent for one, he thought, if he somehow knows we have found him out; perhaps Anomius, if he lives. Perhaps others, and that the case we had better start sailing north to Tezin-dar. He moved to rise, surprised by the weakness of his legs, his swimming head, Bracht's arm a welcome prop.

'My thanks for what you saw,' he murmured, bowing.

Ellhyn smiled, a wan expression. 'I think you go to your deaths,' she said, her dark eyes enfolding them all three, 'but you go with true companions and I wish you success.'

He nodded, turning, feeling Katya close on his right, and smiled at her, this time true warmth in the expression.

'You stand ready to sail?'

She ducked her head, smiling back.

'On the tide. Or sooner, if we must.'

'Sooner, I think,' he said, and gently removed Bracht's arm, finding his own feet as they paced slowly down the corridor, into the heat and light of the jungle-scented afternoon. 'As soon we may.'

Katya nodded, accepting the stones Jirrhun offered, passing the cord of his over his bowed head.

They walked towards the harbour, hands ever close to their swords, for now Kharasul seemed a place of danger, the threat of the Chaipaku joined by that darkness of which Ellhyn had spoken. The very air seemed thicker now, as if the wind that blew across the Ty river bore hint of menace. Calandryll examined the faces of the passersby, wondering if their expressions, some bland, others curious, hid darker feelings, wondering if those eyes that met his recognised him and marked him as victim. He quickened his step, the Vanu warboat a refuge now, an escape from assassin's vengeance and sorcerous retribution alike. He glanced at the stone, relieved to see it dull, and braced his shoulders, finding renewed determination.

Dera, but Reba had spoken truth when she foretold his travelling. There would be no return to Lysse now, no delivery of the Arcanum into Varent's hands, but a journey to Vanu, that land no less fabled than Tezin-dar. To Gessyth first, then into the swamps to find the legendary city, take the book and bring it to the holy men of Vanu, that they might destroy it. Varent - Rhythamun - should not have it! Not while he lived: before that liar should set hands on it, he would lay down his life.

He realised that fewer people thronged the streets and saw that they approached the harbour, passing down a narrow alley, its farther exit marked by the blue mingling of sea and sky. The afternoon was advanced now, the sun far out over the western ocean, shadows lengthening as they emerged from the passage and strode purposefully across the cobbles of the wharf, the air loud with the clatter of marching men and the cries of the gulls disturbed by such activity. The craft anchored in the estuary ran down like grains in a sand-clock, fewer now than had rode the waves at noon, another departing even as they watched, only three Lyssian vessels remaining, and far fewer of the Kand warboats. Soon, he thought, there would be none, and grinned, thankful for Katya's presence.

She brought a silver whistle from inside her shirt as they reached the water's edge, raising the little instrument to her lips to emit three shrill blasts that brought a flurry of activity to the boat. A dinghy was lowered, manned by two tall men, their sweeps propelling the craft to the wharf. An officer - a lictor by the badge on his puggree - looked towards them, his face thoughtful as he recognised their intention, and barked an order that formed a squad of six pikemen about him.

Dinghy and soldiers reached them at the same time, the lictor raising an imperious hand, bidding them halt. Calandryll eased his blade in the scabbard, unwilling to be thwarted now.

'You have permission to leave?'

'We need none.' Katya's tone was brusque, prompting

the officer to frown. 'My boat is out of Vanu; my companions from Cuan na'For and Lysse. Thus we are not subject to seizure.'

The lictor's frown deepened. He said, 'All who anchor in Kharasul's harbour are subject to the Tyrant and the laws of Kandahar.'

'Indeed,' Katya agreed, 'but not to impression into his navy.'

The lictor shrugged, studying the warboat with speculative eyes before returning his gaze to the woman. 'You command a fine vessel,' he announced, 'Such as could find use against the Fayne rebels. I think you had best delay your departure whilst I enquire of the praetor, whether we have need of the boat.'

Calandryll said, 'I am Calandryll den Karynth, son of the Domm of Secca in Lysse,' drawing himself up to his full height, seeking the tone his father used in dealings with functionaries, 'and I have commissioned this boat to bring me home. I have urgent business and I would not be delayed.'

The lictor eyed him for a moment, then shaped a doubtful bow. 'You will forgive me ... my lord ... but you do not look much like a Domm's son, and we have need of sound warboats.'

Calandryll affected the impatience his brother found so natural, returning the officer's dubious stare with a cold gaze. 'I travel incognito,' he snapped, 'but I assure you neither my father or the Tyrant will thank you for delaying me.'

An element of confusion entered the lictor's frown and he cleared his throat. Calandryll said, 'You have need of warboats? Then take those corsairs out there - at least that would leave our sealanes safer.'

'I ...' the lictor cleared his throat again, 'I think I had best ask the praetor's judgement.'

'I think you had best prepare to find yourself stripped of your command,' Calandryll barked. 'Secca does not take kindly to minor officers hindering her ambassadors. The Tyrant shall hear of this!'

The lictor took an involuntary step back, for the moment lost for words. Calandryll seized the advantage, beckoning Bracht and Katya.

'Come, we've delayed long enough.'

He went down the steps and clambered into the dinghy. Katya followed and then Bracht; the lictor stared at them, face flushed, then shook his head and spun on his heel. Calandryll breathed a sigh of relief as he led his men back across the wharf. 'Dera!' he murmured, 'I thought us lost then.'

'We've still to clear the anchorage,' Katya said.

He nodded, watching the sleek lines of the warboat grow as the dinghy drew steadily closer. The oarsmen rowed in silence, tall, slim men, much like Katya in appearance, but muscular, tunics stretched across their shoulders, their near-white hair cut short at the nape, broad-bladed knives sheathed on their belts. More waited to bring them on board, the dinghy rapidly hauled up, the fore and stern anchors stowed, the great sweeps running out on Katya's word, the prow turning south as the helmsman swung his tiller and the warboat moved, darkly majestic, towards the open sea.

Katya led the way to the stern, that raised some little way above the central planking that divided the rowing benches, overshadowed by the curling dragon's tail that formed solid mounting for the tiller. On board, the craft seemed larger than it had appeared, viewed from the poop of the *Sea Dancer*, with storage space between the benches and small cabins at bow and stern. Katya spoke with the helmsman in a language neither Calandryll or Bracht could understand, and he ducked his head, smiling broadly at the two newcomers.

In accented Lyssian, he said, 'So you're the one who near-sank us. I thought we must find the bottom when you brought that maelstrom against us.'

'This is Tekkan,' Katya informed them. 'It was he who saved us then.'

'More luck than I,' Tekkan smiled, and turned to his task.

He was clearly skilled, the warboat gliding smooth between the larger merchantmen, driven by the rhythmic sweeping of the oars. The rowers needed no time beat, it seemed, for there was no drum master to maintain their stroke, only Tekkan shouting from his vantage point, and a man posted to the prow to warn of obstacles the helmsman might miss. Thirty oarsmen, Calandryll counted, fifteen to each side, and all with pale gold or near-white hair, their bare backs tanned, lighter than the Kands or Bracht, and all their eyes grey like Katya's or a blue so pale as to seem mesmeric. They chanted as they worked, not loud, but in perfect unison, their voices melodic, the song strange, unlike any he had heard. And amongst them sat women; the archers, he presumed, tall as the men, but their hair longer, tailed or wound up in knots. Beside each station, against the bulwarks, hung a round shield, hide-covered against the salt spray, and beneath each bench was a locker. The central deck overhung the benches enough that hammocks might be slung there, sheltered somewhat from the elements, and there he saw equipment, sheathed swords and the shapes of wrapped bows, filled quivers, and axes of unfamiliar design. The Vanu-folk were well furnished for the quest and he felt his rekindled confidence mount as the boat moved rapidly past Kharasul, starting to buck a little as the incoming tide met the outwash of the Shemme.

He heard Bracht groan and turned to see the Kern clinging resolutely to the taffrail, face paling, his eyes fixed on the open sea ahead, filled with apprehension.

'What ails you?' asked Katya, moving to his side.

'That.' Bracht jerked his chin to indicate the ocean, groaning afresh as the warboat lurched and he clutched the rail as if his life depended on it. Katya chuckled, setting a hand on his shoulder. 'Come,' she said, 'I've a cure for that below.'

Warily he let go his hold, staggering as the boat shifted again, clutching at her for want of other support, his arms about her so that for a moment they stood pressed tight together. Calandryll saw Tekkan cast a swift and not entirely approving glance in their direction, and then Katya disengaged herself, an unfathomable expression in her grey eyes as she took Bracht's arm and led him from the raised deck. Calandryll followed, seeing that low doorways were cut to either side of the ladder, Katya opening the left and motioning Bracht inside.

It was cramped with three bodies filling the space, a single bunk against the stern, a narrow window above and a cupboard beneath, another built into the partitioning wall, and a third, open and filled with charts, facing that. Katya brought out a flask and silver cup, glancing enquiringly at Calandryll, who shook his head, smiling, and said, 'I've sea legs. Bracht is more accustomed to a horse.'

'Would that we might ride to Gessyth,' the freesword moaned. 'We folk of Cuan na'For are not made for the sea.'

'Drink this.' Katya filled the cup, passing it to him. 'This and a night's sleep and you'll walk a boat like a sailor born.'

Bracht's eyes said that he set no faith in her promise, but he grinned wan thanks and drained the cup, grimacing at the taste.

'You'll sleep now,' Katya informed him. 'And when you wake, the malaise will be gone.'

'Your word on it?' Bracht asked, stretching willingly enough on the bunk. 'And whose bed do I take?'

'My word on it,' she smiled. 'And the bunk's mine.'

'The sweeter for that,' the Kern yawned. 'Though I'd . . .'

What he intended to say was lost in the sigh that followed. With the heavy deliberation of a man close on slumber's verge, he loosed the fastenings of his scabbard and cradled the sheathed falchion in his arms, turning drowsily on his side. Another yawn and he slept.

'It works swiftly.' Katya stoppered the flask and returned it to the cupboard. 'He'll not wake before dawn, but he'll suffer no more. Now come, we've things to talk of.'

She beckoned Calandryll from the cabin, leading the way along the deck to the forecastle, where they leant against the rail, watching Kharasul slide away to starboard, the mouth of the Ty river beyond, and beyond that the dark jungles of Gash.

'Do you trust me now?' she asked, her eyes frank.

'Aye,' he nodded, answering her gaze. 'I was a fool.'

There was bitterness in his tone: Katya shrugged, head turning to observe the jungle.

'I think not. But tell me how you came to this quest.'

They hung close to the coastline, beating north against the wind, foetid now with the reek of the vegetation that clung in hues of livid green to the shore, no beach discernible, only the great mass of exotic foliage. He began to speak, openly, holding nothing back, the telling a kind of absolution, and a commitment to trust. He told her of how his father would make him priest, and of his hopes for Nadama; of Tobias and the meeting with Varent, the ambassador's promises and the finding of Orwen's chart. He spoke of his meeting with Bracht, and Varent's magic, that had brought him out of Secca; and of everything Varent had told him. He spoke of the encounter with the demons and of the *byah*; of Bracht's misgivings, and of the stone; the crossing on the *Sea Dancer*, she chuckling at this, saying how the wind he had somehow conjured came close to sinking them, and of how they had beaten steadily south after, counting on his arrival in Kharasul. He told her of the first Chaipaku attack and the escape from Mherut'yi, of Sathoman ek'Hennem and Anomius, their flight from the wizard, her face clouding then; and finally of their coming to the square where she had met them.

She was silent for long moments when he was done, her eyes fixed on the passing jungle, then she said, 'I think that this Varent must be Rhythamun; and he will not let go easily.'

'That so,' he murmured, watching dark birds wheel above the trees, 'How old is he?'

'Azumandias saw Thomus crowned,' she answered, 'and Rhythamun saw him die.'

'Five hundred years?' His voice was hushed, awed. 'How can that be?'

'There are ways.' She shook her head in distaste. 'They are not pleasant and known to few.'

'How?' he insisted.

Katya turned towards him, then away, her eyes troubled. 'It is a matter of assuming another's life,' she said softly. 'It is not easy; nor without danger, but it may be done. By such as Rhythamun. Likely he stole this Varent's life - and in time will seek another.'

Calandryll shuddered, horrified; worse as a further thought entered his mind. 'Then he can pass unrecognised,' he gasped. 'He is able to assume what form he chooses.'

'Aye,' Katya nodded, 'but I think he has reason to remain as Varent for now - you say he has the trust of Aldarin? In such office he wields considerable power, and that must suit him well. The raising of the Mad God demands more than grammaryes - sacrifice is called for; spilled blood beckons him forth.'

'The fleet?' he asked, staring at her.

'Likely,' she nodded. 'You say this brother of yours spoke for war with Kandahar; and he is to command -

should Rhythamun persuade Aldarin's Domm to war, would Secca follow?'

'Not my father,' he said, 'but Tobias, yes. Tobias would welcome such a venture.'

'And already Tobias employs the Brotherhood.' Her meaning lay tacit between them, an ugly thing. His eyes widened in disgust. 'To slay our father? No! Surely not that! To murder me, perhaps; but not our father.'

'It is not unknown,' Katya said quietly, 'and should Tobias heed Rhythamun's blandishments ... You know him for a persuasive deceiver.'

'Dera!' he groaned. 'He would bring Lysse and Kandahar to war? To further his own ends?'

'To raise the Mad God,' she said, 'aye - to win the power he seeks. He'd need find the lost places, and possess the spells of raising to achieve his purpose. But were Lysse and Kandahar embattled, that letting of blood would make the raising easier. Rhythamun seeks power infinite; and madman that he is, he'd bring the world down to gain that end.'

'That cannot be. *Must* not be,' he said.

Katya smiled then, her expression minding him of Bracht's, when the Kern faced swordplay. 'We have Orwen's chart,' she said, 'and in time we shall reach Gessyth. We need but seize the Arcanum and bring it safe to Vanu. There, it may be destroyed forever.'

'A long journey,' he muttered; doubtful. 'And its return by Lysse's coast. What if Varent has Tobias's ear by then? We'd surely face the fleet.'

'There's a chance of that,' she agreed, 'But what other course lies open? We lack the means to destroy the book.'

'Such was not given you by these holy men?' he asked.

'No.' She shook her head, the long tail of her wind-swept hair tossing. 'I have no magic save this stone, and that only a guide to you. To destroy the Arcanum calls for great power, for occult knowledge possessed by few.'

'Then why do they not accompany you,' he demanded, 'these holy men?'

'They have no power beyond Vanu's boundaries,' she said. 'Their choice is to leave the world to its own devices, and to that end did they limit their power; of their own choosing. Only when they read the augury did they choose to intervene in these affairs, knowing that else they must watch the world brought down in bloody ruin.'

Off the port bow the sun touched the western horizon, a vast disc of crimson that painted the ocean with its fire. Calandryll looked in that direction and it seemed to him that a wound opened in the sea, a livid gash awash with blood. He shook his head in silent rejection and turned once more towards the forbidding coast of Gash. The jungles were dark now, already tinted with the shades of descending night, and from them, faint on the wind, came strange, shrill cries. The full moon hung low to the east, cold as the sun was hot, and although the air was yet warm he shivered, weighted by the immensity of all they attempted. He looked back along the length of the warboat, seeing the women setting braziers on the deck in preparation of a meal, bringing food from the lockers as the oarsmen held their pace, driving the sleek craft steadily northwards into the wind, tireless it seemed, moving like cheerful automata.

'These are warriors?' he asked.

'All,' Katya answered, 'Women and men, both.'

Suddenly they seemed too few to attempt what they attempted, for if what Katya suspected should prove true, on their return they would likely face odds far greater than any he had anticipated.

Perhaps his doubt showed on his face. Or perhaps Katya read his mind, for she said, 'We must find the

Arcanum before we concern ourselves with what might be, and I think that will be hard enough.'

'Aye,' he agreed, smiling tightly. 'What knowledge have you of Gessyth?'

'It lies to the north,' she said, 'and Tezin-dar stands inland, deep in the swamps. Beyond that - nothng.'

'And on that you sailed from Vanu?' he stared at her, amazed at such daring.

'You come with little more,' she shrugged, 'You and Bracht.'

'We have Orwen's chart,' he said, 'and the stone to lead us to the book.'

'Little enough.' White teeth flashed in the fast-dying light. 'But I'd study that map. Shall you show me while we eat?'

'And will you tell me of Vanu?' he asked. 'The land beyond the Borrhun-maj is a mystery.'

He thought she paused then, as if reluctant, but her face was in shadow and he could not read her expression, only see her nod as she beckoned him towards the braziers, the smell of food reminding him of hunger so that he quickly forgot that small hesitation.

SIXTEEN

NONE on board save Katya and Tekkan spoke other than their own tongue, and that a language unlike any Calandryll had heard, a lilting, almost musical confusion of sounds of which, try as he might, he could make little sense. The crew made him welcome enough as he settled on the boards, a smiling woman passing him a bowl piled with a stew of fishes and vegetables, a man handing him a mug that another filled with pale wine, but when he sought to converse with them they only smiled the broader and shrugged, returning him words like a song, pleasant to the ear but leaving him none the wiser. Katya and Tekkan joined him then, the sea anchor dropped to hold the boat against the wind as the oarsmen took their rest, settling cross-legged beside him as, between mouthfuls, he plied them with questions about their homeland and they enquired of his.

Of the two, the woman was the more fluent, trading him question for question, often pausing to relay his words to Tekkan and the others who listened and awaiting their response before replying, so that he became unsure whose answer he received, though that seemed of little moment. Vanu lay, as he knew, beyond the Borrhun-maj, where, did he accept the fables, the First Gods, Yl and Kyta, had withdrawn. Katya laughed at that and told him the land was peopled with human folk, not gods, translating for her fellows, which set them to laughing. It was a lonely place, she agreed, the great mountain chain a barrier to the south, and more ringing the land, cutting it off from outside contact. Sometimes, she admitted, seafarers travelled to Nywam, on the Jesseryn Plain; but seldom, the Vanu preferring to keep to themselves, the mountainous coastline deterring much seagoing. There were cities, he learnt, in the mountains and the grasslands of Vanu's centre, and commerce between them, the metropolises each governed by a council, each of those electing three representatives to attend what passed for central government, which met twice a year, in spring and autumn. So loose an arrangement surprised Calandryll, himself more accustomed to the autocratic rules of Lysse's Domms, or the singular prominence of Kandahar's Tyrants. Did the cities of his homelands not fight, Katya asked, and what of the civil war brewing behind them in Kandahar? In Vanu there was no such conflict, she said, though he wondered at that, seeing warriors all about him. He could not press the point, for she subtly changed the direction of their conversation, steering it to matters more mundane, speaking of the mountains and the harsh winters, the forests and the plains, and he grew sleepy before she was done, accepting readily enough the pallet that was spread for him on the deck.

He woke with the sun hot on his face, rising to eat bread and cheese, washed down with cool water, and as he finished, Bracht emerged from the little cabin. The Kern approached warily, eyeing the ocean as if in anticipation of attack or a return of the malaise, but his pallor was gone and he braced against the warboat's rolling like a seaman born.

'Ahrd, but whatever Katya gave me works well,' he declared cheerfully as he settled beside Calandryll, proving the point by consuming a loaf of bread and a sizeable wedge of cheese. 'Where is she?'

Calandryll pointed to the stern, where the woman stood in conversation with Tekkan. Bracht nodded, taking more cheese, and looked to the east, where the coastline of Gash sat livid in the early morning light. 'You spoke last night, whilst I slept?' he asked, and when Calandryll nodded, 'Of what?'

Calandryll told him and Bracht grunted thoughtfully, his natural pragmatism dismissing idle speculation for the hard facts of their situation.

'I'd know more of the holy men,' Calandryll murmured. 'They chose to intervene in this - so they must be aware of the outside world. Can they truly destroy the Arcanum?'

Bracht shrugged, rising to clutch a line, no longer daunted by the sea, and said, 'The spaewife advised us to trust her, and I do. So we have no alternative but to trust them.'

Calandryll studied his face, thinking that such unreserved faith was out of character. Since they had first met it had been Bracht who doubted, he who trusted. The freesword's nature was, it had seemed, to cast a suspicious eye on whoever crossed their path, but now he appeared committed to Katya - even before Ellhyn had scried their joined destinies he had shown a willingness to believe in the warrior woman. He wondered if Bracht's obvious admiration clouded his customary scepticism, then cast the thought aside: Katya had intervened on their behalf against the Chaipaku, and the spaewife had declared her comrade - likely his own judgement was affected by the disconcerting knowledge that Varent had seduced him so successfully. And yet he could not entirely shake off the feeling that Katya held things back. She had spoken openly enough, or so it had seemed last night, and yet there remained questions he would have asked had she, or some comment of Tekkan's, not turned the conversation into another direction.

'I'd speak with her.' Bracht's voice brought him to his feet and he followed the Kern along the deck to the low poop, where Katya stood with the helmsman. 'You slept well?' she asked, smiling.

Calandryll glanced at his companion as Bracht ducked his head in agreement.

'I did. And now I feel settled.' He swung an expansive arm, the gesture embracing warboat and ocean. 'I'd never thought to feel at home on the sea - I owe you thanks.'

His eyes were on her face as he spoke, his smile as much in compliment as gratitude. And she was, Calandryll could only agree, a sight to stir the blood. The sun struck silver sparks from her hair, its binding emphasising her proud features, dominated by the grey eyes. She had shed her breeks, her tunic kilted by her swordbelt, the white cloth vivid contrast to the dark tan of her long legs, her feet bare for better purchase on the deck. She was lovely - and challenging, her eyes darkening an instant as she recognised the import of Bracht's smile, her own faltering. Beside her, Tekkan frowned briefly, and murmured something in the Vanu-tongue. Katya nodded.

'I'd not bring you sick to Gessyth,' she said. 'And it may well be your swordskills will be needed before we reach that place.'

'You anticipate attack?' Calandrull peered sternwards: the sea stood empty. 'Are we pursued?'

'The danger lies there.' It was Tekkan who spoke, leaving go his tiller to point landwards. 'In Gash.'

'We must take on fresh water,' Katya expanded. 'Our supplies cannot last; nor our food. Eventually we must anchor and go into the jungle; and the folk of Gash are not noted for their hospitality.'

'Ambush?' Bracht's smile did not waver. 'Against an armoured landing party?'

'Perhaps not,' Katya shrugged, 'but the danger is there.'

'And there,' Bracht declared, pointing ahead, and then astern, 'and there. Danger surrounds us, I think.'

'I'd not lose men,' Tekkan said. 'Nor time battling the creatures of Gash.'

Bracht laughed carelessly: Calandryll wondered if his confidence stemmed from the effects of the nostrum or a desire to impress the woman. 'How long before we shall need attempt it?' he asked.

'Ten days if we drink sparingly,' Tekkan answered. 'And ten after that, all the way to Gessyth. This boat was built for coastal waters, not the deep sea.'

There was a hint of disapproval in his voice, suppressed but discernible, his eyes flickering to Bracht as he spoke.

Perhaps the Kern heard it, Calandryll could not tell, but he saw Bracht's smile fade, his expression serious as he looked to the helmsman. 'My blade is at your command,' he said formally, that eliciting a nod from Tekkan. Then, to Katya: 'I robbed you of your cabin - my thanks for that. Shall I sleep elsewhere tonight?'

His gaze fixed frank on her face and Calandryll thought he saw a blush suffuse her cheeks, the tan an instant darker. He saw Tekkan's lips purse, the helmsman's stare cold.

Katya said, 'Your need was greater than mine - last night. Tonight you have choice of deck or hammock.' Her voice was cool: Bracht bowed, grinning. Tekkan spoke again in their own language and Katya nodded.

'There are charts I must study. Do make yourselves at home, I shall speak with you later.'

She passed them, they stepping back to afford her access to the companionway, Bracht's eyes on her as she descended the ladder, hers passing briefly over his face, the grey cloudy, his gaze not leaving her until she disappeared into the cabin. Tekkan said, 'You'll not disturb my crew on the foredeck.'

It was a clear dismissal and they made their way to the bow, that space empty, the oarsmen again at their benches and the women busy about the small tasks common on any vessel. Bracht lowered himself to the sun-warmed planks and set to drawing a whetstone along the edges of his blade. Calandryll sat beside him, troubled; unsure whether silence or speech was the more advisable. There was too much time, he decided, between them and Gessyth, and too much at stake: best therefore to speak out and have done with it.

'You press too hard,' he said.

Bracht glanced at him and grinned.

'Was your gaze not transfixed you'd have seen Tekkan's face,' he insisted.

'I saw only Katya,' Bracht returned. 'And that a more sightly study.'

'Like a lovestruck boy,' Calandryll retorted.

Bracht returned him a quizzical look, then nodded. 'Ahrd, but is she not beautiful?' he murmured. 'And a swordswoman to boot - a rare prize.'

Calandryll sighed patiently. 'Your sallies earned Tekkan's disapproval - would you make an enemy of him?'

'I'd know our new-found comrade better,' Bracht said, undeterred. 'Would she but allow me that pleasure.'

'Some bond exists between them' Calandryll said, 'Perhaps they are lovers.'

'Do you think so?' Bracht turned from his sword to peer thoughtfully at the helmsman. 'Do you say I have a rival?'

'A rival? Dera!' Calandryll lowered his voice as several crew members looked towards them. 'We sail unknown waters - in search of the Arcanum; the cannibals of Gash off our bow; Varent behind us; the goddess alone knows what ahead – and you think to bed Katya!'

'The journey will be long,' Bracht said mildly, 'and likely boring. And I've not met a woman such as she.'

'Would you hazard our quest for that?' Calandryll demanded.

'No,' Bracht replied in more solemn tone. Then grinned. 'But I'd lief claim that woman.'

Calandryll stared at the freesword, angry until he saw Bracht's face and recognised that the Kern was serious. He shook his head, modulating his tone.

'Whatever lies between Katya and Tekkan, our helmsman takes unkindly to your advances. Should that become something more ...' He left the sentence unfinished and Bracht nodded. 'I'd not make an enemy of Tekkan,' he agreed.

'Then curb your ... enthusiasm.'

Bracht met his stare and asked bluntly, 'Do you desire her?'

'No,' he answered. The Kern's eyes held his, speculative, and he shook his head, saying again, 'No.'

'Good,' Bracht said softly, 'Then there will be no rivalry between us.'

'No,' he repeated. 'But nor should you chance Tekkan's anger with your ... compliments. I advise that you walk soft about him - and her.'

Bracht exaggerated a sigh. 'A difficult thing - but, so be it.'

Encouraged, Calandryll said, 'This is unlike you. In all our journeying I've not seen you smitten so.'

'In all our journeying have you seen any woman like Katya?' came the response. 'But set your mind at rest - my tongue shall be curbed and no offence given.'

'The wiser course,' Calandryll said.

Bracht grunted an affirmative and sheathed the falchion, busying himself with the edges of his dagger, a contemplative smile tugging at the corners of his mouth. Calandryll rested back against the curving neck of the figurehead, content with the Kern's promise, content for now to stretch in the sun and listen to the slap of waves against the prow. He was not sure what he had seen in Tekkan's eyes, save that Bracht's advances had irritated the helmsman, nor how he should interpret Katya's response. That something existed between the two Vanu-folk he was sure, but not the nature of it. That Bracht should so suddenly - and seemingly with honesty - become enamoured of Katya surprised him. The Kern had taken his pleasure with Varent's serving wench casually enough, but this appeared a vastly different matter, for all Bracht's blunt approach - it was as if the Kern had arrived at some abrupt decision, a certainty born of instinct and beyond plain desire. And it could, he felt, remembering Tekkan's face, set their quest in jeopardy.

What further thought he might have given the matter was set in abeyance by the helmsman's shout.

He sprang to his feet, Bracht at his side, hearing Tekkan shout again. Orders evidenced by the way the boat gathered speed and the archers set to stringing their bows. He looked astern, at first assuming some Kand vessel hove in sight, then saw that all attention was directed to the shore and swung to face the jungles.

Three huge canoes lay off the starboard bow, hidden at first against the camouflaging backcloth of vegetation, but clearly visible now as they drove rapidly towards the warboat. Great tree trunks formed the bodywork of the craft, bright-painted and hollowed to afford places for the oarsmen, whose paddles churned water with furious energy, archers crouching between them, howling as the dugouts sped to intercept the Vanu craft. Their skin was black, Calandryll saw, but so heavily decorated with colourful tattooing they appeared bright as the multi-hued birds that thronged the trees along the shoreline, faces and chests, arms, legs, all covered with lines of brilliance. Their long, glossy hair was dressed with feathers and shells, and white bones transfixed nostrils and earlobes, more hanging in necklaces or clattering against the breech-clouts that were their only garments to add to their barbaric splendour.

Katya appeared from her cabin, casting a single glance at the canoes as she sprang to join Tekkan on the poopdeck, the helmsman putting his tiller over, seeking to gain distance from the dugouts. The rowers bent to their sweeps, the Vanu craft picking up speed, but matched by the lighter canoes, the yammering black oarsmen fresher, their vessels flying over the water on a course that must, Calandryll thought, bring them into collision.

He moved to the rail, the dugouts as yet out of bowshot, but the archers there already nocking arrows, one or two sending ranging shafts arcing high through the hot morning air, the missiles landing useless in the sea. One canoe drew ahead of its companion craft and he saw the warrior standing at the prow flourishing a wickedly barbed spear, as if he urged the rowers to greater efforts, a necklace of tiny skulls about his throat, the feathers in his hair more colourful than his fellows'. He turned to see Katya join the Vanu archers, who held their fire, though he guessed their more powerful bows might reach the cannibals now. Tekkan swung his helm a degree or two farther over, angling away from the canoes: looking to outrun the pursuit, rather than fight. Had the wind been from the south and the sail up they might have left the dugouts behind, but they drove into what wind there was and the warboat sat heavier in the water than the canoes: the howling savages began to overhaul them.

'I think we earn our keep now,' Brecht said beside

him. 'Katya's archers are not enough to hold them off.'

Calandryll nodded, fingering his sword, less enthusiastic for battle than his comrade.

Tekkan had the same thought, it seemed, for he shouted again in his own language and the warboat heeled suddenly to starboard. Calandryll felt the rail hit his belly, clutching urgently for a handhold as the bow wave churned white beneath his startled eyes. He felt Bracht's hand lock on his belt, dragging him unceremoniously back, then thrust him down as a volley of green-fletched arrows whistled towards them. A shaft stuck quivering in the figurehead a handspan from his face and he heard a great shout of alarm rise from the dugout as the cannibals recognised Tekkan's intention. Too late, they sought to alter course. Calandryll saw the canoe veer desperately away, the dragonshead prow looming like some avenging sea beast over the slighter craft. Then there came the crash of timber against timber, a wilder shouting and a grinding sound as the Vanu craft rode over the dugout.

Black bodies tumbled into the water. Bracht shouted gleefully. The warboat shot forwards, the great sweeps like bludgeons, battering men down, some seeking that precarious refuge, only to lose their hold and fall away, tossed in the wake of the black boat's passage.

A snarling face appeared at the rail, a demonic mask of colour and glaring eyes, hand clutching a spiked club. Bracht swung the falchion and the cannibal screamed, dropping into the water. Others gained the warboat's starboard side and were despatched by the women, their bows dropped now in favour of swords and axes. Tekkan shouted and the oarsmen renewed their efforts, seeking to regain the momentum lost in the ramming.

The damaged canoe floated keelside uppermost, its bow shattered, the hull refuge now for the survivors. They were ignored by their fellows, the two remaining dugouts racing over the waves parallel to the larger vessel. A second volley hummed, answered this time by the warboat's archers, black bowmen tumbling beneath their accurate fire.

'They care little for their lives,' Bracht remarked grimly as the women reaped further toll.

Calandryll found no heart to answer, could only stare as he watched the ranks of the cannibals decimated. He heard Katya shout, and saw the fire of the Vanu archers redirected at the painted oarsmen. The dugouts fell away astern as the cannibals lost their rhythm, dead and wounded rowers entangling those about them, Tekkan bringing the warboat back on course, the angry shouting of their attackers gradually lost in the distance.

Bracht sheathed the falchion, his expression fierce still. It seemed to Calandryll that he regretted the brevity of the fight; for himself, he was glad it was done. He realised he held his own sword and slid the blade home, seeing Katya approach.

'You are unhurt?' she asked.

He nodded. Bracht said. 'It was a poor enough fight.'

'Better that we had not fought at all.' She tugged the green-fletched arrow from the figurehead, examining the tip with distaste. 'These are ugly things - and make ugly wounds.'

Calandryll stared at the barbed head, reminded of how close the shaft had landed, and asked, 'Why did they attack us? We offered them no threat.'

'They need none,' Katya said. 'It is in their nature to attack.'

She tossed the arrow overboard, smooth brow creased in a frown. Bracht stared at her, eyes moving over her bare legs, the thin material of her tunic, his face troubled.

'You wear no armour,' he said; accusingly, almost.

Katya shrugged. 'I had thought to avoid conflict.'

'It seems conflict follows us,' Bracht said, 'And you should wear armour.'

She smiled briefly. 'Look to your own protection,' she advised. 'I am well enough able to defend myself.'

'Against arrows?' Bracht shook his head; bowed curtly. 'Lady, I have seen your swordskill - and I admire you for that - but if we are to face arrows, I'd see you in armour.'

For a long moment their eyes locked. Katya's expression was unfathomable, Bracht's easy to read; then she laughed, somewhat nervously, Calandryll thought.

'You presume much,' she said, but gently.

'Aye,' Bracht replied, his own voice soft.

'We embark on a quest, we three.' She paused, her gaze encompassing Calandryll. 'And we are not alone.'

She paused again, as though seeking words. Bracht said, 'No. But if we were ...'

'We are not,' she said, quickly, grey eyes hooding a moment. 'And this ... your ... *concern* ... is more likely to hinder than help.'

Bracht nodded and said, 'I gave my word that I would endeavour to bring Calandryll safe back from Gessyth - that stands, still. Even though the one who hired me has proven traitor, that stands. Now you are a part of that warrant and I would not see you harmed.'

'Is that the whole of it?' she asked, and Bracht shook his head and answered simply, 'No.'

'Then I ask that you put ... what else there is ... aside.'

She faced him square, her look solemn. No less serious, he said, 'Until we have brought the Arcanum safe from Tezin-dar I will. But after - there are things need be said between us.'

'The Arcanum will not be safe until we bring it to Vanu and it is destroyed,' she said. 'Do you give me that?'

He looked into her eyes and ducked his head.

'Until that is done.'

'Your word on it?'

'My word on it.'

'Then - my thanks.' She smiled again and Calandryll thought he saw relief in her look. 'We eat soon. And should examine those charts you carry. Our own are perhaps not so reliable.'

She turned, making her way back down the deck. Bracht stared after her and sighed. 'Can you hold that promise?' Calandryll asked.

'For her, aye,' Bracht smiled.

Calandryll grinned, thinking he saw what Bracht had not. 'It was a ... large ... promise,' he murmured.

'How so' asked the Kern.

'Your warrant was to ward me until our return to Lysse, no farther. It seems now you extend that to the very boundaries of the world.'

'For her,' Bracht nodded, smiling. Then clapped a cheerful hand to Calandryll's shoulder. 'And for you, my friend. Did you believe I'd leave you to end this quest without me?'

'No.' Calandryll shook his head; and grinned, realising that he had never doubted but that Bracht would stand beside him to the end. 'No.'

They ate on the foredeck, Katya and Tekkan joining them, the helm relinquished for the time it took to another. The maps by which Tekkan steered were spread between them, and those Varent had supplied Calandryll. His proved the more reliable, being of more recent production and indicating more accurately where water might be found along the coasts of Gash and Gessyth. The closest lay some three days off, by the helmsman's reckoning, and they decided to put in there and send a party ashore.

'Armoured,' Bracht said, glancing at Katya.

'Armoured,' she agreed.

'Had we the choice,' Tekkan said. 'I should avoid all such conflict.'

His weatherbeaten features darkened then, a depression settling on him. It was not, Calandryll thought, studying his face, that he feared combat, but that he regretted the loss of life entailed. Bracht chuckled and said, 'A little fighting will serve to hone us for what lies ahead.'

Tekkan favoured the freesword with a dour look and shook his head. 'I take no pleasure in spilled blood, Bracht. Ours nor others.'

Bracht frowned, curious. 'And yet you sail where danger must lie,' he said, mildly, so as to avoid affront. 'And you ran that boat down skilfully enough.'

Tekkan nodded. 'I'd as lief have outrun them - they left me scant choice in the matter. And at least that way fewer died.'

Bracht's frown grew deeper. 'We are different, I think,' he said softly, 'You folk of Vanu and we of Cuan na'For.'

'We sail the same course, though,' Tekkan answered, looking sidelong at Katya, 'and not all of us are so different.'

'No,' Bracht agreed cheerfully, 'and I think that as well - I think we shall have our fill of fighting before this quest is ended.'

'Aye,' Tekkan murmured, sadly, 'on that I think you right.'

A little time proved the point.

Towards dusk of that day two more canoes emerged from the canopy of the jungle, not seeking to intercept them, but flanking the warboat as it moved steadily up the coast. They held their course until full night had fallen and only then did Tekkan drop anchor, farther out than before, and with lookouts posted. The cannibals ventured no assault, but at dawn the canoes still hung off the starboard beam, like wolves trailing a beast too large to attack, and at noon a third joined them, late in the day a fourth, so that they travelled with a flotilla. The rising of the next day's sun revealed a fifth dugout, and by its setting there was a sixth.

As they closed on the egress of the fresh water stream the intentions of their pursuers became obvious: seven dugouts stood between them and the spring, effectively denying them access. Against such odds not even Bracht could urge an attempt to land and they continued north escorted by the canoes.

After seven days even Tekkan's patience was tried and he ordered the mast stepped up, the sail raised.

'What good?' Bracht asked. 'With the wind against us, how can the sail help?'

Calandryll explained the basics of tacking as the warboat moved out to sea, the manoeuvre slowing their northwards passage, but at least ridding them of their pursuers. They held that course until the water barrels stood near-empty and their replenishment became imperative. The charts showed another spring two days distant and - with little other choice - they drew closer to the coastline.

A conference was held on the poopdeck, Calandryll and Bracht joined Katya and Tekkan, a woman - Quara - and a man - Urs - with them. It was decided that they should put in under cover of darkness and at dawn the longboat would go ashore. It could carry no more than three barrels at a time, and several journeys would be needed to restock their dwindled supplies. At the same time a hunting party would seek game, for fresh meat, too, was growing low. Katya was to lead the hunters.

'I'd accompany you,' Bracht declared. 'I grow stale, idling here.'

Katya and Tekkan exchanged glances and the helmsman shook his head.

'There is too much danger.'

'Then let some other than Katya go,' Bracht said.

'I cannot,' she explained. 'I lead these people far from their home and I cannot ask them to do what I will not.'

Bracht shrugged, accepting that but still protective. 'Then I go with you,' he said doggedly, and turned to smile at Tekkan. 'Nor shall any argument dissuade me.'

His tone brooked no disagreement; Tekkan nodded reluctantly. Calandryll said, 'Then I, too, go.'

'There is no need,' Bracht said. 'Not for you.'

'You forget the spaewive's words,' he returned. 'Are we not bound, we three?'

'You need not,' the Kern argued, gesturing at the empty sea. 'Likely there is no danger.'

'And if there is?' Calandryll demanded, looking to each in turn. 'Should we become separated? The prophecy spoke of three - do you go, then I go with you. Or we risk the quest.'

'I must,' Katya said, 'but neither you nor Bracht need take this chance.'

Bracht barked a laugh and chopped air: a dismissive gesture. 'I will not argue this - I go with you and there's an end to it.'

'Then it is settled,' said Calandryll. 'Three, or none of us.'

Katya and Tekkan spoke with Quara and Urs, then the helmsman nodded. Katya said, 'So be it,' and turned, grinning, towards Bracht. 'But armoured.'

They prepared for the foray as Tekkan brought the warboat in, gently under sail, the moon a paling silver above, not bright enough to betray them they hoped. Shirts of fine mail were found to fit them both, and breeks of thick leather, sewn with mail, helms for their heads. It felt strange after so long a time unhampered to wear that weight, and despite its flexibility, not very comfortable, but faced with the threat of arrows neither argued such precautions.

They waited, Calandryll affecting a calm he did not

feel, as the black outline of the jungle bulked higher before them, Tekkan calling soft orders that brought down the sail, the sweeps running out to bring them closer, halting them finally to ride the tide, awaiting the darkest hour between the setting of the moon and the rising of the sun.

The night was still, the wind that blew steadily throughout the day died away now to no more than a fitful breeze, redolent of the lush vegetation, but far from silent. Shrieks and chatterings rang from the jungle, the challenge of hunting beasts and the cries of their prey; the sea lapped softly about the boat, which creaked and groaned, those sounds seeming the loudest, for all - save, perhaps, Bracht - hoped that they might approach unseen, unheard. The minutes dragged slowly by and then the boat was lowered, Urs and his men slipping silently to their places, Quara and four archers following, the boat filled then, moving to the shore. It returned and Katya swung down, and then Bracht, Calandryll the last. Urs murmured a single word and the oars dipped, carrying the boat away from the larger vessel, towards the shoreline.

The odour of the jungle grew stronger, thick and hot, and all their eyes probed the darkness for sight of canoes or waiting savages.

The scrape of timbers on the narrow strand that flanked the stream rang loud in Calandryll's ears. He lowered himself over the side and waded to shore, straightsword in hand, feeling sweat run down his ribs, the armour an unpleasant weight across his shoulders, the helmet hot upon his head. Bracht joined him, his blue eyes seeming to gleam with anticipation beneath his helm's beak. Katya waved them further up the shore, Quara and the other women flanking them.

Urs and his crew dragged the longboat beneath the shelter of a tall palm and manhandled the barrels clear. He and Katya spoke briefly and then the woman beckoned her party about her, translating her instructions for Calandryll and Bracht.

'Urs and his men will fill the barrels and ferry them back. We press inland. Likely we shall find game using this freshet. Stay close.'

'At your side,' Bracht whispered.

Katya looked to Quara; pointed at the trees. Silently, the Vanu archers drifted into the jungle.

The night grew blacker there, what little light the sky offered dimmed by the overhanging trees, the stream their compass. They moved along its bank, hampered by vines and great roots, thick stands of exotic plant life scenting the air so that sweet perfumes merged with the reek of decay. A game trail crossed their path and they traversed it, seeking to come on the watering place downwind of whatever animals might drink there. It was slow going, the ground beneath their feet spongy, the trees close-spaced and hung with lianas, those decorated with spiders' webs, the strands sticky and unpleasant to the touch, but at last they saw the stream widen to a pool, fed by a spring, the surrounding bamboo cut with trails, the soil around the water bare of vegetation and muddy where hooves and paws had cleared a space. Unbidden, Quara and the others ranged themselves windward of the water. Katya settled beside a tree, Bracht and Calandryll to her left.

Time passed and darkness with it, the patch of sky above becoming grey announcement of impending dawn. A troop of monkeys swung down and drank, scampering back to the safety of the upper branches when a great striped cat padded to the waterside. That regal beast drank in solitary splendour, fading back into the jungle as suddenly as it had come. A long-tusked boar appeared, snorting, two sows behind, and then nine fat deer emerged nervous from the shadows, led by an antlered buck. He sniffed the air, scut twitching, and walked daintily to the pool. His harem followed.

Five arrows flew across the water: five deer fell. The herd scattered, the pigs with them, and the jungle was abruptly, ominously, silent.

The Vanu women moved swiftly, splashing through the shallow water to retrieve their shafts and hack lengths of bamboo to which they lashed three of the deer. Bracht and Calendryll sheathed their swords and slung the remaining animals across their shoulders, following Katya down the course of the stream, anxious now to regain the shore, careless of the noise they made in their urgency.

Five deer seemed little enough to feed the numbers of the warboat's crew, but already the sky brightened, the grey fast fading, glowing with the promise - the threat - of the rising sun, and they moved as swift they could along the stream, unpleasantly aware of the arrows that might greet them were they found by the inhabitants of this hostile land.

They encountered Urs and his men towards the shore, labouring under the weight of filled barrels, and splashed past them to deposit their game in the boat. The sky by now was silvery and the warboat clear upon the sea, a marker to any observers. Urs and his men came with the water and stowed the barrels on board. Three, Katya told them as the longboat made the crossing, were already taken back, and one more trip would see them stocked sufficiently.

'Then we've time to hunt again,' Bracht said, grinning as doubt showed on Katya's face. 'Come - there's no sign of danger and those five deer are scarce enough.'

She thought for a moment, torn between remaining on the shore and the prospect of more meat.

'Urs must fill his casks and return with them,' Bracht urged, 'and we must wait for that - we have the chance to take more meat.'

Katya's wide lips pursed, but then she nodded,

speaking with Quara, and the hunting party returned into the jungle. Four pigs rewarded their venture and they found Urs awaiting them, his barrels loaded. The pigs were rapidly tossed into the scuppers and the longboat pushed off, too heavy laden to carry the archers. They remained on the little strand, arrows nocked, as the sky became blue and the wind rose again, Quara and her women watching the brightening jungle, Katya and the two men the sea. The longboat moved, it seemed, with painful slowness. Calandryll felt apprehension mount, staring to north and south, convinced that on the moment dugouts must appear, or arrows fly from the undergrowth. He watched as the dinghy reached the warboat, ropes tossed down to haul the barrels on board, the pigs passed up by hand. It seemed a horribly slow process, measured against the urgent beating of his heart, sweat an irritation on his face, joined now by the insects that swarmed with the burgeoning day. At last the longboat was emptied, turning towards shore, the oars dipping fast; and Bracht cried a warning.

From the south came two dugouts.

From behind came another cry; that and the rush of arrows.

Calandryll turned, sword useless in his hand against the volley of green-fletched shafts that whistled from the undergrowth. A blow knocked air from his lungs and he staggered, seeing a missile drop, blunted on his mail. The Vanu archers returned fire, but blind, their assailants hidden. A second arrow glanced off his helm, the metal protecting him from serious hurt, but ringing with the impact, his head spinning. A woman screamed, falling as a shaft pierced an eye. Quara shouted and the archers fell back, grouping defensively on the shore. Longboat and canoes raced to reach them, the victor unguessable. The dinghy was closer, but only four men manned the sweeps; the dugouts held twenty or thirty oarsmen and sped swifter towards them. He heard Katya mouth a curse, in her own language but its import clear, and Bracht shout again as the arrows ceased and tattooed bodies erupted screaming from the jungle.

The Kern met the onslaught with his own charge. Calandryll was vaguely surprised to find himself at Bracht's side, unaware that he ran with sword upraised until he saw a black face confront him; and the spear that thrust for his belly.

He twisted in midstride, trapping the lance against his ribs as his blade slashed across the savage face. The cannibal fell and he turned, countering the jagged club that arced at his head with a sweeping, upwards cut that near-severed hand from wrist. He brought his sword down across the man's chest and parried a second spear, skewering his attacker. A blow landed against his back and he tottered forwards, dragging his blade loose as he side-stepped, avoiding the viciously-spiked mace that swung at his ribs. Three savages rushed him and he retreated before them, seeing one fall to Katya's sabre, another to Bracht's falchion. The Kern cut the third down and for an instant there was a lull. Calandryll saw a semicircle of tattooed faces, their decoration grotesque, bones clattering about the necks, on wrists and waists. He realised, horrified, that most were human. He risked a backwards glance and saw the longboat closing on the shore, the canoes a little farther south. Beyond, the warboat turned, the manoeuvre ponderous, the sweeps bringing her slowly around landwards as archers grouped on the foredeck and between the oarsmen.

Tekkan sought, he saw, to bring the dugouts within bowshot. It was impossible: the canoes would beach before the warboat could reach them, before Urs could land the dinghy. There was no chance of escape and he knew that he was going to die; that soon his bones would hang from a cannibal's necklace. He felt a strange calm: he had died before, or so he had thought, and suddenly the fact of it seemed immaterial, only the manner important. Perhaps Tekkan would go on to Gessyth, to Tezin-dar, and bring the Arcanum to Vanu. He hoped it might be so.

He raised his sword and shouted and charged headlong into the savage ranks.

Surprise showed then on the barbaric faces, and a kind of grim respect; and pain on some as he cut to right and left, carving a path through them, possessed by berserk fury. He heard a familiar shout and knew that Bracht was at his side, and saw through the flailing clubs and thrusting spears that Katya fought with them. Saw, too, that black-shafted Vanu arrows sprouted from chests and ribs as the archers used their bows. The madness gripped him, dulling the pain of the blows that crashed against his mail shirt and the helm, the straightsword light in his hand and bloodied down all its length. Then Bracht was before him, shouting something, gesturing at the sea, and he felt Katya seize his arm and turn him round, propelling him back towards the ocean.

The longboat floated a little way off, and from the warboat archers flighted shafts into the cannibal ranks. The tattooed men fell back and Calandryll allowed his comrades to urge him into the water. He clambered over the gunwhale, and crouched on a thwart as the others came on board, the boat laden heavy with all their weight, slow as Urs bellowed orders and the sweeps dipped, carrying them towards the dark bulk of the warboat, that turned now, arrows raining on the approaching dugouts.

He saw there was a chance he might live and felt the madness drain away, replaced with fear as hope rose tantalising. Along the shore the cannibals stood watching, fallen back to the shelter of the jungle. He wondered if he should reach the warboat before the canoes came, or if, at the last, the savages would take the victory. He felt suddenly weary. His head ached now and dull fire throbbed along his ribs and through his swordarm. On the beach he saw three bodies, armoured amongst the black corpses, and felt sorrow that they had died.

The warboat drifted closer. The canoes veered off, seeking to come around beneath the bow, one deterred by the Vanu archers, the other succeeding, hurtling closer, spears and arrows arcing dark against the azure sky. He saw the warboat, black against the blue of sky and sea, a promise of safety, could they but reach it, and the fear rose up, a swelling tide as he realised the dugout must reach them first. He raised a hand: an ineffectual protest. And saw the dugout lifted from the water, savages spilling screaming as it rolled over, a twig blown on a silent wind, buffetted in the soundless gale, driven back towards the shore. That same impossible wind caught the other, men flying helpless in the gusting, the dugout spinning, rushing landwards. Tattooed faces bobbed in the water, no longer threatening but terrified now, staring awe-struck, then turning to swim desperately to the safety of the land. From the beach came a howling, not challenge but lament, the savages there retreating into the jungle as their fellows dragged themselves ashore and scurried for the trees.

Calandryll smelt almonds on the wind, fading now, as did his fear, leaving only the weariness. He sank back, unaware of whose shoulder pillowed him, and closed his eyes.

They reached the warboat, Urs steering past the sweeps to come around the stern, the welcome bulk between them and the shore, and he was hauled on board, slumping on the deck as Tekkan roared orders and the sweeps reversed, the tiller thrust hard over. The dragonshead prow turned north again, the little beach left behind them.

Calandryll slipped the latchings of his helm and set it on the planks. He saw that the metal was dented in three places and when he touched his head - with his left hand, for his right arm was stiff and he could not raise it - he felt painful swellings beneath his hair. His ribs ached and he saw his hands painted dull crimson, blood drying fast in the hot morning air. He began to scrub at them, horrified, less for the lives he had taken than the knowledge that he had slain men without compunction or thought. He closed his eyes, then opened them as his throbbing head spun and he felt a hand on his shoulder. A woman passed him a flask and he drank, gasping as fire coursed his throat. He coughed, and the woman gestured, motioning for him to drink again. This time he sipped and the fire dulled, becoming a pleasant warmth that filled his belly and flowed outwards through the tissues of his aching muscles. He felt the pain ease and smiled his thanks, returning the flask. Beside him, Bracht sipped and wiped blood from his face.

'For a moment there I thought us lost,' the freesword said, blue eyes intent on Calandryll, curious and admiring, 'But then you ... did what you did. Ahrd, but you frightened them!'

He shook his head, not sure what he had done, memory of the battle fading like a dream.

'The spaewife - Ellhyn - spoke of power in you,' Katya murmured, respect in her voice, 'and I saw it used before, but I thought us lost then. It is a frightening thing.'

He nodded, too weary to speak, nor knowing what to say; not knowing how he called up such magic, nor much liking that he could, for all it had saved them. It seemed - as Bracht had said, on another boat - that only in direst peril was he able to unleash those forces. He did not want to think about it and began to fumble at the fastenings of his mail, seeing that it was, like his hands, all splashed with blood.

Bracht came to aid him, unmoved by the carnage, pleased even with the battle, or so it seemed to judge by his cheerful smile.

'Your lessons were well taken,' he grinned. 'Ahrd! When you charged them - what possessed you then?'

He shrugged, the answer unknown, and winced as his shoulder throbbed. Bracht eased the mail off and slipped the lacings of the shirt beneath, studying the bruises that purpled on his ribs and back with an efficient eye, probing for broken bones, that ministration elicting a groan of discomfort.

'You'll heal soon enough,' the Kern said briskly. 'A little stiffness for a while, no worse.'

'I fear that Tekkan's temper will be worse,' Katya remarked, easing out of her own armour. 'He will have things to say on the matter.'

Bracht grinned. 'But it was a fine fight, was it not? And we filled both the barrels and our larder.'

'We lost three,' she said, sadly. 'Three who need not have died had we returned sooner. I mourn them.'

The Kern's face grew solemn then and he set a hand on hers.

'That blame lies with me. Had we not returned into the jungle ...'

Katya shook her head, gently extricating her hand.

'I need not have listened to you - their lives were in my charge, not yours.' Her eyes were sad, the grey clouding to stormy darkness. 'The fault was mine.'

'I swayed you,' Bracht said, 'do not hold that guilt to yourself alone.'

Katya sighed, resting back against the stepping of the mast, a tired smile fleeting on her lips. 'Three were lost,' she murmured, 'and I cannot undo that.'

'No,' Bracht said, 'and likely more will die before this quest of ours is done - shall you mourn them all? Shall each be a weight on your conscience?'

The grey eyes turned to his face and Katya nodded. 'Aye - each one,' she said sadly. 'That is the way of Vanu, and as you said to Tekkan, our ways are different. Do you not mourn your fallen in Cuan na'For?'

'We do,' Bracht said, 'but we do not carry them with us. A warrior knows that death walks at his shoulder and he - or she! - accepts that dark friend. That is the way of it, and who cannot accept that should not take up a sword.'

A shadow fell between them then and Calandryll looked up to see Tekkan standing over him. The helmsman's face was flushed with anger and he gestured peremptorily in the direction of the foredeck, snapping something in his own language.

'Tekkan would speak with us,' Katya translated. 'And what he has to say he prefers be private between us.'

It was an effort to stand, but Calandryll forced himself to rise, following the helmsman to the bow, Bracht and Katya close behind. Tekkan stationed himself by the figurehead, the wind whipping his silvery hair, his eyes near-black with anger, a flush suffusing his tanned cheeks. He spoke in his accented Lyssian, his voice harsh.

'Had you returned with Urs and not gone back into the jungle Yvra, Tomel and Ayrtha might live still.'

Katya nodded sadly and said, 'Their deaths rest on my shoulders and I grieve for them.'

'To go back was my suggestion,' Bracht said. 'Katya would have waited on the shore. Do you have blame to lay, let it be with me.'

Tekkan made an abrupt, dismissive gesture. 'Katya led - the fault is hers. This is a thing of Vanu - and we do not risk the lives of comrades without good cause.'

'We sought fresh meat,' Bracht answered, anger straining his voice now.

'Costly meat,' Tekkan snapped, 'Paid for in Vanu lives.'

'How could we know the savages would attack?' Calandryll interposed, recognising the tensing of Bracht's shoulders and seeking to avoid more open conflict. 'It was a risk - yes - but such danger was there from the start.'

'A needless risk.' Tekkan swung to face him, the anger in his eyes startling Calandryll. 'We had deer on board, and they will see us through a while. Had you returned then, none need have fallen.'

'Perhaps,' Bracht said, 'or perhaps the dugouts might have found us sooner; perhaps the savages attacked us in the jungle and we all fallen there.'

'Do you of Cuan na'For deal in *perhapses*?' Tekkan retorted. 'Or does reality have some place in your dealings? The *reality* of these events is that three Vanu-folk lie dead. And that blame rests with Katya.'

Calandryll saw Bracht's hand clasp the falchion's hilt and stepped closer. Katya moved between the Kern and the helmsman.

'The blame is mine,' she said softly. 'I accept it.'

'Better you listen to your own conscience than the persuasions of this warrior,' Tekkan advised coldly. 'Do you heed him, we'll likely reach Gessyth crewless.'

Bracht's jaw tightened: Calandryll clasped his wrist. Tekkan saw the movement and smiled bitterly.

'Do you answer all argument with a blade?'

'I answer insults thus,' Bracht said.

'Bracht sought only to furnish us with more meat,' Katya said, urgently now. 'Sufficient taken here negates the chance of further danger. I weighed that and chose to heed him. That decision was mine alone, and I grieve that it was wrong. But do not lay the blame on Bracht. Nor let this come between you.'

Tekkan studied her face for long moments, then ducked his head; a single, curt nod.

'So be it. May your conscience resolve the matter - but there will be no more forays save in numbers. Nor shall you three venture shorewards again.'

He turned then to Calandryll, the anger faded a little from his eyes, and said, 'You threw those canoes like feathers on the wind, as easily as you turned us back once - why did you not use that power earlier?'

'I do not command it.' Calandryll shook his head helplessly. 'I do not understand it. Not then, on the Narrow Sea, nor here; nor any time it has come to my aid. It comes - I can say no more.'

Tekkan grunted, his face thoughtful. 'You at least saved lives,' he said. 'More would have died had you not summoned that power.'

Calandryll nodded and looked to Bracht, seeing the Kern still tensed with anger, then to Tekkan. 'Is there peace between you?' he asked. 'What lies ahead leaves no room for anger, I think.'

The helmsman favoured Bracht with a speculative stare and slowly ducked his head. 'Words of wisdom,' he allowed, 'I would not have this between us. We are different, I think, and that is an ... obstacle. But I'd see it removed. Shall we agree on that, warrior?'

For a moment Calandryll thought Bracht would disagree, would seek redress for what he saw as insult, but then he, too, ducked his head, hand leaving the falchion, the tension his face.

'We shall agree.'

Tekkan smiled then, shortly and with little humour, his eyes moving to Katya where she stood at Bracht's side, their expression doubtful. 'Best see those hurts tended,' he grunted, and left them.

Calandryll relaxed, watching the helmsman stride back to his tiller, taking the beam from the golden-haired man who held it as might a parent take a child from one entrusted briefly with its care.

'He's a prickly conscience,' Bracht murmured.

'He cares for all on board,' Katya said, her voice defensive. 'Each loss cuts him deep.'

'He need not have rebuked you so,' Bracht said.

'I led,' she answered. 'He had the right.'

'The helmsman commands the captain?' Bracht frowned. 'The ways of the Vanu are, indeed, strange.'

This vessel is his command,' she told him, looking to where Tekkan stood on the low poop. 'The securing of the Arcanum is my task; this vessel his.'

'Even so,' Bracht said, 'he presumes much.'

'Fear edged his tongue,' she murmured. 'He was afraid harm had come to me, and that sharpened his temper.'

'I'd not see him test it on you.'

Bracht's voice was soft: Katya turned to look into his eyes, her own troubled; as though, Calandryll thought, she wrestled with some inner problem, indecision creasing her brow. Then she sighed, reaching up to smooth long strands of pale gold hair from her face, the slight movement of her head both resignation and a negative.

'You do not understand,' she said quietly. 'You praise my sword-skill, but in Vanu that is unusual. In Vanu I am considered ... different.'

'In Cuan na'For you would be admired,' Bracht declared gallantly.

'You do not understand,' Katya repeated. 'I have told you that we fight no wars in Vanu - peace is prized higher there than battle skill. We fight only when we must; when we are forced to it. Quara and her archers? They are hunters - they would sooner use their shafts on game than men. And none can use a blade as well as I.'

She paused, looking out over the sunlit ocean. Calandryll watched her face, sensing inner conflict.

Bracht studied her in silence, waiting for her to speak again. When she did it was in a low voice, tinged with sadness, as though the very talents the Kern had admired caused her regret.

'I was chosen for this task because of that skill,' she said at last. 'Because it suits me better for what needs to be done. That alone causes Tekkan ... discomfort. And fear for my safety adds to his concern.'

'Even so,' Bracht said, 'What right has he to speak thus?'

'Tekkan is my father,' she replied.

SEVENTEEN

'**LITTLE** wonder he's chary of you.' Calandryll's gaze swept back from Tekkan, standing at the tiller, to Bracht's face. 'He finds an outland warrior paying court to his daughter, that same warrior persuading her to risk - can you wonder he shows concern?'

'Do you say I am unworthy of her?'

Bracht stared moodily at the shoreline, the trees there dark as his expression in the fast-waning light. Calandryll shook his head. 'No, I do not say that - I say only what you have said: that your ways are different, and so it is understandable that Tekkan should view your hopes with some alarm.'

'I have given my word,' Bracht returned stiffly, 'and I have not reneged on that. Have I made any further advance to her? Have I said anything untoward?'

'No, you have not.' Calandryll sighed, leaning on the rail, feeling the unguents applied to his bruises do their work, the aches receding. 'But it is in your eyes. In the way you seek to ... defend ... her.'

'I cannot help that.' Now Bracht shook his head. 'And why should Tekkan object to that?'

'I think that he is afraid.' Calandryll frowned,

pursuing a thought that had grown since that angry conversation on the foredeck. 'Not of physical danger, but of what you are - of what you represent.'

'*He* considers me unworthy?'

The risen moon, the accompanying stars, limned the Kern's hawkish features with silvery light, stark-planed and accusing. Calandryll said, 'No, not that - but a danger, yes. These folk of Vanu are very different, I think. Did Tekkan not say he would sooner avoid conflict than fight? Did Katya not tell us there are no wars in Vanu? And that because she shows skill with a sword - and a willingness to use it - that she is considered different? I think that Tekkan had sooner this quest not arisen - that he undertakes it because he knows he must; not from any love of battle, nor desire for adventure. But you - you glory in the danger; and that is a temptation for Katya. I think Tekkan fears to lose his daughter.'

Bracht's face brightened at that, teeth white in the tropical darkness. 'You think she shares my feelings?' he asked.

'I think she is attracted to you,' Calandryll nodded. 'And Tekkan sees that - and fears that when this quest is ended he may see his daughter foresake the peaceful ways of Vanu for a life with you.'

'That, surely, is the way of the world,' Bracht said. 'Parent must bid child farewell.'

'And peace? To forsake a land where there is no war to go with a warrior whose people always fight?'

'That is the way of Cuan na'For.' Bracht's tone became defensive. 'There is honour in battle.'

'Why did you leave then?' asked Calandryll.

The Kern's eyes hooded at that and he turned his face away, staring intently at the shadowed jungle, the phosphorescent patterning of the waves that broke along the narrow strand.

'There was a matter of some horses,' he said at last;

slowly, his voice low. 'A ... disagreement.'

'And more,' Calandryll prompted.

'Aye.' Bracht snorted soft laughter: a self-deprecating sound. 'More that I would not discuss. There was a woman involved.'

'You loved her?' Calandryll insisted. 'Did you quit your homeland for that? As I quit Secca, because I ... thought ... I loved Nadama?'

'You press me hard,' Bracht murmured, 'and I should not allow that from any other, but - yes: for ... similar ... reasons, and I departed Cuan na'For much as you departed Secca. But that is in the past - like your Nadama! - and I do not choose to speak of it further.'

'I'll not ask you further,' Calandryll promised. 'But do you not see Tekkan's doubt?'

Bracht's head bowed, chin to chest, the long tail of his hair hiding his expression. Then he nodded: 'I can see it. But it will not sway me - what happens when our quest is done must be Katya's choice, not his.'

'Until then,' Calandryll advised, 'walk wary around him. We need this boat. Remember that - this boat and the boatmaster.'

'You think Tekkan likely to betray us?'

Bracht's head rose, blue eyes fixing on Calandryll's face. Calandryll said, 'I do not think it likely, but even so ... Should we bring the Arcanum out of Gessyth, does Tekkan need us still? His part in this is to bring the book to Vanu; and for that he has no great need of us.'

'Katya would not permit that. And you forget the augury.'

'What Tekkan knows of that he has heard from Katya and from us,' Calandryll retorted, 'not with his own ears. And should he consider you a threat, what better way to end it than leave us in Gessyth?'

'You grow mightily suspicious.' Bracht chuckled, grinning at his companion. 'I had thought that my province and you the innocent.'

'I learn,' Calandryll replied, face clouding as memory of Varent's betrayal stirred. 'I learn that trust is better earned than taken on faith, and that it may be an exchangeable commodity.'

'You grow cynical,' Bracht murmured.

'I think I grow up,' he said.

The Kern studied him a moment, then nodded. 'That, too. Still, no matter what Tekkan feels for me, I do not think he will betray us. For all he holds no love for me, I believe him an honourable man. And I say again that Katya would not permit it.'

'You have much faith in her,' Calandryll said in a neutral tone, 'and in her influence.'

'I do,' the Kern agreed equably.

'Likely you are right,' Calandryll allowed, 'but I still say that you need show Tekkan a respectful face.'

'As you command.' Bracht flourished a bow that was not entirely mocking. 'I defer to your wisdom.'

'And in the matter of Katya - it would be as well were you to make your admiration less obvious.'

'That,' Bracht said lightly, 'will be harder.'

'Less so than to find ourselves stranded in Gessyth,' Calandryll returned, unaware that his tone was edged until moonlight revealed Bracht's face. He shrugged, forcing a smile: 'I'd not see this quest needlessly jeopardized.'

'Nor I.'

The Kern spoke gently and Calandryll was abruptly embarrassed. 'Forgive me,' he asked.

'There is nothing to forgive,' Bracht said mildly. 'Rest easy - I'll avoid offending Tekkan.'

Calandryll ducked his head; yawned. He felt the warboat alter course, headed for deeper water, away from the shore to where the canoes were loath to follow. In time the jungle faded to a dim joining of ocean and sky and the sweeps were brought inboard, the sea anchors dropped. The slight swell rocked them as the Vanu-folk slung their hammocks and he stretched on the planks, the night air warm as he lay staring at the blue-silver panoply of stars.

He found himself surprised - alarmed, even - at his words, at his doubts. Did he truly believe Tekkan might betray them? He was not sure, only of the ugly fact that since Ellhyn had scried Varent's treachery he looked on all about him with a new-found suspicion. Bracht he trusted without reserve; and Katya, for the spaewife had vouchsafed her integrity. But Varent had used him; and Tobias had sent out the Chaipaku to kill him; and that, yes, prompted a cynicism he had not known. Likely Bracht judged Tekkan aright, but even so, he preferred to take no chances, and he had seen genuine rage in the helmsman's eyes and Katya's revelation had given the reason for that rage. Better then to have spoken with Bracht as he had than risk affront, for once they had the Arcanum on board they would be dependent on the boatmaster. There would be no other way to depart Gessyth until the seasonal winds shifted and the traders came, and should Tekkan seek to separate his daughter from Bracht no better way than to leave the freesword stranded. Him too, for he knew he could not leave his comrade.

He watched a shooting star arc across the heavens. A portent, the palace soothsayers claimed, and he wondered if that was so; and if it was, of what? Did civil war now tear at Kandahar? Would Tyrant or the rebel Fayne lord prevail? And how might that effect his return - to where? Vanu or Lysse? For either destination the warboat was needed and Tekkan, therefore, must be assured no threat existed to sunder Katya from her people. Did Sathoman ek'Hennem carry the victory, he and Bracht might well return to Kandahar to find themselves outlawed; and still the danger of the Chaipaku existed. In Kandahar and Lysse, too, for Tobias must surely still deem him enemy. Secca, then, was no refuge for him; nor Aldarin, once Varent should learn of his intent and doubtless poison that city's Domm against him. He was, he realised with sudden shock, homeless. All his dreams of glorious return, of heroic welcome, were no more than the fancies of a naive youth. And he was no longer that: he was a man with blood on his hands, alienated now from all he had known. No longer the callow youth who had gone so readily - so trustingly! - with Varent, dreaming dreams of high endeavour, but a man grown cynical, just as Bracht had said; a man unwilling to trust even those allies sworn to aid him. He needed Tekkan, he realised, smiling grimly at the stars, simply because he needed the warboat. Without that he was prey to whatever events unfolded in the world behind. Civil war in Kandahar; perhaps war between Kandahar and Lysse. Vanu must be his destination. The taking of the Arcanum and its safe bringing to the holy men of Katya's homeland. After ... that was too far in the uncertain future: he would worry at that bone when it lay before him.

He sighed, and yawned, and closed his eyes, letting sleep assuage his troubled mind. He did what he could: he could do no more.

Dawn brought a resumption of their northwards journeying and an end to doubts. The sun rose ferocious over the jungle, the wind strengthening as the oarsmen ate a hurried breakfast and returned to their benches, Tekkan at the helm once more, conferring with Katya. Calandryll joined Quara and the other women, unashamed to help them gather up the platters and cleanse the dishes in sea water hauled up in canvas buckets before joining Bracht on the foredeck.

The Kern seemed cheerful enough, though several times Calandryll saw him glancing sternwards, where Katya stood beside her father, and finally, when it became obvious she did not intend to join them, Bracht suggested they practise their swordwork.

'We've no practice harness,' he objected. 'Nor blunted blades.'

'There's armour,' Bracht replied, 'and perhaps the Vanu will loan us weapons. Do you approach Tekkan, and if he's no objection we can borrow what we need.'

He nodded and made his way to the poopdeck, voicing the request. Tekkan murmured agreement and turned to Katya, suggesting that she find them what they needed. Father and daughter, Calandryll surmised, had engaged in some debate similar to his with Bracht, for Tekkan's face remained calm and he raised no objection when Katya declared her intention of joining them in practice.

'Tekkan - your father - seems in better humour,' he murmured as they walked towards the forward lockers, where the armour was stowed.

'We spoke,' she replied, 'and I told him of Bracht's promise. He accepts that.'

'And what Bracht is? What we are?'

Katya favoured him with a smile. 'And what is that, Calandryll?'

'Different,' he answered, then grinned as he saw she teased him. 'I think your father has little love for folk such as us - we use a blade too readily, and he fears we might ... taint you.'

Still smiling, she nodded, though her voice was solemn.

'You are perceptive. That is exactly what he fears - that I forget the ways of Vanu, attracted by your stranger habits.'

'And are you?' he wondered bluntly.

Her smile faltered then, but she said, reluctantly, 'Aye,' then grinned, choosing to understand the question as banter, 'But I told you I was thought strange by my own folk.'

He would have spoken with her more, and perhaps

more openly, but they reached the locker then and Bracht stood on the foredeck above, inclining his head in courteous greeting.

'Your father does not object to this?'

'He is a practical man.' She brought jerkins and leggings from the locker, passing them to Calandryll. 'He accepts that skills likely needed to survive must be well-honed.'

Bracht's eyebrows rose as he saw that three lots of armour, three swords, lay on the deck.

'Nor to your joining us?'

'Whatever he thinks of my ... abilities ... he would see me survive.'

'The ends, then, justify the means?'

Katya sprang limber to the foredeck, busying herself with buckles and lacings, avoiding the Kern's eyes as she replied.

'Not that, no. That is the argument of the ruthless - and Tekkan is not ruthless - the means must surely shape the ends. But to attempt what we must attempt unprepared is foolishness - and nor is Tekkan foolish.'

'I did not mean that he is,' Brecht said quickly. 'I intended no disrespect.'

Katya looked up then, smiling, and laughed. 'Do we debate philosophy or practise our swordwork?'

'Swordwork,' Bracht grinned. 'At that I am more adept than at wordplay.'

He drew on the thick leggings and the jerkin, Calandryll following suit. The swords Katya had found them - to avoid dulling the keen edges of their own weapons - were of the type she favoured, seemingly the common sword of Vanu. Sabres, they were, deeper curved than Bracht's falchion and somewhat lighter than Calandryll's straight Lyssian blade, intended, he thought, for use off horseback, but still useful enough on foot. He hefted the blade, accustoming his arm to the weight and the swing of it, that testing instinctive now, born of the experience that had changed him.

'So,' Bracht said, smiling at Katya, 'Do you attack, and we shall see if you've the means to survive. Calandryll shall call the hits.'

Calandryll stood back as they faced one another, their duelling, he realised, a form of courtship, that realisation amusing him, for he suspected that Katya had known it from the start. Bracht sought to impress her - and with a lesser opponent would have succeeded, but Katya was his match and for some time Calandryll only watched, each attack of Katya's parried by Bracht, her riposte deflected, the Kern's counter-attack turned, neither blade touching the other's armour. He saw, his amusement mounting, the Kern's expression shift from casual confidence to determination, and then to genuine surprise, Katya smiling the while, clearly delighted by her ability to hold off so skilled a swordsman.

Sweat began to bead their faces and an audience gathered, seemingly less apprehensive of such talents than Tekkan, whose face, when Calandryll glanced that way, was stern and not entirely approving. Finally Bracht scored a hit, using his greater strength to turn Katya's blade and bring his own in and across, tapping her ribs. She readied instantly for another bout, but the Kern raised a defensive hand, breathing hard as he grounded his sword.

'There's little enough I can teach you,' he declared admiringly. 'Ahrd, woman! In Cuan na'For you'd bring your father a herd in bride-price. And prime horses, every one.'

Katya's face was already flushed with her efforts, but Calandryll thought he saw a deeper blush suffuse her cheeks. She frowned, however, asking, 'Are brides bought then, in Cuan na'For?'

Bracht's tan darkened then and his smile thinned somewhat. 'It is customary that bride-price be paid, yes.

And a dowry given,' he murmured.

'In Vanu a man and woman choose for themselves,' Katya said, that brightening the Kern's smile.

'And fathers?' he wondered. 'What say do they have?'

His eyes fixed frankly on her face; she met his stare and said quietly, 'Their approval is sought.'

'And if not won?' he asked.

Katya's gaze faltered, her eyes lowering to the deck, then rising again to find his. 'It is better won,' she said.

Bracht nodded, his features grave, his reply no less solemn: 'So be it.' Then, to Calandryll, as if he recognised the delicacy of the moment and sought to avoid its turning: 'Now do you try your hand?'

He was, he recognised in moments, an inferior swordsman; at least, faced with an opponent of the Kern's skill, or Katya's. He was good enough - had Torvah Banul, or even his father, been present to witness his bladework they would likely have applauded - but whilst his defence was sufficient to hold off most attackers, Bracht had soon scored three hits to his one. He bowed to the freesword's greater talent and they rested a while, then he faced Katya, against whose flickering blade he fared little better, though he succeeded in delivering two blows to the three she landed.

Panting, they lowered their swords as the braziers were lit for the midday meal, aiding one another with the latchings of their armour until the leather and mail lay heaped upon the foredeck. Their shirts were moist, clinging to their bodies, and Katya went to her cabin to find fresh clothes, her receding figure watched fondly by Bracht.

'You've the look of a love-struck boy,' Calandryll murmured, jutting his chin to the stern, where Tekken studied them, frowning.

'I am,' the Kern sighed; then grinned, 'but I do not forget my promise.'

'Remember Tekkan,' Calandryll warned.

'Aye.' Bracht nodded, his face abruptly serious. 'I think it time we spoke.'

Calandryll opened his mouth to advise against such conversation but the Kern was already on his feet and striding purposefully along the deck, leaving him no alternative save to hurry after, ready to mediate should argument arise. He reached the companionway as Bracht gained the poop, bowing formally to the helmsman.

Tekkan appeared surprised by such obeisance: more by the Kern's words.

'We should lay this in the open,' Bracht said, 'that there be no doubt between us.'

'What?' asked Tekkan bluntly, though the clouding of his eyes said that he knew.

'I had not known you were Katya's father,' Bracht said, 'though had I, I should not have done otherwise. Not in the matter of the savages, nor in other things.'

'You are at least ... ' Tekkan smiled slightly, '...honest.'

'It is the way of my folk to speak openly.' Bracht faced the bulky helmsman, his gaze unwavering. 'And I believe you know of my ... feelings ... towards Katya.'

Tekkan nodded.

'And of my promise,' Bracht continued, 'that I shall not press further on the matter until we have brought the Arcanum safe to Vanu.'

'She spoke to me of that,' Tekkan confirmed.

'I would ask her then to be my woman; and it must be her word that says me yea or nay. That you would have it otherwise is a matter between you and her - but I would have you know that until then I shall neither say or do anything to offend her or you. Until then - when we come safe to Vanu and the Arcanum is destroyed I shall speak openly.'

Tekkan remained silent, staring at the Kern with

thoughtful eyes, his face unreadable. Then he ducked his head.

'You follow the way of the sword, Bracht, and I cannot tell you that I would choose you for my daughter, but you are an honest man and I thank you for that honesty. Let me return mine - should Katya seek my advice in this matter I shall tell her, nay; but it shall be her choice, not mine.'

'And there shall be no ill-feeling between us?'

Tekkan smiled again, warmer now, and shook his head.

'No. We make strange bed-fellows, you and I, but we travel the same road and our purpose binds us – there shall be no ill-feeling.'

'That is good.'

Bracht extended his hand and Tekkan took it. Calandryll felt himself relax; and saw Katya watching from the lower deck, smiling. She had heard enough, he thought, to understand the gist of what had transpired, and it appeared to please her. Certainly it pleased him: he felt a clearing of the air, his own doubts dispelled, the faint, lingering fear that Tekkan might leave them helpless in Gessyth dismissed by Bracht's honest words, the Vanu's honest response. Just as Tekkan feared that the Kern's ways might, in his estimation, taint his daughter, so had Varent's duplicity tainted him. He saw that now; saw that he had seen shadows where none existed, save those cast by Varent's lies. But those were behind him: he was amongst friends, comrades dedicated to the denial of Varent's mad ambition, whilst ahead lay honest toil. Dangerous, certainly, but not tainted with fell magic, or the soft persuasions of an ages-old wizard bent on the insane resurrection of the Mad God. Varent - Rythamun - sat safe in Aldarin, a spider lurking in his web, awaiting the return of the flies he had tempted with false promises; but unaware the flies saw his strands and could avoid them. Varent was behind him, could not touch him, not here on the Vanu warboat, nor in Tezin-dar.

He smiled his relief, not knowing then - not knowing until much later - how wrong he was.

They continued along the coast of Gash, sometimes trailed by dugouts, but those never venturing close enough to attack, as if word had passed amongst the jungle-dwellers that this was no easy prey they stalked and better left alone. Three times landing parties rowed in to shore, to refill the water casks and hunt what fresh meat might be found, and no assault was made, the hunters returning safe with deer and pigs to augment their diet of fish and the rapidly-dwindling supplies taken on in Kharasul. They saw no other vessels as the summer aged towards autumn and their greatest threat was the tedium induced by the unchanging days, that alleviated somewhat by the sword practice that became their routine. Calandryll's skill increased under Bracht's tutelage, and in time - and with Tekkan's not-quite grudging approval - other members of the crew took part, though none of the Vanu-folk approached Katya in ability or enthusiasm.

Bracht, as Calandryll had known he would, remained true to his word, saying nothing to the blonde woman of his hopes. He showed her an oddly formal courtesy that often elicited her smile, that answered by the Kern's, whose eyes said what his tongue held back. Such words were reserved for Calandryll's ears, and he found himself often struggling for the patience needed to hear out the eulogies Bracht was wont to weave as they lounged in the sun or lay watching the pattern of stars spread across the night sky. He wondered if he had piled such enconiums on Nadama, whose face he now found difficult to recall, she a part, he realised, of the life he left behind. That love, if love it had been and not simply a youthful infatuation, belonged to a time lost, shed as a snake sheds its skin, discarded in the rebirth. And he was, he knew, reborn. What small regret he felt at the knowledge that he might likely never see his home again was compensated by what lay ahead. Tobias was welcome to Secca - that had never been in doubt - but now he was welcome to Nadama, too - and should Bylath go to the vaults beneath the great temple of Dera not knowing where his younger son might be, well, he had chosen that fate when his uncaring hand lashed out to firm Calandryll's resolve.

He could accept such things in his rebirth: he changed. Physically, too. His body hardened, the muscles firmed by boat-work and swordplay; Bracht taught him to wrestle, and in that the oarsmen joined, pitting their strength against his, such friendly combats, Katya informed him, enjoyed in Vanu. Quara schooled him with the bow, until he was able to use the barbed fishing arrows near as well as the women, reeling in his share of the catch to the accompanying chorus of praise sung in the soft Vanu tongue that he struggled to master. That was harder, but he found, in time, that he understood simple phrases and could make himself understood were the listener patient enough, practising with Katya until she laughed and threw up protesting hands, claiming that he must wait for a better teacher, perhaps in Vanu itself.

He learned more of that mysterious land, wishing that he had the means to write down what he learnt - perhaps his only regret: that he had no books or writing materials, but that small enough as he gathered knowledge.

He came to understand that Vanu was, truly, without conflict such as racked the southern kingdoms, the folk manning the warboat oddities amongst their people, for whilst they seemed mild-mannered to such as he and Bracht, to their fellows they were unusually bellicose. It seemed an idyllic land, a peaceful haven in a world much given to ambition and struggle, and in only one area did he find doubt. Katya spoke only vaguely, and with scarcely concealed reluctance, of the holy men whose augury had sent her forth, and not at all of gods. It seemed none existed in Vanu, save perhaps as concepts, more embodiments of notions of good and evil than the clearly-defined deities of Lysse or Kandahar or Eyl, and the holy men seemed less priests than sages, concerned as much - or more - with the physical well-being of the people as with matters spiritual. In this Bracht accepted more readily than did he, for the tree god of Cuan na'For was a deity little given to intervention in the ways of men, and the Kern maintained that the appearance of the *byah* had been occasioned only by the enormity of Varent's evil, that so great it had called forth a warning in much the same way as Vanu's holy men had scried their augury. Calandryll found he must be content with this, for when he pressed Katya on the matter she grew increasingly ambiguous and sought to shift the direction of the talk; subtly, but not so well that he failed to notice her reticence. He chose to respect it, suspecting that some admonishment forbade her from speaking more deeply on the subject, and told himself that when at last they came to her homeland he would question the holy man himself, directly.

He remembered vividly Reba's augury: *You will travel far and see things no southern man has seen, perhaps no man at all.*

That came daily true as he travelled northwards, farther than any Lyssian craft had sailed since Orwen. And Orwen had not witnessed the appearance of a *byah*, nor, as best he knew, fought with demons or seen the raising of such fire-creatures as Anomius had brought forth to sack Kesham-vaj. None had journeyed to Vanu and he held that land promise to his hopes, the ultimate goal of the quest begun in that other life. That he should, with Bracht and Katya, reach Tezin-dar and bring the Arcanum out he did not doubt as they closed on Gessyth's coast.

They found themselves, suddenly it seemed, crossing open water, the jungles fading steadily into the distance behind, ahead only the empty sea. The charts revealed this as the great inlet, unnamed, that divided Gash from Gessyth, and after two days they had had their first sight of the land they had come so far to find.

It was a forbidding vista.

No discernible shoreline existed, sea and swamp merging, the blue water of the ocean darkening, becoming a peaty brown on which floated vast fields of lilypads, viridescent and decked with flowers of livid yellow or leprous white. Distant beyond these strange floating fields stood massive trees, great grey mangroves hung with gloomy moss, and between them ran channels of sluggish water that marked the courses of the torpid streams that fed the marshes. Day after day that glum horizon stood to starboard of the warboat, unchanged by the shifting season, the boredom of the lily fields sometimes broken by the appearance of meadows of reeds and rushes that swayed languid in the hot wind, rustling softly, noisomely redolent of fecund decay, thick and rank. They saw birds of brilliant plumage and creatures that combined the aspects of both avians and lizards, things with feathers and scales both, and saw-toothed beaks; and the swamp dragons that furnished the soldiery of Kandahar with their armour. These seemed, often, no more than logs floating amongst the lilies and reeds until they rose up to bay stertorous challenge, vast jaws all set with jagged fangs opening wide as spiked tails lashed, stirring the gruel of the swamp to brown foam. The smallest were long as a a tall man, and the larger of the beasts three times that size, but it seemed they had no love for the saltier water of the ocean for although several charged noisily towards the passing warboat - none ventured far into the sea, instead turning back to roar their displeasure from the safety of the reeds and lily meadows.

It was an uncomfortable time, the air hot and moist and stinking, so that shirts hung damp and irritating to skin that seemed never dry, the daily tasks rendered the harder for the growths of moss and algae that sprang up overnight on ropes and canvas and cloth. Food spoiled faster here, and metal required constant oiling; leather threatened to rot and wind-borne insects assailed them, stinging and sometimes bringing fevers. The Vanu-folk, more accustomed to their high, windswept homeland, suffered the worst, but in that thick, insect-filled atmosphere even Calandryll and Bracht recalled almost nostalgically the cleaner discomfort of the gaheen and the days spent following the jungley coastline of Gash.

At last, their water near-gone and their food running low, they saw the headland that marked the site of the hide hunters' outpost. It thrust dramatically from the vast expanse of swampland, as if whichever god had shaped this desolation had allowed one single nub of solid ground to remain; or omitted to reduce it to miasmic bog. It was a grey thumb stuck across their course, raised up a little above the surrounding swamp. Low huts stood along the headland and shallow boats floated on the turgid water, moored to ramshackle jetties raised up on mossy piles above the reeds. As they drew closer they saw the huts, too, were built on piles, ramshackle, stilted structures of wood and hides and rushes, seeming almost to have grown there rather than been built by human hands, and the foetid scent of the swamp was joined by a ranker odour. Calandryll, standing on the foredeck, came close to gagging on that stench and pointed in silent disgust at the bloody hides stacked about the buildings. Bracht, his own mouth clamped tight, nodded and indicated the dragon carcasses that floated on the tide. Katya, standing beside them, said nothing, winding a cloth about her face, masking nose and mouth.

Tekkan ordered the longboat lowered and soundings taken, bringing his craft in as close as he dared while a crowd gathered, watching this unexpected arrival with the wary enthusiasm of folk too-long accustomed to their own company and consequently suspicious of newcomers.

The anchors went down, holding the warboat, and Tekkan summoned Calandryll, Bracht and Katya to the poop, to hold brief conference there. They had already agreed a simple plan: those three, with eight of Quara's archers and as many oarsmen as they might need, would journey inland to Tezin-dar, using Calandryll's chart. They would endeavour to hire a guide from amongst the hide hunters, someone familiar with the swamps; and Tekkan would await their return offshore with the bulk of the crew.

'These are mostly Kands here,' Tekkan said, studying the swarthy faces lining the headland, his own creased in distaste, 'and Calandryll speaks their language better than any of us - let him negotiate for a guide and a boat. And Katya - I'd wager these hunters have few women present, and have likely never seen any such as you. Warn the archers to tread wary around them; as should you.'

'None shall lay hand on her,' Bracht said promptly, that gallantry eliciting a brief nod from Tekkan, and a warning.

'Ward your temper, Kern - they outnumber us.'

Bracht grunted assent. Calandryll, impatience growing, said, 'Do we go ashore now?'

'Aye,' said Tekkan, and they clambered down into the longboat.

Their arrival at the closest jetty brought the crowd of hunters surging around them, filling the air with shouted questions. Calandryll answered them as best he could, waiting as the boat ferried more of the Vanu-folk ashore.

They were neither merchants nor corsairs, he informed them, but adventurers bent on journeying inland, that news bringing a howl of derision from the assembled Kands. Why, they wanted to know; there was nothing inland save more swamp and the promise of an ugly death. Worse than dragons inhabited the inner swamps, they said, stranger creatures than any man had seen. He noticed then that on the fringes of the jostling crowd there lingered figures he could not swear were entirely human, thrust back by the Kands as might be children, or curious animals. He saw a man - he thought it was a man - whose face appeared scaled, like a lizard's; a woman whose skin was a greenish colour, the bunching of her skirt suggestive of a vestigial tail; another, whose sex he could not define, showed a face flattened, porcine, like ill-moulded clay. There were more, but hidden by the humans, themselves barbaric in high boots of dragon hide, necklaces of teeth, and patchwork garments, with broad-bladed knives and heavy swords much in evidence. Many, he realised, were female, but dressed as the men, and like them, giving off an odour of sweat and blood; and many, male and female both, were missing parts: fingers or whole hands, some with peglegs, others with empty sleeves.

One pushed to the fore, a short, broad-shouldered man, his beard a striation of black and silver, three fingers missing from his right hand, a thong heavy with dragons' teeth about his thick neck. He announced himself Thyrrin ek'Salar, and when he raised his hands for silence, the throng obeyed, as if he held some office amongst them, or was their acknowledged spokesman. He suggested that all should repair to what he called their inn, that all present might hear what word came from Kandahar, and, seemingly accustomed to obedience, led the way to a long building of wood and reeds hung with hides for walls, half its floor jutting out over the swamp, a deck beneath which floated the detritus of the place, the water alive with small scavengers squabbling over the corpses of flayed dragons and the offal that was spilled there. It stank, to which the hunters appeared oblivious, its furniture a motley collection of carpentered pieces and makeshift, bones as prominent as wood in construction. Calandryll saw that the halflings made no attempt to enter, gathering instead about the foot of the ladder as the human folk crowded inside.

They were brought mugs of some sharp liquor, distilled, ek'Salar advised them, from one of Gessyth's few edible plants. He owned the inn, he told them, and was disappointed to learn they carried no wine or ale to trade, his stocks run out and not replaceable until the merchants came north. They drank his home-made brew for appearance sake while the hunters quaffed eagerly, welcoming this interruption of their lonely routine.

Questions were shouted until ek'Salar imposed some semblance of order, requesting Calandryll to rise and impart his news. He climbed to his feet, doing his best to ignore the insects that buzzed about his face, and told them of events in Kandahar, of the uprising in the Fayne and the Tyrant's seizure of available vessels, that producing shouts of outrage and alarm. He said nothing of the founding of the Lyssian fleet, and deemed it the wiser course to allow the hunters their assumption that the Vanu-folk were of his country. Finally he was free to speak with ek'Salar.

'You would travel inland?' the Kand demanded, fixing Calandryll with a dark gaze rendered disturbing by the cast that distorted his left eye. 'Why?'

'Gessyth is uncharted,' Calandryll declared, telling the tale agreed earlier on the warboat, 'and I am a scholar. I would map the interior.'

Laughter greeted his announcement as those closest relayed his words to the rest. Ek'Salar waved his two remaining fingers in the direction of the swamps, his smile exposing blackened teeth.

'There is nothing to map, my friend. There is nothing save what you see - swamp and more swamp.'

'Legend tells of a city,' Calandryll replied. 'A fabulous city deep in the swamplands.

Ek'Salar snorted laughter and shook his head: such a gesture as might meet the telling of a tale so improbable as to place the teller's sanity in doubt.

'Legend tells that the cities of Lysse are walled with gold,' he said, 'but you, as a Lyssian, likely know better.'

Calandryll smiled agreement: this man, he decided, was the one who held the key. Should he argue against their going, they would find no support: he must win ek'Salar's support.

'You are clearly travelled,' he said, 'and so know better than to believe each legend you hear.'

'Indeed, I do,' ek'Salar nodded, pausing to crush an insect that landed on his cheek, idling wiping the smeared remains against his tunic. 'And so I know that Tezin-dar does not exist.'

'You know the name?' Calandryll said.

Ek'Salar chuckled and sipped the fierce liquor. 'I know the name,' he grinned, 'and I know that men have gone seeking that place before. I know that none have returned.'

'Ortan!' called a hunter. 'Tell him about Ortan!'

'Indeed,' said ek'Salar, 'the tale of Ortan is a salutary lesson. He was one of us, Ortan - a hunter of dragons, and a good one. But he dreamt of Tezin-dar, which - as you, a scholar, doubtless know - is reputed to be paved with precious metals; gold and silver and others unknown to man, with priceless jewels set as ornaments in the walls. Windows of gems so large and flawless they form the panes. All there for the taking, Ortan said, and him the one to find it. Well, Ortan persuaded several others as foolish as himself to accompany him on this madman's journey - nine of them, with Ortan the tenth. Good men, all of them: they knew the swamps. Yet not one came back! Though we did see Ortan again ...'

He paused, chuckling, and raised his mug, straight eye fixed on Calandryll. 'At least we guessed it was Ortan because he wore a ring we recognised on the hand we found in the belly of a dragon. That and his knife, which was also in the dragon's belly.'

Fresh laughter met the telling. Calandryll held his face straight and said, 'Even so, that does not prove the city does not exist.'

'Perhaps not,' said ek'Salar mildly, 'but it proves that any man who goes seeking it is a fool.'

'I do not think I am a fool,' Calandryll said, and glanced at his companions, 'Nor are my comrades fools.'

'If you go seeking Tezin-dar,' said ek'Salar quietly, 'you are all fools. And you will die out there.'

'We have come far,' Calandryll returned. 'We have fought the cannibals of Gash to come here.'

'The painted people?' ek'Salar flourished a dismissive hand. 'They are nothing. You have seen the dragons?'

Calandryll nodded.

'You have seen the younglings - the mature dragons inhabit the deep swamps, and they can swallow a boat whole. They have a taste for human flesh.'

'You survive them,' Calandryll said.

'We know their ways, and we do not venture where the full-grown dragons hunt.' The Kand shook his head, his swarthy face abruptly serious. 'I tell you, my friend, that only death awaits you in the swamps. The dragons are hazard enough, but there is more - a great deal more. Out there are living trees that feed on flesh; insects that find a man's - or a woman's,' this with a look to Katya, 'body a most excellent place to lay their eggs. And those eggs hatch grubs that eat you - a most painful death! There are creatures in the swamps such as make those things outside look human - and they are no friends to men.'

'I should be willing to pay a guide,' Calandryll said, 'handsomely.'

'My friend, my friend,' ek'Salar sighed, 'Have you heard nothing? There is no one here will take you into the deep swamps. Your Lyssian gold is insufficient - listen to me! You have coin? Then buy our hides! You come here ahead of all the rest and so have the chance to take your pick of the prime skins. Take those back to Kandahar and you can dictate your price in the market. If what you say of this civil war is true, Kandahar will have need of armour and you shall return to Lysse wealthy. Wealthy and alive still.'

'I thank you,' said Calandryll gently, 'but I am no merchant. I came to find Tezin-dar, and that I shall attempt.'

Ek'Salar shook his head wearily. 'You name yourself fool, my friend. And you will die a fool's death if you attempt this.'

'Even so,' Calandryll murmured, smiling that the Kand should know he was not insulted, 'I would hire a guide. A guide and a boat suitable for the swamps. Will you help me in that? For which service I should, of course, be willing to offer a fee.'

'I require no fee,' said the Kand, 'for you will not find a guide. But I will ask.'

He rose to his feet, gesturing the crowd to silence.

'Listen to me! These folk are come seeking Tezin-dar and require a guide. One who knows the deep swamps. They will pay - handsomely! - for this service. Indeed, I believe the man who undertakes this commission might name his own price. Will any here go with them?'

There was a long silence, then a man laughed, echoed by another and another until all were roaring mockery. Someone called, 'Tezin-dar? I'll show those women sweeter dreams than that.' Another shouted, 'Better slice your wrists now - that's an easier death.' Most shook their heads in negation and disbelief, studying the newcomers with pitying and puzzled eyes, as if they recognised madness.

Calandryll looked to his companions. Bracht sat stone-faced, staring at the laughing hide hunters; Katya's eyes were troubled above the veil of cloth; Tekkan clutched his mug, grimly, his weatherbeaten features stolid. Ek'Salar turned to face them; sat down, smiling.

'You see? And these men are no cowards - they face death when they hunt the dragons, but they know better than to die in pursuit of a dream.'

Calandryll nodded reluctantly. 'A boat then?' he asked. 'Can we purchase a boat?'

'You intend still to continue?' The Kand was incredulous. 'Without a guide? After all you've heard?'

'We have come too far to turn back now,' Calandryll advised him. 'Guide or no, we shall go on.'

Ek'Salar reached forwards, settling his good hand about Calandryll's wrist, the fingers digging deep, as if with that pressure he sought to impress his warning, his good eye fierce on Calandryll's face.

'Are your wits lost, my friend? Are you gone so far into madness you cannot hear what I tell you?'

Calandryll fought the desire to turn his face from the man's sour breath. 'I have my wits,' he said, 'And I shall go on.'

'You!' Ek'Salar released his hold, head swinging to encompass Tekkan with his distorted gaze. 'You are older - and so, perhaps, wiser - do you support this insanity?'

'I do,' said Tekkan solemnly.

The Kand sighed noisily, looking to Bracht, seeing the impassive stare that met his unspoken enquiry and turned to Katya.

'You are, I think, a prize amongst women. Would you have that face eaten by worms? Would you die between a dragon's jaws? Or find yourself the plaything of the swamp folk?'

'None of those,' she answered, her voice even, her eyes steady on his face. 'But still we must go on.'

'Burash!' Ek'Salar raised his eyes to the rush matting of the roof. 'Are you all mad?'

'Will you sell us a boat?' Calandryll pressed.

'If I cannot dissuade you,' the Kand shrugged, 'then, yes. I will sell you a boat and the supplies you will need. But later - tonight you dine with me.'

'You are kind.' Calandryll inclined his head politely. Ek'Salar chuckled, shaking his, and said, 'You shall at least go to your deaths with full stomachs.'

There was more conversation then, and more of the bitter liquor pressed on them, the hunters, their initial curiosity satisfied, clustering about the women with rough compliments and crude invitations. Calandryll saw Bracht tense angrily as several men gathered about Katya, and was pleased that the freesword held tight rein on his temper as the woman adroitly fended off the unwanted attention. Tekkan negotiated a refurbishment of supplies and a refilling of his water casks, all promised for the morrow, and in time ek'Salar announced that they should eat.

Calandryll had anticipated dining where they sat, and did not much relish the prospect of such fare as the inn would seem to offer, so he was pleasantly surprised when ek'Salar rose, leading them from the place.

The sun was almost set now, the swampland assuming a weird beauty as red-gold light sparkled on the brackish water, the moss that festooned the mangroves like golden filigree, the trees themselves burnished. Frogs croaked a chorus of farewell and dragons bellowed far off as a flight of birds - or creatures akin to birds - winged towards the refuge of the branches. The halflings gathered about the inn parted silently, studying them with strange, expressionless faces that seemed to Calandryll to hang on the very edges of humanity, some animalistic in their deformity whilst others appeared merely malformed, their physiognomy misplaced. Ek'Salar paid them no heed, no more than would a man walking amongst cattle, as if they were beneath his consideration: merely present and expected to remove themselves from his path.

He brought his guests to a building on the very edge of the headland, set a little apart from the rest, built all of wood, with some yellowish membrane stretched over the windows in lieu of glass and a covered verandah along two sides. He mounted the ladder, beckoning them on, and opened the door with a grandiose flourish.

They found themselves in a room large enough to accommodate the full party, the walls hung with hides painted in approximation of the tiles favoured in Kandahar, a long wooden table with ominously large rib bones for legs at the centre, chairs of bone and hide set down its length. Girandoles of polished brass were mounted along the walls, set with tallow candles whose flames were reflected in the mirrors, filling the chamber with warm light. Ek'Salar suggested they refresh themselves, indicating a door granting ingress to a bathing chamber, a well at its centre.

'The water is fresh,' he assured them.

'You live well,' Calandryll complimented, glancing about the room.

The Kand shrugged modestly. 'I have done well here,' he murmured, 'and these people regard me as their leader. They are simple folk for the most part who would be cheated by the merchants did I not negotiate on their behalf.'

He clapped his hands and a halfling woman emerged

from a door at the rear of the room.

'Guests.' He enunciated each word carefully. 'Food for all.'

The woman bowed, strands of pure white hair that seemed to move of their accord falling about her face, and disappeared. Ek'Salar opened a cabinet of some reddish wood, decorated with ornate figures, and produced goblets of carved bone and two flagons of wine. 'Saved,' he explained, 'for some suitable occasion. Such as the settling of a contract.'

'We would not rob you of your last wine,' Calandryll protested. 'And the purchase of a boat seems hardly to merit your loss.'

The Kand smiled, filling goblets. 'How many of you venture inland?' he asked.

'We three,' Calandryll indicated himself, Katya and Bracht, 'and eight archers. As many more are needed to handle the boat.'

'A single boat will carry no more than twelve,' ek'Salar said, 'and should you purchase two, that leaves a goodly crew still on board your vessel. Who commands there?'

'I command,' said Tekkan.

'And you will wait for their return? For how long?'

Tekkan shrugged.

'No matter.' Ek'Salar stroked his beard, his voice casual as he said, 'They will not come back and in time you will accept that and depart. If the Tyrant seizes merchantmen in his war with the Fayne, few will venture north - but you will be here. You can carry hides south. And while you wait for them, we can amuse ourselves negotiating a price - let us drink a toast to that.'

'I drink to their return,' Tekkan said.

The Kand shrugged and raised his goblet. 'No matter - you will learn. The lesson will be sad, but you will learn.'

'To a safe return,' said Tekkan.

'To profit for us all,' said ek'Salar; and lower, 'Who live.'

The toast was inauspicious and Calandryll said a silent prayer to Dera as he drank, savouring the wine, for he thought it likely the last he would taste in some time. It seemed ek'Salar took their deaths for granted and that set a gloomy note until the halfling woman and two others appeared with laden platters and the Kand bade them be seated and eat.

The food, to his surprise, was good, ek'Salar explaining that the halflings furnished the settlement with vegetables from the swamps and fish from the sea in return for trade goods. The meat they ate, he told them, was dragon flesh, the hunters' staple diet, and that, Calandryll found, was palatable as good beef. The Kand talked throughout the meal, clearly delighted by the change of company, and whilst much of his conversation seemed designed to deter them, he furnished them with knowledge of the forbidding territory they must soon enter. It was alarming, his talk of burrowing worms and lethal insects, of the swamp dragons and flesh-eating trees, no less so the changeling creatures of the deep swamp, but he promised to furnish them with transport and gear suitable to their venture, and the night was old before they left his home.

None spoke much as they rowed out to the warboat, nor as they prepared to sleep. There seemed little to say: they were committed.

Dawn found them ready. They went ashore, greeted by ek'Salar, who brought them to yet another building, where he kitted them with high boots of dragon hide - waterproof and able to withstand the lesser creatures that inhabited the swamps, he explained - and tunics of greenish fibre, loose woven and light, that would, he said, resist the decay afflicting cotton and similar materials. He sold them foodstuffs and waterbags; ointments to deter insects, and salves for those undeterred; harpoons to use against the dragons. Then he brought them to a jetty, where several boats were moored.

They had decided to distribute their party over two boats. Calandryll, with Bracht and Katya in the first, accompanied by Quara and three of her archers, with four of the sturdy Vanu oarsmen; four archers and four oarsmen in the other, which would bear the bulk of their supplies. The boats were wide-beamed and of shallow draught with low gunwales, more raft than dinghy and propelled with long poles, but suited to the negotiation of lily meadows and reeds. Tekkan examined them both, minutely, and declared himself satisfied. Calandryll gave ek'Salar the price he asked and the Kand ordered a group of watching halflings to load the craft.

The strange creatures obeyed in silence, shuffling back and forth from the storehouse to the jetty, four of them dropping into the water, impervious, it seemed, to the swimming things there. With ek'Salar shouting instructions, they loaded the boats and clambered back to dry land, standing indifferent to the insects as they watched the Vanu-folk descend.

Calandryll, Bracht and Katya stood with Tekkan and ek'Salar, anxious to be gone now.

'You have farewells to say,' the Kand declared, 'and I shall leave you to that. I wish you well.'

He bowed formally: a man convinced they went to their deaths, and walked to the inn. Tekkan sighed, looking them each in the eye, his face grave.

'May your gods be with you,' he said, his voice husky. 'Find the Arcanum and bring it out. I await you here.'

He took Calandryll's hand, and then Bracht's; Katya he embraced, murmuring something in their own language too soft to hear. Katya nodded and went swiftly to the ladder. Bracht followed on her heels.

Calandryll moved after, then halted as a hand touched tentatively at his sleeve. He turned to find a halfling standing close, a hairless man with yellow eyes set too wide apart, and overhung with a ridge of bone, his nostrils flared and flat, the mouth a lipless slit tugged down by the near-absence of a chin. Calandryll thought instinctively of a fish, and indeed there was a hint of scales on the pale green skin, and the fingers that touched his sleeve were joined by webbing, tipped with sharp, curved nails, like claws. The creature - it was difficult to think of him as a man - wore a loose tunic of the woven fibre, sleeveless, exposing powerful arms, kilted with a belt of rope, the legs muscular. He let go Calandryll's sleeve as though afraid of reprimand, but his strange eyes remained fixed on Calandryll's face, intense.

'You go swamp.' The words came sibilant, said slowly, as if with effort in a hard-learned tongue. 'You look for guide ... I hear you talk ... with ek'Salar ... He say no ... No guide ... but I take you ... show you way.'

Calandryll's face reflected his uncertainty: ek'Salar had told them the halflings served the hunters; they cleaned and cooked, acted as porters, flensed the dragon carcasses. Nothing had been said of their use as guides.

'I am called Yssym.' It sounded like Yssym: he was not sure. 'I guide you ... I know swamp.'

A hand pointed to the boats, to the swamps.

'Can you trust him?' Tekkan asked.

'Trust me ... Yssym guide you,' said the creature. 'Yssym know swamp ... Trust Yssym.'

Calandryll studied his face. It was impossible to read, the shape, the colour of the eyes, too alien; it was not made to express human emotion. He stared into the yellow orbs, uncertain.

Then the halfling said, 'I bring you to Tezin-dar ...

Yssym know how ... Bring you to Tezin-dar ... Yssym promise.'

Calandryll turned to the raft-like boats, looking down to where Bracht and Katya waited. 'A halfling - Yssym - offers his services as guide. Do we accept?'

The two exchanged glances; Katya shrugged, Bracht said, 'He may well know the swamp - bring him.'

'Come then,' Calandryll said, hoping he did the right thing.

EIGHTEEN

YSSYM swung fluidly into the foremost boat, Calandryll close behind, and the husky Vanu men took up the poles, propelling the flat-bottomed craft smoothly along the slender ribbon of reed-free water that wound inland towards the distant line of mangroves. The halfling crouched at the prow, touching the harpoons with a nod of approval. Calandryll realised he gave off a faintly piscine odour: it was no worse than the stink of the hunters and he settled beside the creature, taking his copy of Orwen's chart from the satchel.

'This was drawn by a man who came here long ago,' he said, speaking slowly in the Kand tongue, touching the map. 'We are here; Tezin-dar is here. You know the swamp between?'

Yssym stared at the map and ducked his strange head, that affirmative accompanied by a clicking sound.

'Old Ones help Orwen,' it sounded like Awhenn 'make map ... No hunters then ... Swamp belong ...' the name was a whistling sound, *Syfalbeen*, as best Calandryll could tell. 'Swamp change ... But Tezin-dar there.'

He tapped a clawed finger to the chart and raised it

to point ahead, indicating a place invisible beyond the mangrove forest.

'You - the Syfalheen - knew Orwen?' Calandryll was surprised, turning to glance at his companions.

'Old Ones know, yes,' Yssym said, 'Syfalheen know all swamp.'

'The Syfalheen,' Bracht spoke over Calandryll's shoulder, 'Are they what ek'Salar warned us against?'

Yssym's smooth-skinned head swung ponderously to face the Kern, his features immobile. 'I am Sylfalheen,' he hissed, 'all swamp people Syfalheen ... Sometimes hunters kill Syfalheen and Syfalheen fight hunters. But Yssym bring you to clan elders ... They help you reach Tezin-dar if you the ones Yssym wait for. Old Ones say men come seeking Tezin-dar ... to find book ... Syfalheen watch for them.'

'You were waiting for us?' Calandryll stared, shocked, at the halfling. 'How could you - how could the Old Ones - know?'

'Old Ones know.' Yssym shrugged, an oddly human gesture. 'Old Ones good, wise ... Send watchers.'

Calandryll heard the plural and asked, 'You were not the first?'

Yssym's mouth moved in what might have been a smile: he shook his head.

'Always watcher. Old Ones say must always be watcher.'

'These Old Ones?' Calandryll asked. 'Who are they? Are they Syfalheen?'

Again the halfling's head moved in a negative circle. 'Old Ones like you, men ... Friends to Syfalheen.'

'Where are they, the Old Ones?'

Calandryll was aware of Bracht and Katya pressing close, intent on this strange conversation.

'Deep swamp.' Yssym pointed ahead again and faced Calandryll. 'Tezin-dar ... Old Ones live in Tezin-dar ... Guard book.'

'You have seen them? Spoken with them?'

'Syfalheen not go to Tezin-dar. That holy place ... But Old Ones speak long, long time past ... Say to my ... father's father, his father ... Before him ... Send watcher. Yssym watcher now.'

'How do you know we are the ones?' Calandryll demanded.

'Old Ones say three come.' A webbed hand rose to angle a claw at Calandryll, at Bracht, at Katya. 'Old Ones say watch for three and bring them to swamp ... Elders know ... I think you the three ... If not, you die in swamp.'

'A test,' Bracht murmured, 'Varent said the book was guarded.'

Calandryll nodded, watching the line of grey trees loom larger, his mind racing. That they must communicate in the tongue of Kandahar was a curse: Yssym was able to make himself understood only with difficulty, his mouth, his tongue not formed to shape the words, his vocabulary limited, whilst what he said held both promise of aid and threat. 'Were we not,' he asked, 'Not the ones - why should we not force you to take us there?'

'You not know swamp,' Yssym answered flätly. 'Not even hunters go into deep swamp where Syfalheen live ... Men die there, like ek'Salar say. You not ones, you die.'

'But we have you,' Calandryll insisted.

'You not force me,' Yssym said simply. 'You kill me, but not force me. Not matter if I die ... You wrong ones, you die in swamp ... Dragons eat you ... Trees ... I bring you to worms ... No man,' Calandryll wondered if the flat, sibilant voice infused the word with a measure of contempt, 'live in deep swamp ... Not without Syfalheen help.'

'Then we are in your hands,' he said.

'Yes,' said Yssym; bluntly.

Calandryll smiled, accepting that finality - it seemed unavoidable - but still there was much to occupy his mind. Varent had anticipated guardians, but not of this kind. Magic, yes; but not that the inhabitants of the swamps should stand vigil over the Arcanum - he had said nothing of this test Yssym spoke of, nor that the mysterious Old Ones employed the Syfalheen as watchers. Who were they, these ancients who lived in Tezin-dar? For how long had Yssym's people waited? The halfling had not been clear, his sense of time unlike a man's - perhaps generations of the Syfalheen had gone to that miserable headland, awaiting the coming of the strangers. The Old Ones had, it now seemed obvious, foreseen that men should come seeking the Arcanum - and prepared the way. But why? If they guarded the book, why did they not simply close the approaches? To penetrate the swamps was difficult enough - did the inhabitants oppose such coming, few could hope to survive - yet it seemed a path to Tezin-dar was left deliberately open. A trap? He glanced sidelong at Yssym, the halfling crouching expressionless, offering no hint of treachery, and felt for reasons he could not define that he should trust the creature. In that he had little choice; but even so, he did not think Yssym intended them harm. He had followed the strictures of the Old Ones - who were men, he had said, albeit he had never seen them - and he brought his charge to his clan, who would test them somehow.

A design existed here that he could not comprehend. It was a web, hung like the moss that festooned the trees, fragile as that gossamer drapery, but far harder to grasp. Three would come, Yssym had said, that suggesting their arrival was foreseen, though he could not understand how. A spaewife, an augur - all the necromancers and soothsayers of his father's palace - could do no more than interpret the immediate future, and that usually only in terms of an individual's future.

Did the Old Ones then cast their net wider? Katya had said the holy men of Vanu had scried Varent's attempt to raise the Mad God and sent her forth seeking the two men seen in that scrying - but that was of the present. Yssym spoke in terms of some ancient prophecy, a thing foreseen long ages past; prepared for - as if the Old Ones sought to bring the three they had foreseen to the Arcanum. He could not understand why that should be so.

'I cannot understand this,' he murmured.

'There is no need.' Katya spoke for the first time. 'We seek the Arcanum - Yssym brings us to it.'

He nodded, frowning. 'But why? How could they know we should come? Why send us a guide?'

'We are players in a game,' she replied, echoing his own thoughts, 'and the game is larger than we may understand. Our task is to bring the Arcanum to Vanu, that it be destroyed forever. We need know no more than that.'

'But Calandryll is a scholar,' Bracht said, grinning, 'and he seeks the reasons for things.'

'You do not wonder?' Calandryll demanded.

'I wonder at this test,' the Kern shrugged. 'I wonder at the dangers ahead, and that is enough for me.'

Calandryll sighed, absently swatting at a bright green flying thing that appeared intent on a detailed investigation of his face despite the layer of ek'Salar's preventive cream smeared there.

'Likely we shall find your answers in Tezin-dar,' said Katya.

'Aye,' Bracht echoed, 'and sufficient to occupy you along the way.'

He nodded, wishing he could share their pragmatism, disturbing thoughts buzzing, like the insects that clouded round, about his mind. He did his best to set them aside, thoughts and insects both, the one, thanks to ek'Salar's ointments, easier to dismiss, the other less so. He stared at the approaching trees, closer now, and lit by the sun, massive trunks standing on wide-spread roots that thrust from the swamp like the legs of gigantic spiders, the boles all grey and green, wound with parasitic plants that displayed lurid flowers, the reek of the brackish water sweetened by their exotic scent. The moss that at a distance had seemed gossamer-fine was now a thick curtain hung from the intertwining limbs, alive with crawling things, draping the gaps between the mangroves as if the inner swamp sought to curtain itself, to shut out the world.

'Small dragons here,' Yssym warned, hefting a harpoon. 'We find big dragons later.'

The boats pushed through the mossy wall into a place of shifting, subdued light, all shadowy green and blue and gold like drifting smoke, ethereal as the panorama of a dream. The air was instantly thicker, warmer and moist, loud with the buzzing and chittering of insects. The sky was replaced with a canopy of moss and vines, the domes formed by the mangrove roots hued green, patches of open water viridescent, others a flickering blue, filigreed where the sun lanced occasional shafts of brilliance down through gaps in the overlay of foliage, painting the turgid water with gold. Dark shapes moved amongst the shadows, floating logs at first, inexperienced, glance; revealed as dragons only when the great tails lashed, frothing the water as the beasts moved clear of the boats' passage, roaring their disapproval.

'Small,' Yssym repeated with ominous confidence. 'Hide from hunters ... Big dragons not hide.'

Calandryll took up a harpoon, seeing Bracht do the same. The Vanu women held their bows ready, arrows nocked. A dragon swam close, cold green eyes bulging from gnarled ridges of reddish armour. Yssmyn motioned the others back, balancing on the prow, and thrust his lance at the beast, not seeking to pierce the hide, but tapping it firmly on the snout. The dragon snorted and submerged, the eddy rocking the boat. Yssym watched intently, pointing as the beast re-emerged some distance off.

'Soft there.' He tapped his own flat nose, barking what Calandryll assumed was his version of laughter. 'Hit there, small dragon go away. Rest hard ... like armour. You leave dragons to Yssym.'

He nodded, squatting with the harpoon braced across his shoulder, reaching out to drive off the more curious of the saurians, guiding the boats steadily deeper into the shadowy interior.

It was as well he did, for soon it became apparent that the landscape was much changed since Orwen had mapped Gessyth. The chart Calandryll had so painstakingly copied showed the location of Tezin-dar, and described the coastline well enough, but the interior was a shifting thing, changed by fallen trees and the islands of matted debris that arose, indiscernible from the liquid surface save where sunlight penetrated to reveal a subtle alteration in the colour of the water. Without the halfling they would have been lost before sunset, unable to distinguish the landmarks he recognised, or the hazards he steered around.

He named them in his own language as they passed. The thick clusters of oily blue flowers that grew on the reedy islands were *feshyn* and poisonous to the touch, he warned them; and where the water showed that leprous yellow colour, flesh-eating worms, *yennym*, swam. The lianas were the habitat of the stinging insects he called *grishas*, their bite often fatal; and the mangrove roots hid the things called *estifas*, that laid their eggs in human flesh, leaving the hatching grubs to eat the host. He pointed out a rippling in the water, telling them it was sign of a swarm of something he named *shivim* that, as best they could understand his explanation, were predatory fish, attracted by blood or movement, and able to reduce even a small dragon to bare bones in moments. Without his aid they would likely have died, just as ek'Salar had promised, poisoned, or stung, or eaten by one creature or another, for it seemed that very little in the swamp was friendly and the inexperienced went in constant danger of unpleasant death.

Landfall, even, proved hazardous, for as the light began to fade Bracht indicated a sizeable island, suggesting they halt there before the sun finally set, and Yssym shook his head, pointing out the holes beneath, where dragons laired. He brought them instead to another mat of jumbled roots and rotting reeds, grown over with a kind of red-brown grass that gave off a sharp odour, which, he informed them, deterred both dragons and insects: compensation for its offensive reek. They poled in, dragging the boats clear of the water, and made camp. Yssym took a knife and set to cutting rushes, spreading them over the grass to use as bedding, the fronds a barrier against the moisture that seeped through the spongy island.

It was an uncomfortable camp, fireless, for the swamp held no timber so dry it would burn, and the island shifted constantly beneath them, prompting them to cluster towards its centre, sweat-soaked, breeks and tunics wet, impregnated with the odour of their surroundings. Guards were posted even though Yssym's promise that the malodorous grass would hold off the dragons and the insects was proven, only the halfling at ease there, settling to sleep after he had eaten as if the night was not aloud with a symphony of alarming bellows and roars, shrill cries and splashings that told of things hunting and dying in the menacing half-dark. All around the water and the trees glowed with a strange phosphoresence, the canopy above lit silver by the risen moon, though that orb remained unseen behind the curtain, whilst between the trees ghostly lights flickered, as if phantoms sought to lure the unwary out into the unknown.

'I have little liking for this place,' Bracht remarked miserably, the understatement prompting Calandryll to chuckle, for all he shared the Kern's discomfort.

'Perhaps it will improve,' he murmured, staring at a green-yellow glow that appeared to dance about the trunk of a silver-lit mangrove.

'It cannot get worse,' said Bracht.

'You forget the dragons,' Katya smiled. 'Yssym promises larger specimens.'

'Aye, I'd forgotten that.' The Kern grinned ruefully. 'Dragons and *yennym*; *grishas*, *estifas* - have I forgotten any of Gessyth's delights?'

'*Feshyn*,' said Calandryll.

'And *shivim*,' Katya added. 'Nor have we encountered the flesh-eating trees yet.'

'Your optimism cheers me,' Bracht grunted. 'I'd almost wished I'd not gone drinking in that tavern back in Secca.'

'Were that the case,' Calandryll grinned, 'you'd not partake of this heroic quest.'

'Destiny brings us here,' said Katya, thoughtfully. 'We three were bound to meet and I do not think it could be otherwise.'

Bracht stared at her, smiling, and said, 'Then I thank destiny.'

She returned his smile a moment and turned her face away, smoothing hair that shone silver in the strange light from a face pale as sweet honey.

'We were - are - anticipated,' said Calandryll, 'and that I do not understand. How could these Old Ones know we should come?'

'Not only we three,' Katya nodded, 'Yssym spoke of others foreseen by the Old Ones.'

'Varent,' said Bracht, 'May his soul rot.'

'The Old Ones must be powerful augurs,' Calandryll

suggested, 'if they scried all this so long ago. I know no soothsayers able to see so far ahead.'

'There are forgotten magicks,' Katya said. 'Arts old when the world we know was young - things of the elder gods. Perhaps best lost.'

'Aye,' Bracht agreed, 'I'd not know my future set out clear before me, but sooner find it for myself.'

'Ours lies here,' Calandryll gestured at the weird landscape surrounding their little island. 'With the Syfalheen and the Old Ones.'

'And sleep,' said Bracht, stretching on the reeds, 'if sleep may be found in this place.'

They did sleep, albeit fitfully, disturbed by the clamour of the swamp and the discomfort, and when dawn came - indicated only by a changing of the light - they rose damp and more than a little miserable to eat a cold breakfast and man the boats again, poling steadily deeper along the tortuous waterway.

The mangrove forest extended deep into Gessyth and for days they moved amongst the great trees, wary of the *feshyn* and the *grishas* that scurried in relentless columns over roadways of vines. One of Quara's archers was stung and fell into delirium despite the plants Yssym pressed to the bites and the infusion he prepared. By nightfall the woman was silent, her breathing shallow and laboured, and by dawn she had died: reluctantly they left her body behind, knowing it must be soon consumed by the myriad predators of the swampland.

She was their first casualty: in a while they lost two more. An oarsmen, careless of the lurid blue flowers that clustered on an outhrust root, ducked too slow to avoid the *feshyn*. A blossom brushed his cheek and he shouted as he felt the venomous petals lay their deadly caress upon his skin. Yssym called an instant halt, checking the water for *shivim* before wading back to gather handfuls of small yellow buds that he ground to a paste and smeared over the angry eruption covering the Vanu's cheek.

'Perhaps he live,' the halfling announced. 'Perhaps not ... must rest ... Not spread poison.'

The oarsman, fear ugly in his pale blue eyes, was settled amongst the baggage and they went on. That night Yssym prepared more of the ointment and the man appeared in better spirits, arguing against his enforced inactivity. Towards noon of the next day Calandryll heard a shout from the second boat and looked back in time to see the man rub furiously at his face as he began to shudder, that trembling becoming rapidly a seizure so that before his fellows had time to hold him, he pitched overboard. Yssym cried a warning as an archer sprang into the water, wading towards the threshing figure, but even as the woman heard him, the surface rippled, churned by the swarm of *shivim* attracted by the disturbance. She screamed as the blue-grey creatures surrounded her, the swamp boiling where she stood, the fish leaping from the water to fasten teeth in her tunic and flesh, others tearing at her protective boots so that even as her companions stared in helpless horror she was covered with a living mantle. The water became red and she fell down. Calandryll stared aghast, his impulse to leap to her aid, that quelled by Yssym's hand on his shoulder and the certain knowledge that neither she or the man could be saved. He could only watch as both were reduced to bare bones, and the *shivim* moved on in restless search of fresh prey.

Their camp that night, on another island of matted debris, was oppressively silent. The Vanu mourned their losses, Katya sitting moist-eyed, staring unhappily into the phosphorescent shadows, as if she held herself responsible. Even Bracht's sanguine humour was dulled, and save for a compassionate hand upon her shoulder he offered no comment.

The next day they moved with exaggerated caution, steering as far as they were able in that maze of roots and vines from the blue flowers and the overhanging lianas, and when, on the following day, they saw open space ahead, all were cheered by the prospect of quitting the mangrove forest. Before them stretched a lily meadow, narrow spaces of clear water amongst the wide green pads, from which grew single thick stalks, each supporting a single creamy blossom, yellow at the centre, the air refreshingly sweet with their perfume. Overhead they could see the sky once more, bright blue, the sun high. After the forbidding gloom of the trees it was a relief simply to be in the open.

Yssym dampened their good humour with a blunt announcement: 'Big dragons here.'

He pointed to the shapes that bulked amongst the lilies and Calandryll gasped at the size of the beasts. They were far larger than any he had seen, several like small islands, with gaily-plumaged birds, or feathered flying lizards, stalking their crenellated backs.

'They sleep in sun,' the halfling advised, 'We wait, then move slow … If dragon attack, put harpoon in nose, or eye … Only belly soft enough you kill him.'

Katya relayed this information to her people and they crouched nervously in the boats, waiting until the sun hung directly above the meadow. Then Yssym gave word they should attempt the crossing and Calandryll and Bracht took up lances as Quara's archers nocked shafts to bowstrings and the oarsmen poled slowly out from the cover of the trees.

The forest seemed suddenly less menacing as they traversed the floating meadow. The dragons there had been dwarfs compared to these monsters, and no cover was offered by that expanse of open water. For all the myriad dangers of the trees, there had at least been islands amongst the mangroves, solid footing of a kind that seemed less vulnerable than the raft-like boats.

'Ahrd,' whispered Bracht, staring wide-eyed at a monstrous red back, 'how do the hunters kill them?'

'Hunters only take little dragons,' said Yssym softly, 'Four boats to one dragon. Not speak now, or dragons hear you and attack.'

His hairless head turned slowly, yellow eyes studying the hulks apprehensively, his muscular arm poised to cast the harpoon. Calandryll hefted his own lance, praying silently for safe passage across the meadow. Sweat beaded his forehead, running in salty channels down his face, and he blinked, knowing that any one of these gigantic creatures could wreck the boat, pitching them all overboard, that thought prompting him to wonder if *shivim* dwelt there, or if this was the province of dragons alone.

Slowly, slowly, they progressed into the meadow. The oarsmen dipped their poles with dream-like regularity, creating as little disturbance as possible. The archers crouched with full-drawn bows, their breathing a soft sighing that echoed like shouting on tensed ears. The lily pads parted with a gentle rustling sound, that jarred like the crash of falling timber, what little noise the boats made seeming unnaturally loud, surely enough to alert the monsters. Calandryll held his breath as he became convinced one round green eye fastened on him alone. It looked large as his palm, cut vertically with a slash of indigo. An armslength distant, craggy nostrils thrust from the snout, and when the jaws opened he saw rows of jagged teeth, long and pointed as dirks. His heart pounded then and he felt his arm draw back unbidden, ready to cast the harpoon. But the dragon merely emitted a stertorous rumble and sank below the surface.

Calandryll heard his own breath come out in a long sigh and glanced ahead, reckoning the distance to the far trees. At the slow speed imposed by the danger it would be dark before they reached that cover, and he realised they faced the prospect of a night spent on the boats. That held scant appeal; but to hurry was to attract the attention of the dragons and he resigned himself to patience, concentrating on the more immediate threat.

Then a murmur from Yssym halted their progress altogether and he felt his heart lurch afresh as a vast reddish bulk showed directly across their path. The dragon was not the largest present, but it drifted between them and their destination, and to pole around it meant the negotiation of the dense lily pads where the creature's larger fellows drowsed: they waited.

The dragon appeared oblivious of their presence, lying like some vast log in their way. Its eyes were open, but unfocussed, staring unfathomably into some saurian dream. Calandryll counted nine birds busy along the monster's spine, beaks delving amongst the wrinkles of its hide, three between the parted jaws, picking at the teeth with avian industry. How long they took to complete their task he could not tell: each moment was drawn out in silence counted by the thudding of heartbeats too long to measure, the slow drip of sweat, but at last the birds completed their task, hopping briskly to the dragon's back. Their arrival seemed a signal, for the saurian's tail waved lazily and the obstructive bulk drifted clear.

'We go.' Yssym's sibilant voice was urgent, his head tilted to the sky. 'Dragons wake soon.'

Calandryll looked up and saw the sun shifted across the heavens, the day lengthening towards dusk. Katya whispered orders and the Vanu-folk set to poling again, driving the boats on across the meadow. His arm began to cramp from the weight of the harpoon and he flexed it a little, not daring to set the lance down, even though he longed to massage muscles beginning to ache. They moved with agonising slowness as the dragons began to stir, ominous fulfilment of Yssym's warning, the lily pads undulating with the ripples started by tails, submerging bodies. The birds took flight with startling speed, a handful lofting from their floating perches to be rapidly joined by the others, the air filled with the flock, shrill cries echoing as it wheeled low overhead and winged towards the distant trees.

Calandryll saw Yssym's shoulders bunch beneath his rough-woven tunic, the halfling rising from his crouch to stand with harpoon upraised as a dragon swam close, the boat rocking dangerously in the wash of the huge tail. His own balance was precarious and he wondered how effectively he might cast his weapon should that become necessary. He prayed that it would not: he could envisage no way they might survive such attack.

The trees loomed closer. Still too far distant to offer hope of refuge should a dragon charge, but an enticing promise, grey-gold across the perimeter of the lily meadow. The oarsmen plied their poles, driving the boats steadily towards that safety, the open channel of the river clear of the monsters. The trees grew more distinct.

Calandryll began to believe they would survive unharmed.

Then the attack came.

A Vanu in the leading boat called soft warning as a hulk swam closer through the lilies, set on a collision course. Yssym gestured for more speed and waved the second boat back, intending to allow the dragon passage between the two craft. Whether the crew of the second boat misunderstood the halfling's gesture, or thought to outpace the dragon, none could tell, but they picked up speed. And so found themselves directly across the dragon's path.

The creature seemed, at first, oblivious of the obstacle, and for a moment Calandryll believed they would escape unscathed. Then the gnarled snout butted wood. The dragon snorted and submerged. The Vanus drove their poles furiously, the raft-like vessel rocking on the swirling water. The dragon surfaced on the far side and turned back. Yssym shouted a warning: unnecessary, for the oarsmen already dropped their poles and took up harpoons, the three remaining archers sighting on the monster. Its tail flicked, awful evidence of its strength as the massive body was propelled like some vast red battering ram at the fragile boat. Arrows flew, imbedding in the snout. The dragon roared, jaws spread wide, hiding the vulnerable eyes and sensitive nose. They closed on the bulwarks, wood splintering to open a ragged gash that let in water. A harpoon stabbed down and the dragon bellowed again. A man yelled, falling overboard, and the dragon took him, screaming as mantrap jaws closed about his waist. Three more of the beasts approached. Yssym shouted, 'Go fast!' and Katya shouted, 'No! Help them!'

There was little help they could offer. Quara and her women sent shafts fast at the dragons. One pierced an eye and the wounded monster roared in pain, rolling, its belly target for the arrows. The rest converged on the damaged boat, more coming now, attracted by the commotion. Another man tumbled into the water, standing shoulder deep to drive his harpoon between the jaws of the saurian that engulfed him, man and dragon disappearing together even as another beast rose up to crash half its length across the stern of the stricken boat. The lily meadow filled with the bellowing of the enraged dragons; the screaming of the Vanu-folk as they were dragged down. Calandryll locked a fist about the talisman, willing its magic to drive the monster back, but the stone remained inert, cold to his touch; useless.

'Not help,' Yssym said urgently. 'We stay, we die, too … Must reach trees fast.'

Bracht said, 'He speaks the truth. Ahrd forgive us,

but we have no other choice.'

Calandryll saw tears in Katya's eyes. A woman began to wade towards them and went under screaming as a dragon took her. Katya nodded, barking orders in the Vanu tongue. The oarsmen dropped their harpoons and snatched up the poles.

They reached the shelter of the mangroves and halted, looking back. The meadow was quiet now. A few pieces of jagged timber floated amongst the lily pads, but of the Vanu-folk and their supplies there was no sign.

'Big dragons not come here,' Yssym said softly.

Katya looked at him and shook her head, her eyes dark grey, stormy with grief. Quara touched her shoulder, murmuring something in their own language, and she answered in kind, slumping forlornly between the thwarts.

'Yssym sorry,' the halfling said.

'How many more?' Katya whispered. 'How many more must die?'

'Easier now,' Yssym offered. 'We find Syfalheen soon ... I bring you safe to clan.'

'Too late for them.'

Katya stared back across the meadow. Bracht said, 'We must go on. Night comes,' and she nodded, not speaking, her eyes still intent on the spot where her companions had died.

'Safe place near,' Yssym offered. 'Find safe place ... You mourn there.'

Katya nodded again, wiping her eyes, and spoke to the oarsmen. They gathered their poles and sent the boat deeper in amongst the trees, leaving the meadow behind, the shadows lengthening as the sun went down and the mangroves gathered thicker about them, funereal, cloaked in grey moss like silent mourners.

More than the loss of brave comrades afflicted them

in the days that followed: the bulk of their supplies had gone with the destruction of the boat and what remained lasted only a short while. Yssym showed them edible plants, and caught some fish, but it was poor fare, and eaten raw for want of combustible wood. They lived in misery, never dry, only the gear purchased of ek'Salar resisting the destructive atmosphere, whilst all else mildewed and began to rot. Verdigris coloured buckles and fungus grew on leather; bowstrings softened and stretched; they oiled their weapons nightly; and tempers frayed. Calandryll wondered that Tezin-dar should need more guardians than the swamps provided, for it seemed they wandered trapped in a limbo of gloomy trees and theatening meadows, where a myriad dangers lay in wait, and that likely they would wander there forever.

Only Yssym retained his optimism - and that a source of some irritation, for it seemed the halfling shrugged off their losses - urging them steadily onwards with promises that soon they should encounter his people and find food, shelter and welcome. Their sole consolation was that no more died: they learnt from the mistakes of others and all avoided contact with the poisonous flowers and the lethal insects, and when they crossed the paths of dragons they went slowly, and with infinite caution. They detoured around the stands of leprous trees Yssym said ate all living flesh that came within reach of the tentacular limbs and in time the mangroves thinned. The lily-filled water meadows became smaller and less frequent, gradually giving way to reeds and rushes, the islands growing larger and more numerous, spreading before them until they had to abandon the boats and move on foot, the surface shifting alarmingly beneath their feet.

'No more dragons,' Yssym promised, 'Worst over now ... Soon find Syfalheen.'

They grunted dubious acceptance, shouldering what little was left to carry as the halfling led them through a monotonous landscape of high reeds that rustled softly in the slight, hot breeze, the path a winding thing of uncertain footing, awash with brackish water for most of its length, the realisation that they finally trod land almost dry startling them.

Calandryll had simply plodded, miserable, not noticing that the path climbed slightly until he found the reeds no longer at eye level, but below him. He halted, staring around, and saw Yssym point ahead, to where a low ridge of greyish-brown traversed the landscape.

'Syfalheen there,' the halfling declared confidently. 'Come.'

They followed him down off the rise, losing sight of the ridge, then finding it again, suddenly before them, a bank of muddy earth, not natural in origin, but shaped, a barrier against the all-encroaching swamp. It was a dyke, they saw, when they climbed it, a long, low hummock that stretched between the reed beds and the dry land beyond. Strange, stunted trees grew there, with avenues between suggesting organisation, a measure of order that prompted Calandryll to think of the orchards of his homeland, that impression confirmed by the fruit Yssym plucked, handing them each a purplish globe that, when peeled, offered a succulent, sweet core. They ate greedily, the fruit all the more delicious after the long days of raw fish and fibrous swamp plants, their spirits lifting.

'Come, we find clan now,' Yssym said. 'Food there.'

He set off at a brisk pace between the trees, anxious, it seemed, to bring them swiftly to the promised comforts, and in a while the orchards gave way to fenced fields where animals such as none of the outlanders had seen before grazed on viridescent grass. Water was still much in evidence, but channelled here, directed along conduits of ancient stone to pools and troughs, spanned by small, arched bridges of antique design. The track became a roadway, paved with great slabs, and Calandryll lengthened his stride to catch the halfling.

'This road,' he asked, 'the channels - who built them?'

'Old Ones,' Yssym said. 'Long, long ago Old Ones build.'

Calandryll studied their surroundings, eyes opened by Yssym's casual words, seeing now evidence of some forgotten civilization. The stone beside the road was no random boulder, but a megalith, time-worn and mossy, but dressed for all it tilted, and set there for some forgotten purpose; the hummock in the field beyond was a dolmen; and beyond - did the walls of some tumbled hall jut from the grass? He was not sure, but he saw around him antiquities beyond the dreams of such historians as Medith or Sarnium, the remnants of a lost civilization. He trod, he realised, a road forgotten by time, hidden by Gessyth's swamps. He touched the halfling's arm.

'Is this Tezin-dar?'

Yssym barked his harsh laughter and shook his head.

'This Syfalheen place, my clan home ... not Tezin-dar. This my home ..., You meet syfaba ... elders ... they show you way to Tezin-dar.'

'How far?' Calandryll asked.

'We find by dark.' Yssym glanced up, gesturing at the lowering sun. 'Sun go down, we there.'

'And face the elders' test,' said Bracht.

'Face test, yes,' Yssym agreed. 'But rest first ... Eat, bathe ... dry clothes.'

'Luxury,' the Kern smiled. 'And ale, Yssym? Shall there be ale?'

'Not ale,' the halfling replied, 'Drink *chrysse* ... You like, I think.'

Bracht chuckled and slapped him companionably on the shoulder. 'After that stinking swamp, my friend, I'd like anything.' His humour was restored by the prospect and he turned, smiling, to Katya. 'Food, do you hear? And something to drink; dry clothes. Could we ask for more?'

'I'd have others share those things,' she said, moodily.

Bracht fell into step beside her, studying her face, his own solicitous. 'Leave the dead behind,' he said gently. 'You've mourned them, but you cannot bring them back. Let them go - we go on, and our success shall be their monument.'

Katya glanced at him, dour for a moment, as though his pragmatism irked her, then her smile returned, broader as he grinned, and she ducked her head.

'I think I learn from you, Bracht of Cuan na'For. You are right - we go on to Tezin-dar.'

'If we pass whatever test the elders set us,' Calandryll murmured.

'We shall,' Bracht declared confidently. 'We must! We've come too far to fail now.'

His good humour was difficult to resist and Calandryll found himself grinning. Bracht was right - Reba's augury, Ellhyn's scrying, even Varent's treacherous machinations, all led them to this place; the mysterious Old Ones had sent Yssym to await their coming and now they were close: how could they fail? They would pass this test and go on to Tezin-dar; and if the Old Ones had anticipated their arrival, then surely they must give up the Arcanum to be destroyed - why else send watchers? He laughed, staring up at the sky no longer hung with moss and vines, but blue, bright as hope, the air, for all it carried a memory of the encircling swamp, clean. They would succeed! It was, now, only a matter of time.

They marched on, past fields and ponds, the sun sinking in the west, and came, as the disc touched the horizon, to Yssym's home.

*

A wall of tumbled stones, suggestive of ramparts, stood in their way, the road passing between the columns of a long-fallen arch, beyond lay a wide swathe of the bright grass and bushes heavy with brilliant blossoms, scarlet and azure and purple mingling in cheerful profusion, filling the air with pleasant perfumes that masked the odours of the swamp. On the far side of that garden stood buildings, ramshackle as the hide hunters' miserable settlement, but here blending with the surroundings in harmonious confusion, at one with the land. Calandryll guessed, from the outlines of the place, that some keep had once stood sentinel over the vale, its walls mostly collapsed now, though some still remained, hung with climbing vines, those thick with flowers, the buildings that replaced those once-great halls smaller, stone and wood and hides following the contours of the ruins, the floors streets now, those filling with halfling folk coming out to greet their visitors.

They were no less strange than Yssym, but his odd physiognomy was familiar now and consequently his people were less shocking to eyes grown accustomed to halfling form. And they seemed a gentle folk, staring shyly from doorways, holding children up to observe the newcomers - and they, Calandryll thought, likely as strange to these inhabitants of the deep swamp as the halflings had at first been to him. He smiled as they passed, following Yssym down a narrow street of sumptuous tiles towards a circular structure larger than the rest, a rotunda of wood and hides hung with gay blossoms, set at the centre of what had once been a vast courtyard.

Five halflings awaited them there. Old as best he could judge, their green-hued skin darker than Yssym's and seemingly drier, exhibiting a hint of wrinkles, their yellow eyes expressionless as they examined the visitors. They were dressed in long robes of white and crimson, and each held a tall staff of dark wood, tipped at both ends with silver. These, he decided, were the elders - the syfaba. Yssym halted before them, bowing his head, and spoke in his own language, gesturing at his companions.

The elders listened in silence, the other folk of that strange place gathering in a half-circle, some little distance off, all quiet, as if all were anxious to hear what news the watcher brought. When he was done the elders spoke, briefly, and Yssym bowed again, and turned to speak.

'I show you place to rest now ... Then you eat, sleep. Syfaba say you be strong for test ... Tomorrow you face test.'

Weary as he was, Calandryll would have rather undergone the trial immediately, but he bowed to the elders' decision, allowing Yssym to lead him away as the five aged halflings stood watching, their gaze impassive. The crowd parted to let the visitors through and Yssym brought them to a structure set between huge slabs of fallen stone, its roof a mass of flowering creepers, filling the interior with a pleasant scent, its floor an exotic mosaic of colourful tiles. A small fire, unnecessary but nonetheless welcome, burned in a pit at the centre, the smoke escaping through a hole in the arboreal roof, and cushions and fleeces were set about the walls.

'You sleep here,' Yssym explained. 'Come, I show you baths. Then you eat.'

They followed him through the village to what had once been a covered bath-house, its roof gone now, leaving the great tubs open to a sky transformed to velvet with the coming of night, the crescent of a new moon bright silver above, shining on the fresh water that spilled from channels in the wrecked walls. The women were directed to a pool modestly hidden from that to which the men were taken by a divide of stone and wicker. Rough soap and soft towels were set out in readiness, and soon the night was loud with their laughter as they luxuriated in the near-forgotten comfort of clean water, scrubbing industriously at sweaty skin and filthy hair.

Their clothing was taken as they bathed and when they emerged they found short robes and sandals left in place, dark blue for the men, white for the women. Their weapons, too, were gone, occasioning momentary alarm, until Yssym explained none in the village bore arms and that theirs were stored in the sleeping quarters. He took them then back to the central court, where fires burned, meat roasting on spits, and all the village gathered, men and women and children in a curious mass, eager to observe the strangers at close quarters.

They were given mugs of the drink Yssym called *chrysse*, a pale distillation akin to wine, but stronger, and platters of clay onto which the halflings piled generous helpings of meat and vegetables. After the poor fare of the past weeks it was a banquet, the better for the cheerful hospitality of their strange hosts, and they relaxed, grateful to be dry and able to eat without fear of dragons or insects or predatory fish. The halfling folk plied Yssym with questions, though Calandryll noticed that the elders, who sat across the circle, said nothing, merely listening, their yellow eyes intent on the strangers. This was perhaps, he thought, a part of the judging; but only a part: tomorrow they would face the test that, passed, should bring them to Tezin-dar.

For that reason, allied with the effects of the *chrysse* and a belly that felt filled for the first time in weeks, he was thankful when the elders rose and the gathering dispersed. Yssym and several others took torches, escorting the visitors to their quarters.

'Sleep now,' he advised them. 'Elders call you tomorrow.'

Calandryll nodded, yawning, and the halfling barked laughter. 'Better than island in swamp,' he said cheerfully. 'You sleep safe here.'

'Far better,' Calandryll agreed, aware that his eyes grew heavy. 'You've our thanks, Yssym.'

The halfling ducked his head and backed out, letting the hide curtain fall into place across the entrance. Calandryll yawned again, hugely, and found a place on the cushions as the rest composed themselves for sleep. Bracht went to the weapons laid out by the door, extricating his falchion.

'Shall you need that?' The cushions were mightily comfortable and Calandryll felt no desire to rise. 'Surely these folk intend us no harm.'

The freesword shrugged, tossing Calandryll's blade to him. 'I sleep the better for sharing my bed - with this if no softer company should offer.'

He grinned at Katya as he said it, and she blushed, prettily now that hair and face were clean, murmuring, 'You gave your word ... bring my own sword if you would.'

The Kern nodded, still smiling, and delivered her blade with a flourish.

'And that word I shall keep. Until Vanu is reached.'

She took the sword and set it on the tiles at her side. 'Until Vanu, Bracht.'

He sighed, shaking his head, and flung himself down, the sheathed falchion cradled in his arms. 'Oh, Calandryll,' he whispered, deliberately loud, 'know you that women can be harder than steel?'

Calandryll heard Katya chuckle and smiled into the shadows, seeking some witty response. None came, his thoughts too soon overtaken by sleep, and he found himself drifting in mellow darkness, dreamless.

He woke not certain where he was, confused by the absence of swamp stench and sound, no longer used to waking dry, on soft cushions. No insects buzzed about him nor dragons bellowed, and he experienced momentary alarm as he sat up, eyes opening on a chamber harlequin-patterned with the sunlight that filtered through the viny roof. Bracht was already awake, stroking a whetstone lovingly over the edges of his sword, and as he stirred Katya yawned and stretched. Outside he heard the sounds of the village, children rattling laughter and the sibilant language of the Syfalheen, he looked to Bracht, who shook his head in answer to the unspoken question.

'Yssym came early - it would appear the elders are in no great haste to judge us and await our rising.'

'I'd not delay,' Katya said. 'We've been too long in the swamp and still there's Tezin-dar to reach - whatever waits us there - and Tekkan must grow anxious.'

'Aye.' Calandryll smoothed his robe, wondering if he should belt on his sword; deciding against it. 'Do we go out to judgement?'

'I'd eat first,' Bracht said.

'And I'd bathe,' added Katya.

The other Vanu-folk woke as they talked, and together they went out into the village, finding Yssym squatting nearby, deep in conversation with the elders.

All rose as they approached, the elders no more communicative, only nodding greeting, saying nothing as Yssym asked, 'You eat now? Bathe?'

Bracht said, 'Eat,' and Katya, 'Bathe,' Calandryll asked when they should face the test.

'Soon,' said Yssym, 'Elders make ready ... First you bathe, eat ... then time for test.'

They went to the bath-house and then to the courtyard. It seemed all meals were taken communally, for halflings sat eating there and when the outlanders arrived they were given bowls of some sweetened porridge and clay mugs of a hot herbal infusion, loaves of something akin to bread, and wedges of sharp-tasting cheese. By day's light Calandryll could better make out the details of their surroundings, convinced now that the halfling village was built amongst the ruins of some vast, and vastly ancient, hold.

'The Old Ones built this?' he asked.

'Old Ones, yes,' Yssym answered. 'Long, long time gone. Old Ones build here.'

'When did they leave it?' He wondered how many ages had passed since the walls stood; and why they had fallen.

'Long, long ago.' Halfling and human concepts of time were different: Yssym's shoulders rose helplessly.

'How did it come to ruin?'

'Old Ones say the gods fight.' Yssym's webbed fingers shaped a design in the air. A warding gesture, Calandryll thought. 'All bad then ... Gods angry ... Father, Mother of gods angry ... They stop war ... but this fallen then.'

'He speaks of the war between Tharn and Balatur,' Katya whispered. Calandryll nodded agreement and asked, 'Did the Old Ones dwell here then?'

'Here, yes,' Yssym said. 'Other places, too ... Swamp not swamp then ... No dragons, no *grishas*; no *yennym* or *shivim* ... Gods make those when fight godwar. Old Ones here then ... after, too, but this fallen ... Old Ones say belong Syfalheen. They go to Tezin-dar ... Say Syfalheen not come there ... better Syfalheen not know men.'

'But they told you to watch.' Calandryll was intrigued. 'They told you men would come seeking the Arcanum - the book.'

'They tell Syfalheen watch for men,' Yssym nodded. 'Say one day men come for book ... Perhaps evil men; perhaps good. They say good be three, like you ... Show elders way to know. Say bring good men to Tezin-dar.'

'And the evil men?'

'They say test all ... If evil men not die in swamp, they die in test ... or die on road to Tezin-dar. Syfalheen guard Tezin-dar for Old Ones long time now.'

'Little wonder the city remains a legend.'

Calandryll spoke mostly to himself, bemused by the notion of such incredible antiquity. If Yssym's account was true, these ruins had stood when the gods fought; and man had dwelt here. Here and across Gessyth, by the Syfalheen's word. He touched the stone at his feet, staring round with reverent eyes: when this was done, when the Arcanum was destroyed, he would write all this down. By Dera's love, Reba had spoken true when she said he should travel far!

A movement across the yard disturbed his musings and he saw the elders come out from the rotunda, two standing to either side of the entrance, the fifth beckoning.

'Elders say you come now,' Yssym informed him. 'Three who go to Tezin-dar.'

Calandryll drained his mug as his mouth went dry and climbed to his feet. Bracht rose beside him, to his right; Katya stood on his left. The Vanu-folk moved to join them, and Katya waved them back, speaking in their own language. They remained standing as the trio followed Yssym across the yard to the waiting elders.

The ancient standing before the entrance spoke to Yssym and the halfling said, 'Elders take you now ... You obey them.'

He bowed and turned away. The foremost elder raised his staff, indicating the black opening of the door. Calandryll glanced at Bracht, at Katya; took one deep breath and stepped into the rotunda.

He was blind, lost in a darkness permeated with the pungency of incense, panic rising, with it the instinctive desire for the sword left in their sleeping quarters. He fought that trepidation, standing still as he heard the others enter, the rustle of the elders' long robes. A flint scraped and flame took hold on wick, the smell of incense growing stronger as pale gold light fluttered before him. It was a small flame, not strong enough to illumine the walls, barely sufficient to reveal the face that studied him across its feeble glow. He glanced sidelong, to left and right, finding Katya and Bracht, their features shadowed, elongated and planed flat, the woman's hair a glowing halo about her head. More substantial shadows moved along the walls and he saw the first elder joined by his companions, their staffs held out, horizontal across their chests. They formed a circle, shuffling softly closer until the silver tips of the staffs touched, surrounding the trio.

Calandryll smelled the fresh-washed scent of Katya's hair; heard Bracht's nervous breath; wondered if they could hear the pounding of his heart. He felt a staff against his back and stepped forwards as the elder facing him retreated and he was herded across the floor of the rotunda. The elders halted; lowered their staffs. They made a soft, musical clatter on the flagstones. One gestured and Calandryll saw an opening at his feet, smooth steps winding down into ultimate darkness. The elder gestured again and he swallowed, commencing the descent.

The flame faded behind. His hand touched cool stone, slick, curving. His eyes saw nothing: he felt Katya's hand on his shoulder; heard Bracht's muffled curse. Warily, he eased a foot forwards, finding the step's edge, the next, the one after that, the wall smooth beneath his nervous palm, his heartbeat a thunder against his ribs. The smell of incense receded, replaced with a musty odour. The stairway wound down, turning around an axis of stone, the walls crowding closer. He looked back and saw only blackness: he continued into the ancient bowels of the keep.

Flat stone was a shock that jarred his spine, Katya gasping as she fetched up hard against him. He heard Bracht say, 'Ahrd, where are we?' and moved forwards, allowing the Kern room.

Then pale light glowed silvery, a will-o'-the-wisp

suspended in the darkness at first, but growing, spreading until he saw that they stood in a chamber of solid rock, circular, walls and floor and roof merged. All around were niches cut into the stone, and in them bones, dull-gleaming in the light. More littered the floor, these ill-ordered and of more recent vintage, some still cased in tattered remnants of long-rotted clothing. At the centre, the light brightest above it, was a bier, a square slab of stone on which lay a body. It had belonged to a man, he saw, but one possessed of more years than any human man might claim. Hair yellowed by age spread over the shoulders and the nails of the hands crossed on the chest were long, curved like some bird's probing beak. The body wore a simple robe of rough blue cloth, belted with a cord of white. The feet were bare, those nails, too, grown long. He stared at the face, seeing a proud nose thinned by age, cheeks sunken by the years, the mouth thin-lipped above a beard that stretched to the belt.

He cried out as the eyes opened.

Katya made a sound half shout, half shriek; Bracht grunted a soft curse.

The body seemed to creak as it rose, as if the joints protested such movement, locked stiff by time. The hair rustled, like shifting spiders' webs; dust fell soundlessly from the robe. Calandryll found himself transfixed by the eyes. Once, he thought, they had been blue: now they were white, the milky stare of blindness, save that he knew, somehow, they focussed; saw him. He held his breath.

The body - the Old One, he guessed - sighed: a whisper, dry as dust. Painfully he - it - eased from the bier, swaying slightly, as if their breath alone threatened his fragile stability, rising to face them with the husks of long-dead insects dropping from robe and hair. The bloodless lips parted.

'I have awaited your coming.' The voice was a rattle,

like shaken bones. 'How long? Does Gess-ytha stand still.

Numbly, Calandryll realised the words came in the Old Tongue. He cleared his throat and said, 'Men name it Gessyth now,' in the same language. 'And it is swamp. The domain of the Syfalheen.'

'Ah,' sighed the Old One, 'so they dwell here still. That is good. And you - Why come you here to disturb my rest?'

'We seek the Arcanum,' Calandryll said. 'In Tezin-dar.'

Laughter like things crawling among the relics of the dead echoed softly.

'The Arcanum, eh? Why?'

'That it might be destroyed. We come to bring it out from Tezin-dar to Vanu, that the holy men there may destroy it.'

'The Arcanum is a thing of power - power corrupt. With the Arcanum the Mad God may be raised. Do you seek that end?'

'No!' Urgently. 'But one does - a mage named Rhythamun, though he goes by Varent now, and inhabits another's body - and he would return the Mad God to life.'

'Insanity!'

'Aye - insanity. And yet he would attempt it. He seeks the book to that end and we three would deny him. He sought to deceive us. To seduce me, Bracht,' he gestured instinctively at the Kern, 'to his purpose. Katya was sent from Vanu by the holy men of her folk, and warned us of his design. We stand together now.'

'Or fall if you lie. Name yourself and your companions.'

'I am Calandryll den Karynth, once of Secca in Lysse. With me stand Bracht of the clan Asyth, of Cuan na'For, and Katya of Vanu.'

'So - it has come to pass, just as we scried.' The milky orbs surveyed them each in turn. 'The three have come. Now come you to me, that I may judge you. But first be warned - are you false, you shall not leave this place! You shall rest here with those other deceivers who thought themselves the equal of our knowledge. That we guard jealously - as they learned.'

A withered hand indicated the confines of the chamber. Calandryll stared at the bones there; and knew other judgements had been passed.

'Judge us,' he said. 'You shall find us true.'

'Do you turn back now you go with your lives. Do you submit to this and I find you false, your fate lies here - your bones shall join these others.'

'We are not false,' he said. 'Judge us.'

'So be it.'

A long-taloned hand beckoned him forwards. He approached the ancient. The hands rose, cupping his face, the dead eyes peering deep into his: into his very soul, it seemed. No breath came from the parted lips, not even when the bone-white head ducked and the lips moved.

'I judge you true, Calandryll den Karynth. Let your companions approach.'

He motioned them forwards, aware that neither of them understood what had been said, watching as the Old One stared into Katya's eyes, into Bracht's, each in turn, and pronounced his formula of acceptance.

'So, it is done. You grant me rest at last, and I thank you for that solace. Go to the Syfalheen and they will bring to you Tezin-dar. The Arcanum rests there and the Guardians will know you. Take that cursed book and destroy it, with the blessing of Yl and Kyta.'

He waved them away. The silvery light began to fade. Bracht urged Katya to the stairs. Calandryll looked back as he reached the well, and gasped as he saw the ancient face fall in, the white robe collapsing, all become dust that swirled briefly in the dying light, drifting on the still air.

Then there was only darkness through which they climbed, back to the dim light of the rotunda and the waiting elders.

NINETEEN

WELCOME daylight illumined the entrance of the rotunda as they emerged from the crypt. The elders stood waiting, greeting them now in the sibilant language of the Syfalheen, touching them each upon the right shoulder as if in blessing, their yellow eyes no longer impassive but glowing with approbation, leading them triumphantly out to the courtyard. All the village stood there, a shout rising as they appeared, Yssym and the anxious Vanu-folk crowding forwards, plying them with questions. Calandryll reported the Old One's words to his comrades and left Katya to pass that knowledge on to her people, himself intent on questioning Yssym.

'We are not the first,' he said as he was brought across the yard, a mug of *chrysse* pressed into his hand.

Yssym's head turned solemnly. 'You not first ... Others come, false ones who not come out ... Old Ones judge and false ones stay with Old Ones.' He barked with laughter. 'But you not false and Yssym have honour now ... Watcher who bring True Ones.'

Calandryll nodded, wondering what manner of death

befell such false questors. He asked, 'Have you seen the crypt? The Old One?'

'Only elders see Old One,' Yssym replied. 'Guard his resting place ... Seal it now.'

'He said you - the Syfalheen - would bring us to Tezin-dar. That the Guardians will bring us to the Arcanum.'

'We show you way,' Yssym confirmed. 'Syfalheen not enter Tezin-dar, but you go there.'

'And these Guardians?' Bracht settled beside them. 'Are they Old Ones, or something else?'

'Yssym not know,' said the halfling. 'Elders not know. Syfalheen not go to Tezin-dar ... Forbidden.'

'They must be Old Ones,' Calandryll murmured. 'But, Dera! How old?'

'How shall you bring us to the city if you are forbidden there?' asked Bracht, pragmatic as ever.

'Show you road,' Yssym promised. 'Safe way ... You go, no harm come ... Road safe for you.'

'When?' Bracht demanded.

'Dawn,' said Yssym, 'This day we feast ... You True Ones ... Syfalheen wait long time for you.'

They were allowed no other choice: preparations for the promised feast were already underway. The fires that had cooked their breakfast - and that likely their last meal had the Old One judged them false - were banked and meat set to turning on the spits. Loaves were baked, and their mugs filled and re-filled with *chrysse* until, laughing, they protested they should be too drunk to travel farther than their beds did the Syfalheen not moderate their hospitality. Small harps and flutes of bone were produced and the villagers began to sing, strange melodies and likely, Calandryll thought, not heard by human ears in long ages.

'I had not thought to be preceded,' he remarked as the feast progressed.

'The bones?' Bracht shrugged, wiping grease from his

chin. 'So powerful a thing as the Arcanum is likely known to others than Varent-Rhythamun.'

'They were old,' Katya offered. Then frowned: 'Though so is he, and he has long sought it.'

'He made no mention of other questors,' Calandryll said. 'Though he spoke of guardians.'

'Perhaps he forebore to warn us,' suggested Bracht. 'From the start he was a deceiver.'

'Likely,' Calandryll agreed after a moment's thought, 'and likely that is why he did not come here himself - he knew he must fail the Old One's judgement.'

'Aye - and knowing he must fail, he sought dupes.' Bracht chuckled cynical laughter. 'Innocents who might pass the test and bring the book from Tezin-dar into his waiting hands. Well, that shall not be!'

'But,' Calandryll frowned, 'the Old One spoke of three - three seen in their scrying - and Varent sent but we two. He could not know that Katya should join us.'

'Perhaps he did not know of that augury,' Bracht said, smiling his thanks as a halfling woman piled more meat on his plate. 'He is not infallible.'

'The gods work in mysterious ways,' Katya murmured, 'and it seems to me there is a pattern, a balancing. The Old Ones foresaw that there should come a time when the Arcanum must be destroyed and set these obstacles in the way of such as Rhythamun - likely they would not make such knowledge public, lest such as he find a way to the book.'

Bracht nodded and said, 'Certainly their plan was set long ages past - and more skilfully, it seems, than his.'

'Aye,' Calandryll allowed, 'but even so we've yet to bring the book to Vanu.'

'We shall,' said Bracht, supping *chrysse*, 'We have safe passage now - we bring the book out of Tezin-dar, Yssym guides us back and Tekkan brings us to Vanu. We cannot fail.'

'We *must* not fail,' Katya said.

'No,' Calandryll smiled, although a doubt still lingered in the hindermost recesses of his mind.

He pushed it back, listening to the strange Syfalheen song, the voices rising bird-like, in unison, then individual singers taking a verse, sometimes the whole village joining in.

'They sing of you,' Yssym informed him. 'The song is very old ... Not sung until now because True Ones not come until now ... Syfalheen happy now ... Listen, they sing of Watcher now ... of me.'

Had his piscine features been capable of human expression, Calandryll felt sure he beamed proudly. He set a hand to the halfling's shoulder, smiling, and said, 'You have our thanks, Yssym.'

Yssym ducked his head, setting his own webbed hand on Calandryll's. 'You True Ones,' he said. 'Syfalheen promise Old Ones we bring you to Tezin-dar when you come ... This good day.'

'And a better when we've the book,' said Calandryll.

'Tomorrow,' Yssym promised. 'Tomorrow you take road ... Tezin-dar at end ... Old Ones await you there.'

The festivities continued throughout the day, more than one of the Vanu-folk succumbing to the deceptive smoothness of the *chrysse*, though the three who were to go on limited themselves, unwilling to face the road to Tezin-dar sore-headed. Torches were lit as darkness fell and it seemed the Syfalheen were bent on celebrating through the night, for their music could still be heard as Calandryll, with Bracht and Katya, returned to their quarters. They found their own clothes set out there, beside their weapons, and as the rising sun shone through the interlaced vines of the roof, they dressed, buckling on their swords.

Outside, they found the village re-assembled, Yssym waiting with the elders by the rotunda. They broke their fast, though after the excesses of the previous night few had much appetite, and they were soon ready to depart.

Katya bade farewell to her people, and each of them came to Calandryll and Bracht, clasping their hands and speaking in the Vanu tongue. 'They wish you well,' Katya translated, 'and say they will await us here.'

Yssym handed them each a pack containing food, and a canteen of fresh water. 'I not go farther,' he said. 'Elders take you to road ... You follow ... Not go off road! ... Road safe.'

They took his hand and turned to follow the elders, the village forming two lines between which they walked, the Syfalheen calling their own farewells, those fading slowly behind them as they passed out of the confines of the yard into the garden-like fields beyond, the elders marching in their customary silence.

Their way went due north, the sun still low on their right, shining out of a sky empty of all cloud and bright as polished steel. For all their vulnerability, the syfaba maintained a steady pace, the silver tips of their staffs clicking busily on the ancient stone of the roadway so that it was little time before they came to the tumbled walls defining the perimeter of the village. They passed beneath another arch, this still standing, a great curve of weathered blocks hanging black against the sky, deep holes on the inward faces showing where hinges had torn loose. A cistern was dug nearby and Calandryll saw that the ancient gates formed its roof, two huge metal slabs, each thick as a man's waist, unmarked by time. He wondered what force had thrust them in, and thought that some day he should return to this strange haven of tranquility and write down the history of Yssym's people.

Some day - on this more pressing urgencies called him on.

Past the arch were orchards and fields and more of the strange beasts, that watched placidly as the travellers strode purposefully by, the road arrow-straight. Had Orwen come this way, he wondered, taking the chart from his satchel as he walked. The map showed only swamp here, and he wondered if the Syfalheen had guided the chartist around their village, or whether he had come to Tezin-dar by a different route. He realised that an elder had slowed, matching pace and staring at the map.

'Ah-when,' said the halfling, and barked brief laughter, gesturing for Calandryll to refold the chart, then pointing ahead, saying, 'Tezin-dar ... Tezin-dar.'

'The map amuses them,' murmured Bracht as the elder rejoined his fellows, speaking low, his words met with further laughter.

'They know Orwen's name,' Calandryll said. 'But why did he laugh?'

No answer was forthcoming and they continued after the syfaba, who showed no sign of halting, even when the sun stood overhead, as though, the ones they had so long awaited arrived, they sought now to dispense their promise as swiftly as they might.

Indeed, they did not slow their brisk pace until late in the afternoon, when the ridge of the dyke surrounding the Syfalheen's haven bulked from the land ahead. The road ended there, spanned by the mound of earth, the ancient flagstones disappearing beneath the more recent structure, the smell of the swamp wafting on the breeze. The elders gathered up the skirts of their robes and proceeded to climb the dyke wall, beckoning Calandryll and his companions after.

They reached the summit and halted. Before them lay a wide expanse of reeds, brackish water visible amongst the thick strands, and no sign of a path; beyond the reeds, hazed by distance, stood a grey line of mangroves. Calandryll frowned, confused. Bracht said, 'Ahrd! Yssym promised us a road to Tezin-dar.'

'Tezin-dar!' The elder who had spoken before

touched Calandryll's sleeve, nodding enthusiastically. 'Tezin-dar!'

He pointed with his staff to the outer foot of the dyke, shadowed now by the lowering sun. Calandryll stared, searching the reed beds for sign of the road; finding none.

The elders began to descend the dyke, scrambling unceremoniously down the steep side until they stood amongst the reeds, the hems of their robes darkened by the water there. The three joined them. The wall of earth curved here, turning to run more north than west, and consequently in deep shadow.

'Something stands there.' Katya pointed, eyes narrowed as she peered towards the rampart. 'I cannot make it out.'

'Whatever, they've not brought us to any road,' grunted Bracht, a hint of suspicion in his voice now, hand touching instinctively to the falchion's hilt. 'Do they intend to send us back into the swamps, guide-less?'

'I think not,' Calandryll said. 'Look.'

The elders waded resolutely towards the pool of darkness Katya had indicated, thrusting through the reeds, their bare feet making soft sucking sounds in the spongy ground. They halted, waving the others onwards: Calandryll moved to join them, Bracht and Katya close behind.

The elders were formed in a semi-circle before the darkest patch of shadow, staring with an odd reverence into the gloom there. Calandryll looked past them and saw a shallow cave, the shape of ancient stones dim within the recess. There were three, he saw, thick basalt pillars standing upright, a lintel stone across them, all mounded round with soil, the wall of the dyke a grey-ness beyond: a blank-faced barrier leading nowhere.

'Do they show us some monument?' asked Bracht.

'Or the way?' Katya wondered.

'I see no road,' the Kern returned.

'Perhaps this is it,' she said, 'a magical road.'

'How so?' Bracht demanded. 'Even be it a portal, it faces the wrong way.'

'How better to conceal it?' asked Calandryll, turning to the elders, brows raised in silent question.

The Syfalheen parted then, two to one side, two to the other, the fifth beckoning them forwards, pointing with his staff to the monument, indicating that they should approach. Calandryll glanced at his companions, shrugged, and stepped forwards.

The elder raised a hand, halting him, gesturing for Bracht and Katya to stand level. Bracht stepped to his right, Katya to his left; the elders moved closer, clasping them each upon the shoulder, as they had done when they emerged from the crypt. Then the five syfaba each turned towards the stones, lifting their staffs high as they commenced a singsong chanting, low at first but rising in pitch and volume as the setting sun painted the sky red and the upper level of the dyke was briefly illumined, fiery. Calandryll heard an answering hum and cocked his head, at first not sure from where it came: realising that the stones themselves sung. He saw light flicker inside the portal; for an instant thought he saw a wide, gold-flagged road stretching away between stately trees, the hint of proud city walls all gold and silver and crimson. Then the staffs pressed upon their backs, urging them forwards. The light died, leaving a darkness solid as the earth. The staffs pressed harder: he took another step; heard Bracht grunt as soil touched his outflung hands, damp and swamp-scented, the air vibrating.

Then the pressure was gone, both that of the staffs against his back and that of the earth upon his face. There was a moment of - he was not sure what: cold, certainly, intense, striking bone deep so that it seemed the very marrow cringed; or falling, as if he dropped through unimaginable distance in a darkness that was simultaneously impenetrable and lit with the swirling lights of a million stars; of unbeing. He thought his lungs must burst for want of air, and then he breathed again, and stood on solid ground, gasping. For all his experience of magic he was still hard put to believe the evidence of his eyes.

He stood upon a road of smooth stone slabs, lit golden by a sun that no longer westered to its setting but hung only a little way above the eastern horizon, a new day replacing the old. Wide as to permit two broad wagons to pass abreast, with space between for walkers, was that road, though no ruts gave evidence of such traffic, the slabs pristine, set so close and dressed so skilfully their joining was such that a hair might not have passed between them. It ran level and straight to the north, if such direction had meaning here, that horizon mist-shrouded, the air there sparkling as if sun shone on droplets of moisture, to either side the swamp, an expanse of reeds and pools of brown water, stirred by a gentle breeze so that the rustling was a soft song of welcome. He turned, seeing Bracht and Katya staring about with awe-struck eyes, and found he faced a dyke - or that he had just gone through, he was no longer sure - grey-walled, the stones within it, dark entrance to the earth. Of the elders there was no sign; nor of the Syfalheen fields.

'I believe,' he said slowly, his voice soft with wonder, 'that we are on the road to Tezin-dar.'

Katya said, 'Little wonder that city is a legend.'

Bracht shouldered his pack and nodded: 'So, let us go on.'

They began to march.

Time and distance were different here, subject to different laws it seemed, for the sun remained stationary above them even when the muscles of their legs told them they had walked long enough that evening should have fallen, whilst the mist-shrouded horizon was no closer and when Calandryll looked back, the dyke and the stones were no longer visible, lost behind a curtain of the same sparkling fog as lay before them. It was an eerie sensation, as if they traversed some limbo, doomed to march forever beneath the unrelenting sun, trapped between that place they had left and that they hoped to gain, the road a mandala looping eternally back on itself amongst the unchanging reed beds.

It was quiet, the only sounds the rustling of the wind and the steady drumming of their boots. There were no insects, nor any birds, no sign of dragons or other predators. No odour rose from the reed beds, nor did clouds disturb the impassive sky: in time such absences grew oppressive, weighing down on them so that, despite being three and sworn to their purpose, they felt lonely, forsaken. And yet, Calandryll told himself, Tezin-dar lay ahead. It must, for they had passed the judgement of the Old One and the syfaba had brought them to the gate. Perhaps, then, this was a further testing, a design intended to deter the faint-hearted and send them back, scuttling for the safety of that passage through the stones to a more familiar world.

And as he thought it - as if in confirmation - a building showed ahead.

It had not, he was certain, been there moments before, unless distance was distorted beyond comprehension in this odd landscape. He looked to his companions, frowning.

'Nor did I see it,' Bracht said, 'but there it is.'

'And hopefully offering rest,' said Katya. 'I grow weary of this interminable march.'

'Perhaps,' the Kern chuckled, 'it has a stable, and three horses waiting for us. Ahrd, but what I'd give for a good horse now.'

'Perhaps it marks the boundaries of Tezin-dar,' said Calandryll.

Bracht grinned and said, 'We shall know soon enough - we've no other place to go save back.'

They strode towards the building, its outlines growing more distinct as they approached.

It appeared a single massive slab of rose-tinted stone, spanning the road like some overlarge gatehouse, its roof flat, a door facing them with windows to either side, those faced with some glass-like substance that glittered in the sun, tricking sight to deny examination of the interior. The door was metal, a single sheet, silvery and black at the same time, its hinges, hidden. There was no indication of latch or handle or any other means by which it might be opened. Calandryll set a hand to the thing and pushed.

The door swung silently inwards, revealing a hall whose interior dimensions contradicted the external. The floor was a geometric patterning of blue and white, the walls unadorned save by the veining of the marble that faced them, the ceiling vaulted, smooth and blue. A second door and two windows stood in the farther wall, and to either side were two more doors. Calandryll entered, followed by Bracht and Katya. The door swung shut behind them, and when Bracht tried it, it refused to open again.

'It would appear,' he murmured, 'that there is no turning back.'

'Would you now?' asked Katya.

'No,' he said, 'though I'd lief know I might.'

'Too late,' Calandryll said, and crossed the empty chamber to peer out the farther windows.

He saw swampland beyond, no longer the reed beds but a gloomy vista of mangroves, all hung with insect-crawling moss and trailing vines, the livid tentacles of the flesh-consuming growths wavering amongst them. Night had fallen there, though a backwards glance told him that day still ruled where they had come from, and he saw the road continuing on through the trees, lapped by moonlit water in which the shapes of dragons moved. The door between these windows had a great ring of silver metal set to one side, and when he tested it, the door came readily open, admitting a sour gust of swamp-stinking air. He pushed it shut and turned to his companions.

'Night rules out there and I think we had best spend it here.'

'Amen to that,' Bracht agreed. 'Perhaps this place has beds to offer.'

'Safety, at least,' said Katya, joining Calandryll by the windows, 'I've seen no dragons so large as those.'

'Yssym said the road was safe,' Calandryll offered. 'We must hope he spoke the truth.'

'Tomorrow's worries,' said Bracht. 'Come - I'd see what other wonders we may find.'

Unwilling to separate, they set to investigating their strange refuge.

One door - this with latches - granted ingress to a corridor off which were revealed sleeping quarters: three chambers with open, arched entrances, a bed in each, laid with fresh linen, and windows that, when Calandryll peered out, afforded view over a landscape of undulating meadows and copses, a stream winding moonlit between. It reminded him of the countryside about Secca for all he knew it must be the product of magic, and he said as much.

'I see the plains of Cuan na'For,' Bracht said, and whooped excitement. 'Look! Do you see those horses?'

'I see the hills of Vanu,' said Katya, wistfully. 'I see the peaks all capped with snow and the rivers tumbling down.'

'We see what the Old Ones wish to show us, I think' Calandryll suggested. 'We stand in a magical place and I think they seek to welcome us.'

'With food, I hope,' Bracht said, turning almost reluctantly from the window.

'And baths, perhaps,' Katya added. 'Shall we find out?'

They left the sleeping chambers and crossed the hall to the second door. This led them to a bath-house, where a pool steamed, another filled with cool water, and marble benches bore soap and towels; beyond was a dining chamber, windowless, but softly lit by candles, containing a circular table and three chairs, the table set with a meal, and wine, three crystal goblets.

'Three and three and three,' Bracht murmured, 'And yet no sign of servants, nor any other folk.'

'We are expected,' said Katya.

'Long expected,' said Calandryll.

'And hungry,' said Bracht. 'Let us eat.'

They dropped their packs and loosed their sword-belts, though those they put close to hand, settling themselves about the table. Bracht poured out a little wine and sniffed it, suspiciously; sipped a little, no less cautiously. 'It appears untainted,' he declared.

'Do you think to find it poisoned?' Calandryll grinned. 'I doubt whoever built such a place as this need stoop to such subterfuge.'

'Likely not,' the freesword admitted, and helped himself to meat and bread, the both somehow warm, as if fresh from the oven.

'I think this must be some manner of waystation,' Katya suggested, 'and marks a boundary of some kind.'

'It surely marks the boundary of night and day,' Calandryll agreed, 'and whoever travels the road must enter here or turn back. And once entered, it would appear impossible to turn back.'

'At least the builders send us onwards with full stomachs,' Bracht said, 'for which I thank them.'

He raised his goblet in a toast, and the others, laughing, joined him.

'To the Old Ones.'

'To a safe return.'

'To the destruction of the Arcanum.'

Calandryll was not sure, but it seemed the candles burned a little brighter then and he thought he heard a murmur of soft, approving laughter, as if the place itself voiced support of their quest. Certainly he experienced a sense of well-being, a satisfaction at having come thus far and excitement at the nearing culmination of their journey. Or rather, he told himself, its first part, for they must still bring the Arcanum back to the waiting Tekkan and sail for Vanu. But that now seemed the lesser burden, the hardest part near done with the legendary city within reach along that strange road. He sighed contentedly, and the sigh became a yawn: he pushed his plate away, replete, and announced his intention of retiring.

'Aye,' said Bracht, 'For all I've no inkling how far we walked today, I'd find my bed.'

Katya nodded agreement and they went back across the hall to the sleeping chambers. Calandryll had thought some small friction might arise then, if Bracht pursued his suit with the woman, but the Kern merely bade her a polite good night and entered his own quarters. Calandryll wondered if Katya's face registered disappointment. He went to his own bed, leaning for a moment on the sill to stare out through the window, once again seeing the familiar landscape, though now, beyond the woodland he thought he discerned the ramparts of a city, like white-walled Secca seen from afar. He was pleased that he felt no melancholy, no nostalgia for his lost home, and stripped off his clothing, climbing gratefully between the cool sheets.

Sunlight woke him and he rose to find the vista unchanged, save that it was now day and the city walls clear. He hid his nakedness beneath a sheet and went to the bath-house, where Bracht already splashed, busily scrubbing.

'I saw horses again,' the Kern remarked, 'a herd of the finest beasts.'

'And I Secca,' he returned, 'At least it seemed it was Secca.'

'Do you miss your home?'

'No,' he said. 'Do you?'

'A little - aye,' Bracht nodded; then grinned, 'But then I think of our quest - and Katya - and I am compensated.'

'Where is she?'

'Abed still,' Bracht said. 'I advised her to sleep on, for modesty's sake.'

'You become the gentleman.'

Bracht laughed hugely. 'A woman's influence,' he declared, and climbed from the pool to plunge headlong into the cold water. Calandryll joined him and they towelled themselves dry, going back to the sleeping chambers to inform Katya that she might bathe without embarrassment as they dressed.

All three refreshed and kitted ready to proceed, they went to the dining chamber: the debris of the last night's meal was gone, replaced with hot bread, a bowl of fruit, cuts of cold meat and three mugs of tisane.

'I also become less apprehensive of magic,' Bracht smiled, 'when it provides fare such as this.'

'Also?' asked Katya, curious.

'Calandryll remarked that I become a gentleman,' Bracht explained. 'I told him that is your good influence.' Katya's tan cheeks darkened a little at that and she busied herself cutting bread.

'Were you ever else?'

'Oh, yes,' said the Kern solemnly, blue eyes fixed on her face. 'I was much else.'

'And I would be elsewhere,' said Calandryll, 'Such as the road to Tezin-dar.'

'Aye,' Bracht nodded, smiling again. 'Do you but finish, Katya, and we'll depart.'

*

Before they quit that odd hostel Calandryll went to the windows looking back down the way they had come. Night reigned there now, the reeds silver under a full moon, the road a golden ribbon running out into blackness. He turned to the second door and dragged it open on day's light, the air instantly hot, steamy with swamp-stink, a massive dragon rising to bellow a challenge that started him back, hand on sword. Bracht was at his side on the instant, falchion drawn, and Katya close behind, her sabre raised defensively.

'I doubt,' Bracht shouted over the dragon's roaring, 'that swords will have much effect on that.'

Calandryll paused within the shelter of the door, staring at the beast. It dwarfed all he had seen, rising up on tree-trunk legs, towering over the road, its red hide glistening, hung with streamers of slime. The jaws were spread wide, lined with fangs more sword than dagger-like, its foetid breath gusting noisome in his face as the great tail lashed furiously, stirring the surface of the water to reeking foam.

'We must pass it,' said Katya, anxiously. 'Though how, I know not.'

'Yssym said the road was safe.' Calandryll returned his blade to the scabbard, pointing. 'And see, it does not touch the road.'

'It need not,' said Bracht. 'It need only reach down to swallow us all, whole.'

'I think not,' Calandryll said. And stepped out, onto the road.

He heard Bracht shout, 'No!' and evaded the Kern's clutching hand, striding defiantly towards the monster. It stared at him from jade green eyes, implacable, still roaring its challenge. A second, no smaller lifted from the swamp, and then a third, all lining the way he sought to pass with cavernous jaws, menacing fangs. He sensed, rather than heard, the steps behind him and glanced backwards over his shoulder to find Bracht and Katya advancing fast with swords still drawn.

'Ahrd grant you right,' the Kern muttered.

Calandryll saw the door that was their only refuge close unbidden, like its mate devoid of means to open once passed through.

'Shall you use the stone?' asked Bracht.

Calandryll had all but forgotten the red stone still hung about his neck and shrugged, not knowing how to utilise that power; nor thinking that it would be needed: Yssym had said the road was safe so long as they remained upon it. 'Have faith,' he urged.

Bracht's reply was lost beneath the dragons' thunder. Calandryll walked on.

Foul breath rendered the already unfresh air noxious. His head dinned with the roaring; he saw the jaws spread wide, lunging towards him, then halt as if some barrier, invisible, interposed between swamp and road's edge. The great fangs clattered together, snapping closed on nothing. Blunt noses probed. The tails lashed angrily, churning waves of swamp water that he saw did not - could not! - reach the road. That remained dry, the flags untouched, stretching onwards between the trees that closed above, hiding the sky. Still he could not help but quicken his pace as he passed beneath the dragons. He sought to walk leisurely, but for all his belief, near-panic gripped his limbs and he began to trot, looking nervously about as the beasts bellowed and struggled uselessly to reach him. Then he was amongst the trees and the dragons too large to venture there, their own massive bulk denying them access: he halted, panting and laughing, together.

'Have faith,' he repeated, 'Yssym spoke true.'

Bracht and Katya sheathed their blades, their faces both pale. 'It calls for faith to risk those,' the Kern said hoarsely. He looked back to where the dragons stood, grumbling like distant thunder, jaws snapping irritably.

'Faith or madness. Ahrd! One wrong-placed step ...'

'I suspect this road is safe passage and test, both,' Calandryll said. 'On it, we cannot be harmed; but do we allow these creatures to panic us ... as you say - one wrong-placed step.'

'Are they then the creations of magic?' wondered Katya. 'Or living beasts?'

'Those jaws look real enough to me,' Bracht grunted. 'But wait - I'll put it to the test.'

He rummaged in his pack, bringing out a piece of dried meat that he flung out over the swamp. A dragon turned its head, attracted by the movement, snout darting towards the morsel, that disappearing between the jaws. 'I vouch them real,' he declared.

'Then is all this real?' Katya gestured at the looming mangroves. 'Do we traverse Gessyth? And if we do, might this road not be found by means other than the gate?'

'Those dragons have substance,' Bracht said, 'and teeth, and so I deem this Gessyth. As for the road - I know not.'

'I think we cross Gessyth,' Calandryll suggested, 'but by some way found only through the gate - and that entered only with the aid of the Syfaba, who in turn show only those judged true by the Old One. I think we pass along some magical dimension.'

'Or stand idling,' said Bracht. 'How far, think you, to Tezin-dar?'

Calandryll fetched out the map, kneeling to spread it on the smooth, dry stone of the road, remembering the elders' laughter. 'I think,' he said, touching the parchment, 'that the Syfalheen village stood here. A day's march would bring us here.' His finger tapped an area designated by Orwen "dyre swampe, where monstyres be an alle manner of foule creationnes moste peryllousse to menne". 'Tezin-dar is here.'

Bracht looked to where he indicated and grunted.

'Winter will be on us ere we walk that far.'

'Save that we tread a magical path,' Calandryll replied, 'which I believe will bring us to the city swifter than we know.'

'Grant that you guess it aright,' said the Kern.

'In time we shall know,' he nodded, folding the map.

They went on, down a tunnel overhung with moss-draped limbs, the light become an insubstantial haze of blueish-green, the water that boundaried the road black, the trees huge columns of grey. The lesser menaces of the swamp were here, like the dragons, magnified: they saw *grishas* large as a man's hand scuttling over the moss, and *yennym* like serpents writhing amongst the spider-legged roots, great shoals of *shivim* rippled the water and where the lovely, deadly flowers of the *feshyn* bloomed, they were the size of platters. But none breached the safety of the road and the three strode on, holding to the centre, marching steadily until hunger called a halt.

They partook of the food the Syfalheen had provided and rested a while before continuing, still amongst the mangroves, still traversing a tunnel that denied sight of the sky, the sun lost and all sense of time with it so that they could judge the hour only by the weariness that assailed their limbs and the growing pangs of hunger in their bellies. Calandryll had hoped to encounter another hostel before they were forced to halt, but of such refuge there was no sign and they finally succumbed to aching muscles, settling at the road's centre to eat and sleep.

There was no indication that night harboured intention of falling, the blue-green haze remaining constant, a depressing twilight poised, eternally it seemed, between night and day, the air busy with the sounds of the giant insects, the tide-like rippling of the predator fish and the far-off bellowing of dragons. Near exhaustion granted them respite from that clamour, but still they woke more than a little stiff, and less rested than before, rising to massage knotted muscles before starting off again through the trees.

They could tell no better here than before how long they marched, allowing their bodies to dictate their halts and counting it a day between waking and sleeping for want of better calendar. By that reckoning it was five days before they came to the second building.

Like its predecessor this stood across the road as though a single block of stone were set in their way, and it possessed the same impossible dimensions, larger within than without. They entered with no hesitation to find themselves in the twin of the first refuge, crossing immediately to the farther windows to inspect the path ahead. They saw a water meadow filled with lilies and dragons spread out as far as their eyes could see, the road a fragile-seeming ribbon of stone still straight across the water, lit red-gold by a sun that fell towards its setting.

'What time has passed?' Calandryll wondered aloud. 'The sun was new-risen when we came on the road and sets now - a day? No more than that?'

'My legs claim longer,' Bracht murmured.

'You said it yourself - we traverse the dimensions of magic,' Katya said. 'Though the dirt I feel is real enough - I'm to the bath-house.'

She left them to explore, finding all as before, and when they, too, had rid themselves of the sweaty detritus of their journey they ate, and drank good wine before retiring, thankful for beds softer than the unyielding stone of the road.

When they awoke they found their clothing miraculously clean and food once again set out. They broke their fast and filled their canteens, then started across the enormous lily meadow, no longer concerned with the dragons that roared all about, but pressing hard onwards, the sun at their left shoulder, agog to know if its imminent descent into night should mark the ending of their journey, or merely the dying of the magical day: the prospect of a night so long was daunting. Time, or distance, or perhaps both, contracted now: it seemed they walked but a single day, though the sun did not shift, before they came to a third marker.

No hostel this, but a dolmen of black stone, two upright pillars rising massy from the fabric of the road, supporting a great cross-member, the passage between narrow, barely so wide as to allow the three to pass together. Beyond that portal was darkness, an absence of light so total it seemed solid. They halted, wary of that negation.

There was, however, no way around the monument, nor, when Calandryll retraced his steps to peer past the obstacle, further sign of the road. It ended there, beyond the dolmen only the lily meadow and the dragons.

'There is no other way,' he said, studying the great black pillars dubiously. 'This must be a second gate.'

'The elders sang us through the first,' said Bracht. 'Shall we pass unscathed without their aid?'

'We must,' Katya said, 'or turn back.'

Bracht's face assumed a pained expression as he shook his head, vigorously. 'Ahrd, no! No more walking, I beg you.'

Katya laughed and said, 'Then onwards - to Tezin-dar, I hope.'

'Aye,' Calandryll declared, 'To Tezin-dar and the Arcanum.'

He moved to Katya's right, Bracht to her left, and together they stepped into the void between the stones.

Dark so cold it cut like knives of ice; and cold so dark it leached breath. Falling: a soft missile flung through eternity. To crash on the hard stone of reality?

Or some softer landing?

Grass?

Aye, sweet-scented grass, and small flowers, their petals a delicate white, veined through with purple, crushed beneath boots translucent with rime of ice that melted, glowing, in the warmth of a new sun suspended in a sky of purest azure, ribboned with pennants of white cloud. Birdsong, and the lazy buzz of pollen-weighted bees, the chirrup of crickets. Calandryll looked about, mouth open, words lost in wonder. Surely not Gessyth? Not reeking, swamp-filled Gessyth, this fabulous place.

He rose from the grass where he had fallen, seeing his companions no less amazed as they, like he, looked on the meadow that surrounded them, the dolmen standing stark behind, a bleak monument in that green sward all decked with little blossoms. His head swung, eyes blinking at the vision that flickered in and out of sight, like a fragmented dream. He saw the spires of a great city, stately and tall, unwalled, serene; and tumbled ruins, the towers bare-ribbed and fallen, the halls rendered down into rubble that spilled over wide avenues filled with laughing, handsome folk; or empty, the stones grave markers of forgotten splendour.

He sighed and shook his head and the vision faltered, shimmering like sunlit water rippled by a breeze or a pebble thrown. It faded, dreamy as evaporating mist, and was gone, in its place that other vision, less welcome but more real: across the meadow - that, at least, corporeal - stood the ruins of Tezin-dar.

It must be Tezin-dar, he told himself, and sighed afresh, for this place was ancient and wrecked, and held no sign of Old Ones; or of men, or Syfalheen, or any other folk. And yet, he wondered as he stared in silence at the fallen walls of once-great halls, the shattered bulk of spires, the road had brought them here; the Old One, back in the village of the Syfalheen, had sent them here;

the syfaba had directed them down that long path to this place: it must be Tezin-dar, and somewhere within its jumbled confusion must be the Arcanum.

'I thought I saw,' he heard Katya whisper, her grey eyes wide, wondering, 'I thought I saw ...'

'What was?' he asked, no louder. 'The city that was once and is no more?'

She nodded, speechless.

'Yssym said the Old Ones dwell here still,' said Bracht, 'yet this is but a ruin ... For all I saw folk parade its streets.'

'Naught but stones,' Katya said sadly.

'We saw a memory, I think,' said Calandryll. 'The Tezin-dar that once stood here, before the gods fell to war.'

'And the Old Ones?' Bracht asked. 'Those who shall bring us to the Arcanum - where are they?'

'Yssym also said the city is forbidden the Syfalheen,' Calandryll murmured, 'and none have seen the Old Ones.'

'Then must we search all this?' Bracht's hand flung out to encompass the dead city. 'Ahrd, we might spend a lifetime at that task!'

'Varent said the stone would guide me,' Calandryll reminded, touching his pendant at his throat. 'That it would lead me to the Arcanum.'

'And Varent said the walls stood still,' Bracht retorted, 'and believed Orwen's map would guide us here - and he was wrong.'

'It must be here,' Katya said, 'and we must find it.'

'In all of that?' Bracht gestured again at the ruined city. 'Save that in this one thing Varent did not lie, we have no hope.'

Katya's eyes grew stormy then, and she clenched her fists so that the Kern raised protesting hands and smiled an apology for his scepticism, saying, 'I had not thought to put my trust in Varent, but so be it - fetch out your magic stone, Calandryll, and let us begin.'

Calandryll nodded, bringing the stone out from beneath his shirt. It hung lifeless upon his chest, no sorcerous fire shining, nor scent of almonds to alert his nostrils to wizardry.

'Likely we must come closer,' he said, cautiously.

'Then come,' Bracht answered, starting towards the ruins.

They drew nearer, finding the grass-grown memory of an avenue leading to a shattered arch, the sundered remnants of the outer buildings beyond, all driven in as if catapults, or thunderbolts, had struck against the walls, stones fused and run in glistening snail-tracks, melted by unimaginable powers. They skirted a barricade of jagged blocks and climbed another, finding themselves in a plaza where once a fountain had stood, now a crack-lipped pit awash with sour water on which green algae floated. About the plaza stood walls like broken teeth, angled chaotically at the cloud-decked sky, the streets between the broken buildings all pocked and pitted, grass and weeds and some few flowers finding purchase amongst the desolation. They wandered at random, for it was no longer possible to discern logical pattern in that confusion where the wreckage of once-proud buildings covered whole streets and avenues ended in gaping chasms too wide to jump. They clambered over walls and crossed courtyards; found paths through houses where charred timber spoke of burned furniture and melted metal glittered, surprised - for all that they were, too, relieved - to find no evidence of human remains amid the waste. The sun, that had not long been risen when they began, traversed the sky and moved towards the west, casting ragged shadows that hid the pitfalls of the broken streets and gaping cellars, threatening broken bones did they continue searching: they agreed, reluctantly, to cease and find shelter for the night.

The overhang of an arched door and what was left of its surrounding wall afforded some shelter and they built a fire, its flames small comfort to their dampening hope. They huddled miserably about the glow, chewing on the cured meat the Syfalheen had given them as the sickle of a quarter-full moon rose and filled the dead city with eerie silver light. A wind got up, sighing through the ruins: a lament for lost Tezin-dar.

Suddenly Bracht sprang to his feet, falchion gleaming in the fire-glow as unexpected sound intruded on their contemplation.

Katya and Calandryll rose beside him, each with sword in hand, moving instinctively away from the revealing flames, eyes probing the shadows as ears picked out the slow drag of footsteps in the susurration of the wind.

'Back,' the freesword urged softly, 'where we may use our blades unhindered.'

They paced warily to the centre of what had once been a stately hall, standing shoulder-to-shoulder, their blades extended to meet whatever menace should appear. The fire shivered in the breeze, sending dancing shadows over the tumbled walls; cloud drifted to obscure the moon, pooling darkness within the hall. Calandryll felt a prickling against his chest and saw the red stone pulse, thrusting it beneath his shirt lest it betray them all. The footsteps came closer, paused, then came on, and a shape filled the arch, halting there.

Eyes pale-lit by moon and uncountable years surveyed the three, the fire's flames lending shadow to a face sunk in on itself, dry lips drawn back from yellow teeth in time's ancient smile, the cheeks hollows, parchment skin stretched thin over clear-etched bones. White hair curtained the narrow shoulders, falling lank over a robe of blue, skeletal hands all mottled with age thrust from the sleeves, one rising to beckon.

Two more figures shuffled slowly into the ruined

hall, one robed in blue, the other in white, both old; so old as to seem beyond age. They aligned themselves before the three newcomers. Calandryll lowered his blade as the central figure spoke.

'Put up your swords - this place has seen enough of bloodshed.'

The voice was dusted with the weight of ages, rustling and dry, and sad as the wind mourning through the city.

'Old Ones,' Bracht said softly. 'Yssym spoke the truth.'

'So the Syfalheen name us,' said the ancient ... man, Calandryll saw as the cloud cleared the moon and he was able to discern the features: both those in blue were men, the white-robed figure a woman. 'And they speak true. This Yssym - he was the appointed Watcher?'

'Aye,' Calandryll said, his voice unreasonably loud against the other's whisper, 'He brought us to his village, where the elders - the syfaba - brought us to judgement by one of yours.'

'Sennethym.' The deathshead face ducked in confirmation. 'His was the hardest part - to wait alone.'

'He sent you out,' said the female of the three, 'to take the road?'

'How else might they come here?' asked the second man.

'By wizardry, perhaps,' she replied. 'Long and long have we waited, and how might we know what magicks pertain in that world, now?'

'None to find the road,' replied the man, 'On that I'd wager. Were that knowledge abroad there'd be others come ere these.'

The central figure raised a hand, stilling their debate. 'You took the road?' he asked.

'We did,' said Calandryll. 'After ... Sennethym? ... sent us forth the elders of the Syfalheen brought us to a dolmen, through which we passed onto the road. Then we walked to a hostel, and then another, and thence to a second dolmen that brought us here.'

'You see?' demanded the man beside the first speaker. 'If wizardry there still be, it is of a younger kind than ours and cannot find that road. Nor should it pass the gates unscathed - Sennethym found them true.'

'Tereus, Ayliss - would you debate their coming, or judge their worth?'

The two fell silent as he spoke. He touched his chest: 'I am Denarus; my companions Tereus and Ayliss. Do you name yourselves?'

'I am Calandryll den Karynth, lately of Secca in Lysse.'

'I, Katya of Vanu.'

'Bracht, of the clan Asyth of Cuan na'For.'

'Time has passed,' said the woman Ayliss. 'Gods, but what time!'

'Lysse - Cuan na'For, they were wild lands when this place stood.' Denarus's voice was oddly apologetic. 'The domain of small, hairy men more animal than human. As Ayliss says - time has passed.'

'Vanu, though,' said Tereus, 'We knew not Vanu.'

'It lies far to the north,' said Katya, 'beyond the mountains of the Borrhun-maj.'

'Did Janax succeed then?' wondered Tereus. 'Gods, did he find his promised land?'

'She has the look of The Folk,' said Ayliss. 'How think you, Denarus?'

'Aye.' The pale head nodded slowly. 'She has the look of the blood. Whence come your people, Katya of Vanu?'

'Some say from wanderers seeking a warless land,' she answered. 'Others that we are the First Folk and all the world our seeding. Whichever, it was long and long ago, and I know for certain only that Vanu is my homeland.'

'I think that Janax did succeed,' Denarus said, 'and

that pleases me. But say you each the why of your coming.'

Calandryll glanced at Katya, but she motioned for him to speak first, and Bracht nodded his agreement: he told the Old Ones his story; of his meeting with Varent-Rhythamun and the quest the sorcerer had set before him, of his meeting with Bracht, and all their adventures both before and after joining forces with Katya.

'Younger magic,' said Tereus when he was done, 'but still strong; and cunning, for all its madness.'

'Might this Varent-Rhythamun find the road?' Ayliss wondered.

'I think not,' said Denarus. 'For why else send these? Were he able, he would surely come himself.'

'We have yet to hear of the woman's reasons,' said Ayliss. 'Speak now, Katya of Vanu, and tell us why you venture so far abroad.'

'The holy men of Vanu scried an augury,' she replied. 'That Rhythamun - of whom they knew down long ages - should seek to raise Tharn by means of the Arcanum. The spells of raising he already had, but those useless without the book to guide him. They scried that he should send forth dupes,' this with a glance to Calandryll and Bracht; a brief smile of apology, 'and sent me out to find them. To dissuade them or slay them, should that prove needful. The talisman they gave me is a lodestone to point the way, linked in a manner I do not comprehend to that possessed by Rhythamun, which he gave to Calandryll. Thus did I find them and persuade them to an alliance.'

'Why were you chosen?' Tereus demanded. 'Calandryll of Lysse, Bracht of Cuan na'For - I see why this wizard chose them; but on what judgements were you sent forth?'

'My folk are - for the greater part - peaceful,' she said, almost hesitantly, as though the admission she made was a matter of some embarrassment, 'and I am deemed strange amongst them as I am ... less peaceful. Few welcomed such departure from Vanu, whilst I was intrigued to see the larger world. And I have skill with a sword. Nor would I see Rhythamun triumph.'

'None save the mad would see that,' said Denarus.

'The blood runs true in that one,' said Ayliss, 'and that is why they chose her.'

Katya frowned and said, 'The blood?'

'In the dawning of the world we of Gess-ytha were the sole true men,' Denarus explained, 'Whilst all around us the world grew, filled with younger folk, we held to our own land, here, the gift of Balatur. When Tharn and Balatur fell to warring, so did Tharn bring all his awful might against our cities and brought them down to what you see about you now. Before Tezin-dar fell one of our number - Janax - spoke for flight. He was the wisest of us all, Janax, for he foresaw what was and what might be, and set out designs that such as Rhythamun be thwarted.

'He gathered about him all those who shared his hopes - few enough, for we were foolish in our pride and thought we should not see so fair a land as ours ravaged! - and went away to find a land free of gods and their ambitions. I think that land was your Vanu, and in your veins runs the blood of Janax - and that is how your holy men augured this quest and why you were chosen.'

Calandryll looked from the Old One's parchment-fine features to Katya. Much was explained, but one thing troubled him still.

'The Arcanum,' he said, 'Why was it created? You saw the gods war and your cities come down in ruin - yet still you made the book. That such as Rhythamun would seek it, did Janax - did you - not foresee that?'

The Old Ones looked one to the other and he thought he saw guilt, or despair upon their faces: it was hard to tell, so aged were those features, stretched so taut upon the ancient bone as to be empty of all expression save the marking of time.

'We did not create it,' Denarus said, 'and its genesis is a thing not even we - for all we've long pondered it - can properly understand. It was not, and then it was. Perhaps the First Gods made it, to mark the resting places of their children; or Tharn himself, against defeat - we know only that it is now, and we guard it.'

'Janax was gone before it came,' said Tereus, 'though he foresaw its coming and warned against it. Nor did we know whether he lived or died; or where he went. Perhaps he might have found the means to destroy it, but we could not, for all we tried - all we could do was set it round with grammaryes, that it should not leave this place nor be found lest we release those spells.'

'But he set designs against its coming,' said Ayliss, 'thus must the wise ones of Vanu have scried their augury.'

'Aye,' said Denarus, 'Once made it was a peril eternal, for all our efforts to destroy it were fruitless.'

'Yet you would entrust it to us,' said Calandryll, 'And trust that it may be destroyed in Vanu.'

'The holy men are confident of that,' Katya declared.

'And your coming speaks for that truth,' Denarus said. 'Listen - we talk here of things beyond mortal comprehension and our only certainty is that the Arcanum *must* be destroyed, for even we grow old and our magic weakens - we grow weary and would rest. Thus, I think, does this Rhythamun seek to trick us into relinquishing our charge, knowing that we grow weary of the burden. In time even our grammaryes must falter.'

'Then why,' demanded Bracht, speaking for the first time, and bluntly, 'does Rhythamun not simply wait and take it for himself?'

'Perhaps he fears another might come sooner,' said Denarus. 'This Anomius you spoke of, perhaps - or that more honest folk than he perceive the danger, such as those of Vanu. Those cut with his cloth were ever hungry and would snatch what they would, sooner than await its falling.'

'We sensed a stirring,' Tereus said when his companion fell silent, 'We felt the patterns shift and knew that forces moved. To that end we worked to bring you here.'

'Katya's coming I understand,' said Calandryll, 'but us - Bracht and I - why were we chosen?'

'Because you were,' Denarus answered, 'I can say no better - the gods work in mysterious ways, and that you are come here says that you are the True Ones.'

'You must take it,' said Ayliss. 'And grant us long-waited peace.'

'Else death claim even us,' said Tereus, 'and the way lie open to folk less honest of purpose. Our time is passed and we would lay down our burden.'

'Come,' Denarus said then, 'we shall bring you to the book and you shall take it from Tezin-dar. Go back down the road to the Syfalheen and they will bring you to your ship - but hurry then, for the road will soon pass after we are gone.'

Calandryll frowned and Tereus said, 'Our existence is bound with those grammaryes that ward the book - when we loose those, we find our rest. The road and all we built will fade then.'

'At last,' murmured Ayliss. 'Oh, how I long for that.'

'Then come,' said Denarus, 'We might talk forever of these things and never find answers - let the Arcanum go from here to its destruction.'

He turned, Ayliss and Tereus at his side, and went out through the arch into a night grown older, the moon cloud-scarred, indifferent. They wound a tortuous way through the city, past tumbled walls and halls ribbed with the shadows of denuded spires, past gaping pits and riven gulleys, coming at last to a plain door of fire-seared metal set in a deep-shadowed niche. The Old Ones halted before the portal, each in turn laying hands upon the surface as they murmured in a language long-forgotten. It opened and they started down a stairway that fell in darkness into the bowels of the city, ending where pale light glowed from runes graven deep in a second door, this of black metal. Denarus spoke again, joined by Ayliss and Tereus, and that door swung inwards on further steps. These fell steeper, but lit with a cold white light no kin to flame that came from sconces set in niches overhead, so that Calandryll, first behind the Old Ones, could see the dappling of age on their skulls beneath their silvered hair, the slow pulse of blood beneath the parchment skin.

They descended to a chamber all writ with runes, blood-black in the strange light, a silver pedestal at its centre, ringed by flames, its burden lost behind the fire.

Calandryll halted on Denarus's bidding, Bracht and Katya beside him as the Old Ones shuffled past the fire to stand facing them. A great excitement filled him, and a sense of dread, for the power that emanated from within the flames was a palpable thing that seemed to vibrate down the roadways of his bones and within the channels of his veins.

Denarus said, 'Do you truly vow that you will take the Arcanum to its destruction in Vanu?'

As one they said, 'Aye, we do.'

Ayliss said, 'Knowing that you are cursed do you betray this trust?'

Again they said, 'Aye, knowing that.'

Tereus said, 'Knowing your souls damned do you fail?'

'Aye, that, too.'

The Old Ones spoke together then: 'Then take the Arcanum hence, and let it be forever lost.'

Denarus stepped a pace forwards, hands thrust out into the flames. Ayliss moved to join him, and Tereus. They spoke together in that same strange tongue that had unlocked the doors and the flames gusted, blinding, rising high against the roof of the chamber. Calandryll started back, arm raised against the sudden heat, and heard Bracht gasp as it faded, Katya's sharp intake of breath.

The flames were gone and the three Old Ones with them, only a slow drift of dust where they had stood, settling leisurely upon the smooth surface of the floor, its only blemish. On the pedestal, revealed clear now, lay a slender book, its binding black, like ancient leather, the single word scribed red: *Arcanum*. It was small, an unimportant-seeming thing, save for that sense of power that oozed from it, an aura, chilling in the heated confines of the chamber.

Calandryll stepped towards it, reluctant now to touch the relic. And shouted as pain lanced his chest, as though a flaming brand pressed there. He scrabbled at his shirt, seeing the red stone burn bright, fire pulsing through it as the scent of almonds filled his nostrils.

'Ahrd!' he heard Bracht cry, 'What is it?'

The Kern's falchion slid swift from the sheath; Katya's sabre glittered. Calandryll moaned, fastening desperate hands on the leather thong that held the burning stone about his neck, snapping the cord to cast the talisman clear, across the chamber.

Where it landed the air shimmered. Inchoate dread gripped him: thinking it likely already useless, he drew his sword.

And saw the shimmering solidify, the scent of magic fading. And recognised the familiar face that beamed across the pedestal towards him, ablaze with triumph, a hand poised upon the book.

'My thanks,' said Varent-Rhythamun, 'You served me well.'

Bracht moved swift as a striking serpent, yelling a curse as he sprang forwards, falchion cutting at the wizard's head. Varent-Rhythamun raised an almost negligent hand, gripping the blade as easily might a man catching a falling feather. Katya attacked on his left and he blocked her blade, too, smiling as both froze, paralysed by his magic. Calandryll stepped towards him, more cautious, and he laughed, flicking out his hands so that Kern and warrior-woman both were flung aside.

'You cannot touch me,' he said mildly, contempt on his aquiline features. 'Think you that mere blades may harm such as I am? No - my power is greater than you know. And greater still, ere long.'

Calandryll drove the straightsword at the mocking face: felt it halted and himself hurled back, clouded round with the dust that was the Old Ones. Stone struck his head and his vision blurred.

'Dera damn your soul!' he groaned helplessly as he saw the mage pick up the Arcanum, long-fingered hands caressing the binding, adoring as a lover's touch.

'Dera?' Varent-Rhythamun shook his head, chuckling: a malign sound. 'That weak mewling goddess cannot touch me now. No more than you three fools! Now I have this, I have all - I have the key that will unlock Tharn and return my master to his kingdom.'

'You are mad,' Calandryll cried, struggling to rise: finding that he could not, pressed down by Varent-Rhythamun's magic. 'You'd visit chaos on the world!'

'I'd return my master to his own,' the mage retorted, 'and stand at his right hand when that day comes. Oh, you poor, sad fools! How well you played my game - without your aid I might never have gained this chamber; never passed the magicks of Denarus and the rest.'

'The stone,' Calandryll gasped. 'You used the stone.'

'Aided by that power I sensed in you,' Varent-Rhythamun agreed, 'Aye - the stone is a focus for my sortilege. I could not approach here myself, but you, you faithful hounds, you brought it here; and once here I needed only employ my arts, knowing the Guardians departed.' He took up the Arcanum, folding it in his black-robed arms, teeth bared in awful smile. 'And now I take it - to find Tharn's tomb - whilst you remain here. Farewell, my friends.'

The air shimmered again where he stood, and once more the familiar - hated! - scent hung on the air. And he was gone, the Arcanum with him.

'Dera damn him!' Calandryll moaned. 'And me for a fool. Oh, goddess - what have we done?'

'Loosed madness on the world,' said Katya, bitterly, rising painfully to retrieve her sword. 'We were pawns in his game.'

Bracht climbed to his feet, taking up the falchion, his face grim, blue eyes cold with rage.

'The Old Ones said the road remains a while,' he grunted. 'Do we take it, or die here?'

'To what end?' Calandryll shook his head, voice sour with chagrin. 'He has the book - you heard what he intends. What matter whether we die here or in a world gone down in chaos?'

'The Arcanum leads to Tharn's tomb,' Bracht said, 'and likely that is in no place easy of finding - he must go to there before he may raise the Mad God.'

Katya turned to fix him with her eyes, hope flickering behind the stormy grey. 'Think you that we might yet halt him?'

'I'd sooner die attempting that than rot here,' Bracht answered.

'Dare we hope as much?' Calandryll climbed up; sheathed his dropped blade.

'I saw him take the stone,' said Bracht. 'Did you not say, Katya, that your talisman is a pointer to that fell mate?'

'Aye,' she said, 'it is.'

'Then we have hope,' said the Kern, fierce. 'And a battle to fight if we've the heart to attempt it.'

She nodded: 'I stand with you, Bracht.'

'And I,' said Calandryll, his comrades' determination infusing him, resolution burning afresh. 'To the ends of the world.'

'Likely we shall see them before this is done,' said Bracht, smiling now, ferocious, 'Come!'

They took the stairs at a run, careless of the rubble that filled the city as they raced into a new-dawned morning, towards the dolmen standing lonely in the meadow, hurling themselves into its darkness.

Into the pursuit of Rhythamun.

THE END, OF THE FIRST BOOK